Men of Albemarle

Inglis Fletcher

BANTAM BOOKS · TORONTO · NEW YORK · LONDON ®

This low-priced Bantam Book
has been completely reset in a type face
designed for easy reading, and was printed
from new plates. It contains the complete
text of the original hard-cover edition.
NOT ONE WORD HAS BEEN OMITTED.

MEN OF ALBEMARLE

A Bantam Book / published by arrangement with
The Bobbs-Merrill Company, Inc.

PRINTING HISTORY

Bobbs-Merrill edition published October 1942

2nd printing......October 1942		4th printing.....December 1942	
3rd printing......October 1942		5th printing........March 1946	
6th printing.....September 1947			

Doubleday edition published November 1951

Bantam edition published September 1970

2nd printing
3rd printing
4th printing
5th printing
6th printing

Bantam Books are published by Bantam Books, Inc., a National
General company. Its trade-mark, consisting of the words "Bantam
Books" and the portrayal of a bantam, is registered in the United
States Patent Office and in other countries. Marca Registrada.
Bantam Books, Inc., 666 Fifth Avenue, New York, N.Y. 10019.

PRINTED IN THE UNITED STATES OF AMERICA

MEN AND WOMEN CAUGHT UP
IN A FIERCE STRUGGLE—AGAINST THE WILDERNESS AND
THE PASSIONS THAT RULED THEIR LIVES . . .

DUKE ROGER—He had paid dearly for the reckless adventures of his youth and had at last found peace in the Carolina wilderness. Now a savage power struggle and a passionate love affair threatened to plunge him into violence and chaos once more . . .

MICHAEL CARY—The fiery young rebel leader whose quick temper, fierce pride and fighting skill were equal to every contest but love . . .

ANTHONY LOVYCK—A disdainful young London dandy who learned that polished manners and a poison tongue were inadequate allies in an uncivilized world . . .

LADY MARY—Her wit and beauty made prisoners of men; her will enslaved them. Yet a tragic secret ruled her life and denied her the one man to whom she could surrender completely . . .

MARITA—She was a gentle, obedient child until a handsome renegade awakened her to the passions of womanhood and forbidden love . . .

ANNE EVANS—as tempting and innocent, desirable and savage as the wilderness that sheltered her. But fear and hatred of men had scarred her as deeply as the "W" they had burned into her flesh—the "W" that stood for Witch . . .

MEN OF ALBEMARLE

Bantam Books by Inglis Fletcher

MEN OF ALBEMARLE
RALEIGH'S EDEN

DEDICATED TO

JOHN FLETCHER

IN GRATITUDE FOR HIS UNENDING INTEREST
DURING THE YEARS SPENT IN GATHERING MATERIAL
FOR *Raleigh's Eden* AND *Men of Albemarle*

AND TO

JOHN STUART FLETCHER, U.S.N.

A SEVERE CRITIC, BUT ALWAYS JUST AND IMPARTIAL

Acknowledgment

TO THE KEEPERS
OF THE GATES

I MAKE my acknowledgment to the men and women who have so carefully collected and so lovingly preserved the manuscripts and documents, journals and private letters that form the living link between the past and the present now housed in the public and private libraries of this country.

In desert lands, in ancient tents, the Guardian of the floodgates stood on the banks of the Euphrates and the Nile, waiting to turn the life-giving water on the arid land. In our times, librarians are the *keepers of the gates*. They stand ready and eager to open the gates to allow a great stream of history to flow from its uncontaminated source.

I express my grateful appreciation to those library friends who were especially helpful and who have shown continued interest in the progress of *Men of Albemarle:*

Mr. L. E. Bliss and Miss Norma Cuthbert of the staff of the H. E. Huntington Library, San Marina, California, where I had the privilege of examining the Sunderland Papers, and items from the Brock Collection that deal with North Carolina of the period.

Mr. David Chambers Mearns of the Library of Congress, for permission to use rare manuscripts and books housed in that great repository of historical material.

Miss Mary Moseley, Nassau, New Providence, Bahama Islands, who unhesitatingly put at my disposal the results of her exhaustive research in England on West Indies Plantations of the Colonial period.

North Carolina Historical Commission, Raleigh, North Carolina, for maps of the period and permission to read Colonel Thomas Pollock's Letter-book in manuscript.

Sir Angus Fletcher, British Library of Information, New York City, for lists of books and manuscript concerning West Indies Plantations and the American Plantations of the period of the Lords Proprietors.

Mrs. Lyman Cotton, University of North Carolina Library at Chapel Hill, North Carolina.

Miss Nannie Tilly, Duke University Library, Durham, North Carolina.

Mrs. Sidney MacMullen, Shephard-Pruden Memorial Library, Edenton, North Carolina.

Miss Mabel Gillis, Librarian, California State Library, Sacramento, California.

Miss Helen Bruner, Sutro Branch, California State Library, San Francisco, California.

Unfortunately, I do not know the names of all the people who have assisted me in my search to discover the past. In this connection I mention the page boys in the Library of Congress, whose duty it is to bring books to the researcher each morning and take them away at night. In that immense library it would be so easy to fall into a routine. I found the opposite to be the case. Never once did they fail me, in interest and helpful suggestion. My experience has been the same in every library where it has been my good fortune to work. No matter what problem the search presented, there has always been some enthusiastic librarian ready to help me, as he is ready and eager to help any writer who asks for trained advice.

Other sources of unpublished material were:

Nassau Library, Nassau, New Providence, Bahama Islands.

Colonial Records, Chowan County Court House, Edenton, North Carolina.

Vestry Records, St. Paul's Espicopal Church, Edenton, North Carolina.

INGLIS FLETCHER

The Fishery
Greenfield Plantation
Edenton, North Carolina

Contents

Silent Leges Inter Arma

Advertisement for Settlement of the Carolinas

IF THERE be any younger brother who is born of gentle blood and whose spirit is elevated above the common sort, and yet the hard usage of our country hath not allowed suitable fortune, he will not surely be afraid to leave his native soil to advance his fortune equal to his blood and spirit. And so he will avoid those unlawful ways too many of our young gentlemen take to maintain themselves according to their high education, but having small estates.

With a few servants and a small stock, a great estate may be raised. Although his birth, as a younger brother, have not entitled him to any of the land of his ancestors, yet his industry may supply him so as to make him the head of as famous a family, in Carolina.

The Chief Privileges

There is full and free liberty of conscience granted to all, so that no man is to be molested or called in question for matters of religious concern; but everyone to be obedient to the civil governor, worshipping God after their own way.

They are to have a Governor and Council appointed from among themselves, to see that the laws of the Assembly are put in due execution; but the Governor is to rule but three years; also, he has no power to lay any tax or make or abrogate any law without the consent of the colony in their Assembly.

Go to Master Wilkinson, Ironmonger, at the sign of the Three Feathers in Bishop's Gate, London, where you may be informed when ships will be ready and what you must carry with you.

Signed by the true and absolute Lords Proprietors of the Carolinas.

THE GREAT DISMAL

THE coach swayed crazily in the rutted road. All day, ever since they had crossed the James, the rain had fallen steadily, until the forest road that skirted the Great Dismal Swamp was a sea of slippery, slimy mud.

The fading October day was chill. Grey mists rose from rotting underbrush and swamp growth; the stagnant black water, pierced by the twisted, grotesque knees of great cypress trees, gave off a thin miasmatic vapour. Dusk fell early in the swamp, blotting out the autumn colours of gum and sycamore and sourwood, leaving only the blurred grey shadows of pine and cypress that rose majestically from the black mirror of the water to pierce the deeper grey of the night sky.

It was October of the year 1710 and Queen Anne sat on the throne of Great Britain. In this year of change and import there rose the hope of a successful conclusion of wars and tumult. Six years earlier Admiral Rooke had taken Gibraltar from the Spanish; the same year John Churchill, with his conquering British cavalry, fought and won the Battle of Blenheim. In the new world beyond the Atlantic the destiny of the Carolinas lay in the hands of eight peers of the realm who called themselves the Lords Proprietors.

Inside the coach a young girl watched the passing panorama of forest through the wavy glass of the little window. She sat quietly, her gloved hands loosely clasped in her lap, her slight body shrouded in the loose folds of her brown woollen cloak. The hood had slipped back, allowing the tawny mass of her hair to tumble over her shoulders. She was young, not over seventeen, and of no particular beauty—she was much too angular and her face too thin, but her wide, generous mouth was sensitive and mobile; later it might become firm and strong, or droop at the corners into petulance. Her slightly upturned nose gave her a childlike look, belied by her jaw which already showed signs of character.

1

It was her eyes that caught and held attention. They were clear amber, their size emphasized by a double row of long lashes, the upper row golden brown, the same colour as her straight heavy brows, and the lower fringe ivory white. This startling feature gave an unusual interest to her immature face. A curious mingling of the past and present shone from her eyes; the mark of wisdom was there, and the mark of youth. In a measure this was, for Marita, a defence of which she was yet unconscious. Even Lady Mary, her aunt, who was not too watchful of her tongue, sometimes paused in the midst of a tirade, wondering whether she was talking to a child or to a person of mature wisdom.

Marita turned from the window and allowed her heavy-lidded eyes to rest for a moment on the other occupants of the coach—Lady Mary Tower, her aunt and guardian, and Governor Hyde's young secretary, Anthony Lovyck. Both were sleeping, worn out by the long ride. They had left Williamsburg, in the Crown Colony of Virginia, at sunup the day before, and had rested the same night at Half-Way Inn, a house of mean accommodations. Today had been the same: an early start, rough roads, long miles between resting places, and an uninteresting journey. Scarcely a house or habitation had they seen since they came to the road that skirted the Great Dismal Swamp. It was a wild, uninhabited country. All day they had had the further discomfort of the rain and a driving wind. Sometimes a deer leapt across the road in front of them, or they glimpsed the grey of a wolf skulking in the forest shadows. Other animals lurked in reeds and the tangled curtain of wild grape and trumpet vines that grew along the edge of the black water. The night before, Marita had not slept for the howling of timber wolves and the weird call of waterfowl. The strange, lonely voices of the wilderness filled her with vague terror.

Behind them travelled the coach in which rode Madam Catha Hyde, the wife of the new governor, and Hyde's two children, Penelope and young Edward. The children's tutor, James Stephenson, and Miss Mittie Hyde rode in the third vehicle. Miss Mittie was a poor relation of the Hydes whose place in the household was as indefinite as her own personality. Captain James Gregory rode ahead on horseback. He had come from England, at the instance of the Lords Proprietors, to organize a militia for the great Albemarle County of the Carolinas.

A fourth coach carried maids and housemen. Then came

2

the luggage carts and waggons carrying Madam Hyde's most valued possessions of wardrobe and plate for the governor's new house, in Queen Anne's Town in Albemarle. The heavy furniture had been sent overland from the James to the Blackwater and down the Chowan River, on one of Colonel Pollock's sloops. For Madam Hyde and her party had sailed from England three months before to join her husband, who had come out to Virginia some months earlier following his appointment as the new deputy governor of the northern part of the Carolinas. Madam Catha was determined that "his Excellency," as she called her husband, should live in a manner suitable to the dignity of a Lords Proprietors' governor. Moreover, she had no intention of letting anyone in the Carolinas forget that Edward Hyde was own cousin to the Queen of England.

With the long cavalcade of vehicles were footmen and outriders and waggoners and carters, a formidable assembly, the like of which had not been seen in the Carolina Province since the day Seth Sothel, one of the true Lords Proprietors, had come out from England almost thirty years earlier to be governor of Carolina. Like a small army, the coaches, waggons and carts crept along wearily, with almost human protest of shrieking wheels and hubs. The Borderers, who lived along the line between the Royal Colony of Virginia and the Province of the Carolinas, had never seen such display of grandeur in coaches and liveried servants. They came out of the forest at every crossroad, some even running along the road beside the waggon train as it moved slowly southward, while others stood, open-mouthed and silent, watching the coaches, each with its six struggling horses, and peering into the windows to see the occupants of the vehicles.

Marita glanced at her aunt. She was sleeping soundly, her head against a down pillow wedged into the corner of the tufted, plum-coloured lining of the coach. Even asleep she made an imposing figure, long of limb, with broad shoulders and a slim waist. Her ash-blonde hair lay in thick curls on her white forehead and against her slim throat—guiltless of powder, a fashion lately introduced by the Queen. Her face had character, her nose was strong, but her full lips drooped discontentedly. Her skin was very fair and the frankly artificial colour showed plainly on her cheekbones. A violet felt robe, lined with the soft fur from squirrel bellies, covered her knees; under the wide fur sleeves of her mink coat were ruffles of fine Mechlin, and a froth of the same lace was

3

pinned at the throat of her blue travelling dress with a jewelled pin.

An open box, with gold-stoppered bottles and toilet appliances, lay on the seat beside her, and in her lap was a Morocco-leather case with gold clasp and hinges, the strap slipped over her wrist. More than once Marita had seen the key hanging on a slender gold chain around Lady Mary's neck. She knew the case contained something too valuable to be entrusted to her woman.

During the dreary voyage from England the girl had spent many long hours, as she sat on the deck of the *Good Intent,* trying to imagine an adequate reason why her aunt had left London and the round of fashion which was her life. Why did she take ship and sail away just at the very moment when the hunting season was coming on in the Midlands? Why did she leave her home in Sussex and her house in town?... Why did she want to journey to the Carolina wilderness at all?

Marita loved her beautiful aunt, even though Lady Mary was constantly hurting her with criticism of her looks and conduct. She had come to realize that her aunt was unhappy about something, and had learned to bear petulant recriminations without any show of feeling. Whenever fits of depression overtook Lady Mary anyone within range of her tongue suffered. Marita was glad her aunt was asleep, for sleeping she could not find fault with her or her speech.

"I declare," Lady Mary had said just before she fell asleep, "you do me no credit with your *gauche* manners and accent of a Sussex milkmaid. How could that creature Weatherby allow you to ride wild over the Downs and pick up the talk of country folk? I can't imagine what the woman was thinking of, not to give you more finish! It is a very good thing, miss, that her Majesty was bedridden with one of her gout attacks when you came to town. If I had been asked to present you, I don't believe you could have got through a private audience without tripping on your frock or doing something awkward." She drew her lips in a thin, cruel line. "I discharged Weatherby without character for her bungling."

Tears came to Marita's eyes when she thought of this; how many times she had cried out her loneliness on Weatherby's comfortable bosom. She could see her now, standing on the dock waving her handkerchief, her usually beaming face curiously working to keep back the tears. Only three month's

4

ago . . . it seemed a century since that drear morning the *Good Intent* had sailed from Bristol, carrying them across the broad Atlantic to the Carolina plantations. Tears ran unheeded down Marita's cheeks.

A firm pressure on her hand roused her. A square of white linen was laid in her lap.

"Take this and mop up your tears, Miss Marita; we will be reaching the Border Inn before long."

Marita looked up. Anthony Lovyck was smiling at her, but his eyes were kind and understanding. He leaned forward and took up the handkerchief to dry her tears.

"When we get there we will have a hot meal and a comfortable place to rest." He paused a moment, then added, "D.V.," under his breath.

Marita dabbed at her eyes.

"Colonel Byrd declared there wasn't a good bed in all the Carolinas," she said. "He told my aunt they were all made of cypress poles, laced with rawhide and covered with corn-shuck pads instead of good feathers."

The smile died from the young secretary's eyes. "I wouldn't place too much confidence in what Colonel Byrd says, Miss Marita. He looks with a jaundiced eye on everything concerning Carolina. I think he is a man of many prejudices, or perhaps he doesn't like Carolina because Governor Spottswood does."

The girl met his eyes. Suddenly she seemed to him very old and wise.

"You did not like Colonel Byrd, did you, Mr. Lovyck? He made you very angry that last night at the Governor's, when he said something unkind about William Penn."

"I don't like gossips and I don't like snobbery," Lovyck answered shortly. Then his face cleared. He patted her hand. "You notice a great deal for a little girl, Marita."

"I'm not little, Mr. Lovyck; I'm almost seventeen . . ." But Mr. Lovyck was not listening. He opened the little window to give orders to his groom, who was leading his saddle horse. When he drew in his head he settled himself back into his corner of the coach, his broad feathered hat pulled down, half covering his thin dark face. In a moment he, too, was asleep. Marita looked at him. He had a very nice mouth, she thought, and a strong, firm jaw. But most of all, she liked his dark eyes. They were sad eyes, but they were always kind when he looked at her. He was a silent person, quiet-

5

mannered, and he fetched and carried for Madam Catha and Lady Mary without complaint.

Her aunt had told her that he was of a noble Welsh family, orphaned when he was a child. He and his brother Thomas had been brought up by a very wealthy uncle, Edward Parr, who lived in London. Parr was said to have great influence with the Lords Proprietors, because he sat with the Lords of Trade and Plantations. Marita didn't quite understand what that meant, though she knew from her aunt's tone that it was something important.

Marita smiled a little as she folded his fine linen handkerchief into its original creases and laid it on the seat beside him. She liked Anthony Lovyck, although she had noticed he was not always as kind to everyone as he was to her. Sometimes he put on the airs of a fine gentleman before lesser folk. Marita did not like that. Weatherby had often told her that one must always be kind to inferiors. She thought shrewdly that he had a hard time ahead of him, between Madam Catha's ambitions and the Governor's easygoing ways. Presently her head grew heavy and her eyes closed. She, too, slept, rocked by the swaying of the coach and the rhythmic drip of the rain on the roof.

The coach stopped with a jerk. Lady Mary opened her eyes and automatically patted the curls on her forehead into place.

"Lovyck, tell that coachman to drive more carefully," she cried, sitting erect. "I do believe he wants to break my neck!" She looked at Anthony accusingly, as if he were responsible for her discomfort.

Anthony opened the door and jumped out. It was almost dusk, but Marita saw that they had come to a crossroad, crowded with milling, bleating sheep. Dogs were barking sharply, men shouting and cursing, while shepherds prodded the bewildered sheep, herding them away from the quagmire that paralleled the narrow road. A tall man rode toward them, guiding his horse carefully through the moving flock.

Anthony Lovyck called out, "Won't you please drive those sheep to the side of the road so that the coaches can proceed?"

The man pulled up his horse. "Sorry," he said. "The herd has the right of way. You'll have to wait, I'm afraid." His voice was strong and full but it had a curious intonation. He spoke carelessly, as if he weren't in the least sorry to hold up the coaches.

6

The coachman leaned from the box, protesting angrily. "It's the Governor's lady who rides here. You can't delay us this way. Get the stinking animals off the road!"

"If the Governor's lady does not like the smell of sheep-dip, let her put her little handkerchief to her nose." A laugh went up among the shepherds.

Lady Mary put her head out the window. "My good man," she said in her fine voice, "can you not divide your flock and let us through?" She held out her hand with a coin in it. "Here, take this and buy your men a pot of ale when you get to the next ordinary." The man on horseback turned to face the coach. He was young, around twenty-four or five, with strong, rugged features. A faint, quizzical smile hovered about his broad, good-humoured mouth.

"Take it," Lady Mary repeated, tossing the coin. "Get your sheep out of the way, like a good fellow." The man caught the coin, dexterously, eyed it a moment, then tossed it over his shoulder to one of the drovers. He lifted his queer round hat with a sweeping bow, his smile mocking.

"Sorry, Madam Hyde, even at the risk of your displeasure, we must go forward. We are obliged to get our sheep to the ferry before dark."

Lady Mary snapped, "I'm not Madam Hyde and I know from your hat that you're a Roundhead! I thought all those wretched Cromwellian hats had been done away with long years ago."

The young man smiled broadly. "Not a Roundhead, madam; just a humble Friend. Quakers, they sometimes call us."

Marita pressed her face to the window so that she could see him better. She had heard of the Friends, but she had never seen one. Parson Urmston, from the Society for Propagation of the Gospel in Foreign Parts, had been on the *Good Intent*. He had told her about the Quakers in Albemarle—"fighting Quakers," he called them. "A poor lot of ill-bred folk, and worse." She had supposed, from his description, that a Quaker would have horns growing out of his forehead. He's not humble, she thought, and he isn't in the least sorry to delay us. Marita was accustomed to country folk of a different order from this man: men and women who stood aside, bowing and curtseying as she and Weatherby drove about the Sussex downs. Lady Mary looked at the man curiously as if he were a new breed to her also.

All at once Marita felt the horseman's eyes on her. He turned from Lady Mary and rode to her side of the coach.

His round dark hat was still on his head and he didn't remove it when he spoke. This was a strange attitude for a drover.

"Thee is weary," he said, dropping his voice so the others could not hear. "Thee has been travelling long?"

"Since daybreak," she answered, strangely roused by his compelling eyes. "We were told we would reach the border long before dark, but we got off the main road after we left the river."

"There's still an hour's drive ahead before you reach the Border Inn. The swamp is vast and the road is full of pitfalls to one who does not know the way." Marita noticed that he sat tall on his horse, a man long of limb, broad of shoulder, with an easy seat, as one accustomed to the saddle.

He raised his voice. "Yaupim! Atonga!" he called. Two red Indians came forward from the roadside. They were clothed in breechclout and hide vest, and wore soft moccasins on their feet. They moved close to the man's stirrup, as though accustomed to his orders.

He spoke to them in a strange tongue, musical and flowing.

"Did you hear me, my man?" Lady Mary leaned over Marita, her face close to the window. She raised her voice to attract the rider's attention. "I tell you I want my carriage to pass!"

The Quaker did not answer. He went on talking to the Indians, then held up four fingers. When he had finished, he turned to Lady Mary, his face unreadable, his mouth stern.

"Cease talking, madam. It is not necessary to give orders. The flock will be held for the four coaches to pass. Not because of thy importuning, madam, but because the little maid is weary."

The hot colour came to Marita's cheeks, but no one appeared to notice. Some strange new emotion came to her at the man's words, choking her. She had grown used to having her comfort unregarded during the long journey. Solicitude was always for Madam Hyde or Lady Mary. She was used to that, living always in the dominant shadow of Lady Mary—a silent, unobtrusive girl, who fetched and carried and spoke only when she was spoken to by her elders.

Lady Mary brushed the man's words aside as if they had not been spoken, but to Marita they rang out clearly, encircling her, making a strong protective ring about her.

By now Anthony Lovyck had made his way around the coach. He stood at the edge of the roadside ditch, his buckled

8

shoes half covered with greyish mud. "Really, my man, this delay is an outrage," he said loftily. "These coaches must proceed at once. They belong to the Governor's lady."

The man on horseback turned his head and looked down on Lovyck from his superior height.

"Better get out of the weather before the rain melts thy fine clothes, Sir Cavalier," he said mildly, but there was a glint of laughter in his deep blue eyes. Marita saw a flush rise on Anthony's face, but he had no time to retort. The man wheeled his horse and rode off into the gathering dusk.

Marita sat back. It had all happened so swiftly. Anthony returned to the coach; the coachman lighted the carriage lamps and drove slowly on through the bleating flock. Lovyck sat gloomily in his corner, his feet, in the muddy shoes, pulled back away from Lady Mary's silken skirts. His dark brows were drawn together, as if some of the swift anger that the rider's words had occasioned still rankled.

Lady Mary glanced at Marita speculatively, but did not speak.

The coach moved slowly. The horses shied away from the sheep, whinnying and stamping. Shepherds and sheep dogs tried to hold the divided flock to the roadside ditches and the swamp crossroad, but the task was all but impossible. Terrified lambs escaped from one side or the other and huddled in little groups in the road. The coachman leaned forward, flicking the long-lashed whip gently. Outriders pushed their horses, endeavouring to clear the road for the coaches. The noise was incessant. Herdsman and outriders shouted. The bleating of the frightened sheep rose in a crescendo. Lady Mary lay back against the cushions, her salts bottle at her nose.

Marita pressed her face against the window. She hoped for another glimpse of the horseman, but he had already disappeared down the road which led to the swamp. She thought, He held his head high, kept his hat on his head when he spoke to us, excepting when he made that sweeping, derisive bow to Aunt Mary. He was very bold. What a strange world this is, where a drover speaks to a lady as to an equal . . .

The Great Dismal closed down upon them, shutting off the waning light. The coach skirted the black water; shadows of tangling vines and branches swung eerily, as if some unseen swamp creatures lay above them, slimy and reptilian, waiting their chance to fall upon them with twisting, crushing embrace. The heavy shadows of the great cypress trees with

9

their spreading buttresses of twisted knees made a world unfamiliar and frightening. In the forest an owl screeched, answered from afar. An evil omen! Marita shivered, holding her hands close clasped, to keep from crying out.

There was not one familiar thing to hold to. Strangeness and danger lay all about them and the deadly cruelty of the unending primeval forest. Plunder and kill with savage claw—stalk and kill to survive. That was the law of the forest and this strange new world.

Chapter 2

BORDER INN

IT WAS black night when they reached the Border Inn. The lights from the many-paned windows of a long low building shone cheerfully through the driving rain. Men darted back and forth from the lighted doorway; dogs barked; horses neighed; harness jingled; rough voices of holsters and grooms rose out of the darkness as the coaches stopped at the relay station on the border between Virginia and Carolina.

"Hand me my tippet, Marita," Lady Mary said, sitting up and straightening her little hat. "Reach over and button my cloak. I can't think why I allowed Madam Hyde to persuade me to let my woman ride in the servants' coach. Now I have no one to carry my dressing bag and help me make myself presentable after this devastating ride." Her voice sounded tired and querulous. "My hair is tumbling down and I can't arrange it myself."

Marita felt suddenly sorry for her aunt's helplessness. "Dear Aunt, let me . . ."

"No, no, Marita. You couldn't possibly arrange my hair; my head is so tender. I never allow anyone but Desham to touch it. Not that it matters in this barbaric country."

"At least we will have a warm meal." Anthony Lovyck's voice sounded cheerful, in anticipation. "We have a haunch of venison in the boot, and a dozen bottles of wine that Governor Spottswood sent down for you, before we left Williamsburg."

"Very thoughtful of the Governor," Lady Mary said, slightly soothed as she was reminded of the delicate attention of the Governor of Virginia. "I am more convinced than ever that one can always count on a Scot. That planter, Mr. Byrd, gave voice to protestations of friendship for us, but the best he did was to give us much gloomy report of the discomforts we were going to encounter. I declare, I almost took ship for England after hearing his talk that day at Westover!"

"I noticed that he didn't do anything to alleviate our discomforts," Lovyck commented drily.

A footman opened the coach door. When they were all safely out of the rain, on the long gallery which surrounded the clap boarded inn, the other coaches were not in sight. Anthony Lovyck suggested that they go at once to their rooms, where they could rest comfortably until supper was prepared. Lady Mary agreed. Marita thanked him wordlessly for his thoughtfulness, for she was almost too weary to speak.

They crossed a long general room, filled with roughly dressed men who stared at them, frankly interested in the advent of two gentlewomen and their escort. A fire of six-foot logs blazed in the crude stone fireplace. At the far end of the room a man in a dirty leather apron carried tankards of ale to the long, uncovered tables, where woodsmen in tanned-leather breeches and shirts sat with drovers and herdsmen. Lady Mary walked with her head high, her wide blue skirts sweeping the rough boards of the puncheon floor; Marita, a shadow, close behind her.

At the hall door, they waited a moment for the landlord to light them to the upper story. Near the door, at a small desk with sloping top, a wrinkled, leathery-faced man sat on a high stool, an open ledger before him. Standing near him was a drover, cap in hand. He was droning out: "Sandy Point Plantation; 300 ewes, no rams; mark, shallow dart on right ear, left ear cut; 200 for Norfolk Town." The clerk dipped his quill pen into the ink. The drover stopped talking. Without looking up, the clerk rasped: "Go on, go on, I can hear you without looking at you."

"Damnation on this toll-tax nuisance," the drover muttered. "No wonder the bold ones run their sheep across the border."

"Hold your tongue," the clerk said sharply.

There was a silence in the length of the room, only the sharp scratch of the quill pen. A moment later the drover went on: "300 sheep; Greenfield Plantation; mark, poplar-leaf on right ear, left ear split."

The landlord, a big man, with deep chest and overhanging jowls, appeared out of the darkness of the long hall. He walked ahead of them, carrying a branched candlestick to light their way. Lady Mary stopped, her hand on the monkey-tailed newel post.

"Where is Madam Hyde?" she asked, suddenly remembering the Governor's lady. "Hasn't her coach come in?"

The landlord shook his head. "No, my lady. Yours is the only coach in this day. A few men on horseback and the waggoners from Queen Anne's Town, with tobacco—" he stopped, suddenly cautious—"with farm produce they are taking into Virginia," he continued, looking at her shrewdly, to see if she had caught his slip. The law said that no North Carolina tobacco could be brought into Virginia for shipment to New England or to the mother country, but that did not keep tobacco from being secretly carried over the border, even though contraband. Neither Lady Mary nor Anthony Lovyck had noticed the slip, for they knew nothing of the Virginia Tobacco Act. The landlord walked on, satisfied, but a ruddy-cheeked man with sparse grey hair, seated at a table near the fireplace, looked after him, a frown on his face.

"The fool," he muttered. "He should have his tongue slit for such talk before strangers. How does he know who they be?"

Lady Mary and Marita followed the landlord up a steep narrow stair, to the floor above. At the far end of the hall he threw open a door and stood back, holding the candle high. The bedroom was large and low-ceilinged, with exposed rafters and walls sealed with cypress. Two little dormers made low cubbies, under which were stored rattan baskets of potatoes and root vegetables. A dozen hams and sides of bacon, blackened from hickory smoke, hung from the rafters. They gave off a tarry odor, strange but not unpleasant.

Lady Mary stopped at the doorway, aghast at what she saw. "My good man," she said loftily, in a voice she used when she was annoyed, "we can't put up with this attic! Show me your best room at once!"

The man hesitated. "We're saving the other room for the Governor's lady," he said. "The Governor's man rode in this morning to give the orders."

"Where is the room?" Lady Mary said, peremptorily. The

12

landlord hesitated. Under her imperious gaze, he waved a pudgy hand towards the door opposite. Lady Mary swept across the hall and went in. The room was the same as the first, with the exception of the root vegetables and hams. It was meagrely furnished. A large bed covered with a pieced quilt, in pink and white with a green border, half filled the room. A dressing table, flounced with a coarse muslin ruffle, stood beneath the dormer window. A strip of ruffle lay on the floor, and a pair of scissors, as if the work of decoration had been interrupted.

"Put my bag on the dressing table, Marita," Lady Mary said. "I suppose this will have to do." She turned to the open-mouthed landlord. "I shall want the room next to me for my woman, when she comes. You can put my menservants elsewhere."

"But, madam! madam! I can not let you have this room!" the landlord cried. "What will I say to his Excellency when he comes? You must not stay here. I have no other room suitable for a governor's wife. Madam, I beg you, please take the room across the hall. My wife will remove the hams and vegetables. Even, she will spread her best quilt across the bed, and there is a trundle underneath for the young miss." He smiled, uncertainly, hoping that he had solved the problem.

Lady Mary did not appear to hear him. She tossed her bonnet on the bed and removed her gloves. "Have a boy bring more wood for the fireplace," she said. "I am thoroughly chilled."

"But the Governor's lady! Madam, what will I do about the Governor's lady?" The man's face had such a comical expression of bewilderment that Marita was forced to suppress her laughter behind her muff.

"The Governor's lady shall have the room across the hall and your wife's beautiful new quilt." Lady Mary replied. "I intend to remain here." She sat down in the goose-necked rocker. "Put the candles on the table and bring up a dozen more. I can't abide a gloomy room. And plenty of hot water, landlord—two big ewers, and have it really hot. I feel the need of a good bath, after today's journey."

The man shrugged his heavy shoulders hopelessly and backed out of the room. Lady Mary laughed suddenly. When she laughed she looked young, almost as young as Marita.

"My dear, I thought for a moment we would have to go back to that wretched room. But we won. Take a lesson,

Marita. You must always be firm if you want to accomplish anything. Firm enough to convince the other person that you will not give way." She laughed again. "That's something my father taught me when I was a child, when he came to visit my mother and me." She stopped suddenly at the sight of Marita's questioning eyes. "It was when we were at Tunbridge Wells one summer, taking the waters," she added.

"Was your father my own grandfather, Aunt Mary?" Marita asked, her eyes alight with interest.

Lady Mary's expression changed. "Certainly he was your grandfather." She spoke sharply. "Marita, I've told you often that when the right time comes, you will be told about your parents. Let's have no more questions. It isn't important who your forebears are ... it is what you make yourself, please remember."

"Yes, Aunt, I will remember," she answered obediently. It is always like this, she thought; a word now and then—never enough.

The clattering of harness, neighing of horses, baying of hounds announced the arrival of the other coaches. Lady Mary looked out the window.

"It's Madam Catha," she told Marita. "Won't she be annoyed when she finds I have taken the choice room! I'm not sorry. I'm weary of her airs. She makes such a fuss about her husband being 'cousin of the Queen.' Why, I am—" She shut her mouth firmly. Marita sighed. Some day she would tell her. Some day all the obscurity would fade—the veil that linked her to the past would be lifted. She was old enough now to know; whatever it was, disgrace or horror, she could endure—surely to know about her mother, her father, whoever they were, was better than this uncertainty. But it was no use to ask. Lady Mary, under her casual indifference, was as firm and stubborn as a man, and as ruthless, if the occasion warranted.

"When they come upstairs, Marita, tell Madam Hyde that I am resting and cannot be disturbed." Fitting her words into action, Lady Mary loosened her bodice and threw herself on the bed. "Send Desham up as soon as she comes. I want her to rub my shoulder. This rain has brought out all the aches and pains."

Marita covered her with a fur cloak and went out. At the foot of the stairs, she heard Madam Catha arguing with the landlord. She peeped over the stair rail. She could see Madam Hyde, surrounded by the children, Miss Mittie and the

14

servants. They blocked the hall and stairway. From where she stood they looked curiously flattened, like big, puffy pincushions. Madam Catha's hoop swayed and billowed as she gesticulated and waved her hands at the landlord.

"It's unthinkable!" she cried, her voice high-pitched in annoyance. "How could you allow anyone to have the rooms the Governor reserved for me? Will you please order the people out at once!" She stamped her foot, angrily. "I shall tell the Governor—"

The landlord held out a protesting hand. "No! No! No! Don't do that, madam. The lady was firm, very firm. I would not want to make any more argument with her. We have another room awaiting your inspection, a superior room, madam."

"I'll look at it, but if I don't like it . . ." Madam Catha marched up the steps, her flounces rattling, her mouth firmly set, showing her strong intent.

Marita stepped forward at the head of the stairs and put a finger to her lips. "My aunt is resting," she said, in her husky voice. "She is very tired. She had no maid to help her, as you know. She asked me to tell you that she is really quite annoyed that her woman was not here when she arrived. She said to remind you that you promised Desham would be here."

Madam Catha flushed angrily, but Marita went on before she had time to speak: "If I were you, Madam Hyde, I wouldn't disturb her before she is rested. You know how my aunt is when she is tired—and annoyed."

"This oaf didn't tell me it was Lady Mary who had my room. It is quite all right, my dear." She turned to the landlord who waited, a harassed look on his red, seamed face.

"There is really no difference in the rooms at all," Marita said, soothingly. She gave a quick glance beyond the door which a slatternly servant held open. The landlord had done what he promised. The hams and root vegetables had been removed, and a blue and green quilt covered the four-poster. Madam Catha glanced in. "This is a pretty place for a Governor's wife to lay her head," she said harshly. "If this is a sample of what we shall find in North Carolina I've a mind to turn back to Williamsburg."

Marita said, "Parson Urmston told us there were some very nice houses in Queen Anne's Town and many large plantation houses on the Sound shore and up the Chowan River."

"Colonel Byrd told me quite a different story," Madam Catha said shortly, but she stepped into the room and allowed her woman to remove her wraps. The children followed Miss Mittie down the hall to their room. After a moment Madam Catha smiled at Marita. "You are a dear child, Marita. I know you are just as tired as we are. We'll all feel better after we have had some hot tea ... run along and rest."

Madam Catha is really nice, she thought. She is kind and sweet when she forgets that she has come into a high position. In spite of her youth, Marita was observing. Since she did not talk much, she had time to listen.

She found Desham with Lady Mary. The maid had already opened boxes and dressing cases and laid out a black taffeta gown with a broad band of Lyons velvet around the full skirt.

"Where have you been, Marita?" her aunt asked when she came into the room. "Come freshen yourself and change your frock. I'm going to allow you to have supper downstairs. Captain Gregory has sent word that his cook is preparing the haunch of venison that Governor Spottswood sent me. We are to have a really decent meal in the little dining-room off the ordinary." She patted Marita's cheek with her cool fingers. "You've been such a good child and not complained, all this horrible journey, so you may ..."

"Come down for dessert?" Marita laughed, suddenly gay.

Lady Mary laughed with her. This had been a little game between them, ever since she was a small child staying at the manor house down in Sussex. Marita always begged her aunt to let her come down from the nursery for dessert. Sometimes Lady Mary was lenient, and she was allowed to sit in a very large chair at a very long table while a liveried footman brought her pudding.

Desham relaxed her grim look as she helped Marita into a simple brown woollen frock and brushed her bright hair into place. Lady Mary sat at the dressing table. She had taken the small key from the chain about her neck and opened the Morocco-leather case. Inside was a little mirror with a carved wooden frame to which the old gilding still clung. It was very delicate and beautiful in design, and there was a carved cipher with a crown at the top. Lady Mary noticed Marita's eyes on the mirror.

16

"It will be yours, one day, my child. Promise me you will take good care of it, always. It is your only inheritance from your grandfather . . . that and one other thing." Her face was very grave as she spoke. "Promise me, Marita, when the mirror is yours, you will never part with it until you give it to your own daughter."

"I promise," Marita answered, catching some of her aunt's seriousness, ". . . but suppose you should have a daughter of your own, one day . . . ?"

Lady Mary drew Marita to her in a sudden rush of tenderness. "If I have a dozen children, the mirror will still be yours, my dear. I have given orders to my solicitor, Mr. Pell, in Lincoln's Inn. When I die . . ."

Martha buried her face against her aunt's soft breast. "Don't, don't say that. It's an ill omen to speak of death. I cannot bear it. I have no one but you—no one."

Lady Mary shook her gently. "You'll have a husband, one of these days, silly girl. Then you'll forget about your tempestuous old aunt." She laughed, but Marita saw her eyes were wet.

"See what you have done! Desham, bring my dressing case; this child has made me weep."

They were interrupted by a knock at the door. The serving girl stood at the door, wiping her red hands with her apron. "Captain Gregory's compliments and will the ladies join him at supper?"

Lady Mary stood up, turning slowly before the dressing-table mirror. She pulled a blonde curl over her smooth shoulder. What she saw satisfied her. "Come, Marita, let us go down," she said.

The dinner was long. The men did full justice to the haunch of venison and the wine the Governor of Virginia had sent to Lady Mary. After the toast to the Queen, the women folk went to their rooms, Lady Mary pleading weariness from the long journey.

Marita went to the bedchamber she was to share with Miss Mittie and the children. She felt strangely exhilarated—the strange country and the people interested her. She did not undress, in spite of Miss Mittie's importuning. Instead she pulled a chair to the little dormer window and sat down.

The rain had ceased and a few stars shone above the trees. The clean rain-washed odour of the pines refreshed her. She leaned her elbows on the sill. She loved the night loneliness.

Her old nurse often told her she was a child of the night, a moon child. Libra born. Libra's children are nurtured by solitude. Tomorrow they would reach the Ablemarle, the great body of water that cut inland from the sea. The name had a new significance now. A great county which bordered on the Sound, named after the warrior duke George Monk, one of the first named "true and lawful proprietors" of the vast land of the Carolinas.

She was roused from her thoughts by men's voices. She heard the clink of a harness and the stamping and pawing of horses, then the tremulous bleating of sheep. She leaned forward. She could see the stockade, and the drovers herding sheep in through the narrow gate. Beyond were the cattle. Men, ill clad in rough-woven clothes, were shouting and cursing.

A moment later she saw two riders approaching from the north, along the road they had travelled. They rode up to the front of the inn and dismounted, tossing their reins to a stable boy. She could see them plainly as they walked up the steps to the ordinary, their spurs jingling. She recognized the taller of the two. He was the blond Quaker with the strange hat they had met on the road that afternoon.

At the door of the inn they met Lovyck and James Stephenson coming out. She heard Anthony's voice, a little thick from wine. "Ah, it's our fine Quaker. I thought you were running sheep across the border, without benefit of tax."

"The sheep are across the border," the Quaker said.

Anthony resented the Quaker's calm. He resented his attitude of indifference, as he had that afternoon. "I don't like the hat you wear," he said, suddenly quarrelsome. "Take it off in the presence of gentlemen."

"I should be pleased to do so, if I were to meet a gentleman."

"By God, you are insolent!" Lovyck's voice was loud and angry. "Put up your sword!"

"I am unarmed," the Quaker said, and to Stephenson, "Better take thy hotheaded friend to bed before I put his head under the pump for cooling."

"I will, I will indeed," James Stephenson said. "Come, Mr. Lovyck. Come with me."

"I don't want to go to bed. I want to fight," Anthony answered.

"Better fight sleep," the Quaker laughed. "Come, Edward, let's get food. I am fair starving."

Marita leaned from the window, hoping to have another glimpse of the tall young Quaker. At that moment he looked up, and she drew back hastily. What if he should have seen her gawking like a country girl, with her braids over her shoulder? A moment later she heard his clear voice saying:

"The fine-feathered fool! I'll cross swords with him one day."

The man with him answered, consternation in his tones: "Michael, thee must not speak such thoughts. Thee must remember thee is now a Quaker, and Quakers do not resort to swords."

Michael's laugh came to Marita's ears, full-bodied and strong. "I'll have to be one of the fighting Quakers, Edward. I can't allow my sword arm to go stiff with disuse."

Marita moved back from the window. Crossing the room in the dark, she stumbled against a chair.

Miss Mittie weakened. "Marita, are you still up? Don't you know you must get your sleep? We are leaving at sunrise. Have you forgotten we are to meet the Governor tomorrow, and sail up the river to Balgray?"

Marita remembered. She crept into bed and pulled the covers up to her chin. She was smiling a little when she dropped off to sleep, to dream of a drove of bleating sheep on the forest road, and a tall young drover with penetrating blue eyes.

Chapter 3

SCUPPERNONG GRAPES

THE two young men, Michael Cary and Edward Tomes, opened the door and went into the ordinary. The air reeked with stale beer and the smoke of strong tobacco. To this was added the steam arising from damp wool, from rain-soaked capes and cloaks drying on chair backs near the fire hearth.

The room was crowded—drovers and herdsmen and trappers, border people with stern, craggy faces bronzed by wind and sun and lined by hard living. Their bodies were hard and muscular, and their eyes keen and wary as are the eyes of men who live in forests or on the sea. Inured to hard usage by nature and their fellows, they looked on strangers with suspicion, as potential enemies. They sat at the long rough tables, drank their small beer and buttered rum, and played at dice, lifting their rough voices to curse their luck or raising their fists in anger at a fancied slight, kicking at the black potboys when overslow to bring their liquor.

Michael crossed the room to an empty table beyond the roaring fire. Edward, mild and soft-spoken, followed him. Many of the men knew Edward as the eldest son of Foster Tomes, the only Quaker leader who sat on the Council as a representative of the Lords Proprietors.

Michael gave the order for their supper to a slovenly black slave, and settled back to survey the room. His eyes fell on a stocky redfaced man dozing on a settle near the fire, a tall pewter tankard on a table at his elbow. From his dress Michael took him for a man of consequence. Buff-coated, with a collar of embroidered linen about his full throat, he wore fine doeskin breeches and well-made boots drawn high above his knees. A short dagger was sheathed at his leather belt, and a brace of pistols lay on the table. His chin was sunk in his waistcoat and his white, full-bottomed wig was a little awry, giving it a rakish look.

Michael turned to Edward and raised his eyebrows.

" 'Tis Mr. Thomas Pollock of Balgray," Edward informed him. "He is a member of the Council with my father, and he owns more than fifty thousand acres of rich land up on the Chowan River at the head of Albemarle Sound." He hesitated, then added, "He and thy uncle are unfriendly."

Michael nodded. He had heard the name of Pollock many times since he had been at the home of his uncle, Thomas Cary, at Romney Marsh. Unfriendly was a mild word to describe the feeling that existed between the two men, for Pollock was the acknowledged leader of the Church faction as Cary was the leader of the Quakers and Dissenters. The controversy had gone on for some years, until his uncle, armed with authority from the Governor at Charles Town, had controlled the Assembly, deposed Pollock's candidate, William Glover, and driven the two men out of the government into Virginia. Since Queen Anne came to the throne, this factional war had gone on, Cary standing for the Quakers and the Dissenters, and Glover, holding his appointment from the Lords Proprietors in London, representing the Government party and the established Church. The people of the Province, unable to decide which man ruled or whose laws to obey, in consequence obeyed no laws at all.

Michael had seldom been in Albemarle since his arrival in the Province. For the most part he had stayed at Romney Marsh, his uncle's seat on Pamticoe Sound, occasionally sailing to the Bahamas or St. Kitts with a cargo of pine poles or tar. He spent his time hunting and trapping, or drilling the men his uncle maintained as a guard. News that a new governor was coming to the Province had brought Thomas Cary in haste to Pequimans Precinct.

"That makes three of us," he said to Michael. "Two too many, to my thinking. If they think to oust me, there will be another fight on their hands." Michael hoped that were true. He wanted a fight. His men were ready and eager.

Now Edward interrupted his thoughts. "Thee has a stern look, Michael, as if thee were again honing for a fight. Sometimes I wonder if thee will ever be a true Friend." There was amusement in his eyes, and a little smile lurked in the corners of his mouth. "My sister Lucretia says it will take thee a long time; thee is more of a fighting Quaker, like thy uncle and Emanuel Low."

Michael laughed. "I notice your sister is usually right, Edward. At that moment I was thinking of fighting."

"It was plain to see," Edward said mildly.

The slave came then and set the meal in front of them: bacon fried crisp, corn made into grits, with a rich gravy to cover it, and little cakes of meal baked in the ashes.

While they were eating, the door opened and a rider came into the ordinary, followed by a Negro slave. The men about the table spoke respectfully; some of them got up from their chairs to bow as he passed.

The new arrival was well proportioned, tall, with an upright carriage. His light brown hair was his own and he wore no wig. His keen grey eyes swept the room as he waited for his slave to remove the long blue cape from his shoulders and spread it to dry.

The newcomer stood for a moment smiling, as he looked at Pollock dozing near the fire.

Edward leaned forward and dropped his voice: "It's Edward Moseley, the Chief Justice."

Michael had never seen Moseley before. The Chief Justice had been at Romney Marsh several times, but always while

Michael was away. He was his uncle's friend, holding office by Thomas Cary's influence, an outspoken man of commanding presence whose plantation, Moseley Hall, on Albemarle Sound, was a few miles east of Queen Anne's Town.

Pollock opened his eyes and saw Moseley. He sat up quickly and straightened his wig. "Ah, Moseley," he said, putting out his hand, "it is good to see you again. I heard in Queen Anne's Town that you were holding court in this district, but I didn't think I'd have the good fortune to see you."

Moseley sat down on the other side of the table. "This is a pleasure, Tom. I had not heard that you had returned after your long absence in Virginia. What brought you back?"

A look of annoyance crossed Pollock's ruddy face, gone in a moment. "I came with the new Governor, Mr. Edward Hyde," he said, a note of triumph in his voice.

Moseley smiled. "I heard Mr. Hyde was on his way when I stopped at Councilman Chevin's in Pasquotank last night."

"Well, it's the truth. We came down the Chowan two weeks ago in my sloop. My wife has opened the manor house at Balgray again, and we are ready to receive the Governor's lady and her party."

"Oh!" said Moseley, "Mr. Hyde's lady is coming? I heard of her from William Byrd when I was in Virginia. He said she was a woman of abundant life."

"And what did Colonel Byrd say of our new Governor?"

"Byrd told me that Mr. Edward Hyde was a pleasant gentleman, but he doubted that he had much ability in political matters."

This reply angered Pollock. "How does William Byrd know about that—whether he has ability or not? There's too much talk going about. Why, North Carolina is the laughing stock of Virginia and all the other colonies! Yes, and England too. If the Lords Proprietors and their man Tynte could agree, we'd have government instead of no government at all." His voice rose in keeping with his anger. "Haven't I been bedeviled enough to know? Three governors in one colony. It's fair ridiculous, Moseley."

"We could get along with less," Moseley answered. "We've had a taste of Cary the Quaker, and Glover the Churchman. Now if he can get himself seated, we will see whether the Queen's cousin can establish order in the Albemarle. I've an idea it will not be an easy task, Pollock. The people have been promised too much and received too little."

22

"At least Glover is honest," Pollock flared. "He didn't use land money for himself or give out false land grants."

"That's what all you Churchmen say . . ."

"Well, it's more than you can say about that damn' rascal, Cary."

At the sound of his name, Michael pushed back his chair. In spite of Edward's effort to prevent him, he got up and crossed the room to the men sitting at the fire. He bowed to Moseley respectfully. His voice was quiet, but his eyes had anger in them. "I thought I heard you call my name, sir," he said to Pollock.

Pollock returned his steady look. There was annoyance on his moody face at the interruption. "I do not know you, young sir; nor have I heard your name, much less spoken it."

"My name is Cary, Michael Cary." He paused a moment. "Governor Thomas Cary is my uncle. I am empowered to speak for him when he is not present." He stood quietly.

Pollock's face crimsoned. "Why, you young jackanapes! How can you have the insolence to speak—"

Moseley interrupted him. He rose to his feet, a cordial smile coming to his lean face. "It pleasures me to meet the son of my old friend Richard Cary." He clasped Michael's hand cordially. "Your uncle has spoken of you, Michael." He turned to Pollock. "Allow me to present Michael Cary. I knew his father and his mother many years ago in Antigua."

Michael bowed stiffly.

"Colonel Pollock lives up the Chowan River at Balgray plantation," Moseley said. "We are the best of friends, although we sometimes disagree on questions of government."

Pollock nodded sourly. He was exasperated at being put in the wrong by the keen-witted Moseley.

Michael refused Moseley's invitation to be seated. "I'm with Edward Tomes," he said. "We've just come down from driving a flock of friend Tomes's sheep over into Virginia."

"Without paying the border toll, I'll warrant," Pollock said.

Michael did not answer. He bowed again, and went back to the table. "I don't like his ways," Michael said as he sat down.

"Thee means friend Pollock? My father says he speaks harshly but his heart is kind."

The scowl on Michael's face faded. "Your father is a good man. He thinks no ill of anyone. I wonder if I can ever be as good a Friend as he. I try hard, but sometimes I forget . . ."

"Do not be discouraged, Michael. Thee has been one of us for so short a time. I think thee knows there are few among the Friends like my father," Edward answered. "Come, let us go to our room. I am weary from all this travelling and we must rise early if we are to meet thy uncle tomorrow morning at Nixon's Ferry."

They paid their reckoning and left.

Edward Moseley watched them cross the room. "That was a sad thing," he said to Pollock. "His father was killed at Antigua while defending Governor Parke from the mob. A fine man and a brave one was Richard Cary."

"Parke wasn't worth defending. Better have let the mob take him at the beginning."

Moseley's face hardened. "There are two opinions on that, Pollock. I knew him in England. I don't hold with your belief that Daniel Parke was a scoundrel. Nor can any thinking man condone mob action. I believe in liberty for the common people, but liberty under the law." He got up. "I'm riding on tonight," he remarked, as he took up his travelling cape. "I have to hold court tomorrow afternoon at Queen Anne's Town. A witchcraft case, I understand. Somehow I don't relish the task. One never knows what will happen with such cases."

Pollock nodded. He rose and stretched his arms. "I'm going to rest here tonight. It was too late to pay my respects to Madam Hyde and her party when I got in. They had already retired."

Moseley said, "Oh, so it's Madam Hyde's fine coach I saw in the stable yard? Is Edward Hyde here also?"

"No. He is to meet us tomorrow at Pequimans Landing, where I have my boats ready to sail up to Balgray plantation."

Moseley clasped his cape and signalled his slave, who was sitting on the floor near the door. "I will come up to Balgray one day soon to pay my respects to Mr. Hyde. Perhaps I can persuade my neighbour, Roger Mainwairing, to sail up with me in his boat. My shallop is on the ways on the Pasquotank being painted and calked."

"We will be pleased to welcome you, and Roger too. The Governor has been inquiring about him"—Pollock's eyes twinkled a little—"and about you also, Moseley. He wants to meet all the Albemarle leaders. I told him it was wasted time to talk with you Caryites, but he insists that he must talk with everyone to hear what they have to say about conditions in Albemarle."

Moseley smiled a little grimly. "He will hear things he won't like if he questions me, Pollock. As much as I want law established in this county, I would not want to stand in Edward Hyde's shoes. I can see dark days ahead of him before he wins the loyalty of our people. He must remember that we are stubborn people. Five times we have thrown out unworthy governors."

"I told him that. I advised him to let you all stew in your own juice, but he will not listen. A fair stubborn man is Governor Hyde, for all his quiet ways."

Lady Mary's coach arrived first at the landing at the Narrows of the Pequimans River. Governor Hyde was waiting for them at the periauger which was to take them up the Sound to Thomas Pollock's plantation, Balgray. Hyde was a tall man, spare of frame, a little stooped. His mouth was half concealed by a small waxed moustache and pointed beard, but his dark, deep-set eyes and drooping lids gave him a startling resemblance to his uncle, whose name he bore, Edward Hyde the first Lord Clarendon. He had an air of quiet dignity and the composure that goes with an assured position.

He assisted Lady Mary from her coach and kissed her hand. The little crowd of country folk who stood on the banks glanced at one another with expressionless faces.

Lady Mary said, "I ought not to speak to you or anyone else at this hour. Fancy leaving one's bed before sunrise."

Hyde smiled at her affectionately. "I knew I could count on you to be on time, Mary. Punctuality is a prerogative of royalty."

"Such gallantry at this hour is incredible." But Marita knew that her aunt was pleased.

Lovyck joined them, followed by the young tutor, Stephenson. They both showed evidence of the evening's dissipation, for they had lingered long at table after the women left the night before, finishing off Governor Spottswood's wine and brandy.

Lovyck said, "I swear I will never drink again. My head is as heavy as lead and fit to burst with aching. Here comes Gregory. He doesn't show any sign of guzzling. I know he drank three glasses to my one."

Captain Gregory laughed. "Remember, I've been to the

Low Country wars, and had my tests. I know how much I can hold and keep my head." He turned to Lady Mary. "These two had a contest last night, trying to recite the names of the Albemarle rivers. You should have heard them struggling with Pequimans, Pasquotank, and Currituck. I was fit to burst with laughter."

Anthony looked annoyed. "You should have seen our brave Captain, Lady Mary, waving his sword, shouting, 'Broadswords and the Queen, to arms! Follow John Churchill, the hero of Blenheim!'" He broke off suddenly as the second coach drove up to the landing.

Madam Hyde and the children and Miss Mittie got out of the chaise. Madam Catha walked mincingly, picking her way over the rough boards of the wharf. She wore a nut-brown woollen gown banded in mink. With one hand she lifted her skirts, and in the other she carried a small barrel muff. Her little bonnet had a mink head set in a rosette of brown riband. To the men standing at the wharf she inclined her head with exactly the right degree of gracious casualness.

"All Madam Catha needs is the red carpet," Lady Mary said, in an audible aside to Lovyck.

An angry flush crept up Madam Hyde's face but her set smile did not change.

"She's quite ready to greet the populace," Lady Mary went on. "She is really very remarkable. One might think she were Queen Anne herself, or Sarah Churchill." Lovyck covered his mouth with his fingers to hide an involuntary smile. Marita was embarrassed. Madam Catha would be hurt at Lady Mary's remarks. No one wants to be made to appear ridiculous, she thought sagely. She didn't understand why her aunt bothered. No matter how hard Madam Hyde tried, she could not acquire Lady Mary's natural distinction or her detached indifference.

Now, wrapped in an old tartan of the Stuart clan, her hair blown by the wind, Lady Mary looked far more the great lady than did the Governor's wife for all her fine raiment.

The loungers around the wharf recognized that. More than one whispered as she passed: " 'Tis the new Governor's lady, the one with the pale gold hair."

Lady Mary heard and smiled wickedly. Marita didn't like her in this mood. Why not let Madam Hyde have her little triumph? Who was there to see? A few rough country folk, yeomen and herders, a dozen red Indians squatting on the river bank, half a dozen Quaker gentlemen in dun-coloured clothes and wide black hats.

Colonel Pollock waited at the float where his periauger was moored, a big, clumsy boat that would hold thirty or forty people. The boxes and luggage had already been loaded on a pontoon. There was room enough in the periauger to take the household servants, but Madam Hyde would not allow that. With the exception of Lady Mary's woman, Desham, and her own personal maid, the servants and slaves were being loaded into a long canoe which carried eight oars and a small sail.

Madam Hyde stepped into the boat gingerly and sat down in the stern, a child on each side of her, her skirts spread, both hands in her little muff. Lady Mary and Marita were in the bow with Miss Mittie, while the Governor and his aide took seats in the center, near Colonel Pollock.

The mate was ready to cast off when Pollock noticed eight or ten horsemen galloping down the dirt road toward the wharf. One of them hallooed and waved his hand.

"It's Colonel Cary and his men," the mate said. "Do you want we should hold?"

"Cast off," Pollock snapped. "I have nothing to say to that rascal."

Hyde got up from his seat and watched the approaching horsemen. "Wait," he said to Pollock, "I've a desire to meet this Mr. Cary I've heard so much about."

"Governor Cary, he calls himself," Pollock was angry. "Governor Cary! A fine governor he makes, robbing the Treasury for his own uses."

Hyde did not seem to hear. He moved over to the rail, waiting. The sun came up, touching the cypress trees on the long point, throwing their dark shadows into the darker water. A blue heron, startled by the sound of galloping horses, rose from the reeds uttering his raucous cry, and planed out of the marsh, long legs dangling. The little crowd on the river bank grouped themselves, Quakers on one side, Indians and slaves on the other.

Marita looked around. Captain Gregory had his short sword halfway out of the scabbard. Anthony Lovyck, close behind Hyde, fingered the grip of his pistol. She turned to Lady Mary to question her. Her aunt was leaning forward, her eyes alight with excitement. Madam Hyde gasped, her little muff close pressed to her full bosom.

What did it mean? Marita, too, leaned forward, watching

the approaching riders, feeling the tension that animated the whole ship's company.

The horsemen clattered down the wharf; the loose wooden planks rattled under the impact. Marita felt her throat tighten. Even at a distance she recognized the man of the Great Dismal and the Border Inn, the man called Michael.

The riders came down to the edge of the water, a dozen in all. The leader, Thomas Cary, was a tall man with a narrow saturnine face and brown hair hanging to his shoulders. He had a broad sash across his leather jerkin, and a silver buckle held his wide leather sword belt in place. His piercing eyes swept over the group in the periauger and came to rest on Edward Hyde.

"Mr. Hyde?" he said clearly.

"Governor Hyde!" Colonel Pollock snapped, stepping forward. "Give his Excellency his proper title, Mr. Cary!"

Cary did not glance at Pollock or appear to have heard his words. "I am Governor Thomas Cary, Mr. Hyde. I have come all the way from Bath Town to welcome you to our Province, but I see Thomas Pollock has already captured you."

Hyde ignored the implication. He remained quiet and unruffled by Cary's words. "I am honoured at your attention, Mr. Cary," he said. "But you have made a slight mistake as to the title. I come into this Province as its governor."

A thin smile crossed Cary's lips: "And your commission, sir? I presume you carry your lawful commission?"

Hyde's dark face turned a dull red. It was plain Cary knew what he had hoped would remain secret. He had no official commission. The Lords had left that to Tynte, who was the Governor of the Carolinas. Tynte had died before Hyde's ship reached Virginia and Hyde had nothing to prove his appointment but an unofficial letter written to him by one of the Lords Proprietors.

At Cary's words Captain Gregory stepped forward, his sword clear of the scabbard. He waited only for the word from the Governor. Hyde waved him back. His face was stern.

"That is a matter to be decided in Council, Mr. Cary."

Cary laughed loudly. "Thee need not think that the question of who is the lawful governor of this Province will be settled in Council. By God. sir, it is thee who are insolent! I say it will be decided by the people of Albemarle, in open Assembly; not by eight Councilmen, paid lackeys of eight

28

Lords Proprietors. The people rule here, Mr. Hyde, not the Council . . .

"I give warning now, sir. Thee will not walk into Assembly here, and make thyself governor. Ask the last Churchman governor, William Glover, why he fled to Virginia. Ask Pollock there why he has lived across the border for two years. Do not think it will be easy to overcome Thomas Cary's power or take authority from him. Good day, Mr. Hyde."

He spurred his horse sharply and galloped down the dirt road, followed by his men; all save Michael Cary. The young man rode close to the side of the periauger, where Marita sat, and dropped a cluster of amber grapes into her lap. He was laughing as his horse splashed into the water. A tendril of crimson vine caught a silver button of his cuff and held, a fragile chain binding them for a moment. He leaned in his saddle. "Eat of our Scuppernongs and you belong to us," he said so none could hear.

Marita did not stir, her great tawny eyes held by his. The movement of the boat snapped the vine; the leaves curled into a circle across her knees. Against the dull green of her gown, the grapes glowed clear amber.

Lady Mary spoke to her sharply. "Who is that fellow? What did he say to you?"

Marita felt the blood drive to her face. She could not answer. How could she repeat those swift-spoken words?

Pollock's angry voice saved her. He was standing in the boat, shaking his fist at Thomas Cary's back. "You impudent rascal! You damned insolent renegade! How dare you! You and your swaggering nephew and your rascally Cormorant's Brood." He sat down, suddenly unbalanced by the movement of the boat. Cary and his men were galloping swiftly into the green tunnel of the pines.

The impact of Pollock's rage and Hyde's complete silence lay heavy on them. Madam Catha's little muff rolled on the floor boards, forgotten. Her face was white, her eyes blazing.

"Edward," she whispered, "Edward, why didn't you strike him down?"

Edward Hyde did not answer. He turned away and took his place forward in the periauger. Marita had a glimpse of his deep sunken eyes as he turned. Her aunt was watching the fast-disappearing horsemen, a slight smile on her full red lips.

"A bold man," she said. "Bold and very handsome."

Marita did not speak. Her slim fingers touched the globes of tawny grapes. She pressed one to her lips. The taste was strange and intoxicating.

Chapter 4

DUKE ROGER

ROGER MAINWAIRING, planter, stood on the gallery of his manor house on Albemarle Sound and watched the shallop, *Golden Grain,* round the point and set a course for his wharf.

The ship was overdue and he had been somewhat worried about the mahogany logs that Captain Zeb Bragg was bringing up from the West Indies. He needed the logs for the flooring of his house, now near completion.

He was not alarmed about the Captain's ability to navigate the stormy Hatteras, or to show a clean pair of heels to any pirate ship that might be lurking in Teach's Hole, or behind the Banks.

His Negro *capita,* Metephele, came out on the gallery to bring Roger's frieze coat and broad hat, for the east wind was chill. "Captain got the logs of the master on the deck," he said.

Roger looked more closely. "You are right, Metephele. Go tell Mr. Vescels to have the oxen sent down to the wharf so the boys can drag the logs to the shop. I want the carpenter to get to work on the puncheons for the great-room floor."

Metephele said, "Hit tak' sharp saw to strip that mahogany. When we live St. Kitts, two, maybe three, boys work dat saw."

"Yes, you are right. Take the Antigua boys for the sawing."

"Dose boys work late cotton—dat field by Mulberry Hill."

"Take the Jamaica boys then. Don't use the Guinea blacks. They don't understand how to work mahogany."

Roger walked through the garden toward the wharf. He was a tall man, several inches above six feet, with broad shoulders, a flat back, and narrow waist. He held himself well, and he had the lean, muscular hardness of a man who lives in the saddle. His blue eyes were clear and direct, the eyes of a marksman, and his high-bridged nose and strong jaw gave character to his face. His light hair was burned yellow by the sun, for he wore no wig, and his skin was bronzed by the sun and the wind.

Captain Bragg was a welcome visitor. Through him Roger kept in touch with the world left behind him when he came to the Carolinas from the West Indies and took up land in the Albemarle some years before. Roger liked to talk of the islands and the island people. Occasionally he would lure the Captain ashore to spend the night at Queen's Gift. They would play at piquet, drink deeply of brandy and the Captain's rum, and talk of the growing trade with Jamaica and the Barbadoes, of pirate ships harboured in New Providence, of tobacco shipments, and cargoes of tar and pitch for the Indies in return for salt and spices, sugar and tropic fruits.

When Roger reached the steps that led down to the wharf, he turned around to view the house. The place looked best from the water, with the forest behind it. He had built the new Queen's Gift on the foundation of the old house that had been destroyed by fire—the same West Indian house with square pillars supporting wide double galleries. The outside of the house was all finished. Some interior work was still to be completed. Now that the Captain had brought the hardwood, the puncheon floors could be laid in the great room.

Metephele came up to him and waited for Roger's permission to speak.

"Well, what is it, Metephele?" Roger said, as the Negro stood, turning his wide braid hat in his hand. "What do you want this time?"

"Hit's the doors, Master. Do the master wish doors to keep out the spirits?"

Roger did not laugh at the question. He did not even smile. He knew the black man's mind too well to make light of his taboos.

"Certainly we will have witch doors. Measure them correctly so that the crosses have the right proportions. We want them exactly like the ones we had at the St. Kitts plantation."

The Negro's face cleared. "Yes, sir. That we do, Master—like the doors at St. Kitts." He reflected a moment. "Recollect the time bad spirits come to door of the master, to lay a spell, but he flew right away on account of de spirit door?"

He remembered. Some disgruntled native on Captain

Haimes's sisal plantation had tried to put a spell on him, so the natives thought, by making a little image of clay in Roger's likeness, stuck through the vital parts with poison thorns so that he would die in agony.

"On account of spirit door, the master lives," Metephele said with conviction.

"That was in the West Indies, Metephele. I don't believe that the evil spirits have jumped across the water to the Carolinas." The worried expression returned on the slave's face. Roger knew what he was thinking. He said, "But we will have witch doors throughout the house, outside and in."

The Negro was satisfied. He squared his shoulders and moved off briskly. At least the house of the master would be protected from bad spirits, the *Mankwala* of black men. There were still the evils of white men but Metepehele did not give any thought to these things. His concern was to protect the house of the master from the black man's evil spirits. The master would have his own ways to protect himself from white men's magic.

Roger watched the ship swing into the protection of the little cove and come to anchor. The water was too shallow for the *Golden Grain* to lie at the float. The deck men could heave the logs overboard and his slaves float them to the sandy beach, where the oxen would snake them up the road to the sheds.

When the unloading was finished the Captain would come ashore to breakfast. After that they would haggle over the inventory and costs of transportation, for Roger now had a share in the *Golden Grain*.

There was a firm friendship between the young planter and the grey-haired old sea captain. The Captain was older than Roger by twenty years, his face seamed with the cross-winds of seas. They had been friends ever since the time Roger Mainwairing was an indentured man serving his bond.

For Roger Mainwairing "rode with the Duke" and for his adherence to the lost cause of Monmouth he had been sent to St. Kitts, there to serve for seven years on the sisal plantation of one Haimes, a planter.

At midnight one rainy night, twelve young gentlemen, Roger leading them, had left their college at Oxford and ridden away in the night to Dorset. What did lads of fifteen and sixteen know of the intrigues of a profligate Court, the plots of unscrupulous ministers, of hatreds between Whigs and Tories? They cared not at all whether King James was

Protestant or Papist. But to a King who meted punishment to one man of seventeen hundred lashes, twice in twenty-four hours, they had no allegiance. Instead they swore to ride with the young Duke of Monmouth, now in exile in Holland. He would come to England and rouse the countryside. He would have their loyalty and the strength of their swords.

And so they rode down into Dorset and foregathered with farmers and country folk and the Campbells under Argyle, the Covenanter. A long ride, to defeat at Sedgemoor. A long ride that led them straight to Jeffreys and his "Bloody Assizes."

And then the King's vengeance. Monmouth beheaded. Argyle beheaded. Three hundred men swinging from the gibbet. A thousand men made bondsmen for seven years.

Roger Mainwairing stood in the dock and heard his own sentence from the lips of Bloody Jeffreys, heard the sentence of the aged Lady Lisle, to be burnt alive for harbouring a fugitive from Sedgemoor. After that sentence to a noble woman, seven years on the sisal plantation of Haimes were reprieve.

But to work in the fields under the broiling tropic sun, to work as a beast of burden, carrying a load as a slave—that was hard for a lad of breeding and spirit.

One day his master noticed the tall blond lad working in a field with blacks. Haimes sent for Roger to question him. Roger was defiant. He stood facing his master, his steady blue eyes wrathful and unafraid.

Said Haimes, "Damnation on an overlooker who will put a lad like you to work in the fields!"

After that the world changed for Roger. He had clean white clothes, work in the counting house, and a master who taught him to love the soil and the product of the soil.

That seemed a long time ago. Haimes had trusted him, trained him, and when his seven years were up, had paid him well. He owned three thousand acres of woodlands and fields, fishing rights and a great plantation in the Carolinas on Albemarle Sound.

But he did not forget Haimes and his kindness. Nor did he ever lose faith in the soil, which had given him strength and protection. Men had failed him more than once; the land never.

The years had not dimmed that awful day when he stood in court and heard Bloody Jeffreys pronounce the doom of a thousand men. Never once did he blame Monmouth—only the people who had promised to support him, to rise to arms when he called, and who were afraid when the time came—people who had thought too much of their security to strike a blow for freedom. For these men Roger had only contempt.

As Roger walked up and down on the float waiting for the *Golden Grain* to anchor in deep water and send a boat ashore, he remembered the day he had first sailed up Albemarle Sound on the *Kentish Maid*. He had stood on the bridge looking with eager eyes on this new land—its blue water, green pines, and dark, rich earth. But as he had set foot on the crude wharf, not even the beauty and fragrance, gaiety and colour could dispel his sudden loneliness. For the first time, the thought of a home for himself had come to him.

At the edge of the village Roger had stopped to lean against a whitewashed gate, watching the rhythmic movement of a Negro working a small patch of cotton. The bushes were heavy with the largest white bolls he had ever seen.

"The land is very fertile," Roger said.

The old Negro straightened himself and mopped his forehead with the back of his gnarled, black hand. "Sir, it is the Garden of Eden."

The Garden of Eden . . . Here Mainwairing had bought his broad acres and established his plantation, Queen's Gift. The years had given him position and wealth.

Roger Mainwairing lived alone in the big new house. The Soundside planters and his friends in Queen Anne's Town, a few miles west of his plantation boundaries, laughed at him for building the double-galleried West Indian house in the Carolinas. For a man not yet married it was too large and spacious. Roger only laughed and kept his silence. The Chowan River planters had a life of their own and there was close intimacy and intermarrying among the families who lived at the head of the Sound and along the Chowan and Roanoke Rivers. Then there were the shy little Quaker girls of Pasquotank and Pequimans Precincts: the Durants, the Phillipses and the Tomeses. The Pequimans Churchmen had large families, too. Roger knew them all: the Saundersons, the Skinners, the Swanns, and the Relfs. He danced with the girls and drank their fathers' homemade wines, but he courted none of them.

Roger remembered an English girl, Rhoda Chapman, a girl he had met in Jamaica. She was the sister of Tom

Chapman, one of the twelve young lads from Oxford who had thrown their fortunes with the Duke of Monmouth. They came from the Midlands of England, not far from his own home near Market Harborough. It was at a ball at Jamaica Government House that he ran across Tom Chapman. They had not seen each other since the days following the Rebellion, when they all but lost their heads. Tom had been sent to Jamaica; he to St. Kitts. While they were talking, a girl came up, followed by a young officer. She was tall and slender, with Irish blue eyes, and her shining black hair was wreathed in white ginger flowers.

She caught at Tom's hand. "Darling," she said, "darling, Captain Disart has asked me to ride in the morning. I told him I had no mount, but he says he will set me up. I told him we were driving out to Ravenwood at dawn, but he won't take no for an answer."

Tom smiled and patted her hand. Roger saw the girl could wind him around her finger. "Do you want to ride, Rhoda?" he asked.

"You know I do." Her voice was deep and a little husky. "I love an early morning ride."

Tom said, "This is Roger Mainwairing, Rhoda. Captain Disart, Mr. Mainwairing. Mr. Mainwairing is an old friend whom I have not seen for years. He came in today on the packet from Carolina."

After the introduction he turned back to Rhoda. "Surely you remember about Roger, darling. We were talking only a few days ago of some of the escapades he got me into when I was his fag."

Rhoda's dark blue eyes met Roger's; hers shone with gaiety and friendliness. "Indeed I remember how you used to tell tales of Roger Mainwairing, who talked you into joining the Duke! I was a little girl then, a very little girl." Laughter lurked in her eyes, and in the corners of her lips. "I think you were my first hero." She turned to include Captain Disart. "You know every small girl has heroes, usually the friends of her older brothers."

Roger said, "I suppose I should feel a certain pride in being a hero, but to be honest it makes me feel like rather an old fellow, tottering to his grave, you know."

"No! No!" Rhoda said, the colour rising to her smooth cheek. "Please, Mr. Mainwairing."

"About the morning ride," suggested the Captain, pulling at his white gloves.

35

"The ride? Oh, yes, of course." Tom turned to Rhoda, patting her cheek affectionately. "I've decided to stay over until Wednesday, so you may have your ride, my dear."

The music started up in the ballroom. The Captain glanced at Rhoda. "I believe it is a contradance. Shall we?"

"Yes. Thank you so much, Captain."

They started toward the ballroom. Rhoda turned and ran back, her white skirts whirling about her slim feet as she crossed the polished floor. "Why don't you ride with us tomorrow morning, Roger Mainwairing?" she cried.

"I shall be delighted," he answered. "I too enjoy my early morning ride."

That was the beginning. On Wednesday Roger went with them to Ravenwood, Tom's plantation not far from English Bay. He found Rhoda delightful company. They had many things in common besides their love of horses. At home in England she hunted with the Quorn. She knew all his people who lived in the Midlands, aunts and cousins he had not heard of for years. The visit passed too quickly for Roger. Rhoda liked him and had no hesitancy in letting him know it. He knew she looked on him as her brother's friend and contemporary. He made no sign that he regarded her in any other way than as the sister of his old friend, but his interest was deeper than that.

He saw her once after the Jamaica visit—this time in England, when he went to his father's old home, the first Queen's Gift, now passed into the hands of a distant relative.

Rhoda was even more attractive than he remembered. A little more mature, after a London season, but her love of hunting had not decreased. Roger saw her a few times, but always surrounded by the gay crowd of young people of the countryside. He did not stay long in England, for the little matter of being a rebel to the Crown had not been formally cleared. Queen Anne was not hard on Monmouth's followers. Churchill, who had put down the Rebellion by arms, had favored mercy for the rebels. Queen Anne had pardoned many, for she was herself a Protestant Stuart. But Roger had no time to go through the formalities. His own plantation in the Albemarle needed him. So he remained a rebel by act of the Crown.

But the impression Rhoda had made upon him the first time he had seen her remained. Roger thought of her now—

a woman a man would like for a friend or a comrade, and perhaps a wife.

Roger got in the boat and rowed out to the ship. The Captain was on deck watching the unloading. He greeted Roger with warmth and took with pleasure the twist of tobacco Roger offered, biting off a great piece. Between vigorous jaw movements, he said, "Well, I've heard ye've got a new governor, Duke. Have you seen him?"

"Mr. Hyde? No, I haven't gone up river to pay my respects yet. He's staying with Pollock at Balgray."

The old man spat expertly over the banister rail.

"You do everything with a vengeance in the Albemarle, don't you? One, two, three governors—which party do you favor, Ma'n'ring?"

"I'm trying to steer clear of their local fights, Captain. You know I'm no politician."

"I suppose it's the same old seven and six. What's your neighbour Moseley now, Surveyor General, or Attorney General?"

Roger grinned. "Moseley's Chief Justice this time—that is, if you hold with Cary as governor. You must say for Moseley that whatever office he fills, he fills well."

Bragg's eyes closed to a slit. "The juidiciary has come to a pretty pass, Duke. Think of naming that bumble-headed, seldom-thinking fool, Porter, Judge of the Admiralty Court! If ever there was a rascal, it's Porter. I had a little clash with him down at Bath Town that landed me in the Admiralty Court."

Roger smiled. Bragg was proud of evading the law, but a hundred others were proud of that in a hundred ways. It was not that the men were bad or evil-doers, but that the laws weren't planned to solve the problems of the new world. The idealistic Fundamental Constitution for the Carolinas, written by John Locke on the commission of the Lords Proprietors, was not all bad. It contained some good ideas about the common man's part in government that had never been tried before. But the men of Albemarle were resolute against it. They didn't want to wait for slow development in government. They were too impatient to give the Constitution a fair trial.

"I suppose you know I've sat on the Council these past six months," he said to Bragg. "I don't like to take the time. It's not pleasant hearing the eternal bickerings between Cary's and Glover's men, meeting after meeting. Perhaps sending Edward Hyde out was a master stroke; at least the people will respect the Queen's relative."

Bragg screwed up his weather-beaten face. "I heard up the James that he's a fair good fellow, and that Madam Hyde is a prime woman. She's brought a deal of luggage and a small army of servants, and intends to set up a little Court in Queen Anne's Town. Why, she's even brought plans to build a fine Governor's House right on the water, along the Common's Green; least that's what the preacher said, and he came on the same ship."

Roger nodded. "So I heard Urmston say."

"It's going to be a prime house with two floors and giant chimneys, and a little cupola house on the top to show that it belongs to the Governor."

"It's not started yet," Roger said. "Moseley's fighting it for some reason. I can't see why governors shouldn't have a decent place to live and work."

"Oh, Moseley's agin' everything, constitutionally agin'. Look how he sided with Cary against his old friend Glover. Some days he's sitting in the vestry and giving a silver service to the church; other days he's grabbing land by the thousand acres and pushing poor men off their holdings. I can't make that man out."

Neither could Roger; he had given up trying. "Moseley's always talking about the law," he said. "We get along pretty well when each planter administers the law on his own land. It's these men who fight over who's to make the laws that make the province weak."

In late afternoon the Captain came to the house, after the day's work was done. It was warm for October. Metephele had instructed the kitchen to serve supper on the gallery that looked on the Sound, for he knew his master liked to eat out of doors, especially on the gallery where he could look at the water and also see the open fields where his slaves worked.

Bragg, puffing a little from the walk up from the float, seated himself at the table and mopped his face. He bowed his head while Roger said grace, then gave himself to a generous helping of hominy grits swimming in butter, and several rashers of crisp bacon. He ate quickly and in silence as one accustomed to eating alone, and drank half a pot of tea before he spoke. Then he leaned back and glanced at

Roger, who sat sidewise in his chair looking out over the water.

"Well, I guess we've about settled most of the business—inventory checked, all squared away, excepting one thing. So, get your oaths ready, Duke, for you'll need them." The Captain braced his elbows squarely on the table, his shoulders hunched forward.

Roger turned from his contemplation of the water. "What's wrong? Another revolution in Antigua, or is the pirate Rackham out again?"

The Captain glowered as he always did at the mention of that particular pirate.

"No, it's nothing about Rackham or about the Indies. It's something that concerns you Albemarle planters. I put into the James before I came into the Sound. I heard in Norfolk Town that Governor Spottswood had issued orders that none of us sea captains would be allowed to move North Carolina tobacco to Virginia ports any more."

Roger turned so that he could see the Captain's expression. The old man was fond of his little jokes, but the twinkle in his eyes always gave him away. A man of almost ruthless strength, as men of his calling needed to be to fight their fight against the sea and the freebooters who raided upon the sea, he had his moments of gaiety. But there was no twinkle in his eyes now.

Roger leaned forward. "They certainly aren't going to invoke that old Tobacco Act now," he said sharply. "It will be the ruin of all of our border people!" Thinking of his own fields of leaf, he added, "Yes, by God, and all the people who are seated around the Albemarle! It would wreck Carolina. You know tobacco is the money crop of half of our planters. It's bad enough to pay their outrageous tolls and taxes; but now the damned fools want to put an embargo on our tobacco."

Captain Bragg hitched his chair forward with his great hands spread on the edge of the table. "Don't blow up a storm, Mainwairing. I'm just telling you the gossip along the James. I heard them say at the Coffee House that Governor Spottswood is preparing to enforce the Act. If ships unload tobacco in the Nansemond or at Norfolk Town, their captains will be hailed up before the Admiralty Court."

"And then what? Pay a fine?" Roger asked.

Bragg shook his head. "You know what kind of a judge you have in Admiralty Court."

Roger nodded. Porter was a neighbour of his whose land lay east of Blount's plantation, Mulberry Hill. But he didn't like the man. He was avaricious and not above taking tribute beyond his perquisites.

"More than that. They'll take away our ship's charter if we get caught," Bragg added.

"It's a rank outrage," Roger's voice was raised. "Damn them for their Tobacco Acts and the Admiralty Courts! We won't stand it! We'll sell our tobacco and be damned to Virginia laws!"

Bragg, unperturbed, looked at Roger shrewdly. He repeated his last sentence slowly: "I said they'd take away our charter if we get caught . . ." He paused significantly.

Roger looked at him a moment. Comprehension began to dawn in his eyes. He banged the table with his clenched fist. "You mean you'd risk your ship to run a tobacco blockade, Captain?"

Bragg shrugged his shoulders significantly. "I've risked my ship running blockades before. I've brought in 'black ivory' under the ban of the Royal Africa Company, so why should I draw back for a few hogsheads of tobacco? Yes, I'd even risk being called up before the Lords of Trade and Plantations. I've given testimony before them more than once, in their grand offices in London." He laughed. "They didn't get much information about the slave trade out of me; that is, nothing they wanted to hear."

Roger Mainwairing would not wantonly break laws had there been any constituted government. But like other planters of the Albemarle, he was a law unto himself. Nor was he a smuggler. But the Virginia tobacco laws were unjust. Why should a Crown Colony set laws for the Province to obey? Lawmaking for Carolina was the right of the Lords Proprietors and the constituted Assembly. Roger didn't in the least mind working out a plan with the Captain that would mean money out of the Virginia Customs coffers. That it would put money into his own was a matter of honest pride.

Roger was not a blind adherent of any side. He had managed to keep clear of taking sides during the Cary-Glover disputes. Whichever man was in power constituted the law. His youthful experience in following the Duke of Monmouth had cured him of half-baked plots against government and law. One thing Roger Mainwairing did not forget for a moment—he was a planter, and a planter's life was to develop, grow and trade. To that end he would devote all his energy and skill.

"I've been thinking over what you propose, Bragg. It's too late this year anyway. Next year we'll break the Virginia Tobacco Act into a thousand bits." Roger spoke with his old easy confidence.

He hitched his chair closer to the table, leaning forward. The grizzled head and the blond were close together. The Captain glanced over his shoulder. There was no one within earshot.

Chapter 5

BALGRAY PLANTATION

THE reflection of the low sun lay on the river, as the Pollocks' boat with Governor Hyde's party found anchorage at the mouth of Salmon Creek. The quiet of early evening was on the water. Fish were breaking near the shore, their curved bodies silver against the black swamp water.

Heavy buttressed cypress marched deep into the water, sending up tangled roots and grotesque twisted knees. Two great blue herons rose from the water, spreading their wings, flying low along the stream; a deer lifted its startled head, stood for a moment, then vaulted up the bank to sanctuary in the deep forest.

Marita caught her breath suddenly. The solitude, the poignant beauty of the dying day, set her beyond known horizons, into a new and unknown world, vast and disturbing.

The double-winged manor house stood out white and glistening against the black pines of the forest clearing. Balgray was well set, placed back from the river. The house held a quiet old-world dignity that seemed at variance with the strength and savagery of the forest behind it, and the broad sweep of the river roadway at its feet.

The voice of the mate, giving a sharp command, brought Marita back to the present. The boat was swinging against the long float. Slaves, Indian and Negro, were on the bank, waiting to carry off boxes and luggage.

Her aunt's voice: "Thanks be to God this jouney is over." She turned. Lady Mary had come up from the little cabin where she had spent most of the day. She was rested and in excellent spirits, her eyes on Madam Pollock, standing on the gallery of the manor house, whose spreading gown made a patch of bright colour against the white clapboards of the house and the evergreen shrubs of the garden.

"I am curious to meet Madam Hester," Lady Mary said, her eyes taking in the house and long stretch of lawn. "She does herself very well, very well indeed, in this forsaken wilderness." After a moment she added, "Madam Catha has told me that she has had three husbands, two of them governors. Not too bad for a provincial, born in the colonies!"

They had time to rest and refresh themselves after the day's journey before the dressing bell rang. Their rooms were in a small cottage close to the manor house. Marita's bedroom was upstairs under the sloping roof. From the dormer windows she could see far up the Chowan, with its deep-wooded shores. When she had finished dressing she went to Lady Mary's room. Her aunt still wore her travelling dress, and a Royal Stuart tartan was pinned at the shoulder with a silver crested pin, set with a cairngorm. Desham had brushed her ash-blonde hair back from her white forehead in curls, which hung to her shoulders without riband or ornament.

"I did not trouble to dress," her aunt said as they walked down the hall. "I'm sure I could never equal the Governor's lady or Hester Pollock. It is better to remain a wren than attempt the plumage of a bird of paradise."

Marita spoke impulsively. "No matter what any woman wears, you are always the most beautiful. No woman I have seen has the elegance . . ."

Lady Mary laughed. She brushed Marita's cheek lightly. "Dear child, you are always a comfort," she said.

There were other guests for supper. Planters from the neighbourhood, who had come to pay their respects to the new Governor: William Duckenfield, whose land adjoined Pollock's on the south, Willie Maule from up the river, and a lovely young girl near Marita's age, Penelope Galland.

The dining-room was large with a domed ceiling and walls panelled in cypress. A painting of Hester Pollock, over the mantelboard, dominated the room. A younger Hester, wearing a scarlet dress, her blue-black hair falling over her shoulders. The artist had limned something more than her features.

42

He had reflected the hard implacable soul in her brilliant black eyes.

Lady Mary faced the portrait from her place between the Governor and Tom Pollock. She is bold and hard, she thought, and very ambitious. She did not know then that the word the village women had for Hester was "brazen." Hester knew of their dislike for her, but it did not disturb her. She was secure, married to the greatest landholder in Northern Carolina, and owner of the finest manor house. She had married Tom Pollock after a short, a very short period of mourning for Wilkinson, her former spouse.

"The winter weather is too cold for widowhood. One must take a husband to keep warm," she had told the scandalized Ann Moseley and Mary Badham, when she met them at service one Lord's day. "It was a question of a new goose-feather bed or a husband, and I chose Thomas."

Hester, once established at Balgray, had made many changes in the manor house and in Tom's way of living. He had been content with pewter and heavy china for the table. Hester bought silver in Maryland and had it cut with the Pollock crest. Chelsea china she ordered from Williamsburg, through Mr. Jenkins, and her linens and blankets from Holland. If Tom would only enclose the frame house with brick, Balgray would be as fine as Westover or the Harrison house. Surely the Chowan was as beautiful as the James, and their hospitality as open and generous as that of the upper James planters!

She looked at her husband, seated across from her at the side of the long table, a smile of satisfaction on her lips. Things were going well. The food was good and well cooked; wild turkey was an epicurean dish. The Governor had complimented her by having a second slice of the breast meat.

She let her eyes roam about the table. The young people at the far end were enjoying themselves. Willie Maule and the Governor's young secretary, Lovyck, were attentive to Penelope Galland's bright talk. Marita Tower was smiling, as if she was amused at something Penelope was saying, Hester thought. Marita seemed a quiet girl but certainly not dull.

A puzzled expression came into her eyes as she glanced at Lady Mary, as if she could not quite fathom her. She had a look of distinction, in spite of the ugly dun-coloured gown and the old tartan she wore. Her hair was too plain, without puffs or ringlets. Hester had spent some time on her own tresses, a fashion book propped up on the dressing table before her. She had boxed Suky's ears and had the woman take down her hair three times before it was done to her satisfaction. She thought it looked quite as fashionable as Madam Hyde's, and the colour of her gown was better. She did not care for the long sacque that the Governor's wife wore, or the velvet rosettes down the front. It would have been handsome if the velvet had been green, the colour of her petticoats, instead of the blue of the sacque. Madam Catha was too short for a long sacque. It was designed for a taller woman. She herself could wear one with better style.

Hester's eyes went back to Lady Mary. Edward Hyde was speaking to her. Was there deference in his manner to her, or did she imagine it? She wondered if she had done the right thing to put Lady Mary and her people in the cottage. Would it have been better if she and Tom had moved over to the small house and given them their bedchamber and dressing room? But what was she to do, when she did not even know they were coming until she saw them on the boat? It required some ingenuity to house all the people who came with the Governor's party. Fortunately, she always kept two cottages ready for unexpected guests.

She heard the Governor ask Squire Duckenfield about the Albemarle planters. The Squire named several leading men: the two Joneses; Frederick, the lawyer who had come recently to the county and was talking of buying Smythwick's land; Edward Moseley, the Justice, at Moseley's Point; Thomas Benbury, who owned Benbury Hall; and the Porters.

"You made no mention of Duke Roger," Pollock broke in. "He is the leading planter in the Albemarle."

"True, I overlooked him," Duckenfield said. "He takes no interest in politics at all. He has only a temporary seat on the Council."

"Who is Duke Roger?" Madam Catha asked, "And why does he have that name?"

"Roger Mainwairing is his true name. The other is but a made-up name that followed him from the West Indies."

Edward Hyde turned to Pollock. "Why is this Mr. Mainwairing not interested in the government?"

"He's taken up with farming," Pollock answered. "He hasn't any concern excepting his place. I admit it shows his care. A better plantation doesn't exist anywhere in the North of Carolina than Queen's Gift."

The Governor dismissed the subject of Mainwairing.

"I was told in London to make inquiry about a man

44

named Tomes, Foster Tomes. I believe he represents one of the Lords Proprietors on the Council. He is a Quaker, is he not?"

"He's a Quaker, but he is not one of the fighting Quakers. We may be able to count Tomes among us," Pollock answered, glancing at Duckenfield for confirmation.

Hester thought the conversation was too dull. Let them talk politics later when the women had left the table and the men were having their port.

"While you are naming the leaders in Albemarle, why don't you tell his Excellency about Tom the Tinker?"

A laugh greeted her words, although her husband frowned. Hester turned to Hyde.

"Tom the Tinker is our village scold. He stands on the Green on market day, haranguing the country folk on our grievances. When he is slightly drunk, he tells of the evils of King William's day. When he is quite drunk, but can still keep himself erect, he shouts about the profligate King Charles the Second. When he is so intoxicated that he is put into the gaol, he makes plans to put the Pretender on the throne in place of our liege lady, Queen Anne."

"Why, that is treason!" cried Madam Catha. "Don't they punish treason?"

"No one takes Tom seriously," Pollock said. "He's a wee bit daft."

Madam Catha was shocked. "But he should be punished for such loose talk. Don't the authorities do anything?"

Hester said carelessly, "Oh, he gets whipped every now and then. He's really not a menace. Once they cropped his ears when he had too much to say about the Pretender."

Lady Mary looked up from her plate. "What did this Tom the Tinker say about Jamie Stuart?"

Everyone turned. It was the first time Lady Mary had shown any interest in the conversation.

"Tom the Tinker said he wanted Jamie the Pretender to succeed Queen Anne," Hester started to answer, but not before her husband had said:

"It was all a pack of nonsense and no one listened to a man who spoke from whisky."

"But there are people who don't believe he spoke from whisky," Hester persisted. She addressed Lady Mary. "Tom the Tinker holds that most of the common people want the Pretender to be King if the Queen should die."

A slave came in and spoke to Pollock. Tom rose from his

place and went around to his wife. "The man says that De Graffenried's boats are at the lower landing," he said.

Hester's face brightened. "Is the Baron with them? Tom, why not send a slave to bring him down here? Have him tell the Baron that we expect him for supper." She turned to Madam Catha. "Baron de Graffenried and his poor Palatines have arrived from Virginia. We have been looking for them for some time."

Hyde leaned forward. "I shall be delighted to see De Graffenried again. The last I saw him was in London not long before we sailed. In fact, it was at a meeting of the Lords Proprietors."

Lady Mary listened, a slight smile on her face. Edward Hyde was already feeling his way, gathering information about the leaders of the Albemarle, laying his plans.

Hester said to Lady Mary, "The Baron is such a charming gentleman. He will be a real addition to our poor provincial society. I just wrote a letter to Tom's dear uncle, Sir Robert Pollock, in Scotland, telling him we were starved for good company. Now suddenly we have a number of charming people."

"But De Graffenried's land is some distance away, is it not?" Lady Mary said, ignoring Hester's reference to Sir Robert. She did not bother to say she knew Sir Robert quite well and had shot over his preserve many times.

"Only a few hundred miles. That is nothing to us here. We consider that New Bern, on the Trent, is really at our doorstep."

Tom Pollock came back into the room. With him was the Baron de Graffenried, a slight young man, blond, with round blue eyes. He was of medium stature, although his soldierly carriage and the way he carried his head gave the impression of greater height. He clicked his heels together and made a stiff bow to the ladies, then greeted Edward Hyde warmly. He refused supper, he had had something in camp, but he would be delighted to accept a glass of wine.

"It is kind, Mr. Pollock, that you have prepared a splendid camp for my Switzers and my poor Palatines," he said, after he had taken a chair next to Hester. "They will rest well tonight, without fear of Indians or marauding animals, and they deserve rest. It is a hard trip that they take here from Virginia, so soon after their long ocean voyage."

After a few moments Hester rose, the women following her. "We will leave the gentlemen to their port," she said, moving towards the door. "Tom, do not stay too long talking government affairs."

Marita noticed the Baron's eyes were following her aunt as she crossed the room, a puzzled look in his light blue eyes. She heard him say to Pollock, "I think I have seen Lady Mary Tower before, in some city—London or Paris. I think of her as riding in a glass coach, dressed in great elegance; not as she is now." Marita did not hear Pollock's answer.

The men sat down again when the women left the room. A slave brought in decanters and lighted fresh candles.

Two hours later they were still at table. Pollock's wig lay on a chair beside him, leaving his head bald. The wine had put a little colour into Edward Hyde's dark face, and his eyes were deep and thoughtful. Squire Duckenfield nodded in his chair. County government did not interest him now. He was sailing next week for England.

The younger men, Anthony Lovyck and Willie Maule, had followed the women into the great room. Captain Gregory remained.

Pollock spoke to his servant, telling him to take brandy to the gentlemen in the great room. He sat down near the Governor and took up the discussion where they had left off.

"Say what you will about bringing peace into the Albemarle, sir, I promise you there will be no peace here until you oust Thomas Cary from this government. Do you not see your way clear to send some of your men, under Captain Gregory, to Bath Town and arrest the rascal? Arrest him for treason. Send him to England for trial."

Hyde was silent, his long fingers tapping against the table. "Treason is a high crime and difficult to prove, Pollock. Besides, that is not my object. I did not come to Carolina with the sword. I came to make peace, not war. To establish a stable government. We have had enough of war in England. Let us make a peace here so that we may go forward."

"By what means, Mr. Governor, do you propose to do that?" Pollock's mouth was set, his features craggy as a rock. "We've tried every means, Glover and I, for the past three years. What has it got us? Nothing but more fighting. I beg your Excellency to be firm. Go into Queen Anne's Town and set up our government there. These are parlous times. We want a strong hand, not the appeaser's velvet glove."

Hyde glanced about the table. Duckenfield's eyes were closed, his head nodding. Gregory's face showed that he

47

agreed with Pollock. De Graffenried wore an enigmatical expression. He broke the long silence that followed Pollock's words.

"I do not understand quite. But you are the Governor, Mr. Hyde. Why do you not exercise that authority given to you by the Lords Proprietors?"

Hyde looked down at his glass to hide the disappointment in his eyes. "That is the difficulty, Baron. Tynte, the Governor of all the Carolinas, was to have given me my commission. Unfortunately he died shortly before I arrived here from England. As it stands, I have no legal authority as governor until my credentials come from England."

De Graffenried's light blue eyes went from one to the other. "But I was at the meeting of the Lords when it was decided that you were to be the governor."

Pollock interrupted. "It is the custom here that the deputy receives a commission from the Governor of all the Carolinas before he takes office."

The Baron turned his eyes to Hyde, evidently puzzled by what he had just heard. "But it was said at the meeting in London that you were to be full governor of North Carolina. I myself heard them make the recommendation to be sent to the Queen in Council."

"That is true, but I have no papers to prove it. I have written to England stating the facts. But until I have full authority I do not intend to challenge Cary. Whatever step I take must be under the law."

"You talk just like Edward Moseley," Pollock grumbled. "He's forever going on about the law."

The Baron said to Pollock, "I must talk with you tomorrow about supplies for my poor Palatines. We are running low on the provisions I secured from Governor Spottswood. We need pork and corn, if I may be permitted to buy them."

Pollock nodded. "I have some supplies on hand but I do not know how much I can let you have until I talk with my steward. We'll speak about that tomorrow. Are your people going to travel on foot, after you cross to the south shore?"

"Only as far as Bath Town," the Swiss answered. "Mr. Cary has kindly offered to furnish boats to take them the rest of the journey."

The Governor looked quickly at Pollock. The old Scot was staring at De Graffenried. The Baron was looking down, his quick, nervous fingers turning the slender stem of his wineglass. "Tom Cary sent word to me in Virginia to offer

48

his help. He will have some of his men at Bell's Ferry to meet my people and guide them by the shortest road to Bath Town. Very kind of him and so thoughtful," he added.

Pollock's eyes sought the Governor's. They were both thinking the same thing. The balance lay here, in the small, almost womanish hands of the Siwss nobleman, De Graffenried. With his Palatine hundreds, many of them trained to military service, he could throw his power one way or the other. Cary had seen that also and had made his plans.

"Do not have a worry about your supplies, Baron," Pollock said heartily. "I have everything you need. My steward will attend to all that tomorrow."

De Graffenried lifted his eyes from his wineglass. There was a look of cool calculation in them which the Governor observed with some uneasiness. The man was not as ingenuous as he appeared. It would be well to have him on their side.

"My cash for the moment is very low." De Graffenried hesitated.

Pollock interrupted. "Say nothing about cash, Baron. A bill on your London agent is sufficient for me. Pay at any time you wish, at your own convenience." Pollock looked towards the Governor and again at De Graffenried. "We want to do everything we can to help you establish your people in Carolina."

The calculating look in the Baron's light blue eyes changed to one of satisfaction. He smiled as he lifted his glass and drained the last red drop of wine.

Hester came to the door. At her signal Tom got up from the table. "We will have brandy with the ladies," he said.

Edward Hyde walked in the garden that night long after the others had retired. The moon was at the half, and the night clear and still. The fires of De Graffenried's camp had died down to embers. The dark form of a sentry moved back and forth along the river bank, the moonshine catching light from the musket over his shoulder.

The Governor's mind was active, sifting the information that he had absorbed since he had landed in Virginia three months earlier.

Governor Spottswood, Harrison, William Byrd and Ludwell had also given him their views of the confused state of the Carolinas. "No government at all, or less than none," was the general opinion in Virginia; a harbour of rogues and

49

criminals, men from gaols and debtors' prison, runaway bondsmen and the like.

Hyde was an astute man. He listened and made his own valuation. He had reached a very fair idea of the situation before he left London, by reading over letters and records. He knew the causes and the results of Culpepper's rebellion. He saw plainly that the present trouble, which dated back to the opening of Queen Anne's reign, could easily flare into open rebellion once more, unless some agreement could be made with the Quakers through their leader, Thomas Cary.

Before he formed an opinion of his own he wanted to talk to all the Albemarle leaders. Hyde assumed that he could count on the members of the Council since each one of the eight members represented one of the Lords Proprietors. Pollock, staunch man that he was, had deep-seated prejudices. Duckenfield was old, and thought more of his contemplated visit to England than of the Albemarle situation. Edward Moseley and the Soundside planters were the men he must meet. He gathered that Moseley, although an adherent of Cary's, had a broad view. "He's always talking of establishing law," Pollock had told him. That was Hyde's idea, but he knew too much of politics to hope for immediate changes. A nephew of the great Edward Hyde, the first Lord Clarendon, he was bred with knowledge of political expediency.

Hyde wanted first to establish the common law; second, to develop trade and make the country desirable for settlement. Trade must be developed with the West Indies—that could be done immediately, because it coincided with the wishes of the Lords of Trade and Plantations. Particularly with Jamaica and the Bahama group. The only thing that stood in the way was the presence of pirates in these waters. These were the drawbacks to colonization, other than the hardships that came with breaking new bottom lands and clearing the forest. Anarchy within, piracy without—and the menace of Indian uprisings.

Hyde set these thoughts aside and turned his mind to the conversation that night at table. He was convinced that De Graffenried was shrewd and energetic in spite of his youthful appearance. He had cleverly put the canny Pollock in a position where the Scot was obliged to furnish him what he wanted in the way of supplies and food, without paying for it. Pollock dared not refuse, after the Baron had intimated that Cary was eager to help his Palatines. De Graffenried must be won over first. Hyde did not think that would be difficult. The man was young and could be played upon by flattering his importance to the colony, with his Palatines and the position as Landgrave which the Lords had generously conferred on him.

Moseley he must have, and the lawyer, Christopher Gale. Pollock had told him that Gale would soon be back from the Bahamas. He must use all his persuasion to attach these men to him, if he was to make any headway in government.

He thought of the settlers who had come early to the Albemarle under the first Charter, during the reign of Charles the Second. Most of the people lived meanly, in log houses and huts with earth floors, when brick-making was only a matter of industry and a little imagination. But these people were without imagination. Runaway bondservants and slaves, rogues fleeing from the established law of Virginia, they had had the habit of poverty for generations. Whether it was the poverty of the lowest depths of London or poverty of a new world, it was the same. Without leadership they could not rise beyond their own thought; without knowledge they could not think beyond the poverty that was inherent. The habit of poverty, of want, persisted in a land of biblical plenty. No strong men rose because there was no strength without knowledge. Leadership is aristocratic; not the aristocracy of birth and position, but the aristocracy of imagination and training for leadership. A man whose belly sticks to his ribs from hunger does not dream of power. The average settler was occupied with his hundred acres of raw land, his long musket and axe. The instinct to survive carried him no further than to assure his daily food.

Head bent in deep thought, his hands behind his back, the new Governor paced along the path by the river. The task that seemed simple when he sat with the Lords Proprietors at their meeting place in Whitehall now assumed a magnitude almost beyond endurance.

The Lords were too deeply concerned in Queen Anne's foreign wars to give much time or thought to the problems of the Carolinas. The list they had given him of his new duties was a formidable one. He could repeat it without reference to the paper, so often had he read it. First, make peace with the Quakers and Thomas Cary. Second, settle the long-drawn-out dispute with Virginia over the boundary line. Third, secure some measure of parity about shipment of tobacco. After that, increase trade, in order to induce new settlement in the rich bottom lands of rivers and streams and insure a stable government. "A small matter," Lord Craven had said, "a small matter, not hard to accomplish if you use diplomacy"—but to Edward Hyde it seemed the work of a lifetime.

Chapter 6

POOR PALATINES

DESHAM was brushing Lady Mary's long hair, preparing and rolling it on strips of linen for the end curls, when Marita stopped at her aunt's door to bid her good night. Lady Mary was seated before her dressing table. She had put off her woollen gown, and wore a blue silken wrapper, cascaded in heavy lace, over which her pale gold hair spread across her fine white shoulders.

She snatched a brush from the table and gave the woman a smart tap on the back of her hands. "Go away, you are murdering me. Go lay out my night rail and turn down the sheets. I'll roll these up myself." She looked in the glass to catch Marita's eyes. "You should be grateful that your hair curls of its own accord and you don't have to wear lumpy rags to hinder your sleep," she sighed. "I do miss Monsieur Pierre. He managed to arrange my curls without all this torture."

"Did you enjoy the supper?" Marita said, to take her aunt's mind off Desham's heavy hands.

"The supper was well enough for plain English cooking," she answered. "But the evening was interminable. I should have perished if I had not resorted to my game of patience. Those women," she said scornfully. "Did you hear them matching each other with 'Sir Robert this' and 'Lord So-and-so that?' Each trying to outdo the other with names of persons in high places. I'll give a week, no more, before they will be scratching each other's eyes out like two cats."

She rolled a long strand of hair into place. "Three strong-willed women under one roof is beyond endurance. After listening to the mighty battles of her Majesty and Sarah

Churchill I do not mean to be bored by quarrels of lesser folk."

"Why should they quarrel?" Marita said.

"My dear child, you are young! Ambitious women, trying to create a place for themselves, always quarrel. Hester was the high lady here until Madam Catha came, and there will be a struggle. I watched them when they thought I was engrossed with my card game."

Marita looked at her aunt, her amber eyes wide. "They are both so pleasant spoken I thought they were already friends." She hesitated a moment. "I think they both envy you."

Lady Mary laughed aloud. "They don't envy me, my dear child. They loathe me."

"I don't understand," Marita said, her smooth forehead furrowed. "Why should they dislike you?"

"Because I disturb them. They cannot quite place me."

Lady Mary tunred on the stool to face Marita. "Do try to remember this, Marita. Never allow yourself to be involved in the petty strife of women. If you fight, let it be over something where the stakes are worthy of the battle."

She signalled to Desham, "Come here, woman, and finish this. Keep a light hand or I'll be harsh with you next time."

Marita kissed her aunt on the forehead and took up her bed-candle.

"Don't sit up reading," Lady Mary said smiling. "Save your pretty eyes for better things. In the morning you may go down by the river to see the Baron's poor Palatines, before they depart from their camp by the river."

It was close to noon the next morning when Marita, dressed in her russet riding habit faced with buff, mounted her horse at the block and, followed by one of Pollock's stable boys, rode to a clearing in the forest that overlooked the beach where Baron de Graffenried's Switzers and Palatines had moved that morning. The day was clear, the water sparkled in the sunlight. She pulled her horse to a walk until she came to the edge of the high bank overlooking the white beach, where in season Thomas Pollock fished for herring. Half a dozen great boats and periaugers were anchored, and the bright dresses of the Swiss and Palatine women and children brightened the white sand as gay flowers brighten an early garden.

Marita dismounted, passing the reins to the Negro boy. She walked to the little lath garden house on the Point and sat down on a bench to watch the people below. Before her eyes the broad Chowan River joined the Albemarle; to the south the Roanoke sent an amber stream deep into the great Sound. The "meetings of the waters," the Indians called it. Many miles above on the Roanoke were the swift rapids which cut deep into the high banks, bringing down the tawny earth, darkening the waters. The Chowan, broader, flowed slowly, deep and quiet as the forests which lined its banks.

A long canoe glided across the quiet water from the south shore, moving slowly, no swifter than the river current. The men bending to the oars were dark, flat figures, blurred into the flat water of the Sound. Across the water little columns of smoke marked the chimneys of Queen Anne's Town. Along the rivers in every direction tall trees followed the banks and led to dark swamps and deeper forests. Evil lurked there. Silent beasts of prey, hidden among the trees. Red men also, as silent, as sinister as the beasts. Marita felt a shiver down the length of her back. She was afraid of the forest, afraid to explore its dark secrets.

A shadow fell across the path. The dark figure of a man standing in the doorway blotted out the midday sun. She rose to her feet, her white hand against her throat. Michael Cary stood before her. He wore a leather jerkin and breeches and was tanned like an Indian, his body lean and hard; his thick, light hair, blowing in the wind; his eyes very blue in his thin, bronzed face. Marita thought that there was some subtle difference in him. He was not bold and audacious as she had seen him that day at the ferry. He was quiet, isolated, stepping out of the deep woods as stealthily as one of its denizens. Looking beyond him, she saw his Indian servant, standing near a great tupelo tree, watchful and waiting.

She struggled to make the familiar effort of steadying speech. But the words would not come. He lifted her hand. She felt his lips against the throbbing pulse of her wrist. She felt the flow of life between them warm and pulsating.

"I knew I would find you like this. Alone, with the solitude of the forest about you."

His voice released her. The magic of the moment passed; a thousand fears came to her. The violent words she had heard; the threats against his uncle. The danger to him if Thomas Pollock should find him here on his land. She could not speak the fears that trembled on her lips. She could only stand silent before him, looking at him.

He put her thoughts into words. "You are afraid for me. I

can read your thoughts," he said. "But you need have no fear. I am quite safe."

He drew her to the bench and sat down beside her.

"I am afraid for you," she said. "Mr. Pollock has told me who you are. You do not know your danger here."

"Danger has no meaning if it keeps me from you," he said, a light glowing in his eyes. "You must have known I would come."

He caught her hands in his and held them closely. "Let them say we Carys are the Cormorant's Brood, that we are linked with the Devil. Do not believe them. My uncle is a noble man. He has fire in him and life, and he fears no one."

He threw back his head and laughed. "They fear him, the Pollocks and the Glovers and their pale-livered followers."

Marita drew back, terrified by the violence of his words and the look on his lean face.

He bent toward her, suddenly contrite. "I have frightened you, little Marita?"

She felt the blood rise to her face. The clasp of his hands was heavy on hers. No man had looked at her like this. No man had moved her so strangely. He did not speak again, only looked at her until her own eyes fell beneath his gaze. In the silence she heard a low birdcall, a little stir in the dried leaves at the edge of the woods.

Michael let her hands drop to her lap. He rose to his feet and moved swiftly to the door. She saw his hand go to the hilt of his sword. The birdcall came once more. Marita rose then and followed Michael outside. She saw that his Indian was no longer standing near the tree. At that moment she heard dogs barking, and the sound of a galloping horse.

"Michael, you must go," she said in alarm. "Please . . ."

His face hardened, his eyes turned to agate. "Carys do not run, my dear. Stand back, or, if you are afraid, seek shelter in the house."

"I am not afraid for myself," she said, catching his hand, "but for you, Michael, for you."

A sudden smile illuminated his stern face. He had no time to speak to her. Instead he stepped forward where he could see down the road. A few moments later Lady Mary galloped into view, her blue velvet skirts whipping, her plumed hat hanging down her back, her pale hair flying. Half a dozen hounds followed her horse, their pink tongues lopping from their open jaws. She drew up sharply when she saw Michael.

55

Her blue eyes appraised him coldly. She waited, without speaking, as if for some explanation.

Marita spoke with an effort to appear casual. "Here is Mr. Cary," she said. "You remember we saw him . . ." She stopped. She did not want to recall to her aunt the scene at the ferry or the time when Michael's sheep held up their coach on the Dismal Swamp road.

"Oh, the herd boy," Lady Mary said. "For a moment I did not recognize you without your sheep."

Marita coloured painfully. Her aunt was cruel, needlessly cruel. She expected Michael Cary would fly into a rage at her words. Instead he laughed and made a low bow.

"I am afraid I made a poor herdsman that day. I let too many sheep stray into the swamp while your ladyship's coach passed by."

Lady Mary did not smile. Instead her face stiffened to a mask. She said, "If your name is Cary I warn you this is not a place for you to linger." She glanced over her shoulder. "Mr. Thomas Pollock is on the way, and several other gentlemen."

Cary did not give ground. "I have a good sword," he said, touching the hilt, an amused smile on his lips. "But I do not think I shall use it today." The smile lingered on his lips but his eyes were hard and angry. He neither liked the words nor the implication. He turned to Marita, dropping his voice. "You have not told me whether you liked our grapes . . ."

"Marita, come here, I wish to speak to you." Lady Mary's tone was mandatory.

Marita hesitated. She glanced at her aunt. Lady Mary was looking straight at her, her face flushed and angry. Marita resented her aunt's speaking as if she were a young child.

She took a step toward Michael. "I wanted to thank you. I thought the grapes were . . ." She paused, seeking a word. "You were kind to give them to me," she said with a rush, "so very, very kind."

She turned. Three horsemen were trotting down the road, Thomas Pollock, the Governor and Anthony Lovyck. Instead of going to Lady Mary she took a step toward Michael. He gave her a quick, reassuring glance, and moved forward to meet the horsemen as they dismounted. He bowed to the Governor as a cavalier should, not looking at Pollock or Anthony.

"I am searching for the Baron de Graffenried," he said. "His people told me I would find him here."

56

Pollock glanced at Michael. "The Baron will be here any moment. He is following us, with Madam Hyde and my wife." He looked more closely at Michael. Recognizing him, he changed his tone. "I think I can settle any matter that you may have with the Baron, Mr. Michael Cary."

Michael bowed. "Thank you, sir, my business is with the Baron. I will wait until he arrives." He moved a little to one side, and stood quietly looking down toward the beach.

Lady Mary said, "Marita, give me your shoulder. I wish to dismount."

Michael stepped across the intervening space swiftly. He spanned her narrow waist with his strong hands and lifted her from the saddle.

"Thank you, sir," Lady Mary said loftily. "It was not necessary for you to exert yourself on my behalf."

"It was a pleasure," he replied unsmiling, "and no exertion." He walked away and stood with his back to the riders, apparently engrossed in the activity on the beach below.

"The man is insolent," Lady Mary said. "Stand here beside me, Marita. It is not necessary for you to speak with him again."

Marita thought her aunt's words were uncalled for. She turned away so that her aunt could not see her face. Michael did not want to speak to her. He was angry. She could tell that by the movement of his shoulders, the way he stood with his feet apart, his stiff, straight back and the turn of his head.

The other riders came up. Madam Catha and Madam Hester were laughing and gay, as if the young Baron had just said something amusing. The Baron saw Michael standing by the bank. His face lightened. He swung from the saddle, walked over to Michael and greeted him cordially. They talked for a few moments, but Marita was too far away to hear them. The Baron's voice was courteous and pleasant. Michael spoke again. The Baron watched, a little smile on his face, as Michael went down the steps cut in the steep bank that led to the beach. A moment later Marita saw Michael step into a canoe. His Indian took up a paddle and pointed the canoe south, toward the mouth of the Roanoke.

When Marita turned she saw that Pollock's face was red as a turkey's wattles. The Governor was thoughtful. Anthony wore an angry look. Only the Baron was smiling. He said, "It was so kind of Captain Cary to come all the way from Bath Town. He says he will meet me and my people tomorrow at the ferry on the south shore and guide us the two days' journey through Bath County to his camp at Romney Marsh." De Graffenried looked from one to the other, his eyes expressionless. "So very, very kind," he added.

Anthony had moved to the summer-house. He paused a moment in front of the door, his bright, dark eyes scanning the ground. Marita followed his glance. In the dust, in front of the door of the summer-house, was the print of Michael Cary's boots. Close to them were the smaller prints of her own buckled shoes. Anthony said:

"What is the matter with you, Marita? You look as white as if you have seen a ghost."

"I think I must be hungry." She managed to be prosaic, hoping Anthony would be put off.

"I invite you to lunch with my poor Palatines, Miss Marita," the Baron said. "You must not refuse me, as all these good people have done." He turned to her aunt. "May she not go down to the camp with me, Lady Mary? I promise to take very good care of this charming child."

Marita waited for her aunt's permission to go. Lady Mary did not answer. She was watching the canoe, with Michael Cary and his Indian, now far out on the water. Her face cleared. She was satisfied that the bold young Cary would soon be across the Sound.

"I think it would be very nice, Baron," she said. "I am sure Marita will be pleased to go to the camp with you. Anthony, if you will give me a hand I will mount."

Anthony made a cradle of his clasped hands and she vaulted lightly to the saddle. She waved to Marita. "Do not stay too long, child. Remember, you must work with your French before tea."

The men had a few words with De Graffenried before they followed. When they had gone, the Baron turned to Marita. "Now, mademoiselle, we will walk down to the beach. I want you to see something of my people. See how many there are. Besides my Switzers I have almost seven hundred Palatines. I want you to talk with some of our *Hausfrauen* and see their children while my man prepares our luncheon." He led the way, steadying her as they descended the steep steps.

They walked across the sand to a little group of women who were sitting on the narrow beach. Children were tumbling in the sand, chasing a small crab that was trying to escape to the water.

The Baron mentioned the names of the women, Frauen Katherine Shaffer and Anna Ponly. He said, "You may have a lesson in French now, Miss Marita, for these good women come from the border country. I will come back shortly. Then we will take the canoe and paddle around that little point." He smiled at her look of surprise. "My man is already busy with the cooking and Michael Cary will join us there."

He went away without looking at Marita, leaving her speechless, unable to move. One of the women broke the silence.

"Will you sit near us, mademoiselle? We are so happy to see a new face. So long we have looked only at each other."

Laughter greeted her words. Marita smiled too, and sat down on the sand, near the kind-faced old woman who had just spoken. She too wanted to laugh and be gay. The old woman looked at her with her dark bright eyes, moving her gay skirts aside.

"If you please," said Marita.

The old woman took up her lace pillow, her bobbins weaving in and out with incredible swiftness, weaving the intricate pattern. "We have only one more moon. Then we will be in our new home," she said, her eyes shining in anticipation. "Mademoiselle will know what that means to a goodwife, to have her house and her little things about her. To spread her beds neatly, with clean, unwrinkled linen. To churn her butter and make her fine round cheeses. That will be living again. The journey has been so long."

Marita felt the quick tears filling her eyes. The old woman watched her over the flashing bobbins.

"You have the kind heart," she said softly, so the others could not hear. "A kind heart is God-given."

Marita and the old goodwife sat in silence while the younger women ran along the beach with the children. There was a common bond between them. After a time the Baron came for her. The old woman smiled and touched Marita's hand. "God with you," she said. De Graffenried watched them for a moment. He laid his hand on the old woman's shoulder. The smile on his lips was gentle.

"We will soon be home, good mother. One day I will give you the thanks of my heart for what you have done...." He pressed her shoulder affectionately.

As they walked down the beach to the canoe, he said, "It takes only one stout heart to rule. That good mother has raised the spirits of my people when they were sunk in despair. Sometimes I think she walks with God."

59

Michael was waiting for them. When the canoe rounded the Point, Marita saw him standing on the beach. The Baron looked at her, smiling a little. "You wonder, mademoiselle, why this thing happens? I will tell you. Michael arranged it. I knew him from Virginia, when he came to meet me and my people, sent by his uncle. I like Michael. When he says, 'I must speak alone to this young lady ...'" He laughed suddenly. "Michael will have his way always, I think."

After lunch they sent their servants back to camp. The Baron sang and gave the calls of his high mountains that echoed along the water and against the banks. For a moment he shed his cares and was young and gay.

Marita said little. She sat on the sand while the two raced along the shore and fenced with their swords. After a time, De Graffenried said, "I shall now take my repose." He hollowed a space in the sand and made himself comfortable, covering his face with his plumed hat.

Michael came to Marita and threw himself beside her, where she sat on the sand, her back against the bank. For a long time they were silent, watching the slow flight of waterfowl. In the distance the sound of the camp drifted toward them. After a time Michael talked to her, telling her about himself, his mother who lived in England now, the tragic death of his father in Antigua. He spoke of his own ambition to come to the New World and make his own place, in his own way, instead of waiting at home for an old uncle to die so that he could inherit his estate.

"I sailed to my adventure," he told her, "with as much joy and anticipation as ever Jason sailed for the Fleece."

"And you found it?" Marita said, watching him as he looked out over the water.

"I don't know," Michael said, "I don't know. I came seeking adventure. Now I am sometimes afraid that it is war I have found, not high adventure."

They sat then not speaking. He took her hand and held it for a moment against his cheek. "I think we must go now. The sun is behind the trees and it grows dark." He rose then and walked towards the sleeping man.

De Graffenried sat up and dusted the sand from his woollen tunic. "You are right," he said. "I promised to have Mademoiselle Marita home by teatime." He walked off towards the canoe.

Michael stood for a moment looking at Marita. "It is the beginning," he said to her, "the beginning. I shall see you again and again. The thought of me will never go from you."

She raised her eyes to meet his. "I will not forget you, Michael," she said steadily.

The Baron and Marita overtook Anthony and young Willie Maule near the manor house. Michael had not come back to camp. His Indian would paddle him across the Sound and he would lie the night at Edward Moseley's plantation, White Marsh. The following afternoon he would meet De Graffenried and his people at the ferry. They would spend that night on the south shore, then a two days' march for them to Bath Town, where a camp had been arranged until they were ready to take the last of their journey by water.

Marita asked him to come in for tea, but the Baron excused himself. He had business with Pollock, and with the Governor also.

Lovyck and Maule went with Marita. They took up an argument where they had left off. It was about the families of the Albemarle. Anthony was inquiring who were of Cavalier descent and who were lesser folk.

"You are too proud, Anthony," Willie said. "You are always thinking about position and money. We are not like that here. We don't question who a man was before he came here."

"Best not," drawled Lovyck. Maule was silent. Anthony continued. "As for pride, why shouldn't a man be proud of his birth and his position? Pride is like dignity. It belongs to the upper classes."

Marita disliked Anthony when he was like this. He was being superior, trying to make Willie feel provincial and inferior. Instead he made Willie angry.

"Don't be an ass, Loyvck," he said. "We don't countenance snobs here in the Albemarle." Anthony's face darkened.

Marita interrupted. "Please don't quarrel," she said in a grown-up manner. "You know my aunt doesn't like quarrelling."

"There's always quarrelling when there are three women together," Anthony said lazily. "I can foresee the explosions that will come one of these days, among Hester and Madam Catha and . . ." He paused, glancing at Marita.

"You were going to say Lady Mary," she said quickly. "I can tell you Lady Mary does not descend to small bickerings. She has witnessed real quarrels between the Queen and Sarah Churchill; all other quarrels are tame affairs."

Anthony's eyes lighted up. "Jupiter! What luck! They say

61

the Duchess' voice carries from St. James's to the Cockpit when she is really angry. Did your aunt tell about the time Sarah broke up the furniture in her apartment?"

Willie looked horrified. "I don't believe that a beautiful woman like the Duchess would do anything so crude. What could she and the Queen quarrel about?"

"They say that the Queen wanted to allow a bottle of wine a day to one of the charwomen, and the Duchess didn't like it," Anthony answered carelessly.

"But why should the Duchess care about that? Surely such a small sum wasn't important."

"It wasn't the amount. You must remember that the Duchess is Mistress of the Privy Purse. She won't allow her Majesty to make any expenditure unless she has given her approval. My uncle told me that. He's often at Court, you know."

Marita, annoyed that Anthony should take that tone again, said, "My aunt lived at Court." She stopped, confused. A slow flush rose from the little white bend at her throat to her cheeks.

The eyes of the two young men turned towards her. Willie was frankly curious. Anthony Lovyck's eyes had a curious glitter, something more than curiosity, almost cunning.

"Tell us more about your aunt, Marita. Is there really some mystery? I heard Madam Catha tell Madam Hester there was."

Marita did not answer Anthony. She said, "Let us go in. I see Desham bringing in the tea-things."

Lady Mary was sitting in the little drawing-room near the window that looked out on the river. She had on a white wool skirt, long and very full. Over it she wore a deep blue velvet bodice and overskirt that touched the floor. Her ash-blonde hair lay in long, loose curls over her shoulders, woven into place with a blue velvet riband.

A lute lay on a low table in front of her, and an open sheet of music. At her elbow was her mahogany reading-box with its protected candle. The English mail had arrived from Virginia that morning while they were gone, brought down the Chowan River to Pollock's wharf. The news was nearly five weeks old when it arrived in Balgray, but Lady Mary applied herself to the latest *Tatlers* as if it were the day of publication.

Marita usually tried to keep out of the way on mail days until her aunt had gone through her letters and laid them aside for the books and magazines. Lady Mary wanted quiet when the post came from home. Sometimes she was quite gay after she had read her letters; sometimes gloomy and very quiet, even sad. But now she welcomed the young men with obvious pleasure. Marita knew from this that the news from England was to her aunt's liking.

Desham came in with the tea-things. Lady Mary lifted the clumsy earthenware teapot with obvious distaste. "I simply can't enjoy pouring tea from such a clumsy pot," she said, addressing Anthony and Willie Maule. "There is really no reason to live so crudely. I think we should go to the other extreme here, in the amenities, to make up for all this." She waved her fine white hand to indicate the room.

"We think we are quite civilized—much more so than we used to be when my father came," Willie Maule said, a little resentful.

Lady Mary smiled. "No doubt a man would feel that way, Willie, but I enjoy my comfort." She handed a cup to Anthony. "I've sent home for a few pieces of furniture—beds and bureaus and my escritoire. They should be here in a month or two . . . certainly by Twelfth Night."

Marita looked up from her tea. Her aunt had told her nothing of her plans beyond saying that they would look for a house on the Sound.

Anthony stirred his tea. "Then you do intend to stay here, Lady Mary?"

Lady Mary shrugged her shoulders. "I think so. Either here or at St. Kitts; one or another of the Plantations. It depends on how the air agrees with me and with Marita."

The idea of dwelling here long was new to Marita. Somehow Marita had thought the journey to the Plantations was to be a venture of short duration—a short interlude in her aunt's crowded life, a relaxation from the cares and worries of society.

"I may buy a plantation," she heard Lady Mary saying. "I rather fancy owning land in this fine new world."

Willie Maule said, "There's no land left on the Chowan or the Roanoke worth owning."

"Perhaps someone will sell," Anthony said easily.

Willie laughed. His was a peculiar laugh, without sound, although it shook his stocky body. "I see you haven't yet discovered what we planters of the Albemarle are like, Lovyck. We take up land—we don't sell."

Lovyck was not satisfied with this explanation. He named

the neighbouring planters. "What about Duckenfield, Bryan, Henderson, or Jonathan Jacocks? Surely they would give over a small acreage if Lady Mary wanted it."

Willie shook his head. "Not one of those men will sell, or my father. I don't believe there is a planter from here to Duke's Mill at the Virginia line who will part with an acre. That's the reason De Graffenried had to take his Switzers and his poor Palatines to the Trent for his settlement."

Anthony turned a bewildered face to Lady Mary. "Can you imagine? He says not one of these men will part with an acre of this wilderness, and it's new land, not entailed like our estates at home."

Lady Mary smiled her little slow smile. "Perhaps these planters love the wilderness, or perhaps they intend to start an empire of their own."

"Or maybe they are obliged to love it," Anthony said, an edge to his voice. "Rogues' Harbour was the name we heard in Virginia. There are enough rogues hiding up and down these small creeks in the back country, God knows; and a lot of pirates and blackguards, from what I've heard—penal colony men, some of them."

Willie Maule bristled. "That's a blasted lie, Lovyck; a tale left over from fifty years ago when rogues and rascals did take refuge here! Some of them were political prisoners or other decent folk who had been thrown in debtors' prison. But many of them were men who wanted religious freedom. Roundheads came here after the Restoration, and Quakers who had been persecuted in Virginia and the North."

"Any regicides?" Anthony asked sarcastically. "I've heard you Colonials gave refuge to regicides."

"No!" Willie Maule cried vehmently. "No, that is not true! The regicides went to New England, not to the southern Plantations."

Lady Mary yawned, bored with the discussion. She signalled Desham to remove the tea-things. A moment later the two young men got up. Before they left, Willie returned to the first discussion.

"The planters who have seated the Albemarle are men who do not want to sell. They take up patents and prove their land and develop it themselves. But I did hear the other day that Tom Pearce, who owns Greenfield, may have to return to England. If he does go, you might buy that parcel."

"Is the location good?" Lady Mary asked, indifferently. "I want something facing on the Sound or a river."

"Greenfield is on the Sound between Sandy Point plantation and Drummond's Point. It has fine cleared fields and good pasture and there is prime timber."

"You know a good deal about the place," Lovyck said, idly arranging the laces of his cuff before a small wall mirror. "Are you thinking of getting married and buying it yourself?"

Maule's face flushed. Marita smiled. Madam Hester Pollock had told them that Willie was sighing for little Penelope Galland.

"No," he said sullenly, "I'm not. Even if I were, I wouldn't have the money to buy a place the size of Greenfield."

Lady Mary drew the reading-box to her side. Lovyck accepted the signal of dismissal and got to his feet.

"Chief Justice Moseley has the letting of the place if Mr. Pearce goes," Willie said. "It would be a place for a lady like you, ma'am. The stockade is already set, and there are good neighbours along the Sound shore, and there's not the danger from Indians that there is on this river."

No one made any comment. Lovyck pulled at Willie's sleeve to quiet his talking, and they made their farewells.

Marita ran to her aunt and knelt beside her. The hard feelings she had had earlier in the day were gone. "Are we going to stay here, Aunt Mary, really?"

Lady Mary raised her narrow arched brows as she ran her white ringed fingers through Marita's tawny hair. "What is this, my demure little Mary! Why are you so excited? Who is it? Not Willie Maule—or Anthony?"

"No, no. Don't tease me. I love it here. It is glorious. The birds—the forest—the great rivers. It is so strong. Oh, I can't say it. It needs Mr. Dryden to put into words what it is like. It is so beautiful."

Lady Mary put her fingers under Marita's chin, lifting her face. "My dear, girls of seventeen don't grow poetic over rivers, or a great forest, unless—" she paused—"unless there is a man."

Marita felt her cheeks flame. She turned her eyes away, unable to meet her aunt's searching gaze. "I love it here." She felt her voice had lost conviction.

Lady Mary said no more. She drew the low table, which held the lute, towards her, and ran her fingers over the strings. "You must take up your singing, Marita. Your voice is too good not to keep in practice." She played an adagio. "This is one of Mr. Handel's new pieces. Abigail Hill wrote me that the Queen is very fond of Mr. Handel's music." She was silent for a time, trying the new piece. "My mother had a beautiful voice," she said suddenly. "I heard my father say it was the most beautiful voice in all England."

Marita did not go to bed at once, as her aunt had told her to do. Instead she sat at the little dormer window and leaned her elbows on the sill, looking out at the dark sky. The clean, fresh smell of pine woods came to her. The stars were brilliant in the dark sky. She thought of the old goodwife, with her wrinkled face and bright eyes and her mouth turned up at the corners into a smile.

Michael. She had waited until she was alone like this to think of him. She would always think of him when she looked at the trees and the water. Other men she knew belonged to city streets, to towns and drawing-rooms, with their elegant dress, and their bright, crisp talk. Michael was different. He was like the forest or the sea. She closed her eyes and put her head on her hands. In the dark she could bring him close to her.

Desham came into the room and found her asleep at the window, her head pillowed in her arms. She lifted Marita in her strong arms and carried her to her bed.

Chapter 7

LEET WOMAN

NOVEMBER came in with rain and chill north winds that soon veered to the east, whipping the waters of the Sound in sharp squalls and sudden gusts. This made sailing of the heavy-laden boats hazardous. The road to the Yaupim was deep in mud, so deep that the high carts rested in the stables, and the Yaupim farmers went to the village on horse or muleback or carried their produce to the wharf of one of the wealthier planters, to be hauled to town by canoe and periauger.

Roger Mainwairing went down to his wharf about sundown to see what progress his slaves were making with the loading. He wanted to get his produce aboard a West Indian packet now anchored in the bay in Queen Anne's Town. They should get it off before cock's crow in the morning. He carried his lists with him as he had kept the habit of checking the plantation work himself, although he had trustworthy overlookers in Watkins and Jeb Vescels. His early training on Haimes's plantations in the West Indies was to trust no underling, indentured white man or Negro slave. "The difference between a planter and a landlord is that the planter looks after his own interests and a landlord trusts his interests to a hired man," he often told his neighbour, Moseley.

Now he stood at his wharf, and watched with a feeling of complacency the loading of the boats. Corn and pork, in barrels coopered on his own plantation, labelled for Bristol by the next ship sailing; poles for Nassau and Kingston. Also on the wharf were forty barrels of tar. In the last year Roger had learned that money was to be made in naval stores. Christopher Gale, the lawyer, had put the idea in his head at a Council meeting the previous spring.

"You planters keep your eyes to the ground," he told Roger. "Tobacco and corn—tobacco and corn! That's all you think about. Why are you letting men in Virginia and the Ashley River Plantation pick off easy money from tar? Don't you realize England is at war and naval stores are all-important? It's stupid to let the Swedes undersell you in tar when you've got the trees and the labour! Raise your eyes above the ground, Roger Mainwairing, and take a look at the world."

Roger had raised his eyes and had acted promptly. First, he bought eight hundred and fifty acres of land on the Yaupim road from Thomas Luten. He made several trips across the Sound and up the Scuppernong River. There was woodland aplenty to be had on the south shore—swamp land and high land. Some open land he patented, paying three shillings an acre. He applied for an eight-hundred-and-fifty-acre parcel already taken up by William Bryan, but lapsed for want of seating. He bought outright from Godfrey Sproull three hundred acres of timber lying between Richard Davenport's middle plantation and Caswell's Red Banks. This land adjoined Edward Moseley's White Marsh plantation on the south shore. Moseley himself had told Roger about the last parcel. He had surveyed the acreage, in the first instance, for Michael Gordon, who had returned to England. The Council was to pass on the application at the meeting in Queen Anne's Town tomorrow.

As soon as the loading was finished, Roger would get on his horse and ride over to the next plantation to have a word with Moseley about that, and about the advisability of going up the Sound to call on Governor Hyde who was now established at Tom Pollock's plantation, Balgray. Roger had a little curiosity about his neighbour's attitude toward the Governor. Since Moseley had allied himself with Tom Cary, Roger had seen little of him. As for himself, he would withhold judgment. Cary or Glover or Hyde—it did not matter so long as they had stable government in the Albemarle favourable to better trade.

Roger had a little contempt for what he called "the political planters of the Albemarle." He was a planter pure and simple. He loved the land and he loved to force its yield to full measure. He knew too much to abuse the soil, or to overtax it. He was a careful master of his acres, and a careful master of his slaves, also. Partly because he had been in bondage himself, partly because he knew that if he kept them well fed and well housed they would be content and give him better service. He kept as careful books on his blacks as he did on his stock. Women who were good breeders got a little the best of it in the way of food and houses. His men he picked for work and disposition and vigour. In this matter he relied on Metephele. Lazy, surly males had no place at Queen's Gift. Roger liked the sound of laughter and singing. The wild jungle sound of drums that came from the quarters line at night, after the day's work was done, made him homesick for the tropic islands and the soft, caressing wind of the Indies.

When work was extra heavy, in the spring planting season or at the harvest, he rode daily over the plantation with a word of encouragement or a jest that brought laughter to the slaves and an increased tempo to the swing of the chopping-hoe. His people knew that the master had a keen eye and knew a day's work. For Roger believed the old adage: "The tread of the master's foot is worth a load of manure." The increase of work in the watched field was the sign of the successful planter.

His people liked him and they worked for him willingly. They knew he gave reward for honest work, and the whip for malingerers. Roger was no better nor worse than his neighbours in his attitude toward his slaves and indentured men, but he was a just man. For extra work at the harvest there was extra grog for the men and a piece of gay calico

68

for each woman. So the people at Queen's Gift were happy, and there was laughter to balance cursing, and rest to assuage the weariness of work from daybreak to nightfall—or as the Negroes said, "from can't see to can't see."

The loading passed the hour of sunset, and the early dusk fell. Metephele sent some of the young boys for lightwood, and the blazing knots of pine, thrust into the ground, cast restless moving shadows on the waters of Albemarle Sound. In and out of the light moved twenty or thirty Negroes, wheeling barrels and crude crates of pork and corn and cotton, while the great hogsheads of tobacco which Roger had held, hoping for a better price, made a barricade along one side of the wharf. The *Jamaica* should be in next week. if she had fair winds, and then he would send the tobacco in her to Charles Town for trans-shipment to Bristol. He was tired of fighting the Virginia Customs about the quality of his tobacco.

Roger walked slowly down the dock to watch the last periauger loaded. He stood looking out across the Sound, his tall, broad-shouldered figure silhouetted against the white-washed boat-house, his dark cape whipped about him like giant wings. Bareheaded, he faced the wind, his blond hair plastered against his bronzed cheeks by the wind and spray.

Vescels, his overlooker, came up to him. "It will take another boat, Mr. Mainwairing. We've got fourteen barrels of tar yet to load. If you want to send the tobacco—"

"Let the tobacco go until Monday, Jeb. It's almost dark and the slaves have already done more than a day's work." He paused to tamp and light a long clay pipe in the lee of the building. "When they have finished, give them another ration of rum. They've earned it."

A sudden hoarse shout went up from the slaves who were poling the pontoons out to load the canoes and periaugers. Roger saw at once what had caused the trouble. He turned swiftly. Somehow the barrels had shifted, listing the flat pontoon on its side. Before he could shout an order, barrels and men had slid into the water. Metephele's voice rose above the cries and shouts of the injured men: "'Fore God, Master, I didn't mean it to happen. 'Fore God!" Slaves on the land ran down to the water's edge and began to wail, "*Ay-ee—ee-ay—ay-ee—ee-ay—ay-ee—ay-ee*."

"For God's sake shut your mouths and help those men!" Roger roared, angered at the blacks. A few of the slaves waded out into the cold water. He saw that it was no more than waist-deep where the boat had tilted, one side on the sandy bottom, the other side rising three or four feet in the air.

Roger cast a quick look at the dock. The tobacco was safe. The barrels of tar would not be injured, but the cotton must be got out quickly to avert serious damage. Some of the blacks were already halfway to the boat, hip-deep in the muddy water but a dozen still stood on the bank hesitating. One of his infrequent bursts of rage overcame Roger. Shouting to the slaves who still held back, he laid on with his riding-crop; booting them forward with curses and vitriolic commands.

Metephele called to him from the water. "Two men caught between the tar barrels, sar," he shouted. "Need poles and rope."

This was what he had feared—the heavy, crushing barrels. Against their weight, arms and legs had little chance. He sent a man to the warehouse for cant hooks and ropes. "Run to the house," he called to Cato. "Have a cask of rum brought down. Be quick about it!"

The man darted off into the darkness towards the house. Roger's great voice followed him: "Tell Primus to ride to the village for the doctor."

When he turned back, he saw Metephele's great bronze body rise from the water, bearing an unconscious man in his arms. The slave's arm was hanging limply, dragging in the water. It was Tom, one of his best field hands. One of the men waded into the water holding a flaming pine knot high above his head to light the way through the cypress knees and the tough roots, half hidden in the water.

"God's death!" muttered Roger, when he saw the blood spurting from a gaping wound in the man's thigh. "God's death and damnation!"

He went quickly to the float and bent down over the groaning Negro. His large, strong hands were very gentle as he felt along the shoulder and collarbone. He was relieved to find that it was a simple dislocation. He would set the shoulder himself, as soon as Metephele had finished dressing the thigh wound, made by a gouging pole.

Slaves came running from the house, rolling a cask of rum. A small boy followed carrying several long-handled gourd dippers. Roger forced a stiff drink through the set jaw of the wounded man. He gulped and sputtered loudly as the raw spirit burned down his throat.

"Give him another drink in five minutes, Metephele;

enough to get him good and drunk so he won't feel the pain when I set his shoulder."

"Yes, sar!" said Metephele. "Yes, sar! It won't take much, 'cause he got religion at revival and hain't had a drink of rum since last August moon."

Roger turned to the other wounded men lying on the float. After they had had their grog they ceased to moan. He turned to the overlooker. "Better send Cato out in a skiff to the men working in the water, Watkins. Tell him to take a bucket of rum and give every man one and a half. They'll need it."

He found three men on the float with slightly injured knees and legs, where barrels had rolled, burning and bruising. Satisfied there was no serious damage that the overlooker and the house slaves could not handle, he turned his attention to the pontoon. The boat was not more than thirty feet offshore, in shallow water, at least twenty feet from the ship channel. The men would be able to load from the spot as soon as the slaves, now working waist-deep in the current, had levelled the pontoon. Watkins would have to rig some kind of a hoist to lift the heavy barrels, but he was an ingenious Scot and would get the whole thing done before morning. As for the slaves, they didn't mind the water. In the fishing season, during the herring-run in the spring, they worked the nets deep in the water, as they were working now.

Roger had a moment's thought of his good hot dinner waiting for him at the house, but instead of going ashore he stepped into a small canoe and called a Negro boy to take the pole. They slid along the edge of the pocosin. Roger liked the softly slurred " 'cosin" which the Indians made of the harsher Indian word for swamp. In and out among the tall cypress trees that grew deep in the water at the point. He stopped a moment to see the condition of the periauger nearest the pontoon. He hoped the hull had not been battered by the barrels on the prow of the pontoon when it listed.

Here, close at hand, it wasn't so bad as it had looked from shore. The black boy, skilful with pole, swept with the current into open water. The yellow moon was rising over Albemarle Sound. In a little time it would give enough light to work by, for it was almost at the full.

The men in the water started up a song to ease their work, a slow measured beat interspersed by exhalations of breath, as they heaved at the ropes and hooks they had forced about the barrels.

71

*"Changua, changua, chamba
Cha-mwera moa."*

("The sand bank, the sand bank,
The Indian-hemp plant has drunk beer,"
i.e., the canoe rocks as if it were intoxicated.)

The moon made a broad path on the water. As they neared the shore he thought he saw a small boat beating along the channel not far below the landing at Moseley's Point, some little distance west of Queen's Gift. It was bobbing up and down in the water.

Empty, he thought, watching the way the boat rode high in the water. "Pull over to that canoe, Cato," he said to the boy. "One of Mr. Moseley's boats has broken loose. We'll catch it and tie it up to the float."

"Mowt be from Cap'n Blount's moorings at Mulberry Hill," the boy said, as he swung the canoe about. "We picked up two of his'n dis mornin' and one of Marster Porter's travil all de way down from Sandy Point. Dat was a strong wind yesserday."

The skiff was farther downstream than Roger had thought when he first sighted it. They had almost rounded the point before he saw that the boat had an occupant. He saw an inert hand lying across the gunwale, dragging in the water—a woman's hand. The thin silver of the moon caught the heavier silver of half a dozen bangles on the slender wrist.

He snatched the pole from Cato's hand and with a few skilful sweeps, brought the cypress canoe alongside the skiff.

A young girl lay huddled in the bottom of the boat, her face upward to the full light of the moon—a pretty face, framed by a tangle of corn-coloured hair. Blood dripped from a wound near her temple, an ugly jagged cut as if from a rock. Her red kirtle was torn and muddied; the sleeves of her white waist were in shreds. Her eyes were closed, her mouth twisted in pain. She moaned a little, although she was unconscious. Roger had never seen the girl before. Her woollen skirt, her heavy leather shoes with wooden soles, and her coarse woollen stockings marked her as a country woman, although her fine skin and clear-cut features belied her clothes. This was not uncommon in the new world. Little was known or inquired of the origin of the people who came to the Albemarle.

The girl gave no indication of consciousness. Cato steadied

the canoe while Roger with great gentleness lifted the slim body from the skiff. They tied her boat to the stern of their canoe and turned shoreward. As they approached the float the girl stirred, opened her eyes and attempted to sit up. Seeing Roger, she shrank back, her hands grasping her torn waist which had slipped, showing the white skin of her neck and arms. With an exclamation Roger leaned forward. In the hollow of the girl's shoulder was a fresh livid burn in the form of the letter "W."

The girl's angry eyes challenged him: "How dare you gape at me! Let me go." She struggled to her feet, tilting the canoe dangerously. Roger caught her slim waist with both hands, settling her back in the bottom of the canoe.

"There is no need to play the fool," he said sharply. "We will be ashore in a moment. The doctor will attend to you." He paused, not wanting to speak of the brand.

"I want no doctor," she said sharply. "I want no favour from you or any man."

"Sit down, please. No one's going to hurt you," Roger said, more gently. "The water is very cold, I assure you."

She sank back, pulling at the dark cloak that was tied about her throat with a woollen cord. Roger leaned forward and covered her shoulders.

Their way was lighted by flares. The slaves were still working in the water. Frequent visits to the rum keg made them impervious to the chill of the wind and the waist-deep water. To keep up their spirits some one started a song.

*"Amai a-da-fa ndi
 Diwa u-chi-kala nsampa
 Ndi-ka-da-mva
 Kuti pu pu pu."*

("The Wood Pigeon's Song:
"My mother died in a diwa trap.
If it had been a tree-trap That catches by a noose
I would have heard her singing.")

Roger knew the song of the wood pigeon. He had heard it often when the Negroes were working in the woods.

As they reached the float, Roger saw that the two injured men still lay on the dock. White bandages stood out starkly against their dark skin. Dr. Parris had come. He was examining the second man. Roger recognized the cut of the Doctor's coat, his loose flapping hat, before he was near enough to see

73

his face. He was glad Parris was there. He was a good man and a skilful surgeon.

Roger helped the girl out of the canoe. She stood, swaying slightly, her lips drawn tight with pain. He reached out his hand to steady her as she slipped to the float. In the light Roger saw that the blood was flowing more freely down her cheek and onto her white shoulder.

"Don't touch me!" she cried hysterically. "Don't touch me!"

The Doctor raised his head quickly at the sound of the girl's voice. He did not seem to notice Roger. His bright button eyes fixed on the girl, he said sharply, "What are you doing here? Where did you come from? Where's your mother?"

The girl turned white, trembling so she could scarcely stand. "I don't know," she whispered. "I don't know."

The Doctor caught her wrist. "You do know, you little devil. You may as well tell me." He paused, then said: "They brought out the hounds not an hour ago."

The girl jerked her arm from his grasp. "No! No! Not the dogs . . ."

The Doctor said, "Don't be a fool, girl. I won't harm her. I want to help her if she's hurt." His eyes fell on her shoulder. "Brutes," he muttered, stirring around the boxes and vials in his saddle-bag. "Here, let me," he said, pushing back the blouse. The girl stood quietly, making no sound, as he applied some salve or unguent on the brand. But Roger saw her hands were clenched and her full lips drawn tight together.

She has courage, he thought, as he watched her. Courage and a stubborn will.

The Doctor finished putting lint on the wound, then addressed Roger for the first time: "Where did you find this girl, and what are you going to do with her now you've got her?"

Roger resented the Doctor's brusque tone. "I don't know. I found her unconscious in a drifting boat. What does that brand mean?"

"What would 'W' stand for? Witch, of course."

Roger was silent a moment; then he asked, "Who is she?"

The Doctor didn't hear. He had dropped to his knee beside the injured Negro. Roger noticed that the slaves had gathered in a little close group. Their faces were blank and expressionless. There was no longer any singing or laughter; their quiet was a hush of expectancy. In the silence the sound of the water lapping against the cypress trees and the sandy beach seemed as loud as the sound of breakers.

Something was wrong. Roger sensed it at once in their strained attention and their blank, unreadable faces.

The Doctor got slowly to his feet. "The man's dead," he said abruptly, a puzzled look in his tired eyes. "A moment ago I could have sworn he would be all right." As he spoke, a clamour arose among the slaves; a weird, pagan sound, half chant and half wail. They stood with their eyes turned to the girl.

"Leet woman, Marster, she kills," Metephele shouted.

The girl shrank back; then she raised her head, facing the angry crowd defiantly. "I had naught to do with it, I tell you." Her voice rose to a shriek. "I did not do it."

The Negroes kept up the chant. One of them knelt, throwing sand over his breast and shoulders; another took a step forward.

"Yaupim witch!" He pronounced the word angrily. A wail rose from the crowd on the shore.

"Mfiti! Mfiti! Mfiti!"

"This is bad," the Doctor breathed. "Let me get her away in the boat while you keep them quiet." He put his hand to the pistol he wore in a holster strapped under his arm.

Roger restrained him. "No, that's not necessary."

He turned to the girl. "If I knew who you were and what you have been doing, I might be able to straighten this out," he said.

"You heard what they called me," her voice was sullen. "Leet woman—do you know what that means? A slave, as low as a serf."

"Mankwala," the Negroes wailed. *"Mfiti! Mfiti!"*

"What is your name?" Roger asked her again.

The Doctor turned to him wearily. "What difference does it make? I thought everyone in Albemarle knew that her mother, Susannah Evans, had a charge of witchcraft against her."

The Negroes in the boats raised a crude chant. Echoed from the water, it rose weirdly, caught by the wind, buffeted by the dark walls of trees. Roger knew it well, a strange savage chant against evil and evil-doers.

"Be silent!" he shouted to the men. "Get back to your work or I'll have Watkins give every damned man of you half a hundred—yes, and twenty-five to the women." He noticed the group of women and children hanging at the back of the crowd. "Go back to the quarters," he shouted.

The men turned away sullenly, but they took up their work with Watkins standing over them, whip in hand.

Roger said to the overlooker, "Have the men carry Tom to the dead house. Send Metephele ahead to tell his wife before the men get there."

Roger was in an ugly situation. He had lost an excellent man, worth fifty pounds at least, and here the slaves were thinking his death came by witchcraft, brought by the shivering girl at his side.

The Doctor spoke under his breath. "We'd better get the girl out of this. Have you any place on the plantation where she will be safe for tonight?"

Roger hesitated a moment. He didn't like witchcraft. He did not want it coming up at Queen's Gift. One could never tell how the Africans would act. But the girl was wounded. He couldn't turn his back on her.

"I can take her to my housekeeper," he said uncertainly.

"Better not take her to the house," the Doctor said, voicing his own thought. "Keep her away from the blacks. They think she's tarred with the same stick as her mother."

"There's an old dairy house. She'd be comfortable there. Watkins can get one of the white bondwomen to look after her." He turned to speak to the girl. An exclamation of impatience came to his lips. She was no longer there. While they were talking, trying to make some plan for her safety, she had slipped away into the deep woods that skirted the shore.

"Damnation!" he said aloud. "Damnation!"

"Gone without benefit of broomstick," the Doctor said grimly. "That settles the problem."

Roger started up the narrow path that skirted the wood, to look for her, but the Doctor restrained him.

"Let her go, Roger. She's as wild as a wood cat. She knows how to protect herself. She's had enough reason, poor creature."

"But she's injured," Roger protested. "I wouldn't allow a wounded animal to crawl into those woods to starve or die."

"Do as I say!" the Doctor's voice was sharp. "There's no good getting yourself mixed up in this mess. It's bad, damn' bad, as you'll find out."

Roger hesitated a moment, looking into the gloom of the

76

forest, then shrugged his shoulders. "Come up to the house. I feel the need of a stiff drink."

"Me, too," agreed the Doctor. "Maybe I could be persuaded to take two. I don't mind saying I feel sick at my stomach when I think of such superstitious nonsense in this enlightened age. But the common people believe it. They see witches on broomsticks riding in the night sky, or stalking through the night forest in the guise of animals, and no amount of explanation could convince them to the contrary."

Roger strode up the path, carrying a lanthorn. When they came to the broad entrance of Queen's Gift, they found Metephele was waiting for them with a ship's lanthorn to light them up the steps. He had managed in that short time to change to his house livery, a long white robe with wide sleeves, belted at the waist with a striped scarf. No matter how many times Roger had told him he was not to wear arms in the house, Metephele refused to give up the habits of Africa. He continued to wear an ivory-handled, two-edged dagger, protected by a sheath of cowhide, at his waist.

A crackling fire of tupelo logs welcomed them to the library, where the butler had already placed a silver tray with decanters and glasses on the falling-leaf mahogany table near the fire.

The Doctor sat down in the great wing chair with his feet to the fender, spreading his hands to the blaze. The firelight accentuated their thinness and the knotted blue veins, yet there was a wiry strength in his hands as there was in his attenuated body, a tough fibre like the unexpected strength in a thin twisted vine.

Roger lifted a decanter. "Whisky or rum?" he asked.

"Rum, thank you, if you have any green limes."

"A large basket," Roger said, crushing sugar and lime together. "Captain Bragg brought them up from St. Kitts last week."

A pleased smile broke over the Doctor's weather-lined face. "I always contend that, given green limes, there's no drink that compares with a white rum cup. You can have your Scotch whisky and your brandy, and that villainous stuff your men manufacture here at Queen's Gift."

Roger laughed as he poured himself a stiff drink from the decanter labelled "Whisky."

"I know you don't hold with our distilling, but it suits me well enough. Perhaps I've a perverted taste."

"An iron stomach, more likely," returned the Doctor,

77

lifting his glass to the light. "Well, here's to Queen's Gift and many years of hospitality to man and beast."

The butler came in with a platter of cold meats and a plate of hot scones made of cornmeal. Roger moved over to the fire, his elbow against the mantelboard.

"To the future mistress of Queen's Gift," he said, raising his glass and bowing towards the dim recesses of the panelled room.

The Doctor looked up quickly. "What's this? What's this? Are you going to get married after all these years?"

Roger stiffened. "I'm not as old as you seem to think!"

The Doctor grinned. He liked his little joke. "No matter. Who is she—Maria Blout of Penelope Galland, or one of the Quaker girls?"

"No. None of them," Roger said, lighting his clay pipe.

The Doctor looked at Roger shrewdly. "Finding it lonesome here in this great house, eh?"

Roger nodded. "Perhaps. Well, after all, any proper house needs a mistress."

"And a man a bedfellow," the Doctor chuckled. "Is there any particular one—in England, perhaps?"

Roger set about making another drink for the Doctor; then he poured one for himself. After he had settled himself in the second wing chair on the opposite side of the fire, he said: "There is a girl. She lives in England. Her brother's a friend of mine, a planter in Jamaica. We were at Eton together. Rhoda is her name, Rhoda Chapman. I've been thinking about her this last year. I haven't seen her for three years."

Roger got up and rummaged through the papers on the table.

Finally he found the one he wanted under the tray with the drinks.

"Here, let me read you this piece in the *Tatler* that came last week," he said. "It may amuse you, as much as it did me. '—My friend the foxhunter has a natural aversion to London. He came up to the city to give testimony for one of the rebels, because he was a fair sportsman. He travelled all night to avoid dust and heat and arrived a little after break of day at Charing Cross, where, to his surprise, he saw a rummy footman carried in a chair, a waterman following. He was wondering at the extravagance of their masters, when he saw a chimney sweep with three footmen running before him.

" 'During his progress through the street, he saw many in rich morning gowns. He was surprised to find persons of quality up so early; lawyers in their bar gowns, though he knew by his almanac the term was ended. Then he was frightened when four bats popped their heads out of a hackney coach, frightening both him and his horse—' "

The Doctor interrupted, "Bats? Bats? I don't understand."

"Maskers," Roger said, impatiently. "Made up to resemble night birds."

Roger continued reading: " 'My friend, who always takes care to cure his horse of such starting fits, spurred him up to the very side of the coach to the great diversion of the bats, who, seeing the fox-hunter with his long whip, horsehair periwig, jockey belt and coat without sleeves, thought him one of the masqueraders on horseback. They greeted him with peals of laughter.

" 'Then a venerable matron rode by in her chair. He took off his hat to her, out of his good breeding. Someone pulled off her mask and 'twas a pock-marked young fellow. A drunken Bishop, playing sweet on an Indian maid, a beautiful female Quaker, so pretty that he could not forbear licking his lips and saying, "It is ten thousand pities she is not a Church-woman." Then came half a dozen nuns, who filed one after another up Catherine Street to their respective convents in Drury Lane. Then came a judge who snapped out a great oath at his footman, and a great-bellied woman, who upon taking a great leap into the coach, miscarried a cushion. All that and a Cardinal who picked his pocket—' "

Roger laughed, and the Doctor smiled at his mirth, but he was not particularly amused at a familiar picture of extravagant and careless London life.

Roger said, "The old foxhunter is from my county; in fact he is the father of the girl I was talking about a moment ago."

"Oh," said the Doctor. "So that is it."

"Squire Tom Chapman. I can see him gaping at the bawdy London merrymakers. He hates the city and holds it all evil. He will be more set than ever."

"And the girl, his daughter?"

"She is one of the Queen's ladies," Roger told him, as if that answered the Doctor's question, which it did.

Roger walked about the room a little. "She's a proper horse woman, Rhoda is, keen on foxhunting. She rides with the Pitchley. She wrote to ask me if we hunted here."

"What did you tell her?"

Roger's eyes crinkled at the corners, as they did when he was quietly amused. "I told her we hunted," he said, without a smile. "I didn't want to make a hazard against her coming out here if she decided in my favour."

The Doctor laughed, thinking of the Albemarle Hunt, made up of all the farmers in the neighbourhood riding any old hack, each bringing a hound or two with him to the meet, and wearing any old coat, mostly fringed leather, Indian style.

Roger put down his paper and grew serious. "But I forgot, you were going to tell me about that girl."

"Oh, yes, Anne's is a particularly sad plight. That Pequimans farmer's wife died, you know, and he accused Susannah of being the cause. Like mother like daughter the people say, and they drive her away from their doors as if she had the plague."

Suddenly there was the sound of a thud and the tinkle of glass breaking in the long window that opened into the gallery. An arrow sped past the Doctor's head to lodge in the rug in front of the fire. Roger sprang to the window.

"Stand by, you fool!" the Doctor shouted at him, sinking into the protection of the winged chair. "It may be Indians."

Wrenching the window open, Roger ran the length of the gallery and stood looking into the dark shadows of the night. In the lower garden he thought he saw a shadow, heavier than the mass, move a little; then he heard the bark of a dog in the distance.

A rustle in the dry grass caused him to jump back. "Dammit! Metephele, don't creep up on me like that!" he said angrily.

Metephele was peering into the dark shadows. Then he walked over to a tall tupelo tree below the gallery, holding a lanthorn close to the ground. A moment later he beckoned Roger. On the ground below the tree was the blurred print of a heavy shoe and the pad of a great dog. The trunk of the tree bore a fresh scar and a few bright leaves were clipped from a limb. Whoever shot the arrow had climbed into the tree and so put himself on the level of the library window.

Metephele nodded his head in satisfaction. "I go," he said, and disappeared into the dark shadows of the trees that led to the shore. Comment was unnecessary. Metephele had forgotten none of the ways of the jungle; he had a genius for tracking.

In the library Roger found the Doctor standing by the table examining the arrow. It was a small dart, almost a toy, but expertly drawn and feathered.

"Not Indian," Roger said, after a careful scrutiny.

"No, not Indian," the Doctor replied. "Look at this." He handed Roger a piece of paper on which some words had been crudely printed. "I found it wrapped around the shaft."

Roger spread the paper to the light. He knew at one reading that it was the leet woman; he was surprised that she could read and write.

"Waste no pity, I do not want it. Nor help. Keep your men and dogs away from me or I will kill them."

"The insolence of that girl!" Roger said, angered.

"The boldness, I should say," the Doctor cut in. "Poor creature. She's bred in fear with her mother's milk. Fear breeds hatred and hatred turns to venom in the young."

Roger still had the angry light in his eyes. "But why? Why? I never saw the girl before in my life, or her witch mother."

The Doctor took a pinch of snuff from a silver box, sneezed violently.

"Perhaps you haven't seen her, but other men have. Men and dogs have been after her like hounds after a bitch in season. Always being pursued, that's her life. Some of your fine gentlemen planters hanker to lie under the hedge with a well-favoured woman like Anne Evans."

Roger moved restlessly about the room. "I'm sorry," he said, after a time. "I would have helped her, but there seems to be no way."

The Doctor said, "If you let me advise you, you won't get mixed up in this. There's bad blood on both sides. Her father's a scoundrel lawyer, her mother bound herself to him, a leet woman under the old law."

Roger said, "But the laws regarding caste have never been accepted here in Carolina."

"That hasn't kept the Lords Proprietors' governors from trying to enforce them from time to time," the Doctor answered drily. He got up and put on his cloak, twisting a woollen scarf about his thin scrawny neck. Roger sent for the Doctor's horse and went with him out to the riding block.

The Doctor took up the reins and mounted his horse, seating himself comfortably in the saddle. "Will you be in the village tomorrow?" he asked Roger as he spread the skirts of his long coat to protect his thin legs.

"I don't think so," Roger answered. "We won't have the pontoons loaded until noon. I think I will send Vescels in with the load, for I want to ride over to Newby's Ferry to look at the Shropshire rams."

"Well, you'll certainly be in to the Muster Day celebration next Saturday at Balgray?"

Roger nodded. "Yes, I've fifty well-drilled men from Queen's Gift. They're hot to get the prize for best-drilled platoon."

"I wish all the planters along the Albemarle could say as much." The Doctor spoke glumly. "I'm beginning to think you've been right all the while, Roger. We've got more politician landholders than we've got real planters."

"What we're going to need is soldiers," Roger said. "Between Tom Cary and the Indians, I believe we'll see trouble in these parts before the twelvemonth."

The Doctor shook his head. "I hope you're wrong. Good night."

Roger stood at the block and watched him trotting down the moon-dappled avenue of magnolia trees. The Doctor's indignation about the girl passed to him. He went back to the library and poured himself a drink. A leet woman! Because she was born the daughter of a leet woman. Hunted and pursued by brutal, bestial men. It was all a part of a greater injustice wrought by that damnable section in Locke's constitution which would set up a caste system here. Well, they couldn't do it. The people wouldn't stand it. Medieval serfdom extended to the New World! The whole thing was an outrage. This country was sanctuary for persecuted people. His resentment rose higher as he sat drinking. The more he drank, the deeper his indignation. Yet all this was no different from Europe or England. Why should he suddenly be so vitally aroused by the injustice of an ancient caste system? Because a girl had angry blue eyes and flaxen hair?

Deep in the night Roger was aroused by a gentle tugging at the bedclothes at the foot of his bed. He knew it was Metephele, for that was his way of waking his master.

"Dammit, Metephele," he shouted, roused by the *capita*'s persistence. "Don't you know better than to wake me at this hour?"

"The woman, master," Metephele said, holding the lanthorn so the light shone directly in Roger's eyes.

"What woman?" he asked angrily. Then he sat up, awake. "Well, why do you stand there gawking? What about the woman?"

"She fly away, sar. She and that great staghound that runs with she. Fly right away to the moon."

"Nonsense! You've been drinking rum. People don't fly."

"She do. With these eyes Metephele see she. I follow she an dat houn' half de night, right down to the Yaupim. She look along de bank for she boat, but thar no boat, so she put she hand on de collar of dat big hound and dey fly right across de water—like dat. After dat, what she be?"

Roger shouted, "Get out of here! And don't go telling the slaves any such story."

The *capita* departed through the door.

Roger tossed in his bed until dawn, unable to sleep. He didn't like the idea of a slim young girl running loose in the woods, pursued by men and dogs. He didn't worry about the blacks. They would give her a wide range. To them she was *Mfiti,* a creature of the Spirit World—therefore taboo.

Chapter 8

THE
RED LION

PASTOR URMSTON had set the night of the full moon for running the Bounds. The Hunters' Moon, the country folk called it, but the old wives spoke under their breath of the Witches' Moon. Evil came with it, to men who slept under its light and to men who sold themselves to the devil by speaking blasphemous words during the year that had passed. "A poor night for churchly work," they said, but the parson would not listen.

In the new world of the Carolinas there were men who were in gaols for evil doings other than murder and thievery and the like—men and women accused of practising black magic, and of laying spells on people they had never seen, for a price, a shilling, or a shoat, or perhaps a young calf.

They were called the "dark people" of the Witches' Moon. They were not the Negro slaves, who practised magic of their own unknown to their white masters, but white people who were said to walk on two feet by day, moving among their fellow men in the village, yet at moonrise could change themselves to wolf or some wild forest animal and walk their dark and evil way.

Jeb Vescels, the overlooker, waited at the gate as Roger Mainwairing, followed by his *capita*, Metephele, and a Negro groom, rode down the drive on his way to Queen Anne's Town. Vescels was a Devon man, determined and strong-willed when he set his mind. It was late afternoon, and Roger was in a hurry. He planned to ride through the piece of timber he had bought a few weeks previous from Thomas Luten, on Queen Anne's Creek and the Yaupim road. There was just time before he went to the village, if he were not delayed. Jeb had a way of lying in wait for Roger at the gate to ask him to add to his list of items to be purchased in the village, and it annoyed Roger. Once started, he wanted to be on his way. Patience was not a virtue that he possessed to any notable degree.

Today Vescels had something on his mind beside supplies for the plantation. "I've planted the north pasture, Mr. Main-wairing, the one that lies against Benbury Hall. The boys did well and laid the seeds in deep, so the grass will take strong root before spring," he said, keeping the heavy gate latch closed. He took a step forward until he stood close by Roger's stirrup, solicitude on his wrinkled face. "The Parson is a bold man to ha' the Bounds run this night," he said mysteriously. "Most like ye'll get yourself into danger, Master Mainwairing. I've brought ye this to put in your wallet." He thrust a hare's-foot into Roger's hand. " 'Tis magic against evil," he said. "I've had it this many a year."

Roger's impulse was to laugh, but Vescels was too serious. He would be hurt. So he pocketed the hare's-foot. "Thank you, Jeb. But why should I be in danger tonight?"

" 'Tis the Witches' Moon, sir, and more than that, there's witches loose about us." He turned and glanced toward the forest. "Ha'n't ye heard that Bourthier's woman ha' died in the night?"

Roger shook his head. He knew Bourthier, a French Huguenot who had a small farm in Pequimans Precinct bordering on Yaupim Creek. "I hadn't heard she was dead."

"She's had an illness this se'night, put upon her by the witch woman, Susannah Evans. I tell ye, sir, it's evil that walks abroad, and harm will come if ye do not have care."

84

He took hold of the stirrup, standing close to the horse's flank. "Death came sudden like. Deborah had refused to lend a horse to the witch woman when she asked for it. Susannah Evans looked at her hard, fixing her with her evil eye. Deborah screamed out with belly pains, screaming and writhing and calling to God Almighty to protect her. But the pain went to her foot an' she couldna hold herself up, but fell on the floor. It was like a thousand awls and nails piercing her. For twenty-four hours she screamed out, and the torment clung to her bowels till her death."

Roger said, "I'm sorry to hear that Deborah Bourthier is dead."

"Yeh, and now her husband is took the same, directly after the burial, and Susannah walked by their house. The witch woman bruised his body with her evil eye, and——"

Roger interrupted the tale. He knew it would be interminable. "Why do you tell me the story now, Jeb?"

The overlooker looked at him strangely. "I tell ye now for you'll be in the forest in the moonshine tonight. I said a prayer that you won't see the witch woman when she stalks at night, sometimes like a wolf, sometimes like a painter. Have care, master."

Roger laughed. "I'll be careful, Jeb. Trust me for that. I'll try to avoid any danger from witches."

Jeb was not satisfied. "It's your boldness, master, that makes you one to run towards danger. Have care of the woman, for she's a black soul." He made a horn with his fingers when he spoke. "She's evil—she and that brat she calls her daughter, you brought to your land this night a week ago, that leet woman. You recollect well enough, master. She had hair like ripe wheat, and she binds it in bright leaves and scarlet berries, and calls herself Anne after our Queen."

Roger lifted his reins. "God knows she's pretty enough to bewitch men without any of her mother's arts," he laughed.

Vescels held up a warning hand. "Don't make laughter, master. It is not laughter but tears these women bring to men who look at them. They're out of the blackest hell—both of them. The old woman and the young one—out of hell!" Again he made horns of his fingers against the unseen evil.

Roger smiled. "I'll be safe enough, Jeb. Remember, I'm in the Lord's work tonight, running the Bounds for the Parish Church."

Jeb was not to be placated. "I've seen work that wasn't the

Lord's work goin' on at the Bounds' running. Lads and maids, two and two like the ark, going off to the woods to lie under the hedges. They won't be running Bounds then, sir." A fanatical light gleamed in his eyes. He turned back to unlatch the gates, swinging them wide open for Roger to ride through, his black boys a few paces behind.

Roger glanced at the sun. It was too late to ride through his new woodland or to look at the timber in the north section. He would have to come down early in the morning instead, when the sun was high, so that there would be light enough in the deep woods to estimate the tar trees and decide whether it was worth while putting a crew in to score the trees this winter. He turned his horse to the path that followed the creek along the edge of the swamp. It was almost dark when he came into the village through the Northern Gate.

He was cold and wet from splashing through the pocosin. He stopped at the Red Lion for a drink to warm his vitals. The tavern was not one frequented by the planters of the Albemarle. It was the haunt of drovers and herders, of men who lived along the creeks that lay hidden from view from the broad waterways of the rivers, and of the low people of the village. Sometimes the place had more sinister patronage—highwaymen and robbers who lurked along the Somer Town road and the post road to Nansemond, preying upon travellers.

Since the border disputes with Virginia had flared up again, border running had taken on new life. Stolen cattle were herded outside the village stockade; brands on cattle and sheep changed as the animals changed hands, to be driven up past Duke's Mill into Virginia. Sometimes when the men carried money to pay the Customs' fee for their animals, the robbers had easy pickings.

Roger threw his reins to Metephele, with orders to wash the horses' muddied legs and give them some food and drink. He walked into the tavern ordinary, ducking his head as he went through the low door. The room was packed with men in butternut brown, buckskin jerkins and heavy boots. An evil-looking lot, he thought, as he sat down at a vacant table near the fire. The talking stopped when he came in. They turned toward him with sullen glances, alive with suspicion. Roger's quick eyes swept the room. Fifty or more men, and not one face did he see that was familiar to him. These were not the men of Albemarle, or of the Chowan or Roanoke country, most of whom he knew by sight. Strangers, all of them. Evilly disposed on evil business, from the look of them.

He ordered a tankard of ale from a slovenly potboy, and turned his back to the room, facing the blaze. It was then that he noticed a printed placard hanging on the wall. He smiled slightly at its title, "The Rules and Regulations of the Two Penny Club." Clubs for men were prevalent over here as well as in England. This one was evidently patterned from a working men's club at some little alehouse where artisans and mechanics met in London. He leaned forward so that he could read the rules:

"Every member at his first coming in shall lay down his two-pence.

"If any member kicks or curses, his neighbour may give him a kick on the shins.

"If any member absent himself, he shall forfeit a penny for use of the club, unless in case of sickness or imprisonment.

"If any member tell stories in the club that are not true, he shall forfeit for every third lie, a penny: and a kick as well.

"If any member strike another wrongfully, he shall pay his club for him.

"If any member bring his wife to the club, he shall pay for whatever she drinks or smokes.

"If any member's wife comes to fetch him home from the club, she shall speak to him from without the door.

"If any member calls another cuckold, he shall be turned out of the club.

"None shall be admitted to the club that is of the same trade as any member of it.

"None of the club shall have his clothes or his shoes made or mended, but by a brother member.

"No nonjuror shall be capable of being a member.

"Tom the Tinker is suspended for a fortnight, for lewd talk concerning our late King, Charles II, of blessed memory.

A pretty picture of low life, Roger thought. Worthy of some of the club rules of higher society in London, as the Club of Kings, or the George, the Hum-Dum or the Kit-Kat, where the select group went to eat their mutton pies and talk over the events of the day. Or the East Gate Coffee House, in Queen Anne's Town, where the gentry of the Albemarle met and argued the matters of interest to the planters and lawyers.

He was interrupted in his thoughts by the sound of chairs scraping on the rough board floor, and loud voices raised in anger. Roger turned in his chair so that he could view the low, smoke-filled room.

Across the room at a long trestle table were seated eight or ten men. They were dressed carelessly, yet they had the look of soldiers. Every man carried a poniard at his belt, and a stack of muskets leaned against a wooden bench close at hand. Roger's eyes lingered longest on a tall young man seated at the end of the table. He was of a different class from the rest, by his bearing and his clear, strong features. He was garbed as a Quaker, in drab smallclothes, but he wore a soldier's leather jerkin and high loose boots on which heavy spurs were visible. He was talking to a strangely attired man, a foreigner, dark and swarthy, with long, greasy black hair escaping from a red Turkish tarboosh. Roger had seen plenty of his like in his tour into the realm of the Grand Turk, when he was yet a boy. The man might be a Levantine or an Assyrian; his tarboosh proclaimed him a Mohammedan. What was he doing here in this far country? A pirate off a corsair ship?

The question was answered a moment later when the man opened his pack and spread its contents of copper and brass on the bench near the muskets. A peddler, one of the breed who travelled from place to place selling household wares and yard cloth to women. The men at the table had no eyes for such vessels.

"The swords! Where are your swords?" one of the men cried, impatiently. "Get out the swords, you swine, or you'll feel this point." He pricked the fellow in the buttocks with his poniard. The Turk cried out, rubbing himself, to the loud laughter of the crowd.

"Gentlemen, gentlemen! For the love of Allah, have a care!" he cried.

The young captain at the head looked up from his food at the peddler's outcry. "Take no more liberties with the old man, Dobbins. Let him have his time to unwrap his swords."

The Turk bowed humbly. "Thanks, kind gentleman. May Allah protect you. It is as the gentleman says. The swords of Damascus are like beautiful women. They must be protected and sheathed and kept free from the rough winds and rains." He went about unwrapping a large package. Uncovering a long slim blade, he held it out to the young man. "Here is something so splendid that it is fit only for a prince. Will your Honour examine the Damascene work on the hilt, the gold and silver design ..." He laid the rapier along his swarthy forearm and presented the hilt to the young captain.

The others left their seats and crowded around to look. Their comments overlapped. "It is too thin...." "I like it not...." "Show us a broadsword with a double edge, or a dagger that will spew out the guts of a man."

"Be patient, sirs," the Turk said smoothly. "I have such weapons—weapons to each man's liking. See ..." He spread some short swords on the table. The men snatched at them, clawing and growling for all the world like a wolf pack.

The Turk turned back to the man at the head of the table and whispered something in his ear. The young man laughed aloud—a strong, youthful laugh, carefree and fearless. Roger had a momentary pang. So he had been ten or twelve years before. Then he could laugh without thought of what might come. A good blade and a good fight were food and drink to him. A passing melancholy came over him.

He called a tap-boy and ordered another tankard of ale. He would have preferred stronger drink, but at this place one could not trust the liquor. It was likely to be green and burn a man's vitals like a swift poison. A small Negro came from the back room to wipe the mud from his boots. A porter spread his cloak on the back of a chair to dry and stood near, waiting to serve him further if the need arose. It was not often that a gentleman came into the Red Lion.

Roger leaned against the high back of the settle, his legs stretched out before him, the earthen mug in his hand, lost in his thoughts of spring planting and plans he had to increase the acreage of his plantation. He was brought back to the present by the noise of a heavy chair overturned, the clatter of falling pots and pans, and a shrill cry of pain.

A soldier had the Turk by the neck shaking him violently. "A shilling, you said. A shilling, not a pound sterling. A shilling is a high price for a dagger."

"Please, sir, please. The sword cost me a pound sterling in Constantinople. How can I sell it to you for a shilling?"

"Because I say so," the ruffian replied, twisting the Turk's neck as he would a pullet's.

"Please, sir, please save me!" the Turk appealed to the young captain. But the Quaker had started towards the door, apparently indifferent to the man's predicament.

Roger pushed the mug across the table. It angered him to

see anyone unfairly put upon. He got up and stepped in front of the young man, so that he was between him and the door.

"You're a stranger here?" he asked, with a show of politeness. The captain stared back at him with arrogant eyes. Recognizing Roger to be a man of condition, he inclined his head slightly.

"I thought as much. That is some excuse for your not knowing the customs of the Albemarle."

"I care nothing for the customs of the Albemarle, and I do not brook interference. I wish to leave the room through that door. You impede my progress, sir!"

Roger's voice was quiet, but it held authority. "A fair fight is one thing, but oppression is another. We do not stand for oppression in the Carolinas. 'Tis not the custom of the Albemarle to allow a weak old man to be robbed."

The man who held the Turk let go. The old fellow staggered to a chair, rubbing his throat with his clawlike hands.

"Will you stop this indignity?" Roger asked, his voice taut. "Or can't you control your men?"

A dark flush rose to the young man's cheeks. "I will thank thee to mind whatever business thee has come here for," he said shortly.

Roger laughed. "Oh, I see you are a Quaker. But not a fighting Quaker!"

The young man's face burned to a brick red.

"I know some Quakers who fight," Roger said, slowly, "and fight well."

"You want we should truss him up, Captain Cary?" a man shouted from across the room. Out of the corner of his eye, Roger saw the soldiers edging forward, leaving the Turk to gather up his swords. Roger thought: I'm a fool! His rapier was sheathed in his saddle; he had only a short poniard at his waist. The men had daggers and their muskets were stacked in the corner within easy reach. He stepped back cautiously, until his elbows were against the high table where the barman served his drinks.

"No!" he heard the young man shout. "I want no help. I'll look after this gentleman myself. Stand back, men, and leave me to settle this in my own way."

"He has a powerful arm," someone called out warningly. "He stands as tall as yourself, Captain Cary."

Cary ... Cary ... It flashed into Roger's mind that this must be a relative of the rebel Thomas Cary. Edward Moseley had told him that Cary had a nephew. Roger had had no quarrel with Thomas Cary so far. He had not taken sides with either Glover or Cary. But no matter who this man was, he did not intend to have the Turk abused by a crowd of bullies. Cary had drawn his sword from its scabbard. He stood easily, with his feet spread, as a fencer stands. He was tall—almost eye to eye with Roger, who was three inches beyond six feet. His body was lithe and sinewy, and hard from riding and the open air.

He is a swordsman, Roger thought, strangely exhilarated at the prospect of a bout. I would like to try his mettle.

"Defend yourself, sirrah," young Cary said, his voice choking with anger.

"I have no sword," Roger replied.

The Turk sidled along the wall until he reached Roger's side. "Here, sir, take this," he said, thrusting the hilt of the Damascus blade into Roger's hand. Then he leapt backward out of range of Cary's hand.

"Strike! In the name of Allah, strike!" he cried, shrilly, dancing up and down in excitement.

One of the soldiers struck the Turk's mouth with the back of his heavy hand and he fell to the floor. The bullies grabbed the Turk's daggers and swords.

"Drop those blades!" Cary shouted angrily. "Keep back, you fools. I'll handle this insolent fellow. On guard!" he said to Roger.

The men fell back. Drovers and shepherds and a few artisans who were having their small beer left their tables and crowded to the walls. Roger's eyes took them in—evil, hard-faced men, but they would take no part in this, he knew. It wasn't their quarrel. It was only young Cary and his followers he must look to. He was not sure of them. He must keep them in front of him, within range of his eyes. Only the Turk was back of him now. He had crawled to his feet, leaning hard against the rough pine wall, wiping the blood from his mouth with a bright-bordered kerchief. The man would be no help, but might be trusted to warn him if one of the soldiers should slip behind him.

"On guard!" Cary's voice rasped. "On guard!" Like a flash, his sword thrust forward, a fair swift blow, caught and parried by the Damascus blade.

Roger laughed aloud. It was good. The hilt of the sword fitted him like a glove. The blade was light in his hand ... light but well balanced. It seemed as if it had power of its own to thrust and parry. He had only to hold it. This was his dream of a sword. It gave him comfort and strength. He eased his body, watching the man in front of him warily. A stern young face—younger than he had thought, in the dim light—with cold blue eyes, a marksman's eyes. He had met such men in battle with muskets and with swords. They were cool and gave no thought to danger.

The barman had come near, holding candles aloft. A high lanthorn swinging from the rafters shed a greenish gleam upon the floor and made a ring of light surrounding the antagonists fighting with swift, keen swords. There was none of the formal ritual that lent grace to a test of skill in sword-play.

"Have a care," Roger warned, as his sword slid along Cary's blade and pinked his upper arm lightly.

"Guard yourself," Cary answered, his voice edged with real anger.

Roger laughed again. He had a better wrist and a stronger guard. He could have cut through Cary's arm, but he held his sword in check. He knew his power. The man was a good swordsman, but too angry now. An angry man loses the advantage in sword-play.

"Behind you! Look behind you!" the Turk's shrill voice came out of the dark corner where he had taken refuge.

Roger did not take his eyes from his adversary but he made a swift semicircle of his blade. A heavy curse followed. One of the soldiers staggered across the room, his hand clasped to his forearm.

"Dammit to hell!" a voice shouted. "It is a devil he is. I swear I saw a blue flame fly from the sword. The Turk has given him the Devil's sword."

A second man dived at Roger's feet, only to get a thrust through the calf of his leg.

Cary shouted, "Damn you, men! Keep back, I say. I'll fight my own fights!"

And fight them well, Roger thought. He returns thrust for thrust, but I'm weary of this. I'll make an end of it before he runs himself on the point of this good blade.

Roger changed from the defensive to the offensive. A few moments later Michael Cary's sword flew from his hand. He caught his arm with his hand as the weapon clattered on the stone hearth.

"Damn everything!" he said through tight lips. "Damn everything!"

The soldiers rushed forward then; some of them had daggers in their hands. Roger backed close to the wall to protect his back. He cut and slashed, using the fine Damascus blade as if it were a two-edged sword.

"Sorry, my beauty," he said, in apology to the blade. "You are too fine for such ignoble work as this." The men grouped closer, more wary now, crouching, knives in hand, waiting for a chance to rush the swordsman.

Roger heard Cary shout, "Back, I tell you! Stand back!" He was leaning against the table, grasping his arm where the blood was dripping from his sleeve to his hand. But his men smelled blood and there was no holding them. Roger was pressed slowly back until he stood against the wall. It was useless to fight longer. There were too many against one. Men who would not fight a gentleman's fight. He had no stomach for dying now at the hands of a band of Cary's ruffians.

He raised his voice and shouted: "Metephele! Metephele! *Menyana-Towana!*"

Almost as his word died, the black giant burst through the door, Cato at his heels. They had their knobkerries in their hands—clubs with heavy knobbed ends, fighting clubs of the Africans. They leapt into the room and laid on the attacking men, shouting their answer to their master's call: "*Menyana-Menyana-Fa!* (Strike to kill!)" Skulls cracked, necks bent, men dropped to the earthen floor. The injured bullies crawled across the floor, hid under tables, fell over each other until they blocked the doorway.

It took little time to clear the room of all but Cary and the Turk and the combatants who lay inert on the floor. The barmen came up from under tables, and the landlord, blunderbuss in hand, ran in through the kitchen door. But there was no need of firearms. Metephele and Cato followed the flying attackers into the darkness of the night, shouting their strange African war cry, "*Umquazi-zee-Menyan-Fa.*"

Roger called to the trembling landlord: "Get hot water and towels! Can't you see the gentleman is injured?" He steadied Captain Cary, helping him to a chair. He slit the jerkin sleeve with his poniard and turned back to the cloth. His sword had slashed a gash the length of the man's upper arm.

"It is not serious," he said, as he stripped a piece of cloth the barman gave him and bound the injured arm. "I had no intention of giving you a permanent injury—just a scratch to give you a lesson."

Michael's voice had an edge. "A lesson?"

"Yes, a lesson. Do not provoke strangers to fight you. They might prove to be swordsmen." He finished off the bandaging and dipped his hands into the basin of hot water a slave had brought for him.

Michael struggled to sit erect, his face a mixture of emotions. His first anger had faded. Humiliation was written uppermost in his eyes. He felt ashamed both of the cause of the quarrel and its outcome. "I suppose I should thank you for not making an end of me." Cary spoke sullenly. "I will, if you give me your name."

"There is no need to thank me. All I ask is that you keep your men away from the Turk. . . . Good night. My compliments to an excellent swordsman." He crossed the room and went out the door, leaving Michael Cary slouched in the chair, his face still sullen and angry. Roger found his men waiting, his horse ready to mount. He realized that he still held the Damascus blade in his hand. He started for the tavern to give it back to its owner.

"The sword is yours." The Turk's voice came out of the darkness. "A brave sword in the hand of a brave man stands as a shield for the oppressed."

Roger was embarrassed by the man's words. "I cannot accept the sword, Turk. It is too valuable. Name your price; I will pay what you ask. I have a wish to own this good blade."

"I will take no money from you, sir," the Turk said with a certain dignity. "To accept a gift well given is to show the fiber of a man. The sword of Saladin belongs to you, else you would not have had strength to hold it. May it be always your friend and your servant . . . never your master . . . by the will of Allah the Compassionate." He laid the Damascene sheath in Roger's hand and disappeared into the darkness.

Roger did not move for a moment. He was strangely affected by the Turk's words: "Your friend and your servant . . . never your master." There was truth in that. He buckled the belt to his waist and slipped the blade into the scabbard. Metephele came to his side. Roger put his elbow to his man's shoulder and swung into the saddle.

A crowd of herders and drovers and common fellows slipped out from the shadows and stood silently watching him mount. One man after another pulled at his forelock, or touched his cap—a salute seldom given by these wild border men. Roger touched his hat with the handle of his riding crop in return. The crowd gave way to let him pass as he lifted the bridle and trotted towards the dark path that led to Queen Anne's Town. As he came to the crossroads, Roger looked back. He saw the tall form of Michael Cary standing in the doorway, silhouetted against the tavern lights.

Metephele and Cato trotted behind him, their black faces set and unreadable, their knobkerries hidden under the skirt of their long robes. They were through with fighting and bent now on a peaceful mission. It was not often that Roger permitted them to "strike to kill" these days, and they were content.

Things had happened too rapidly for Roger to do much thinking about the incidents that led up to the brawl. It was only as he came in sight of the Coffee House at the East Gate that he began to wonder why Cary's men were in Queen Anne's Town. For Queen Anne's Town was the heart and centre of Glover and his men, and Glover was Cary's mortal enemy.

What disturbed him was the exhilaration he felt when his sword crossed Cary's blade—a sensation he had not had for some time. He said aloud, "Have done with thoughts of fighting and sword-play! No credit to you to prick the young captain in his sword arm. You are a planter now and a man of peace."

He touched his horse's flanks lightly with his spurs. The mare increased her stride. He wondered whether, when he withheld his sword this night at the Red Lion, he had made a friend . . . or an enemy?

Chapter 9

RUNNING
THE BOUNDS

ROGER opened the door of the East Gate Coffee House and stepped into the warmth and light of the entry. Tossing his cloak and hat to a black slave, he walked to the general room and stood for a moment in the doorway, looking about him. The contrast between the East Gate and the Red Lion, which he had just quitted, struck him with full force.

Here was warmth and light and a pleasant orderliness. The pleasant odour of meat and poultry, roasting on the spit, filled the nostrils and tapped at the stomach of a hungry man. Great roaring fires burned in the stone fireplaces at either end of the room. In contrast with the rough board of the log building of the Red Lion, here were panelled walls of black cypress, mellowed by time and the smoke of the many long pipes of the planters who raised the dark leaf.

Seated at the table and standing in small groups were his friends and his neighbours, for the Coffee House was to the planters of the Chowan Precinct as their club to the men of London. Only here in the Province there was no bright, scintillating talk of a Swift, an Addison or a Pope. Nor were these men discussing the latest play at Drury Lane, the auction at Tattersall's, or the races at Epsom. The scene lacked wits and men of fashion, Roger thought as he stood looking about him, shadowed by the door: We are sterner stuff, more concerned with raising food to sustain us and making a safe land for the people who may come to join us in planting a new world.

It was typical that Roger Mainwairing thought first of the products of the land. That was his life and his chief interest. Yet he knew that most of these men were not concerned with planting. They were concerned with gaining a short cut to wealth which they did not possess in England; or with making a place for themselves through political offices that gave them a standing which would be impossible at home.

It did not take him longer than the time his eyes swept the room to note that the men seated at the tables were allies of Glover. The running of the Parish Bounds was a very good cover for a meeting of Glover's men, for the Churchmen all stood with him against the Quaker, Cary.

Seated at a long table, tankards of ale in front of them, were the Jones brothers, Frederick and Thomas, together with Beasley, Luten and Porter. A green baize cloth had been spread over the oaken table and they played at hazard with the dice while young Tom Benbury kept the score. Porter was dark-faced, scowling. He's losing, thought Roger, knowing his neighbour's disposition; he'll be fighting before the night's done.

Another neighbour, John Blount of Mulberry Hill, was standing near the fire, his thin, stooped figure outlined against the blaze, a tankard of ale in his hand. With him were Tom Pearce, who owned Greenfield, and Christopher Gale of

Strawberry Hill. Roger had not heard that Gale had returned from Charles Town and the Bahamas, where he had been the past six months on matters concerning trade between the Provinces. Near by, at a small table, Nicholas Crisp and Nathaniel Chevin sat, their heads bowed over a map.

He heard Chevin say: "I've made up my mind to ship my tobacco in the *Mermaid*. She sails from the Pequimans Thursday week and goes by way of Jamaica to Bristol."

"But why around Robin Hood's barn? It's quicker if you send your tobacco by pontoon up the Chowan, overland to the James; from there by packet to England. That's what I plan to do with my crop." Crisp traced the route on the map. "See here—look at the difference in miles of sailing."

Chevin grunted. "I've lost two shipments by using that route. One was seized by the Spaniards off the Virginia capes; the other held up by the Virginia Customs. They said my leaf wasn't up to their standard, blast them. That's why I ship the other way. There's an advantage, even though it's leagues longer. We pick up a convoy of ships of war off the Bahamas that takes us right to English waters. I'll tell you it's far safer."

Chevin looked up and saw Roger. "Here's Mainwairing, just come in. He'll tell you the same thing. You're sending your cargo to join the Jamaica convoy, aren't you, Roger?"

Roger nodded. "I can't stomach the attitude of the Virginia Customs," he said. "Now if we had a properly run Customs . . ." He paused as he glanced at the long table, his eyes focussed on Porter. "But we haven't."

The two men looked their agreement. The inefficiency of the Northern Carolina Customs was an open scandal.

Roger moved across the room to join the men at the fireplace. They greeted him noisily and called the potboy to bring drinks. Roger ordered a cheese savoury and a pot of ale. He felt the need of food beneath his belt.

"I'm hungry," he said, sitting down at a table. John Blount joined him. "What time are you running the Bounds?" Roger asked.

"In an hour, when the moon comes up, Mr. Mainwairing."

Roger turned. He had not noticed Parson Urmston sitting in the shadow of the fireside settle.

"In an hour we're going out again," the Parson continued. "We ran the Bounds with the old men before dark. Old men don't want to be out in the moonshine. It went as well as usual. We had a proper fight between Kent, the cooper, and

97

MacTavish, the smith. Kent said the northeast corner was at the big red oak by the creek, and Mac said it was the gum across the road. They were at it hammer and tongs, just as they were last year. I had to break them or it would have been fisticuffs." Mr. Urmston lifted his tankard and took a long draught.

"Where did you finally set the boundary?" Roger asked, attacking the big dish of melted cheese the Negro set in front of him.

Urmston's lips turned in the shadow of a smile. "The middle of the road," he said, signalling for another pot of ale. "There's already one fight over that road between Vaile and Mr. Bount here."

Old John Blount looked at the Parson, started to speak, but decided to hold his peace. It did no good to argue with the Parson, for all the bitterness of his twisted foot and his thwarted life came out in him when he had too many pots of ale.

"Middle of the road will do well enough," Urmston said. "Nobody comes down the road; anyway, nobody finishes my chapel. A fine place it stands today. Walls up, but no roof. Windows set, but no glass in them. The floor—why should I bother about puncheon flooring rotting at Moseley's wharf? Earthen floor is good enough for the swine and calves that take refuge there."

"An earthen floor was sufficient for the Saviour," John Blount said mildly.

A dark flush covered the Parson's cheeks. For once he had no answer. John Blount was a silent man, given to few words, but he was an important man in the Albemarle, and he sat on the Vestry. Many a time he made up the deficiency in the Parson's small salary, and he seldom made comment on Urmston's many complaints.

The dicing game at the long table broke up, and the men came to join the group at the fire.

"Who is the winner?" Roger asked.

Beasley was stuffing papers in his pocket. "I've got I.O.U.'s for some of Porter's prime tobacco crop," he said with his big laugh. "Why don't you ask who's the loser, Duke?"

"I don't need to," Roger said, looking at the scowling Porter. Porter, seeing the crowd laughing at him, tried to remove the frown from his face.

"I don't mind as long as it's Beasley," he said, with an

98

attempt at jocularity. "I'll get it back from him before the month's out."

Beasley laughed ruefully. "I'm sure you will. You'll take it out of my hide the next time I ship indigo. I know . . ."

A baleful glint shone for a moment in Porter's eyes. Roger thought: That young fool, Beasley! He's put an idea into Porter's head. For Porter had the Customs for the Port of Roanoke and could make things very unpleasant for the planters of the Albemarle when he chose.

The tall clock by the door chimed eight. Urmston reached for his cane and got painfully to his feet. "I'm to meet Mr. Glover at William Badham's house," he said. "From there we are riding out to the northwest corner of the Parish land. The young folk will be gathered there. After they finish the Bounds we are invited to Smythwick plantation for supper and dancing, for those who like that sporting."

Roger hooked his arm under the Parson's and walked to the door, followed by the others in groups of two and three.

The Commons Green was illuminated. In front of each house that faced it the owners had set up poles of iron, with lanthorns hanging from them. Some were plain, some ornamental work, like the signs that swung from the East Gate Inn. Housewives had set candlesticks at the small-paned windows. Gaiety, a feeling of festivity, was in the air.

Young voices shouted and laughed in the darkness, and lights bobbed up and down like long irregular rows of fireflies in midsummer, moving across the Green and out to the bridge that crossed Queen Anne's Creek. The night was soft and warm for early winter. Some of the young people walked; others were on horseback. They went gaily, half a hundred or more, escorted by small boys and dogs. The villagers of the middle years, who still had stomach for the sound of a fiddle, tramped along, for after the work the time for play would come.

Running the Bounds was a custom carried from the old home to the new land. Once every year the ancients of the village walked the boundaries of the Parish land, remarking each signal tree, tying in the east-west lines with the north and south, blazing trees, recording, making clear the ownership. Each year the old men showed the boundaries as they remembered them to younger men. They, in turn, showed the lines and marks to the youths of sixteen and seventeen, so that they, too, would remember.

It was like an odyssey, or tales of early Britain, kept from dying by word of mouth, told by the bards and strolling minstrels. Only these folk made boundaries of land to protect ownership, instead of singing songs to keep alive tales of valour and high deeds.

The young folk walked the Bounds by the light of the moon, hand in hand, in twos and fours, skirting swamps, swains lifting maids over small creeks or muddy roads and paths. A kiss was the reward for such courtesy—a kiss and sometimes more.

The work completed for the lesser folk, there was singing and dancing in an open spot in the forest near Urmston's unfinished chapel, or by the sandy shore of the Sound where Negroes fried fish and made cakes of cornmeal in the ashes of the fire. Barrels of home-brewed ale were a part of the feast, or cider hardened to prime potency.

Flambeaux and flares stuck into the ground formed the race path for the runners, ringed a wrestling bout between two young giants, or made a circle for the contradancing. The tinker and the smith, the cooper and the merchant, the yeoman and the drover, all ate and drank and played at sports. The small farmer and the owner of the great plantations mingled among the crowd, not as onlookers but as part and parcel of the whole.

Roger liked that. He liked to see the freedom with which the lesser folk addressed their wealthy neighbours. It gave him pause and he sometimes wondered if some new thing were growing here, coming up out of the virgin soil. Some new, strong growth like a great tree that had its root and foothold deep in the soil; something new to make a balance in the lives of these people. What it was he had not yet divined, but he was conscious of it now as he watched the crowd tonight. Some great force was at work, driving men forward. Every man had a part to play to keep this new land clean and strong, to develop unity and strength.

Here it was before his eyes. Village girls and youths from farms and plantations, young and eager. Laughter that came easy, unafraid, undaunted and carefree. No oppression kept them from their fun and merriment.

The bondslave or indentured man might, after the years of his bond were served, become a smith or a tinker, a weaver or a small farmer. He might even in time have his voice in the affairs of the village. He could look forward to something beyond his own lowly condition.

These thoughts raced through Roger's mind as he leaned

100

against the stout trunk of a giant gum tree and watched the dancing. Buckled slippers tapping; gay petticoats whirling; the scrape of the fiddle and the beat of drums. Not orderly thoughts, but flashing fragments, aimless as a bank of cumulus clouds floating across a midsummer sky. He had never taken time to think it all through, nor put his feeling into words, for there was no anchor to tie to, no comparison in history. It was all new; all new like a great, nebulous, unformed world, as if God were creating anew in this wilderness of Carolina.

He was roused from his thoughts by a broken exclamation, and a girl's voice, throaty and dark: "No! No! I'll not! Go away!"

A man's voice, eager, husky: "Oh, Anne, let me. You are beautiful. You drive a man out of his senses."

"I will not. No!" the girl answered.

Roger smiled. The "will not" was not as firm as it had been in the beginning. Repetition did not give it added strength.

"I tell you to go away—"

"But I love you, Anne. I've told you over and over, as often as you will let me get near you."

"I hate men! I hate all men! They are all beasts; no, they are less than beasts!"

"Anne, I beg you—"

"You are all alike, with your hot eyes and drooly mouths and seeking hands. I despise all of you. I know what you want."

"I swear I will marry you. Listen! I'll take you away in my ship to the Indies—to New Providence ... or the Leeward Isles ..."

There was a silence. Roger turned to move away but the path was blocked by the shadowy forms of the lovers.

There was eagerness in the girl's voice. "The Leeward Isles? What are they like?"

"Beyond my poor speech—so beautiful! The seas are like nothing you have ever seen; the flowers brighter. Their fragrance sets a man's pulses reeling. Come with me. I will show you." Roger knew the girl was weakening. If the fellow were wise, he would leave off love talk and speak only of tropical isles and the sea. "Sometimes there are hurricanes," the man spoke hesitatingly, "but not often."

"I love the wind and the storm. I love the sea whipping about my face, and the sails flapping, and the crash of masts on the deck. Then one can fight—you against the storm—your will against the wind." Her voice was vibrant with excitement. "I will go with you," she said suddenly, "if you take me to the islands of the storms and the great sea. But you must promise on oath—on your knees—swear that—swear!"

"I swear," the man's voice broke. "When?"

"You said your ship sailed on Sunday. On Sunday I'll be at Bat's Grave. I will row out with my small boat when you lay by for fresh water at the Yaupim."

"Anne, you do love me! Must we wait? Lie with me tonight—my blood is hot for you!"

There was a moment's silence, then sound of the flat of the girl's hand on the man's face.

"Beast! Beast! You are like all the rest."

There was the sound of scuffling, followed by a sharp exclamation from the man. "You devil! You little devil! You've bitten my hand!"

A Negro, carrying a torch to light the way for the slaves who were bringing food to the long tables, came up the path. By the light Roger saw the angry, tempestuous face, the sullen mouth, of the girl the village called the leet woman, the daughter of the witch. Before he had time to move, the girl flashed past him with a swirl of skirts and running feet, down the path that led to the forest along the shore. Instinctively, he put out his hand to stop her, but she was gone in an instant, into the deep forest that was sanctuary to all hunted creatures.

Roger turned to look for the man, set on thrashing him, but he had disappeared in the other direction. He made his way down to the table where supper was being spread by the village women. There he fell in with Christopher Gale.

"Duke!" Gale called. "Well met. I'm going over to Smythwick's for a drink. Come on with me." The two fell into step. "I want to visit with Glover. He told me he wants to talk with you. He's going back to Virginia tomorrow. There are some things that ought to be settled before he goes. I think most of the Council are to be there."

Roger followed him to where the horses were tied. There he found Metephele and Cato with the other grooms. He sent them home. It was no use to keep them up. He knew this would be an all-night session if the planters got to wrangling over political matters.

At Smythwick's house they found the others had already assembled. In the big room young people were dancing to the music of banjo and fiddle, played by two Negro slaves. He looked in for a moment. Maria Blount, John's daughter, ran over to speak to him, her eyes shining, her cheeks pink with the vigour of Jonathan Vaile's dancing.

"Ah, Mr. Mainwairing. It is so much fun!" she said. "I had forgotten how nice it is in the Albemarle; much, much nicer than England."

Roger patted her hand. He felt himself aged beside her, this tall girl who had grown up almost under his eyes. He had not seen her for a long time, for she had been away in England with her father's people.

"How did you leave your beautiful aunt?" he asked.

"Which one?" Maria challenged. "All my aunts are beautiful."

"I mean Martha, Mr. Pope's sweetheart, of course."

"I knew you did. I was only teasing a little. She is really lovelier than ever, Mr. Mainwairing. Every time she rides out in the Mall, or drives in Hyde Park, it is always the same. The beaux surround her to the exclusion of all the other ladies."

Roger said, "Do the crowds still wait for her chair to be carried through the streets when she goes to a ball?"

"Yes, and they shout and laugh and clap their hands. She is a favourite, I tell you, at Court too. The Queen must have her company very, very often."

Roger nodded.

"And did you know that Mr. Byrd had Sir Godfrey Kneller paint a portrait of her to hang in the new house he is going to build at Westover?"

Roger hadn't heard that. He knew Mr. Byrd had ordered many portraits painted of great folk in England to grace his Virginia manor house.

Maria was dragged off by her partner, who was tired of hearing about the beautiful aunt. He preferred Maria herself to any fashionable lady of Queen Anne's Court.

Gale joined Roger and they went into Smythwick's office in the west wing of the house. Here they found Nathaniel Chevin, Nicholas Crisp, Frederick Jones, Will Badham, Churchmen all, the former supporters of Glover. They were standing around, drinking hot toddies. A moment later, their host came in, accompanied by William Glover, once Deputy Governor of the northern end of the Province. Roger looked at the strong, pugnacious face and wondered if the man might have in mind to feel out Hyde's strength and his chances to get back the power he had lost to Thomas Cary.

Glover was a stocky man, with heavy, strong features, not unlike Tom Pollock in build, but younger. He was Pollock's man, in reality; stood for Pollock's ideas and moved when Pollock gave the word. Since Hyde's advent, Pollock had withdrawn his active support of the Glover program to make another fight to defeat Cary and his Quakers by backing Hyde. Glover had come down from Virginia, where he had been living ever since Cary two years before had won control in the Assembly and made himself Deputy Governor of Northern Carolina. Now his morose expression told Roger that he was not happy over the Chowan situation, and his first words bore this out.

"I've asked you gentlemen to come here tonight to try to get an idea of how things stand in the Albemarle," he said, when all the men were seated. "I think I can count Cary's strength, but I'm not sure of my own. I'll be frank with you. I think I should make a fight, for we cannot count on Hyde as governor until his credentials arrive, if he ever had credentials."

Roger noticed that John Blount, and other Chowan men had come in in time to hear Glover's plea for support.

Christopher Gale got up from his chair and poured another toddy. Glass in hand, he stood by the fire looking down at Glover. "Have you met Mr. Hyde?" he asked, in his even, quiet voice.

"No, I haven't; I understand from reports I heard in Virginia that he is a good enough man, but a mighty poor politician."

"You heard that from Byrd, no doubt," Gale said, setting down his empty glass and taking a clay pipe from the rack near the fireplace. He went to the table and helped himself to a leaf of tobacco from the long box. Crushing it in his fingers, he filled the bowl. Then he lighted it with a sliver of lightwood ignited from the blazing log.

Glover said, "Yes, I believe it was Byrd who told me. He met Hyde at the Governor's Palace and dined with him there."

The room was silent. The men were waiting for Gale. It was always so. Men waited for Gale to speak and they took heed of his words.

"If I were in your place, Glover, I wouldn't put too much confidence in William Byrd's opinion, nor would I underestimate Mr. Hyde. I wouldn't be fooled by what people in Virginia or Carolina say about Hyde, nor would I be fooled by his easy manner, or his lively sense of humour. Hyde comes of a family noted for their political sagacity, their honesty and their loyalty. It's bred in the bone and taken with his mother's milk. No, I wouldn't underestimate Mr. Edward Hyde."

Glover looked uncomfortable. He glanced at the others but could read nothing in their faces. The barrister, Frederick Jones, spoke to Gale.

"You think he really had his appointment?"

"I would believe Edward Hyde in any circumstances," Gale answered. "But in this instance, I do not have to rely on his unsupported word that he was to get his commission from Governor Tynte. De Graffenried was at the meeting of the Lords Proprietors in London when the question of Hyde's appointment was presented, and when it was unanimously confirmed. De Graffenried told me himself when I saw him at New Bern last week."

"I wouldn't take De Graffenried's word," Glover broke in, "any more than I would the unsupported word of any foreigner."

"You're done, Mr. Glover," Gale said, blowing a puff of smoke from his pipe. "You can't defeat Cary or Hyde. I think it would be the point of wisdom to withdraw with what grace you can muster."

Glover did not give in easily. He turned to Nicholas Crisp. "What do you think, Crisp? Have I a chance?"

Crisp shook his head. "I agree with Chris. Better withdraw your claims. Fighting among ourselves is bad for the country."

Chevin leaned forward, shaking an accusing finger at Gale. "You can't speak for us all, Gale. You don't know the feeling of the country. You've been away too long—London, the Bahamas, the Ashley River Settlements, one after the other, going to Court, meeting great folk. You've lost sight of our problems."

John Blount took up the argument. "There may be truth in what Chevin says, Chris. You are losing sight of one fact. The Church people are with Glover, and if we lead the way they will stand with him against Cary."

"They may back him against Cary, but will they back him against Hyde? I think the situation changed the instant Hyde set foot over our borders. As the Queen's cousin he has the backing of the Whig Government, strong Tory though he may be himself."

Roger said, "Why must we consider the Whigs and Tories in this? We have two parties of our own—the Government and the rebels. Let us fight out our own battles here in Carolina."

Gale smiled. "That's the crux, Roger, but our problem is not the choice of a Government man or a rebel, but a choice of who is to represent the Government, Glover or Hyde."

That brought Glover to his feet. "Dammit, gentlemen! I thought I was coming to my own, to my friends and loyal supporters, but I see I'm mistaken." He looked angrily at Gale. "There is one way to settle all this, and that is by vote, first by the people, then by the Assembly."

Gale laughed. "Better keep to the Council, Glover. You know Cary will manage to carry the Assembly, by either fair means or foul."

"Where does Moseley stand?" someone asked.

"With Cary, of course. Hasn't Cary made him his Chief Justice?"

Blount spoke up. "The Vestry is going to ask Moseley what he has done with the money that the Secretary of the Society for the Propagation of the Gospel sent out to buy the church silver."

"I think he used it up, if you ask me," Glover growled. "I know he's short of cash. He's spreading his money too thin, buying up land."

"Buying!" someone laughed.

"Taking, you mean. Grabbing more land than he can survey," Chevin said meaningly. There was bad blood between Chevin and Moseley. . . .

This talk was leading nowhere, Roger thought. Now it was descending to gossip. Roger had no desire to defend Moseley. It wasn't necessary. Moseley could always defend himself when the time came. Roger had heard rumours before about the church silver, but he was sure there was some explanation. If Moseley had been given money to buy it, it would be bought, he was sure.

His seat was near the door and he slipped out into the hall. He had had enough of Glover and footless argument. Three men fighting to be governor of one small section of this wilderness—it was ridiculous. It confirmed his old belief that he was in no way fitted to politics. He hadn't the patience. He realized that Gale's words made a marked impression on the group. If Hyde were the man he described, there should be no question who should be the governor. Tomorrow, or the day following, he would sail up the Chowan and see for himself. Too long had he put off paying his respects to the Queen's cousin and his family. Besides it was time the Province united again under one leader. These quarrels among themselves weakened the white men and invited outside attack.

One of Smythwick's slaves brought his horse to the steps. He mounted and started for home. As he cut across the field and took the bridle-path to the Shore Road, he heard the scraping of the fiddle. The shouts and laughter of the merry-makers seemed to be growing noisier and more lusty. A chant rose, repeated over and over by fresh young voices. The young folk were chanting the Bounds:

> "In the beginning
> A road leading from Thomas Gilliam's
> House in the woods
> And follows the old grant
> Of 1697.
> Beginning at the Red Oak
> Standing by the River
> North 400-East 300
> Poles—to a Tall Gum tree
> South 36-East 170
> Poles to the great
> Red Oak
> Standing by the banks
> Of the River.
> So are the Parish Bounds
> Run by us, so all will remember,
> In the year of our Lord
> 1710—the eighth year
> Of the reign of our gracious
> Queen—Anne."

Roger had no feeling for that now. He felt depressed over the spectacle of Glover hanging onto his tenuous and uncertain hold in the office. Why didn't he and his followers give way? It was plain they were thinking only of themselves. How could the Province survive this long-continued fighting and turmoil of factional war? Wasn't there a single politician among them who thought of the good of the country?

One only. Gale. He was their hope. He had the long view. Christopher Gale had the strength and foresight to work his way through the seeming impasse; the vision of the others was dimmed by their own misguided interests. Yet, knowing all these things for the truth, Roger had not opened his mouth in protest. It was not his affair. It was the affair of the politicians. His affair was his plantation; his affair was to supply food, to bring money into the Province through his tobacco, his indigo, his cotton and tar. That was now his major concern—more tar, and yet more tar, for naval stores were sorely needed for a country at war.

He rode across the triangle of Moseley's plantation to the Point, skirted Benbury's south cotton field. From there he could ride along the narrow beach to Queen's Gift. The rattle of oarlocks made him pull his horse back into the deep shadow of the bank.

A rowdy voice came clearly over the water. "Ahoy! Throw down a rope."

Roger's eyes strained into the darkness. In the channel he saw the riding lights of a barkentine.

Another voice answered. "That you, Will? It's fair good you got back this night. Captain's sailing within the hour."

The first voice answered: "I'm willing. Nothing to keep me in this goddam hole."

Then louder:

> "Oh—it's off to sea we go
> For a merry life and a sail-ho
> For the girls of Pamticoe."

He broke off with a sudden hiccough.

> "Oh, the girls of Valpariso
> And the girls of the Spanish Main . . ."

"Keep quiet, you fool!" the other man broke in. "Here's the rope."

Roger rode on. He had recognized the voice. It was the man he had overheard earlier in the evening, pleading with the leet woman to sail to the tropic isles.

Metephele waited for him at the door of Queen's Gift. In the library a fire burned. Decanters of port and brandy were on the candle-table. Roger threw off his coat, which Metephele caught dexterously. Then he poured himself a glass of

108

brandy and sat down in the elbow chair, his feet on the brass fender. Metephele, after hanging the coat in the hall cupboard, came back with a bootjack to assist his master with the heavy, long boots and to put on his red Morocco slippers.

"Go to bed," Roger said. "It's past midnight and I want you up early in the morning. We are to go across the Sound to the middle plantation."

Metephele hesitated.

Roger's voice was gruff. "Go on, go on. I'm not going to drink any more. I'm in no humour to get myself besotted tonight. I want to think."

"It's not that the master needs watching, but it is the new sword. Will the master look at it closely?"

Roger sat up. "By Jupiter, I had forgotten. Bring it in. It's tied to my saddle."

Metephele went out into the hall and returned with the sword. "It is here, master."

Roger took the weapon and held it to the light.

"It is a magic sword," the slave said, his voice filled with awe. "It bears no blood from the wound the master gave."

"Nonsense, you cleaned it!"

Metephele shook his head solemnly. "No, master. It was as you see it now. Nor yet did any bloodstain rest in the scabbard."

Roger did not reply. He was examining the hilt, set with uncut stones, red and green. Arabic characters were engraved on the upper blade. He tried the blade, bending it almost double. It sprang easily into place.

"God's death, what temper!" he said aloud. Perhaps the Turk had told the truth, that it really was a Damascus blade. He wished he were able to read the characters to see what the inscription on the upper blade meant. He would ask Moseley, who read in many languages and had books in his library that might be a help. The Turk's curious words came back to his mind—"A sword should always be the slave, never the master of man." Those were well-spoken words. True enough, but in his earlier days Roger had not followed that rule.

He laid the sword on the mahogany table. The light of the candle fell on the jewelled hilt. He thought of the encounter at the Red Lion and felt a little ashamed. The lad was no match for him. He had known it in an instant of sword-play. He should have disarmed him without shedding any blood or wounding the man's sword arm. But the old spirit to fight had swept over him like a torrent. It was as it had been when he rode with the Duke, not caring for anything but the fight and his joy in the battle. He had thought he was done with all that, with war and sword-play and the lust to conquer, but here he was with his blood warm and racing over a meagre encounter with an inferior foe. He knew that hot blood and the sword should be behind him. The Biblical admonition to beat the sword into a plowshare was the advice he had chosen to follow.

He got up to pour himself another brandy and drank it quickly, not slowly as becomes a man settled in his ways. "God's death," he muttered, "does a man never cleanse himself of violence?"

He sat down in the wing chair, a fresh-poured glass in his hand. Metephele came quietly into the room and stood with his arms folded over his chest waiting for permission to speak.

Roger had just enough brandy in him to be irritable. "Get out!" he said crossly. "Get out! Damn you, I won't have you watching to see how much I drink. Get out, I say." He kicked at the Negro, who easily stepped back out of reach of his master's foot. "Go to bed!" Roger shouted.

Metephele shut the heavy door carefully behind him. But he did not obey his master. He squatted down on the floor outside the door, waiting.

Roger moved around the room, walking restlessly up and down. What life was this for a man of spirit if the New World was to be as rife with politics and schemes for power as the Old? He had better be in England, or fighting in the Low Country. He forgot for the moment that he was still an exiled man with a price on his head, for the Queen's amnesty did not extend to his case. His mind surveyed England's struggles. If he held to his old beliefs, he would be a follower of the Pretender, not of the Queen. There were plenty of men who shared that idea. . . . He shook himself out of this contemplation. He had determined against getting himself involved in any more plots.

He went to the window and looked out. The moonshine touched the trees along the shore, turning them to silver. The water rippled with a little breeze—an east wind. He wouldn't be able to get a Negro to seed the west field tomorrow unless the wind changed. They would have some excuse —"plant in the east wind and the worms will devour the crop"—planting would be taboo. He stepped through the long window onto

110

the gallery. God, how quiet it is! he thought. A forest stillness that struck into the very marrow of one's bones. He shivered and went back into the warm library, lighted new candles and kicked the logs into a fresh blaze.

He looked at the decanter. It was still half full. He poured another glass. There was nothing like brandy to take away the chill and put fresh life into a man. After a time, his head dropped onto his chest. The glass fell from his hand and broke into a hundred fragments on the stone hearth.

Metephele rose from his crouching position beside the door and came silently into the room. He stood for a moment looking down on his master, his face inscrutable. Then he leaned forward and slipped his long arms under Roger's torso, lifting him from the chair. With little effort, he carried his master's heavy body across to his bedchamber, as easily as if it were only an ordinary weight. There Metephele laid him on his great mahogany bed. With the skill of long practice, he undressed Roger and pulled the cover over him.

Outside the door Cato waited to help if need be. Together they left the house and walked through the darkness to the quarters line, without words. At the door of his hut Metephele paused.

"The house needs a woman," he said to Cato in his own tongue. "The master needs a warm woman to take away the restless feeling."

Cato grunted. When he grew too lonely, a man must go forth looking for a wife. All native men knew that. Among the Negroes it was a matter for tribal consultation and the time was now ripe. Their master needed a woman. Not a woman of the village to go to now and then, but one that came to the house and stayed day in and day out, sunrise to sunset, moon to moon.

Metephele gave the order. Was he not a chief in his own land and the master's *capita* here? "We will call old Sochi, the Ancient One. She will make sacrifice. Go now, Cato, and bring her to the sacrifice tree. Within the hour of the moon set, we will make *Mankwala*."

By the time appointed, all the Negroes of the plantation were at hand under the sacrifice tree. Half a hundred or more, as the children were left to sleep. This was not the business of children. It was the business of men, and women who understood the needs of men.

The Ancient One, Sochi, wrapped in her calico, with her necklace of leopard claws about her scrawny neck, was waiting under the sacrifice tree, ready to make her medicine. She had her antelope horn ready to whirl and the powder with which she must fill it: dust of the entrails of a fox caught in a trap; the liver of an unborn lamb, dried and powdered; the tail of a wolf, stripped and dried; and other obscene articles necessary to the medicine making.

Under the tree she went, and with her double-bladed knife gashed the gullet of a live pullet so the blood flowed freely. The others moved slowly in a circle, depositing offerings of maize and beer. A fire was lighted, a small fire, over which the Ancient One crouched, ready to twirl the antelope horn with its potent powders when the omens were favourable. Men and women crouched near, waiting for the drum to sound at the Old One's signal.

She began by dropping the meal on the ground slowly, so that it formed a cone, intoning softly as she worked. Now she gave the drum signal to Metephele. Over the meal she poured the beer from an earthen pot. It made a round hole in the meal cone. All the time the drum was beating softly under Metephele's strong fingers. Suddenly, the Old One rose from her crouched position and whirled the antelope horn around her head by its rawhide thong; round and round, until the double thong was twisted tightly. Then, with the horn suspended perpendicularly in front of her, the thong weighted by the heavy horn began to unwind.

Lifting her voice, the Ancient began her chant. Metephele's drum beat the increasing tempo. On the left and right women knelt, pounding maize in mortars with stone pestles.

"Pound!" she shouted. Her voice, cracked with age, was very shrill.

"*At home I do not pound*," answered the chorus of kneeling men and women.

"Pound to celebrate a wedding," the Ancient wailed.

"*Yepu—Yepu*," was the answer.

"Call a crane, call a crow, call a quail, let us hear from the doves," Sochi chanted.

"*Pound, pound, pound*," intoned the chorus to the beat of the drum.

"To bring a woman from the dust.

"*Pound, pound, pound*."

"She who nurses the sun is gone."

"*Pound, pound, pound*."

"She who nurses the moon is here."

"*Pound, pound*."

112

Men and women rose then, beating the air with switches made from the tails of calves, circling slowly around the old woman under the sacrifice tree. Faster and faster, the drum beat increased its tempo.

"*Pound, pound,*" the chorus was slower.

"I chant for a wedding," the old woman intoned.

The antelope horn had ceased to move and was pointing toward the east. The chanting seemed to come now from under the ground. Metephele leaned forward as if listening. The Old One raised her voice again.

"It is the child crying out, a maiden for my master. A child comes from the wedding of the maize and the beer ..."

The women threw themselves upon the earth on their backs, clapping their hands.

"Mulungu is speaking! Mulungu is speaking."

The earth moved. Metepehele saw it crack open. The head and shoulder of a new-born babe came into view. He quickened the drum. The men shouted and danced around the prostrate women. All the time their eyes centered on the little mound of maize and the broken earth at the Ancient's feet. The thong that held the antelope horn was almost untwisted. Slower and slower went the drum and the dancing.

"*Pound, pound,*" the chorus wailed.

"I pound for a wedding." The old woman's voice was high above the din of shouting and clapping.

Suddenly the drum stopped. Without speech, like shadows, the dark people faded into the heart of the swamp. The *Mankwala* was finished.

In the plantation house Roger Mainwairing moved restlessly in his sleep, and dreamed a dream of hunting in the Midland Country, near his old home. He heard the baying of hounds and saw the flash of the fox brush as the hunted animal fled into a hollow log, the field following at breakneck speed. A woman, mounted on a strong bay horse, vaulted a high stone fence. She turned her head as the horse skimmed the barrier, following the hounds in full cry. He saw her face, alive with the excitement of the chase. Rhoda, Rhoda Chapman ... He knew her in an instant.

He sat up in bed wide awake. Then the dream came back to him, vivid and real.

"Rhoda," he said aloud, "Rhoda."

He got out of bed hastily and began to dress himself,

shouting to Cato to bring him a fresh linen shirt and hose. What a fool he was for not thinking of it sooner! Why was he waiting to go to England to get her? In the back of his mind the thought of her had lain for the past two years. He knew she was not averse to coming to the Albemarle. He had planned to wait until he completed Queen's Gift, a home that was suitable for her. Now the house was all but finished. He would write to Tom Chapman that very day. He would ask permission to marry his sister, Rhoda.

He dressed hastily, clattered down the stairs, shouting to Metephele to bring his horse. The house servants poked their heads out from doors and windows, and the little boys ran with all their might to the kitchen. Master was in a humour, and when he shouted and stomped about the house it was best to be busy at their appointed tasks. A procession of small boys left the kitchen for the dining-room, each carrying a covered dish or plate, with his breakfast of porridge, hickory-cured bacon, and lamb's kidneys. Cato herded them across the garden at double-quick, shouting at them to mind their step. Cato himself, in his capacity as butler, carried the teatray, the pot covered with a great wadded cozy of flowered calicut, to keep the contents hot.

Roger had no time for breakfast. He waved them all back to the kitchen house. He mounted his bay gelding from the ground and trotted down the river road. He could think clearly on the back of a horse, with the tawny water of the Sound at his feet and the great dome of the sky overhead.

When Roger came back half an hour later, he ate his breakfast without speaking. Now that he had cleared his mind he felt strangely quiet and at peace. As he pushed back his chair and rose from the table, he glanced at Metephele's dark, impassive face.

"Metephele, I have decided to go to England when the seeding is over," he said. "When I return, I will bring home a wife . . . a new mistress for Queen's Gift."

Metephele concealed a smile as he bowed his head, his arms crossed over his white robes. "It is well, master," he said. "I myself, I say it is well."

That night the drums beat again down in the quarters line. This time there was no supplication to the spirits in their rhythm—only rejoicing.

Chapter 10

MUSTER
DAY

Miss Mittie rose early on Muster Day. She had work to do, and whenever there was work, her idea was to get about it. Madam Hyde had decided that her servants, both white and black, must be in distinctive livery before the festivities. She had consulted Miss Mittie and they had settled upon the design. Madam Hyde chose red and purple—red trunks, and purple coats with braiding on the arms.

"Almost as gay as the Guards," her husband exclaimed, when he came into the sewing-room and saw the design Miss Mittie had sketched. He turned to his wife. "Do you think it proper for us to use purple, Catha? Isn't it a little too—well too royal, for simple folk such as we are?"

Madam Hyde flared at that, her eyes glazed over with tears. "Edward! How can you be so dull as to pretend that we are not—that is, I mean you do stand in lieu of royalty here. In this Province you are the Queen's representative, aren't you?"

Edward Hyde smiled, ruefully. "If you asked Thomas Cary or William Glover, my dear, they would say no."

"But I can have my livery, can't I, darling? Then when the Lords send that silly old commission of yours, we will be quite ready. Did the Council pass on the plan for Government House yesterday?"

Hyde walked about the room nervously. His wife watched him anxiously.

"No. They laid it on the table. They were polite, but I could see that it is not their intention to go ahead with any plan to build a house for the Governor until my case is proved. They formulated a resolution that they did not have the authority in Council. It must be done by Act of Assembly."

Miss Mittie glanced up from her sewing. She wished the Governor and his lady would go away. The tailor from Queen Anne's Town, who had cut and stitched the garments, had left much to be desired. Then there were the buttons to be sewed on. Madam Hyde had brought them with her from London, silvered buttons, almost as large as a shilling, with the Hyde crest.

The Governor had moved over to the window, and stood there lost in his thoughts. Madam Catha was turning over a box of silver and gold braid.

"Oh, here are the frogs," she whispered to Miss Mittie. "I was afraid they were lost. They are to go on the butler's coat—or shall I make him a majordomo and give him more gold braid?" She busied herself, pinning the gold ornaments on a purple coat.

"They are quite the rage in London. The Duchess of Derwentwar had them on all her lackeys' liveries. I saw them one day in the park. I didn't see the Duchess, though." She spoke with regret. "She was sitting so far back in her coach. They say she is a beauty."

"I've never seen her, either," Miss Mittie murmured. "She has lived most of the time in France with the household of the Pretender. The Queen doesn't like her, they say."

Madam Catha laughed.

"Indeed she doesn't. The Duchess is a Papist, like the Pretender. They say she's too outspoken to please the Queen. I've heard she—" She broke off. The Governor had stepped in from the terrace. His usually amiable face showed his anger.

"Catha!" he said sternly, "I have told you not to discuss the Duchess' affairs with anyone."

"But Edward, Mittie is Family; surely you don't object."

"I do object. When I told you to talk with no one, that is what I meant."

He turned to Miss Mittie "Not that I think you would repeat anything you hear under our roof, Mittie."

"Indeed I will not, Edward," Miss Mittie said hastily. "You can trust me."

The Governor turned and went out of the room, the frown still on his face.

"He hates gossip," Madam Catha said, unperturbed by the Governor's outburst, "but I confess I like it. That's why it was such fun to be in London—" she sighed—"but we never had much chance; we were too poor. We have always had to stay at the old Priory down in Devon."

She got up and moved around the room restlessly, picking up a length of cloth and putting it down again.

"Do you think you can have them finished by noon? I did want to put the liveries on the servants for Muster Day. Hester Pollock says the Baron de Graffenried has yellow livery for his men. . . ." She looked at Miss Mittie with raised eyebrows. "The Baron thinks himself vastly superior to anyone here because the Proprietors have made him a Landgrave. I can't see why . . ."

Miss Mittie bent over her work. In her quiet way, she missed nothing that went on. She understood Madam Catha perfectly. The Governor's wife was jealous of De Graffenried, because he lived with a certain amount of show, in the same way he lived on the Continent. Madam Catha would have liked to do the same—after all, who had a better right?

At least she was happier now that they had moved from Balgray to Squire Duckenfield's house, Scots Hall, while he was in England. Living under the roof with Hester Pollock had been a sore trial to Madam Catha, and she had been relieved too when Lady Mary Tower had elected to remain in the small cottage at Balgray.

Here, at least, she was mistress. She could make no complaint of the house or the furnishings. While it was not so elegant as she would have liked, the living was not unlike most English country homes in Devon or Sussex or Kent. When the Government House, in Queen Anne's Town, was built after the plan she had had Mr. Seigal draw up for her before she left London, she would have things as she wanted; until then, well, she had resigned herself to be content, without resorting to vapours to get her way.

"They say the Duchess of Derwentwar had lovers when she lived in France at Jamie's Court, even though her husband is still alive," she said, taking up the gossip where her husband had interrupted. "Maybe that's why the Queen doesn't favour her."

"Many a lady of quality has taken a second husband before the death of the first."

"Mittie!" Madam Catha cried, "Mittie, you scandalize me!"

Miss Mittie's smile cracked into broad mirth. "Nonsense, Catha. You know that is true. It isn't for such a cause that the Duchess of Derwentwar is out of favour with the Queen. It is for a different reason, quite."

"What is that?" Madam Catha hitched her chair forward, her face alight at the suggestion of a tidbit.

Miss Mittie glanced over her shoulder, but there was no

117

one on the terrace. "They say she's mixed up in some plot to bring back the Pretender."

"Mittie! How can you say that? Why, that would be treason!"

Miss Mittie shrugged: "I said 'they say.' After all James Stuart is as much her cousin as Queen Anne. They say also that the Duke and Duchess of Marlborough are in the same conspiracy."

Madam Catha rose majestically. "That is enough, Mittie. I will not listen to such talk. Why, it is like treason to my Queen." She stalked out of the room with the tragic mien and step of a Mrs. Oldfield.

Miss Mittie went on sewing, unimpressed by Madam Catha's heroics. She bent her head over her work. She must hurry if she was to have the last inch of braid sewed on the last coat by noontime.

A sharp tap on the window made her raise her eyes from her sewing. She saw the laughing face of Marita through the glass. The girl was mounted on a black horse that she was trying to bring closer to the window. Miss Mittie laid down her red and purple livery and went to open the casement.

"Come for a gallop," Marita said. "I've brought a nice, safe old nag of a mount for you." She nodded her head towards the end of the garden. Miss Mittie saw a black groom leading a sorry nag, not unlike Don Quixote's steed. Marita seemed to read her thought. "I've named her Rosinante," she laughed, "but she is safe as can be."

Miss Mittie shook her head. "I can't go, Marita. I've got all this sewing to do before noon."

"Oh . . . those liveries. Aren't they finished yet?"

"No. Not yet. There's yards of braid to put on."

Marita jumped down and led her horse to the end of the terrace, beckoning the groom to take him away. Then she went around the house, unbuttoning her safeguard skirt as she ran.

Into the room she came, her cheeks glowing, her eyes bright. She tossed the Holland safeguard on a bench, and snatched up a coat and a length of braid.

"Show me. I'll help you so you can get them finished. There's no sense in your being here all morning, when everybody is out getting ready for the Muster. Now hurry and get into your habit. Put on a warm vest under your coat, so you won't be cold."

Miss Mittie hesitated. She wanted to go to the Muster but

Madam Hyde had made no provision for her and she hesitated to ask a favour.

"Lady Mary sent me. She wants you to sit in the little kiosk with her," Marita said, as if that settled everything.

Miss Mittie's little face brightened. "How nice of Lady Mary! Do you think she really wants me?"

"Of course she does. Don't you know that my aunt never does anything unless it pleases her?" This settled the matter.

"Just follow the outline of the frogs," Miss Mittie said. "I'll be back in a moment."

"Don't hurry, Miss Mittie. There's plenty of time and I can sew like a flash."

When Miss Mittie came back, Marita was on the last piece, her head bent over her work, her dark blue riding skirt tucked into her lap, her coat on the chair.

"It's hot, if one is working," she said, tucking her full linen blouse into her belt. "Did you tell Madam Catha you were going?"

"Yes, she—she was pleased. She said it was very civil of Lady Mary to ask me, but she had intended to have me to sit with them." Miss Mittie stuttered over this little lie. Madam Catha had been quite cross. She wanted Miss Mittie to watch the children so that they would not run out onto the field when the soldiers were drilling. She had given permission reluctantly, saying she supposed one of the slaves could be trusted with the children.

"Perhaps I should have . . ." Miss Mittie hesitated.

"Nonsense," Marita laughed, as she walked out on the terrace and signalled the groom to bring up the horses. "You are to come with us and have a good time for once."

"I always have a pleasant time with you, Marita," Miss Mittie said wistfully. "You are so gay in your heart, and so young."

"I'll get over that," Marita said, as she boosted Miss Mittie up to Rosinante's broad back, "being young, I mean. Come, we must make haste. Auntie is to meet us on the field. She rode out with Anthony, and Willie Maule. Now have no fear; Rosinante is as safe as an elbow chair."

They rode down the Hall drive to the road and crossed the wooden bridge over the fork of Salmon Creek. From there the wood road broadened and led them to the great field that bordered on the Chowan River.

The crop had been harvested and the stalks of maize had been trampled down by the grazing herds; an early rain had

119

come and where the ground had dried out, the earth was hard and firm. The field clearing was surrounded by heavy forest on three sides, on the fourth by the Chowan River, but there was room in plenty for a parade ground to accommodate three regiments of foot, if there had been that many soldiers in the Province.

Muster Day was a new thing in Chowan Precinct. The idea was Governor Hyde's. While he lingered in Virginia, as the guest of Governor Spottswood, he had attended the Virginia Muster Day at Westover and at Mr. Randolph's Pleasant Mill, where he watched the companies exercise and perform their manual.

Colonel Pollock had seized on the idea with a will, and worked out the details. Each planter on the Roanoke, the Chowan and the Sound was to undertake to drill his men, indentured or free tenants, in companies. Once every six months a general Muster would be called, with drill and inspection.

The Governor would give a prize to the best-drilled—a gilt caudle-cup, with fine figures of saints on the lid, the cup to stay with any company able to win it three times running, so the Proclamation said. The townsfolk, too, could enter a company. There would be other prizes, of kine, or sheep, or a calf; and there would be plenty of home-brewed small beer.

The burley farrier, MacTavish, had growled, "Small beer! Rotgut!" to the men who stood about in his smithy, talking over the plan.

"Have done with complaints," Barstow, the wheelwright, remonstrated. "It's a rebel you've become, MacTavish, ever since you served your time in the stocks for drinking and talking bawdy in the Nansemond coach. Before your betters, and ladies, too. It's a kind judge it was, not to have your tongue cut out instead of pinning your ears to the post."

The farrier gave him a black look and spat. "I bain't radical. I be a plain-spoken, honest man and I don't hold with no Whigs. I bain't goin' to drill for no governor sent out from England. I be drilling for some other people."

"Shame on you. You're gettin' critical—like Tom the Tinker," the shoemaker said, "and you a soldier with Marlborough in the long campaign."

"That campaign and others," the farrier said, laying the red-hot iron on the anvil. "And I know my arms, and I know the drill of an honest soldier, not these sons-of-whores militiamen."

120

He brought his hammer down on the glowing metal until the sparks flew and the onlookers scattered. "I'll be drilling all right, but not for no Whigs," he repeated.

Marita and Miss Mittie rode down through the river road and came into the clearing. Already a hundred or more men were there talking in little groups and crowds, some on foot, some on horseback riding back and forth. In the far end of the pasture a platoon of Captain Gregory's militia was drilling, their muskets on their shoulders, stepping out to the beat of a snare drum and a trumpet. Some marched in step, smartly, others shambled awkwardly on their feet—but no man was awkward with his musket. Firearms they handled as part of themselves. For there was need of skill in the forest after game, or for protection from skulking Indians of the Northern tribes, who sometimes found their way down the broad streams to cut and crosscut the land.

Most of the men wore butternut-dyed woollen, with leather jerkins and caps made of fur. But the planters who had been officers at home wore the uniforms of their own regiments. They gave colour and substance to the scene.

On the side of the field near the river broad planking had been set up on stumps, to make seats for the womenfolk of the farms and village. A striped canvas marquee covered the chairs reserved for use of the gentry. Down toward the shore, an ox was roasting in a big pit, and half a dozen pigs and lambs were skewered ready for the revolving spit. Slaves ran back and forth carrying food and dishes, busy with the preparations for the feast.

Thomas Pollock was a hospitable man; he wanted food in plenty for every man, woman and child who came to the Muster Day—and drink, plenty of drink. What if they did get to fighting? "A good fight is like a surgeon's blood-letting; it improves the stream," he often said, quoting a pawky old Scottish saying.

The officers and the planters would take supper at the manor house, and many would stay the night. Madam Hester had been planning the meal for a week, and the manor house kitchen swarmed with slaves and half-grown pickaninnies hastening back and forth from the cook-house to the ballroom where the banquet would be served.

In all this Hester was in her element. She wanted Balgray to be the centre of hospitality of the Province. No entertainment was permitted to surpass hers. Neither Colonel Hecklefield's feasts to the Assembly, nor Chevin's meals for the

Council, were comparable to those at Balgray. As for the Albemarle planters—it was true John Blount had a brick house, but Elizabeth Blount's linen did not compare with Hester's, nor was her food as well prepared or as plentiful.

Hester moved about the house, putting the last touches to the decorations of grapes and persimmons, apples and late pears, which covered the centre of the long tables. Suky and Deb and old Moll jumped at her slightest word, for did she not carry her rawhide whip at her wrist? It was small, and not lashed like the overlooker's, but it was supple and could curl about bare legs and shoulders with a stinging rebuke. She had a temper, had Madam Pollock, although she had never burned any of the slaves with a hot poker as had one of the fine ladies of Virginia.

She would not ride to the Muster Field and sit all afternoon in the raw wind. Let the women go and be dishevelled and blowsy from the wind and the sun. She would dress leisurely, in her yellow paduasoy, and be fresh to greet her guests in the great hall when they came in at sunset after the Muster Ceremony.

She stopped a moment, a bunch of bright green leaves in her hand; a thought struck her. What would Lady Mary wear? Would she come dressed in her habit, or would she go to her house and bathe and dress for the supper?

Lady Mary's presses were full of beautiful clothes. Hester's maid had described them after Desham had given her a peep at them one day. Hester wished she could examine them herself. Perhaps there was something the dressmaker in the village could copy—with changes, of course, so it would not be recognized. That was the trouble with living like this. One never knew about the new styles unless one went to Williamsburg or up home in Maryland—for Hester had no woman correspondent in London to write her about the changing fashions.

She put a cluster of bright leaves into a brass bowl on the mantel and straightened the brass candelabra. She wished they were plate—the service, too. She had wanted silver but Thomas was obdurate. He wouldn't give her the money for plate—well, at least it was the best pewter, from the best pewter-maker in Philadelphia.

She gave a last look at the tables and went up to her sleeping room. She could have an hour's rest. Then a leisurely hairdress—and the yellow paduasoy, which she had never worn except at Williamsburg. Still and all, she wished she

122

knew what Lady Mary would wear. She hoped it would not be some colour that would dull her gown. Yellow hadn't much life in candlelight.

She glanced out the little window at the curve of the stair. The housemen were stirring a hogshead of punch while the overlooker stood by to see that they drank none of the brandy or wine. She glanced into the open doors of the sleeping rooms. The beds were all dressed and in order, the valances and testers fresh and starched, her fine Holland sheets lavendered and spiced. A glow of satisfaction came over her. The fine hospitality of Balgray would not be wanting this night.

Governor Hyde and his lady rode onto the field shortly after Miss Mittie and Marita. The Governor was well mounted on a black horse, and made an imposing figure of great dignity. Madam Catha came in her chaise, with her two children on their little ponies as escorts.

The chaise was driven across the field to the canopied stand where the horses were unhooked and taken away, leaving Madam Catha's chaise to become a box from which she could survey the scene, a step above the gentry on benches. She wore a fine blue gown, a step with a furred coat and a blue velvet hood. Her hands were hidden in her little fur muff—the muff that had already caused comment in the village, not because it was costly, but because in England a small muff worn either by a man or a woman was considered the symbol of foppishness and extravagance.

The crowds were gathering. Every moment brought new people to the field. The planters along the Chowan River were the hosts. Robert West, Daniel Henderson, Lockhart and Jacocks did the honours. Pollock missed old Squire Duckenfield who was on his way to England, for the Squire was in his element on occasions like this. "Militia and more militia!" was his constant cry. He would have been pleased with Muster Day.

"Drill the old men, drill the young men; let every man be fit, ready to take the field." The Squire had harped on this one story for so long that he had converted Thomas Pollock as well as Bryan and Maule and Thomas Hill, from up the river. They all were here today riding around the field, going from one group to another, greeting the Albemarle planters from down the Sound. There was a little good-humoured rivalry between the Chowan River planters and those who

123

lived on Albemarle Sound. Queen Anne's Town, too, joined the rivalry.

William Badham had had the Queen Anne's Town company outfitted in new uniforms, bright blue coats, and black hats with red feathers. He had mustered up thirty men of the town: the butcher, the cooper, the joiner, as well as the young sons of lawyers and doctors and merchants. They made a good showing indeed, as they stepped off the pontoon and came up the field in formation.

The Soundside planters were not to be outdone. Thomas Luten had six men of his own, while Frederick and Thomas Jones, Vaile, Benbury, Beasley, and John Blount of Mulberry Hill had fifty men entered as a unit. They were good, vigorous white men, mostly indentured, but they were not uniformed.

The two Porters from Sandy Point had six men, indifferently trained; and Pearce of Greenfield had five.

The best showing for the Sound planters would come from Queen's Gift. Duke Roger had thirty men, well drilled and uniformed, besides ten Negroes, trained under Metephele and armed with bows and arrows and stabbing-spears like African warriors.

The young belles of the village and their mothers came over in the Badhams' yawl, with them the Chevin girls and Prudence Crisp. The Jones girls and Sarah and Maria Blount came with their people. They were presented to Marita as soon as they arrived, and they glanced shyly from under their bright-coloured hoods at Anthony Lovyck. Marita introduced them. Anthony was in good form today, handsome in his riding-coat of scarlet and his plumed hat. He held his head high. Marita smiled a little; Anthony was amusing when he preened himself like a male pheasant.

Sarah Blount, an Irish beauty, with violet-blue eyes and blue-black hair, managed to be near Anthony when he dismounted.

"Oh, Mr. Lovyck!" she cried, flashing her eyes and dimples. "Who do you think will win the Governor's Cup?"

Anthony tugged at his long gauntlet gloves and looked pleased at her interest. "I have scarcely given it a thought," he said, trying to assume a casual air. "I've never seen any of these—these—" he hesitated for a word—"these militamen drill."

Sarah laughed. "You almost choked over 'militia,' Mr. Lovyck. I don't wonder. Our men are quite unmilitary—
124

but," she said, shrewdly, "I fancy they can outshoot some of the Queen's men, even if they don't drill as well or wear as fine uniforms."

Maria Blount chimed in. "But wait until you see Mr. Roger Mainwairing's company. They can drill. You know, Sarah, that they will win the cup! Don't you think so, Miss Marita?"

Marita said, "I have never met Mr. Roger Mainwairing, but we hear he is very, very nice."

"Nice?" Sarah raised her black arched brows. "That is hardly the word to describe Duke Roger."

"Duke Roger?" Anthony asked, not wanting to be left out of the talk.

"That is the name they call him here, and in the Indies. He's had the most adventurous life.... Fancy! He rode with the Duke of Monmouth. He all but had his head ordered cut from his body by Bloody Jeffreys."

"Really, and he lives here, in the Albemarle?"

All the girls answered Anthony at once. "Oh yes! ... He's building a lovely house at Queen's Gift ... that's his plantation.... You know he is our neighbour.... He's very well born and so handsome...."

Willie Maule put his hands to his ears. "Now, now, now! One at a time."

Anthony laughed. "I take it your Mr. Mainwairing is a favourite with the ladies."

"We all love him. But he is old—and nobody has won his heart," Sarah said, with devastating frankness. "Look! Who is that riding across the field? Did you ever see such a beautiful woman?"

Marita did not need to turn her head. She knew it was Lady Mary.

"Lady Mary Tower, Miss Marita's aunt," Willie Maule told them. "She looks as if she were the queen of a tournament, in olden days, doesn't she?"

Lady Mary rode slowly across the field, as if she were riding to greet Queen Anne at the Great Parade. The bright blue velvet skirt of her habit swept the side of her horse almost to the ground. Her broad velvet hat was turned up on one side and a brave white plume fell over her shoulder. Her light gold hair was close to her head, confined by a net, and she wore her black patch low on her right cheek.

Almost as Lady Mary greeted Madam Catha, the bugle sounded and the five-piece band began to play. Marita, quieting her horse, was suddenly conscious that an Indian was standing by her side looking at her, gravely and intently. She caught her breath. She had seen this Indian before; he was Atonga—Michael Cary's man. She dropped her whip in her agitation. When he handed it to her, he put a piece of paper into her hand and slipped away into the crowd.

She closed her fingers on the note, afraid to look at it. Anthony Lovyck was too close to her. One never knew how much he saw, with his clever roving eyes. She hoped her cheeks wouldn't turn red and give her away.

Feeling her uneasiness, her horse fidgeted and she turned him and walked him up and down behind the line to quiet him.

Miss Mittie started to follow with Rosinante, but Marita waved her back. In a moment she had three or four horsemen between her and Anthony Lovyck's penetrating eyes.

Swiftly she unfolded the bit of paper. Two words, only, were scrawled on half a sheet of paper, torn hastily from a ledger or book:

"Sunset tonight."

Marita shivered as though a chill wind had caught her. How could he be so bold? With all these people here. Today of all days! Many times she had gone up to the little belvedere on the bank. Day after day she had ridden home, saddened because he did not come. Now today, with all the people of the Albemarle here, he chose to come!

She unhooked a button of her habit and thrust the paper inside, against her breast. How fast her heart was beating! One word from him—and all her world turned upside down.

The trumpets sounded! Drums were beating. Men began to march and countermarch, wheel and turn, arms to the shoulder, carry and trail—an ill-kept line, and lagging footsteps. She glanced at Anthony. He was pulling at his tiny new moustache with an air of supercilious hauteur, for all the world like the portrait of King Charles the Second. He fancies himself superior, she thought. She didn't like Anthony when he acted this way. She liked the other Anthony, gay, laughing, almost a boy of her own age. Why did he want to be superior? Could it be because he was born under the sign of the Gemini? He had told her one day: "I'm twins, Marita— one side of me is ambitious and grasping, eager for money and position; the other side is quieter, satisfied with little. I never know which one I am."

126

"I know," Marita had answered sagely, "the laughing twin is nicer. He is the one I like."

"He will always come out when I am with you, I promise," Anthony said, serious for a moment.

But now he sat on his horse proudly, as if he felt himself grander than anyone, even the Governor who was always kind to everyone, even the slaves.

Suddenly the bugle sounded sharply, blowing a quickstep. "It's Duke Roger's men!" someone shouted. "Three cheers for Duke Roger!"

Marita turned her horse and rode up beside her aunt. Lady Mary smiled at her affectionately, then turned back to watching the field.

There was no question now who would win the Governor's caudle-cup.

Mainwairing's thirty men were well uniformed in leather jerkins and brown breeches, with wrinkled jackboots of brown leather, broad belts with great buckles, and well-set firelocks. Quickly and with precision they went through the manual, called by Duke Roger himself dressed in the uniform he wore when he fought Monmouth's battles. The rich cloth, high wrinkled boots, the braided collar, the wide beaver, with its drooping plumes, made him an outstanding figure—"the handsomest man in the Albemarle," Willie Maule said to Madam Catha, "and rich in land. They say he is going back to England to marry an heiress from the Midlands."

"He is not married?" Madam Catha asked, watching Duke Roger's men.

"No, ma'am, though every girl in the north of Carolina has turned her St. Anthony on his head to get Duke Roger for her husband."

"How can you speak lightly of such Papish nonsense?"

Willie glanced over his shoulder, his eyes on Lady Mary on her tall black horse. "They say Lady Mary says her Aves every morning."

Madam Catha looked flustered. Edward had warned her against any comment on religious matters when she came to the Province. "Never speak of denominational affairs, Covenanters, Quakers, Papists or Churchmen. It is not for you to criticize any person's choice of religion," he had said in his severest tone.

The blast of a trumpet called their attention to the parade. Duke Roger's black men had finished shooting their arrows and throwing their spears.

127

Shouts of approval and violent hand-clapping followed, showing the onlookers' choice. The judges put their heads together only as a matter of form. In truth, there could be but one winner of the Governor's Cup.

Just at this moment there was a little disturbance at the edge of the field and a strange horseman, wearing a mask, rode up in front of the Governor. Saluting, he said, "I beg permission to enter my company of dragoons in the Muster Day competition."

Pollock wheeled his horse beside Hyde. "What skulduggery is this? A masked man! Certainly it is not the custom in this Precinct for a man to cover his face from the world. Get you gone!"

The Governor raised his hand. "Wait, Pollock. Do not be too hasty. Let us hear what this young man has to say." He turned to the masked rider.

"You say you have dragoons? How many?"

"Thirty riders here, your Excellency."

"Where are they?"

"In yonder wood."

The Governor looked at the judges; he saw curiosity mirrored in their eyes, and some disapproval.

"Bring your men out of the woods to the parade ground," he said. "It will add zest to our muster to see what a troop of dragoons will do. They must be good, young sir, for I am a cavalryman myself."

The young man bent his head. "It is for that reason that I wish to enter my troop, your Excellency."

Thomas Pollock said, "I trust they are not all masked."

The young man laughed aloud. "No, they wear their own faces, Colonel Pollock." He wheeled his horse and galloped across the stubble.

"Your Excellency is ill advised to allow a stranger to enter the lists," Pollock said. One or two of the planters agreed. The muster was for the Albemarle men—not for any soldiers from Virginia.

"Who is he?" Bryan asked. "Some rider from Virginia, or from the Ashley River Settlements, do you think?"

"It may be one of De Graffenried's men. The Baron has a liking for the dramatic."

Across the field people wondered what was going on.

"What have we here—dragoons?" Anthony Lovyck said to Marita. "A masked captain, with a vizard, or do I see aright?"

128

Marita looked across the lower end of the field. It was Michael! How like him to throw himself into danger. It was foolhardy to put himself in the hands of his uncle's avowed enemies.

She was frightened. Desperately frightened. She turned her horse away. She would go away out of this crowd. She could not bear to see him unmasked, before all these people. How could he have been so reckless?

She tried to leave the field but she could find no way to force her horse through the closely packed crowd. People on horseback and on foot had pressed forward to see the dragoons. For a few minutes they manoeuvred. Then at a signal a dozen horsemen joined them, Indians, bareback, on small horses from the Banks. Their oiled bodies glistened in the sunlight. Galloping back and forth, wheeling and turning, the riders vaulted on and off their ponies with lightning speed.

Lovyck said, "The cup will go to them. No question. What will the fine Mr. Roger Mainwaring say to that?"

"He will say, 'Bravo! and well done!'" a strong voice answered. Both Marita and Anthony turned quickly. Beside them was Roger Mainwairing, a broad smile on his face, his eyes shining with laughter.

Anthony stammered something and spurred his horse, causing it to rear and engage its rider's attention.

Roger Mainwairing reined his horse next to Marita. "Your squire seems to be in a hurry to make his exit." Marita smiled. One could do nothing else in response to such a warm, friendly voice.

"Mr. Lovyck is embarrassed," she answered.

"He need not be. I should be the one to feel embarrassment. What is it they say about eavesdroppers hearing no good of themselves? But I must not take your eyes from the spectacle. You see before you excellent riding and good drill. Do you know the name of the captain?" Roger thought he recognized his antagonist at the Red Lion, but at the distance he could not be sure.

Marita hesitated. She hated a lie. She said, "By his mask, he prefers to remain unknown, don't you think?" Instantly aware, she said, "Oh, Mr. Mainwairing, I did not mean to be rude. I do not know what to say."

"You are quite right, Miss—" he hesitated.

"I am Marita Tower. I am here with my aunt, Lady Mary Tower."

Roger bowed. "I am very pleased to meet you so informally. I had intended paying my respects to your aunt this very evening."

"She will be delighted. Perhaps you will have tea—" She stopped, suddenly remembering. At sunset she would ride to the tryst with Michael.

Roger thanked her. "It is kind of you but I must see to my men. After that I promised Tom Pollock to help him take care of this multitude."

A shout rose from the crowd. The Indian riders were leaning low, snatching a small object from the ground as they rode past at a gallop. It was the last act of a dramatic performance in horsemanship.

Roger made his adieux, and rode away. Marita found herself on the edge of the crowd making its way towards the judges' stand where the awards were to be given.

The Governor's voice carried clearly. "The cup goes to the unknown contestant and his dragoons." She did not hear his next words. Then she heard Michael's voice.

"We are visitors, not Albemarle men, therefore we do not qualify." He gave a signal to his men. They wheeled and galloping across the field, in a moment were lost to sight in the deep woods.

"I wager they are up to something," a man near her said. "Who do you think they are? Border people, or Virginians?"

Another answered him. "They might be Cary's men, but he wouldn't be so foolhardy as to send men here."

Marita's heart missed a beat, startled and alarmed by the farmer's words, but she was somewhat comforted. Perhaps no one would recognize Michael. But he must go away at once. She glanced at the sun; it was getting low. She must get out of the press before her aunt saw her. Long ago Miss Mittie had joined Madam Catha's party. She saw that Willie and Anthony were up near the judges. She put her horse through the crowd cautiously, and took the narrow path to Balgray. From there the old wood road would take her directly to the Point.

As she was leaving the far end of the field, she noticed a girl dressed in a blue kirtle. She was barelegged, though the day was chill, and she stood leaning against a sapling, looking out toward the Parade. Her head was bound in a triangle of scarlet cloth and two long braids of flaxen hair fell over her shoulders. She saw Marita suddenly, glared at her a moment with angry, sullen face, and vanished into the bushes followed by a great staghound.

Marita was puzzled by the venom in the girl's eyes; then, immersed in her thoughts of Michael, she forgot her and galloped down the quiet road that led to the river. She had but one thought: to convince Michael that he must go away—at once—on the instant. She knew it would be hard to persuade him—he was stubborn. But for his own good— Then for a moment she allowed herself to think of something else. Suppose he didn't go away? Suppose he was waiting for her now in the dusk of the forest?

A picture rose to her mind. She could see him lifting her from her horse . . . feel the hard strength of his body as he held her against him—Michael—oh, Michael . . .

Chapter 11

ROAD TO
ROMNEY MARSH

THIS whole business of Muster Day was a stupid performance, Michael Cary knew, but his orders from his uncle had been explicit:

"I want these Churchmen, especially old Tom Pollock, to get a little idea of our strength, guess more and then worry."

"But, if I'm to be masked how will they know whose men they are?" Michael asked.

"They'll find out quick enough," Colonel Cary told him.

"But the masking, that's foolish."

A dark look came over Thomas Cary's face. He was quick to anger and his temper was violent. "I give the orders, not you, Michael. Don't take advantage of our relationship," he said harshly.

Michael had a short temper also, but he swallowed his wrath. His uncle was being unfair and he hated unfairness in any form. But it might be that Colonel Cary had some plan that justified the means. So he held his peace.

Now the order had been performed. If it was dramatic effect that Thomas Cary had wanted, he had gained his end. After Michael left the field he saw his men to the ferry that ran from the long point below Scots Hall to the south shore. It would take some time to get them across as they must go in relays. He saw the first ferry off.

Then, followed by his Indian guide, he rode through the woods towards the confluence of the rivers. All was bright there, although the sun was dropping low and it was already dusk in the forest. In a little time the sun would be lost behind the trees. His spirits rose as he made his way along the path. Marita would come, of that he was certain. Women always came when he wanted them. Young as he was, he had had his experiences. The blood flows hot in the warm tropical islands and the opportunities were many. Creole girls developed early and it wasn't hard on a moonlit night for them to escape from their duennas to jasmine-scented gardens and white beaches swept by the soft wind.

In England, like the other lads at his college, he had known every parish by its impurities and the streets of lewdness in London, although he had never, like some of his companions, frequented the haunts and resorts of female nightwalkers. Nor had he indulged in the midnight masks where the "ladies of quality" of Bridewell mingled with the ladies of the West End, each conveniently hidden by a tiny mask of velvet or silk. He could not stomach these congregations which ended in intrigue and assignations.

But his thought of this girl was different, somehow removed. His pulse quickened at the image of her. He wanted to look into her eyes—those clear eyes, tawny as topaz. Never had he seen such depths in a woman's eyes, or any eyes set with a double fringe of lashes such as Marita's, either in England or in the Golden Isles where women were beautiful and entrancing.

She was so young, so virginal and untutored. If he could only wake her to life with his kisses. That thought had burned in him when he had last seen her, but something held him back. It was as if she were surrounded by a protecting unseen force. Would it guard her tonight? Or could he step past the invisible barrier that sheltered her?

He thought of the blue shadows under her eyes, the delicate flush on her smooth cheek. Her mouth, which held so much promise, was firm, and her little jaw was strong. She could be stormy and he smiled at the thought of her stubborn loyalties.

"By the living God, you're in love, Michael!" he said aloud. The sound of his voice brought his Indian up to him.

"No. No. I don't want you," he said. "Stay back, Atonga, I do not need you now."

He found the little house deserted. A swift glance at the ground and the path leading to the belvedere showed no marks of her little shoes. A woodsman, he read the signs quickly. No one had been there this day.

He walked out to the edge of the bank. All was silent; even the waterfowl were motionless on the water. At the foot of the path that led down the high bank to the beach a small boat was moored, swinging slightly with the current. The quiet of the sunset and the forest swept through him, as it always did. He was young but he loved solitude. A long time he waited, but at last he grew impatient and walked back to the bank, his heavy boots breaking the pine needles.

By God, she knew how to keep a man on tenterhooks, he thought, angered. He was a fool to let a chit of a girl ensnare him.

A few tiny white clouds turned gold with the setting sun. The tenuous scents of the forest filled the air: dried leaves and bracken, the damp earth of the swamp. He made up his mind not to hurry matters. Let her come to him in her own way.

The breaking of a twig set him alert and he stepped behind a tree to watch the slight stirring among the low bushes. A woman moved, shadowlike and veiled, beyond the tangle of vines.

"Come out," he said, a laugh in his voice. "Come out."

A girl stepped from the screen of vines, a white staghound by her side. She had not seen him nor had the dog scented Michael, for a north wind blew off the water. His heart contracted in disappointment. It was not Marita but a strange girl with flaxen hair in great braids over her blue kirtle. Her legs and arms were bare, scratched by briars and brambles. A long knife in a leather sheath hung from her belt. She wore rough dress and heavy shoes; obviously a common wench for all that she had grace of movement. Her face aroused his interest; it was turbulent—passionate and bold. Like a startled animal she was poised ready for flight, her hand on the collar of the dog, but he was too quick for her. He caught her wrist and hindered her.

"Spying," he said.

"Leave go!" she said, dragging at her wrist.

"Spying," he repeated at her. Her breast rose and fell under her light bodice. The dog growled and bared his great

133

fangs, but he did not move; he was waiting for a word from his mistress.

Michael dropped her wrist. The girl rubbed it. His hold had been heavier than he had thought.

"You are strong," she said.

"And you are pretty."

"Have done with such talk," she said shortly. Michael was piqued by her words and the contempt in her voice. She looked at him from under half-closed eyes.

"Art a stranger here?" she asked.

Michael nodded.

"A sailor from a ship?"

Michael shook his head; the girl looked disappointed. Michael laughed aloud.

"What's wrong with a landsman?" he asked. "Do you like only sailors?"

" 'Tis not sailors I like; 'tis the ships they sail in. I thought mayhap ye'd take me away in a ship with tall masts and great billowing sails."

Michael looked at her more closely. The girl was overbold but she had a way with her. "Well, I haven't a boat. I live in a camp."

"Camp? Then you're a soldier? I will go with you to your camp."

This has gone far enough, Michael thought. "We want no camp women," he said shortly.

The girl stamped her foot, her eyes blazing. "I'm not a camp woman; I would cook and sew."

"And sleep in my tent at night? No thank you," Michael cut in. The girl stood looking at him for a moment with angry, sullen eyes. Suddenly her face changed. Two tears fell from her wide blue eyes. "Oh, I say." Michael was suddenly remorseful.

She drew her coarse linen sleeve across her eyes and sobs shook her body. "What's wrong with you anyway?" Michael, like most strong men, was dismayed by tears. Her sobs continued. He threw one arm about her protectingly.

The dog stiffened and growled; his head turned toward the wood road.

Michael turned to look. He dropped his arms from the warm body of the girl. "Marita!" he called, "Marita!" but it was too late. She had wheeled her horse and was galloping down the road at breakneck speed.

"You wanton!" he shouted as he pushed the girl from him.

"Damn you!" She swayed a moment and caught herself against the trunk of a tree.

"Damn you!" she shouted back at him, her eyes blazing. "Art shamed to be caught with a leet woman? One day you'll wish you had more kindness in your veins." She turned and raced down the little path to the beach, her staghound at her flying heels. She jumped into the boat he had noticed before, and took up the oars, the dog crouching beside her.

He did not wait to see what direction she took, but turned his eyes to the wood road. Why hadn't Marita waited? He could have explained so easily.

He took a few steps. He would overtake her, bring her back to his kisses. Then his wrath rose. No, by Jupiter! She expected him to follow her, to explain. He would never explain! If a woman had no trust, he was through with her—through!

He flung himself on his horse and took the path that led through the swampland, his Indian close behind him. He crossed the ferry in silence, without talk for old Jephthah, the ferryman.

The road from Hill's Ferry to Romney Marsh was long and not without danger from skulking beasts of prey or from warlike Indians. But Michael was too angry to exercise caution as he made his way through the forest. He pushed his horse, riding hard to the accompaniment of his own hard thoughts. It was almost daybreak before his anger died. There was nothing left but the ache of having lost her. "Marita," he said aloud, "Marita!"

Michael reached the stockade at Bath Town at sunup. The sentry let him through and he rode directly to the home of Tobias Knight, where he thought it likely his uncle might be. There was little activity in the village. Most of the shops were shuttered and only a few Indians, servants of the village, were stirring, making small fires to warm themselves and cook their frugal breakfasts.

Tobias Knight was having early tea when Michael arrived. He was seated at a window looking out on the broad prospect of Bath Creek; the table was spread with papers, and a horn inkwell and a sanding-box were close at hand. From here he could watch his slaves working at the great stone vat where his tar was being boiled for caulking the vessels that sailed into Pamticoe Sound, through Ocracock Inlet.

Michael did not think too well of Tobias Knight, who was most affable to him because of his relationship to Thomas Cary. For the moment Knight was on excellent terms with Cary, but he was a man of variable moods. In his capacity of judge of the Admiralty Court he had many and important decisions to make over vessels sailing into the Sound. Some said he was not above taking a bribe, if it were of sufficient size, from the masters of vessels who wanted to make speedy disposal of cargo and stand out to sea the same day.

The Judge called to a slave to bring a chair for Michael, who had refused tea although he had not yet broken his fast. He preferred to ride on to Jewell's plantation rather than to eat under Tobias Knight's roof.

"Your uncle rode to Romney Marsh last night," Knight told him. "There is some little difficulty with his command, I believe." He looked down his long nose, a peculiar smile on his thin lips and in his light blue eyes.

He looks exactly like a fox, Michael thought, crafty and sly. He started to get up from his chair.

"No, no, now. Wait a moment," Knight said. "I need some advice." He pushed some charts and papers about until he found the one he was looking for. "I'm making up directions for navigators. They have grave trouble entering Pamticoe and Albemarle Sounds. Your uncle says you are familiar with every league of water from here to the Bahamas. Is that true?"

Michael said, "I've sailed these waters a few times."

"Good! Then listen. Don't mind making suggestions; Tobias Knight has always an open mind, don't forget that."

Michael nodded.

"I've had soundings taken," Knight went on, "but one can never tell if these rascally bondsmen are accurate."

He spread the chart on the table, using the earthen teapot and his cup and saucer to hold the corners, while he read. "'Directions to Sail into All the Navigable Inlets.' ... Let's see—Fair Cape, Bear Inlet, New Topsail, Currituck Sound— where in confusion is Ocracock?" He turned over a page to write. "Here it is—Ocracock. Listen well, Michael, I want no mistakes here." He cleared his throat and set his steel spectacles atop his long nose. "'Make toward the Bar and you will see a flagstaff, or flag, hoisted, which the pilots generally display on the west end of the island when they see a ship off, then make towards Ocracock Island and bring Beacon Island to bear west by north. That course will lead you close

136

to the breakers in seventeen feet. Keep close to the Island till you come to the north end, then steer an East-Northeast course for the Hole in four fathoms. Come to anchor and take on a pilot.'

" 'This harbour serves for Pamticoe and Albemarle for the largest vessels. Ships' officers are not to be trusted, therefore a pilot is necessary. Fee for taking ship over the bar, twenty pounds sterling.' "

He pushed the chart towards Michael when he had finished.

Michael glanced at it briefly. He was quite familiar with that inlet, as well as with Hatteras and Roanoke.

Knight looked at him. "Well," he said, "am I correct in the soundings?"

Michael nodded. "But no navigator who has good charts needs a pilot," he said.

Knight's face darkened. "The fee goes to the government," he said shortly.

Michael got to his feet. "I must get on," he said. This time Knight let him go without protest.

I wonder just how much of the fee the government really receives, Michael thought, as he rode along the shore. He passed Adams' place and Ottiwell's and turned into Jewell's. Jewell was not there, but a slave served him breakfast of bacon and corncakes.

It was ten o'clock when he reached Cary's camp at Romney Marsh. Here they had snug harbour. Surrounded by marsh on three sides and water on the fourth, he was well hidden and protected. Only men who knew the marsh knew the secret paths and dry islands of the vast pocosin. Beyond there to the east were the Wild Deserts, extending to the sea. There they were safe, but Cary had one uneasiness. No one had the key to his marsh kingdom save the Quaker Porter, once his friend, now his enemy. So always there was a strong guard at the land entrance, and sentries, well concealed, watched the water for ships. There were men in the Albemarle who had fears about Cary's camp and about Cary's army. It was an army such as the old Barons had, to go out and wage war, and take slaves, a menace to the government and to the peace of the country.

Michael was aware of this. Foster Tomes had spoken more than once to his uncle about the danger of setting up a marsh kingdom of his own. "There will be no peace in this Province until Thomas Cary rids himself of his worldly ambitions, and sees the Light," Tomes had told Michael when he last saw him. "Friend Thomas has let hate and envy and pride enter his soul and crowd out love. There is danger in that."

Michael came on the sentry and gave the word. The man, a toughened, hardy Yorkshireman who had run away from his bondholder in the border counties, grinned, for the word was "Victory."

"Victory," the sentry repeated as he grounded his musket and stepped aside to let Michael pass on the narrow neck. "Mayhap we will be riding again soon." Michael did not answer; he did not know what their next move would be.

His uncle was seated on a stump in the centre of the compound, watching two Indians make shot. The method was crude in the extreme, yet he had managed to build up a supply. Powder he had in some quantity, taken from a ship wrecked off Nag's Head. The men from the Banks whispered to each other that the ship had been lured to its doom with false lights. They resented Cary and his encroachment on their domain, for had they not been wrecking ships these many years? But Cary's soldiers were in force and they had arms, so all the Bankers could do was to whisper among themselves.

In build Thomas Cary was not unlike Michael. Both of them were well above six feet, broad of shoulder and flat-waisted. They were of the same colouring, blond and blue-eyed Saxons, but here the likeness ceased. Thomas' eyes were a cold pale blue and his high-bridged nose larger and his lips thinner. There was strength in his face, but there was cruelty also, and his eyes lacked the clear candid look that made Michael's eyes his best feature.

He led the way into his bell tent before he asked any questions.

He wanted minute detail of the occurrences on the parade field, and he was well pleased, particularly when Michael told him how he had outdrilled the soldiers trained by Roger Mainwairing.

"Good! Good!" he said, rubbing his hands together. "That pleases me. I've more than one score to settle with Duke Roger." Michael had a score to settle also, but he said nothing about that. He hoped his uncle would not notice that his arm was stiff from the wound Mainwairing had given him when they fought in the Red Lion. But the Colonel was too engrossed with his own affairs to think of Michael.

"Did Knight tell you that Edward Moseley was in Bath Town yesterday?"

"No, sir, he did not mention it."

"Moseley thinks we should make peace with the new Governor," Thomas Cary said after a moment. "He tried to get me to sign a paper. Why should I sign away my power to Hyde unless it is to my advantage?"

"But I thought Moseley was on our side?" Michael's tone showed his surprise.

Tom Cary laughed. "So he is, after his fashion, but Edward and I disagree sometimes. He has great ideas about men's rights and law enforcement. I don't think this country is civilized enough yet. You can't set men in a wilderness and give them law. You have to hold them in check by force rather than law or government."

Michael was startled at this answer from his uncle. "But I thought—"

"It is not for you to think, Michael." Cary's voice was sharp. "It may prove to be good sense to make a truce—it will give me time to build up my little army." He laughed without mirth. "Yes, perhaps a truce would have advantages."

Michael left his uncle then and went to his tent. "Atonga!" he called. The Indian came from behind the tent; in his hand he held a basin of hot water.

Michael's face cleared. Atonga knew what was necessary. The wound was aching painfully. He had had no time to take off his jerkin or change the rude dressing the Indian had put on the day before. Now he found the cut had opened and a heavy blood clot had formed. The sleeve had to be cut before they could get it clear of his arm. The wound was angry and red, and his upper arm swollen. What if the wound should mortify? It might leave him with a stiff arm.

Atonga cleaned away the clotted blood and stood looking at the arm attentively. "Wait," he said, and went out of the tent.

Michael had taken off his boots and changed into fresh clothes before the Indian returned. With him was an Indian woman. "Atonga's wife," the guide said, by way of introduction.

The woman said nothing, but came over and took hold of Michael's arm. She pressed the red, angry flesh between her fingers, shook her head and said a few words to Atonga. He took his knife and held it for a moment in the blaze of a candle.

"Very still," he said to Michael. In an instant he had made a crosscut in the wound. The woman pressed again and white pus squirted out. She nodded with satisfaction, as she proceeded to clean the open wound carefully. Then she took several leaves of tobacco from a bag and laid them across his upper arm, binding it with a clean white cloth. "All well," she said, and without waiting for Michael to thank her, she left the tent.

Michael breathed a long sigh. The throbbing had gone. The leaves felt cool and soothing. He yawned widely. How long had it been since he slept?

"Sleep is good," Atonga said, reading his thought.

Michael threw himself on the pine boughs that made his crude bed. In an instant his eyes closed.

Atonga stood watching until Michael's breathing came slow and regular. Then the Indian covered him with his cloak and went out.

At the manor house the feasting and dancing went on from sundown far into the night. Hester, with cheeks flushed, black eyes sparkling, played the great lady with a will, as if she were bred to courts and palaces, accustomed to spending her nights at theatres and assemblies, masquerades and routs.

Madam Catha was gracious, and if there was a little hauteur in her manner, who could criticize? The Governor led out Hester Pollock, when the Negro musicians played a contradance, while Thomas danced with Madam Catha.

A Councilman, Nicholas Crisp, bowed before Lady Mary, but she begged off. She still wore her riding garb—and who could dance in heavy boots? But she pleased Nicholas by brushing her skirts aside so that he might sit beside her to watch the others dance.

Marita found her way to the small parlour with the young folk. She had no heart for the gaiety. She danced with Anthony, but she could think only of Michael. How could he have treated her so rudely, making love to a peasant girl! It was the same girl she had seen when she left the field, slinking from tree to tree, hiding—from what? Perhaps she was not hiding, only watching for Michael, to keep an assignation. Or perhaps the girl had mistakenly come too soon. Perhaps Michael had intended meeting Marita first, then, with her kisses warm on his lips, to make love to his lowly mistress.

She tried to harden her heart against Michael, to be gay

for other men, but she could not. As soon as the dance ended she made some excuse to Anthony and went out to the terrace. The moon was riding high, sending its thin glow to soften the landscape and to lie, a veil of silver, on the water. For all her effort to hate him, the want of Michael was heavy on her.

"Wish on the moon?" A deep voice broke her melancholy thoughts. She turned around. Roger Mainwairing was coming towards her, a glass of port in his hand.

"I saw you from the window. I thought this no time for a young maid to be lonely." He put the glass in her hand. "Drink it," he said firmly. "No 'buts.' It will bring the colour to those pale cheeks."

Marita obeyed him. Who would not? For he was a strong man, stronger than Michael and taller. She wondered if he would do to any woman what Michael had done to her this night.

"May I take you to your aunt?" he asked, after she had finished the drink. She nodded. She did not feel inclined to speak, nor did she feel the need to. This man looked at her so warmly, so understandingly.

Lady Mary dismissed her partner with a nod of her head when she saw Marita. Her eyes had been on the tall figure of Duke Roger moving with easy natural grace among the dancers as he guided Marita across the dancing-floor.

"Madam," he said, "my service to your ladyship. I have brought you a weary child,"—he smiled down at Marita—"a tired, weary child."

Lady Mary made a place for Marita but she did not look at her. He eyes were fixed on a riband across Duke Roger's chest from which hung a golden decoration. "Mother of Mercy," she whispered. "I did not think to see that here, at the end of the world."

Roger touched the golden bauble with his strong brown fingers, almost a caress.

"Mr.—" She paused. "I think I do not know your name."

"Roger Mainwairing, at your ladyship's service," he answered, bowing.

"Mr. Mainwairing, you must pardon me if I seem rude, but tell me why—how—you wear a decoration bestowed only by King Charles himself?"

"The riband came to me, not from the King, but from the King's son. He pinned it to my cloak at Sedgemoor, after the battle and we were hiding in the ditches from King James's soldiers."

"Monmouth," she said, her face very white. "You rode with the Duke? I should have known from your uniform. Monmouth," she repeated. "Monmouth."

Roger looked at her but asked no questions. Marita saw her aunt's hands were trembling as she clasped them in her lap. She did not take her eyes from Roger.

"He was my—" Lady Mary stopped, as if she were having difficulty in speaking—"my dear—my beloved friend," she finished.

Then she pulled herself together, rose. "Come, Mr. Mainwairing, let us get out of this room—I am stifling—I can't stand the voices and the noise. Come."

Roger offered her his arm and the two walked across the floor and out on the terrace, leaving Marita sitting on the bench. She went to the window. They were walking down the garden, across the greensward to Lady Mary's. There was something in her aunt's voice, in her white face, that Marita had never seen there before. She looked stricken, as if she had been dealt a blow; yet there was something else, some hidden fire that flared at the sight of Roger Mainwairing.

Marita was suddenly very lonely. She sat quietly, her hands folded, looking at the floor. Thomas Pollock found her a little later. "What! Not dancing?" he said in his hearty voice. "Where are the lads that they are not at your feet?" he drew her to her feet without waiting for an answer.

"Come. Hester needs you. She is going to serve supper and she wants everyone in the ballroom. It is the moment of her big surprise."

"A surprise?" Marita forgot her momentary loneliness. "What is it?"

"I cannot tell you. I am sworn to secrecy." His round red cheeks glowed, his light blue eyes danced. "Really it is my surprise. Come. I want you to be there."

Marita grasped his arm with both her hands, lifting her eager eyes, caught up by his excitement. "Oh, Mr. Pollock, let us go quickly. I don't want to miss your surprise."

The revelling reached its climax when the pipers Pollock had brought down from Williamsburg entered the room, to "pipe in the haggis." That was the Pollocks' surprise. Round and round the room the pipers went—past the high table, weaving in and out among the little tables where the lesser people sat—their pipes skirling, their kilts swinging.

Old Thomas was mellow from wine and the success of the first Muster Day. He stood up and proposed the toasts: To the Governor; to the Governor's lady. With each successive drink the burr of his tongue had become thicker, his cheeks more rosy and shining.

He called for a special cup of silver. The slave filled it to the brim.

"Do ye realize to what extent we are indebted to the Scotch Covenanters for our civil and our religious liberties?" Pollock cried in a loud voice. "A glorious day it was when there was union between Scotland and England, for there is strength in that Union. My Lords and Ladies and Gentlemen, I give you a toast: To The Union Treaty, may it last forever!" He nodded to the pipers and the bags began to skirl:

"Thus spake Britain to the Royal Pair:
One stem the Thistle and the Rose shall be
The Thistle's lasting grace; thou, oh my Rose, shall be
The warlike Thistle's arm, a sure defence to thee."

Pollock lifted the silver cup, touched that of the Governor and drank deep.

The Governor gave the toast, "Her Majesty the Queen," and the guests drank, standing.

The seat beside the Governor, where Lady Mary Tower should have sat, remained vacant. Vacant too was the seat at the right hand of Hester Pollock reserved for Roger Mainwairing. Hester glanced at Madam Catha and the vacant chair beside Governor Hyde, raising her eyebrows significantly. A slow smile crossed Madam Catha's lips, as if she understood and was diverted by the implication.

Lady Mary and Roger Mainwairing moved across the dappled carpet spread by the moonlight through the heavy darkness of the trees. She turned her face to him. The intensity of her emotion puzzled Roger.

"I want you to tell me all of it, everything you can remember of Monmouth."

"I was with him to the end, Lady Mary, to the tragic end, until the beautiful head of our leader of the Western Protestants was cut off at the Tower."

Lady Mary caught at his arm to steady her halting steps.

143

"Tell me—how was he at the end—did he die with courage?"

"Believe only this of him, Lady Mary. He faced his death bravely, with steady eyes and steps that did not falter."

"And Argyle?"

"Died bravely, too. He was an old man. It did not matter—he had lived a full life. But the Duke was young and before him stretched a glorious path, if only—"

She buried her face. "Yes, I know . . . 'if' . . . but it was his destiny. He could not escape the destiny of the Stuarts." She brooded for a little time before she spoke again. "The time was not ripe; there was waiting to be done and preparation."

Roger spoke sharply. "What do you mean, Lady Mary? No, do not answer me. I do not want to know. I've done with such things, with conspiracy and intrigue and another man's ambitions."

"Do you regret following Monmouth to his doom?" she asked harshly, scornfully.

"No, madam. I regret nothing. I would follow the Duke's banner as I did before—but I was young then, and hot against intolerance and oppression. Now, I am content to work my land and live my life quietly."

There was a silence, then she said, "You are young to have the ideas of an old man. You will find that you cannot escape. You are near my years, I think. I would not hesitate to throw my life and everything I hold into the vortex, if right could be done."

They came to the door of her house. The candles shone through the windows and a fire burned on the hearth. She said abruptly, "I must know more of Monmouth."

Roger hesitated. "Why live again the old bitter story? It will do no good to remember the eight hundred simple godly folk of Dorset and Somerset who were sold and sent to West Indies plantations. I was one of them, Lady Mary. I know their heartaches and their tragedy."

She held up her hand to stop him but he went on, his voice bitter at the memory. "Surely you have not forgotten the three hundred hanged by Judge Jeffreys at the Bloody Assizes? Men and women of the west of England who saw the dismembered remains of their dear ones displayed upon their own market places, and on the highways. . . . Do not ask me to talk of it. I have forgotten." His countenance had changed. He was another man, with set, hard features, his eyes, blue ice.

"Come," she repeated, "we will not talk of Sedgemoor—nor of Monmouth. Instead we will talk of the Albemarle, and of ourselves." Her voice was rich and deep, her eyes were warm and inviting.

Roger hesitated a moment, then followed her into the house. Desham was waiting to take her mistress' cloak and her plumed hat.

"Have Scipio bring brandy and some cold meats," she said. "Let him fetch the rose glasses for the brandy. We will sup before the fire."

"Your ladyship—" Desham hesitated—"I—"

"I shall want you no more tonight. Go to the manor house. The servants will feast and you will enjoy the gaiety."

The maid curtsied. "Thank you, my lady, you are very kind."

Scipio set the decanter on the table. Lady Mary dismissed him.

"Pour a brandy for me, Mainwairing," she said. "Do you know the meaning of these glasses—the Stuart rose of four petals and the bud? Four Stuart rulers and a bud for the Pretender. Let us drink to the past, and to the future, and to Jamie over the water."

Roger gave her a sharp look. To speak of "Jamie over the water" was treason in England. But what matter? England was far away and so was France, where the Queen's half brother, the Pretender, dwelt.

The woman was beautiful, her small head, held high, rising from the ivory column of her throat—a proud woman, he thought, proud and desirable. He raised his glass. "Let us forget the Stuarts and the Old World we have left behind. Let us think of the New World, and the present. To you. To your warm red lips—." He emptied the glass.

Lady Mary glanced at him. A strange, almost wanton, look came into her eyes. She moved a little so there was room beside her on the fire bench. Her long lithe figure, the curve of her breasts, her slender waist were accentuated by the close-fitting habit. She lifted the glass to her lips, watching him through half-closed eyes.

After a moment she said, "I came here to this place because it was wise for me to leave England for a little while. I thought of myself as a woman worn out, done with living. I thought myself a dispassionate onlooker of life, amused by the human comedy." She paused.

Roger did not speak. He stood close, looking down on her lovely face, her lithe, desirable body.

Her words came swiftly then. "To think that I should find a man like you in this Godforsaken wilderness."

Roger leaned forward and took her hands, drawing her to her feet. "You are beautiful," he said abruptly. "You have all the arts to turn a man's blood to fire." He put his arm about her and drew her body against him. "Like calls to like," he said. His low voice held a challenge. "Let us think only of your new life in a bold new world."

Chapter 12

MADAM CATHA MAKES A DECLARATION

NOVEMBER and December passed rapidly. The Hyde children had been sent to Williamsburg, to live at Parson Blair's, the boys' tutor, James Stepehenson, with them. Penelope and young Edward did not want to go; they much preferred riding wild over the plantation on the little Banker ponies, or shooting rabbits and gray squirrels in the woods. Once the Governor had taken Edward with him on a wild turkey shoot, and as the boy conducted himself well, had promised him that he might go 'possum hunting after Christmas; but Colonel Pollock was taking a sloop up the river and it seemed a good opportunity to send the children, since Hester was accompanying him.

Edward was nine and arrangements were made for him to have his lessons at William and Mary, where young Stephenson had been engaged to teach Latin. Madam Catha objected violently. She had heard that the college was enrolling Red Indians from Nottaway Town in the classes. But the Governor was firm and young Edward was entered. Penelope was too young for school, so a governess would continue her lessons. It was arranged that she would have dancing and deportment with Colonel Byrd's young daughter and the Harrison children from the James River plantations, and she would spend part of the time at the home of Colonel

146

Ludwell, where Madam Catha would visit the children at the Easter holiday.

Marita and Miss Mittie went down to the wharf to wave them all farewell. Madam Catha was in tears but the children were gay and excited to be going on the shallop up the Chowan River.

"Children are so brutal," Madam Catha sighed, as she dabbed her wet eyes with her handkerchief. "They show no affection whatsoever."

"Aren't they young for that?" Miss Mittie ventured.

"Certainly not! What do you know about children, Mittie? You've never had a child."

"I should hope not!" Miss Mittie said, aghast at the suggestion. "I'm an unmarried woman."

"There has been many an unmarried woman who dropped a child," Madam Catha said. The Governor joined them and they walked up to the manor house, where Madam Catha's chaise waited to take her home. After she and Miss Mittie were seated, she remembered something and called Marita back.

"Please tell your aunt that we are all to go over to Queen Anne's Town on Monday. There is a Council meeting that day and I must declare the persons I brought into the Province with me. Your aunt is to be signatory to some papers, also. Too silly, I think, but it will give me time to see the foundations of the new Government House and show my plans to Mr. Whiting who is to overlook the building." Marita promised not to forget to tell her aunt, and the chaise drove away.

The wooded pasture ground that lay between the manor house and Lady Mary's cottage was bare and brown. The bright autumn leaves had gone from the trees, but the dark green pine and the cypress along the water kept their vigil in their own colour. The desolation of Hester's garden suited Marita's mood. Alone she lost the smile that she had forced to her lips, and she gave herself over to melancholy.

No matter how often she told herself that she would not go to the trysting place at the confluence, day after day found her waiting at sunset.

Michael did not come. Nor anyone. Only the silence of the deep woods. Today it was the same as other days. A fine mist lay on the water; it veiled the trees and the swamp, making a world unknown and eerie. Today would be the last time. She would come no more. What did it bring her? A passing

147

return of the golden moments? She was no longer a child to be lured by a bright object. She was a woman; she must have a woman's will and courage.

She turned away with a heavy heart, and walked slowly homeward. She had gone over every moment she had been with him; now she would lay all thought of him aside. She must learn to live without that bright memory. Unconsciously she squared her shoulders, quickened her steps. She had laid a ghost. She would look forward, not back. Life was ahead of her, not behind.

She ran up the steps to the gallery and into the house. She found Lady Mary in the drawing-room, having her tea. Captain Gregory stood by the fireplace and Anthony Lovyck was pacing about the room, cup in hand.

"Ah, there you are," her aunt said, as she entered the room. "I'm glad you came; Anthony was about to ring the plantation bell and call out the slaves."

Marita laughed. She was surprised it came so easily. "I've been for a walk in the woods," she said.

Lady Mary glanced at her boots. "Tell Desham to bring your slippers. I declare you are more like a dairymaid than a young woman of fashion."

"She has a blooming look," Gregory observed, "blooming and very vivid; 'pon my word, I believe the gal is growing up."

Marita laughed again. "I am grown up—quite grown up."

"Nonsense," said Lady Mary sharply. "You're a young girl, a very young girl."

Anthony, too, scrutinized her face. "I believe you're in love, Marita, you look so—well, so joyous," he said. "Tell me who it is that takes your fancy. I'm sure it isn't I, for you never give me the favour of a glance these days." There was a little pique in his voice.

Marita turned the attack, lightly. "How would you know, Anthony? You have eyes for no one but Penelope Galland."

"Penelope?" Gregory asked. "That won't do. She's Willie Maule's inamorata."

"Marita is just talking," Anthony muttered, gulping his tea, his face brick-red. "I've no time for women. I mean to do nothing but work until I amass a fortune. After that I can choose where I will."

Marita said, "That is not true, Tony. Love doesn't come for a shilling or a pound. It comes—for nothing at all."

Lady Mary interrupted. "What wisdom for a child! But let

148

me advise you that love for love, if it dwells in a cottage, is not very lasting. In a palace there is more room to spread and keep out from under each other's feet. There is a chance for happiness if one does not see too much of one's mate."

Anthony laughed. "I did not know you were a cynic, Lady Mary."

Lady Mary smiled slightly. "Knowing the world does not necessarily lead to cynicism," she said, signalling Desham to take away the tea-tray. "Bring me my patience cards," she said to Marita, "the Tory cards, my dear." She smiled a little secret smile. "I've about worn out the Whig pack that Lord Clarendon gave my father. It's time for a change, I think."

Anthony looked at her keenly. "What are you saying, Lady Mary? If I did not know your complete boredom with politics I would think you were making a prophecy of sorts."

Lady Mary shuffled the cards expertly, with her long white fingers, the secret smile still on her lips. "What interest could one have in English politics in this far-off wilderness?" she asked.

Anthony looked at that aristocratic face, the well-placed head on her fine white throat. How curious it was that she was here. How meaningless her life now, contrasted with what it must have been in England and in France. She had wisdom and spirit and worldly poise. Was it all drowned by her utter indifference to people, to the world about and beyond her? He had asked a cautious question or two of the Governor when they were in his office, busy over letters and the confused affairs of the district. The usually kindly expression left Hyde's face. His answer was short, so short that Anthony had not the courage to reopen the subject.

Beyond the fact that Lady Mary had spent much of her life in France, Anthony had gained nothing. He had set himself to extract what he could from the Governor's wife.

"She uses a false name," Madam Catha had told him one day when she was piqued at what she called Lady Mary's superiority. "Some people think her name isn't Tower at all."

"Surely your husband knows all about her," Anthony said slyly.

"Certainly he does," Madam Catha retorted, "but you know him. He's stubborn as a mule. You'd think he'd confide in his lawful wife, wouldn't you now?"

He thought of that conversation now as he watched Lady Mary, wrapped in an old Stuart tartan, engrossed in her patience game.

He reached the end of his speculation. Here she was, at least, on equal footing with them all, and she made no effort to prove herself a great lady. It was only Madam Catha and Hester Pollock, by their curiosity and secretive questionings, who placed the halo of mystery about her. But he could not help but feel there was something about her. Her bearing, her detachment, her over-fine skin, her long narrow face with its high-bridged nose, the elegance of her long body—where had he seen them before, in some person, in some portrait by Sir Peter Lely or Godfrey Kneller?

He himself had never been to Court or attended any of the Queen's levees, although his uncle went regularly to St. James' Palace and attended the Queen's hunts in Windsor Forest. He must remember to write his uncle.

"Whatever are you dreaming about, Anthony?" Marita said, from her stool by Lady Mary's side.

Captain Gregory said, "I was going to ask the same question, Tony. You look as though the cares of the world were on your shoulders. Surely his Excellency isn't working you that hard yet?"

Anthony got up and went over to the fire. "No, I wish I had more to do. I wouldn't be half busy enough if I had not offered to write Colonel Pollock's letters and copy them into his letter-book. He is a writer with great attention to detail."

"Political letters?" Lady Mary said, not looking up from her cards.

"Yes. To the Lords Proprietors, about the state of the Province; to Lord Carteret, in particular, Pollock represents him, you know."

"Pollock is a good man," Lady Mary said.

"Yes," Anthony hastened to agree, "yes, very kind but awfully stubborn, sometimes."

Lady Mary laughed aloud. "We Scots are like that."

Marita started to speak, but thought better of it. It was the first time her aunt had ever said anything about being a Scot. Still she should have known. Didn't she always wear a tartan, or a brooch with Scotch pebbles in it and a thistle in the border?

Gregory said, "I must be going. I'm riding to Queen Anne's Town tonight—a meeting of sorts on this idea the Governor has about organizing the militia."

Anthony glanced at the older man, a thin smile on his lips. "Your men did not show up so well beside the stranger's dragoons."

Gregory's red face grew redder, if possible. "God's truth!" he exploded. "What devilment there was astir that day."

"Did you ever find out who the masked man was that drilled his men so well on Muster Day?" Lady Mary asked idly. Marita's throat constricted. She held her hands tight together in her lap, waiting tensely for Captain Gregory's answer.

"Obviously one of Cary's followers," the Captain replied. "What a devilishly ingenious way to show the superiority of his soldiers! If it hadn't been for Mainwairing's men, we would have a cut a sorry figure indeed."

"Your men were a little rough," Anthony said.

"Yokels and bumble-heads!" Gregory snapped. He took up his cape from a chair. "I think I'll be moving on, Lady Mary. Thank you for the tea and your charming society."

Lady Mary extended her hand, which the soldier raised to his lips. "Don't be discouraged, Captain Gregory," she said kindly, "I've often heard John Churchill complain about the stupidity of his men, but see what he's managed to do with them."

Gregory laughed, his ill humor instantly gone. "I'm afraid I'm not the soldier the Duke of Marlborough is, but none the less it's a consoling thought that even our great generals have their difficulties."

Anthony said, "I believe we are to go to Queen Anne's Town on Monday to make our declarations."

Lady Mary nodded. "Marita told me that Madam Catha was to make the official declaration for herself and the members of the party which she imported into the Province."

"Why did we wait until now?" Marita asked. "It's more than five months since we arrived."

"I'm sure I don't know," Anthony said, getting into his coat which a slave held for him. "Perhaps it was the Council. You know it meets only occasionally, and its time may have been taken up by other and more important matters."

Marita laughed. "What could be more important than our arrival in this colony?"

"Our departure from it," Lady Mary answered.

Monday was a fair day, so Madam Catha, Lady Mary, Anthony and Marita sailed over to the village in one of Colonel Pollock's shallops. The Governor did not accompany them. He had never gone into the village, nor did he intend to go until his appointment was duly accredited. When necessary he sent Captain Gregory and Anthony Lovyck as his representatives.

In spite of this, many people accepted him as the true Governor, and while he had no voice, he sat in the Council when it met at Balgray. He was conversant now with most of the problems of the government which was, in reality, no government at all. Cary administered, after a fashion, in Bath and the Pamticoe Districts; and Glover, although he dwelt in Virginia most of the time, had Pollock as a staunch advocate in the Albemarle.

They landed at the long wharf, at the west end of the village. Mrs. Badham met them with her chaise. Madam Catha and Lady Mary drove through the muddy streets with her to the Government House, on Queen Anne's Creek. Marita walked with Anthony and Captain Gregory. The villagers along the way stopped their work or came to the windows to see the gentry go by.

"By Gad, they have an undue amount of curiosity," the Captain muttered, but Marita noticed that he stiffened his back and tilted his plumed hat at a rakish angle. Anthony was picking his way along the path, finding the dry spots for Marita. He was dressed in fine clothes, a long coat of dark blue wool to his knees, and a gay striped waistcoat. He did not wear tall boots, as Gregory did, but he had stout shoes with silver buckles, and his heavy silk stockings were held in place by the lower cuff of his doeskin breeches. His wide hat had two dark blue plumes and he looked the picture of a London gentleman of quality.

Marita held her full woollen skirts high above her buckled shoes, and her hunter's-green bonnet fell back from her curls, held in place by the riband ties.

By the time they had reached the temporary building on Queen Anne's Creek, half a hundred small boys and old men and a few straggling women made up a gallery which followed them to the doors of the building. The bailiff had his men at the doors to keep out the villagers, and had set a guard. These were the men who had drilled rather badly at the Balgray Muster Day. But Captain Greogry had a kind word to say to the young commander, who stood at the door in his new uniform consisting of a brown leather jerkin, nankeen breeches and jackboots. He wore an iron helmet which was much too large for him and doubtless had belonged to his father, once one of Cromwell's men.

When they entered the chamber, the Council was in session. Christopher Gale sat in the place of Thomas Pollock, who had not returned from Virginia. Nathaniel Chevin was there, also John Blount, and Foster Tomes the Quaker.

The clerk was reading the list of freeholders on the south shore who were memorializing the honorable Council for the right to build roads and set bridges along the Scuppernong.

There was some discussion over the width of the road. The south-shore men wanted it to be ten feet wide, while the Council thought three feet would do, for there was nothing there excepting horseback travel.

"But we must think of the future, gentlemen," Dr. Sproull insisted. "The time will come when coaches and two-wheelers will be plentiful for the farm people and not a luxury for the gentry alone. Let us have our roads not only wide enough for the farmers' two wheeled carts but for the larger vehicles."

The discussion went on for some time, and the memorial was finally laid on the table for the next meeting. Then came half a dozen petitions for land which had been taken up by grant or patent and not seated according to the law. Edward Moseley's name was on one of these petitions. He asked for a patent on one thousand acres of land near his White Marsh plantation on the south shore for himself, and one thousand acres for Roger Mainwairing, whom he represented by power of attorney.

An objection was voiced by Nicholas Crisp. "I think we do wrong to let all the desirable bottom lands and water lands go out in such large parcels. Why, in no time we will have no decent land left in the Albemarle. I think we should pass a law that no man will be allowed to own more than eight hundred and fifty acres in one piece lying against a principal stream, either on the Sound, the Roanoke or the Chowan."

There was a hubbub over this. Most of the Councillors owned large holdings and were looking about for more. Pollock had over fifty thousand acres, not counting his land on Pamticoe, and Moseley had almost as much.

Said Nicholas, "Do we want this country to be like England, with the land in the hands of a few nobles?"

"For shame, Nicholas," said Moseley. "Land should always be in the hands of men who can make the best use of it. What could our friend Mainwairing do with eight hundred and fifty acres? With that amount he wouldn't be a planter; he would drop to the status of a small farmer. He might as well be a tenant."

"Well, I still think I'm right," Crisp said, giving way reluctantly.

"Why should we argue the point now?" Moseley asked suavely. "It isn't in the province of this body to set such a law. We have only the right to assign the patents for seating."

Crisp settled back in his chair. The other men about the table did the same.

Christopher Gale looked through the paper on the table. "The next business before us is the declaration of Madam Catha Hyde concerning the people she has imported into the Government. The Clerk will please read the petition."

The Clerk read: "Madam Catha Hyde comes before this Board and is admitted to prove, upon oath, the importation of eleven persons, into this Government: Edward Hyde, Penelope Hyde, William Clayton, Anthony John Lovyck, James Gregory, James Stephenson, Debby Desham, Mistress Mittie Hyde, Lady Mary Tower, Mistress Marita Tower, and herself."

He set down the paper and took up a Bible that lay on the President's desk. "Madam Hyde, are you prepared to take oath on this?" he asked.

Madam Catha, with a rustle of silk and a nodding of her plumed bonnet, moved majestically up the aisle, escorted by the bailiff and his two assistants. She slowly stripped her glove from her hand before she lifted it to take oath. Repeating each word clearly, she made an appreciable pause before she said, "So help me God."

"And now, if you will be so kind as to step into the small Council Chamber, we will have the signatures affixed to the papers."

Lady Mary and Marita, followed by Captain Gregory and Anthony, made their way across the back of the room to join her. At the door they met Roger Mainwairing. His face lighted when he saw them. Lady Mary paused a moment. "Good day, Roger. May we see you after we have finished this—say in half an hour, in the ladies' parlour of the East Gate Tavern?"

"It will give me pleasure to be there," Roger said. "I have only to set my name to this land patent, and I am at your service, as always."

Lady Mary said to Marita, as they entered the room, "He is a pleasant person and has the grace of a gentleman. I am

154

glad he is here. He will be a comfort to us when we go to live at Greenfield."

"Are we going to Greenfield to live?" Marita asked, suddenly excited.

"That is why I am here today, my child. I am to meet Mr. Pearce at the tavern after we have finished with this formality."

"And when will we go there to live?" Marita persisted.

Lady Mary, smiled at her excitement. "As soon as our goods come from home, my dear. I've had word that some of the household pieces are already at Williamsburg. Tom Pollock will see to the transport for me. Now do not ask any more questions." Lady Mary moved up to the table where Christopher Gale was seated with William Reid.

Madam Catha signed for herself, the children and her people who were absent.

The bailiff pulled back the chair for Lady Mary and handed her the pen. Lady Mary started to sign, then glanced up. Madam Catha was leaning forward, her eyes fixed on the paper. Lady Mary turned in her chair, so that her body was between Madam Catha and the document.

"I will sign for you, Marita, since you are a minor and I am your legal guardian," she said over her shoulder. Her eyes slid over Madam Catha with slow deliberation. The lady moved back quickly. Then Lady Mary turned and wrote in her large vigorous hand; she had almost finished when her pen caught in the paper, splattering ink over the signature.

"Oh! I'm so sorry," she said to Christopher Gale. "It was the pen; it is dull. It needs cutting."

Christopher Gale looked at the document. "I think it is quite legal," he said, smiling into her clear blue eyes, "quite legal, even though it looks a little like Tudor, instead of Tower."

Lady Mary laid her slim white hand on his arm for a moment and looked into his eyes, an ingenuous smile on her red lips. "It is of no moment really, is it, Mr. Gale? I am loath to think of that nice clerk having to have to copy so long a document."

"Of no moment, Lady Mary," he assured her as they walked across the room. "I am delighted to hear from Tom Pearce that you are going to take over Greenfield and live on the north shore. We Albemarle planters will all approve of that. You've been too much of a prisoner up on the Chowan."

Lady Mary smiled dismissal graciously. She said to Marita, "Another delightful man. I feel that our life at Greenfield will be very pleasant. Not without companionship."

Madam Catha rode off with Mrs. Badham in her chaise. Lady Mary and Marita walked over to the East Gate Tavern, accompanied by Edward Moseley who was to handle the transaction and papers concerning the sale.

The villagers still lingered, waiting to see the gentry pass by. The women took interest in Lady Mary. "She's a fine figger of a woman," one housewife said, "but she's nae so handsome dressed as the Governor's lady with her fine blue gown."

"Have done wi' such talk. Ye ken nae difference between a brand new gown of London stuff and an elegant bit of woven goods from the highlands. Her ladyship wears the tartan—and they's nae better than that anywhere. So quit your talkin' blitheration."

Lady Mary smiled at the woman and spoke to her in broad Scots. "Dinna ye yaff the puir woman. She dinna ken a tartan from a bit o' linsey-woolsey." She took a piece of money from her reticule and placed it in the goodwife's hand. "Here, take this an' the both of ye buy a tass o' ale."

"God be praised! She speaks our tongue!" cried the delighted woman. "Come, Jessie, make you bow to her leddyship—an' we'll tell the toon Jinnie MacTavish kens a gra' leddy when she see one."

There was laughter among the people as they crowded near to hear what Jinnie MacTavish was saying to the fine lady, for Jinnie was quick with her tongue.

"MacTavish is a guid, proud name," Lady Mary said. She dipped into her bag again and brought out a gold piece. "Take all your friends, Jinnie MacTavish, and buy ye a great tass o' ale to drink to the Union of Scotland and England."

A cheer went up from the crowd as they moved off across the Green.

Marita smiled; her aunt always had a way with the commonalty. She noticed Edward Moseley had been an interested spectator of this little scene.

"You know the right thing to win the people, Lady Mary," he said, admiration strong in his voice.

Lady Mary laughed. "A good drink and it is easy to win people."

Moseley shook his head. "It's more than that, if you allow me to say so. I believe you really like people."

156

"Why not," said her ladyship, "why not? We are all the same, stripped of external embellishments." She laughed lightly. "You are surprised to hear me say that?"

Moseley nodded. "Yes, I am. It is the first time I ever heard a woman express such an opinion."

She glanced at him shrewdly. "But it is your belief, is it not?"

Moseley inclined his head. "Yes, but I get little support from men or women in this Province."

Lady Mary laid her hand on his arm for a second. "I know what you are working towards, Mr. Moseley. One day you will build a following who believe as you believe."

Moseley said, "I had not hoped for understanding in a woman."

Lady Mary smiled but said no more.

They crossed the bricked courtyard of the East Gate Tavern and went in by the side entrance to the small ladies' parlour, which Lady Mary had reserved.

Mr. Pearce awaited them with his lawyer. They talked for a moment about the weather and the Council meeting. Then Lady Mary said, "Have you brought the papers, Mr. Pearce?"

The solicitor stepped forward and handed a bundle to Moseley. Lady Mary unhooked her fur cape and gave it to Marita before she sat down at the round table covered with a green baize cloth.

She read the transfer papers which Edward Moseley spread before her, with some care, reading each page, asking a pertinent question now and then.

"I am delighted to see you take so much interest in such a dull document," Moseley said.

"It is my father's teaching," she replied. "He told me more than once always to read documents that I was to sign, and no matter what amount of money I spent, to know what I was spending it for."

"Ah, your father was a frugal man," Pearce remarked.

Lady Mary's clear laugh broke in. "Quite the contrary. People accused him of the greatest profligacy."

"Then he was a solicitor, accustomed to legal documents?"

"Not a solicitor, but he signed many legal documents and charters."

"Ah, a magistrate," Moseley said, well satisfied that he had gone to the root of her extraordinary ability and understanding.

Lady Mary did not answer. She saw Roger Mainwairing coming down the hall, and rose from the chair. "Ah, there is Mr. Mainwairing. I have asked if he will be so kind as to go over the list of stock with Mr. Pearce. I'm sure he can tell me what I must add to give myself a model small farm."

"You could not go to a better man for advice," Moseley said, gathering up the papers and putting them into his case.

"One thing more, Mr. Moseley," Lady Mary said: "I want one other deed to be drawn up to transfer Greenfield to my—my niece, Marita. I have really bought Greenfield for her." She smiled, as the surprise gave way to delight in Marita's candid eyes.

"Mine? All that land is mine?" she asked in a hushed voice. "Oh, Aunt Mary, I'm—I think I'm going to cry."

"Not here, my dear! Not in a public room. Save tears for the privacy of your bedchamber." But her voice was kind, and she patted Marita's soft cheek.

"It is a very handsome gift," Moseley said, watching the young girl's changing expression. "Shall we say it is her dower—her little dot, as the French put it?"

"But I don't want it for a dower. I want it to grow things on," Marita cried. "I want to have dogs and horses and Shropshires to nibble the lawn and keep it short, and I want shaggy highland cattle, just like they have in the North."

"Well, well, you are quite ambitious, Miss Marita."

Marita turned. Roger Mainwairing lounged in the doorway, almost blocking it with his tall, elegant figure. "A real farmer's program," he said, looking down at her.

"Is it too much?" Marita murmured, turning to her aunt. She was trembling with doubt now lest her sudden dream might fade.

"No, I think not, but we must consult Mr. Mainwairing. He has so much experience."

Marita looked at him, her eyes wide. She said in a solemn voice, "I would like two of each, just like the ark." She hesitated and looked from one to the other. "It would be like the Bible, wouldn't it, to see your flocks and herds multiply and grow?"

Roger laid his hand on her shoulder. "You're a real farmer, Marita. We'll have to see what can be done."

Moseley tucked his portfolio under his arm. "I see that the work of the lawyer is over and the planter comes into his own." He turned to Lady Mary. "I'll have my clerk draw up the papers. If there is any way in which I may serve you, please let me know. I, as well as Roger, will be your neighbour when you move to Greenfield."

After he had gone, Marita threw her arms about her aunt and kissed her on the cheek. "You are so kind, so kind," she whispered.

Lady Mary kissed the top of her shining head. "Now run across the Green and join Madam Catha at Mrs. Badham's house, my dear. Mr. Mainwairing is going to help me make out my lists."

She turned to Roger. "We will be finished by five, don't you think?" She had to repeat the question before he heard her.

"Yes, certainly. It will not take more than an hour to make out the list." He looked past Marita to Lady Mary, his eyes strangely bright in his bronzed face.

He waited until the hall was clear, then closed the door. Crossing the room, he took Mary into his arms. After a little time she stood off, so that she could look into his eyes.

"I wanted you to come back," she said. "Why did you not come?"

Roger caught her hands and held them close. He was smiling as he looked down at her. "I was afraid," was his answer.

She laughed aloud, a gay reckless laugh. "Are you so timid?"

"It was not timidity that kept me away. It was wisdom."

She pulled her hands from his, her mouth petulant. "Wisdom? A dull word for dull people who do not know what living means."

Roger turned her chin upward and kissed the hollow of her throat. "You think we know what living means, Mary?"

She came close to him and put her lips against his.

Chapter 13

LETTERS
TO LONDON

NEWS that a Jamaica packet would sail for England in a week's time was brought to Balgray by Thomas Pollock when he returned from Williamsburg early in March. From the plantations along the Chowan the news spread to the plantations on the Sound and to the village itself. Quills were pointed, shot and sand made ready, writing papers spread on knee-desks and tables. Everyone wanted to get letters off before the new post rate went into force. A shilling and three pence would be a high sum to pay for a single-sheet letter. That made three shillings an ounce, and the frugal men and women of the Albermarle hastened to beat the rate with one crowning effort at letter writing.

At Scots Hall Anthony Lovyck laboured day and night with the Governor's letters to the Lords Proprietors and the Lords of Trade and Plantations, for Hyde was sending his first official report on the situation in the Carolinas.

In her morning-room, Madam Catha toiled and struggled. She was not so ready with the pen as she was with her tongue, and her letters were copied more than once on the thin paper Anthony had accommodatingly lined for her the night before. She was writing to Lady Anne Hyde, her husband's cousin, who occupied a high position as lady-in-waiting to her Majesty Queen Anne.

"My dearest Lady Anne:

"What would I not give to have a dish of tea with you at your charming rooms at St. James's Palace, and a good long gossip! We are so out of touch in this Wilderness that I have lost all sense of time, and one day is much like another. We have little news of what is going on in London and at the Court—it is like another world. However, one must do one's duty for one's Country; and I, as the wife of the Governor of North Carolina, will do my part in keeping up my spirits and showing a serene face to the world.

"The situation here has been very embarrassing for us both. To come out with such glowing hopes and to have such bitter disappointments meet us; for as you know when we got to Virginia Colony, we found that the Governor of South Carolina, who was to issue Edward's Letters-Patent, had died, and that left Edward without authority to take over the government.

"We enjoyed the hospitality of Governor Spottswood of Virginia. You know him so you will relish the gossip that his cousin, Mrs. R., who presides over his house, is said to stand in closer relationship to him than that of hostess.

"On the James River are many very fine seats; the Byrds' and the Harrisons' and the Carters' among them. Colonel Byrd you know from his exploits in London. But I find him a most charming and delightful gentleman. His wife is very high spirited and people say they quarrel incessantly. She is the daughter of that Colonel Parke,

160

who was Marlborough's aide at Blenheim, so frightfully massacred at Antigua this year. The Harrisons and the Hills and the Randolphs are nice people, and in Williamsburg, the Blairs. He is the rector and she was Sarah Harrison. I like them much, though she tipples a little too much for one in her position.

"While we were still in Virginia, Colonel Thomas Pollock asked us to be his guests at Balgray, until things were adjusted. For a time Edward held back, not wanting to go into this Government until he had his Letters-Patent from the Lords Proprietors, but he was finally persuaded to go. He went down with Colonel Pollock, who is a cousin or a nephew of Sir Robert Pollock at Balgray in Scotland. They went by shallop by way of the Chowan River, but we journeyed overland by coach.

"The responsible planters are standing by Edward, for they want a good government. But there is a rascally man by the name of Colonel Thomas Cary who has caused much disaster and bloodshed in this land, and he insists he is the rightful Governor. However, I have no fear but that we, with the help of God, will wrest his authority from him. I wish you could tell us something about his career in London, something that would be a help to Edward.

"Anthony Lovyck, Edward's secretary, the nephew of Edward Parr, is agreeable enough, but I think he is becoming very ambitious. He talks of taking up land patents. Just now he is paying suit to Sarah Blount, the daughter of Captain John Blount, of Mulberry Hill, one of the richest and most influential planters in the Albemarle. You know their connection in London—the beautiful Martha Blount and her sister Teresa. That is quite all right. A young man should think of his future. I know he comes from a fine Welsh family, and they are noble, but I think his mind should be on his work and his usefulness to Edward.

"This is a little gossip. You know that a Lady Mary Tower joined us when we sailed and came out with us? They say here that Tower is not her real name. Edward knows, but he won't tell me, and I had not the honour of being very well acquainted with Court Society, as we were a Devon family, and came not often to London, so I do not place her. She says she spent much of her life in France, but she takes upon herself the airs of Royalty, an absurd affectation. She says plainly that she doesn't care for the society of women and prefers men. Now she has quite a passion for a bachelor planter here by the name of Roger Mainwairing. He goes every day, they say, to Greenfield plantation on the Sound which she has recently purchased. He is supposed to be advising her about stocking her place with cattle. She is there all alone with her servants and overlookers and slaves, with the exception of her niece Marita, a lovely innocent young child of eighteen. Not that Duke Roger, the name they call him, is her only male caller. Half the men of the Albemarle are at her tea table or dining and supping with her, or sharing her bed—who knows? Do tell me what you can about her. Tower being not her real name adds to the mystery that surrounds her. She carries herself with a great air and the men think her beautiful. I don't see it myself. Edward says she has wonderful intelligence, however that may be. But why she is here in this Godforsaken world, no one knows. I think she is a Catholic, and may be in some Papish plot. . . .

"You remember the Lords Proprietors promised Edward that he was to have a house, a suitable Residence in Queen Anne's Town. I had a young apprentice architect in London draw a design for me for a suitable Residence. The Council says it is too ambitious, that they are simple people and want a simple Government House. I have had to give way in some things, but I'm determined to have a cupola, for it adds dignity and anyone can see it is the house of the Sovereign's representative. Then, too, we can look for a long way down the Sound from that high point and see what ships come in. God knows when it will be finished. Time means nothing to these people.

"There are *some* pleasant people here, but so many rogues that the Virginia people call it Rogues' Harbour. These rogues and lawless men are constantly at outs with people of higher class and authority. In fact, lowly people demand a higher place for themselves than they had at home. Many of them do not know their place and speak to their betters without touching their hats or pulling their forelocks. I hope Edward will change all of that. I want him to put into effect the Fundamental Constitution, which Mr. Locke wrote for the Lords some time ago but which has never been administered properly. Edward says he won't do it—that people came to the Carolinas for more liberty, not for less; and he talks a great deal about the Magna Charta. I think it all very silly and stupid. How can people rise above a station to which they are born?

"Do write me the latest creations of the London mantuamakers. How wide are the petticoats, and is there still much lace trimming? I must have something very special when Edward is invested.

"Who is sitting to Kneller these days? Tell me, has Sir Christopher Wren completed St. Paul's, and is it very beautiful? Does the Queen still hunt for stags in Windsor Forest in spite of her gout? And what are the Freeman-Morley letters? We hear sly comments that they have something to do with the Queen.

"I've heard rumours that Sarah Churchill is quite out of favour in the Queen's household. How can that be when the Queen has given her all of her affection almost to the exclusion of everyone else for nearly thirty years? Tell me what kind of person the new favourite is. They say in Williamsburg that her name is Mrs. Masham, and she is a cousin of that arch-Tory, Harley. If he is to form a Government, there will be a wailing among the Whigs. That will please Edward. You know he is a great Tory. Did the Queen touch for the King's Evil this year? In truth, write me at length about everything.

"Fancy, I have already written three shillings' worth of paper

162

according to the new regulations, and have told not the half! The children remain in Virginia. Young Edward is at William and Mary's School, and Penelope stays with the Blairs and has private instruction.

"Naturally, all this is in confidence. As one of the family you will understand.

"Believe me your devoted relative,
"CATHA HYDE

"CHOWAN
"IN NORTH CAROLINA
"MARCH THIRD 1711/12"

Down the Sound at Greenfield, Lady Mary sat at her escritoire writing a letter in her strong, bold hand. The letter, addressed to a man high in Court circles, Henry St. John—sometime Lord Bolingbroke—was marked "Private and Confidential."

"MY LORD:

"You asked me to keep you advised of the situation here in Carolina. I have not before written to you for the reason that the affairs of this Province are in such confusion as to be laughable, if they did not harbour a tragic portent.

"Edward Hyde has just visited me, and I think the weight of all this unrest lies heavy on him. However, he has at last received his commission from your honourable body, the Lords Proprietors, so at least he has authority. Whether he has the power to enforce that authority is another matter. Certainly he has not the arms. Whatever he does must be from the diplomatic side.

"You know the situation after these several years of bickering and fighting between the factions, so I will not go into that. What he has before him is first to take over from Glover. That should be simple, as Thomas Pollock—the strongest factor for the Government side, the Church party and the conservative people—will stand by Edward, which at once sets Glover into the background. Then there is 'that rascal Cary,' to use the mildest terms applied to him. I have seen the man but once, but I'm inclined to believe there is something to be said for him. At least he is a man of action.

"It is true that Cary hangs onto the quitrent money or some of the other tax money, but so far as I have been able to find out he does not use the money for himself, but to run the Government he has set up, and, I suppose, to maintain his fighting men. I understand he is a man of some means, so he has not personal gain to consider. I think he loves to fight, and he has well-trained fighting men under his nephew Michael Cary. These are bold men, not afraid of man or devil. Cary has several vessels at Bath Town, where he makes his headquarters, and he has considerable fighting force at a place not far from there called Romney Marsh.

"If his men are anything like those Romney Marsh men in England, they are a formidable lot. If the Free Men of Kent have their prototype in Cary's army, then Edward Hyde will have to look out, for Captain Gregory's Militia is as yet very meager and ill trained, with the exception of the soldiers trained by a planter of Albemarle named Roger Mainwairing, who was with the Duke of Monmouth's Army.

"Edward's idea is to unite the warring factions as soon as possible, for he feels that the real danger is from the Indians. But with Cary he has so far made little or no headway. His only other chance is to get your friend, Baron de Graffenried, and his Switzers, on his side. That will throw the balance of power to Edward. However, De Graffenried is being wooed by Cary's men also, and he is nobody's fool. He understands exactly what the situation is, and he will throw his power and his trained soldiers to whichever side he thinks will be of the most benefit to him and his people.

"Edward is dubious about him, but I think he will join Edward eventually, for he is somewhat of a snob, or perhaps I should say that he is always on the side of 'great' people. Knowing your lordship and so many of the True Owners and Proprietors, and having that 'awe-full' respect for Edward as a close relative of her Majesty, he will, I think, throw his weight on the side of the Government and not to Cary's rebels. I may be wrong in this.

"My solution of the Cary situation is to reach him through Edward Moseley, another strong man in the Albemarle. A barrister and a surveyor, at the moment he is the Chief Justice under appointment by Cary. He is of a slightly rebellious turn, although he comes from a Cavalier family. Perhaps he is a Jacobite in his heart. That I do not know. But he has influence with Cary and he is respected by the others too. Pollock fights with him about his ideas, but they remain friends. Moseley talks about 'the rights of the people,' and the 'liberty they deserve'—whatever that means. I agree with him in everything because we need him but his ideas annoy me. People are as they are born. It's nonsense or worse to put other ideas into their heads. If you're born a slave, you are a slave and that's all there is to it.

"The other real leader, besides those whom I have mentioned, is Christopher Gale, a lawyer and a very civil gentleman. He will be made Chief Justice when Edward takes the Government. He has already had much political experience here in South Carolina and the Bahamas. I think he has had something to do with the Customs there, and he has acted as the Carolina agent in London. You may know him, as his father still lives down in your County, the Reverend Miles Gale of Kingley. Mr. Gale will be in London soon, for he is to appear before the Lords of Trade and Plantations. Perhaps you sit on that board. I have forgotten. Anyway, I want you to be kind to him and take him to call on Lady Elizabeth Blake. What I would like to see happen is that she appoint him to represent her son as a deputy on the Council of Albemarle. It would be a very farsighted move on her part, for she can be sure that her interests will be well looked after by Mr. Gale, a man of integrity. I'm surprised that there are so many cadets of noble families who have come here to make their fortunes.

"As for my own affairs, I understand that the ———— still is suspicious of my intentions, and it is best that I stay here for a little time longer. I have been very bored with the life until recently, but now that I have bought a plantation I'm quite taken up with the idea of managing it. Mainwairing has been very helpful, and has sent me a well-trained overlooker. By the way, will you see that an old sentence against Mainwairing, for treason or something, is quashed, or whatever the term is? He served his sentence by working out his bond on a plantation in the West Indies and is clear of it on that count. This is nothing against him except that he took part in Monmouth's Rebellion, and that was long ago, when he was a mere child, and you know the way Monmouth could influence people to do as he wished. Roger tells me he has already gone to England once, taking a chance that the old charge had been forgotten. But if you will kindly, in your official capacity, see that it is righted, I will be pleased, or as they say here, it would pleasure me.

"On the other matter—the very important and secret matter— Governor Spottswood is naturally interested in seeing Carolina a Crown Colony. He has already talked to Edward Hyde about the Boundary Line dispute. He thinks it must be settled at once so that the Albemarle becomes a part of the Virginia Colony, but the people here are set against that.

"What is in the rumour that Churchill is losing power? If it is true, I'm sure it is through some of Sarah's temper. It would be the direst loss that England ever sustained, to lose the services of our greatest general. The greatest loss save that one thing: selling Dunkerque to the French. I suppose I shouldn't say this, since my father was instrumental in that disgrace. But I still remember the crowds on the streets of London when they found out that Dunkerque was lost. My family has not always meant good fortune to the people of England, but we have loved them and wanted their welfare. I am talking of these things when what I mean is that if anything happens to Churchill, we are undone, and Harley will have the opportunity to make the threat of the Hanoverian succession an actuality.

"Now tell me about my good husband. Does he still loathe me? I'm sure he does. Dear God, how he hates me! I'm sure he is the most resentful and vicious man who ever lived. Why, he was even jealous of you! Did you know that? Such stupidity!

"I suppose the ———— still thinks I'm plotting against her. I wonder who it is that keeps that flame alive? Someone close to her, of course. Please give my felicitations to your good lady and I hope God gives her health and good spirits. Have you read Mr. Swift's latest effusion? I suppose he is still deeply infatuated with his Stella.

"I'm enclosing a letter, as this comes to you through a person I can trust. Please send it over the water as soon as possible. This is the only way I have of communicating at the moment. We have no direct post with France from here except through the Indies, and letters are likely to be opened, unless they are sent by private messenger.

"That reminds me. We have now heard all the details of the killing of the Governor of Antigua. A most horrible and ghastly thing, which proves beyond a doubt that the people should never have been given power.

"My best friendship to you and may God guide you and help you in these uncertain times. I would be happy if you would send me six or seven mezzotints. Hunting scenes, if you are able to find them. My walls are so bare.

"MARY"

On the confluence of the Neuse and the Trent at the newly seated Swiss Colony of New Bern, the Landgrave Baron de Graffenried wrote to one of the Lords Proprietors living near Whitehall:

"MY LORD:

"The report of the settling of the Switzers in New Bern went forward in a packet which sailed last night. There was not time to include this personal letter to you, giving you a confidential report of conditions here and in the Albemarle.

"The Earl of Pembroke ordered Knight Norris, a Rear Admiral, to escort our two vessels with his squadron as far as the latitude of the Azores, which was on account of privateers and pirates.

"I found my people, who arrived here earlier, in bad case. The poor Palatines were much worried, and all fell sick on the voyage because there was too little space on the ships, and the salted food did not agree with them. More than half died at sea, and many died from drinking too much water and eating raw fruit to excess after landing. Then one of the vessels was plundered by a French Captain at the very mouth of the James River, in sight of an English Man-of-War, which was anchored and partly dismantled so it could not come to help.

"After the landing of the Switzers in Virginia, they started with goods and chattels a distance of twenty miles by land. That took time and money, but they dared not go by sea on account of the privateers. Besides, the waters were so low at the mouth of the Carolina Rivers that a ship could not cross their openings. So they went by the River Chowan into the county of Albemarle, to the residence of a rich settler, Colonel Pollock of the Council of North Carolina. He took care of them and supplied them with all necessities and put them in great boats to cross the Sound. From there they entered the county of Bath and went to the end of their journey, where the Surveyor General of Northern Carolina, Mr. Lawson, had located for them a tongue of land between the Neuse and the Trent Rivers.

"The Surveyor General put these poor people in his own land on the south side of the River Trent, in hollows, a most unhealthy place. This was another mishap, for we paid him a heavy price for that tongue of land, in advance. The poor Palatines suffered and were ill.

"On my arrival, I found my poor people in a wretched and sinful state. Nearly all were sick and at the last gasp. The few who had kept their health despaired, and they are fearful of Indians who are a savage and warlike people. God knows what a labyrinth! Even in danger for my own life I found myself then.

"Finally Colonel Cary has for some years led an open rebellion and brought together a party and a force of armed men by means of promises and plenty of good drinks to which he treated them. So that the new Governor, Mr. Hyde, dare not undertake to put himself in possession of big Government by force, all the less so that his Letters-Patent were not yet ready. Although orders had already been issued on the strength of which Governor Tynte of South Carolina was to install him, and had already written to that effect to the Council of Northern Carolina, when he suddenly died. This fact was the cause of some of these disturbances.

"However, this inter-reign did not suit me—such pressing need among my people. The question was, would I leave all that colony to wrack and ruin; or let them starve; or should I run into debt myself to relieve them buying provisions from Pennsylvania and Virginia?

"I forgot to add that when we arrived in a village on the frontier between Virginia and Northern Carolina called Somer Town, a small crowd of inhabitants of Northern Carolina came to greet me. They offered the Government to me. They insisted, among other methods of persuasions, that it was due to me, since, in the inter-reign and in the absence of a Governor, Landgrave occupied first rank and held presidial. I replied that though I was duly invested with the title of Landgrave, I would not avail myself at the moment of that title. I thanked him for the honour and pointed to the following consideration that Governor Hyde was already in Virginia and I had an ocular witness to his election as such by the Lords Proprietors and congratulated him in the rooms of these distinguished gentlemen. That furthermore, he was a near relative of the Queen, and had been confirmed by her Majesty, that it would be ungracious in me to meddle in such business.

"As these persons did not like to have such a great Tory for their Governor, my answer did not please them, but they partook of a collation with me, and returned home.

"This is the situation as I see it. Later I will write more when I have again seen the Governor and Colonel Thomas Cary.

"Until then

"I am, your Lordship, your obedient servant and friend,
"DE GRAFFENRIED"

By the same packet went a letter from Parson Urmston to the secretary of the Society for the Propagation of the Gospel in Foreign Parts. Urmston's letter was full of complaints. He was already worn down by his duties, a sick man, barely able to cover the great territory which had been assigned to him. After the business of the Vestry had been reported, he turned to personal things.

". . . I at last have bought a plantation, situated on the north side of the Sound in Chowan Precinct, between some of Mr. Vaile's land and Mr. Moseley's. I found a new house and kitchen half finished, a dozen acres of ground, the rest woods; a horse, three cows and calves, five sheep and some fowls. The serving wench my wife brought from England is sorry help.

"This is not a good Country to promote religion. In the village are men of many crafts: wheelrights, joiners, coopers, tinkers, butchers, tanners, and shoemakers, carpenters, watermen. Women make the soap and starch. The posterity of the old planters or those who have been very fortunate, have a great number of slaves, who are wonderfully understanding of handicrafts. Thirty or forty families live at Alligator and Scuppernong River, about thirty or forty miles down the Sound toward the south. Most of them have never seen a Muster. Colonel Hyde has already done all he can to encourage good order in the country and to promote religion. He is, therefore, hated and threatened with "fire and sword.' Even some of the Quakers bear arms.

"This is a nest of the most profligate and notorious people on earth. Women forsake their husbands and come here to live with other men. They are sometimes followed. Then Madam gives a price and stays with her Gallant. A report is spread abroad that the husband is dead. Then these people become man and wife, make a figure and pass for people of worthy reputation, and arrive at first rank and dignity.

"What to do with such, I do not know, or how reformation can be hoped for! Libertines and women of loose and dissolute, scandalous lives and practices. Some say our colonies are chiefly educated at the college of Bridewell or Newgate, or the Mint.

"I have spoiled a good horse, enslaved myself, hazarded my life to little purpose.

"About this Cary, who leads the Quakers. Madam Knightly, a lady of known worth, can give you account of him. She lives at Kensington. Another known villain here is Porter, a son of a Quaker. Mr. Glover is discreet, a man of parts, but the Quakers dislike him.

"Our churches at Pequimans and Chowan are ready to drop down. The latter has neither floor nor seats, only a few loose benches on the sand. The key being lost, the door has been open ever since I came to the country. All hogs and cattle fled there for shade in the summer and warmth in the winter—a loathsome place with their dung and nastiness.

"Please order me two Negroes from the Barbadoes—born there, who speak English.

"In a very long time, the Vestry of Chowan has not met at all.
"Your Worship's humble servant,
"CHOWAN"   "JOHN URMSTON"

At the end of a long letter to Lord Carteret, Edward Hyde wrote:

"I beg your lordship to use every endeavour in your power to have the Admiralty send us a guard-ship, such as they have now in Virginia, or H. M. S. *Garland,* to be used in Albemarle and Pamticoe Sounds, and with it a company or more of marines.

"I am very fearful of what will happen with the Coe and Tuscarora Indians. I pray you to remember the weakness of our defences and our poor soldiering—only farmers and planters and their slaves. So illy outfitted with arms as to be almost no defence whatever. A good company of marines and a guard-ship with great guns and mortars would make us secure from invasion by Spanish and French pirates, and from the Indians as well."

The last letter slipped in the pouch was the shortest. It was addressed to Miss Rhoda Chapman, Gouldsborough Hall, Northamptonshire.

"DEAR RHODA:
"When I wrote you and your brother I thought I should be able to leave here late May after the Spring planting was over. But I find now that it will be impossible to come over before the Harvest. That will make it late in October, when the last of the cotton crop is in.

"Perhaps you will like that—we can hunt together once more, before you say good-bye to the Quorn and the Pitchley and the Melton-Mowbray. When you get to the Albemarle you'll find hunting and fox-hunting is done very differently than in England, but I think you will like it.

"You ask if you can bring your hunters to the Albemarle. I think it a good idea, but I will talk to you about it when I arrive

"I'm sorry not to be able to come now. But conditions have changed.

"Always your obedient servant,
ROGER MAINWAIRING

"QUEEN'S GIFT
"ALBEMARLE COUNTY
"CAROLINA"

Chapter 14

GREENFIELD

THE country was growing green again, and every day the slaves turned more earth for the seeding. The forester's axe sounded hollow through the great aisle of trees that led from the manor house to the Sound. Slaves and indentured men felled trees and cleared land, and made ready for pasturing the herds of cattle and sheep which Lady Mary had bought for Greenfield. She had had her estate manager in Scotland send over sturdy highland cattle and sheep, herd boys and their sheep dogs. The native pasture was good and soon the bellowing of cattle would join the early morning chorus of birds and the call of the wild turkey gobbler to his bronze harem.

Two new tenant houses were built, part log and part clapboard. They would house the overlooker and Captain Bragg. Captain Zeb had started his garden down by the shore. "All my life I have followed the sea and longed for the land," he told Marita one morning when she rode her bay mare down to watch the work on the new fishery.

Marita had made a great friend of Captain Zeb since he "blew in with a storm one night," as the old sailor put it. His boat had been wrecked off Bat's Grave. Now he proposed to take advantage of misfortune and find the cottage and garden he had long talked of, to live ashore. Roger Mainwairing had advised Lady Mary to let him have one of her two new houses, and he had settled in comfortably with his Algerian "cabin boy" to look after him.

The overlooker, Watkins, had started work on a large fishing shed just below Zeb's house, for it was almost time for the spring run of herring and sturgeon. The horses and fishing were in Marita's charge and she wanted to know everything that was done, every step that was taken.

She got off her horse and walked up to Captain Zeb's cabin. The old seaman was in duck breeches and worn blue pea-jacket, with a sailor's cap set jauntily on his grizzled fringe, the visor pulled low over his weathered face. He was seated on the stump of a great pine tree giving orders to a Negro slave who was making mounds to plant melons. Captain Zeb was hard to please. "The mounds must be just so," he told Marita, "for these seed are something special. Melons from Persia can't be found on many farms hereabouts, no more can rice from Madagascar, or seed cotton from Egypt."

Captain Zeb took a clay pipe out of the pocket of his jacket.

"I've been getting seeds all my life, from every corner of the globe where my ships put in," he said, tamping the dark tobacco into the bowl. "I had a great chest of seed packets waiting for a place to plant them. I'd a mind to take a patch of land off Gilliam's plantation, but I like this better." He took off his cap and mopped his bald head with a large handkerchief of bright Indian cloth. A scar ran half across his bald pate, and another across his forehead down to his eyes, causing the eyelid to droop at one corner. This gave him a sinister look which quite belied his real nature. The scar was the result of a fight with pirates.

"I'll tell you the whole story one day," he promised Marita, proudly displaying the scar. "It's a long one, and a little gory for a young miss to hear." He puffed vigorously, sending out a volume of smoke. "Yes, I like this patch of land better than Gilliam's. The trees are larger, and the forest deeper. I've found a place to anchor a sailboat in that little cove, and with the 'cosin there at the east, I'm protected from the wind. So if you and her ladyship have no objection, I'll just settle here for a spell."

Marita hastened to assure him of his welcome.

"Oh, we love to have you, Captain!" she cried. "My aunt says that she likes having you here. It makes her feel so safe."

"That's mighty fine of her ladyship," the Captain replied. "Mighty fine." He had a little twinkle in his eyes as if he had a secret he would like to share, but he did not confide in Marita or another person that it was Roger Mainwairing's suggestion that he take up his abode in the old house.

"I'll give you a couple of slaves and you can plant that garden you're always talking about, Captain," Roger had told him. "I'll feel safer knowing you're there. You and Watkins and the two indentured men could keep off a parcel of Indians if need be, or get the women up to Mulberry Hill by water if there should be an alarm."

Mulberry Hill was the designated "fortress" for all the planters along the Sound shore. There were always extra food supplies stored there and extra arms. In case of Indian trouble, the strongly built, heavy-walled manor house of the Blounts was readily accessible to all the plantations because of its location. The stockade was stout with loopholes for observation of the water and the forest, and the open field around the house afforded extra protection. The plans for such an event were made down to the last detail and could be used either in an Indian attack or slave uprising.

"We sit on a powder keg," Roger Mainwairing had said at a meeting of the Sound shore planters earlier that year. "It may go off at any time. We must not be found napping." Most of the men agreed with him but many laughed at the idea. "We are as safe here as if we were in the heart of England," one planter said. Others concurred: they were safe; no Indians had risen against the English for a long time. Roger did not press the point. It was enough that some provision had been made.

Balgray was the fortress for the Chowan and Roanoke planters, and the stockade of Queen Anne's Town was large enough and strong enough to accommodate the other families whose plantations were near the village, along the smaller streams.

"There are things I can teach you," Zeb said to Marita. "A lot of things. For one, I want that you should come here every day and take a lesson in pistol shooting."

"Pistol shooting!" Martia exclaimed, opening her heavily fringed lids wide. "Why, I couldn't shoot. I couldn't kill anything!"

"Who's askin' you to kill?" the Captain demanded. "You shoot at your mark for the present." He waved his arm in the direction of the Sound.

Marita looked. She saw a small keg floating in the water— on it had been painted a white circle.

"When you've got so you can hit that bull's-eye every time, I'll let you begin on a musket." His eyes twinkled.

Marita's expression showed her dismay. "I can think of pastimes I'd like better."

"This isn't a pastime," the old man said. "Every woman here in the Province must know how to shoot—and shoot to kill."

Marita suddenly understood what he meant. This land was not always a benign land, soft and lush and fertile. There was something sinister here also. The land could be hard and cruel, not always sunny and warm and peaceful. Danger lurked in the deep forest, on the broad rivers, and along the sandbanks tha ran like a chain into the ocean.

"I want to learn," she said simply.

"Good girl," the old man said, patting her soft hand with his horny hand. "I told Duke Roger you would understand."

Marita looked at the Captain's guileless eyes; he was not so guileless after all. All this had been talked over between the Captain and Mr. Mainwairing. They were preparing for some unknown danger. She had no sense of fear but she would have liked it better if they had talked to her frankly. She was no longer a child to be kept in the dark about things which concerned her. She got up and walked towards the bank looking out to the Sound. The water was sparkling and beautiful under the warm spring sun. The tall pines along the wooded shore on the south were clearly etched against the bright blue sky. Beyond were the great swamps, and not so far away to the south was the Indian village of the Tuscaroras. King Blont, their chief, was friendly now. But could he be trusted to speak for all his people? There were other dangers. She turned a little. To the east where the great waters of the Albemarle went to the sea, were the Banks, the long strips of sand that protected the coastland.

But there were inlets—seven in all, where pirate ships could enter from the ocean and raid the rivers and the river plantations. Danger lay to the east as well as to the south and the west. She walked slowly back. Captain Zeb watched her with shrewd, kindly eyes.

" 'Tain't a country for weaklings—male or female," he observed, tamping his pipe. " 'Tain't very easy to make a new world out of a raw wilderness. Land don't give way easy, no more than varmints can be moved from their burrows or their lairs."

Marita did not answer. The Captain smoked in silence. Then she saw his body stiffen as he stared out toward the Sound. She turned to look. Two Indians, skilfully handling a hollowed-tree-trunk canoe, were approaching the shore. Captain Zeb shouted to one of his Negro boys, who ran to the house and returned almost at once with the Captain's long gun.

They watched the slow approach of the canoe, the smooth poling of the standing Indian. When the canoe touched the float, the Indian raised his hand in the sign of peace. Zeb walked stiffly toward the shore with his musket in the crook of his arm. Marita got up to follow him, but he waved her back.

"We'll find out who he is first," he said. "Can't tell about these red Indians, and I don't propose to trust no one. Mungo, we'll go down to the float and ask a few questions. Miss Marita, you just step inside my cabin there, and if there should be trouble, my cook boy will bar the door. There's an extra musket inside and the boy knows how to use it."

Marita went to the cabin reluctantly. She had no longer the fear of red men she had had when she first came to the Albemarle. There had been many friendly Indians at Balgray and at the village on the Chowan, and many of the planters had Indian slaves as well as Negroes.

Marita had not been inside the cabin since the Captain had moved in. She smiled a little as she glanced around. The room was as much like a ship's cabin as he could make it, a long low room, ceiled in pine with a chimney in the center. Off the main room was a shed-kitchen, where Bingo presided. The Captain had built bunks against the side of the wall, ship fashion. A hinged table stood near the bunks, with a ship's lanthorn above it, and over the fireplace were a compass and wheel. The north wall was covered with charts of the routes from Plymouth to the Cape of Good Hope, round the Indian Ocean to India. A great map of the West Indies islands, with all the intricate passages, bays and inlets and small islands, occupied one wall, with red marks showing where Zeb had met pirate ships. One larger red cross, off the Canary Islands, had a legend under it, "Captured here by Pirates," and the red line followed the course of the pirate ship to its haven in Tripoli. "Here is where I was prisoner for a year and a half," read the legend at that spot.

The sound of voices broke on her ears. Marita went to the door. The Captain was approaching the house, followed by two Indians, a man and a woman. Mungo was at their heels.

The Captain had a letter in his hand, which he waved when he saw Marrita. "Duke Roger has sent you these people," he called as he came up. "Quis-la-kin is the man's name. He is to be your hunter and fisherman. His wife's name is Kikitchina. She will dress the hides and be a slave for you, if you need her."

Marita looked at the Indian woman. She was young and very erect. Her skin clothes were soft and well tanned, heavily embroidered with coloured beads. Her dark eyes met Marita's levelly, without a change of expression, but there was no unfriendliness in them.

"I'll have Mungo take them to the house," the Captain told her. "Watkins will know what to do with them. Roger says he hopes you will allow your women to train Kikitchina to do things for you, Miss Marita. He says she is very deft with her hands and learns quickly."

"My aunt's woman will teach her," Marita said, quickly, at once eager to follow Roger Mainwairing's suggestion. "I think it will be very nice to have her." She smiled at the girl in her warm, friendly way. "She can show me about the plants and flowers that grow in the forest and tell me the names of the birds."

"I doubt that you can learn to speak the Indian names," the Captain said dryly.

Marita blushed, embarrassed that she had been so eager. "I suppose not," she said, slowly. "I suppose it would be hard, but some people must have mastered their language."

The Indian woman nodded. "I show," she said, and picking up her bundle, she started off for the manor house. The man quickened his steps, and passed her on the road, so that he walked first, after Mungo.

A smile crinkled the corners of the Captain's farseeing, blue eyes. "That is as it should be—the woman the burden-bearer, following the master, but I never got one trained to do it," he said regretfully. "I tried it three different times with three different kinds of woman, but it always turned out the same. I had to wait on them, even when I had a harem."

Marita spoke hastily—one could never tell where Captain Zeb's amazing frankness would lead him. "I had better go now. Watkins may be surprised if I do not tell him the

Indians come from Mr. Mainwairing. He might send them away."

She stepped onto the stump and mounted the mare, Blenheim. At the bend of the lane she looked back to wave to the Captain, but he had already returned to his melon mounds.

When she passed the stockade that surrounded the manor house she saw two horses hitched to the rack. A strange man, a servant by his garb, stood near by watching half a dozen small Negro children playing the stick game. Two of the boys got up quickly and ran to take her horse. Marita kicked her foot clear of the stirrup and stepped to the riding block. Pausing for a moment to button her long skirt over her doublets, she ran up the wide steps to the gallery and entered the house.

Desham was waiting for her in the hall. Finger to lips, she tiptoed past the drawing-room door to the little office back of the stairs. "Her ladyship has been looking for you, Miss Marita. She wants you should go to her directly you came into the house. She has visitors."

"Who are they?" Marita asked, taking off her cap and tidying her braids.

" 'Tis the Quaker women from across the river, and her ladyship is fair wore out with them. They sit and sit and never a word do they say."

Marita giggled, knowing how little her aunt would care to make conversation with anyone, much less two strange women.

"Not a word, Desham? Surely they say something."

Desham shook her head vigorously. "I've served them morning tea. They drank the tea and ate the little cakes, but they had naught to say. Her ladyship is fair wore out, I can tell you."

"I'll go in. Perhaps they may talk a little. Two women, you say?"

"One woman and a young person no older than yourself, Miss Marita. They are dressed most queer, in starched grey petticoats and little white fichus over their plain bodices—and the strangest bonnets."

Marita had never seen Quaker women but she recognized the costume.

The bell rang—jerked would be nearer to the word for the discordant jangle that pealed through the hall.

"It's her ladyship," the maid said. "She must have heard you come in. She'll be wanting you."

Marita put out her hand. "I'll go, Desham," she said.

Marita walked into the quiet room. At a glance, she had taken in the attitudes of the two women and her aunt. Lady Mary was seated by the fire, her two little spaniels lying on the voluminous folds of her rose-coloured petticoat. The look of boredom on her face gave way to relief, when she saw Marita. "There you are, my dear. I thought Desham would never find you."

"I've been down to the Sound," Marita said, glancing at the two guests.

"Madam Tomes, this is my niece, Marita Tower; and this, Marita, is Madam Tomes's daughter, Lucretia."

Marita bowed to the elder woman. Madam Tomes was seated on the edge of the high chair, her feet close together, her hands folded primly in her lap. The young girl with bright dark eyes and rosy cheeks sat at her side.

The elder woman was dressed in some grey stuff, a full and round skirt, and plain buttoned bodice with a small fichu of crisp pleated lawn around her neck. On her head, completely concealing her hair, was a grey bonnet, like a great scuttle. The young girl was a duplicate of her mother in her clothes and posture, but her bright dark eyes were alive with curiosity, darting this way and that. She looked as if she might speak, but a side glance from the elder woman stopped her.

They both looked so prim, so fresh and clean, so spotless, that Marita involuntarily put her hand to her wind-blown hair.

"Perhaps you would like to see our garden," Marita suggested after a few moments. Her aunt gave her a grateful look.

"Thank thee, no," the elder woman said: "I should like to see thy dresses."

For the first time that Marita could remember, Lady Mary looked nonplussed. "My dresses?" she managed to say.

"Yes. It is said that thee has half a hundred of silk and satin and wool."

"Indeed I have not," Lady Mary said shortly, annoyed at the strange request.

"Then show me what thee has," the Quakeress said serenely. "My daughter would like to see. She has never seen aught but Quaker dress," she explained.

Marita saw the slow flush rising to her aunt's cheeks. Lady Mary was angered, and there was no telling what she would do when her temper rose. But suddenly she threw back her head and laughed.

A faint smile came to the Quaker's woman's lips.

"Go upstairs, Marita, and have Desham bring down some clothes. The cherry-coloured petticoat with the white over-dress, and the blue embroidered in silver."

"And hoods! Has thee any bright hoods?" The young girl's voice broke a little in the embarrassment of speaking. A pang shot through Marita's heart. The poor child always dressed so drably, never a bright colour to bolster up low spirits.

She held out her hand. "Come with me, Lucretia. You can help me decide what to bring downstairs."

The girl looked at her mother, waiting for her consent. The older woman nodded. Lucretia rose eagerly, but she walked across the room primly, with small steps.

As she reached the door Marita heard Madam Tomes say, "It is not well for a young girl to see only drab things."

Lady Mary leaned forward. "You have not long been a Quaker, Madam?"

"Since before Lucretia was born, but I have not forgotten."

Lady Mary nodded, as if she quite understood. "Did you live in London?"

"Yes. In London and in the provinces."

Marita heard no more. She led the way up the stairs to her aunt's room. Desham was outraged by the request. She set her lips firmly as she opened press and cupboard.

Lucretia stood still in the middle of the room, her face radiant, her eyes eager, as Marita laid dress after dress on the bed. Timidly she advanced and ran her fingers lightly over a brocaded petticost. "I did not know cloth could feel so delicate," she said in a low voice. Desham looked at her, her face softening at the girl's expression.

Marita went to her own room and came back with a bonnet-box. She took out a gold-coloured hood, quilted, and trimmed with a tiny edging of swansdown.

The girl clasped her hands together. "How lovely!" she exclaimed: "How lovely!"

"Try it on," Marita said, "I'm sure it will become you. It is just the colour to go with your dark eyes—and your hair—is it dark, too? Let me take off that bonnet."

Lucretia protested feebly, but Desham was already untying the grey strings and taking off the heavy stiff bonnet.

"What lovely hair!" Marita exclaimed. Plainly parted in

the centre, the long brown braids encircled the small head with a sculptured beauty.

"I must not. It is frivolous," Lucretia murmured. But Desham paid no attention to the feeble protest. She tied the ribands under the girl's soft chin.

"Look, miss," she said, pointing to the long mirror. "Look."

Marita smiled at Lucretia's changing expression—timidity, surprise, and a little satisfaction. Suddenly she began to untie the ribands with trembling fingers. "I must not! I must not! Vanity is a sin," she repeated breathlessly.

Desham was about to protest, but Marita gave her a swift look. "We will go downstairs, Lucretia. Desham, bring the gowns."

Lucretia put her bonnet on her dark braids and tied the strings without looking in the mirror. Together they went down the stairs, followed by Desham, her ams a cascade of laces and satins, brocade petticoats and basques. At the door Lucretia paused, her hand on Marita's arm. "Do not tell Mamma that I had the gold-coloured bonnet on my head," she whispered.

Madam Tomes did not change her position; her features remained serene, but her eyes sparkled when she saw Desham.

Then began a strange showing of feminine belongings. For a long time the two women sat quietly, almost stoically, unmoved by the glitter of brocades and the rainbow array of silks and satins.

The shy, sensitive face of the girl was alight. The older woman said to Lady Mary, "It is said in Pequimans that thee has petticoats that measure twenty-four yards in circumference, that thee cannot enter a room unless it has two great doors to be thrown open at once, and that one of thy frilled lace-trimmed skirts was pulled up on a pulley and used as a canopy over a judges' stand."

Lady Mary's musical laugh filled the room with merriment. "My good woman," she said, trying to compose herself, "your informant in Pequimans has been misinformed. He has been reading Mr. Addison or Mr. Steele in *The Tatler*. It is one of them who has made up that ridiculous story."

"And thee doesn't have to lift thy petticoats on a pulley, to get them over thy head?"

"No, no. Desham manages very well without a pulley,"

Lady Mary said, drying her eyes with her lace handkerchief. "Nor have I a skirt like the cupola of St. Paul's," she added, "nor do I wear my hair towering to the ceiling. Everything is just as you see here."

She pulled a cherry-satin skirt out; it fell in billows around her. "How wide is this one, Desham?"

"Twenty-four yards, your ladyship."

"You can see for yourself how light it is," Lady Mary said, dropping the satin on Mrs. Tomes's lap. The Quakeress drew backward, allowing the shiny skirt to slip to the floor. Desham snatched it hastily, a horrified look on her broad, rosy face.

"No, no. It is the lure of the Devil," the woman muttered. "Thee must take it away. I do not know what I was thinking of. My child must not be tempted. . . . My husband will be sadly annoyed. He says, 'Youth is devoted to lust.'"

Lady Mary looked at her, her eyes full of pity. "You have given up a great deal, my poor woman."

"No, no. It is not too much to pay for tranquillity," Madam Tomes said quickly. "Not too much for a quiet conscience."

She rose to her feet, her heavy grey cloth gown hanging limply about her well-shaped body. "Come, my child. Make thy farewells to this kind woman."

Lucretia gave a little curtsy to Lady Mary, and they moved slowly across the room to the door.

"Please come again," Lady Mary said, without rising from her chair. "Lucretia would be a good companion for my little Marita."

Madam Tomes bowed slightly. "Thank thee for thy hospitality."

Marita went to the riding-block with them. Lucretia said timidly, "We would be happy to have thee come to us one day. Perhaps when the Assembly meets next month? It is very active then, with many people coming to stay with my father and Mr. Hecklefield."

Madam interposed: "Our rooms will all be occupied, Lucretia. Thy father told me ere we left home this morning that Colonel Cary and his party would be quartered with us."

A flush came to the girl's already bright cheeks. "Michael," she said, "is Michael coming?"

Her mother gave her a quick glance: "Why should thee be concerned with the comings and goings of Michael Cary, Lucretia?"

"No reason, Mamma; no reason, only for my brother's sake. He is happy when Michael comes."

Marita felt the hot blood pounding in her veins. Michael came to their house. Lucretia loved him. She could read it in her eyes.

Madam Tomes was pondering something; a slight crease shadowed her serene forehead. After a moment's thought she said, "Perhaps it would be pleasant if Marita did come. She could have thy bed and thee could sleep in the trundle."

"Oh, yes, Mamma. Yes, I could sleep in the trundle. Thee will come?" she asked Marita, her eyes shining and eager.

Marita would not give an answer. She must have time to think it over. She said, "I thank you for inviting me, Madam Tomes. I will have to consult my aunt. I do not know how I could go away and leave her alone at Greenfield." But all the time she was thinking, "Miss Mittie will be staying here while Madam Hyde is in Virginia. Aunt Mary will not be alone if I go."

The servant led up a fat bay mare. Madam Tomes, with a surprising degree of agility, put her foot in the stirrup and seated herself firmly in the saddle, man-fashion. The servant pulled her skirts into place, securing them with a black band around her heavy shoes. Lucretia got up behind her mother and rode postilion, her full skirts flapping around her ankles. Down the driveway they rode at a fast clip, the manservant following, his long coat-tails flopping.

Marita did not smile at the picture. She had already forgotten the bobbing grey figures on the fat bay mare.

All the old hurt came back to her. Michael's name on the lips of the Quaker girl brought it back to her with a sudden rush. She had been so sure she had put him away from her, far, far into the remote recesses of a heart quite numb. But now that heart was alive again, alive and aching. She stood there, her arms tightly folded over her chest, her mouth trembling. Dark thoughts drove away her newly acquired peace. She stumbled forward, into the hall, up the stairs to the sanctuary of her bedchamber.

When Desham came into the room an hour later she found Marita lying on her bed asleep, the trace of tears still on her cheeks. She stood for a moment looking down at Marita, her hard face gentle. There was not much that escaped Desham's sharp eyes, though she said little. After a moment she touched the girl's shoulder to waken her.

"Her ladyship says to tell you it is time for your tea, Miss Marita," she said.

Marita sat up. She did not speak. She felt Desham looking at her. She raised her hand to her eyes, to shield her ravaged face. "I will come," she said, sliding off the bed.

"There is warm water in the ewer, miss," Desham said. "Do you want me to bathe your eyes?"

"No, thank you. No."

The hurt and doubt and longing had all come back: He does not love me. He never loved me. It was only I who wanted him. All women come to him—had she not seen him in the forest with his arms around a strange girl, with bright autumn leaves in her hair?

And now this girl, quiet as a dove, with her soft cooing voice and her bright birdlike eyes. Marita thought of the dove that wore a bright red wound over its heart. Was Lucretia like that—with a wound in her heart?

The golden sunset entered the room and lay all about her, touching the bed and the dark polished floor. She wished for a moment that she had no power to feel, that no one could hurt her, that she could be strong—and remote—like her aunt.

She walked downstairs, her head erect, her cheeks flushed. Roger Mainwairing rose from a seat near Lady Mary and held out a chair so that she could take a place at the tea table. She smiled at him gratefully, not for that little act of courtesy, but because he was there to claim her aunt's attention.

She had noticed that when Duke Roger came Lady Mary did not pay any heed to her. Sometimes she scarcely knew Marita was in the room. Sometimes it hurt Marita and made her feel like a very small child, but now she was glad. She could sit quietly and pour the tea while Lady Mary and Roger sat close together, their voices dropped to low, intimate tones.

She could sit in her place at the table and think of Michael—no, she must close her heart to him, now and forever. But somehow that determination would not stay with her. It was crowded out by another and stronger one. If she should go to Pequimans to visit Lucretia . . . if her aunt would consent . . . if Miss Mittie would come . . . if . . . Presently the ifs grew dim and faded completely. The new thought was affirmative, not negative—"when I go to Lucretia's . . ."

Roger Mainwairing's voice brought her up with a jerk.

182

"Lady Mary would like a cup of tea," he said. She noticed he had placed himself between her and her aunt. As she lifted the silver pot he said, "Do not go so far away, little Marita; save dreams for your solitary moments."

She looked up and found his eyes were kind and understanding. "Thank you, Mr. Mainwairing," she said, in the same low voice. "Thank you for reminding me."

"What are you two talking about?" Lady Mary said.

Roger answered as he took the cup from Marita, "About your tea. Whether to add hot water or not—"

Marita thanked him with her eyes. A moment later she slipped out of the room. Taking up a cloak from a hook, she ran out of the house. She would walk down the lane to the water.

She was deep in her own thoughts but even had she looked about she would not have seen the Indian Quis-la-kin, who followed her at a distance gliding through the forest. In sight of the fishing hut she stopped. A few slaves were there, trying out the small nets. Like statues they stood knee deep in the water between her and the sinking sun.

How silent it was, how tranquil! If only she could gather to herself the quiet strength of the earth and the trees.

Suddenly she was at peace with herself. She would see Michael Cary once more. Though Lucretia loved him, Marita would visit her, share her room, and hide from her that Michael—that she—She would look at Michael with her new knowledge; surely now she was older, wiser. She could tell if he was untrue, unstable ... she must see him, hear him speak, judge him herself.

The sun was down, leaving a blood-red reflection in the still waters of the Sound. Marita turned to the darkened path, her mind at peace again.

Chapter 15

THE TURK AND THE CYLINDER

ROGER stopped at Mulberry Hill on his way home. Americus, the black houseman, ushered him directly to the dining-room where John Blount was just sitting down at the long mahogany table. Roger always enjoyed a visit with the big Blount family. For a lonely man it was heartening to see John and Elizabeth Yelverton Blount with their brood. They had just taken their places at table tonight, all the nine children, including the elder sons, John, Thomas and James, almost men grown. They were seated near their father while the daughters, like a bouquet of spring flowers, surrounded their mother, who looked almost the age of Maria, the eldest girl. Maria had only lately returned from a long visit in England, and all the graces of confident young womanhood enhanced her blonde beauty. Roger had heard that she was being wooed by one of the young Jacocks lads from up the Chowan. A good match, although her father would have preferred her to choose a planter of the Albemarle, particularly one whose land joined some of his holdings.

Sarah, the second girl, was only a little over a year younger than Maria. She was casting timid eyes toward Anthony Lovyck. She was as dark as Maria was fair, with the deep-set blue eyes of the Blounts. Elizabeth was a small edition of Maria, whom she adored and copied even to inflection of speech and the colour of ribands in her hair. Martha was nondescript at the moment, very shy and self-effacing. She seemed almost younger than Hester, the next girl, who at twelve was bursting with individuality and as vital as her curling red hair. Charles, the very little boy, was the youngest of all, but even he had a place at the table.

Hester was first to discover Roger as he stood in the doorway. She bounced out of her chair and rushed to him, slipping and sliding across the polished floor.

"Mr. Mainwaring has come to supper!" she cried. "Mother, it's my turn to sit by him."

John Blount rose from the table, a warm smile of welcome on his thin face. In a moment all was confusion; chairs were pushed back or slid along to make room for one more. The younger children crowded around Roger, each one begging to sit near him. To end the confusion, Elizabeth Yelverton had Americus put a place for Roger between herself and Hester, who had won first privilege by virtue of her claim that she had seen him first.

In a moment they had all scrambled for their places, to the annoyance of Maria who raised her arched brows to her mother. She said in her new, fine-lady manner, "At Aunt Teresa's house the younger children have their meals upstairs in the nursery, so that the grownups may have a little peace at their supper and some quiet for conversation."

At her words a new commotion arose. Hester wailed, "Mother, is Maria going to be like that? Is she going to be dic-a-toral all the time?"

Everybody laughed at Hester as she stumbled over an unaccustomed word. Elizabeth Yelverton quieted her brood, but Hester clung with both hands to Roger's arm until Americus and one of the coloured housewomen brought a place service to him and she was quite sure that he would not be snatched away and seated beside one of the older sisters.

Elizabeth Yelverton looked around the table. "Charles, will you please say grace?"

All the other children folded their hands and sat with their eyes cast down, while little Charles, important at having been chosen tonight, folded his plump little hands one over the other and began, "O Lord, in thy good mercy, bless thou this food." Here he ran astray and instead of ending the grace, he rambled into bedtime prayers, blessing each member of the family in turn, and all the dogs and cats. The older children began to glance sideways at each other in consternation, and at their mother, but her eyes were closed as Charles rambled on. From cats and dogs he started on horses. Thomas nudged him and young John lifted his long leg and gave him a gentle kick under the table. But Charles had a good start and was down to the mules and old Ezra. This was too much for his father. He broke in on the long prayer with "In the name of Almighty God the Father. Amen." Everybody chorused "Amen." All but little Charles, who opened his blue eyes wide and wailed, "But I haven't blessed my pony yet—or old Tige or Sarum—" Tears filmed his eyes, ready to tumble down his fat, rosy cheeks.

"There, there," said his mother, soothingly, "you can bless them all tonight when you go to bed."

"Well, it's high time," Hester said loudly. "Since Charles has made up his mind to be a preacher like Parson Urmston he wants to make sermons at us all the time."

Elizabeth Yelverton said, "I think it is very fine of Charles to choose the Church as his calling. I don't want you children to annoy him if he wishes to preach a sermon."

"Oh, Mother," Martha cried, "isn't it bad enough to listen to the Parson on Sunday without having weekday sermons?"

"I don't know why you should squawk, Mathy—you need somebody to preach about sin. You told a lie yesterday."

"I did not tell a lie, Master Thomas!" Martha cried. "I just said I thought Marita Tower was much, much, much prettier than Clorinda Vaile."

Thomas' face burned. John Blount's lips pressed firmly, his face hard.

"There, there," Elizabeth Yelverton broke in. "What will Mr. Mainwairing think if you children make so much noise? Hester! You are not to help yourself to English bread until your elders are served. How often have I told you to wait until Sybana serves you?"

Hester put the bread back on the dish. "Sybana's too slow and I'm hungry," she muttered.

Sybana, big, fat and very black, paused in the middle of the floor, a plate piled high with boiled muton and dumplings poised precariously over Thomas' head.

"Dat child she eat all de time, lak she got a worm. Just a little while since she come out to de kitchen and she drink one big jug of milk, fresh outen de cow."

"That will do, Sybana; put Mr. Thomas' plate on the table." Mrs. Blount looked helplessly about the table, her grey eyes coming to rest on Roger. "I don't know what Mr. Mainwairing will think of you children with your chatter; you make so much noise. He is used to having his meals in peace and quiet."

"Too much quiet," Roger said laughing.

Throughout the long, bounteous meal, made up entirely from the products of the plantation, the conversation concerned itself with Mulberry Hill and its neighbours, with a few exceptions: Maria's continued references to her life in London, and John Blount's talk of Virginia political affairs.

He had just returned from a visit to Williamsburg and he was full of news about the fleet which had just been sighted off the capes. Two ships-of-war had already come up the James, and others would follow, more than twenty sail besides the ships-of-war, he told them with some satisfaction. "Now we can be sure we will get out crops across, with a proper convoy to guard them."

"It would be better for us if they didn't have to split the fleet and send part of them to join the Jamaica convoy," Roger said glumly. He had just had word that day of the loss of one of his cargoes, taken by pirates off the Bahama Islands. "We should have that many sail right on this coast all the time. Hatteras is the most dangerous cape on the whole shore line. There are hundreds of lurking places for French and Spanish privateers in the Pamticoe and up the Neuse and the Trent and the Ashley. Along the Banks, too. Any of the sandy islands offer shelter and hiding places for enemies to lurk. If we had the ships to clear out those nests we could have some degree of safety for our cargoes. Four ships-of-war besides the guard-ships would be somewhere near what we need to protect our trade."

John Blount did not share Roger Mainwairing's anxiety. He did not have so much land for crops nor had he gone so heavily into trade with England and the West Indies as Roger had. The Blounts had most of their money in England in securities and shares, some in the newly organized Bank of England, and some in Mr. Law's South Sea Company. The owner of Mulberry Hill raised ample crops to supply the household and to do a little trading with Virginia merchants and the New England captains who brought their ships to his own wharf.

After the womenfolk and the young people had left the table John Blount and Roger lingered over their port, talking plantation affairs. John had brought down fifty black cherry trees from Virginia, and Mrs. Harrison had sent his wife some crepe-myrtle trees for ornamentation in her garden. He told Roger about the sickness that was so prevalent among the Negroes along the James River Plantation, vomiting and a looseness, for all the world like a plague. It was helped somewhat by blood-letting, but many of the slaves were dying, a great loss to the planters. He was in Williamsburg on the thirtieth of January, he told Roger, the day of fast proclaimed by the Governor to commemorate the martyrdom of King Charles the First. Governor Spottswood and all the ministers of churches and chapels made prayer that day, imploring Almighty God to forgive them their sins and to prevent the grave sickness now raging among them.

"I hope the plague doesn't get to us," Roger said, remembering that he had not had his people up to the dispensary for some time. "If we should have a contagion, I don't see how Parris could handle all the plantations, with King far too old to go beyond the village. I think I'll give all my blacks wormseed and oil of croton whether they are ailing or not."

John Blount's thin face wrinkled into a smile. "You are ?

bad as Porter with his blue mass and Peru bark. He gives it indiscriminately from May until November."

Roger took the clay pipe Americus handed him and tamped it with leaf. "That's not such a bad idea, John. I notice Porter's field hands have less ague than my men. I believe I'll start his cure-all this spring."

John did not comment. His mind was on something else. After a few moments' silent puffing he said, "Governor Spottswood is bringing some of the young Nottaway Indian braves to school at William and Mary. It seems a useless waste of the people's money."

"God's death, is the man crack-brained?" Roger exclaimed. "You can't civilize an Indian by book learning. Better buy powder and shot with the money. Fear of musketry is the only thing that will hold a red Indian in check." After a moment he added, "That reminds me, how much powder have you on hand in your magazine?"

"I don't know just the amount. I haven't opened the powder house lately," John answered indifferently.

Roger frowned and laid down his pipe on one of Elizabeth Yelverton's fine silver salvers. It irked him when any of the Albemarle planters were indifferent to the Indian situation. "If Mulberry Hill is to be the fortress for the protection of the women and children of the Sound plantations, you will have to know what you have on hand in the way of ammunition. I tell you, John, you can't shut your eyes to the unrest of the northern and western Indians. Every time one of my trappers comes in he tells me of some new deviltry or atrocity. It's no longer safe up the rivers or at the outlying farms. I saw Lawson last week. He says the 'Cores' are restless. Their warriors are getting insolent. They thieve and pilfer among De Graffenried's settlers without punishment. What's wrong with our men? If our government is so weak that it can't suppress thieving by Indians, then it's time for the planters to take the law in their own hands."

John Blount shook his head. "You're always suspicious, Duke. You're still a soldier at heart, wanting to shoot and kill. I say we must be friends with the Tuscaroras. We have a peace treaty, signed by Chief Blont, and I hold that we must abide by the treaty."

"You are closing your eyes, John. You desire to feel secure and so you assert you are. I believe so little in that security that I sold off every Indian slave I have on the place. There are only two Indians in the Province that I would trust."

"And I suppose you have sold them also?" John asked, sarcasm in his question.

"No, I gave them away," Roger said shortly, thinking of the Indian couple he had sent to Greenfield. "I saved the man's life once and even an Indian respects that bond."

He scowled unconsciously. To try to convince John that he was mistaken in his ideas was too much for Roger. These planters had no worries. He glanced at the remains of the feast on the table, the plate marked with the Blount crest on the sideboard. They lived in plenty, for the land was rich and lavish for the working. The streams abounded in fish, the forests in game. Slave labour was plentiful for planters who had gold to buy them.

"I've asked Bragg to bring me six field men," John said without answering Roger.

"I gave Bragg an order for some blacks too," he told Blount. "But I won't have any of his Guinea-men. They're too bad a risk. They have mean dispositions and they won't work unless you stand over them with a whip."

"I've given my overlookers orders not to use the whip except in extreme cases," Blount said.

"God's death, John, whatever has come over you!" Roger exclaimed. "You can't run a plantation unless you lay on with a lash and a strong one. Why, I've just finished a dungeon where I can throw the rascals until they come to heel. What's got in you to be so lenient?" That was the question he asked aloud, but in his mind was another which he did not put into words. All the Province knew that John was at outs with his son Thomas because he paid court to one of Vaile's daughters. A feud between the Vailes and the Blounts was of long standing and so deep-seated John had had a road made side by side with the river road, that he might not have to ride on the same earth Vaile travelled. But he was so soft that he would not flog his slaves. There was no sense to that.

"The Bible does not hold with flogging," Blount said slowly. "Love thy neighbour is what it says."

"You'd better tell that to the Parson," Roger said grimly. "I rode by there the other day when he was flogging that white wench his wife brought over. It was no light lash that he laid on, let me tell you."

"That's different. The woman is going to have a bastard child. She won't give the name of its father," John said harshly. "We're going to have her up before the Vestry next meeting. She'll tell then, never fear."

"By the living God, John, you're crazy! Can't you let the poor wench alone? What if she does bear a child out of wedlock? Plenty of her betters have committed that crime—if it is a crime."

John Blount's lips made a straight line. His usually mild blue eyes were hard. "She is the minister's servant. That makes a difference. She should set an example."

"I can't see the difference," Roger said heatedly. "I flog my slaves because they are lazy or sullen and won't do an honest day's work. They are my property and I govern them. I do what I think right with them. You won't agree with that, but you—"

"You are a hard man, Roger," John interrupted. "A hard man in your ways and your living. You don't follow the word of God."

"Maybe I don't," Roger replied heatedly. He knew the wine was speaking, but he didn't care. "But I'm a fair man and I treat my people according to their deserts. If they are good and do their work well and faithfully, I reward them; if they don't, I punish. They know this and I have little trouble. But I'd shoot any overlooker of mine who would flog a woman that was with child."

"I repeat, you are a hard man with a soldier's view of punishment and discipline."

Roger didn't answer this. What was the use of arguing with his neighbour? He would only let his temper get out of control and that would get him nowhere with John Blount. "Every man to his liking," he said, as he drained his glass. "Are you going to the village tomorrow?"

It was raining when Roger Mainwairing left Mulberry Hill. He drew his heavy cape close around him. There was still a few miles' travel ahead of him through the woods before he would reach his own land. The wood path was as dark as Pharaoh's heart. It was well that his horse knew its way in the dark; else he might have lost the path and wandered into the pocosin and mired down. It was a lonely night and the wind was from the northeast, raw and blowing hard. Far off he heard a wolf cry and the lonely call of a waterfowl rose from the lower bank. Once he heard a dog bark sharply in the distance, then a sudden hush as if the animal had been quieted. He wondered about that bark. It was not the bay of a hound. Suddenly a thought flashed into

190

his mind. The witch's daughter! Was she roaming the woods with her great staghound?

Metephele had come to him more than once with some weird tale about the girl and her dog. Th Negroes had seen her time after time on the shore road, or gliding through the wood in the moonlight. Once when the hounds had treed a 'possum, it wasn't a 'possum at all but the witch girl peering down at them from the branches of a great sycamore tree. "She put de mouth on us'n and Primus he can't mak' it to shoot he musket noway," Metephele told him. "What business had Primus with one of my muskets?" Roger had said angrily. "I told you to keep the arms-room locked day and night. I don't want to hear of your letting any of the Negroes have fire arms, do you understand?" Metephele had promised. "Primus he got the gun from Mr. John Blount to shoot a deer that was eating the young grain in the east field."

Metephele had been so concerned to clear himself of the charge of giving out a weapon against orders that he said no more about the girl. Roger wondered if she really did live in the forest, or if the Negroes had already created a legend about her.

He turned from the Yaupim road to a lane that led to the water. From there he could make time by following the sandy shore to Queen's Gift. Suddenly he heard the sharp bark again. This time it was close, not more than a quarter of a mile away. The animal seemed to be paralleling him. For a moment he thought it might be the bark of a fox, but it was too heavy and full.

He slowed his horse down to a walk, listening intently. If the dog and the girl were following the middle road, they would have to drop down towards the water when they came to the Vaile pocosin. He would wait at the fork of the road to see what happened.

Hidden by a thicket of myrtle and bay, he waited at the side of the path. Five minutes or more he stood quietly, his hand on his horse's neck to quiet the animal. There were no sounds but the washing of the water on the shore and the twittering of some night bird disturbed by his presence.

The rain had checked. After a time his eyes, grown accustomed to the darkness, made out the outline of the small trees and bushes along the shore, and the differences in the shadows. Then he saw a small animal, the size of a hare, run distractedly along the edge of the sandy shore as if pursued. A moment later came the shadow of a larger animal, hot on the trail. Roger recognized the great hound he had seen with the girl Anne on Muster Day at Balgray.

Almost in front of his eyes the dog made its kill. Roger heard the pitiful little scream of the hare as the great jaws cracked its bones. A moment later there was a shrill whistle and the dog bounded away. Roger swung onto his horse. That whistle told him something. The girl was near, out in the rain, waiting for the dog to bring home his quarry. The action told him something else: how she managed to live in the forest. The dog was trained to hunt and bring home the kill. All Roger had to do now was to find where she had her camp. He would wait for the glimmer of a fire through the trees, then circle and come on her, upwind. He had a feeling he would find her on his own land, not far from where a little stream flowed into the Sound. There was an old tumbledown hut there that had been built for a drying house for the slaves when he had used the Point for fishing. The hut had a stone fireplace and chimney. It was a proper hiding place, far from the fields where the blacks worked, shut away from the house by a dense growth of forest and a small pocosin. He chuckled to himself. A very proper hiding place, indeed; one he would never have thought of searching. The girl might have remained undiscovered if he had not seen the shadow, caught the baleful gleam of her dog's eyes when he leapt on his prey, and heard the whistle from the direction of the abandoned fishing hut.

He tied his horse to a sapling and moved off in the darkness. Once he found the beginning of the path it would be easy for him to follow through the centre of the swamp to the hut. Fortunately the wind was blowing against him. With luck he would be able to get to the place without the dog's scenting him. He had given no thought to what he intended to do once he got within range of the hut. The idea of a young girl, any girl, living alone in the forest, subsisting on God knows what food, was abhorrent to him.

A bit of moon slipped out from behind the flying clouds, casting a dappled light on heavy swamp shadows and the dark mass of the half-demolished building. The place was worse than he had thought. There was a grey miasma in the air, the heavy smell of putrid, decaying logs in the dark swamp water. He told himself that he must get the girl away from here whether she wanted to go or not, yet all the time he knew her hiding place was safe—as far from the travelled roads as could be found anywhere in the Precinct.

He reached the hut without being discovered. From the shadow of a great cypress he could see inside through a half-open door that sagged crazily on its rusty hinges. A small fire burned on the hearth. The girl was moving about, sometimes in the light, again in the shadow. The great dog lay exhausted by the fire, its head dropped on its paws. The girl knelt on a bench before the long table the fishermen had used for cutting fish. Her lovely hair, the color of ripe flax, was unbound, falling in a bright cascade to her waist. Her face was hidden, but he caught the flash of a long knife as she worked, skinning the hare her dog had fetched in.

After a time she moved to the hearth, holding the skinned animal by the tips of her fingers, as if she disliked touching it, and dropped it into a blackened pot which was hanging from a crane. She knelt before the fire and began to blow on the coals. A small blaze puffed up and ignited a handful of twigs she threw on the embers. Something about the skill with which she accomplished her object caught at Roger's throat. How long she must have been living this way! She was as skilled as any trapper or hunter. A pretty thing in this new world, where all folk were to be given an opportunity to live. Why had she not gone to the Vestry for help? But even with that thought came another and a stronger one. Short shrift would be given to the daughter of a proved witch, and the woman was coming up for trial tomorrow.

His heart warmed to the girl. He took a step forward. The dog raised his great pointed ears as if he were disturbed by some vague dream.

"Rest well, Royal," the girl said quietly. "No more hunting tonight."

At the sound of her voice the dog quieted. For a moment Roger hesitated. Then he turned and slowly retraced his steps, careful not to make any sound.

He could not disturb the girl now. What could he offer her that equalled her present sense of security? She was sure of her safety, so sure and untroubled. If he spoke to her, even if he offered to help her, he might send her roaming through the woods again seeking new shelter.

He found his way back to his horse. He was depressed by what he had seen. The lonely girl caught his imagination and left him disturbed and uneasy. Certainly it was no good to go any further at present. Now that he knew her hiding place he could help her if the right time came.

A sharp gust of wind greeted him as he left the shelter of

193

the pocosin. In a few moments the rain came—heavy, driving rain that stirred his horse to a swift trot. One good thing: the rain would drown his footprints by morning.

A sleepy stable boy took Roger's steaming horse. Metephele waited for him on the gallery, to take his hat and sodden cape. Roger sat down on the hall settle while the *capita* pulled and tugged at his muddied boots.

"Dark man waiting for master," Metephele said when Roger stood up.

"Dark man? What do you mean—a Negro waiting for me tonight?"

Metephele shook his head. It was not a Negro but a strange dark man with *ntola* and *mkwisa*.

"Pots and kettles?" Roger repeated. Then light came to him. What the devil did the Turk want of him this evil night? "Bring him in," he said, walking through the door into the lighted library.

Metephele lost his usual calm. He followed Roger, protesting in a mixture of English and his own tongue as he did when he was excited. "*Iai, Iai,* Master, *nsanza chi'gudu.*"

"I don't care if he is in rags," Roger said truculently. "Let the man inside. Wait. Have Cato bring something to eat— cold turkey or chicken." He remembered the man wore a tarboosh. "I don't want ham. How long has he been waiting? When did he come?"

"He comes through the storm, a *kale kale*, a long time ago," the *capita* said.

What could the Turk want of him that he journeyed six miles on a rainy night? His eyes sought the wall where his rapiers and small arms hung in a rack. The Turk's sword had not been disturbed. Well, if he wanted money for the blade, he should have it. A full price, for it fitted his hand as no sword had fitted it before. He had distrusted the gift from the first. One always paid in the end. When he turned his eyes, the Turk stood in the doorway. He made a swift movement of greeting with his hand. "*Bis'millah, Bis'millah,*" he murmured.

Roger knew the greeting well. Many times he had heard it when he journeyed in the East. "Enter, in the peace of Allah," Roger replied, knowing the greeting from his days on the Bosphorus. A swift smile came to the swart face of the Turk, and was gone.

In the light he saw that the Turk's *aba* was muddied, the wide sleeves torn and frayed. There was a great bruise above his temple and a cut on his cheek on which the blood had dried. He crossed the room, but instead of taking the chair Roger indicated he sat down near the fire, his legs gathered up under his wide robe.

"The *Effendi* will pardon that I come without permission, and in disarray?" he said in a quiet soft voice. "I know not where to go other than to the *Effendi*."

"You are in trouble?" Roger asked.

"Sore trouble. The low people of the village have set their dogs on me. They have stoned me. They have shot at me with muskets and said I must leave. But how can I leave, when there is no ship to take me?"

"Take you where?" Roger asked, watching the man warily. He looked harmless—aye; pitiful—so small and shrivelled a creature, so abased.

"To Jamaica, or St. Kitts, or, with good fortune, to Martinique."

"How did you get here?"

"On a shallop, down the Chowan from Virginia. They told me I could take ship here for the West Indies." Suddenly his eyes flashed with a fanatical light, and he rose beating his breast with his fists. "They spit upon me, me—a follower of the Prophet—and stoned me!"

"Why?" Roger asked quietly. "There must have been some reason."

A torrent of words came piling one on the other, Arabic and English, a polyglot profusion of words.

"Wait, wait," Roger said, stopping him. "English only, if you want me to understand and help you."

First it was the small boys calling indecent names, snatching at his copper pots and kettles; these he let go, but when it came to his dagger and small arms, he defended them! Then older men had come, no one with the heart to defend a stranger, as Roger had defended him the night at the tavern. These laughed at him, and spat, screamed words that defiled a true believer. The Turk's dark face grew livid at the memory.

"Then?" Roger said.

"I defend myself as a man defends, with a dagger. Ah! The *Effendi* knows our people are not without skill. A man fell to the ground, blood splashing from his gullet."

"That is unfortunate," Roger said gravely, "very unfortunate."

"Yes, *Effendi*, for the man wears a bright coat, with buttons."

"A militiaman! Did you kill him?"

"He will not live the night."

Roger got up and walked the floor. This was bad, indeed. By morning they would be after him. What should he do? The Turk had no defence if he had killed a man. "Resisting arrest" would be the charge. No one would listen to what went before.

"I have a shallop leaving for Pamticoe in the morning. I'll put you aboard."

The Turk shook his head. "I have found a way to go," he said. "It is of another matter that I wish to speak to the *Effendi*."

Suddenly Roger said, "How did you find your way here?"

The Turk hesitated only a moment. "The girl, the girl with the hair of sunshine, with kindness in her eyes. She found me hiding near the stream at the edge of the village."

Roger did not comment. He could not imagine kindness in the leet woman's cold blue eyes, but he could imagine her helping another hunted creature.

A tap at the door interrupted them. Cato came into the room carrying a platter of food and a decanter. He set the tray on a table and poured two glasses of wine. The Turk shook his head. "We of the faith are not drinkers of wine," he said.

"I'm sorry. I'd forgotten." Roger turned to Cato. "Bring a jug of milk and quickly."

The Turk ate slowly. Roger had the feeling that he would have been glad to wolf the meats hungrily, if he had followed the dictates of his belly. Cato returned with a jug of milk. "You may go for the night," Roger said. "Tell Metephele to make a bed in the south room."

The Turk stayed Roger with a gesture. "I must not trespass. They will come looking for me, with the light. I must be far away by daybreak."

"How can you?" Roger ejaculated. "How can you be far away before morning?"

"There are ways," the man said. "You will pardon if I do not tell you? It is not that I do not have faith, but it is better that you say to these people, 'I do not know the way he goes.'"

Roger nodded.

The Turk finished his food and drank the milk, mumbling some prayer before he broke bread. He got to his feet and placed the dishes on the table. Facing Roger he said, "The request I make of the *Effendi* is one of some importance."

The sword, thought Roger. I knew it would come. "The sword suits me well," he said aloud. "I will be glad to pay any reasonable figure."

The Turk shrugged his shoulders and spread his hands in negation. "Already I have forgotten the sword of Saladin, knowing it rests in worthy hands. It is another matter, *Effendi*."

He walked swiftly to the door. Opening it suddenly, he looked into the long hall. Then he crossed to the windows, latching each one, before he came back to the hearth.

Roger watched him, his eyes alert. He was beyond amazement. The whole action was too strange, too inexplicable. "What villainy is this?" he said sharply.

"No villainy, *Effendi*, only grave necessity, for I have a favour to ask that wants no listener save yourself."

"How do I know I will grant this favour?"

"I swear by Allah the All-Merciful that there is no harm in it, unless it fall into wrong hands."

"God's death, I like it not!" Roger said roughly. "What is it you are asking? Who are you?"

The Turk met his eyes squarely. "What matter a man's name, or whence he comes? A man is a man who does the thing he has to do."

He rolled up the sleeve of his *aba*. On his thin upper arm Roger saw a small box, held in place by a strap. He had seen these amulets often before in his Eastern travels: boxes in which the Mecca pilgrims used to carry a few pages of the Koran or a bit of cloth from the covering of the sacred stone. The Turk unstrapped the box with his thin, clawlike fingers, and took out a small metal tube, sealed at each end with bright red wax. He put the cylinder in Roger's hand. "Will the *Effendi* place this in the hands of the Lady Mar—ee—"

Roger knew at once he was speaking of Lady Mary. What had this Turk to do with the Lady Mary Tower?

"You will give it to the lady? Quietly, when you are alone?"

"Quietly and alone?" Roger repeated. He had not yet taken in the whole implication.

"As soon as may be. Say to her, 'It is easily destroyed once

197

it is read. The writing is on very thin paper, so thin it can readily be made into a pellet—and swallowed.' "

Roger jumped to his feet, towering over the little man. "Before God, what mystery is this? I do not like it!"

The Turk's answer was quietly spoken. "The Lady Mar-ee can tell you, not the Turk. He is a messenger, nothing more." He stood before Roger, meeting his eyes calmly. Somehow he had grown in stature and in dignity.

"May the sword of Saladin rest firmly in your hand when drawn in a worthy cause. *Bis'millah.*"

Roger took up the sword to examine the hilt more closely.

The Turk left the room, so swiftly, so silently, that Roger was unaware of his departure.

"It is sorcery!" he cried. He snatched up a candle and rushed to the door. There was no one in the long hall. When he reached the turn of the stairs he saw the great front door swing shut, slowly, without sound. His candle sputtered and went out.

He groped his way back to the room he had just left, the lead cylinder warm in the palm of his hand. "A pox on the fellow!" he muttered. "What devils work is this?"

He stood for a moment looking at the inanimate thing. Why should a man risk his life to carry it to Lady Mary Tower? When he thought of her his pulse quickened.

Evil dreams had their way with Roger Mainwairing that night, dreams in which the Turk ran before a pack of maddened dogs with wide, killing jaws and foaming mouths, and the girl Anne threw her fine young body in front of them to save the desperate, fleeing man.

He sat up in bed. Somewhere in a distant part of the house a door creaked on its hinge and a shutter banged back and forth in the rising wind. Full awake, he felt for the little metal cylinder he had put in the pocket of his night clothes. It was still there. Not a safe place, if he should forget it in the morning when he dressed.

He lighted a candle and got out of bed. Rummaging in a drawer of the walnut tallboy that stood between the windows, he found a knitted garter. He strapped it about his upper arm and wound the metal case into a safe cradle. It would be secure there until he rode to Greenfield in the early morning.

He could not sleep. He walked along the upper gallery off his bedchamber thinking of her. The constellations swung across the dark dome of the sky. He searched for his lodestar. The mystic white light of Vega shone clear and steady following its eternal path. But tonight it brought him no tranquillity. When he thought of Mary his own path was not clear to his eyes.

He did not want to know the secret the cylinder held. He did not want to know anything that would draw him closer to her. As it was, she had become so much a part of him that he could not put the thought of her out of his mind. This disturbed him. Women he took as he wanted them, or left them alone. There had never been a woman before who could satisfy his body, his mind and his heart. The idea of "consuming passion" he had treated with disdain. Now he felt that it was possible for a man to lose himself, to forget everything but his desire for one woman.

Chapter 16

QUAKER HOME

A COUNTY meeting had been called by Thomas Pollack to be held at the house of Colonel Hecklefield in Durant's Neck. It was expected that there would be few absentees, for it was known thoughout the Province that the lines were now drawn and the opposing factions ready to try the outcome.

Every plantation house in Durant's Neck, as the settlement was known, was full to overflowing, as many as four members to one bedchamber in some of them. But no one minded that slight discomfort for there was always food in plenty and drink in quantity, although the quality of the latter might be dubious.

Thomas Cary came up a few days before the Assembly "to get the lay of the land," he told Michael, with a sly twinkle in his keen blue eyes. "I'll stay at the inn at Newby's Ferry for a few days. It's easier for me to hold meetings there."

Michael said, "I thought we were going to lodge at friend Tomes' house."

"You are. I'll come over there the day the meeting opens and stay from then on through the session." He smiled a little. "You've earned a little holiday, Michael. You can enjoy yourself with the young people of the Tomes household—young Edward and the pretty, demure Lucretia."

"But I don't want a holiday. I want to be of service to you."

Colonel Cary shook his head. "I can handle this part better alone, nephew. I have other work for you. Make yourself agreeable to Tomes and his womenfolk. That will be a service to me."

Michael did not reply. He realized the implication. Foster Tomes was a powerful figure in the Quaker world, and for some few months past he had been cool to Cary. In fact the Colonel had reports that he was friendly with William Glover. This was something that could not pass unchallenged, and the senior Cary, with the subtle intrigue of which he was master, would find some way to counteract Glover's growing influence.

Michael was not happy about the plan. He did not want to stay under the hospitable roof of the Tomeses in such conditions. He liked the family too well. He respected the elder Tomes, and his wife had made a place for Michael in their household. He felt more at home there than at any house in the Carolinas. Although he would not admit it to himself, Michael was lonely. The life he was leading now, under the direction of his uncle, made for adventure but not for happiness. The wound dealt him by the tragic death of his father had gone very deep, too deep to heal quickly. He missed his mother and his young brothers whom she had taken back to England with her. This life was of his own choosing, yet there were times when he wondered if he had taken the right turn in the road.

The motherly Martha Tomes had sensed this. Without words she had supplied the friendly warmth so lacking in Michael's present life. He was companionable with Edward. He loved the little boys, Jack and David, who were near the age of his own brothers—eight and nine years. For a moment he hated his uncle for his sly insinuation that he should court Lucretia because it was politic to gain the friendship of her father. Lucretia was so shy, so gentle and trusting, he could not hurt her. How could he trade on their hospitality because of doubtful loyalty to his uncle and his uncle's cause?

Now that the first glow of the adventure was fading, Michael had begun to doubt Thomas Cary's honesty. At the beginning it was a great cause, a quest. He had thought of him as another Arthur, with his knights, lifting the shield in defence of the wrongs of innocent people. Now he was not so sure. Whatever his doubts, he thrust them aside. He believed in Fate as directing all men—one must follow one's star to whatever destiny it points. This had been the fixed faith of his proud and turbulent young nature.

Then Marita came, with her thoughtful deep eyes, her gentle but spirited responses. From the moment he saw her he had felt there could be no other like her. She had become his star—even when she did not trust him. He did not like to think of the day she had seen him with his arms about another girl. She had turned and run away down the path. For a moment he thought he must overtake her—tell her the girl meant nothing to him—but pride and masculine stubbornness held him back.

A woman should trust the man she loved. That was her part. She should have discerned his devotion, the quality of his feeling for her. But she had run from the sight of another woman in his arms. That told him something, when his anger and dismay had subsided. She loved him or she would not have fled! She would have been indifferent had he not been already her lover in her own thoughts.

He had wanted to go but there had been no opportunity. As soon as he returned to Romney Marsh his uncle had sent him in his barkentine to the Ashley Settlements for arms and powder. Michael's trip had been successful. He had purchased two four-pounders to mount on the deck of the ship, and some barrels of powder and round shot.

"Why do you want all this ordnance?" he had asked his uncle when he returned to the marsh.

Colonel Cary smiled. "One never knows when a cannon will be needed to fend off pirates." Michael was not satisfied with the answer.

He rode up to the Tomeses' house shortly after breakfast. It was early, but already everyone in the household was up and dressed. As he rode up the driveway he saw Edward starting for the woods, his broad axe over his shoulder. With him were two Negro men, his helpers. When young Tomes caught sight of Michael, he let out a loud halloo and ran towards the road, Michael dismounted quickly and went to meet him.

"Thee is very welcome, friend Cary," Edward said, grasping Michael's hand with more than the customary Friends' greeting. "My mother is looking forward to thy visit. She is baking molasses tarts filled with hickory nuts against thy coming."

Michael laughed. "I have brought my appetite, Edward. I've eaten nothing but salt meat for these many days, until my stomach rises against the thought of it."

"Our father is in very excellent health," Edward said in answer to Michael's query. "And so is my sister, Lucretia, although thee has not asked after her health." There was a laugh in his eyes.

Michael flushed. "I was going to inquire," he said.

Edward thumped him across the shoulders. "I know, I know; I am but teasing. My mother tells me I will get in trouble one day. Come, I think they are in the kitchen. For two days there has been cooking going on here. Hams baking in the outdoor ovens and wild turkeys in the smokehouse. Now it is pie-baking and churning fresh butter that occupies them." They opened the door of the milkhouse and stood for a moment without speaking.

Lucretia was seated on a three-legged stool, a wooden churn bound in copper held steady between her knees. She was churning vigorously, both hands grasping the churn stick, her cheeks pink with the effort. Little splashes of cream had reached her face, and tiny globules of golden butter dotted her bare forearms. Strands of soft brown hair had slipped the confining braid and straggled down her cheek.

She stopped churning. She pushed down a little ridge of butter that clogged the round opening where the churn stick entered the wooden lid, then looked up, her buttery fingers halfway to her lips. Her face crimsoned, her black eyes were wide with surprise.

"Friend Michael," she said softly, "thee is welcome to our home."

Michael walked across the low room to take her hand.

"No, no, thee must not—my hands are thick with butter."

Michael laughed. "No matter; I like butter." He lifted the cedar lid of the churn. "See, it is almost finished. If I finish it quickly may I have a cup of milk?" He moved Lucretia aside and sat down on the stool, his leather-covered knees firm around the churn. A few vigorous strokes and it was finished.

"I'll go to tell our mother that thee has come, Michael."

Edward left the room and walked quickly cross to the

kitchen, a separate building that stood well behind the broad, low house, where the Tomes family had now lived for twenty years. For they had been long in the Albemarle, arriving shortly after the Phillips family settled in the late sixteen hundreds—not long after the great Edmundson had visited the Quakers in America, to help them and bring his message of peace and freedom for all people.

Lucretia sat on a step while Michael drank the milk left from the churning. She sat very quietly, but the quick rise and fall of her round breasts gave evidence of her feeling.

Michael did not notice. He was enjoying the drink to its full. Ten days in the woods, with only camp food prepared by his Indian, Atonga, whetted the appetite for good eating. "Come," he said, wiping his lips on the back of his hand. "Let us go to see your mother." He caught at Lucretia's hand to assist, but she got up quickly, apparently not noticing his proffered assistance.

"My mother will be waiting, friend Michael. Thee is a favourite of hers."

"That pleases me, but it would also please me if I were a favourite of yours, Lucretia."

A painful blush covered Lucretia's face, rising from the little starched collar above her simple grey wool dress to the braided band of brown hair on her smooth forehead.

Michael could have bitten his tongue, once the words had escaped him. The quiet confidence in her dark eyes hurt him, for he saw that she had taken his light impulsive words more seriously than he had intended. "Your family is my refuge," he said honestly. "Your home is the only home I have. Edward is my brother. You are my very dear sister."

"We love thee, friend Michael," she said steadily, using the word "love" as the Friends used it, with its all-abiding and encompassing interpretation.

Michael breathed easier. In spite of the talk he had had with his uncle, he was determined not to let himself be drawn into any involvement that would be misconstrued by these dear people.

Aside from the quick rise of colour to her smooth cheeks, Lucretia was apparently undisturbed. She was serene and tranquil; her eyes, when she returned his look, were calm and steady. Michael was satisfied with what he saw—but he could not hear the swift beating of her heart, or know the pain his words brought.

Madam Tomes met him at the door of her kitchen. "Ah!

friend Michael," she said, her blue eyes beaming with pleasure in her round, rosy face, "I hoped thee would come early. Sit thee at table with Foster. He has not yet has his second dish of tea."

She patted the hand that grasped hers so firmly, and gave him a gentle push towards the house.

"Stay here, Lucretia," she said sharply as the girl started to go with Michael. "There is work for thee with twenty at table for supper. Thee must help the maids with preparations."

Lucretia turned and went back to the kitchen. Michael heard her mother say, "Be ashamed, Lucretia! Thee is now too much grown to tag young men about. Come, we have the bedchambers to air and spice and beds to make up for thy father's guests. We will show them what Quaker housekeeping is like."

Michael found the Quaker leader, Foster Tomes, in the dining-room seated at the end of the long stretched table. He was a man of past middle years. His shoulder-length hair was streaked with grey, and his mild blue eyes were steady and confident. There was strength in his face and his firm jaw and chin. Not a man to trifle with in spite of his professed faith. A man of importance in the Pequimans Precinct. Michael had heard his uncle call him, often enough, a natural leader. At the moment the senior Cary was not certain how the Quaker would vote in the Assembly. Should Tomes go over to Glover he would carry a following with him.

Tomes welcomed Michael with gentle cordiality. "Sit at table, friend," he said, as he seated himself at the end of the table. Michael sat down. Tomes clasped his hands and looked downward. Michael bowed his head. "To thee, O divine Lord, we give thanks for these our blessings."

Madam Tomes came into the room followed by two buxom Quaker girls, daughters of near-by farmers, whom she was training. One girl carried a pewter platter with crisp bacon and fried eggs, the second had hot bread made of corn, and pats of golden butter. Madam herself carried a silver teapot of goodly size, her most prized possession. Sometimes her conscience hurt her for being vain of it, since that was worldly vanity, but she argued that the silver was left to her by her own mother, so she could not well part with it. It was polished to the brightness of a French mirror, and when she sat down Michael could see her distorted reflection in the bowl.

Tomes talked of crops, of the weather, of the Indians of Tuscarora Town, of the preparations for the seine fishing, but said no word of the county meeting or the problem that would be fought out when it met tomorrow. Michael was well pleased with that. He did not want to discuss political matters. So he talked of hunting and fishing and of a barkentine which his uncle had brought up from the West Indies.

Michael loved sailing. Since he was a boy in Antigua, he had owned a small sloop, large enough to sail in and out of the small islands. He had even sailed from Antigua to the Barbadoes—and St. Kitts, and once as far as St. Croix. That was before the islands were harried by the Spanish and the French. But once he had been taken by Rackham the pirate, who allowed him to go free when he saw that Michael's little sloop contained nothing of any value.

Edward came in to ask his father some question about the wood cutting, and went away directly. Lucretia slipped in and took a seat at the far end of the table near her mother. She sat quietly, listening to her father's questions about the West India trade and Michael's ready answers.

"I'm of a mind to ship my pork to Jamaica or Antigua," Tomes said. "Friend Mainwairing has had success in that trade. If I had a proper cargo boat—"

Michael said, "My uncle is having one built in Pasquotank, a beautiful ship of eighty tons. They have excellent boatwrights there who came up from the Barbadoes."

Tomes nodded. "Yes, and good carpenters came with the Bermuda Hundred, but I never thought to build a ship large enough to go beyond the Banks into the great sea. I have been content to take my shallops up the Sound and the rivers that empty into it, to serve the farmers on the Pequimans and the Little River, or up the Chowan to the Blackwater. I have no ambition to become a seaman, friend Cary. I had enough of that when I became Collector of her Majesty's Customs for thy uncle, Thomas Cary."

He gave a signal to his wife, and rose from the table. "Thee will excuse me, friend, if I leave thee. Today I have a meeting of Friends of Pasquotank at Symonds Creek. We must consider the gross and vile aspersions that Thomas Rawlison hath spread abroad against Matthew Pritchard, tending to defame the truth."

His wife came to his side. "I hope thee will let someone speak for friend Rawlison. Thee knows there are always two sides."

The Quaker smiled lovingly at his plump rosy wife. "Thee always has a good word for the sorry sinner. Rest easy. Zachariah Nixon and James Davis speak for him and John Holmes and Henry White speak for Pritchard."

He turned to Michael. "Does it seem a small matter to thee, when other great issues will be our talk on the morrow? We deem it not so; the small matters grow into large when the question of truth is involved."

Lucretia brought her father's wide black hat. Tomes set it firmly on his head, and strode from the room, a sturdy figure of a man with justice sitting on his broad forehead and his strong kindly features.

Michael joined the womenfolk as they stood on the stoop watching the old Quaker ride down the path to the main road.

"God go with him," said his wife.

"With God," added Lucretia.

Michael made his farewell. He had promised to meet his uncle at the inn at Newby's Ferry.

"Thee will be here by sundown," Madam Tomes said. "Bring thy uncle with thee. I have never seen a man who thought so little of food and bed when he can gather men about him."

Michael smiled at her shrewd comment. Talk and argument were breath to Thomas Cary's nostrils. He was happy if he could but rouse a crowd, and he would stand for hours putting forth his ideas and answering hecklers.

"I promise you that I will bring him back for supper."

Martha Tomes shook her finger at him. "Many times I have told thee to say 'thee'—not 'you.' If thee is to become a true Friend, thee must speak the language of Friends."

Lucretia said, smiling, "Once I heard my mother forget and say 'you' as worldly people do."

Her mother's fair skin flushed faintly. "Get thee to thy ironing, miss. Thee has two Holland shirts of thy brother to press and has thee forgotten thy father's fine lawn falling-bands for his coat? I found them this morning misplaced behind the jars in the pantry. Thee knows they were yesterday's stint."

Lucretia retreated rapidly through the door, not forgetting to wave a cheerful farewell to Michael as he mounted his horse.

"Thee is to sleep with Edward and the little fellows,"

Madam called after him. "I will have the man carry your saddle-bags to the room and unpack *your* belongings."

"Thank thee so much," Michael said with a grin. "It is so kind of thee."

"Get thee gone!" Madam shook her finger at him. "I declare, thee brings more levity into this house than all my children together."

At the barn-lot, Michael found Atonga waiting for him. Together they cut through the woods towards the Yaupim road that led north to Nixon's Ferry. It was ten miles or more, even by cuting short through Pritchard's and Skinner's fields, and Thomas Cary would not like it if his nephew kept him waiting.

Lucretia ironed the fine lawn falling-bands and the Holland shirts. When she carried them up to the boys' room she found the man had dumped the contents of Michael's saddle-bags and left them on the middle of his bed. She frowned and started to put them in order, when she noticed his shirts were wrinkled and needed pressing. More than that, they were in need of washing. She gathered them up into a bundle and carried them downstairs and out to the washhouse.

Old Cush, who did the washing, was nowhere about. With a little smile on her curved red lips, Lucretia rolled up her sleeves and took off her ruffled fichu. Surely her mother would praise her for such a housewifely act. But her heart beat a little faster because she could do this small thing for Michae, even if he never knew.

The water was hot in the great iron pot that swung over a fire pit in the lower garden. A few minutes' boiling in a lather made of Old Cush's soap rendered the yellowed linen white and fresh. The shirts looked as if they had been washed in the yellow waters of the Albemarle, thought Lucretia, as she hung them over a myrtle bush where the sun would dry them. It was quite warm. The bulbs she had planted last year in the borders of the flower beds were bright with bloom. Along the streams the redbuds were showing. A week or two more of warm weather and the waxy petals of the dogwood would turn the deep green woods into fairyland.

Suddenly she came to herself. She had almost forgotten. This was the day Marita Tower was coming, and her sheets not yet out of lavender! What was she thinking of to forget? Perhaps she had the spring fever Old Cush talked about, when the sap ran swiftly.

She picked up the grey shirts of her linsey-woolsey gown

and ran up the path to the house. Her mother saw her as she whirled onto the stairs, her hands clasped about the newel post as a pivot.

"Lucretia, thee is forgetting thee is grown up and no longer a child with child's prankishness. Walk slowly, daughter, with a dignified mien."

"Yes, Mamma," she answered, walking up the steps one at a time.

"See that thee puts the cut-work pillow shams on Marita's bed, and the best bolster off the bed in the north guest room."

"But that is Colonel Cary's room!" Lucretia said aghast. "How ever can we do that?"

"Do as I say. Men have no feeling for fine linen and hand work, while—" She did not finish the sentence. Lucretia, out of sight of her mother's watchful eye, was running down the hall.

It was a lovely day. She was going to have a guest of her own, and Michael was here. The image of his lean brown face held her thoughts. She dressed the bed mechanically, pulling the sheets this way and that—an unaccountable thing. Even the glossy silk puff made from soft goose feathers gave her no satisfaction. If only Michael—but why dream? Michael thought of her as a sister, a dear, dear sister. She must remember. She gave the counterpane a jerk to put it straight and stood off to look at the effect.

Everything in the little room was clean and in order, the crisp chintz curtains, the white linen valance, the little ruffle on the dressing-stand. She sighed a little. She wished the valance and ruffle were of silken taffeta, the colour of an apple blossom in spring. But she must not think these thoughts; it was a sin to be so worldly. After all, everything was fresh and clean. Clean! She had heard that word so often she hated it!

Marita came shortly after dinner. She brought her serving maid with her, an Indian woman, and with her came also an Indian man who acted as groom and cared for the horses. Two saddle-bags on her horses were stuffed as tight as drums.

Lucretia ran down the steps to meet her guest, and Madam Tomes, cool and fresh in a dove-grey gown, came to the door, her hands extended in welcome.

In Lucretia's room, where her bags were carried by one of

208

Dame Tomes's stout women, Marita stood still and looked about her.

"It is as sweet as a spice garden, Lucretia," she said, smoothing the soft Holland blanket on the foot of the bed. Then she went to the window. Like her own room at Greenfield, Lucretia's was under the eaves, with little dormer windows to give light. But here they looked directly on the river, for the house and garden were set close to the bank.

"And see, your garden is all in order. I wish mine were as well kept. I want the one at Greenfield to look just like yours, with a sundial, and little walks to cut the beds."

"We can give thee some cuttings," Lucretia said, "and my mother has some boxwood bushes, only they grow so slowly."

"Yes, I know, but I want them just the same. Oh, Lucretia, isn't it wonderful to dig in the ground and put in seed, then see it grow? I've never had so much pleasure in anything."

Lucretia looked at Marita's bright eyes wonderingly. "Did thee never have a garden before? In England do they not have great gardens?"

Marita shrugged her shoulders. "Of course, we had gardens down in Sussex, but they weren't my very own. The gardener cared for them—a cross old fellow he was. Why, he wouldn't let me cut the flowers. He always did that himself, for fear I'd step on some little plant, but now—" she threw her arms open wide—"now the garden is my own, and the fields too, and the cows and the little new calf, and all the fishing for three miles from the shore." She laughed and sat down on the bed only to bounce up, instantly smoothing the crease with both of her hands.

Lucretia laughed. "I know! Mamma is like that. She says ladies don't sit on beds; they sit on chairs."

Arm in arm the two girls walked down the stairs, leaving Kikitchina to finish hanging up Marita's dresses on pegs on the wall. The room already looked like a tulip bed, bright with colour. "It has never been so gay," Lucretia said wistfully.

The house was quiet and empty. They looked into the long room, and into the dining-room across the hall. The table was set, a long stretcher table of oak that would seat twenty people.

Both rooms were simple, but they gave Marita a sense of substantial living. She longed to ask Lucretia if Michael Cary would be there to eat at the long table tonight, but something kept the words from coming.

Suddenly Lucretia clapped her hands together. She had just remembered Michael's shirts still hanging on the myrtle bush. "I have a task to finish," she said to Marita. "Sit here and read a book, or would thee like to walk in the garden?"

Marita preferred the garden and said so.

"Thee is sure the air is not too chill?" Lucretia asked. "Here, take this." She took a grey cape from a rack under the stairs.

Marita walked along the river path. The sun was behind her, reflected low on the water. A fish jumped, rippling the quiet water, followed by another and another; silver shadows lay just below the surface. Marita moved closer and stepped to the sandy shore. Was it the first of the herring run? The "advance," Captain Zeb had told her, was due to come up the Sound shortly.

Intent on watching the water, she did not notice the long shadow cast on the shore or hear the footsteps on the path. A voice broke the silence. "Little sister, what are you gazing at so intently?"

Marita whirled around. He was standing beside her—Michael, Michael Cary!

As she turned he stepped back, surprise and wonder in his eyes. "I thought it was Lucretia," he said. "The cape——"

He came close to her, and caught her hands, holding them close. Whatever had been before—all her doubts—left her with his nearness. What if he had held another woman in his arms? Today he was here looking at her, his eyes warm and loving.

"Little maid," he said, "what good fortune is mine to find you here!"

Marita for a moment could not speak. She could only look at him, at the bronzed face, at his lean, strong body. This time he did not wait. He put his arms about her. Never in this world was there anything like the strength of his arms or the pressure of his lips against hers. How long she clung to him she did not know. It was their moment—at sunset, as he had told her it would be.

"Marita, Marita," Lucretia's voice floated down from the garden. "Where is thee?"

Marita broke away, and stood for a moment, uncertain.

"Answer her, darling," Michael whispered. "Answer."

Marita could not. It was Michael who answered. "We are here, by the river," he called.

How could he be so calm, when her heart was beating so violently?

"Wait, I'll come for you," he called.

"See, I have made myself acquainted with your visitor, Lucretia. Come present me properly."

Marita watched him fall in step with Lucretia. There was no sign on his countenance of the brief moment that had been theirs. This puzzled her. How could he change so quickly? They were coming down the path before she found herself.

"I think the herring run has started," she said quietly. To her surprise her own voice was steady and quite natural.

Chapter 17

I AM
A JACOBITE

IT was late morning and the sun well up in the sky when Roger Mainwaring left Greenfield, headed for Yaupim Road. He had several hours' ride ahead of him before he came to Nixon's Ferry, where he was to meet some of his neighbours who were members of the Assembly. A meeting of prime importance would be held on the morrow on Little River, a meeting where the more cautious men of the Albemarle would try to bring the warring factions together so that there would be a stable government in the land.

It was early April and the season advanced. The air had the smell of spring and Roger had noticed a few azaleas blossoming on low bushes in the burned-over areas of the forest. He loved the spring—the overturned earth in straight furrows ready for planting, the earth warm with the sun, fecund and waiting. May peas and black-eyed peas should soon be in the ground, and the new red beans that had been sent to him from Jamaica. He would test a few rows below the lower pasture, where the soil was rich and unused.

Then his thoughts went back to Lady Mary, whom he had just left. It was a strange interview.

Impressed by the Turk's warning, Roger had felt the necessity of haste in reaching Lady Mary and putting the cylinder in her hands. He was dressed for riding almost before sunup. Metephele packed his saddle-bags while he breakfasted, for he would ride on from Greenfield to the ferry.

When he arrived at the manor house, Lady Mary was still "abed," the Negro gardener told him, and Miss Marita "gone off to the Quaker folks in Pequimans, for to make a visit."

Roger dismounted and tossed the reins to Metephele. He went quickly up the broad steps that led to the gallery and into the hall. There he found the slave Beulah flirting a dusting cloth over the oak settle that stood near the door. She repeated the gardener's words. "Her ladyship she rest in the baid. She stay up late las' night playin' on the little music."

"Tell Desham I want to see her."

Beulah wandered off to the back of the house. In a few minutes Desham came into the hall, her fluted cap slightly awry, her skirt looped back over her petticoats.

"Desham, I want you to waken Lady Mary. I must see her at once."

Desham's eyes popped. "Mr. Mainwairing, I could never think to do that. I can't aggravate her, so early."

Roger looked at the woman without smiling. "Call her now, Desham. I will take the responsibility. As soon as she is awake, tell her I have a message that I want to deliver to her in person. In person, do you understand?"

Desham, caught on the horns between Lady Mary's anger and Roger's severity, hesitated, her face a curious mixture of uncertainty and fright.

Roger allowed a fleeting smile to cross his lips. "If you don't waken her, I will." He took a step towards the stairs. Desham raised both her hands in a gesture of protest, pretending to be shocked to the depths of her spinster soul. Roger laughed aloud.

Desham gave him one quick look. Satisfied that he would do as he said, she picked up her wide petticoats in both hands and ran up the stairs without thought of her round legs, clad in unbecoming thick white wool stockings.

Roger grinned. The little ruse had worked.

Desham's entrance was followed by an angry voice, and the sound of something falling. No doubt her ladyship had flung some handy article at her woman. The small display of temper amused him. He liked the natural reaction in her.

Women should be natural, not hold their emotions in check at all times.

In a very short time he heard Lady Mary's voice calling to him. "Roger, how outrageous of you to come at this hour! You knew I would not be presentable."

He advanced a step or two so that he could look up the stairs. She was standing at the banister looking down. Her ash-blonde hair was bound in a riband; curls hung about her shoulders. She wore some rose-coloured silk garment, wrapped about her, revealing the soft curves of her body.

"Wait a moment while Desham puts something on me so that I can come down."

"Come as you are, or I'll run up and bring you down," Roger answered.

He could hear Desham gasp. "Your ladyship, you can't go down, you have no petticoats!"

"Nonsense! Mr. Mainwaring has seen women without petticoats before, I'll be bound! Quick, tie that sash around my waist and bring me my Spanish slippers. No, stupid, the rose-coloured ones to match this wrapper."

Lady Mary was laughing when she came down the stairs, her Spanish mules clattering with every step. Roger had never seen her lovelier or more alluring, her fair skin flushed with sleep, her eyes so deeply blue. Without the concealment of the half-dozen petticoats that fashion demanded, the long-line of her limbs and the perfection of her rounded breasts gave her the look of a fine sculpture. He lifted her extended hand to his lips, and followed her into the little parlour, closing the door behind him.

Something in his face drove the smile from her curved red lips. "What is it, Roger?" she said alarmed. "Marita! That wild horse has thrown her!"

Roger led her to a chair and sat down opposite her. Briefly he told her of the Turk and his message and his sudden, almost fantastic disappearance. Her expression changed as he talked from gaiety and laughter to apprehension, almost fear. Her body became tense, her fingers closed on the arms of the chair.

"Give it to me," she said, without moving from her chair.

Roger rose, unbuckled his sword belt and laid it on the long seat. He slipped off his leather jerkin, and pushed the wide linen shirt sleeve to his shoulder. Then he unrolled the long knitted garter that held the metal tube, and put it

213

into her hand. Her fingers closed over it, holding it tight as if it were too precious to be exposed even for an instant.

Roger rolled down his sleeve and buckled his sword belt. He took up his wide hat ready to leave the room. Lady Mary had not stirred. She seemed to have withdrawn herself, oblivious for the moment of his presence. He waited, hat in hand, for her to speak again.

"Please do not leave me," she said, without raising her eyes from the cylinder. He laid his hat on a chair and sat down again, facing her. Lady Mary scrutinized the seals carefully. Satisfied they had not been tampered with, she tapped the wax with a metal paper knife, and broke them.

Roger turned in his chair. He did not want to watch her while she read. He did not want to know by the changing expression of her face whether the news was good or bad. But his eyes kept coming back to her. She read through carefully by the help of a reading-glass that she took from the table. She puzzled him by her quiet, so that he was not prepared for the hopelessness in her fine blue eyes when she raised them from the paper.

"The letter brings evil news," she said abruptly. "Churchill is without support. He will not be able to hold out against his enemies at home for long, no matter what victories his armies win for us abroad. I would not believe the rumours I heard from Virginia, because I did not want to believe such a calamity could happen to my country."

She got to her feet and began to move around the room aimlessly, not attending what she was doing ... picking up a book, laying it down again, the thin paper still in her hand. After a time she moved to a chair by the hearth, where a small fire burned.

Roger said nothing. He knew she was scarcely aware of his presence. He might have been a piece of furniture in the room for all he entered her thoughts. She was so still, so silent, the life gone out of her. He had the feeling that there was something more personal than the removal of the Duke of Marlborough from his high office that weighed her down. He would not question her. She would tell him what she pleased. He was seeing her now in a different aspect, as a person who has received a mortal blow, trying to adjust herself. She was meeting her trouble as a strong man meets adversity.

"Let me read you something," she said abruptly. Spreading the page on her knee, she began:

214

"England will lose her strongest man and the greatest general in all her history, before the year is over. Short months ago the nation was crying for him to lead them out of the darkness of war and conflict. Now his weary feet may lead him toward the Tower. You and I, Mary, will grieve for our friend, but our greatest concern is for our ally, and he was the strongest one we had. They say in London that he was disloyal to the Queen and plotted against her. We know that is not true. He spoke only the truth, fighting against the Hanoverian succession.

"The politicians are in the saddle again. Harley comes now into power. Tory that I am, I cannot see good in this. Churchill's is a universal genius which we will not match in our times. As a general he could circumvent without loss of men, and snatch victory where a lesser man could win only with great loss of life. Once he drove sixty thousand Frenchmen before him, and seized half the Duchy of Brabant without the loss of eighty men. Do the people of London remember that? Or Malplaquet, or a dozen other victories? He has a gift for statecraft. He is suave, affable and patient. Who but Churchill could have held together the ill-assorted allies that combined to attack Louis XIV? He has intellectual greatness, but he has one weakness, and that will defeat him: his inordinate love and admiration for his wife. Sarah can do no wrong. Two women have been his undoing: one whom he loved, his wife; the other to whom he gave his loyalty, his Queen. Could anything be more tragic?

"I wish I could speak my full mind to you, Mary, face to face, but alas, that cannot happen, for a great ocean separates us. Only a short time ago, those women whose quarrels will cause the downfall of a great man, were writing daily letters to each other like lovesick school girls, under the names of Mrs. Freeman and Mrs. Morley! The whole of London rang with the silly story.

"The Queen sits in St. James's Palace overlooking the Orangery. From there she can watch the companies of red-coated soldiers and pikemen pass on their way to Westminster Hall. I recall I stood behind her that day when her soldiers marched by carrying thirty-four standards and one hundred and twenty-eight colours Churchill had captured at the battle of Blenheim. Ten thousand of her rapturous subjects stood in Pall Mall to see them pass, and went mad with cheering. And now she fights for the keys of the office with the hero of Blenheim, and orders Sir Christopher Wren to hold up the completion of the palace she is building for him. When Harley takes the office he will be given a peerage. Between us, this comes through the intrigues of the new favourite, Abigail Hill, now Mrs. Masham. The irony of it is that Mrs. Masham is Churchill's cousin, and Sarah herself put her in as one of the Queen's ladies. Now Marlborough will doubtless lose his head if he doesn't flee England. As for us, we will have to begin all over.

"I suppose you realize that every day we feel the loss of Dunkerque more deeply. Whenever England has occasion to transport armies to the Continent, it will always be in support of some ally whose town will serve the same purpose as Dunkerque would had it remained in the hands of the English."

Her voice left off. She leaned back in the chair, her hands grasping the carved wooden arms. She was spent, as if the events her correspondent described had driven the life from her body. The clock on the mantel became dominant, and the soft-throated laughter of the slaves working in the garden floated in from the open window. She raised her head and looked at him.

"I am a Jacobite." She spoke dully. When he made no answer she added, "Now you know why I am here."

"You need not explain to me, Mary. I would never ask."

"I know. That is why I can talk now. The Queen has intimated that she is happier when I am away. Someone has convinced her that I am plotting with Jamie . . . with the Pretender."

Roger spoke quickly. "Please say no more. Long ago I told you I was done with plots and intrigues. I've paid my forfeit for rash youth. I do not want to know who you are or where your loyalties lie. I want you here, as you are, in the Albemarle."

She did not seem to hear him. "I have some enemies who are powerful and unscrupulous. I am not disloyal. Like John Churchill, I am afraid for our country when the Queen dies. I have no anxiety while she lives, for she is a good woman and a faithful queen, devoted to her people."

For a moment Roger saw Lady Mary struggling under the shadow of an ominous mystery, bowed down by events beyond her control. Whatever these events were, she had accepted them without protest. Whatever resentment may have held her in the beginning, today she was quiescent. She raised

216

her eyes and looked out the window. The sun shone, birds were singing, the song of the slaves and their careless laughter brought her back to the present. She took up the paper once again, and read it through, memorizing it, then shredded it into streamers, dropped the pieces on the red coals, watched them take fire, blaze, then die into grey ashes.

"There is only one hope left," she said, more to herself than to him. "One hope—Bolingbroke; if he should come into power . . ." She left the sentence unfinished. Roger knew that she had met the blow, parried it and put it away from her. From now on she was looking ahead, to the future. The past was done with and it must be forgotten.

"You have a stout heart," Roger said, rising to his feet and looking down on her, his eyes filled with admiration. "The oak bends to the wind but does not break," he said.

A little smile came to her lips. She held out her hand. "Do not go," she said. "I think I need you."

"No," Roger said slowly, "you do not need me, or any man. You have your own reservoir of strength that will sustain you. I think you have never needed to lean on any man."

She did not answer. She seemed suddenly aware of the disarray of her wrapper, her unbound hair. She looked up into his eyes as she pulled the silken garment about her throat. There was a slight smile on his lips when he kissed her hand in farewell. "You will be disillusioned now."

"You have never been more desirable," he said. He took up his hat and left the room without waiting for her answer. As he passed the window he had a glimpse of her leaning against the high back of the chair, her fine sensitive hands idle along the arm of the chair.

The picture would not leave him as he galloped his horse swiftly along the road. It did not take much imagination to go on from where she left off. He noticed that she had not read the letter by half. Whoever wrote to her stood high in the Court and knew the situation there. It might even be Bolingbroke himself, or someone near to him. There was no question in his mind now that she was deep in a Jacobite plot. She was not one to stop short or consider the cost. He remembered words she had spoken the first time he had met her on Muster Day: "To throw my life and everything I hold into the vortex, if right can be done." The very fact that she had said that the Queen preferred she remain out of England was the key. If she were not a person of consequence, the Queen would not trouble herself.

The more he thought of Lady Mary the more his admiration grew. He had been on the losing side of what he counted a great cause, and he knew the bitter disappointment that filled her mind and heart. Marlborough's character was all Lady Mary's correspondent had said. Roger had never believed him to be unscrupulous or a lover of money; of power, perhaps.

No explanation was necessary. "I am a Jacobite," Mary had said. Roger knew how people at home feared the Hanoverian succession. With all their faults, the Stuarts were their own people, their vagaries known. To exclude Anne's half brother from the throne for a distant cousin, a Hanoverian, was to deliver the Throne to an unknown man, apart from the religious question. The Pretender, James, was a Catholic Stuart, son of the Catholic James II. He could have had the succession had he been willing to give up his Romanist religion and become a member of the Church of England.

What surprised Roger was that there should be a following of the Pretender in the Carolinas—a man had been arrested in the Ashley Settlements for expressing such views.

Lady Mary had not asked him about the safety of the Turk, or even asked how he had come by the cylinder. She must have known that even to carry a message that contained talk of the Pretender, no matter how veiled and cryptic, was worth a man's life. There was something almost royal in her acceptance of this, as if she were used to having people do things for her that involved risk and danger. Nor had she asked secrecy of him; she had taken his loyalty for granted—to her and to her cause. Roger liked that. It showed the strength of her mind and character.

The thing that lay heavy on Roger's mind was Rhoda Chapman. He had allowed his voyage to England to be postponed for one thing after another. First he had written her he would come in the spring. They could be married and come directly home to Queen's Gift or spend a month by the sea at his lodge on Ocracock Island. The next post he had written that he could not leave until after mid-summer harvest. Now he thought he must set his departure in October, after the cotton was picked.

Whenever he tried to imagine Rhoda walking down the broad halls of Queen's Gift or out on the wide galleries that gave on the gardens and the Sound, his vision blurred and he saw, instead, the slim elegance of another woman moving from room to room, gracing his table, lifting the night candle from the niche on the stairs; another woman lying in the great bed he had brought from St. Kitts, waiting for his coming, with her shining eyes and passionate mouth. From the first night they had met at Balgray, he had felt the strength of his passion for her rising. They were of a kind, the two of them; in each life flowed strongly. He wanted strength in a woman, one who would walk beside him with mood to meet his own in anger and in love. This he had never found until now, and for that reason he had until now gone his solitary way. Women he had used as a necessity and no more.

He faced the facts now. If he married Rhoda Chapman it would be what was named a suitable match. She came from his own class: country families of such age that they thought little of titles or the new order of nobility. She had wealth, inherited, in land and great collieries. Their lands in England lay close. Their people were neighbours for more generations than he could think.

He had no doubt of her. If she came to this new country she would bring something that he needed, the flavour of old settled living, of order and worldliness. She would do it without ostentation. Easily and naturally the standard of their living would be lifted to her level of life. That was what he wanted now. That was what the Albemarle lacked. It wanted order and good living in the home the same way that it needed order and law in government—to have done with log houses and earth floors of pioneer living, to move on to a more decent life.

Roger knew this was behind his desire to marry Rhoda Chapman. He had never before admitted it though, never until he suddenly realized that he loved Mary Tower, longed for her love as a traveller lost in the desert longs for food and water. She would love him; he would hold her by the very strength of his ardour.

"Best make up my mind, while I still have sanity," he heard himself say aloud.

Two horsemen turned from a lane into the road ahead of him. He recognized Crisp and Nathaniel Chevin. They were riding towards Nixon's Ferry and the meeting at the inn. All the leaders of Pequimans and Pasquotank would be at the inn and there would be bickering and wrangling and trading of political perquisites. He need not have come, except for

Moseley's importuning. There would be quarrels and fights and fisticuffs as men got deeper into drink. He thought Cary's method of buying barrels of whisky was wrong. It brought the rogues and the lowest class of men from their hiding places up the small creeks and streams. If there was real leadership, it must come from men of better education and breeding—men who knew the value of the law. The whole thing suddenly became distasteful to him.

Men talked loosely of freedom and liberties. Liberty for what? To hide in forest and swamp from the officers of the law? To refuse to pay taxes? To escape punishment for petty crimes or worse? That was not Roger's idea of liberty. Freedom must be for every man alike. The only way it could be had with any degree of equality was freedom under the law. Could they have that if the leaders continued to fight for supremacy as they were fighting now? It had to be done another way. There must be some united action of law-abiding leaders, so that the common men had confidence that their leaders were worthy and their laws for the defence of all.

Roger came in sight of the river, a noble prospect of large and spacious water; fine meadows with the young, tender grass showing; stately laurel, bay and myrtle; dark towering pine and cypress.

Another thought came to him as he looked across the river. The only men fit to govern should rise in nobility to meet the demands of this far land. It was time to finish with intrigue and war. Leave that to the Whigs and the Tories and the Jacobites in the world they had left behind. This was a new world, with new problems. To meet these problems would take courageous, steadfast men who were willing to assume responsibility.

In this mood, he lifted his reins as a signal to the mare. She broke into a swift trot. In a little time he overtook the horsemen, and with them rode on to the ferry.

Chapter 18

QUEEN'S
PEACE

ROGER tossed the bridle to a hostler, and made his way across the stable yard. The post chaise had just drawn up at the front stoop of the Ferry Inn and was discharging passengers. When he saw the crowds he was glad that he had sent Metephele on ahead to engage a room. A motely gathering it was. Men of all classes and condition. Tom Cary's free drinks were the attraction for some of them. They remembered how lavish he had been when the Assembly mèt at Hecklefields two years before—that famous Assembly which still remained a byword, a blot on the Albemarle's political escutcheon. The whisky had no doubt helped Cary garner the votes, for he came out of it holding the power and the seals of office, while Glover and his chief supporters made haste to escape from the Province, Thomas Pollock among them.

When he reached the inn he saw that his suspicions were well grounded. On one side of the house was a barrel of whisky, completely surrounded by planters from Currituck, Pasquotank, Pequimans, and Chowan. On the opposite side was a barrel of beer for lesser folk—drovers, herdsmen, growers and the like.

Tom the Tinker, from Queen Anne's Town, lurched through the gate that led from the stable lot, holding his saddle in one hand, the stirrups dragging the ground. "He doesn't trust his own kind," thought Roger, looking at the saddle. A bird of ill omen was Tom the Tinker. Whatever he showed himself there was strife. He was like a bustard flying over a battlefield waiting his turn to pick the bones.

The tinker had a following of sorts among bordermen of ill repute who would, for a few shillings, smuggle goods across the line between the Province and the Crown Colony. Some claimed he knew where the pirates hid gold and loot. Roger had never seen any pirate ships in the Sound. But it was rumoured that ships of light draught, flying the black flag, made their way up even into the smaller streams. Safe hiding places were many up Bennet's Creek or Sarum, cool dark creeks where drooping vines masked the entrance to sweet black water of the deep swamps.

As Tom came near he pulled at his red forelock. "Good day to ye, Mr. Mainwairing, good day."

"Good day, Tom. What are you doing with that saddle?"

Tom swayed a little on his feet, and put one grimy finger to his lips. "Hist, hist—it's the Governor that wants it. I can't leave it on my mule lest he come out of the inn and steal it."

"Which governor do ye mean, Tom?" some one asked.

"Any of them, any of the three of them. They all want it." He leaned over, leering up at Roger. "I'll let ye have it for a farthing, Mr. Mainwairing."

Roger tossed a coin to the fellow. "Here, get yourself a dish of hot tea inside, and ask the innkeeper to lock your saddle in a cupboard."

Tom bit the coin, put it into his pouch; then he went to the pump and stuck his head under the spout, calling to the Negro boy to give the wooden handle ten strokes.

"Have done, Hocus," he cried as the cold stream flowed over his head and down his open shirt to his belly. "Have done, I say." He kicked out but the boy was too agile. Shaking the water from his red head, like a spaniel that has just come out of a stream, he broke into a song, in a high raucous voice:

> "For a man like me
> That's stout and bold
> A ghost is no' as dreadful
> As a scold."

The crowd which had gathered around him broke into a laugh. Tom the Tinker, the man who stood on the Green and harangued the crowds on market day, had a wife who had been known to chase him with a broomstick—or leave him to sleep on the stoop on a cold night when he came home late from a meeting of the Two Penny Club at the Red Lion.

Now that he had the wastrels and the men of ill condition around him, he began to speechify and run a counter-show to the one under the great tree where Thomas Cary stood, greeting his supporters.

Roger went in the side entrance and up the rickety stairs.

222

Metephele was waiting for him, standing guard outside the door. His fresh linen was laid out on the bed. By the time Roger was undressed the slave had brought hot water and poured it into a wooden tub he dragged in from the hall. Dressed decently in a brown cloth coat over his leather riding breeches, Roger felt himself a new man. He buckled on his sword belt, pulled the Turk's blade from the Damascene sheath and whipped it through the air.

"Master feels the sword's strength," Metephele observed, standing well out of reach. "He cuts the air like swift lightning."

"Never was a better blade," Roger said with satisfaction.

He stopped on the stair for a moment on his way to the ordinary. Angry voices came from the little room below. He recognized Thomas Cary's strong, confident voice. "Dammit, you are insolent, handing a gentleman a charge before the day is over! I've a notion to lay my sword on you for that."

"Your worship, I waited a full twelve months after the last Assembly. Six times I sent the account to you. Six times you sent word that the money would come by messenger, but the money did not come until I went to Bath Town to collect."

"The bill was outrageous. I should never have paid it if it hadn't been for Mr. Low taking your side. Now get out. I'll pay for the whisky when I'm ready. Get out if you don't want to feel this blade in your fat stomach. . . ."

There was the sound of a scuffle. The door burst open and a man catapulted from the room and ran down the hall, his fat body rolling from side to side. Roger had a glimpse of Thomas Cary, sword in hand, doubled up with laughter.

Roger stepped across the hall quickly and opened the door into the ordinary. He didn't want Cary to know that he had heard the discussion with the landlord about payment for the whisky provided for men who might turn against Cary for a higher price.

The room was crowded, as the yard was, with half-drunken men from every walk in life. Voices were rough and high; even laughter had an edge to it. He crossed the ordinary to a small dining-room, thinking to get away from the press of people, the smell of stale beer and whisky and smoke of many pipes.

The small room was occupied. Around a table were seated half a dozen men he knew: the Quaker Tomes, his own neighbour Moseley, and Lawson, the surveyor. Tom Pollock was there, and the Governor's secretary, Lovyck. It took only one glance to know that this was a meeting of importance, since all factions were represented. He opened the door to leave. Tom Pollock stopped him.

"Oh, here you are, Mainwairing. Come in, come in."

Moseley made a place at the table for him. "I stopped at your float, but your man said you were off before sunrise. So I brought him along in my boat."

"What is this, an extra Council?" Roger asked, looking around the table.

The men laughed. "We don't know what it is yet. Come in and sit down. We don't know yet whether this will be a peace meeting or an open ruction. But a little blowing off may ease matters."

Pollock got up from the table and crossed the room to bolt the door. "John Blount will be here presently. I dinna think we need wait." He spread out the tails of his bottle-green coat and sat down again. "I take it that you all agree that this is a secret meeting. Whatever is said here goes no farther than these walls. Lovyck, no need to take notes for Governor Hyde until we come to some decision."

He glanced around the table, his bushy eyebrows close together. Roger had in impulse to get up and leave the room. He had no stomach for secret meetings, nor for quarrels. He was about to speak his mind when there was a knock at the door. Pollock let John Blount in and a moment later the meeting was in full swing under the guidance of Pollock.

"It's better that we know what we are aiming at before we come to the full meeting tomorrow," he said. "I want every man to speak his mind frankly, and let there be no angry words. We've had enough of that. I've talked with Glover. I've convinced him that he must waive his claim." His face wrinkled in a wry smile. "I'll confess it was no easy task to make him give in. I've seen Thomas Cary. I invited him to sit at this table, but he refused. He is more interested in currying popular favour through his own methods than talking things out sensibly and quietly."

Pollock took a bright blue handkerchief from his pocket and gave his great nose a blow that sounded like a bugle. Lovyck, who was drawing little figures on the paper before him, jumped uneasily and the others smiled. Roger thought Pollock had interrupted himself as if he were determined not to apply any of the names he usually mentioned when he spoke of Thomas Cary.

"I don't claim to be a barrister or know the law, but if we

224

can convince both Glover and Cary that they should withdraw their claims in favour of Edward Hyde, it would solve some of our difficulties. What do you think, Moseley? I believe you are a fair man and will give us your honest opinion."

Moseley's thin, aristocratic face showed some surprise. Pollock had gone straight to the crux by calling on him, the only one present at the meeting who had stood for Cary.

Moseley said, "One thing I want to make clear. I have supported Cary in the past because I believed that he would give us the law and government we need in this new land. I believe that we have come to the place where we must lay aside all personal feeling and think of this country. In law we have a term called the Queen's peace. That is what I want. I believe every man present has the same idea. What good is Magna Charta, the Petition of Right, and Coke's pleading for the Common Law, if we do not use the power we have won for the benefit of all the people? Everybody's responsibility is nobody's responsibility. If we try to escape responsibility we are no better than Tom the Tinker, or those poor border men who hide from the law.

"I have come to the parting of the ways with Tom Cary on this point. I believe we must settle differences, cease factional warfare, and put the government into capable hands, and I will use all the influence I have to work towards the Queen's peace in the Albemarle, no matter who heads the government."

Moseley's statement created some surprise and a little doubt. All the men of the Council were not ready to accept his declaration without reservation.

Pollock nodded assent and turned to Foster Tomes. "May we have your opinion, friend Tomes?"

Tomes pulled his chair closer to the table, his broad benign face serious. "All of thee present know that the Friends call me a moderate Quaker. I am not a fighting Quaker. So I speak not only for myself but for a large majority of my sect. Therefore my words must come not from myself, but from the Spirit that guides us all. ... Let us have peace. Our land is bountiful and overflowing with plenty. Let us make it the Harbour of Peace, not a Rogues' Harbour. We have room here for thousands of settlers. But can we expect men and women to come here when we cannot offer a safe government?"

"Hear, hear!" John Blount called out.

"What I have to say is little enough, but it comes from the heart. We must have love, not hate, among us." He paused, looking around the table with honest eyes. "Love is what we Friends live by, if we are true Friends."

Lawson, the Surveyor General of the Colony, followed Tomes. "Friend Tomes has spoken wisely, but he stopped short when he spoke only of the room we have for settlers. I have just come from New Bern, where I have been visiting De Graffenried's Palatines. They have made progress, but they are beset by fears because they have no security by law to take up the land they have bought from the Lords Proprietors. And because they fear the depredations of the Indians they will not till lands that are most fertile. They must stay close to one another, not daring to move outside their houses unless they have a musket in their hands.

"We fight among ourselves. The Indians know we are without authority or power." He paused a moment, then went on, his slight, almost delicate body tense, his dark eyes burning. "Indians are kindly folk, if they are not harmed, and when they know the white man has power. I have travelled among them for months at a time, knowing only friendship and kindness. But things are changing. We have in our own people those who make prisoners of them, even slaves."

No one spoke for a moment. Every man present owned Indian slaves with the exception of the Quaker and Roger Mainwairing.

Pollock's face grew crimson above his broad Dutch collar. He spoke stiffly. "I do not think the question of Indian slaves enters into this discussion, Mr. Lawson."

Lawson's eyes blazed a moment, then went dull. "We shall see . . ." he said quietly. "Friend Tomes spoke of peace. It is peace between the whites and the Indians I want most to maintain."

John Blount spoke shortly and to the point. "We must have peace, no matter who is hurt," he said. "If it means we give up Indian slaves, then we must do it. Mainwairing thinks, too, we should do it. If we are to have a strong government and militia to keep peace, we must do that and at once."

Roger knew it would soon be time for him to say his say. He would speak out and be done with it. When Pollock nodded to him, he was ready.

"We are living in troublesome times. Let us be through with trying to fool ourselves. We are a set of numskulls, too selfish, too intent on our own interests to think about the country. These things we must do. First, since Hyde has his proper papers, acknowledge him as our rightful governor. Let Cary and Glover withdraw. Second, let us settle the dispute over the boundary. As long as it remains we'll have rascals and trash within our borders because we have no law. Third, let us set about making laws to help trade and encourage our planters to grow crops. It isn't enough to supply our own wants and sell a little produce to Southern Carolina and Virginia. We have the Indies at our doorstep. With a little encouragement by way of navigation and trade laws, our people would enlarge their acreage—yes, and new settlers would come. It seems the height of stupidity to continue these petty quarrels. And let the new Governor move quickly to increase our defences. We are at the mercy of attack when we have no union among ourselves."

Roger left the room. Now they would settle down to making plans for the meeting tomorrow. He wanted no part in that. It was not his business. He had the feeling that good would come of it, and that satisfied him. Let the politicians think out the ways and means.

When he stepped outside of the door he heard Cary's voice. The Quaker stood under the great tree in the yard, haranguing a crowd of silent countrymen:

"We are not in England," he shouted with vehemence. "We are in a new country. We have new problems belonging to a new country. Our problems are not those of pocket-handkerchief fields surrounded by hedgerows of may. Ours are the problems of vast untouched forests and land yet to feel the weight of a man's plow."

Moseley stood beside Roger in the doorway. He stood looking at Cary, shouting and waving his arms at the crowd, who cheered at every pause. "He doesn't know yet that that sort of thing will no longer serve," Moseley said.

"How will you gain his consent to withdraw in favour of Hyde?" Roger asked.

Moseley shook his head, a look, almost of pity, reflected in his eyes. "I can do nothing. I have tried and failed. Tonight Foster Tomes and Phelps will watch up with him."

"Watch up?" Roger asked.

"A Quaker custom, Roger. Two men will sit for hours trying to make the sinner see the light and turn him to the path of duty." He stood for a moment, his eyes on Cary. "Let us hope his faction will give way without bloodshed," he said.

He turned around and went back into the inn. Roger thought he had never seen Moseley so concerned, nor had he ever heard him speak more feelingly.

He heard the rattle of dice on a bare table, the husky, strident voices of men calling for whisky. That was why they all were here in the Albemarle. He was like the other planters, no better, no worse. Tarred with the same brush. Hard drinking—hard riding—each man for himself and his own law.

He found himself walking rapidly down the path that ran along the bank of the river. To take on responsibility that belonged to maintaining law was not to his taste. He wanted only to live his own life in his own way. To plant and harvest his land; to keep his people fit and well; to accumulate land and more land, fields and forest. What more could a man want? But in his heart he knew Moseley had gone to the very root of their trouble. Everybody's responsibility was nobody's responsibility. And there it stood.

He was out of sight of the inn now. Below him was the sandy shore line, half hidden by a tangle of vines, of grape and trumpet, wild smilax and honeysuckle, all in the first faint green of the bursting leaf.

A dugout canoe, tied to a stake, swung lazily in the sluggish current. A fish-line hung over the side and a sturgeon flopped in the bottom of the boat, at its dying gasp. The fisherman was not there. No doubt he was lower down with another line, hoping to gain enough fish for his family for the evening meal.

Roger walked on, occupied with his thoughts, until he came to a fork in the path. One branch continued along the bank, the other descended to the river level.

He heard voices, a man's, then a woman's raised a little. The next step brought him to a bend in the path, obscured by the hanging moss and vines. He looked down and recognized the leet woman.

She was standing in the centre of the path that led to a broken-down float, to which her boat was tied. A man blocked the way, standing with feet wide apart, as if more accustomed to the quarterdeck than to the shore. He wore a small cap set jauntily on his head and a gaudy sash about his middle. The man's back was towards Roger, but he could see the glint of gold in his ears, and his thick swarthy neck rising from the open collar of his shirt.

The girl broke the quiet. "Stand aside, so I can get to my canoe."

"No, I can't do that, my little dove."

"Let me pass, I am in a hurry."

"No, my little turtle, my little duck. You do not pass until you give me a rousing kiss."

"I say let me pass." Her voice was not loud but it carried.

"My humble service to you, madam. I'll be hanged if I do. We sailors want obedience. Come here!"

There was a lull. In a changed tone she said: "Did you say you were a sailor?"

"None better on Spanish waters. Come, my angel, give us a kiss and I'll tell you a tale of Rackham and the Brasiliano and how we outwitted the French men-of-war."

"Rackham's a pirate," the girl said. "I want no truck with pirates."

"I swear on the Throne, he's no pirate. A freebooter. He's got honour, he has. He won't let a woman aboard his ship. He'd skewer a man with his sword if he raped a captive. Give me the kiss and I'll tell you a tale to make your hair rise on end."

There was another silence, followed by a muffled curse.

"I said one, not more," the girl said. "A bargain's a bargain, so keep your distance or I'll claw you again."

"Blood of Mary, you're a cat!"

"Cat or not cat, sit where you are and tell me the story of Rackham."

Roger was out of earshot now. He walked on the upper path smiling a little. For a moment he had thought to go down and send the man about his business, but there was no need. She could take care of herself in her own way. It reminded him of the night the Bounds were run and he heard her talking with the sailor. This man had more finesse. He traded a tale of the high seas for a kiss. Why was the girl so eager to learn of the sea? And how dared she hang about when her mother had been heard by the Court and bound over for trial and perhaps death by hanging.

It was almost dusk when he returned to the inn. Near the ferry he caught sight of the leet woman standing close to a tree, her face turned towards the noisy, boisterous crowd in the yard. She turned quickly at his voice, ready to rush away into the forest.

"What are you doing here? Don't you know that half the men there would put the dogs on you for a witch?"

"They'll never see me," she said shortly.

"You are a long way from your shelter," he said.

She turned quickly. "I have no home. They burned it when they took Susannah Evans to the gaol in Queen Anne's Town."

"Best go back to Queen's Gift. You are safe there."

The girl's eyes blazed blue fire. For a moment he thought she was going to claw him. "Safe?" she cried angrily. "With that man there?"

"What are you talking about?"

"Lovyck, that fine gentleman Lovyck. He's a devil. He came upon me unexpected. He tried to turn my petticoats. He said he wanted to see if my legs were as pretty as my face!"

Roger remembered the day Anthony had stopped in, as he rode home from Sandy Point, with one cheek scratched and bleeding. "He told me he had run into a thorn bush."

She laughed harshly.

"The fine gentleman, with his brocade coats and his lace cuffs, hunting down a leet girl as he would hunt a vixen! 'Come on, my dear,' he says in his sugar voice. 'Lift up your petticoats and I'll give you a flourish.' "

"The contemptible ass," muttered Roger.

The girl did not hear him. She was trembling with anger at the very thought of Lovyck. "I went at him and scratched his pretty face. May the black death destroy him!" She turned and rushed off into the dusk of the forest as if she were pursued.

Roger went into the inn. He was angry at himself and more angry with Anthony. He had had some satisfaction before this revelation in seeing that the girl was left in comparative safety on his place. He had ordered a fence put up to keep the stock from wandering in that stretch of wood, and made the few little changes that were possible to make without alarming the girl. All she needed was a small sense of security. Now that had been taken from her by Lovyck. He felt like wringing the coxcomb's neck. But as he walked on his anger cooled. Lovyck was young, the girl was pretty, and a wild one. The attempt on her virtue was not unnatural.

When he got to the inn yard he saw the swarthy seaman. The man was at the pump washing his wounds, two long gouges where the skin was broken and bleeding. Roger smiled grimly when he heard the fellow explaining to his companions how he had walked smack into a thorn bush in the dusk.

All the following day men talked and wrangled and got into fisticuffs. Once Roger stopped a more serious disturbance when Emanuel Low, Cary's brother-in-law, and one of Gover's men were drawing swords.

The day wore on without anything being settled, although most of the leaders of each precinct in the county were in favor of accepting Hyde. Cary and some of his adherents held on; Low, and Porter, and one or two others. Then suddenly Cary abandoned the meeting and rode away, carrying the seal of office.

There was no hope left except in Foster Tomes. Even that was a remote possibility. For Cary had, unexpectedly, received reinforcements to his side in Roach, who had recently come out from England. He had, at the request of Danson, the Quaker Lord Proprietor, landed at Bath Town with an armed brigantine. Then there was Cary's barkentine, ready to leave the shipyard in another week. The Cary Rebellion might flare into civil warfare at any moment. The outlook for Albemarle was very dark indeed.

Roger sent his horse home by Metephele, and accepted Edward Moseley's invitation to go home in his periauger. He didn't want to make the long ride home with Lovyck.

It was good to get away. The impact of strong will against strong will had become almost physical. Rancor and bitterness were hate breeders, slow poisons, injuring men and leaving them unbalanced. Roger was glad to leave them behind, to feel the sharp cleansing air sweep over him as the shallop cleared the bar at the mouth of the river and entered the heavier wind that was blowing up the Sound.

Moseley lay back against the rim of the deck. His face looked drawn and tired. He spoke little, his mind refusing to turn from the unsolved problems.

A light fog close to the water shut them off from the familiar shore, set them adrift on a sea or desolation. Great cypress trees cut through the vapour. The grotesque, slimy knees rising from the clouded water were redolent of decay, an abomination of desolation. Sky and water met, only to be blotted out by the murky mist. The sails were lashed to the masts, useless.

The rowers laid their oars clumsily. The steersman, poling his sweep, peered ahead into the gloom. The heavy fog cut off the man at the prow. Far away, the heard the weird call of a low-flying heron. There was something sinister in the oppressive thickness that fell upon them.

Moseley's voice spoke in the gloom, a disembodied voice out of the grey mist. "There must be a way to keep the Queen's peace. Our people will have to learn that if they want to preserve their freedom they must have freedom under the law; that none of us is above the law."

Roger thought a few moments. "That will be hard to make our border people understand. They have made their own law for so long a time. They tell me that none will pay taxes on land. When the Virginia collector comes, they claim their land is in North Carolina; and the other way around when our collectors go there—they say they come under Virginia jurisdiction."

Moseley laughed. "And so escape all taxes. Yes, I know. That is the reason we should set about getting this boundary dispute settled as soon as we can."

Roger said, "Don't you think Tom Cary's day is past, Moseley? He can't go on forever, now that Hyde has his Commission. Surely he doesn't intend to use powder against adherents of the Queen's representative."

"That's what I told him today," Moseley said, noncommittally. "By the way, I suppose you know where we are. I don't."

Roger listened for some sound from the shore to give him bearings. The boat scraped against a stub of cypress. It must be either Bluff Point or the pocosin at the south end of Porter's plantation, Sandy Point, for they had passed Bat's Grave at the mouth of the Yaupin some time ago.

A familiar sound came to his ear, now sensitive and attuned, the shush of water against the blade of a paddle, rhythmic and even as the flow of water. Indians! he thought, instantly alert. He could not see the canoes but they were passing downstream from the Roanoke, keeping the channel. Not one canoe, but several.

The men heard also, and stopped their pull on the oars. The periauger lay silent, swinging a little with the current. It must be Indians from the village on the Chowan, or Tuscaroras from the south shore moving eastward, stealthy as the flow of the river.

Roger thought, Why are we men struggling and fighting for supremacy in our ill-starred government? The real danger lies to the south—even though King Blont swears everlasting friendship for the white man. . . . A repugnance, almost physical, came over him, directed towards Cary and Pollock and Glover and all their sort. How could they be blind to the danger that was lying in wait, there to the south, in the Indian villages?

The boat scraped against a staub, swaying a little. A point of light showed to the north, fluttering and diffused against the heavy, lazy fog. Roger's spirits rose. Let them wrangle and fight and babble of Queen's peace and the law. Beyond the shapeless mass of shadows were great forests of pine and gum, oak and cypress; the majesty of Nature was in the wilderness and in the strength and fertility of the Albemarle. In land was the strength and the hope of the future, not in men.

Across the water he heard the beat of a drum and a bell ringing. His people were sounding the drum and ringing the great plantation bell to guide him to his home.

Here ahead of him lay his own kingdom, won from the forest by the work of his hands. Labour and toil and then hope of the harvest—that was enough for any man. He cupped his hands and hallooed, his voice full and eager.

Chapter 19

TO YOUR LOVELY EYES

THE tables were set, the flowers in place, the dining-room ready for the guests. Marita stood back from the table and felt pleased with her part of the work. It was the first time in her life she had ever arranged a table. She was so slow and exact, laying out the pewter spoons and the two-tined forks, that Lucretia had finished one side before Marita had completed a single service to her entire satisfaction.

Lucretia laughed at her awkwardness. "Has thee never set a place before?" she asked, her bright, birdlike eyes full of laughter. "Thee is so slow. See, this way." She took the cutlery from a case and began strewing it about the table, her small, capable hands flying. Marita watched her dejectedly.

233

"It is hard to remember whether the tumbler goes at the head of the knife or the fork." She leaned over to straighten a knife. The bottom of her cuff caught the rim of a tumbler and it crashed to the floor.

Both girls stood looking down at the pieces, dismay on their faces. The noise of breaking glass brought Dame Tomes in from the pantry. She looked from the frightened girls to the splintered glass. "Get a brush broom, Lucretia, and sweep up the pieces. It would be bad if the little fellows should get slivers in their bare feet."

Dame Tomes turned to Marita, a gentle smile on her lips. "There is no need to worry, Marita. It is good that I never bring out my best glass for the menfolk. It is easily replaced."

Tears came to Marita's eyes. She rushed across the room and into Martha Tomes's arms. "I am so sorry, madam. How can I learn not to be so awkward?"

The older woman patted Marita's shoulder. "There, there, thee is not an awkward child. Is this unfamiliar work? Has thee had no training for house duties?"

Marita shook her head. "No, madam. There was always some one . . ." She paused a moment.

Martha Tomes eyes widened. "How can thee hope to have proper servants if thee does not know how to instruct them?"

"The housekeeper . . ." Marita began.

Madam Tomes nodded understandingly. "True. I had forgotten. In England it is different from this new world. Look, I will show thee." Her plump, capable hands spread the white serviette into a fan and set it into the tumbler. She laughed at Marita's attempt to fold the linen. "Who sees to the training of thy servants at Greenfield?" she asked, without pausing at her work with the linen.

"Desham, my aunt's woman," Marita said. She felt suddenly ashamed of her ignorance in these vital matters. "Do you think I could learn?"

Lucretia answered instead of her mother. "A Quaker girl must learn everything about a house—to make the beds properly with stiff folded corners; to lay the table for serving; to order the meals, and give out supplies to the cook. Yes, she must even know how to cook, so that her man will have decent food when he comes in worn and tired from his work in the fields."

"Lucretia, do you know all these things?"

"Naturally, from twelve or thirteen years. By sixteen we

234

can weave cloth and sew our clothes; at seventeen we are ready to walk out."

"Walk out? What do you mean, Lucretia?"

"She means betrothal," madam said, amused by Lucretia's gentle boasting.

"I am ready for marriage now," Lucretia said, not noticing the little gleam of laughter in her mother's eyes. "I have my quilts pieced and my goose-feather pillows. I plucked the down myself and made the ticks out of strong, heavy calicut. I have the bolster for my marriage bed, and I have a woven a dozen linen sheets and two dozen slips. They are put away in my marriage chest."

Marita looked downcast.

Madam, intent on checking Lucretia, said, "What has been thy teaching, child?"

"My teaching? Oh nothing, nothing important. Of course, I had my French to learn, and a little Latin, and how to compose a letter. Then I must read the classics. My aunt insisted on that. And do my figures, because some day I might have to go over the rents with the bailiff. Then there was dancing, and deportment, and how to curtsy without getting caught in one's frock. But the most fun of all was riding lessons—how to sit when I rode in the park, and how to ride to hounds, how to put my horse over a fence or a hedge without tumbling off." She laughed aloud. "I've had many a tumble, I can tell you."

Dame Martha was watching her daughter's expression with deep amusement. "You see, Lucretia, thee has had good training for thy station in life and Marita has had good training for hers. It does not become thee to be prideful."

"Yes, ma'am," Lucretia said meekly.

When madam had gone back to the pantry, well satisfied with the little lesson she had given her daughter, Lucretia turned to Marita. "How does thee say when thee walks out with a young man?"

"That you are betrothed when you wear a ring."

"That is what worldly people say?"

"Worldly?" Marita questioned.

"People like thee who are not Friends we call worldly. Some Quaker people will not let their children know any worldly folk."

"You mean that you could not be friends with me?"

Lucretia nodded. "Yes, but my father is a moderate Quaker. He has said that I may have thee for a companion." She smiled a little as she worked, a pleasant, secret smile.

"Why are you smiling to yourself, Lucretia?" Marita demanded.

"At something my father said about thee. He loves thee, Marita. He says thee has quiet, modest ways, almost as if thee were born a Friend."

Marita was pleased. "Oh, I am glad. I like your father and your mother and Edward, and your house. I feel at home here, so much at home." she added.

Lucretia smiled again. "We love thee. Best watch out, Marita, else we have thee an acknowledged Friend one day!"

"But I belong to the Church of England!" Marita exclaimed quickly. "All my people . . ."

Lucretia touched her cheek gently. "So did my mother. She was a worldly woman when she met my father and love came to them."

"Oh!"

"Yes, and she stood up in meeting and acknowledged herself a Friend before ever they were married. She has often told us about it—how frightened she was, and how she cried all night before, when she put aside her worldly raiment. But love is stronger than the world." Lucretia spoke the last slowly, a little secret smile on her red lips.

"Why did she have to give up her church and her pretty clothes?"

Lucretia set the glass tumbler she had been polishing on the table. "It is a law of Friends that we must marry a Friend. We cannot marry a worldly man, or a worldly woman. It is a law."

Marita turned away so that Lucretia could not see her face. An unknown fear clutched her heart. He was a Quaker, Michael. She remembered how he had spoken the first time she had seen him that evening near the Border Inn, when he had his men drive the flock aside so that their coach could pass him. "It is not the hat of a Roundhead, but a Quaker's hat," he had said.

"What is wrong?" Lucretia asked. "Thee looks so white, Marita."

"I think I am a little tired," she answered dully.

Lucretia was at once all solicitude. "Come, thee must rest on the bed. Thee is not accustomed to work. Run upstairs and lie down."

Marita shook her head. "I am all right," she answered.

Lucretia took her by the arm and led her to the stairs. "Come, go up to thy bedchamber and rest, for tonight we must help my mother serve the supper."

Marita slipped out of her dress and put on a wrapper. She wondered where Kikitchina was that she was not on hand to help her. As she unbound her hair she stood by the little window, looking out.

Activity extended to the kitchen garden. Neighbour women in their wide-skirted grey frocks were standing over the great black kettles. A pleasant odour of spices floated upward.

The air was mild and soft. Beyond the garden was the river where little canoes were moored. The quiet river made no impression on her. One thing filled her mind, crowding out all other thoughts. Michael was a Quaker, and Quakers did not marry worldly women. She moved slowly across the room and threw herself face downward on the bed.

The work of serving the supper was over. Dame Tomes sent Marita out of the pantry where she had been helping Lucretia all evening. "Go into the parlour and take thy rest," she said kindly. "After we have finished we will join thee. The men will sit for hours with their talk."

Marita slipped off the encompassing pinafore, and went out through the back hall to the parlour.

Voices of the guests came to her as she sat alone in the great room. Sometimes loud words spoken in anger, sometimes conversational tones. She could imagine men sitting at ease at the table, smoking their long pipes or sipping Dame Martha's wine of the Scuppernong or wild fox grapes.

"How do we know that Hyde isn't here for another purpose?" Thomas Cary's full voice rose above the others. "How do we know he isn't sent here by the Queen to gather the Carolinas into the fold of the Crown Colony?"

"Nonsense," a voice she did not recognize answered. "You're talking nonsense!"

"Oh, am I? Well, listen to this letter from Spottsswood, the Queen's Governor in Virginia. I'll read it to you. It's dated Williamsburg on the sixth of March. It's written to the Lords of Trade and Plantations in London."

"How did you come by it?" someone asked.

"How do I come by many things I know?" Cary's voice had an edge. "We have Friends in Virginia, have we not?"

Marita could not hear all that followed, just a sentence now and then. She moved over towards the hall and sat down near the door just inside the great room. She heard him read:

". . . I have made the Government of Carolina a suggestion for obtaining a speedy settlement of the boundaries. I have not been able to bring them to concessions . . ." His voice died down for a few moments, then rose again:

". . . But Hyde is upon so precarious a footing and his authority so little that he is forced to submit his own judgment . . ." His voice again died away.

A chair scraped on the floor, as if its occupant had moved hastily. "Did Spottswood write that letter?" a man asked, his voice raised.

"Who else?" Cary's answer was cool. "What does he mean by 'to others whose interests are likely to suffer by an equitable distribution?' What does he mean, fool? What, but one thing? Spottswood seeks to get Hyde to interest himself in throwing the boundary south of the Albemarle so that all the north of this county is annexed to Virginia, and therefore becomes Crown territory. What is wrong with you that you cannot see . . . ?"

"Friend Cary, I think thee is reading too much into these words. We must not jump at conclusions."

Marita recognized Foster Tomes's strong, quiet voice. "Now let us consider . . ."

She heard another chair being moved, and the sound of someone walking across the dining-hall towards the doors that opened onto the entry. She had no desire to be caught eavesdropping. She got up quietly, crossed swiftly to the fireplace and sat down in an elbow chair, her eyes on the blazing logs.

The door opened and closed. Someone walked across the hall and into the room where she sat. She looked up. Michael was standing in the doorway, a glass of wine in his hand. Seeing Marita, he moved swiftly across the room. For a moment she was unable to draw breath or to move. By the flickering light of the mantel candles she saw his face was flushed, his eyes unnaturally bright. It is the wine, she thought, remembering that Dame Tomes had said it was old wine and very heady.

"I wanted to come back," he said, "but my uncle sent me to Emanuel Low's house with a message. I could not refuse."

238

He put out his hand and touched hers. "Come, let us walk in the garden," he said abruptly.

Marita glanced towards the door.

"Do not be afraid," he smiled. "The women are in the pantries and the kitchen, and the men will sit at table for hours."

"I think I must not go," she said, remembering Lucretia. "I must stay here."

"Do not be timid. You are not a Quaker girl."

She said nothing. She could not speak for the swift pounding of her heart. She knew she would go with him. She could almost feel his lips on hers as he smiled down at her. She rose slowly.

He held the wineglass towards her. "Drink, little Marita. Taste the wine that is the color of your eyes." He put the glass into her hand. "Do you recall the day you sat on the boat? Do you recall what I said? 'Eat of our grapes and you belong to us forever'?"

"Yes," she whispered. "Yes, I remember." She touched the wine to her lips. It was as sweet and intoxicating as the grapes had been.

He took the glass from her and drained it. "To your eyes, Marita, to your lovely eyes."

He put the glass on the mantel and caught her arm. "Come," he said. "Come with me."

They walked into the quiet of the garden, down towards the river. The moon was at the half and the path veined with silver where it fell upon the leafless trees. No word was spoken between them. She knew when they came to the shadows he would put his arms, his strong arms, about her. She knew this must not be, for he was a Quaker and she was worldly. Then there was something else that troubled her: Lucretia. She was sure that Lucretia loved him, Lucretia with her chest of linen and her piece-quilts, ready for the marrage bed. She tried to remember this as they walked swiftly down the path towards the river. It was Lucretia he must walk with, Lucretia who had had her spiritual awakening, who was full of godliness. She herself was rootless and unhappy, with only a shell of faith to sustain her. Salvation was Lucretia's, hers by divine grace. So Lucretia had told her. She was ready and waiting for marriage.

These thoughts, formless and vague, flashed through her mind, but her heart and her emotions sang another song.

Halfway across the garden she found tongue. "I cannot go with you, Michael," she said, stopping short.

He did not loosen his firm hold on her arm. Gently he propelled her forward down the path. "Why can't you?" His voice was husky. It had lost its firm ringing quality which was so much a part of him.

"I must not go with you. I must not. It is not—good."

They had come to the river. At their feet the water lapped against the narrow sandy beach. The boats swung at anchor. The landing float loomed dim in the moonlight. The shadows lay thick here from evergreens, pines and cypresses.

"What is not good?" he repeated. He drew her to him suddenly. His lips against hers were cold and hard. "This? And this?" he asked, and released her.

What was it she was going to say to him? What was it? That Lucretia loved him and was a Quaker? She felt the strength of his arms, felt his lips on her throat. It was easy now to forget. "Michael, Michael," she spoke his name to stay the turmoil in her.

"My little Marita," he said, "do not think of other things. Think only of this moment which belongs to us."

There was no need to tell her. She no longer had will to think, only to feel.

After a little he released her and held her away at arm's length, his hands on her shoulders. "Stay there, my dear, stay there. If you are close I forget what I must say."

Marita put her hand over his. There seemed to be a sombre gentleness in him now. She wanted to listen but was afraid.

"I am going away tomorrow. The barkentine which my uncle has been building up in the Pasquotank is almost finished. First I must take her to Bath Town to be outfitted. Then I must sail her to the Indies."

"Do not go!" she cried suddenly afraid. "Do not go!"

He put his arm about her, quietly now, speaking gently as to a child. "When I come back, I will come for you. I will go to your aunt and say: 'I am home from the Indies. I have been to Antigua and brought back my rightful inheritance. Now I am ready to ask for Marita's hand in marriage.'"

"How can you?" she said, her breath coming fast. "You a Quaker and I a worldly woman They will not let you."

"We will find a way," he said harshly.

"My aunt will not permit it . . ."

"Why not?" His voice rose a little as if he were angered.

Marita had no answer to give him. She could not tell him the many times her aunt had told her that she must marry in England, a man of her own class. "A woman must never marry beneath her," she had so often said. "A man can raise a woman to his station, but a woman raise a man—never."

"I am not of age and I must do as she bids me. She does not like Quakers," she said, her voice very low.

Michael dropped his arms to his side and stood away from her. A curtain of darkness settled down upon her world which had been so shining and so happy.

"I have not been a Quaker very long. I forget to say 'thee' for 'you', and I still like to use my sword in a fair fight, but I would not allow anyone to change my faith. No matter what my religion might be, a man worships as he chooses. That is one reason why we came to a new country."

The impact of his words shook her profoundly and left her bereft of speech.

"Come, we must go to the house. They will miss us." They moved slowly, side by side. He did not touch her arm nor speak until they were close to the light from the window. Then he laid his hand on her shoulder for a moment. "There must be a way, but I do not see it clearly. One thing I know: I will see you once again before I sail for the Indies. I do not give up so readily. No other woman has ever moved me so strongly as you. I will not let you go without fighting to hold you."

He turned and walked quickly away into the shadows of the garden. She ran up the path to the door. She encountered no one on the way, or in the hall. A few moments after she had seated herself by the fire Lucretia came into the room.

"Where has thee been, Marita? I have been looking for thee."

Marita's answer came readily, as if the lie lay ready at the tip of her tongue, though she hated herself for the half-truth. "I walked in the garden. The night is very quiet." She stopped, aware that Lucretia was not attending to her words. She was looking at the wineglass Michael had carelessly left on the mantelboard.

"It is nice in the garden in the moonshine," Lucretia said, but her voice was flat and lifeless.

Marita wondered if Lucretia had missed Michael, if she knew they had been together. Was she hurt? Marita did not want to hurt Lucretia, but she would not give up Michael—not even if she lost Lucretia's friendship forever.

After a few moments Marita got up. "If your mother does not need me I think I will go upstairs, Lucretia. I find myself very weary."

Lucretia let her go without protest.

Outside the door of the bedchamber, Kikitchina was waiting. She held the door open and followed her inside the room. Quietly, without words, she helped Marita undress and drew the covers up over her.

"Thank you, Kikitchina," she said. "I think we will go back to Greenfield tomorrow. We will go early, quite early."

The Indian woman nodded. She crossed to the window and drew the curtain so that the moonshine would not fall on Marita's face. A moment later she had gone from the room.

Below, the rumble of men's voices sounded dimly. After a time she forgot Lucretia and the sorrowful look in her candid eyes. She could remember nothing but Michael and the strength of his arms. "Once more I will see you," he had said. The remembrance of his words comforted her.

Chapter 20

THE COUNCIL
SITS AT BALGRAY

ANTHONY LOVYCK sat quietly looking out the window, his quill poised, waiting for the Governor to clear his thoughts and continue his dictation. They had worked long, since early morning. Now Hyde had news of importance to send to Governor Spottswood in Williamsburg, and to the Secretary of the Lords of Trade and Plantations, in London.

It was some weeks now since the meeting at the Hecklefield farm. The Governor had not been too pleased with the outcome. He would have preferred a unanimous vote of confidence in him. Although it was not an official meeting, the inference would have been helpful and comforting to him. As it was now, he had his official status, but the seal to stamp the official papers remained in the hands of Thomas Cary. There had been only one thing to do: avoid signing papers and land grants that required the seal. His letter to the Lords of Trade and Plantations required some thought.

"I want to bind a stronger link between the Bahamas and this colony," he said aloud. Anthony took up the writing where he had left off. "Since six of the Lords Proprietors are also the Lords Proprietors of the Bahama Islands, I should think something could be done at once to increase our trade with them and with Jamaica. We need salt and sugar. They need naval stores, particularly Jamaica. We have pitch, tar and turpentine. We have also cotton and pork and tobacco. If you will take this up in your next meeting we may be able to plan for the year following."

He paused again, sitting quietly in his tall-backed chair, his thin delicate hands resting on the table in front of him. Anthony thought the Governor had aged in the months they had been in Albemarle. No wonder. There was worry enough to age any man. A governor without authority was bad enough. A governor without troops was even worse. He turned his eyes to the window again. The broad sweep of the Chowan lay before him, beyond the long garden. The trees were in full leaf and the early dogwood was gone and the azalea that grew rank on the burned-over ground had gone. Across the river, to the north, thin spirals of smoke rose over the trees, marking the Indian village above the mouth of Rockahock Creek. He stared at the cooking fires for some time before he noticed how numerous they were. Idly he began to count, to twenty-eight, thirty, before he came to a full realization that this was an extraordinarily large number. The village must have been increased considerably since yesterday. He was on the point of calling it to his Excellency's attention, but at that moment the Governor resumed his dictation where he had left off.

"I have recommended the appointment of Mr. Christopher Gale as Chief Justice of the whole Province. It is my understanding that he is also to be appointed Chief Justice of the Bahamas, so that will bring us in closer contact with the Island of New Providence and its chief city, Nassau. Mr. Edward Moseley, who now holds that position as an adherent of the Cary faction, will doubtless use his influence to be appointed Surveyor General, if Mr. Lawson does not want the position. I hope you will lay all these matters before the Lords and use your own vast influence for the welfare of our Province."

Anthony's pen scratched over the paper. After a few

moments he sanded the whole and handed it to the Governor.

"You make an excellent copy, Anthony," he said, after he had read the letter through. "Perfect, in fact. I have never had a secretary who was so faithful and loyal, and did such excellent work."

Anthony's dark face lighted at this unexpected praise. His quick, facile mind told him this was the time to strike a good word for himself and his future.

"I thank you, Excellency. I am happy to have a humble part in your great work of reconstruction here in Albemarle. Sometimes I have thought . . ." He paused, as if his embarrassment would not allow him to continue.

The Governor smiled. "Go on, go on."

Anthony still hesitated. Then he said: "Sometimes I have thought I could be of a greater service to you, sir."

"How is that?" Hyde asked, turned his deep-set eyes on his young secretary.

"If I had an official capacity; that is, if I were the Secretary for the Province." Anthony stopped short. Had he said too much? He bit his lip, hoping he had not been precipitate.

The Governor fingered a paper cutter, tapping it quietly on the edge of the table, a habit he had when he was thinking deeply. Anthony could read nothing from his expression. After a time he said, "That is something which requires thought," and turned to the mass of papers on his table.

Anthony breathed again. At least the Governor had not dismissed the idea as one of no moment.

Hyde took up a paper, turned it over once or twice, until he came to a marked passage. "You may prepare a letter to Governor Spottswood. Open in the usual way. Now say:

"Relating to our boundaries, I shall have all regard possible for the issue and will lay the plan of a permanent Commission before the Council, as I hope, next week. I have forwarded your letter to our Surveyor General, Mr. Lawson. I am sorry that any act by our temporary Commission is not approved by you.

"On the other hand, I hear great complaints of how, in Virginia, they drive over the Meherrin Rover great stocks of cattle, and when they return to Virginia drive great stocks of this Colony along with them. If their owners go after them, they are upbraided, and charged with thievery. The Meherrin Indians are very insolent and abusive to our border people; kill hogs and cattle of ours, hoping they will have protection

244

from you. I hope you will not countenance anything of the sort, but hereafter there may be decorum kept until bounds are determined.

"I hope also that you will not proceed in drawing the Line until the Commissioners of this place, Mr. Lawson and Mr. Moseley, are able to join your own appointees. I am, et cetera, et cetera."

Lovyck wrote busily for some time. The Governor smiled a little when he read the completed letter. "It is well for us to throw in a complaint or two," he said, as he wrote "Edward Hyde" across the bottom of the page. "We hear altogether too much about the depredations of our border people, and too little about the marauding Virginians. Now that the Lords Proprietors have made me full Governor of North Carolina, we may as well let our neighbours know that we are prepared to stand on our rights."

Anthony laughed outright. "I'm sure, your Excellency, that Governor Spottswood will be a little surprised. Usually we are busy defending our people, with no time to make attacks. The last, about the cattle, is a master stroke."

Hyde smiled. Then his face relaxed into its accustomed gravity, "I can lodge a complaint, Anthony, but they all know we haven't the strength to carry it through. Our friend Cary knows that, for he holds the great seal of Albemarle. . . . The Indians know it, the Meherrins, the Cores and the Tuscaroras. If we had one hundred seasoned, well-trained soldiers, and a guard-ship, we could protect our women and our children. When I get full power, someone will pay for all this anxiety."

There was so much bitterness in his usually quiet voice that Anthony looked up quickly. The Governor was staring straight ahead, his face set in a mask. His dark, deep-set eyes held tragedy in them as if he were seeing into the future and what he saw was not good. Never had Anthony admired him so much—his fortitude, his never-ending patience.

"That will be all for today, Anthony. You have worked hard. All this confinement is not good for a young man. Go for a canter, or take a canoe on the river."

He got up and walked across the room and stood looking out the window. "It is very quiet, now that Madam Hyde has gone. Let me see. How many days is it?"

"Three weeks, your Excellency. Three weeks yesterday."

The Governor sighed a little. "It will be another three weeks before she can take ship for England. The sinking of

245

the *Four Winds* by the pirates just off the Capes set back the sailing until another ship can come from Jamaica."

"Why don't you go up to Virginia for a few weeks, sir?"

The Governor shook his head. "No, I must stay here. There is much work to be done and so little time."

He took a turn about the room, walking quickly. "I believe we do well to have her carry our secret report to the Lords Proprietors."

"Indeed, yes. Just think, it might have gone down on the *Four Winds*."

The Governor stopped his nervous pacing and put his hand on Anthony's shoulder. "And all your good writing lost. That would have been a heavy blow!"

Anthony smiled at this.

"If Parson Urmston sails at the time, Madam Hyde will have company," the Governor continued.

Anthony gathered up his papers and the letter-book. "As for me I could think of better company. I've never seen a man so sour on the world as Parson Urmston."

"He has had many disappointments," the Governor said quickly.

"Yes, I know, and his lameness. But I have known people with heavier handicaps who have borne them cheerfully," Anthony said quickly. "He is unkind and harsh. He offers no salvation for repentant sinners, which is Christ's first law."

"A man's nature cannot easily change," the Governor said. "Don't be too hard on the man. He's gone now, and the new man will have a fresh paper to write on."

"I hope he writes with a clean hand and clear head," Anthony grumbled as he crossed the room. At the door he stopped, his hand on the door knob. "Wouldn't you enjoy a little trip upriver in the canoe, sir? You've been working hard all day."

The Governor smiled, pleased at Lovyck's thought of him. "Thank you, no, Anthony. Pollock's sloop should be putting in any time now, and I have matters to take up with him when he comes."

Anthony thought of this as he paddled upstream close to shore. "H. E. is worried. I wish to God Cary would betake himself back to the West Indies and let us get on with the work."

He dipped his paddle into the water. The little skin canoe that one of Pollock's Indians had made for him shot ahead, gliding over the water.

It was easy paddling here on the edge of the channel—almost as easy as on the Thames. His face broke into a grin. What would his fine friends in London think of him now, dressed in tight breeches of doeskin, and a doeskin jerkin? They wouldn't know him! His skin was almost as brown as Duke Roger's, and his shoulders were widening. He was a little sick of his days in the house, writing letters for H. E. and Pollock. Next season he would plant the land he had bought on the Kesiah, and next year Anthony intended to buy a plantation on the Albemarle, and he had his eye on Sandy Point. After all, he was getting no younger, and he must think of the future.

Thinking of the future meant that his thoughts would stray to Penelope Galland, who lived not so far upstream. But she was engaged to his friend Willie Maule, therefore not for him. He gave a deep sigh as he bent to the paddle. There were always other girls, he thought. His mind turned to Sarah Blount. She was attractive although a little delicate.

After a time he looked up. He was almost opposite the Indian village across the river. What he saw made him drive his canoe towards the bank. There, behind overhanging bushes, he could look without being seen.

The village must be increased twentyfold, he thought, as he watched from behind the screen. He could see them moving along the beach. A dozen big canoes with warriors drove down the river and came to rest at the long beach. What did it mean? It was not the harvest, nor had he heard of any big hunt. Some kind of a conclave was going on, and he didn't like the looks of it.

Lovyck was too far away to see more than the silhouette of the Indians on the water and those on the beach. He gave the village a wide berth. He had heard enough of the earlier times in Virginia, and the dangers of the western wilderness, the horrible, barbarous massacres of women and children. The thought of it made his blood run cold. Anthony Lovyck was no woodsman. He was handy enough with his light rapier, a gentleman's weapon, but a long musket, or a heavy sword—that was a different thing.

He eased his canoe out from its protective screen and headed back towards Balgray. The sun was low in the west, and along his side the river bank was in deep shadow. Once or twice he turned his head, startled by the lonesome cry of a loon. Fish were leaping from the water, falling back into it with a flat splash that seemed to break the silence into many

247

fragments. Once, as his canoe rounded a little point of land, he startled a buck and two doe, drinking at the water's edge. They bounded up the bank and crashed into the deep forest almost before his eyes could focus on them. The stillness and the loneliness hung down on him like a pall. Unconsciously he raised the beat of his paddle, quickening the rhythm. He knew no one was following him—no Indian canoe in the water. He had made certain of that; yet he was relieved when his canoe swung around into the little bay at the mouth of the Salmon River.

The sun was gone from the south shore and the manor house at Balgray was in shadow when the canoe touched the float. He put the canoe under the boat-house and walked briskly up the path to the house. He and Hyde had moved back to Pollocks' when Madam Catha left for England and Hester went to her people in Maryland. Soon they hoped to find a place in Queen Anne's Town suitable for the Governor and his official family, so that they could oversee the building of Government House, which had been slow in starting.

When he opened the wide front door he heard men's voices in the library. Slaves, carrying trays with glasses and decanters, were hurrying across the hall. He heard Thomas Pollock's strong voice, shouting to his house slaves to get rooms ready. The Council was to sit tomorrow and some of the members had already arrived.

Anthony went back down the steps and around through the garden to the small cottage he occupied, his thoughts distracted from the Indian gathering. He was too dishevelled from his long canoe trip to meet Mr. Pollock's distinguished guests. He must bathe and change first. A dark blue worsted coat and doeskin breeches, black silk stockings and silver-buckled shoes. He called to the black boy he was training to lay out his clothes.

He had almost finished dressing when a slave came to tell him that his Excellency asked him to come to the manor house and bring his quills and paper with him. Anthony was in front of the small, wavy mirror settling his wide white collar into place when the message came. He knew what that meant and he was not too pleased to be called to sit up half the night, writing down the conversation of half a dozen men whose tongues were limbered with wine, only to have them order it all destroyed by morning when their heads were cooler and caution was to the fore.

He finished tying the stock to his satisfaction and screwed

a pair of golden globes in his ears. Without doubt, the earrings gave a fillip to the costume. Reluctantly he unscrewed them and dropped the little ornaments into a leather case. A French fashion would look out of place among these plain people.

Satisfied with his appearance, Anthony pointed a few duck quills and took up his writing case. Fortunately he had some ruled paper on hand. He hoped he could make out without having to line more that night. One thing was certain, he would allow himself only one glass of port, so his head would be clear for work. He had neither the hard head for drink nor the strong stomach of these Albemarle men. A strong, sturdy lot, these men of Albemarle. He wondered if the time would come when he would be able to follow their lead, drink for drink, without finding himself under the table.

He made his way carefully along the dark garden path. When he neared the kitchen he saw the slaves were cooking something outdoors in one of the big iron pots. They had stuck blazing pine knots into the ground near the cooking fires, to give enough light to work by. The odour that came to him was tantalizing and whetted his appetite, already hearty from his paddling on the river.

"What are you cooking?" he called, as he passed by.

The Negro jumped back, waving a long spoon in the air. " 'Fore God, Master Lovyck, I thought you be a ha'nt risin' right up outen the ground!"

Anthony laughed. "A hungry ghost. What are you cooking that smells so appetizing?"

"Hit's venison, sar. Mr. Maule he sent a young un down. We pack in vinegar and hit lay two, free days, and now we cook he."

Anthony looked into the pot; a pleasant odour of spices and vinegar rose with the steam that was released when the Negro lifted the lid. "Hit's all ready now," he added. "Whenever de gen'man they finish with they drinking. I worry 'bout Master Tom. He ain't et no thing. Just doin' steady drinkin'."

Anthony entered the little room that Tom Pollock used as an office. The smoke was so heavy he could scarcely make out the features of the men. After a moment the draught from the open door cleared the air.

Nathaniel Chevin, Nicholas Crisp, and William Reid. Only a few members were absent: Foster Tomes, Roger Mainwairing, and Swann from Pasquotank.

Ebenezer, the slave, handed Anthony a glass half full of

249

spirits. He sniffed it and set it down. He had no thought of burning his innards out with whisky made that autumn in a still on the place. He didn't share the natives' enthusiasm for corn liquor, fresh from the still. He wanted good whisky aged in the wood.

Pollock saw him. "Come, come, my lad, where is your drink? Ebenezer, bring a glass for Mr. Lovyck."

"I gave he one and he set hit on the table."

"That's right, Lovyck," Chevin said ponderously. "The young don't need liquor. Leave that to the old ones."

"Moderation is a good thing," the Governor said. Anthony noticed he was drinking Madeira, not raw whisky.

"Wait until you've been out in the Carolinas a couple of years; you'll be able to down corn liquor with the best of us." Chevin drained his glass and reached for a decanter.

"Does one lose one's taste for good wine in so short a time?" Anthony asked pedantically.

A laugh went up. "Strong drink for strong men. That's the Albemarle!" someone shouted.

Pollock stood up and drained his glass. "Drink, men. Toss off your whisky. My boy tells me that supper is spread on the table."

The men finished their drinks and straggled into the dining-room. A good drink and a gusty appetite and plenty of plain food to eat were the rule at Balgray when Madam Hester was absent.

In the morning, before he was out of bed, Anthony heard loud halloos from the landing. He got out of bed and pulled the heavy curtain. The sun was well up. A mocking bird was singing in the myrtle thicket. The air was soft and fragrant, and all the world was gay and full of promise—all excepting Anthony Lovyck.

It had all happened as he expected. Until two o'clock he had been writing a full record of the night's discussion. With all the talk back and forth, opinion and fact, one thing came out: They were all afraid of Thomas Cary. They did not know his strength or what he intended to do with the seal of office. "Set up a government at Bath Town," a councilman said, "and defy us to come down and take it away."

"We can never fight him on his own ground," the Governor said gloomily. "I will have to ask aid from Spottswood."

A shout of protest arose at his words. No one wanted help from Virginia. And so it went, hour after hour, until between drink and weariness old Thomas went to sleep in his great chair.

Now by seven they were at it again. He stood for a moment watching the skilful manoeuvring of a sloop tacking up river to the landing. He recognized Roger Mainwairing at the helm. With him was Edward Moseley and a man he had never seen before.

Anthony called for his boy, who must have been waiting outside for he came at once, carrying a copper ewer of hot water. A quick sponge and a shave, his hair well brushed, and Anthony got into his clothes. He was out of humour with himself and the world. A scrivener—that was all he was—a fine calling for a young man of ability and ambition!

All morning the Council sat, carrying on routine business of their office. The erection of a permanent residence for the Governor, so long delayed, was discussed and laid on the table as a matter for the Assembly. Tom the Tinker's case was also laid aside. "He had devilishly and maliciously, in the presence of divers witnesses, shouted 'God damn King William—and all their Majesties—and God damn him again! I drink to the health of Jamie, the rightful King!' John Philips and others in Pasquotank had heard him, all contrary to the peace of the lady our Queen and her crown and dignity."

"The fellow must have been drunk again," said Roger Mainwairing, "if he didn't remember King William has been dead all these years."

"No matter!" snapped Councilman Boyd. "The idea is the same. He is a Jacobite and holds with James, the Pretender."

"It is a matter for General Court," said the Governor, and passed on to the next item.

"Magdalene Corrier, delivered of a bastard child, which she did kill and bury," was also a matter for the Court of Oyer and Terminer or General Court.

Boyd had something to say about this. "I believe we should recommend the Assembly to pass an act on regulation of the procedure in our private burial grounds. Something like this can happen—people be murdered and laid away, without any the wiser. With every plantation having its own burial ground, there may be things happening that would bear investigation."

"You're right, Boyd," barked Nicholas Crisp. "We had a

case—" He went on to illustrate. Anthony stopped writing and waited.

"My idea is," said Boyd, when he could get in a word, "my idea is that it should be a law that two or more witnesses should view every corpse before burial, witnesses outside the family—and as many attend the burial."

"A matter for the Assembly," the Governor said again without comment. "Next item."

"It's about Jeremiah Hogan."

A laugh went up. The Governor rapped the table with his gavel. "Order," he said. "Order, gentlemen."

Anthony read the charge: "Jeremiah Hogan, of Chowan, speaking profane and irreverent words to great scandal of the Christian religion. He is accused of saying that he never had good thoughts following the sermons of the parson, and all good he ever had was not from any sermon in church but what he thought by himself."

The Governor smiled and the Council guffawed.

Roger said, "Do we always have to punish a man for speaking his mind on matters of religion?"

"There is yet another charge," Anthony said. "Jeremiah Hogan is charged with cohabiting with his neighbour, Sara Golightly. This charge has been repeated several times and a fine paid. The condition has continued in spite of orders of the court to the contrary. We recommend that said Jeremiah be sentenced to punishment not exceeding four hours in the pillory and Moses' law of forty lashes, one withheld, on his naked back, if the court so wills."

"I hope the game is worth Moses' punishment," Roger Mainwaring commented.

"Mr. Mainwaring, I consider such levity in Council is reprehensible."

Roger smiled as he watched Anthony busily recording the little interchange.

Other things moved swiftly. Nicholas Crisp's Negro slave, Quashy, had run away, "after stealing one coat, one shirt, one new rug, a pair of breeches, stocky shoes and twenty-five shillings—a reward offered for his capture and the same posted."

"That will be no use," said Chevin. "The man is in Pennsylvania by now. The underground is working freely these days."

"Thomas Cook has filed against Thomas Heath, planter,

one thousand pound weight of brick work, damage ten pounds sterling."

"I wish cases that belong to the courts would not be brought in Council," the Governor remarked.

"We have always encouraged such, your Excellency. That is the way the Council knows what is going on in the Province. We sift the cases and send them to the Court or Vestry as the case may be," Pollock explained.

A list of the new churchwardens of St. Paul's parish was read: John Arden, Esquire, John Blount, Captain Thomas Luten, Captain Nicholas Crisp, Captain James Long, Thomas Garret, Edward Smythwick, William Benbury, William Charleton and Edward Moseley.

Again the Governor passed the list to the table, and nodded to Anthony to proceed.

"The next is definitely a court case," Anthony said, hesitating.

"Read it," Hyde ordered.

"John Collins, marshal in Charles Town. Body of Thomas Nairne brought in to this present day and charged with high treason in endeavouring to disinherit and dethrone our rightful and lawful sovereign Lady Queen Anne and to place in her room the Pretender. Signed by Nathaniel Johnston, Governor."

Hyde held out his hand for the paper and read it over carefully.

Roger Mainwairing listened to the reading. Not a muscle in his strong lean face moved. His mind pictured again the Turk and his message to Lady Mary, and the proud, unhesitating declaration she had made: "I am a Jacobite."

Until she had spoken these words the pretensions of James Stuart had seemed to him of small account and very far away. What had the people in the Carolinas to do with plots that concerned princes? This was a new world, fighting to take toe hold on forest and stream; to conquer a lush, open land; to live, as the Proprietors had said in the Charter, in a newer, wider freedom than had been granted to any men since the days of Magna Charta.

Now in one morning, here, sitting in Council, two cases had been presented naming people in the Province who would have done with the Queen and set Jamie in her stead. Was Mary Tower in correspondence with these plotters in the Ashley Settlements, or were there plotters in Martinique or the French Islands?

He had no thought of Tom the Tinker, a drunken man, but Nairne—that was different. All this disturbed him. He recognized that his uneasiness was not for the Province but for Mary Tower.

The Governor had finished reading the charge and risen to his feet. He stood a dignified figure in his dark clothes with his full-bottomed wig. "I do not know how many of you have knowledge that I have just received a full Commission from the Lords Proprietors," he said. "I think it proper at this time to mention one clause that has bearing on this case. I have been duly appointed Governor of North Carolina. You, as Councilmen, know that in the past the Governor of the northern end of the Province has been a deputy governor, serving under the Governor of all the Carolinas stationed at the Ashley River Settlements, although the courtesy title of governor has always been in use in the Albemarle. Now that is changed. The division has been approved by the Queen's Council and the Lords Proprietors. We now have a Governor of North Carolina."

There were cries of "Bravo!" and "Hear! Hear!" from the delighted group. Long had they felt the need of a governor of their own—now independence was accomplished.

Hyde bowed slightly. "The seat of government will be in Queen Anne's Town, as it has been for some time. I hope we shall be able to proceed with the erection of a proper building for the Governor's residence and to house the government offices. We may not be able to build a courthouse, or a governor's palace as fine as the Williamsburg buildings, but I hope they will be adequate. If they follow plans we have had made in London, I think they will. Small buildings may be as perfect in design as great ones."

Without waiting for comment, he tapped the table with his gavel. "Council adjourned until after dinner," he said, as he laid down his gavel.

While they dined, a slave ran into the dining-room to say that a sloop was pulling into the mouth of the Salmon River.

Thomas Pollock rose hastily and went out to the gallery and took the spyglass his servant handed to him. He recognized Foster Tomes. With him were several men whose faces were indistinct.

He sent word to have a table set for six men, and made his way down to the landing. Only one man came ashore. Pollock recognized the sombre Quaker garb, the strong, fine figure of Foster Tomes. The others were hidden by the slack sail.

"I am late," Tomes greeted him. "I was delayed at the village. There was news there of a pirate ship wrecked off the Banks, and the people were troubled."

"I hope we won't have them up in our waters, hiding up our creeks," Pollock said gruffly. "We've worries as it is without adding pirates and buccaneers to the dish."

Tomes said, " 'Tis said they hide gold at Bat's Grave, but no one has found any."

"That's because everyone in Pequimans is afraid to go there—afraid of the spirits that keep tryst with the evil one," Chevin said with a laugh that disclosed nothing of his own beliefs.

"They've a Frenchman in irons, and other prisoners. I did not stay to find out. Maule's boy, Willie, brought the news when he came up from Bath Town."

"I suppose they will be tried before the Admiralty Court," Pollock observed.

"Aye," said Tomes, "Porter will try them. But I have other matters to bring before Governor Hyde and this Council."

"They are at table now. I have had places laid for you and your friends." He indicated the men on the boat.

"My friends have dined," Tomes said, "but I will be glad to break bread with thee."

Tomes ate a substantial meal before he broached his purpose. Then he pushed back his chair and rose. "If your Excellency will permit me, I have a matter of some concern to bring to the Council."

"Shall we adjourn to the great room?" Pollock asked.

"No, not at the moment, with thy permission, friend Edward."

Hyde bowed. "Please proceed, friend Tomes."

Tomes glanced about the table. Then he said, "Thomas Cary is in my boat. He has words to speak before the Council."

There was a sudden hush. The clatter of dishes ceased, glasses were set down. Every man was looking at the Quaker. His expression told them nothing. The Governor half rose from his chair, then sank back. A strange expression crossed his stern face and lingered in his sunken eyes. "What has Thomas Cary to say to this body?" his voice rasped.

"Perhaps thee will allow him to speak in his own way."

There was a quick break in the silence. "No!" Chevin shouted. "No! No!" echoed the others.

Pollock looked as if he would burst a blood vessel, so red was his face. "The insolence of that damned rascal!" he barked. "This Council will have no words with a rene-gade."

The Governor glanced at Pollock. The older man sank back, muttering.

"Gentlemen, gentlemen, let us have order. Let us not be narrow in this matter. Colonel Cary is seeking the Council. Let him know that we are broad enough to listen to what he has to say." The Governor turned to Foster Tomes. "Bring Thomas Cary before us, in the great room."

Tomes bowed slightly and walked out. The Governor drummed on the table with a knife for a moment, while the men watched him and waited for some expression of opinion. Instead he said, "Mr. Lovyck, since you are not a member of the Council, perhaps it will be best if you absent yourself. I will ask Mr. Crisp to record the proceedings."

Anthony got up and left the room. He was annoyed at being dismissed in such a cavalier fashion. It was true he was not of the Council, but he would have liked to hear what was said at a meeting between the arch-rascal and the Council of North Carolina. As he went out the side door to his own quarters, he saw Tomes and Cary walking up the path. On the shore were four or five men. He didn't like that. What if it were a ruse, and they were here with evil intent?

He hurried into the house and put on his sword belt. At least he would be well armed. He went out again and walked towards the shore. Standing near the deep well, he saw Michael Cary. Anger rose in him. He remembered his first encounter with this man and his insolence at the Border Inn. He distrusted the fellow, and he didn't like his bold ways. Without thought of consequence he walked quickly down the path that led to the boat. There was anger in him and an urgency to provoke a quarrel.

The Council had moved into the great room and the Governor had taken his place behind the long table. His face was grave, and his eyes were guarded. The others stood around the room talking in little groups, their voices low and guarded. When Tomes and Cary came to the gallery and entered the hall, they all found seats and sat down, their faces expressionless.

Thomas Cary paused for a moment at the doorway, his

hawk glance sweeping the room with a deliberate challenge. His pale blue eyes were cold and penetrating as they rested on each man in turn with studied indifference. He made an impressive figure, taller than any man present except Duke Roger. He wore a uniform of his own design, a bottle-green coat, braided in gold, with tan leather breeches, and his broad beaver had a sweeping green plume. His high wrinkled boots were spurred and he wore a long dark cape that almost concealed his crossbelt and heavy broadsword.

Every man in the room thought of arms at that moment and remembered the sword belts and swords that lay on the wooden bench near the front door.

Roger sat near the door. In an instant he could be in the hall and have his blade ready to draw. He smiled to himself. What was it about this Thomas Cary that put caution and fear into the hearts of men less bold?

Cary walked across the room to the table where the Governor sat waiting. He removed his hat and flung it carelessly in a vacant chair. Smiling a little he stood before the Governor. "May I have permission to speak, your Excellency?"

"You have the permission of the Council to state your case."

Cary let his gaze drift around, a slightly cynical smile on his full lips. "This is not a court of law, gentlemen," he said. "Do not wear the expression of judges or jurymen."

He moved a step closer to the table, his hand resting lightly on the hilt of his sword. Roger slipped into the hall and buckled on his sword belt. It took only an instant but Cary had noticed the act.

"It is not necessary to arm, Mr. Mainwaring. This time I come in peace and not with the drawn sword." He paused to let his words sink in. Roger thought, He is as great an actor as Betterton when he is playing in Mr. Shakespeare's plays at Drury Lane.

"I have little to say, and it can be said briefly. Last night friend Phelps and friend Tomes watched up with me, twelve hours on end, until I could no longer stand against them." He glanced towards Tomes, a fleeting smile on his lips before he continued. "Since your Excellency is not familiar with the custom of the Friends, I will explain. We watch up with recalcitrant members in order that they may see the Light."

With a quick movement of his arm he threw his long cape over one shoulder. Roger saw he had a long packet under his arm, wrapped in a piece of red baize, which he put on the table in front of the Governor.

"Your Excellency, I have the honor to present you with the seal of our great County of Albemarle."

The silence spoke as he drew the red cloth, and the silver seal of office lay shimmering on the dark surface of the walnut table. A long-drawn sigh, almost a gasp, came in unison, as every man in the room leaned forward, his eyes on the silver emblem of authority.

The Governor was first to recover his composure after the first shock of Cary's unexpected action. He bowed graciously. "As the legal representative of the true Lords Proprietors of the Carolinas, I accept the seal of office from your hands, and the implication which the act connotes. In the name of the Council, I thank you."

Cary, not to be outdone, made a deep bow. "I had thought to dicker and trade with you," he said, relaxing a little. "I had thought to demand an oath, before witnesses, that as Governor of this land, thee would never plot to betray Carolina to the Queen, to be turned into a Crown Colony."

He stopped a moment to let his words sink in. "But friend Tomes convinced me that what was done must be done freely, without bargaining, and so I have subscribed to his wishes." He took up his hat and stood at ease. "There is only one condition. Twenty pounds sterling I ask for the seal, the same amount that I forwarded to their lordships for engraving the seal, and the weight in silver."

Roger noticed a shadow spread over the Governor's eyes. His lips tightened. He remembered then the rumours that the Governor was not a man of wealth and that he was sometimes embarrassed for ready funds. The idea came to him that Cary hoped to embarrass him now, before his Council. Without hesitation Roger rose.

"Your Excellency, with your permission and the permission of this body, I ask the privilege of reimbursing Colonel Cary for the weight of the silver and the engraving."

Hyde bowed his head slightly. "A generous gesture, Mr. Mainwairing. You will be thanked in Minutes of Council."

Roger looked at Cary. "If you will accept a draft on the Bank of England . . ." he said formally.

"As you wish, Mr. Mainwairing; in whatever form is convenient for you." Cary wheeled suddenly and fixed the astonished Councilmen with his eyes narrowed. "I am returning to my plantations on Pamticoe Sound, but I will not dismiss my army. I have followers waiting for me to give the word. They will come up the creeks and rivers, Sarum and Bennet's, up the Roanoke and Meherrin. You who have called me a rascal and a traitor have that hanging over your head like a drawn sword. If you make laws unjust to the Friends, or to any man, take one hair's breadth of freedom from the Quakers of this Province won for them by my father-in-law Governor Archdale, you will have to deal with Thomas Cary and his men."

He gave one quick look at Pollock as he left the room, as if the challenges were directed at him and not the Governor or the Council.

Roger followed him out of the room and overtook him on the gallery. He intended to speak to him of the money but he had no time. One of Pollock's black slaves was running up the path, his eyes rolling in fright. "Fore God! That giant man done kill Mr. Lovuk. He batter he down with he sword, jes' like nottin' a-tall."

"Shut up, you fool," Roger said, "and go about your work."

Down near the landing they saw two men in white shirts, their swords flashing in the sunlight. A little group of men stood near watching, and half the plantation slaves were on the river bank.

Cary cursed roundly. "It's Michael, God blast him! How often have I told him he is too ready with his sword!" He strode off down the path, his face as black as a thunder-head.

Roger stood on the steps watching the sword-play. He had been moved to a reluctant feeling of admiration for Cary as he stood before the Council. His words were those of a strong man. It was not easy for a proud, arrogant man to give way. One thing was evident: Cary had been in complete command of the situation from the moment he stepped into the room until he left it.

Foster Tomes went by him, walking swiftly towards the boat. He passed without a word, a look of anxiety on his usually placid face.

Before either Tomes or Thomas Cary got to him Roger saw young Cary lunge forward and Lovyck's rapier make a shining arc in the air before it hit the ground. He saw Lovyck clutch at his arm as he stood swaying before the triumphant Cary.

He heard Thomas Cary's voice, "Have done with your

259

brawling, Michael, and get on the boat. Today we come in peace, not with a sword."

Chapter 21

JOY RULES THE DAY
AND LOVE THE NIGHT

POLLOCK'S voice came through the open door as Roger entered. "He's a rascal, I tell you, as slippery as oil. I put no trust in his smooth lying tongue. Dinna' ye see what he did? He put the Council, aye, and the Governor himself, in the wrong. I say he's fair steeped in iniquity. Curse his black heart, walking in under my roof and laying the silver seal on the table like he was conferring a favour. You'd ha' thought it was his own property. The devil take him!"

"He paid for it," Roger said, a twinkle in his eye at the sight of Pollock's rage.

"Yes, and don't you be thinkin' the seal yours, because you laid down twenty pounds for it."

Roger laughed. He rather enjoyed Pollock when his temper got the best of him. It was then he dropped his English speech, and the burr on his tongue was thick.

"What could I do with the seal?" Roger asked. "Stamp some new land-grants for myself?"

"It wouldn't be the first time that has been done in Carolina," Pollock said gloomily.

"For shame, Tom," Crisp said. "Give the Devil his due."

" 'Twas what I was doing," Pollock said, his anger subsiding.

At that point Lovyck came in holding his arm, leaning on the arm of one of Pollock's house slaves, the blood heavy on his white shirt. He sat down suddenly as if his knees would no longer hold his shaking body erect.

Pollock called for hot water and fresh clothing in a loud, angry voice. Black faces appeared at every door. "Body of Christ! Can't a man get anything in his own house?" he bellowed.

The shoulder was only scratched, for all the blood. Roger soon attended to the wound. Lovyck lay on the couch, shaking violently. Roger carried a certain rancour towards Lovyck, because of what the leet woman had told him. There was contempt in his voice. "God's wounds! I believe Michael Cary has put the fear of death in you."

Anthony raised his heavy eyes. "Dammit, can't you see I've got my ague? Leave me alone, won't you?"

"If that's your trouble, you want a good sweat and a purge. I'll send my man to fix you a tea that will sweat the fever out of you quick enough."

"Go away," Anthony muttered. He closed his eyes. Roger threw a rug over him and went to find Metephele.

By the time his servant brought in the tea, Lovyck's fever was on him. His eyes were glistening, his face flushed. He had dozed off but his lips moved, muttering uninterruptedly. Once he sat up and spoke clearly, "It is my writing arm, I tell you . . . my writing arm."

The Governor stopped his pacing about the room. "The poor lad," he said, his face relaxing a little from the mask he had worn ever since the advent of Cary. "I did not realize he took his work so seriously."

"He's had no holiday this six months," Pollock said, pouring a glass of whisky. "Why don't you take him to Queen's Gift when you go home tomorrow, Roger? That is, if the Governor can spare him."

Hyde came out of his abstraction at the sound of his name. Pollock repeated what he had said.

"Yes, yes, of course. I can make out for a fortnight."

"The lad needs young folk," Pollock confided to Roger after Lovyck had been taken to his quarters by Metephele and his own servant. "One of those fine daughters of John Blount might hasten his healing. I've a mind how my young lads were at his age. Looking about at the maids, and wanting to dance and gad about visiting. It's a dour place here, Duke, with all the womenfolk away. I'll be glad when my wife has had her fill of her family and her Maryland friends and turns homeward."

Roger found no objection to the proposal. They got off to an early start the following morning. Anthony's boxes were packed and in the boat by breakfast time. He made some remonstrance about leaving, with the Governor's work piling up, but Hyde soon reassured him. He had plans of his own. He would work over some ideas he had, to be put before the next Assembly, which Anthony could copy later. The fever was gone but the weakness was still upon him. He lay on the deck of the little sloop and basked in the warm sunshine, idly watching Roger swing the tiller to catch the light morning breeze. The sail flapped dismally, and the two blacks pushed the vessel along with long poles until they got out of the Salmon. At the river they caught the wind and the sails spread as Roger manoeuvred his boat out into the Chowan.

Roger handled the boat skilfully, and with ease—as he did everything. Anthony thought, He is a strong man, strong in body and mind. He would never have let himself into a position where he was not the master.

That brought back the humiliating experience of yesterday. He must have had his fever upon him when he told Michael Cary that he did not like the way he wore his hat on his head. Nor had he liked it when Cary called him a "City cockalorum." I know your kind," Michael Cary said. "London is full of smart young blades who take out in talk what they don't care to put to the sword."

That had angered Anthony beyond telling. Looking back, he must have been secure and self-satisfied. Certainly he had not acted as a polished man of the Court would have done. He had allowed himself to drop to vulgarity. The fever must have been already on him when he said, "I do not like the way you fling grapes into the lap of a young woman of my acquaintance."

"So that's at the root of it!" Cary said, his eyes narrowing. "I've a good mind to slit your foul tongue for venturing to speak of that occasion. On guard, sir! I'll teach you to bring a young woman into men's quarrels."

Before he knew it, swords were out. Never had he been so outplayed before. The humiliation of it was beyond endurance.

"What disturbs you so deeply, Sir Knight of the Rueful Countenance?" Roger's voice broke into his gloomy thoughts.

"My arm pains me," Anthony answered, his face sullen.

"I fancy the fact that Michael Cary's sword pricked your shoulder hurts more than the wound."

Anthony said nothing. Roger went on: "No doubt he felt the same towards me when I disarmed him not so long ago at the Red Lion Tavern."

Anthony's long face brightened. "Did you disarm Cary?"

"Yes, and gave him a slight cut in his sword arm." Roger did not mean to boast of his skill. He only wanted to cheer the disconsolate Anthony. "When your shoulder heals, I'll

262

teach you a trick or two to use on a man who has a longer reach."

"You will? I will be glad to improve. I've had no practice since I came to the Province. I've heard you are a master," he said.

Roger smiled and shook his head. "Indeed I am not, but I was trained by a master. I wish I did him more credit."

Anthony, his mind cleared, lay back in the sun and slept. When he wakened the boat was tacking into the little bay. The white houses of the village stood out from the thin green foliage of the trees. Numerous fishing boats lay along the wharf, and there was activity in the long sheds by the dock.

"They are cutting fish," Roger observed, as he let the sail run. "The herring run is at its peak this week."

Anthony sat up and gazed at the fishermen. They were standing at the long tables, slashing at the fish with long bloody knives, throwing the cuttings into a trough. "What a disgusting sight! The smell makes me ill," he said.

Roger paid no heed to his words. He was watching the men, a look of interest on his face. "It takes skill," he said. "Watch that Indian at this end. Two movements of his hand and the fish is scored, the roe out, and the fish into the vat."

Anthony lifted his eyebrows. He was a little disdainful of Roger's interest in the skill of the lower classes. A few moments later he went down to the little cabin to put on his coat and freshen up. He was smiling as he looked at himself in the glass. His discontent had vanished with Mainwairing's words. Michael Cary had been disarmed, even as he had been, by a more skilful swordsman. Let him watch out. The next time it would be different. He said to himself that he loathed Michael Cary. Devil take him, he would get back at him one day! He went on deck and stood at the bow.

As they made the turn, they saw a strange ship was anchored out by the Dram Tree, the *South Wind*, from Jamaica. Roger observed that she carried a deck gun, and one mast had been shot away. He wondered if this was the ship that had fought the privateer off the Banks.

Roger left Anthony at the Green. He was going to call on Dr. Parris while Roger went on to the Coffee House at the North Gate. When he crossed the upper end of the Green he saw a great press of villagers in front of the long tobacco barn that was sometimes used as a courthouse. He was too far away to see what they were about, but he had an idea that they were up to no good. The villagers, like the rest of the county, were divided in their political affiliations, and riots were frequent between factions.

Instead of going direct to the Coffee House, Roger remembered that he wanted to consult McTavish. The farrier looked up from his anvil when Roger Mainwairing dismounted at the door of his shop. He had stopped to see MacTavish about shoes for his mare. The bay had developed a bad habit of throwing her front foot sidewise, which changed her gait unpleasantly, Roger told the farrier. MacTavish was a grumpy fellow at times, who spoke his mind freely, but there wasn't a man in the county who could equal him in shoeing a horse.

"What is going on down at the courthouse?" Roger asked.

The farrier banged down on the anvil and the red sparks scattered from the blow of his hammer. "They're having a drumhead court—that's what they're doing—and the sheriff's not stopping them. I told Tom the Tinker that I was agin' what they're aimin' to do. I don't care a tinker's dam if the heathen did stab a militiaman in a fight at the tavern. The man's got rights, he has. Every man's got rights to fair trial. But you can't stop them. They're fixin' to tar and feather the fellow and set him loose in the forest to fend for himself, without givin' the law a chance at him."

Roger knew at once what that meant. They had caught the Turk and they meant to punish him in their own way. He stepped to the door and looked across the Green. "Where have they put the man?" he asked.

"The Constable's got him locked in the barn, but he won't be there long. They'll break down the door. Damn them for fools!" he said angrily.

Roger did not wait to hear more. He ran out of the shop towards the barn. Small boys were singing and shouting, dancing around a black kettle which swung over a fire. He made out the words of the song as he neared the crowd.

> "Pitch, tar and turpentine
> Make an awful plaster.
> The more you try to pull it off,
> The more it sticks the faster."

The young devils! He'd like to butt their silly heads together. When he got to the corner he saw Tom the Tinker standing on a stump waving his arms and crying, "Hang the heathen! Hang the bloody heathen! Hang him high as Haman!"

"Can't anyone stop this?" Roger said to a man on the outskirts of the crowd.

The man looked at him, a fanatical gleam in his eyes. "It won't hurt a heathen, tar won't. They got no feelin' in their skin."

Roger pushed his way through the crowd towards the door of the building. There he came across Edward Moseley who was coming from the opposite direction. Moseley's face was white with anger. "We must stop this," he said to Roger. "We must protect the Turk no matter what crime he committed. Do you know what they're going to do? Tar and feather him!"

Roger said, "No telling what a mob will do when it gets out of hand. It may be more than tar and feathers before they're through."

"They're in a mind to hang the Turk. Listen to them now," Moseley said.

The crowd on the Green was shouting and cursing, the noise growing in volume. Some of the older men had pikes and staves in their hands.

"The guards won't be able to hold them back," Moseley said. "I swear I won't allow an unlawful hanging here. I've looked everywhere for the Constable but he's not to be found."

Roger said, "You're the Chief Justice. Talk to them. Make them listen to you. Hold them as long as you can and I'll try to get the fellow out of the barn the back way and into the gaol."

"It's worth trying, Duke. I'll see what I can do." Moseley walked away swiftly towards the crowd.

Roger ran around to the back of the building and pounded on the door, shouting to the Constable to let him inside. After a moment the door opened a crack and the frightened face of the guard appeared. When he recognized Roger he loosened the chain and let him inside, banging the door shut and slipping the great bar into place.

"Where's the Constable?" Roger asked, looking about the cavernlike room.

"He's gone out there," the guard said, "out there." He waved a flaccid hand in the direction of the front door. "Out there," he repeated again, stammering in his fright.

Roger saw he would get no help from the man. "Where is the Turk?"

"Over there in that corner. I've chained him to a post."

Roger took the keys from the guard's belt. The man made no protest.

He found the Turk in the far corner of the room. He was backed against a post, his legs and arms chained. His eyes were glazed and dull. His face was bruised and gashed where a stone had cut him, and the scar on his temple had not healed.

Roger put the key in the lock and released the man's hands, thrusting his shoulder under the Turk's arm to keep him steady while he unlocked the rusty gyves that bound his ankles to the post. The man was ready to drop of fatigue.

"Move your legs a little to bring the blood back. Can you walk?" Roger said. After a moment he was able to move.

"In a moment," the Turk said. "I feel life in them again."

Roger said, "Keep moving them. I want to see if there is anyone in the rear of the building. If it is clear, I am going to try to get you up to the gaol where you will be safe from the mob."

"Mr. Mainwairing, you are very kind. But do not expose yourself to danger."

Roger said, "Do not worry about me. Think of yourself. You are the one who is in danger."

He walked quickly across the loose board floor and cautiously unbolted the door that opened out to Queen Anne's Creek. Two sturdy guards, one on either side of the door, turned quickly when he appeared, and pointed their muskets at him. They dropped them to their sides when they recognized Roger Mainwairing.

The crowd was occupied on the Green. Roger heard Moseley's voice, but he could not understand what he was saying. The path to the creek was clear. At the foot of the steps was a small landing place, and several row boats were tied to the piling.

"I'm going to take the prisoner to the gaol," Roger said to the guard. "Have a boat ready to cast off when I come out. Keep your muskets ready to cover me if anyone comes around the building."

"Do you want that we go with ye, Mr. Ma'n'ring?" one of the guards asked.

"No, I don't think so. I believe it would be better for me to take him alone. Be ready. I'll be out in a moment."

When Roger went back the Turk was walking about, stamping his foot softly on the floor. "Come," Roger said. "We've no time to lose."

He threw his cloak over the man's shoulders to conceal his torn clothing and they went out together. Roger helped him down the steps, for the Turk's legs were stiff.

"The first boat," the guard said, closing the door after them. "Best make haste, sir. No tellin' when someone will come down the road."

The Turk got in and crouched in the bottom of the skiff. It was wet and had an evil smell from rotting fish. Roger took the oars and pushed off. He saw two men come around the corner of the barn. A guard challenged them, his musket held against his shoulder ready to fire. "Stand back," he called sharply. The men protested, but the other guard ran up to reinforce his comrade. Using his musket as a club, he set the men running.

Roger glanced over his shoulder as he pulled upstream. The intruders had disappeared. No one had noticed their flight save an old Negro working his mule on the opposite bank of the stream, turning the earth for summer planting.

Roger pulled the boat briskly. It would be well to go some distance upstream, he thought. He would leave the boat, cross the fields, and come back in the rear of the gaol. He must get the Turk safe inside before the crowd undertook to batter down the doors of the barn, if Moseley was not able to hold them.

When they had rowed some distance upstream, he pulled across the stream to shore. He put his hand under the Turk's elbow and helped him out of the skiff. Walking was hard for the man. He was weak and exhausted, and the gyves had cut into his boots driving the rough leather into the flesh. They encountered no one. Most of the village was on the Green by now—some to make trouble, others to prevent it.

"I gave the cylinder into the proper hands," Roger said as they made their way across a plowed cornfield.

A slight smile came to the Turk's lips. "It is well," he said.

"I hoped you had made your escape and were well out of the country by now."

"I got away on a boat, but there was a sea fight off th⸱

267

Banks and the ship had to put back into the Sound to escape the pirates. The boat is in the harbour now."

"I will see that you are defended at your trial," Roger said, when they had reached their destination. "If you had not been taken by the law, I might have hidden you and helped you make your escape, but now I have no alternative."

The Turk nodded. "You are kind, Mr. Ma'n'ring, but it is of no use. I shall die if it is my time. That is the will of Allah."

Roger did not reply. This was the Turk's faith and his firm belief.

The turnkey let them in and led the Turk away to a cell. When he returned Roger gave him money to get food for the prisoner.

"He will be safe now," the man said, pocketing the coins. "I have locked him in a cell by himself, next to the witch woman, Susannah Evans!" He gave Roger a toothless grin. "They're afraid of her, they are. No one but me goes near those cells." He touched a charm that hung from his neck and ambled away.

Roger walked down the street to the Coffee House. The room was deserted. He ordered whisky and drank it off quickly. By good fortune he had the man out of harm's way. He felt certain the mob would not go so far as to storm the gaol. He had ordered a second drink when Moseley came in. He had his hat in his hand and was mopping the perspiration from his forehead although the air was cool. He sat down at the table, his long, thin legs stretched out before him.

"It was close," he said, after he had drained the cup of toddy the boy brought to him. "Too close for comfort. Tom the Tinker was burning for a hanging. The crowd was burning for a tar and feathering, and I was burning to uphold the law." He laughed mirthlessly. "The court will hang the man, that's certain," he said, "but it will be by legal process, not by the will of a mob."

"What court?" Roger asked.

"I don't know. He may come under the Admiralty Court, if they prove he's a pirate as they are saying. Then Porter will get him, because he was on a ship. You know Porter. He has an eye on the fees."

Roger was thoughtful. It had not occurred to him that the Turk belonged to the pirate ship. "I am going to employ Gale to defend him," he said.

He felt Moseley's keen dark eyes on him. "Why do you do that, Roger? It will cost you something."

"I know that. You lawyers have your methods of gouging a man. I don't know why I have this idea. Perhaps the Turk is my responsibility, now that we've saved him from the mob; or perhaps it is because I also believe that every man has a right to trial. Have it any way you will."

Moseley smiled at him and leaned forward over the table. "Of course you do. You and I, Roger, can't escape what we are. Our ancestors were at Bury St. Edmonds and at Runnymede. Our kind of folk have held to their rights ever since that time. No man arrested and tried without a jury of his peers. That alone should make us forever proud to be Englishmen."

Moseley sat looking out of the window, his glass in his hand. The crowd had gone from the Green. Roger thought of all the men in the Province Moseley held the broadest view of what lay ahead.

Roger took up his hat and went over to the doctor's house, a block down King Street beyond the Green. He rang the bell. The doctor himself opened the door. Roger said, "Will you look in the gaol tonight? There is a prisoner there—a Turk. He has some cuts and bruises that need attention."

Parris looked at Roger. A slow smile crossed his fine-wrinkled face. "So you're the fellow?" he said. "I might have known you'd have a hand in the rescue."

Roger's answering grin was a little embarrassed, but he made no admission. "About the reckoning," he said, "I'll stand for it. I don't think the poor devil has a tuppence."

The doctor asked him to come in. "One of those rascally fellows of mine will bring tea presently," he said.

Roger declined. He wanted to be home in time to see what his men were doing with the north field.

"By the bye," the doctor said, "I am keeping Lovyck here a few days. He needs rest and nursing."

Roger inquired, "Is he ill?"

"No," Parris answered. "Ague. But I want to look after him."

Bidding the doctor good-bye, he rode down the street to the East Gate.

Roger saw Lady Mary and her groom trotting along the River Road, her blue velvet skirt flapping against the sweating flank of her horse. He touched his mare lightly with his spurs and overtook her near the bridge.

She flashed a smile over her shoulder and pulled her horse to a walk to wait for him.

Roger's hand closed over hers. "Mary, what a pleasure. I was sunk in dejection, thinking what a sorry world we live in. Then I find you."

She laughed aloud. "We were well met. For two days I have been talking to a barrister on legal matters and my mood was alternating between anger and boredom, and then by chance I look over my shoulder to see—"

"Your lover, your devoted and eternal lover."

"Do not use the word lightly, Roger. There was a time that I could say it easily, but not now." She leaned across her horse and touched his hand. "I have been thinking of you so much these past days," she said.

"You did not answer the letter that I sent you."

"I know. I did not feel inclined to set my thoughts on paper. The things I have to say to you must be said when we are together."

A cart, pulled by a mule, came into sight. The blue-smocked farmer looked at them from under the wide brim of his hat and smiled. Roger waited until the cart jogged down the road and turned into a lane, hidden by the hedge.

She said, "I want to kiss you, Roger. No, no, not now," she laughed, when he pulled over until their horses were side by side. After a pause, she said, "You are quick to take fire."

"You kindle fire," he answered. "You know how to drive a man to madness."

"Is it madness to love?" she asked as they rode on. "Is it madness to live again?" She turned to him. The expression on her face was profoundly sad. "We have talked little of ourselves, Roger. We do not speak of what has gone before. That is right, I think ... because living began for me when I saw you that first night."

"And for me, Mary. When you look at me—when you touch my hand—something goes from my heart to you. ... There have been women—"

She laid her fingers to his lips. "Let us not speak of other women—or of other men. That is the past. We are alive now, and we love."

Roger drew a deep breath. "Let us gallop. If we don't I shall—"

"Scandalize my groom?" she asked, laughing now.

They rode on to the gate of Queen's Gift. Roger said, "Metephele will give us tea."

Lady Mary said, "That would be nice. I want my tea, and it is another five miles to Greenfield, and too, I have a woman's curiosity about Queen's Gift."

Roger was quiet when they rode up the long tree-lined drive. He lifted her from the saddle, holding her an instant before putting her down.

She stood for a moment looking about her before they entered the house. What she saw pleased her, the house and the garden and the broad expanse of the Sound at their feet. Roger had little to say. Lady Mary glaned at him once or twice, puzzled by his changed mood.

Roger opened the door to his library and stood aside while she entered. He called Metephele to bring tea, and followed her into the room.

She raised her arms slowly to take off her hat—her lithe figure outlined against the window behind her.

Roger wanted to put his arms about her. But that must wait. Metephele came in with tea. Lady Mary sat in an elbow chair. She talked lightly of inconsequential things as she poured tea from the squat silver pot. Metephele served the bread and butter and carried a cup of tea to Roger.

He spoke sharply to Metephele in his own tongue. The *capita* left, closing the door behind him. Roger set down his cup. He crossed the room and took Mary in his arms. His passion for her flamed in his eyes. The words she would have spoken died under the pressure of his lips.

After a time Mary released herself and straightened her hair. "You are very strong," she said, her eyes meeting his in the mirror, "very strong. You make me forget." She tried to speak casually but her voice shook.

He watched her, his eyes sweeping the long line of her body. The look in his eyes made her turn to him.

"Roger," she said, "you care for me so much?"

He did not seem to hear her question, although his eyes remained fixed on her. He got up from his chair and stood before her. He laid his hands on her shoulders. "I have seen you here in this room night after night when I sat alone. A thousand times I have imagined you walking from room to room, bringing life to this house, meeting my need of you with your beauty and your passion." His hands slipped from her shoulders down the curve of her breast to her waist, his strong fingers closed on her wrist. She followed him across the room and into the hall. "I will show you the house," he

271

said. "Come, let us go upstairs before the sun sets." He spoke to Metephele as they passed him on the way upstairs.

Roger opened the door to his room. Her eyes swept over it—the great canopied bed, the divan near the long windows that opened on the upper gallery.

Roger closed the door and came toward her. His figure darkened the light from the window and the world outside. She could no longer see the green of the waving treetops or the placid waters of the Sound, turned to crimson by the last light of the sun. She could only feel the strength of his lean, hard body against her and the passion in his eyes.

They walked out on the gallery. They stood for a long time without speaking, lost in the vibrant, moving silence that belongs to lovers. Dusk had fallen; the fireflies made little points of light in the fragrant darkness of the garden. Roger's arm was about her shoulders.

Mary turned to him. "I must think of the long ride home," she said.

Roger tightened his arm about her until she was close against him. "Not tonight, Mary. Tomorrow you will ride away. Tonight you belong to this house and to me."

Down in the Quarters a drum was beating and the slaves were singing a happy song at the end of the day. Mary turned her face so that her cheek rested against Roger's shoulder. "It is good to live again, Roger—to live and find love."

Chapter 22

MIGRATION

THE sun was well toward the zenith when the slaves, who were in the south field chopping May peas, stopped their work and, leaning on the long handles of their hoes, looked fixedly at the sky.

A heavy cloud was showing above the pine trees that rimmed the south shore of the Sound. The Negroes watched the black cloud anxiously, talking among themselves.

It was late for a seasonal blow, and there was no feeling of hurricane weather in the air. The light wind that was blowing came from the west, not the direction from which a hurricane could be expected.

Marita, seeing them shout and point upwards, galloped over to the field on her black mare, Blenheim. She found the women frightened, preparing to throw down their hoes and run for shelter as they did when a big wind came. The men kept their eyes fixed on the cloud, but they were uneasy. Marita had been long enough with blacks to know how frightened they became at the time of some natural phenomena. She remembered their fear at a quarter eclipse of the moon— a mass fear that was contagious.

She began to feel the unrest. If it were a seasonal storm, they would rush to close shutters and openings in their huts, battening down anything that would blow, chasing fowl and young biddies into their huts along with the children and the ancients.

Instead, led by an old woman, they dropped on their knees in the field, the children close beside them, their dogs crouched at their feet. Facing the rising cloud, they raised their hands toward the heavens. The old woman began a chant, a supplication to their unknown gods. The others joined, clapping hands to keep the rhythm.

"Ko-Kwe-Ko-lo-le
Ko-Kwe-Ko-lo-le
M'bvula-ya kuno
Si-Ku-dza
Ko-Kwe-Ko-lo-le."

("May there come a sweeping rain, Sweeping down.
The rain has been restrained, Sweeping down.")

Blenheim pawed the earth, his ears erect, his nostrils quivering. He reared his head, sniffing the air. Marita felt helpless and a little alarmed. Once or twice she called to the leaders but they did not hear her. She had turned to ride to the house for help when she saw Watkins galloping across the field on the grey mule. He was shouting and waving his arms.

"Pigeons, pigeons! Run to quarters. Get brooms, cloths, anything to keep them from coming down."

"Njiwe, njiwe!" they cried, looking into the sky.

"What is it?" Marita called, racing along after Watkins.

"The migration, passenger pigeons. Millions and millions of them. I've sent the Negroes for brooms and cloths to wave

273

above the rows. If the birds settle down they will ruin the young grain and the peas."

"What will we do?" Marita said in despair.

"Get in the house and close the windows. The smell of them isn't nice, and their droppings cover the whole earth."

He galloped on to the stables. A moment later the plantation bell began to ring violently, calling in the herd boys and the hands from the lower fields.

Excitement had entered the house before her. Shutters banged, maids rushed outside, gathering in clothes from the line and covering the iron kettles. Lady Mary was coming down the stairs. "What in God's name does this mean?"

Marita told her. "What will we do?" she cried. "We will lose all our crops! 'Millions,' he said, 'millions of passenger pigeons flying north.'"

"Be quiet, child. It won't be your death if you do lose a few rows of peas."

"But the young grain—" Marita wailed.

They ran out on the gallery. All the house servants were there. Miss Mittie was looking at the sky with a spyglass. She handed it to Lady Mary. The birds were flying high, still far to the south, but the cloud was spreading.

The plantation bell rang again, sharp, quick sounds. Marita ran into the office. There was a card on the wall with the signals recorded. Watkins was calling for the boys to house the cattle. When she went back to the gallery Lady Mary was seated in a chair gazing through the glass at the sky. Desham hovered about, alternately wringing her hands and crying. "It's a sign, a sign sent from heaven! A warning from God himself. Oh, why did we come!"

"Quiet, you brainless fool," Lady Mary said.

Watkins galloped up the drive, his mule covered with lather from hard riding.

"What are you going to do about it?" Lady Mary asked the harassed man.

"I'll have fires built around the outside of the grain field and set the slaves to work waving cloths and brooms. We may keep them from lighting here."

"How long will this keep up?"

"I've seen them fly for three days and three nights, your ladyship—so many of them they hide the sun and the moon."

He spoke to the mule and galloped off towards the fields

where the Negroes were gathering around with brooms, limbs of trees and long pieces of calico. Marita saw little fires starting up along the edges of the field where the tender young grain was just showing.

Marita stood without moving, a sinking feeling at the pit of her stomach. The birds were a menace, even a scourge, like the biblical plague of locusts. She went into the house, out to the kitchen building. There she found the house servants in a small group standing near the well, watching the sky.

"Cover the well," she called.

"Kikichina has already covered he," one of the Negroes said. "Missy want me go to the fields?"

"Yes, all but cook. She must stay to cook food and make tea for the workers."

One of the older men came over to her. "Three days and three nights, missy, bird droppings come out of the sky like rain." He ambled off to the quarters.

She went around the house and met Captain Zeb hurrying up the walk. He had brought his men along. He knew what it meant, he told her. Had he not seen thousands and thousands of rosy flamingoes and snow-white egrets on an African lake, tramping down young plants, seeking for worms?

"What can we do to keep them from flying down?"

"Dunno, nothin' more 'an Watkins done. Might fire a big cannon into the air, if we had a cannon." Then he added, "They look for water. They might make a landing near our Sound."

"Oh!" said Marita. Again the sick feeling hit her at the pit of her stomach. "Oh!"

Captain Zeb patted her arm. "Now don't you give up yet. There's things in nature ye jes' naturally got to take as they come. A big wind, or a hailstorm, or big waves piling up on the beach." He squinted up at the sky. "They're getting closer. Mighty soon they'll fly across the sun. Better get under cover. You won't like bird whitewashing."

"But my crops?"

"Come, come! If you're a proper farmer, you've got to be a farmer. A wind can flatten the corn, or too much rain rot it at the roots; or if you plant in the east wind the worms will eat it."

"I know," Marita said disconsolately. "I prepared myself for all these things but not for birds."

The old fellow laughed. "There is one thing you overlooked. Pigeons make an extra good potpie—most as good as green turtle."

But Marita was not to be comforted. While she was looking at the migration with the glass a great din rose in the fields. She ran to the edge of the gallery. Some of the Negroes were jumping up and down waving brooms and streamers of cloth, branches from trees, while others were beating on pots and pans. A moment later a deep booming filled the air.

"Good," Captain Zeb shouted. "They've got out the big drums." He turned away towards the fields. The birds were overhead now and the sky was growing darker. A cock began to crow.

"I told your ladyship," Desham cried, "it's a sign from heaven!"

"Go in the house, woman, and light candles in my morning-room," Lady Mary ordered. "Call me if anything else happens, Marita."

Miss Mittie laid the glasses on a table. "I wouldn't object to going out to the field, Marita. I could put on a Holland coat, and a big hat and veil." She screwed her little wrinkled face into a smile. "I never have had a chance to make a really big noise," she said. "I think I'll ask cook for a pan. I'd like to beat a pan and scream as loud as ever I wanted for once!"

Marita laughed. She too wanted to beat a pan or a drum, and join the noise-makers.

Lady Mary refused to stir. "Shout and yell as much as you like. It will loose your pent-up feelings. As for me, I have none to release, no energy or emotion."

Dressed in riding doublets and boots, covered with a Holland dust coat, Marita put a wide seaside hat over her hair and tied it down with a veil. Miss Mittie was lost under an old beaver of Cavalier vintage which had belonged to some former occupant of the house. She, too, covered herself with a dust coat. Her fine-wrinkled face was bright with colour and her eyes shining. She pulled on a pair of heavy gauntlets.

A small Negro boy brought a pan and a lacquered tray. Miss Mittie chose the tray as giving out the louder sound.

Bright fires were burning along the length of the fields, small Negro children were carrying sticks and limbs of trees to stoke the fires. The whole field took on a strange pagan look. The fires lighted up the dark faces of the Negroes, catching the whites of eyes and gleaming teeth. Many of the women had their heads bound in bright calicut. They had cut holes in tow sacks to admit their heads, which gave them a strange, formless look.

Captain Zeb was horrified when he saw Miss Mittie and Marita coming across the field. "You can't stay here." He spoke to Marita, but his eyes were fixed on Miss Mittie "Bye and bye it will smell to make you disgorge. You'll be sick of the odour of birds and feathers. Bah! You can't stand it."

Miss Mittie smiled at him. "I want to stay. I want to strike a big gong and make a great deal of noise."

"God love the woman, what is she saying!" The Captain was aghast at Miss Mittie's words. "So small, to fit under a man's arm, yet she cries to make a noise like an Ashanti warrior."

"I am not going to the house," she said. "I shall sit down under that little shelter by the fire and beat this tray until I frighten all the birds in Christendom."

She walked over to a small shelter made of four poles with the branches of trees forming a roof. She sat down on a stump and began to bang. Captain Zeb sat on the log, stretching his bad leg out in front of him. "I find myself weary," he said. "I think I'll have a pipe and spell ye when your little hands get tired beating that plate."

Marita smiled as she looked at the ill-assorted pair, but they were oblivious of her and of the moving figures of the Negroes. The giant, Ebon, near by, had straddled a big drum and was rubbing out a heavy warning swell of sound. Marita walked over to the old man, so intent on his drumming. The black children crowded around him, keeping the rhythm with their thin swaying bodies.

"What do you call it?" she asked, indicating the drum made from a hollow log.

"*Ng'oma*," he said, without pausing or changing the rhythm of the beat. "*Ng'oma—Koka*—the big drum."

"*Ng'oma*," Marita repeated. "*Ng'oma*." The word had a musical sound. The drum was larger than any she had seen when the slaves were dancing. The drumheads were stretched over both ends of a hollowed log, held in place with pegs. The rim of skin was rolled above them. The Negro rubbed the vibration from the drumhead with the heel of his heavy black hand. It seemed to her that the vibration came from the ground, not from the drum itself. When she stood near the drummer, the sound was not loud. Yet one could hear it for a long distance—several miles, the drummer told her.

The Negro looked up at her, his white teeth showing in a broad smile. "*Ku omba ng'oma*," he said. "To beat the drum."

Marita tried to phrase after him.

The man nodded his head, smiling broadly. The little children chanted, clapping their hands in unison: "*Ku omba ng'oma—Ku omba ng'oma!*"

Marita smiled also, caught up in their laughter. How carefree and gay they were, these dark-skinned people. How quick to break into laughter!

All about her they took up the words, singing and shouting with laughter until the whole field rang with their merriment.

"That is good, Miss Marita. A song always helps the slaves. It makes them forget they are tired." Marita turned about. Watkins, the overlooker, was smiling at her through his begrimed face. Through the night he was everywhere, directing the slaves. Marita found him beside them again hours later. He pointed towards the east. A faint streak of light lay above the horizon.

"It's almost dawn. I don't believe the pigeons will come down in the daytime." He turned his horse and rode along the field, with a word of encouragement for each group of slaves.

Marita slipped away and sped to the house, out to the kitchen. She roused the cook, who was asleep in a chair near the ovens. "Tea," she said; "make a great kettle of tea."

The old woman nodded toward the hearth. "Hit ready, miss. Tea and corn cake. I'll call Matt and young Eb. Dey carry the kittle to de field."

She clapped her hands and two half-grown black boys came from the woodshed, rubbing their eyes sleepily.

The cook put the lid on firmly and packed a big basket with little hard corn cakes baked in the ashes.

Marita followed, stopping only to drink a cup of tea. When she returned to the field Captain Zeb had set the kettle under their shelter and was ladling out tea with drinking gourds the Negroes produced from somewhere.

The sun came up over the horizon. It was good to see the red glow and the ball of fire giving light after the hours of darkness. The birds were flying high, still a dark cloud in the blue bowl of the heavens. There would be light until almost noon, the captain said. She would take Miss Mittie and go home so they could snatch a little rest, a few hours at least. "How long will they be migrating?" she asked the Captain.

"God knows," he said, getting up stiffly. "God only knows, two days—mayhap three—there must be millions of them."

"I wonder where they came from and where they are going?" Marita said, looking out at the flight from the shelter.

"I don't know where the birds are going, but I'm going to bed." Miss Mittie stood up, flexing her wrist. "I haven't any feeling left in my arm. If I have to beat the gong all night again tonight I'm going to get some sleep now."

"You're a strong, brave woman," the Captain said, making a stiff little bow.

A faint flush crept over Miss Mittie's face. Marita wondered if any man had ever complimented her before in all her long life. "Thank you," she said in a low voice. "That was very nice of you."

The second night went by, and the third day began, without cessation in the great migration. If they could only pass this third night, it must come to the end. Not one of the slaves could remember a flight that lasted longer than three days.

Marita wondered once or twice what had become of her Indians. She could not remember having seen either of them since the first day. Perhaps they had gone away in the forest hunting. Quis-la-kin sometimes stayed away two or three days at a time but Kikitchina seldom was gone more than a day.

It was almost sundown of the third day when she noticed she could make out the wings of the birds. It took her some time to realize what this meant. They were flying lower. Did it mean they would settle down in their fields?

She looked for Watkins. He and the Captain were looking at the sky. No need to call to him, for he had seen. She heard him shout, "Get to the grain field. Let this one go." She saw what his intention was—to place all the slaves around the grain field. The peas and small cornfields would have to be sacrificed. She turned away and walked to the house. She remembered what they had said: "They are likely to come down at sunset."

Lady Mary was seated in the morning-room with windows closed. Desham was walking about the room carrying a shovel of hot coals, from which rose the pleasant odour of spices.

"I thought we could try to clear the air," her aunt said, as she appeared in the doorway. "It's been like sitting in a fowl coop for the past three days." She looked Marita over with her china-blue eyes. "I think a good bath and a fresh gown would probably help."

Marita nodded. There was no need to tell them that the flight was winging its way down to earth. They would know soon enough.

She bathed and put on a fresh cotton frock, with little sprigs of gay flowers sprinkled over it. She was braiding her tawny hair into a flat coronet when Kikitchina knocked lightly and came into the room.

The Indian woman was dressed in the skin dress she wore in the woods, with moccasins on her feet. She made no explanation for her absence. She came across the room to the dressing-stand where Marita was sitting and laid a folded paper on the table. Marita's hands dropped to her side. She recognized Michael's writing. Her heart beat violently and her hands trembled.

"Where did you get this?" she asked the Indian woman.

"Atonga brings. He waits by the fishing place for answer."

Marita broke the seal. "It has been overlong, but there was no way to come sooner. My boat is in Yaupim Creek, well hidden. My Indian will show you the way. At sunset."

She sat for some moments without moving. Then she raised her eyes to the Indian woman who stood waiting. "Tell Atonga I will come."

"No more?" Kikitchina asked.

"No more."

The woman left the room silently. Marita sat looking out of the little window toward the Sound. The flight had changed direction. The sky directly over them was almost clear of birds. In the west the colour flamed and deepened against the whirl of fluttering wings flying downward.

Michael was waiting for her at the end of the lane. Her pulse quickened at the sight of him. He did not touch her hand, but the look in his eyes gave the greeting she wanted. When she was away from him, she was assailed by doubts and fears. When she was near him, they slipped away and became nothing.

"I have a boat here," he said, guiding her along the narrow path that led down the bank to the sandy shore. They made their way across fallen logs. The pine needles crushed beneath their feet. When they came to the water, Marita saw that Kikitchina and Quis-la-kin were in the skiff with Atonga. Michael looked at the Indians, raising his eyebrows. "You have brought your guard," he said.

Marita didn't tell him that she did not know they were coming.

"Maybe it is better," he said after a moment. "Come, let me help you across."

He lifted her lightly as if she were no burden, and carried her across the shallows to the boat. Atonga threw a cloak over the seat in the prow and Marita sat down, Michael facing her. He said something to the Indians in their own language, and all three of them took up oars, Atonga standing, using his oar as a sweep.

The water was smooth, almost without a ripple, so quiet that the reflection of the trees along the bank lay clear green upon the water.

The migration was thinner, and there were bits of blue sky to be seen. No birds were flying over them; their flight was farther north now. The trees cut her vision so Marita could not see whether they dipped toward her fields or not. She did not care. She could think only of Michael sitting before her looking at her.

"It is a night for lovers," he said, dropping his voice. How warm it was. It enveloped her as completely as though he had put his arms around her.

"I am your lover, Marita. In all my life I have never given thought to a woman as I have to you."

"Oh, Michael," she said, quickening to his words. "Oh, Michael, I love you so much, so very much. But I know it is wrong."

"Why is it wrong? I will marry you. I swear it; as soon as I come back from the Indies. I will have gold then. We will build a house in Bath Town on the water. I have found the place—across the river from the village. A point of land, with great trees, where one can look down the river and see nothing but the water and the trees."

Marita sat with clasped hands, listening raptly to Michael, looking with his eyes into the future. He was strong. How could she remember her fears when he sat close to her? His strong face turned to her. His firm, hard body had likeness to the trees that grow in deep soil. He had the strength of the vast out-of-doors and his own hard living. She had never s a stronger man, except Roger Mainwairing, and he was old—in his thirties. ... She closed her eyes, afraid that she would show too plainly where her thoughts were straying.

"Don't!" Michael said, laying his brown hand over hers. "Don't close your eyes. I like to look at them, and your lashes. Never before have I seen anyone with lashes that were bronze and ivory."

"My grandmother's eyes were like mine," she said. "My aunt told me. Men wrote sonnets to her lashes." She laughed, a little embarrassed under his unfaltering gaze.

"I have no facility with my pen," he said regretfully. "But I can defend you with my sword."

"Michael, oh, Michael, you must not, you must not say things to shake my resolve."

He threw back his head and sat erect. "Marita, nothing can come between us. Nothing! I have made up my mind. I shall take you away from here. Why should we stay? We can sail to St. Kitts or Antigua or Jamaica. We will buy a land by the blue sea; or we could take a salt cay. You would not mind living far from neighbours, with me?"

"I would follow you to the end of the world, Michael, if it were right. But it is not right. The wall is too high." She did not say to him that she knew her aunt would not let her marry him. Lady Mary had other plans.

"'I am a ward,' she said, when he did not speak. 'I cannot marry without the consent of my aunt.'"

He swore a round oath, fit for a men's camp, not for a woman's ears. He was so quick to anger. "She would have you marry a cockalorum like Lovyck, I suppose. I wish I had run my sword through his silly body instead of pricking his shoulder!" His fingers closed on her hand with such force she could have screamed. "I won't let him have you, the pale-faced scrivener."

"Don't, Michael. You hurt me," she said.

He dropped her hand quickly. "I'm sorry," he said sullenly.

"Anthony is my friend," she said after a long silence.

Michael was not listening. He turned to the Indians. "Atonga, swing the boat sharply and nose it into the pocosin along the black water of the deep swamp." After a time they came to firm land. "We must walk a little now, across this neck to the river."

They moved along a narrow path in the gloomy shadows

that were cast by the tall cypress trees, Michael walking before her, pushing vines and briers aside. In a short time they came to the river.

A trim ship with tall masts and furled sails rode at anchor where the river flowed into the Sound. Michael cupped his hands, shouting. A moment later a boat put off.

"I want you to see the *Willing Maid*." He could not keep his pride out of his voice as he looked at the trim beauty of the barkentine. "It is my uncle's boat, but I own a share in her, and I am to sail her and be her captain."

"She is so large!" Marita exclaimed. "As large as the ship in which we sailed from England."

"She is staunch and seaworthy. She could sail in any ocean," he answered proudly. "Come, we will go on board. I want you to see the ship. Can you climb the ladder, or shall I have the men sling a chair over the side?"

Marita laughed. "That is for old men or admirals. I will go up the ladder."

The sailors looked curiously at Marita when she walked across the deck. Half a dozen seamen were busy with the brasses and the ropes. One man with black, scraggly hair, and a dark, bold face, touched his cap. "The gear is stowed in the hold, sir."

"Did you get the salt fish loaded?" Michael stopped to inquire.

"Aye, sir. The fresh-water cask is filled and stowed, sir."

"Right. You can portion out the grog to the men, Diego."

The sailor touched his cap. Marita saw he had two long scratches along his swarthy cheeks.

Michael threw open the door to the little cabin on the forward deck. He stood aside. "Enter, mademoiselle," he said, with an exaggerated bow. "Enter the world of Michael Cary."

Marita looked about the compact little room. The panelled walls were lined with charts and maps; two chairs and a heavy table made up the furnishing, with the exception of a berth built against the wall.

She walked across the floor to look out of the open porthole. Bat's Grave, the small wooded island beyond the mouth of the river, was framed by the opening. It lay like a green jewel in the tawny water. A boat with a lone oarsman caught her attention. She wondered who it was that fished so close to the haunted island. Roger had told her that it was guarded by the restless spirits of an Indian girl and her white lover, avoided by the people who lived near its shores.

Herons were flying low over the water, and a few pigeons straying from their flight. Over the island two eagles hung suspended in the air, motionless, as if caught in the great solitude of approaching night.

She heard the door close. Michael crossed the room. She turned to meet his enveloping arms.

A few moments later there was a knock at the door. Michael dropped his arms and called, "Come in."

A slave carrying a tray with tea came in.

"On the table," Michael said briefly.

Marita had not moved. When the Negro came into the room she turned and looked out the porthole. Their brief moment had passed.

Michael went with her to the spot where the Indians waited in the boat. He took her hands in his. "I want you to promise me one thing: that you will come back tomorrow. Here at this spot, in the morning early, before midday."

Marita hesitated. How could she get away without their knowing at the manor house?

"You will come," he said, watching her face. "You will come because I need you. Do not think I am afraid to go to your aunt and speak to her. But I am not free until this journey is finished."

He lifted her chin with his fingers so that her eyes met his. "You will come? You will give me the day as my own?"

"Yes, Michael," she said. "Yes, I will come."

The canoe moved swiftly through the darkening water. It was almost dusk when they landed on the sandy shore at the foot of the lane. She walked quickly towards the manor house, her Indians behind her. She noticed that the woman carried a string of fish, as if they had been down at the nets.

Subterfuge was foreign to Marita but she made no protest. Lady Mary would lock her in her room if she knew. Michael had only one day more before the long journey. She would go. A few hours together and that was all. She had forgotten Lucretia. She had forgotten the young green fields, smothered and flattened by the beating wings of the passenger birds. She had forgotten how terrible Lady Mary's wrath could be. What did it matter? Tomorrow was Michael's.

She walked swiftly, almost running, never noticing the birds that lay in the path, the small weak birds that had not strength to stay with the flight.

Chapter 23

GOD GAVE
THE DAY

THE companionship of the trees quieted Marita, as she sped lightfooted and sure along the narrow path which skirted the pocosin.

She had slept little the night before. Twice she had risen from her bed, without a shawl to cover her thin shoulders, and sat before the open window. Elbows on the wide window ledge, she watched the midnight stars. After a time Kikitchina, whose ears were as sensitive as a forest animal's, slipped into the room and covered her with a bed blanket. "Better the bed at night," she said, as she wrapped Marita's bare feet in the corner of a blanket. "Better to sleep and dream."

Marita could not. The happenings of yesterday came between her and the oblivion of sleep. Michael, tall and proud, standing by the river; Michael's penetrating blue eyes questioning her; the steady beat of his heart under her cheek, as he held her against him; Michael, strong-willed, asking her to come to him. "What is one day out of all the days?" he had said. What did he mean? Were they to have only one day that belonged to them? She was numb with anxiety and dread as she thought of his words. Why had he made himself so dear to her, so necessary to her happiness, only to leave her?

A dozen times she told herself that she would not go back to his ship, yet when the morning came she knew she must go. She must see him to set her mind at rest. She would say to him aloud the fears that beset her when she was away from him. Did he love her? Or did he think of her as of some wanton girl, ready to throw herself into his arms?

When she awoke at sunrise she found herself lying on her bed. The Indian woman had carried her there in the night. Now it was day, and with the light came all the old fears. She wanted to go to her aunt and tell her about Michael, but she dared not. If Lady Mary did not know, she could not forbid her seeing him.

Her aunt would not be out of her bed for hours. Marita wrote a little note saying she would be gone for the day. She was taking the Indians to fish up the river. "Perhaps we will have sturgeon for supper!" She added the line as an afterthought. It will look natural, she argued to herself. Then she won't worry about me if I am late getting back.

She was really clearing the decks, making ready to fight. The thought terrified her. She had never once in all her life gone against her aunt's wishes. But even this thought did not halt her hurrying feet.

She liked the early morning. Sometimes when she rode down to the water a deer would raise its startled head and look at her a moment before it leapt into the tangle of the thicket; or nesting birds rise from the trees; or a hare scuttle across the path. Once she had seen a bronze gobbler spreading its wings before it made its awkward flight. The air was soft with the fragrance of spring. The sky was cloudless and a wren sang in the high branches of a tupelo, as if to burst its little heart with joy.

She came to a little pool of dark water where the Sound had cut deep into the swamp. The shadows were deep and cool, for the sun had not yet slanted down through the dense crown of the trees. Suddenly she stopped. Almost overnight the dogwood had bloomed, great clusters of waxy white petals, set against the deep green of the forest. A cardinal bird flashed by, paused for a moment on a myrtle bush growing on the rim of the blackwater. Marita stood motionless, but the bird only lingered a moment, then skimmed its jewelled way into the deeper shadows of the forest.

The sight of the flowers made her remember it was May Morning, the day in Sussex when lads and lassies carried May flowers in little baskets and hung them on the doors of the cottages in the village. At night they danced Morris dances around the beribbonned maypole.

She would carry May flowers to Michael to dress up his little cabin. Standing on a log half sunk in water, she broke a branch of dogwood. A hoarse croak, followed by a heavy splash, frightened her for a moment. She laughed aloud when she saw the pop-eyes and the green body of a bullfrog.

She hurried on, carrying the great sprig of snow-white blossoms in her arms. Her wide hat had fallen back on her shoulders, held by the long brown ribands, and her tawny hair lay in soft curls about her neck.

Michael saw her coming down the narrow path between the pines. She came to him swiftly, her wide skirts fluttering, a little smile on her lips, carrying the great branch of white blossoms.

"I would to God that Sir Godfrey could paint you as you are at this moment, in your yellow gown, your arms filled with alabaster flowers."

"Wouldn't you rather have me than a piece of painted canvas?" she said, trying to appear at ease. But her heart was beating too swiftly. "Oh, Michael, I have brought you May flowers as a Sussex lass brings flowers to her lover on May Day."

When they reached the river bank she saw that her two Indians were there ahead of her, sitting stoical and silent in the little boat.

"Your guard of honour again?" Michael said, turning his head slightly.

"Do you want me to send them away?"

"No, it is better this way. They can row us up the river. I want to make a call on a friend this morning."

A little disappointment clouded Marita's amber eyes.

Michael laughed a quick, joyous laugh, that made her laugh also. "After that we will go for a sail in my boat," he promised, as he would a child.

"But, Michael, I don't think I should go on the boat again." She was remembering the almost unbearable emotion of yesterday.

"You may take your slaves," he said. He lifted her up and carried her to the boat.

"Careful of your flowers," Marita warned.

"I'm being very careful," he answered. He raised his voice and shouted. A seaman, evidently waiting for Michael, came down the beach. Marita saw that one of the ship's small boats was pulled up on the sand.

"Take these and have Ramon put them in the ewer in my cabin. Tell the cook I will not be back for dinner, but we will have guests for tea. Let him do something extra." He laughed as he gave the order. The sailor touched his cap and carried the flowers to the little boat, holding them as if he thought the task beneath him.

The two Indians knelt in the prow of the canoe, their paddles dipping, first one side, then the other. They were looking ahead, their black eyes focussed on some distant point upstream. Marita was in the stern, while Michael sat in the bottom of the canoe, his broad, firm back touching her knees. The high banks were covered with wild grape vines and little thickets of bay and drooping willow, the soft yellow green of early spring clear-cut against the heavy blackness of pine and cypress. A quiet stream, solitary and still; deep running water, without ripples.

"It is as if we were going into a world where no one has ever been," Marita said. Michael turned his head a little. She could see his profile now—his straight nose, the strong, lean jaw, and the sweep of his heavy brow.

"I wish I could say we were," he said, "but I'm afraid we will come to the road to Nansemond before long, and the little inn near the ferry."

"Oh, I don't want to see people!" she exclaimed. "Must we go?"

"No, my dear, we will stop short of the inn. But it has its uses, you know. I've sent Atonga up there to have them pack a basket of food for us."

"Michael, you think of everything!" she exclaimed.

Michael did not answer for a moment. When he spoke his voice was low and quiet. "I never want to forget anything that will bring you happiness."

She laid her hand on his shoulder and kept it there. It was comforting to feel his nearness. Perhaps it would help her to remember in the long days ahead.

They came presently to a little clearing in the wood. There was a small float in the water and a landing place. Michael gave some order in the Indian tongue, and the canoe pointed towards the bank. Michael stood up, pulled the canoe against the float, and stepped out. "Step from the middle of the canoe to the float," he warned her, as he steadied her with his hand. Marita balanced herself and made the float without mishap.

He led the way up the steps cut in the bank to the clearing above. She saw a little log house in the mist of the trees, so diminutive, so neat and fresh, it seemed almost a play house. A path bordered with green bushes led to the door.

"This is the path we take," Michael said, walking toward the house. The door opened at his knock, and an old slave looked out. He smiled when he saw Michael.

"Master says to step inside. In a little while he will come

from the ferry." He went off moving slowly, his back bent almost double.

Michael stood aside for Marita to enter. She looked about curiously. The house had only one room. Its floor was of earth and there was a great stone fireplace at one end. A table scrubbed white stood near a window. A wooden bench by the fire hearth and one by the table made up the furniture, with the exception of a bed built of saplings held together by braided rawhide. On the table lay an open Bible. A small candlestick with a half-burned candle was beside the book.

The windows had no glass or paper to cover the opening. But withal the room was spotlessly clean. Marita saw the old slave stirring something in a kettle set over a little fire, not far away.

Michael led her to the bench by the fire hearth. He loosed the ribands that held her hat, took it off and laid it on the table. She felt his hand on her hair for a moment, a tender caress that made the pulse quicken in her throat.

Michael did not sit down beside her. Instead he moved about the room restlessly. Yet she felt at peace—a strange, almost positive peace, in which there was no thought of the morrow. The day was enough with its bright spring beauty.

After a time he crossed the room and stopped in front of her, looking down, his eyes pleading. "Marita, there is something I want to say to you now. Please hear me through until I have done. This house is the house of a Friend, James Thurlow. He is an old man, who has travelled afoot through this whole land from Massachusetts Colony to the Carolinas, preaching the doctrine of the Friends. When he returns I want you to stand up with me before him, and repeat the words the Friends say, to make us man and wife."

Marita heard his voice from a great distance. Her world was whirling about her. How could she speak, tell him that she could not do what he asked? She could not do what he asked for it would hurt her aunt too deeply. She seemed to be thinking with two minds at once: one with great clarity which told her that she could not—could not; the other with no clarity, no will, only a blinding love for the man who stood before her.

"Don't, don't look that way," he said, catching her hand. "Marita, do not think me a coward because I have not gone to your aunt and asked her for you, as I should. There are reasons which I can't tell you now. You must trust me." He

289

raised her hand and held it against his heart. "You know I love you," he said. "Do not sit there so white and still. Marita, answer me."

"Yes, Michael, I know."

"And you love me?"

"Yes, Michael."

"Then there is no other way out. All last night I walked the deck of my ship. I could think only one thing. You must be my wife before I leave. Without that I cannot go away or fulfill my man's word." He sat down and put his two hands before his face. After a time he turned to her. "A man's word means something, and I have given my word to take my ship to the Indies and bring it home again with a cargo. That I have promised on oath to do before another day goes by. I gave my promise willingly." He got up and began pacing the floor again. "That was before I held you in my arms yesterday. I knew that you were dearer to me than anything in the world—anything—"

"Michael, you must not set me before honour. The good God might hear you and strike you down!"

They were silent for a long time. Sounds came to her: the old man stirring the kettle, scraping a spoon against the iron sides; a bird singing a small faint song, trying his newly found voice. A boat scraped against the float and she heard steps on the wooden planks. She saw a thin man with long white hair coming up the path. He stopped a moment and bent down to look at a small flower growing near the walk. His face was seamed and brown, but it was a good face. When he stepped into the room she saw how kind his eyes were, candid and steadfast. He stood at the threshold looking from one to the other, a kindly smile on his lips.

"Thee has brought her to me, Michael," he said. "When I look into her eyes I find her worthy of thee."

Marita's heart swelled, tears rushed to her eyes. Worthy of Michael—pray God that she would be worthy of him! She put out her hand blindly. Michael's strong fingers closed over hers.

They moved over to the table where James Thurlow stood, his thin hand touching the pages of the Holy Word. The old slave shambled into the room and stood at the door wiping his hands against his leather apron.

"Friend Marita, say the words after Michael." The words came from a long distance rushing towards her, enveloping her. "You are here in the presence of God and his word." The old man's voice died away.

Michael's voice, firm and steady: "I, Michael Cary, do take this maid, Marita Tower, to be my loving and lawful wife, promising to be a true and faithful husband unto her, till death do us part."

There was a long silence, and the old man's gentle voice: "Repeat after Michael."

She heard a woman's voice saying: "I, Marita, do take this man, Michael Cary, to be my loving and faithful husband, and I do promise to be a loving and faithful wife, until death do us part." It was her own voice that said the words. Marita Tower had promised, had given her word.

The preacher was writing something on a little slip of paper. The old servant was making a cross on it.

Her knees trembled, and she groped for the table to steady herself. Michael took a golden chain from his neck, where it lay concealed under his leather jerkin. It had heavy links, and a jewelled locket swung from a clasp. "My father gave this chain to my mother," he said. "I want you to wear it all the time, day and night, and let it bind you to me."

"Her words have made that bond," the old man said. "And yours to her."

The old Quaker gave the strip of paper to Michael. He looked at it a moment; then folding it into a small space, he placed it inside the locket. A moment later he lifted the chain and clasped it about her throat. It lay heavy, with the jewelled locket against the curve of her breasts. She looked up then. Michael was watching her, his eyes tender. He leaned down and placed his lips against her forehead.

They ate their wedding breakfast under the great sycamore at the edge of the bank, waited on by Atonga and Marita's two Indians, with the old servant hovering in the distance. The hamper of food from the inn was adequate: cold chicken and mutton, and a deep-dish pie of apples, drowned with fresh milk.

The old man lifted his glass. "God gave the day and God will take it away. To your long life together! To your happiness," he said, "under God's love!"

Marita felt Michael's hand closing over hers as she bowed her head.

Michael stood up. He was in haste now to get to his boat. "We will sail across the Sound to the head of the Alligator River. There will be time." Marita followed him down the

291

path, turning to wave farewell to the kind old man, standing in the doorway.

The journey downstream was swift, with the current. When they came in sight of the barkentine, the swarthy seaman with gold rings in his ears was leaning over the side. Seeing Michael, he shouted some order. A moment later the ladder was over the side.

"Let the Indians come aboard and be fed in the forecastle."

Michael said to the mate, "Get under way. We will sail across the Sound, to the Alligator Point."

Marita stood at the rail, her eyes on the widening strip of water. She was conscious of canvas flapping as the seamen ran up the sails. Michael stood beside her, his hand firm and strong over hers. After a brief time they were in the river current, abreast of the wooded island of Bat's Grave. She saw a boat close by them, and a woman standing at the bow, poling with a long sweep. A great staghound was crouched in the bottom of the boat. Marita remembered. It was the girl she had seen on Muster Day in the Balgray forest. The leet woman, someone had told her, the daughter of the witch woman they held at the gaol in Queen Anne's Town. The girl's eyes were fixed on her with almost savage intensity. Marita turned to Michael. His face was dark and he cursed under his breath.

He took her arm and guided her away from the rail. The boat was listing a little as it swung to catch the down-river breeze.

"You had better sit down," he said, pulling a canvas stool toward the wall of the cabin. "It may be a little rough as we cross the channel." He moved off down the deck, raising his voice to shout orders to his mate.

A moment later, Marita heard the woman's voice calling to one of the seamen. "You lied to me, Ramon! You said you couldn't bring a woman aboard this ship."

A man's voice answered forward. Marita could not catch his words.

The girl's were clear enough when she replied, angry and filled with scorn: "You lie. I saw a wench of the afterdeck, talking to your brave Captain!"

Marita felt her face crimson. Now the whole village would know that she had sailed in Michael's boat. There was nothing she could do about it. When Michael returned she showed nothing of the fear the girl's angry words had caused.

292

"The wind is coming up and the air is chill," he said, drawing her to her feet. He put his palm under her elbow to steady her as they crossed the deck to the cabin.

The faint perfume of the flowers met them as he opened the door. A cloud of white blossoms spread from a copper bowl onto the dark wood of the table. All the long years after, the scent of spring flowers and the pale alabaster of dogwood brought him back to her, the light in his eyes as he closed the door and took her in his arms.

Chapter 24

HANGMAN'S NOOSE

ON SATURDAY, Roger sent Vescels into the village to bring out supplies. A slave drove the high, two-wheeled cart, and the overlooker led a saddle horse for Anthony Lovyck.

Anthony had quite recovered from his ague and the shoulder wound was healing properly. He was full of talk about the village. He had been at the Coffee House playing at dice and cards, and lost aplenty. There was much talk about the escape of the heathen Turk from the mob, but no one knew who it was that had spirited him away. Some of the low class believed he had been helped by the witch woman, Susannah Evans, who had turned herself into a black cat and guided the Turk out of the warehouse through a chimney.

"The chimney was wide enough," Anthony said soberly. "I examined it and measured the breast with a rule. A man could have escaped that way readily enough."

"By the aid of a black cat?" Roger asked, slightly amused by Lovyck's earnestness.

"That I don't know," Anthony replied. "I wouldn't like to encounter the woman unless I wore a charm against witchcraft and all evils."

Before he caught himself, Roger said, "I hope you had the same charm in your pocket when you encountered the woman's daughter."

They were seated in Roger's study at the time. They had finished supper, walked along the shore for a mile or so, then settled down for an evening of talk, and perhaps a game of chess later. At Roger's words Anthony looked up from the wineglass that he had been holding to the light. He set the glass on the candle table carefully. He did not speak for a moment, but a slow flush crept up his cheeks, showing the shot had gone home.

"I did not know I was infringing on your preserves," he said sulkily. "It was but an impulse of the moment—a pretty wench, and a lonely spot."

Roger kept his voice even, although he felt his anger rising at the implication. "The leet woman is nothing to me. Nothing at all except that she is a poor creature, hounded by ignorant men because she has the misfortune to be the daughter of a woman whom our courts have branded a witch."

"I didn't know she was the woman's daughter! She might have put evil upon me—"

"Don't worry, the girl will not harm you or leave a scar. It appears that she sought sanctuary on my land, and sanctuary she will continue to have as long as she remains." He paused a moment, allowing the words to sink in, before he got up and pulled the bell cord. "I'll have the chessboard brought in," he said in a normal tone. "I feel lucky. Perhaps I can beat you, to make up for last night's defeat."

They were still at their game when Metephele came in with the light supper he usually served his master around midnight. Anthony was winning and his usual good humour had returned. A toddy of rum, and the two men said good night and each took up his lighted bed-candle.

Roger did not undress. He felt restless and in no mood to sleep. He picked up LeBlond's quarto volume on gardening which Moseley had sent over to him. But the print kept fading between his eyes, and his mind kept wandering to the plantation. He had been away too much of late. Things were getting out of hand. The rain had held up seeding corn in the south field. The May peas were ruined when the migration settled down on the field. Vescels had told him it was the best crop they had had in years. The young beans also, but that was farmer's luck, or bad luck. His mind wandered off. He intended to get some indigo plants the next time he was at Ashley River. If they could raise it down there he saw no reason why he couldn't have success in the Albemarle. That would be another money crop. He could use the cut-over land, near the lower cornfield, for the experiment.

He got up and walked to the window. It was dark. The moon was in the first quarter, but heavy wind clouds were racing across the sky. He stepped out on the upper gallery. He could hear the soft lapping of the water against the bank at the edge of his garden. In the far distance a dog barked. It made him think of the leet woman, with her great hound. He wondered whether she was roaming about the forests, or whether she had found another sanctuary.

Once he had thought of speaking to Lady Mary about the girl. Perhaps there was something he could do—take her in, give her some training so that she could find a place in Virginia. He wondered who owned her. He must ask Moseley.

Lady Mary. He tried to avoid thinking about her, because he found he could not think clearly where she was concerned. No matter what his resolves, the thought of her persisted, standing between him and the path he must walk. Tonight he faced that thought. What had he to offer Rhoda? Any less than he had had before? Or would he have more to give her, because he had found himself capable of a deeper emotion than he had experienced before? He wanted no situation to arise of which he was not master.

He did not know how long he had been on the gallery, thinking of the problems that had arisen to complicate his life, when he heard the plantation dogs barking sharply. A few moments later a horseman galloped up the drive and ran up the steps at the side entrance. He heard a sharp rap on the knocker, followed by a door opening and Metephele's voice, "Who is there?"

"One," Roger heard a Negro answer, "one has arrived."

Roger walked quickly to his bedroom. A messenger at this hour of the night boded no good. He met his slave running up the stairs, a paper in his hand.

"Mr. Moseley sends slave. Brings *Kalata*."

"Give me the letter," Roger said. Holding the twisted paper near the light from the candelabra, he saw it was sealed with Moseley's crest.

"There is trouble in the village. I've had word that a mob is attempting to break into the gaol. The Turk, I suppose. I'm leaving at once with my men."

That was all Moseley had written, but Roger knew it was an appeal. He strapped on his sword belt while he gave orders to Metephele. "Get my pistols; see that they are ready. Have Primus raise half a dozen of our best fighters, and get the horses saddled."

"Fighting spears?" Metephele asked, his eyes gleaming. "The master goes forth to battle."

Roger laughed shortly. "Arm yourself. Pikes will do, or whatever you want."

Metephele had already left the room, running down the stairs, his long, white robe flying. Roger smiled grimly. He would have six good fighting men by his side tonight.

When he was at the landing a door opened and Lovyck put his head out. He had his boots on and was thrusting the tail of his nightshirt into his breeches. "I'll be with you," he said. "Have you extra pistols?"

He galloped down the drive, Anthony abreast, Metephele and his men close behind. The horses knew the way to the village even in the dark. They needed no guidance. Once they reached the main road they settled down to a long, swinging trot that ate up the miles.

They were splashing through the upper ford of the creek when Anthony saw the glow of fire in the west. "What's that?" he shouted, calling Roger's attention.

"Good God!" Roger's voice carried across the water. "I'm afraid we're too late."

The horses quickened their stride. The North Gate was open. No sentry opposed them as they galloped inside the stockade.

At first Roger thought the fire was at the gaol. As they neared the commons, he saw it was beyond. The air was heavy with the acrid smell of smoke. They saw flames leaping between the trees, and sparks scattering. Men were running along the road carrying lanterns. Here and there he saw the glint of firearm or sword.

A man shouted to them as they rode by, "They've got them surrounded at the Red Lion." He recognized Will Badham's voice.

"Where's the fire?" another voice called.

"A tobacco warehouse," someone answered. "The girl set it afire. It's witchcraft. I saw the fire flash from her fingers."

Roger cursed aloud. The leet woman again. What was she doing here, getting herself into more trouble?

They had come to open commons. Across at the north end a frame building was blazing, throwing a fantastic glow on the dark moving figures. Militiamen were trying to hold back the crowd with bayonets. He saw other riders. In the glow of the fires he recognized Smythwick and Beasley. A moment later he came up to Moseley.

"We're too late," Moseley said, his voice hoarse with anger. "They've run them both up on a gibbet . . ."

"Who?" Anthony cried, his voice shrill with excitement. "Who?"

"The Turk and the witch woman. God blast their souls, they've hanged them without process of law. They've set us back fifty years."

Roger saw that Moseley wasn't concerned with the poor wretches who were swinging on a gibbet. He was outraged only with the lack of process of law. "Who is responsible?" Roger asked.

"We don't know. The mob, wearing vizards, broke into the gaol. They took them out, and brought them here. They had pulled the ropes before the marshal got here. See, there they are."

The smoke drifted with the changing wind. Roger saw two dark figures hanging limply from the gallows tree. Anger surged over him. He had no time to question further before the marshal and a deputy rode up.

"We've got the leaders inside the tavern. They've barricaded the doors."

"Why don't you go after them?" Moseley's voice was sharp. "You've got them surrounded, haven't you?"

"Yes, but I've not enough men."

Roger put his horse over to the marshal. "I'll go after them," he said, dismounting.

"I'm with you!" Anthony cried.

"Good fellow," Roger returned. "Metephele and his men will batter down the front door. Stand ready to rush in, Lovyck." To the marshal he said, "Is the back entrance covered?"

"Yes, we've a ring around the place."

"Then find some heavy sills over there." He pointed toward the gallows tree. The Africans ran to get the timber to use as a battering ram.

"Cover my men with your muskets, while Lovyck and I make the door," Roger said to the marshal. "Anthony, take your place against the side of the house near the door, out of range of the windows. I'll take the other side of the door. Pistol primed?"

"Yes, and sword loose in the scabbard," Anthony said briefly.

Roger saw he was cool, and his hand steady. "Good fellow," he said again.

Roger crouched low and ran across the intervening space, flattening himself against the logs at the right of the door. Anthony followed as Metephele and his men rammed home the great log. Roger noticed they carried heavy knobkerries in their belts, but Metephele had a stabbing spear in his right hand.

The heavy oak door stood the first onrush. The second did more damage. On the third thrust a lower hinge gave way. Roger heard a window back of him open. He wheeled, ready to use his pistol. A scream followed his shot, and the thump of a body. The next few moments were confused. He could never quite remember what happened. He found himself inside battling with a dozen men. He used his second pistol on a man levelling a musket at Lovyck. His men were inside now, shouting and yelling and laying on with their stout clubs. Anthony fired his pistol and whipped out his sword. Metephele was loading for Roger. The men were pouring in from the back of the house while the marshal's men were smashing at the door. One man picked up a heavy oak chair and hurled it at Roger. He went down with a crash. His pistol went off as he hit the floor. He saw the ruffian fall.

"All out!" the leader shouted. "Grab horses!"

That was all Roger remembered. When he came to he was at William Badham's house, lying on a couch. He sat up; his head felt light. The doctor came in from the hall. "Lie down, Roger. You had a nasty blow on your head." Roger put up his hand and felt a bandage.

"I'm all right," he said. "Did they get them?"

"Some of them; but the leaders got away."

"Know who they are?"

The doctor shook his head. "No. Strangers, the marshal thinks. Drovers, no doubt, or some of those rascally border people."

"I'm glad it wasn't Tom the Tinker," Roger said, getting to his feet. "I'm getting fond of that rascal. I'd hate to have him gaoled for murder."

Moseley came into the room. "Nobody can identify the dead men," he said briefly. "Your man Metephele got the one who was about to shoot you. He slung that spear of his clear across the room and pinned the fellow against the wall. He

298

died screaming imprecations against the witch woman and her brood."

Roger said, "We must be going. Where's Lovyck?"

The doctor said, "I've sent him to my house. That wound broke open again while he was fighting. I'll have to catgut it."

"Better stay here the night, Roger. It's raining hard." Will Badham said. "We've room for you. Moseley is staying."

Roger shook his head. He had other things to do which he did not mention. "I'm going on to Queen's Gift," he said.

The doctor said no more, knowing Roger.

Metephele and his boys were waiting with the horses. Roger rode out towards the North Gate. At the head of the commons, he wheeled his horse. "Let your men wait at the stockade," he said to Metephele. "You can follow me."

They rode across the commons to the gallows tree. The fire was still burning, not flaming now, for a steady rain was falling. A few guards, silhouetted against the glow, moved back and forth. The people of the village had returned to their homes, sent there by the marshal and his men.

No one had troubled to cut down the two corpses. They hung, limp and desolate, lighted by the fading glow of the fire. The wind had risen, blowing the body of the Turk, giving an almost lifelike movement to the thin legs.

Metephele hung back. *"Mankwala,"* he said in a sibilant whisper. *"Mankwala,* Master."

"Get out your charms," Roger said. "I'm going to cut them down."

The rain beat against his face as he made his way to the gallows. He knew Metephele was close behind him; no matter what his fears, he would follow his master, for that was his code.

"Look for a ladder," he said. "There must be one here. Perhaps they carried it over to the tobacco barn."

Metephele moved away and was lost in the shadows.

Suddenly Roger heard someone sobbing. Deep, soul-racking sobs. He walked over to the second gallows. Crouched at the foot, he made out the figure of a woman, her arms clasping the limp, lifeless feet of the witch woman. He did not need to see her face, or hear the growl of the dog, to know who kept vigil that night.

He spoke quietly. "Do not weep. She is better off. Life had nothing for her."

299

The girl sprang to her feet and stood defiant, backed against the frame of the gallows.

"It is I, Roger Mainwairing. You need not be afraid. Speak to your dog, I don't want him at my throat."

"What do you want?" she said angrily. "Can't you leave me be alone with my dead?"

"I will take her down," Roger said. "Where are you going to put her then?"

"I have a place," the girl said, "a place where she can lie."

Roger threw his cape over the girl's shaking body. "First I must cut down the Turk."

"Why do you do that? Are you a werewolf? Do you devour bodies of gallows birds?" Her voice rose shrilly.

"Be quiet woman. Don't speak nonsense. I will bury the Turk on my own land, so that he may rest in peace, according to his belief."

The girl quieted then.

Metephele came back carrying a ladder. Together they cut the rope, the fine slick rope that had tortured the doomed man. They laid him out on the damp ground.

"Wait, I will cut down the woman," Roger said.

Metephele held the ladder while he mounted, the Negro uttering strange words, protecting himself and his master from evil.

"Carry the Turk across your saddle," Roger said. "Ride directly to Queen's Gift. Set the men to digging a grave in the burial lot. He must face the east, for this is his law."

"Yes, Master," Metephele said, relief in his voice. He did not mind carrying the dead man. It was the woman who had strange powers.

The girl had wrapped her mother's body in her cloak. Roger was glad that the darkness hid her poor swollen face from her daughter's eyes.

He carried the corpse to his horse and laid it across the front of the saddle, easing himself into the seat, so that the limp body lay across his knees. The girl did not move.

"Step on that pile of planks and get up behind me," Roger said.

The girl did as she was told without protest.

The dog lifted his head and howled, a long, dismal wail. "It is her soul, seeking rest," she whispered. He felt the girl's thin body tremble.

So they rode out of the village through the North Gate, Duke Roger, the leet girl, and the woman who was hanged.

Chapter 25

QUEEN ANNE'S
LACE

SUMMER came. Queen Anne's lace grew tall and rank along the roadside, and spread its lacy white bloom on hedgeways and pasture land.

The June moon was a wet moon. Seeds rotted in the ground, and corn planting was late. The first hot weather brought a plague of small insects in the swamps.

Roger Mainwairing found sickness among his slaves. Their ague came on them and they lay ill "of the bed" in increasing numbers. He opened his dispensary at the manor house and ordered every man jack of them up to be dosed with bitter milk, made from camomile flowers and ginseng root. Those that developed coughs he dosed with honey and butter. And those who were too ill to come to the great house, he visited at the quarters line.

When the doctor could not come out to Queen's Gift, because of the run of sickness in the village and the near-by plantations, Roger took a lancet and let blood, to try to cure his sick people of the fever.

The blacks were afraid of blood-letting, and it tested Metephele's hold over them and the fear of the overlooker's whip to get their consent. Sometimes Roger called in the Ancient One, and allowed her to make a protective *Mankwala*, while he performed the minor operation of bleeding them.

With all his care he lost five field men and one good breeder. Other slave owners fared worse than he. Moseley and Vaile and Frederick Jones, who had bought Smythwick's plantation near the village, doubled his score, and Porter's Sandy Point people were almost in a panic over the scourge.

Roger worried. He had heard that smallpox was raging in Virginia, along the James River plantations. Seamen had been taken off the ships in dying condition, and the plague could easily spread to the Albemarle either by ship or by the travellers between Williamsburg and Queen Anne's Town.

The doctor wanted guards set at the main roads leading from Virginia: the road to Somer Town, the road to Nansemond, and Norfolk, and the road along the Great Dismal. He brought his plan before the Council when they sat early in June, but he could not obtain the consent of the members. "A scourge is the will of God," Reid said, and others concurred with him.

The Governor was not too interested. His mind was concerned with legislation he had urged passed in the spring Assembly. The reaction had not been what he expected or hoped. People complained that he was throwing his power against the Quakers and toward the Church party, and the long-hoped-for peace and amnesty were again threatened.

This was a bitter disappointment, for much had been expected of Hyde's administration. "He is a good man," Moseley told Roger, "but he is under Pollock's eye and you know what that means. All the old hatreds will blaze up and we will be no better off than we were under the 'bad Governors,' or the time of the Culpepper Rebellion, when Culpepper and Durant and Captain Gilliam threw out Governor Miller and Governor Eastchurch, with the help of Valentine Byrd and Thomas Relf."

The idea of watching the borders for pox victims did not take hold, and the doctor worried along, taking care of those sick with ague and fever, and the new babies.

In the town there was fear that a doom was upon them, cast by the witch woman and the heathen Turk. Had not Tom the Tinker seen her, with his own eyes, spirited away in the black sky on a bolt of jagged lightning? The commonfolk believed him. When he first told his tale at the Two Penny Club, half the members were afraid to go home that night until they were fortified with double their usual allowance of small beer or rum.

The tale grew with each telling until now it was a village legend. It was not only the lower class who believed it, but many better balanced people carried their witch charms when they walked out at night. Even those who scoffed remembered that the body of the woman Susannah and the body of the heathen had disappeared from the gallows tree in a thunderstorm. That was in itself something to give pause to the bravest. Everyone knew that no villager would touch the body of a witch, even after it had swung for hours. As for the Turk, He had not a friend in the country to step forward to claim his lifeless body for burial.

Roger Mainwairing had heard this discussed many times in the Coffee House and at the homes of his friends. He said no word of the carefully concealed grave at Queen's Gift which faced the east and the Mecca of the Turk. He did not know where the leet girl had taken her mother. When he wanted to help her the girl had opposed him so vehemently that he did no more than place the corpse in the small boat she had hidden in the lower swamp. Nor had he seen her since that night more than a month ago. He had thought of her more than once, kneeling in the frail boat, the body of her mother beside her as she paddled swiftly from the shore. It was like an ancient lay or Viking tale—the girl with her bleak white face, in the early light of false dawn, the rain beating her wretched garments close to her body. Desolation was in her pale blue eyes, despair, and some other thing he could not fathom. Was it the fierce flame of revenge?

It was the busy season now. The loss of his early crop through the passenger pigeons was almost forgotten. New seeds were sown. The young cotton was up. Today Vescels had sent half his people to chop in the north field. Roger rode along the path towards the water. The wind had swept the water far out. Tomorrow he must send men to clear up the hidden logs and staubs, so that boats could get to his float without danger of having their sides stove in.

Roger had not been to Greenfield for some time. He had made up his mind to stay away. He had come to that decision the day he had a letter from Rhoda, in answer to the one he had written early in the year. She wrote:

"Do not think of coming to England for me. I have about determined to go out to Jamaica to be with my brother Thomas. I will stay at his plantation for a time. Then I will come to the Albemarle or perhaps you will meet me at Charles Town?

"I have taken your acceptance of this idea for granted. I have already shipped my horses and some pieces of furniture that your aunt is sending to you from the Old Queen's Gift, a table or two, a dozen stout chairs, and a beautiful escritoire that belonged to your mother. Your aunt told me that it was presented to her by King Charles, and it was willed to you. These pieces went out last week on the *Dra Castle*. My grooms and a stable man will look after the three hunters. They told me at Mr. Lloyd's office that the ship would stop first at Virginia, but since it is a small boat of light draught it will then proceed up the Albemarle Sound to Queen Anne's Town.

"I do not know how far you may be from the village, but I have asked the officer to send a messenger from Virginia so that you will know when my hunters arrive."

A postscript followed:

"I shall stay with Tom three months at least. That would bring me to the Albemarle about Christmas or the Twelfth Night season. If this plan does not suit you, will you write to me in care of Tom at Ravenwood plantation, Kingston, Jamaica? I will not take it ill, Roger, if you have changed your mind. It has been a long time since we have seen each other—almost three years. You and I are civilized people and we can make adjustments. For that reason I think we can make a success of marriage, without that first passionate emotion which belongs to extreme youth."

After this letter there was no need for Roger to concern himself with the decision whether or not he should go to England. It had been decided competently by Rhoda. He smiled a little when he had finished the letter. He had an idea that it would always be that way from now on. Rhoda would arrange matters of his household, and perhaps his life, cleverly and completely. This was not a disturbing thought. Roger was a little weary of an empty house. He could not always rely on his neighbours for entertainment. Moseley was often away—his wife was at her father's home, waiting to die. He knew he was welcome at John Blount's, at Christopher Gale's new place, Strawberry Hill, or at half a dozen houses in the village. But these did not answer his need. He wanted a home. A wife and children were something to think about in the long, lonely evenings.

He shouted for Metephele to have a horse saddled. He would ride to Greenfield.

Roger swung into the saddle and trotted as far as the gate, when he saw Edward Moseley coming down the road. He pulled up his horse and waited, knowing that Moseley was on his way to Queen's Gift or Mulberry Hill. "Coming in?" he called, as Moseley drew nearer.

"No, I'm on my way to Blount's, but I'll ride with you if you are going that way."

"That far and beyond," Roger answered, putting his horse abreast with the other. "I'm on my way to Greenfield. I haven't been down for some time and I want to see how my student farmer is progressing."

"And play a game of piquet with her charming aunt?"

304

Roger laughed. "I might be persuaded. Why don't you ride with me? Is the Mulberry Hill visit important?"

Moseley said, "No, not particularly. I wanted to talk with John before the next Vestry meeting."

Roger glanced at him. He recalled the rumours in the village that there had been trouble in the Vestry over some plate which the Society had ordered for the Church and that members had gone so far as to say that Moseley had received the money, but no altar silver was forthcoming.

Moseley looked up suddenly and met Roger's intense gaze. He smiled wryly. "Yes, yes, I know. They're saying in Queen Anne's Town that I've taken the money."

Roger, being a forthright person, said, "Why don't you blast the lie in their teeth, Edward? There are a lot of scandal-mongering people around here that deserve to be set in the ducking stool or have their ears cropped."

Moseley's saturnine face took on a look of despondency. "I can't blast the lie. That is the answer."

Roger said, "Why not? I could never believe that you have stolen Church money, or any other money."

"Thank you, Roger. It cheers me to have a good word now and then. Between the Vestry trouble and Pollock on my heels for Cary's misdoings, I'm in a fair way to lose heart."

"Come now, tell me. Sometimes it eases one to speak out."

Moseley did not answer at once. Roger knew he was turning the idea over in his mind. He was a cautious man, never one to go off hastily. After a moment his face cleared. "You are right, Roger. Sometimes it eases a load to speak out to a good friend. There was a sum of money sent out from London by the Archbishop for the purpose of buying the plate for the chapel. But it was not sent to me, nor was it in my custody at any time. It was sent to my wife's first husband, Henderson Walker."

"Oh!" Roger whistled. "So that is the story!"

"Yes, and when his effects were settled that sum was not accounted for. I am trying to get enough cash together to send to Boston to buy the silver and have it made up to design." He gave a wry grin that made his thin face sardonic. "You know what it is to get hold of any sterling."

Roger knew. Every planter was in the same condition. Land and produce, but no money to speak of, unless they were fortunate enough to own paying shares and stout investments in England like John Blount.

"You can understand why I can't stand up in meeting and explain, can't you?"

Roger understood. A man couldn't very well say that the money had disappeared while it was in the hands of his wife's first husband, especially when that man was dead and bore an honoured name.

"I knew there was some good reason, Edward. You may have some strange political views, but I'd never question your integrity. I'd let you have the money myself if I had cash at hand, but I'm rather strapped until I realize on my tar this autumn."

Moseley laughed. "I heard you paid Cary for the silver weight that is in the seal. Isn't it a slough of despond when a Governor hasn't the money to pay for a seal of office?"

"Or a government," Roger added. "That's even worse. We ought to sell land rights, as Byrd does for Virginia. We might get something in the treasury."

They rode on in silence, each busy with his own thoughts.

"I look forward to the day when we'll have a stable government, Roger, but somehow I'm disheartened. Perhaps it's my own depressed thought that colours my feeling. I had great hopes in Hyde."

He pulled his horse to a walk. They were approaching the manor house at Mulberry Hill. "I've fought to get Albemarle on a sound footing. We can never hold our place until we quit this haggling and backbiting. As we stand, it's every man for himself, and a devil's tattoo for the rest. Sharp-toothed unkindness, instead of the milk of human kindness—that's our way. Each man fights his own fight, with his fists or his sword, according to his station in life. I tell you, Roger, we must have law to settle disputes, not each man to his sword, or by bell, book and candle."

They had reached the gate. Moseley reined his horse to a stop. Roger did likewise. Moseley was looking at him with a deep burning light in his eyes. "The English common law is our basic law. It is elastic enough to last this New World for centuries to come. I hope I see it evoked here in my time." He laughed shortly.

"Don't you think Hyde sees it that way?" Roger asked.

"I'm afraid not. He is too close to the Crown. He is more the Queen's Governor than the Lords Proprietors'. Hyde is

306

bred in another school of governing than I have in mind, Roger. Divine right of kings and party rule of the ministers. Playing one faction against the other. I am more interested in the rights of men, through courts of law."

Roger said, "The Governor will be at Greenfield on his way to Virginia. Why don't you come with me and talk to him. I think he has an open mind."

Moseley said, "Perhaps I will when I finish the business I have with Blount."

He turned his horse and galloped up the long cedar-lined drive to the manor house. Roger watched him for a few moments. Whatever others said of Edward Moseley, he knew him for an honest man, sincere in his desire to be of service to the Province. Politics brought an assortment of queer companions and strange ideas. Perhaps the radical Moseley, as Pollock called him, was right, and the rest of them were wrong. Perhaps he was looking ahead, while they held back, digging their heels into the soil, serving with their stubborn strength but inaccessible to reason. Pollock was a grand, good man, honest and upright, but not flexible. A stalwart Scot. And such men were needed to give depth and strength, as a broadsword, to this great new adventure in government. But the other kind was necessary also, the men fused of keen rapier steel, flexible and bending but not giving way.

Roger sighed as he rode through the forest. He understood Moseley's problems. In a way they were his own, only his were of the land, not of government. To get the planters to see beyond their own acres, towards the future of the land, was what was needed here—men who had the long view. Until that time . . .

He put spurs to his horse and galloped down the narrow road, lined with tall white spikes of Queen Anne's lace. Enough of problems of land and corrupt government. If only stiff complacency could be conquered, they would go forward, reaching out to the future as men of first quality should, instead of hanging to a feudal past.

At Greenfield he found other guests had arrived before him. Captain Zeb met him near the gate. He had walked up the lane from his place to take the air. "The Governor and Tom Pollock are inside, and that young sec'tary. Miss Marita wants me to come to dinner, but I've no mind to eat with great folk."

"Why not?" Roger said. "Why not come for dinner when a lovely young maid invites you?"

"I've a far better notion," Captain Zeb said, with a twinkle in his eye. "I'm going to get the cart and carry Miss Mittie down to my place to eat a fine dish of green turtle and rice I've cooked special."

"Oh, so that's the way the reeds fall?"

"That's the way, as far as Zeb Bragg's concerned. But I've not got around to letting the lacy know yet—mayhap never will fetch up the courage to say the word."

"Nonsense," Roger said, trying not to smile. "Nonsense. A man who has your record for killing Barbary pirates certainly has the courage to speak to one woman."

"I d'know. Anyway, we're to come back later. It seems they want to know about me being took off the Morocco coast by the pirates. But I told Miss Marita I never told that story unless I had a punch, a good strong punch made of proper rum."

"I'm sure she promised you could have what you like."

"That she did. She's a fair, fine maid, she is, and she knows a man must wet his whistle once or twice when he tells a good yarn."

He went off towards the barn lot with a wave of his hand. The old man was in fine fettle. Roger supposed he would be driving up with the old black mule hitched to a high-wheeled cart to carry Miss Mittie down to the shore. It was amusing, but it had something of pathos, this late autumn romance of two lonely people.

Roger went into the house. He found the Governor and Thomas Pollock in the little morning-room. Anthony Lovyck was with them. A slave, dressed in livery, brought in a tray set with decanters of whisky and rum. A few moments later Marita came into the room. She greeted the guests, her pleasure showing in her mobile face.

"My aunt asks you to please make yourselves comfortable. She will be down shortly. Beulah will show you to a room if you care to freshen up."

"Beulah has already done the honours, my dear," Pollock said. "We were just complimenting you on the progress you have made here at Greenfield."

Marita's eyes lightened. "Oh, do you think so? We did have bad luck with the pigeons, but now everything is popping up out of the ground again."

The Governor smiled at her enthusiasm. "I believe you really like it here."

"Indeed I do, your Excellency." She smiled at Roger. "Mr. Mainwairing has given us so much help."

Anthony said, "I'm sure you are an apt pupil, Marita. I may ask your help when I buy Sandy Point from Porter and become a farmer."

Pollock glanced at him. "I didn't know you were thinking of that. You said nothing to me about such a plan."

Anthony said, "I found out only today when the English mail came. My Uncle Parr sent me the authority to buy."

"What of the parcel you have on the Kesiah?"

"Oh, I'll deed that to my brother when he comes out." Anthony was trying to be casual, but Roger saw there was a suppressed excitement in his voice. He noticed the Governor was smiling.

"I don't believe Anthony can keep his secret much longer," Hyde said.

Anthony's face grew red. "Do you think I should tell them, sir, or would it be better to wait until Sarah—" he stopped.

Marita's eyes sparkled. "Oh, Anthony, you're going to marry—"

Lady Mary came into the room in time to hear her words and stopped her. "Marita! Why don't you let Anthony tell us himself in his own way? I can see by his face that he has a surprise."

Marita leaned back against her chair. "Yes, of course," she said.

A moment later Anthony's secret was no secret. They all knew that he and Sarah Blount were to marry in July, and John Blount and his wife had given their sanction.

Roger glanced at Lady Mary. She sat near the window, indolently waving a fan made from a palm leaf. She was white and there were dark shadows across her eyes as if she had not slept.

Roger went over and sat down beside her. Pollock and the Governor were talking with Edward Moseley, who had just arrived. The talk had changed in character. From the easy flow of banter and good-humoured conversation, every paragraph, every sentence had taken on meaning. Pollock was wary of his words, the Governor almost judicial. Moseley was blunt, an unusual attitude for him to take. He was inclined to conceal his thoughts behind a suave, courteous behaviour. Now he was challenging.

"I suppose your Excellency has given thought to what such a stand will involve?"

Roger knew he was talking about the new laws the Governor proposed that were detrimental to the Quakers.

"Laws should be made to apply to all the classes and all the denominations," Hyde answered without enlarging.

Moseley spoke warningly. "The Quakers are powerful, and Tom Cary still has followers—not only his men at Bath Town and Romney Marsh but there are farmers and drovers who live up the rivers and creeks from here to Virginia who will come to his side if he gives the word."

Lady Mary's voice interrupted Roger's thought. He looked up to meet her eyes. She was smiling, a little, detached smile. A different woman from the one she had been that day he had brought her the Turk's message. He didn't like her thus, remote and uninterested, the surface smooth and hard as porcelain. He wanted to say something to bring a shadow to her calm brow, a tremor to her firm wide mouth.

"The Turk took his punishment without question." He spoke quietly, so that no ears could hear save hers. There was no break in the slow indolent motion of the fan, or in the calm opaque look in her blue eyes. "It was not a pretty death," Roger was suddenly cruel. He wanted to hurt her. Why should she take death so lightly, with such casual indifference? "Strangulation," he said, giving the word an implication, wanting her to see the Turk, as he had seen him, swinging limply, pathetically, tragically alone.

"One must keep one's thoughts clear for the ultimate thing," she said quietly, by inference denying his implied accusation. "If we stopped to think of the details we would be overwhelmed by doubt. A cause may be lost by such indecision."

Roger showed nothing in his face. Her eyes searched his, but he gave no sign to help her. He felt her eyes leave him and wander to the other end of the room where the three men were engrossed in their task. Marita and Anthony had vanished.

"Roger, you are very cruel," she said. Her voice trembled. "I hoped you would understand and not judge me. " The detachment had left her eyes. "I have missed you," she said quietly.

After a moment she leaned back in her chair wearily. "I have had letters from home. The Duke of Ormond will have command in France in place of Churchill," she said. "He was

310

given secret orders by someone not to advance his armies to aid Austria. Now the Ministers are in negotiation with the Electress Sophia of Hanover. The Queen's health is poor. If she should die, the old Act of Settlement will be in force, and England will pass into the hands of the Hanoverians."

Roger did not ask from whom she had received this information, but he did not question its authenticity.

"The Stuarts carry a doom with them," she said, not trying to hide the bitterness in her voice. "It is always so. They cannot escape it."

The Governor got up and walked across the room. Roger rose, offering him his chair. Hyde sat down. By his expression Roger saw he was not pleased with the talk he had been having with Moseley. Hyde had aged in the months he had been in the Albemarle. His dark cloth coat, the wide white embroidered collar, made his face sallow, almost jaundiced. Roger bowed and left the room. A moment later Moseley followed him.

He walked to the riding-block where Old Cush, Moseley's groom, was allowing his horse to graze on the grass of the little greensward. "It's no use, the Governor's as stubborn as all the rest of the Hyde family," Moseley said, dispirited. "I tried to show him that he would have a real rebellion on his hands if he persisted in making hard terms for the Quakers. And trying to make them take the Oath. He is doing just what the others before him have tried to do. I told him what I thought about that. I did not spare words. Cary has more power than Pollock has informed him, both in men and ordnance. Roach, a merchant from London, has come recently to Bath in his own ship. He brought cannon and round shot and small arms. No doubt Danson, the Quaker, sent him to strengthen Cary's cause. Danson is a Lord Proprietor, sitting in the place of Archdale, who was once our governor. I called Hyde's attention to the relationship of Cary and Emanuel Low and Danson. They are all three sons-in-law of Archdale. I laid stress on Cary's ambitions. He is as courageous as he is arrogant and ambitious. I told him also that we could not hope to enforce the Lords' 'Grand Model' that Locke wrote for them as our Constitution. The people of Carolina have always been violently opposed to Locke's class distinctions, and they will fight for any infringement on what they think are their rights as free men."

"And how did the Governor answer?" Roger asked.

A thin smile crossed Moseley's firm mouth. "I think Edward Hyde is no mean diplomat," Mosely said. "He said very little—asked a few questions—then he asked me to sit on the Commission to represent North Carolina in the dispute with Virginia over the dividing line; and gave me a hint that I might be the next Surveyor General, as Lawson wants to be relieved of that position soon."

He swung into the saddle. "Mr. Edward Hyde is no mean diplomat," he repeated, "but I hope he doesn't think that this New World will be satisfied with the ways of the Old. Our people have had a taste of freedom, and they are not likely to give back what they have won."

When Roger went back into the house the Governor and Mary were alone. Lady Mary was saying, "I've ordered the cypress planks cut. Watkins tells me that we can have the log part of the house covered over without too much trouble or cost." She glanced about the crudely panelled walls. "I don't mind this; the wood is mellowed and not bad. But the log exterior—" she lifted her long hands in protest. "I want a little comfort while I am in exile." She laughed. "It's bad enough to be here, God knows."

The Governor nodded. "I can see how you feel, Mary. I hope you will not have to stay too long." He got up. "With your permission, my dear, I will follow Pollock's example and retire to my room for a little nap. We started out very early this morning. That is, if there is time before dinner?"

"We dine at two o'clock," Lady Mary said as Hyde was leaving the room. "I'll have the bell rung at a quarter before two."

The room was silent, the air was heavy with the heat of mid-summer. The bright, gay song of a mocker in a laurel tree broke the quiet.

"I do not know how I can endure the heat," Lady Mary said, fanning herself.

"This is only the beginning of summer," Roger answered, offering no comfort. "August is really hot. It is hot in London too this season, or have you forgotten?"

"I've never been in London in summer. We were always at the shore."

"You might go to the Banks for a month or two. The sea air is cool and refreshing. I have a small lodge on Ocracock Island. You are welcome to it, although it is rather crude."

Lady Mary glanced about the room. "I can stand almost anything after what I've experienced in this country."

Roger thought a moment. "Moseley has a better place on

312

the Island. He does not use it except for fishing, late in the season. I'm sure you could arrange to have it. I will take you down on my boat whenever you wish."

"You are kind, Roger," she said absently. "I'll think it over. Perhaps we might sail down one day soon to look at the lodge to see if I like it."

"It is a long sail, not one to be made in a day."

Something in the tone of his voice made her turn her eyes from the fields. Roger was staring at the floor, apparently in deep thought. For a moment his guard was down. What she read there puzzled and piqued her.

The drone of the bumblebee, drawing honey from the long tube of the scarlet trumpet, sounded loud in the room. Lady Mary got up from her chair and crossed the room. The soft white mull dress flowed behind her, and the ribands of the blue sash that girdled her slender waist drooped over the lace flounce. She sat down on the sofa bench beside him. The scented lace of garments touched him as she leaned forward.

"Would that be so unendurable?" she asked, rousing him from his abstraction.

He looked at her blankly for a moment.

"Am I so unendurable?" she repeated. "Are you loath to take me with you—to be alone with me on your boat for a day or two?"

His face changed. The rugged tightness broke down. His strong hand closed on her wrist. "You know how to break a man's will, Mary." There was a savage intensity in his low voice.

She had a sudden feeling that this man could destroy her, turn her from her purpose. His will was stronger than hers—his determination greater. She moved her hand slightly. He released his hold on her wrist, as if he had not been aware.

"We cannot go on as we have been. I've tried to think it out. You know I am bound to Rhoda. I have asked Tom to bring her here, so we can be married."

She started to reply, but he went on, speaking rapidly, his eyes holding hers. "I have given my word. Before I found you, Mary, that seemed the wise thing. I wanted a home."

"And then?"

"Then you came." He got up and took a turn or two about the room. He stopped in front of her, looking down at her, his eyes sombre. "My passion for you is strong enough to make me break my man's word. I will write to Tom. I will explain to him. Tell me what it is you want of me. Do you want a lover or do you want me for a husband?"

She was silent. The room was silent. His eyes did not leave her face.

"What will you have of me, my dear?" he repeated, his voice harsh. "Do you want me for a husband or a lover?"

She was silenced by his words; she who knew every trick of parry and thrust, was silenced by his direct attack. "I have a husband," she said at last, forced to truth by his steady eyes.

Roger got up and walked toward the window. Lady Mary sat, unmoving, staring at his straight flat back. "I have not seen him for years. He loathes me and I despise him, but I am tied to him as tightly as if I loved him."

She could not read his face. His eyes were hard and cold. She must go on—she must make him realize. "I was very young to marry. He was already known as a roué in a court that was filled with profligate, licentious men. He was jealous of me, accusing me of wrong-doing before I scarcely knew the meaning of passion. He came into my room the day our child was born. He swore before the servants that the child was not his." She did not move, but her hands that lay in her lap were clenched tightly. Her voice was very low. "I went away as soon as I had the strength to travel. I had a chateau in Normandy my father had given me. I hid there until he grew tired of searching for me. I never saw him again." She caught her breath to gain composure. "The child died," she said firmly.

Roger said nothing. He did not meet her eyes. She leaned toward him and put her hand over his. "There can be nothing but the truth between us, Roger. I—I care for you so deeply that I must give you the truth." She broke off. She put her cheek against his. "You are my lover, Roger. Must I give you up, now that I have found you? In a few months I will go back to my own country. You can come home. I have a house in Kent, not far from the channel. We can live there, or after the war is over we could live in Normandy—"

He broke in, his voice scornful. "And act the part of your man, waiting your pleasure, eating out my heart when you turn to a new lover?" He unclasped her hands from his arms. "No, it will never be that way between us. I had a different dream, but I have been a fool. I see now that you could never be anything but what you are—a woman of fashion.

For a little time you may have amused yourself with a provincial—"

Lady Mary rose suddenly, her face white with anger, "Stop, Roger, that is not the truth." She went to him and put her arms around his neck, her body pressed against him, her lips hard against his mouth. For a moment he was implacable, resenting her embrace—then his arms went about her. "Roger," she said brokenly, "Roger."

Marita's voice came through the open window, answered by Anthony's gay laughter. They were crossing the lawn from the farm lot.

Roger released Mary slowly. He crossed the room and sat in a chair by the open window. When Marita and Anthony came in Lady Mary was swinging the palm fan back and forth indolently, complaining of the heat, and the sultriness in the air.

Chapter 26

BAT'S
GRAVE

ROGER made his excuses and left before dinner. He was too profoundly moved by what had transpired to sit through dinner, or to listen to the Governor and Tom Pollock discuss their plans for travelling on to Kiquotan to inspect the Virginia militia with Governor Spottswood on the morrow.

Nor did he care to ride home, there to sit alone, his mind dwelling on Mary Tower. It was better not to think of the disclosure she had made. It was also better for his peace of mind not to dwell on another thing which had forced itself upon him as she was talking—the truth that she did not belong here in the country he loved—not because she had a living husband, but because Mary herself was so much a part of the Old World, a world with which he had come to grips and cast away for new, more robust living. It was not a man who separated them but a stronger force that he could not combat. He had not lost her. He had never had her—not even when she was close to him, lying in the circle of his arms.

He would ride down to see Captain Zeb. He would talk to him about taking the *Golden Grain* to the Bahamas with a cargo of pitch and tar. That was something solid and real to help him close his mind and keep him from thinking.

Roger made the turn to the lane below the overlooker's house. Two Negro herdboys were in the lane, grazing their sheep along the ditches. He slowed his horse to a walk as he went through, not to frighten the lambs.

Even in the shadow of the forest the heat was oppressive. He stepped under the shadow of a giant sycamore tree and took off his leather jerkin. Riding in his white linen shirt was more comfortable. He came to the clearing where the Captain's house stood on the shore of the Sound. There he got the full sweep of the water and the horizon. Great caravels of floating white clouds sailed across the sky, moving eastward. It might be a weather breeder if the wind turned before night.

The Captain's hearty voice greeted him as Roger rode in sight of the house. " 'Light and tie," he shouted jovially. " 'Light and tie, Duke, and join me in a fine Jamaicy punch I've just brewed."

From the colour of his face, Roger thought the Captain had been sampling his brew more than once. He was not averse to a drink. He turned his horse over to one of the Captain's slaves and walked around the corner of the cypress-boarded house to the bank. There he found Miss Mittie in the shadow of a great holly tree, taking her ease. A small Negro boy stood behind her, waving a myrtle bough to keep off flies and small insects.

"The girls are down on the float," Miss Mittie said. "The young gentlemen have gone for a bath in the cove beyond the fishhouse." She put her thin hand over her eyes and looked out across the water. "I hope it is quite proper," she said, her forehead furrowed by a frown. "I'm not sure that Lady Mary would approve." She looked anxiously at Roger, waving her hand vaguely in the direction of the cove where the young gentlemen were bathing.

Captain Zeb brought Roger a glass of Jamaica punch. "Now don't trouble your pretty head about that. The young ladies can't see beyond the cypress swamp, even if they peeked," he said to Miss Mittie. "There's not a thing wrong or indecent in a young man swimming in his underbreeches. Even if they went stark naked they are out of sight." He sat down on the stump of a big pine, his glass in his hand.

"Oh, Captain, you do say such dreadful things," Miss Mittie cried, a tea-rose blush spreading over her face.

The Captain doubled with laughter. "She's no more than a child about these matters," he said to Roger; "as innocent as a babe. Why, you should have seen some of the sights these old eyes of mine have beheld. Now in Madagascar, when the brown women swam out to our vessel, I'll swear they had nary a stitch to cover their hides but a big scarlet flower behind their ears. They swarmed up the ropes to the deck like a pack of monkeys."

"Whose shallop is that at the float?" Roger interrupted what promised to be a lusty tale of the brown ladies of Madagascar.

The Captain glanced over his shoulder. "It's Blount's *Brown Betty*. Young Tom sailed her down. His two sisters are with him, Miss Maria and Miss Sarah. They're on the float with Marita. As I was saying, naked as Eve before the serpent beguiled her—"

Roger interrupted. "I really came here to ask you to take a cargo to the West Indies for me."

Zeb set his glass down and took up a pipe. He broke up the long leaf, rolled it to powder in his horny palms, and filled his pipe before he answered. "I'm not a-yearning to go to sea," he said, blowing a cloud of smoke in the air. "I'm a landsman now, and my garden's doin' fine."

Miss Mittie looked at Roger, her pale eyes troubled. "Mr. Pollock said that Rackham's ship was seen anchored in the deep water behind Ocracock Island shortly after a merchantman was looted off Cape Hatteras."

"There's always some pirate anchored at the Hole," the Captain said. "That old fire-eating devil Teach hangs about Bath Town most of his time when he ain't raiding." He winked at Roger. "Some say he keeps rendezvous with one of our good citizens there."

Roger had heard of late that Tobias Knight had been accused of buying goods from pirates, but he gave the story no credence. "There are plenty of pirates infesting the Bahaman waters and Mono Passage, Captain."

"Rackham and his cutthroats," Zeb said angrily, "lying off the Carolina banks, waiting for merchantmen that stray from their convoy."

"I didn't think you'd be afraid of Rackham." Roger knew his words would be a challenge.

The old man's fist came down on the stump. "No, God

317

blast his skin, I'm not afraid of him or any other damned freebooter—not even François l'Olonnois, if he were alive!" He got to his feet shaking a gnarled forefinger at Roger. "I'll take your damned cargo out and get it safe to Jamaica. But you'll have to mount a swivel on the deck and give me plenty of round shot before I set sail."

"The cannon is mounted now." Roger lifted his glass. He was satisfied. "We'll drink to a safe return," he said. His eyes turned to Miss Mittie. She put her hand to her mouth to hide her trembling lips. A momentary twinge of remorse came over him, gone instantly. Ships must sail, and cargoes be transported. A woman must have strength to stand on the Captain's Walk and watch his ship sail with a smile on her lips. If she hadn't that courage, she had no place in the life of a seafaring man.

Roger's thoughts were interrupted by the arrival of the young folk. They were racing up the slope from the water, Maria Blount well ahead of her sister and Marita. When she saw Roger she settled down to a sedate walk, her white hands busy with her dishevelled hair. Anthony and Tom Blount followed, their hair damp from the swim, their faces shining and fresh scrubbed.

"We are going to sail to Bat's Grave," Maria Blount said to Roger. "Won't you go with us?"

"And you, Miss Mittie?" Sarah cried. "And Captain Zeb? We want to see if the pirates have hidden any gold on the island."

Captain Zeb looked from one to the other, his eyes twinkling. "I'll tell you what I'll do. I'll have my cook bring supper, and we'll eat turtle potpie on the shore. You'll need food if you dig deep enough to unearth pirate gold."

"I believe you are laughing at us, Captain Zeb," Maria Blount pouted. "My father said two strange ships sailed up the Sound last week. They didn't put in at the Bay, but went up the river to Bennet's Creek. Some say they bury gold up there."

Zeb gave a mighty laugh that shook his stocky body. "I dare say those ships wanted no more than fresh juniper water for their casks, my young lady."

"I prefer pirate ships hiding loot," Anthony said, looking at Sarah Blount. "If we unearthed a chest of gold, doubtless we could build a brick house at Sandy Point."

Sarah smiled happily. "I like the house as it stands, Anthony. I am quite content."

Her sister interrupted. "Sarah is always content. I think it is silly. I'd like to find a casket of pearls and rubies from Cartagena or one of the other rich cities of the Spanish Main."

Roger turned to speak to Marita. She was a little apart, looking out across the water, her tawny eyes inscrutable. She was not listening to the gay talk. She was far away in some world of her own. When she looked at him, Roger saw her eyes were filmed with tears. He moved a little so that he stood between her and the others. What disturbed Marita he could not fathom, but he did not want Anthony Lovyck's quick, sharp eyes upon her until she regained her composure.

The wind was light, but enough to fill the sails. Roger sat at the tiller, Marita near him. They passed Drummond's Point. Near the mouth of the Yaupim River he saw Skinner's manor house, and the open clearing of the old Durant place. He steered towards Harvey's Neck. With the light wind he would have to tack to reach the island.

Marita touched his arm. "Could we stop at Tomeses' landing? Perhaps Lucretia and Edward would come with us."

Maria Blount interrupted. "Lucretia is so quiet. Do you think the Friends make good company for a picnic?"

Roger let the sail run as he bore down on the tiller. "The best company in the world is a good listener," he said with a laugh. "We will stop at Foster Tomes's and pick up Lucretia and Edward. That will give me a moment with their father. I want him to sell me some of his fine Shropshires."

Marita gave him a grateful look. "You are so kind," she said. He knew she was not thanking him for putting the boat in at Tomeses's landing.

The interest in searching for buried treasure on the Island of Bat's Grave soon slackened. Anthony and Sarah sat apart on the sandy beach, talking in low tones. The others walked along the shore, then wandered back to the spot where Captain Zeb and his black boys were preparing the turtle pie.

Miss Mittie sat near by. She was watching Marita as the girl talked with Lucretia and her brother. "I am troubled about Marita," she said to Roger when he sat down on the sand near her. "She is not herself. She is daydreaming half the time. That's not natural for Marita. She's a quiet girl, but she is always happy."

"Perhaps she longs for her old home."

Miss Mittie shook her head. "No, it is something else. I think she is in love," she said sagely. "That makes people moon about, doesn't it?"

Roger laughed at Miss Mittie's inquiry. "So they say," he said. "But who?"

Miss Mittie didn't know. "I hope it isn't Anthony Lovyck," she said, dropping her voice. "That would be sad."

"Perhaps it is the weather," Roger answered.

Miss Mittie gave him a scornful glance. "I know a lovesick lass when I see one." She leaned forward so that her voice would not carry. "I hope it isn't any young man from the Albemarle that she is dreaming about. Lady Mary wouldn't permit it. She has other plans for Marita. A suitable marriage in England . . ." The little pines of worry deepened about her eyes and the corners of her mouth. "I pity her if she displeases Lady Mary."

"Marita is a young woman and should know her mind."

Miss Mittie gave him an impatient look. "You don't know Lady Mary. She has a will of iron. I shouldn't say this, for she is very kind to me. But I love the child. I do not like to see her hurt."

Roger turned his head to look down the beach. Marita was laughing as she walked along the sand, arm in arm with Lucretia Tomes, Edward by her side.

"I think you are imagining things, Miss Mittie," Roger said.

"I hope I am," she answered, but her voice had doubt in it.

Captain Zeb banged a pan with a long stick. He shouted, "Mess call!" in a booming voice.

Anthony and Sarah came in first. "We found an old boat around the point, and the pad of a great panther on the sand." Anthony told Roger, "If I had a fowling piece I'd go hunting after supper."

Edward Tomes said, "We did better than that, Lovyck. We found a grave with a little cross above it made of sticks, hidden under the trees. We think the pirates buried one of their men here."

Captain Zeb held a ladle suspended over the iron pot that held his turtle dish. "Pirates don't put crosses over graves." His voice was filled with scorn. "They don't bury their dead on a beach either. Like as not they throw the bodies overboard for the sharks to gnaw at."

"How horrible!" Marita exclaimed. "How horrible!"

320

"Piracy isn't a lady's game," Zeb said, turning back to his task of filling plates with the savoury dish.

Roger did not enter the discussion. Edward's words had meaning for him. A grave, hidden on a lonely island, a place taboo to the black people and many white because it was haunted by the spirit of an Indian maiden and her white lover whose grave was here.

"Perhaps you stumbled onto Bat's grave," he said to Edward.

The Quaker shook his head. "No, this was a new grave, not one sunken into the ground with age."

Roger took a plate of food from Captain Zeb. He was satisfied now. This was the leet woman's refuge. He must keep these people from further search.

"Why are you so stern?" Maria Blount said, taking a place beside him. "You look like my father when he is angry with Tom or one of the boys."

Roger smiled. "I'm sure I don't mean to look stern. On the contrary, I should be gay, with such company and such excellent food."

"And drink," Captain Zeb interrupted the sentence. "Good old Jamaicy. Nothing better for a summer drink. Eat your food and after supper I'll give you the tale about the time I was captured by the Barbary pirates."

The supper was cleared away by the black boys. They loaded the pots and kettles into a skiff and departed. Captain Zeb mixed more Jamaica rum in a large bowl he had brought for the purpose. First the toddy was too strong, and he weakened it with spring water. Then it was not sweet enough, so he put in more cant sugar. Then it was too weak and he poured in more rum from the jug, sampling it each time.

Miss Mittie was anxiously watching Zeb's face, as it grew redder and his eyes more filmed. Anthony was urging him on, for the old man's fancy ran best as his tongue loosened. He sat on the sand, the bowl at his elbow, and told him how in his young days he had been caught by the 'press gang and put aboard a man-of-war. Wrecked on the coast of Morocco, he was captured by the Moors. Chained to a barrow, by day he was forced to roll earth to build a great mound, so that the Sultan could grow tropical plants beside the fountains of the courtyard.

Captain Zeb took up a stick and began to draw a diagram of the Sultan's garden, stopping now and then to "likker up,"

321

growing bolder and bolder with his descriptions of the Sultan's garden, his palace and at last the harem.

Marita was troubled. She said somethng to Anthony Lovyck that Roger did not hear. Anthony's reply was audible enough. "Don't be prudish, Marita. The old man is funnier with every cup—let him tell about his houris."

But old Zeb had sampled too often. His voice trailed off and he began to nod. Anthony got up and dusted the sand from his breeches. "Too bad," he said. "I thought we were going to be amused and enlightened." He turned to Edward. "Come on, Tomes. Show me the grave you found. It may prove no grave at all, but a hiding place for gold."

Roger rose quickly. He had no intention of allowing them to go to Susannah Evans' grave.

There was a sharp sound of breaking twigs on the bank behind them. A moment later an arrow sped from the tangle of vines and branches. A sharp cry of pain, followed by a curse, came from Anthony's lips. Roger saw that the arrow was embedded in the fleshy part of his leg.

"Indians!" shouted Zeb. "We are attacked!" He tried to get to his feet but his legs would not hold him. "God damn Jamaicy!" he cried, struggling to his knees.

Edward Tomes started for the bank. Roger restrained him. "You have no arms," he said. "Get the women over to the boat."

Roger knelt by Anthony. The wound was very slight. The arrow had been nearly spent. He removed it without trouble and ordered the white-faced Anthony to help the Captain to the boat. Roger waited until they were all on their way to the boat before he went up the bank. He knew for certain now that it was the leet girl. The arrow was like the one he had found in his own room. He called, not too loudly. He did not want the others to hear. When there was no answer, he repeated, "Anne, it is I, Roger Mainwairing. I will take the people away. They will not disturb you." The wood was silent. He turned and walked down the beach. When he was halfway to the boat he saw the leet woman running towards them, her long, flaxen hair flying behind her, her bow in her hand. She wore a white linen shirt and a pair of sailor's breeches cut off at the knees. She had bound her waist with a bright scarf of calicut. Behind her loped the great dog, growling, his heavy jaws extended.

Maria Blount screamed when she saw the wild figure, and splashed into the water in her rush for the boat. Sarah and

Anthony followed. Lucretia and Edward were already aboard. Marita stood on the beach near Miss Mittie. The Captain had recovered his balance. He stood with his legs wide apart, watching the flying figure.

Roger ran. No telling what the violent woman would do. "Anne," he called, "Anne Evans!"

She glanced at him, but did not pause until she was within arrow shot.

"Oh, it's the leet woman!" Anthony jumped out of the boat and waded ashore, oblivious of his hurt. "Damn you for this! What do you mean by it?"

The girl stopped and took careful aim. Anthony ducked and the arrow went harmlessly over his head.

"You devil!" he shouted. "You devil!" But he did not advance.

Roger had never seen such rage in the face of any woman. Her pale blue eyes were ice, hard and glassy as obsidian.

Anthony shouted, "Leet woman, I'll have you whipped and your ears cropped for this."

The others were galvanized to silence. Roger tried to reach the girl before she lifted her bow again. Miss Mittie and Marita were directly behind Anthony, in range of her arrow. She had missed once. She might not miss again.

Roger called out, "Anne Evans! I want to talk to you."

The girl raised her bow. She was close to them now. She looked from one to the other, defiance and anger in her face. Her voice was controlled.

"Anne Bonney is my true name," she said, facing Anthony, her lips drawn like an animal at bay. "You will have cause to remember Anne Bonney, Lovyck." She lifted her voice so that it could be heard on the boat. "Lovyck, women hunter, chasing girls under hedges ... I dare you to call me leet woman again." She faced him squarely, her bow drawn taut. "Let me hear you call my name properly."

Anthony hesitated a moment, then said, "Anne Bonney."

A protest escaped Marita's lips. "You poor girl!" she cried, advancing a step, her eyes full of pity.

Anne Bonney wheeled about. "I want no pity from you, my lady trollop. I saw you meeting Michael Cary in the woods. I saw you go aboard his ship to rest the afternoon in his cabin." She laughed shrilly. "Mayhap you rested—mayhap you—"

Roger saw Marita's white stricken face as he dashed by

her and caught the leet woman's shoulder. "Have done with your talk," he said harshly. "Have done, I say!"

The dog crouched to spring. Roger caught up a piece of driftwood washed clean as a bone by the current. "Call him off or I'll brain him!" he said.

The girl caught at the dog's collar.

"Get out of here," Roger's eyes were as hard as her own. "Get out. Don't let me see you again."

The girl's face twisted in rage. For a moment Roger thought she would set the great dog at him. Suddenly she dropped her eyes and turned away. A moment later she was running down the beach towards the cove where her boat was hidden.

They sailed home in silence. Anthony was in a sullen rage, angry at this encounter before Sarah. Marita sat silent. Roger saw Miss Mittie clasp her hand under the fold of her skirt. Roger glared at the others. Lucretia Tomes was staring at Marita, her dark eyes hard with anger. Once he saw Marita look at her, but Lucretia turned away, refusing to meet her pleading eyes. Roger thought, Miss Mittie was right. The girl is in love with Michael Cary. . . . What would happen when Lady Mary discovered this? He glanced at Marita's white face and her trembling lips. He felt sorry for her but there was nothing he could do.

Roger swung the tiller and let the sail run. The wind was shifting. He sighted Tomes's float and set his course.

A shutter banging wakened Roger Mainwairing from a heavy sleep. He sat up and struck a flint to light his bed-candle, but the wind from the open window blew out the flame as fast as it was struck. He cursed when he hit his leg against the sharp corner of the tallboy as he made his way to the window. The wind was high, almost hurricane strength. In a flash of lightning he saw the trees in the garden bent almost to the ground. He shouted for Metephele to latch the storm windows, but no answer came. His head was bursting. He remembered that he had sent the *capita* off the night before when Metephele tried to take the whisky away.

The happenings of yesterday came before him. If he had stopped to think he would have known Lady Mary would not remain long in this new country. It was so contrary to her life. The thing that attracted him to her was her worldliness. Only a woman of experience could have awakened such deep passion in him. The thing that attracted him made the barrier that would keep them apart. Other men had loved her. That was the way of the Court where she lived. He remembered well enough her talk of Monmouth—himself a bastard son of King Charles, whom Charles had delighted to give honours and titles and legal status—as he had all his natural children.

He walked out on the gallery. The wind was rising. Limbs and branches of trees were whirling through the air. He hurried back into his bedchamber and put on breeches and boots. He thought of his shallop that was anchored at the float. He must get it inside the boathouse. He must get someone to help him. He raised his voice and shouted again. His voice beat back against him, flattened to nothing by the wind.

The sultriness had gone from the air. It was clean and cool. He found his way down the path without trouble. The lightning was far off now, but it gave him light to reach the boathouse. He groped his way to the door. Inside was a hurricane lanthorn and a flint box. The cavernlike gloom of the boathouse absorbed the faint light. Roger saw then that his boys had pulled the boat under cover and secured the canvas over the cockpit. "Good fellows," he said aloud. "Good fellows."

He felt wide awake now, his brain cleared from last night's drink. He sat down on the bench outside the boathouse, the water lapping at his feet. Here he could see the noble outline of Queen's Gift, shadowy against the heavy blackness of the trees behind it. It was finished, the last puncheon floor laid, both wings roofed over. He must plan a little now—some furniture from Williamsburg or maybe Philadelphia to go with the pieces Rhoda was sending over. How could he think of Rhoda when the long, pliant body and the lazy eyes of another woman came before him. He turned his mind resolutely. The stables would please Rhoda, the stalls for her hunters, the tack-room lined in a red-heart cedar. Tomorrow he would have a place sodded for a tennis court, and a green for bowls.

He picked up the lanthorn and started up the path that led to the manor house. Halfway he saw a shadow move from the shrubbery. He stood still. It might be one of his boys, taking his sleeping mat to lie outside the master's door, or it might be some marauder. Roger did not like the stories he had heard in the village about strange ships sailing along the southern shore. The shadow was lost in the darkness. He ran forward swiftly. Turning the corner of the house, he threw the light of the lanthorn, focussing on the shrubbery under his window.

There was a muttered imprecation, and the figure turned swiftly, blinking in the light cast by the lanthorn. It was Anne, the leet girl.

"What are you doing here?" he said harshly.

The girl put her hand up to shade her eyes. He saw the lines of weariness about her scarlet mouth. Her white blouse clung to her shoulders and her long braids straggled down her back. He noticed she still wore blue cloth breeches cut off at the knees, and her legs were bare, scratched by briers and brambles. He felt suddenly contrite. "Come into the house," he said. "I will get you a glass of toddy. You look beat."

She did not speak but walked ahead of him in the glow the lanthorn spread on the grass. He noticed she moved silently, easily. He saw her as she had been that afternoon, shrieking her defiance to them all, hitting out, wanting to hurt. He realized now that it was from fear—fear that they had come to disturb the grave of her dead.

His voice was kinder now. "You must be weary, you have rowed far tonight." He lighted a candle and preceded her to his study, standing aside to let her pass in before him. She glanced up quickly, a strange look in her face. She moved into the room with a certain conscious dignity that took no cignizance of her outlandish clothes.

He pulled a chair forward. She stood for a moment, her eyes taking in the room, the books, the tall mantel with pipes and jars of leaf, the red Morocco chairs. She spoke abruptly. "My father had a cabinet like this. Only his books were of laws and cases, and documents."

Roger looked at her. He remembered old Evans who died soon after he came to the Albemarle, a small farmer with no learning.

The girl read his thoughts shrewdly. "Him? He wasn't my father. No more was Susannah my mother, but she treated me kind, kinder than my own mother."

Roger poured out a drink and handed it to her. "Don't talk if it distresses you."

"It don't distress me. I told my name today: Bonney, Anne Bonney. My father was a barrister in Cork. My mother"—she stopped a moment and took a deep breath—"my mother was a serving wench in his own house. That's why they say true when they call me a leet woman."

326

She took a deep drink. The wine brought colour to her face. "My father left his wife and his children and fled to Carolina with my mother. I was born here," she added. "I think he hated her but he couldn't leave her. When she died he put me out to a foster mother, and went away—to Jamaica, some say—I don't know."

She spoke dispassionately. "It's always been so—there has been no one to want me but Susannah. She was kind . . ."

Roger filled her glass again. She was not so bad looking with colour in her thin, gaunt cheeks. "Why do you hate everyone?" he said, knowing the answer well enough.

"Hate? Why shouldn't I hate? Boys and men chasing me like hounds after a bitch. But I can scratch and kick or use my knife. I've done it more than once. I can fend for myself."

Roger poured himself a drink and sat down, staring at the girl. She took a long, tired breath and touched the rim of the glass delicately with her firm red lips. Her voice was low, not harsh, and when she wanted to, she spoke without dialect. He could understand men and boys chasing her. She was desirable. He realized she was talking again, quietly and dispassionately.

"Man are all beasts. They want to lay foul hands on my flesh and drag me under the bushes like that filthy Lovyck, telling me that my breasts are round and firm and my thighs . . ." She looked steadily at Roger, meeting his eyes with a passionate desire for him to believe her words. "I am virgin still," she said with startling frankness.

She set the glass down on a table. Rising to her feet she took a step toward him. "Show me to your bed," she said, so low he could barely hear her words.

"My bed?" he said, astonished. "God's death! What are you talking about?"

"You want to lie with me. I see it in your eyes. I wish to make myself ready."

"You don't know what you're talking about," Roger said.

She met his eyes unfalteringly. "It is said that a virgin brings a high price in the brothels, that gentlemen pay well for fresh girls from the country."

Anger rose in him. "You don't know what you are talking about," he said again gruffly.

She came closer to him. "I am grateful to you, Duke Roger. I wish to pay."

"God damn! I don't want gratitude from a woman. I don't

want your body. You may have the King's Evil for all I know." He wanted to hurt her, to send her away. He wanted no gratitude from the girl, or from any woman.

She faced him, her hands clenched, her eyes venomous. "You lie!"

"Or you may be thick with vermin, sleeping as you sleep . . ."

She tore at her blouse, showing the fine white skin of her shoulder. The red scar shone out, the red brand burnt deep in her flesh. "I am clean!" she said, her lips drawn taut. "I wash and scrub my body clean with sand." Her voice broke. "You are a beast . . . like the rest!"

"No, not like the rest. I don't run after you."

"But you hurt deeper," she said, her voice husky.

He got up from his chair and stood beside her. "Men will always run after you, Anne, because your body is for love, and your mouth for kissing. They do not trouble to look into your eyes, or they would not seek you. Your eyes are hard and cold and full of smouldering hate. You could kill a man as he slept."

The girl stood motionless, her arms hanging straight at her side. Roger thought, I must make her angry again so she will go away. The lines that ran from his nostrils to his lips were scornful. "I would not take you. Even in the dark I would remember the hate in your eyes and your body would repel me."

Roger expected another outburst of violence from her. He was not prepared for the silence that followed. She did not move. She seemed suddenly to lose stature, to become small, almost childlike. "I will go," she said submissively. She lifted her head. Her eyes were not cold or pale. Without reason he thought of blue windflowers on the northern moorland. She stood quietly, but he saw the swift rise and fall of her breasts under her thin shirt . . . the slim grace of her firm body.

She made a swift move forward, pressing her lips against his hand. For a moment she was desirable in his arms. She broke away suddenly. A moment later he heard the great door slam violently. Perhaps he was a fool to send her away. He was lonely enough tonight to have given something for companionship and the comfort of a woman's body, but he thought of the girl. It was far better for Anne Bonney to hate him as she hated other men. Her hatred was her strength and her protection.

328

He opened the window to look out but the night was too dark to see beyond the shrubs that bordered his garden.

A great lunar moth, driven by the wind, clung to the window sill. Attracted by the light of the candelabrum, it spread its delicate green and violet wings and floated into the room. Roger watched the moth as it fluttered towards the light. Before the gossamer wings touched the flame, a sudden gust of wind left the room in darkness.

Chapter 27

TOLL HOUSE
ROAD

THE Two Penny Club was playing at ninepins at the Red Lion. There was plenty of buttered ale, and as the evening progressed the landlord had a candle made to treat the players. Tom the Tinker was reinstated that night, after having been suspended for two weeks for his uncomplimentary remark concerning King Charles the Second. It was a big night at the Red Lion. Tomorrow was market day, and the Great Court sat

Tom was a "wee bit sad the night," MacTavish, the farrier, remarked Tom sat in a corner playing his flageolet, only stopping long enough to sing a few verses of "So and Be Hanged and That's Good-bye," a weird dirge about a man hanging on the Green, his flesh shrunk to bones. He left his corner briskly enough when the pullet was off the spit and the supper on the table. Before he sat down he took his cap from his tousled red hair and got down on his knees. He lifted his mug of buttered ale and cried in a hearty voice, "God bless King Charles. May his soul be at peace!"

Every man at the table looked at Tom the Tinker in astonishment until MacTavish explained. The judge had so sentenced him. Every night for thirty-nine nights must Tom fall on his knees and drink to the late King—instead of thirty nine stripes, since his back was not healed well from the last beating.

"'The drinking comes easy!" Tom exclaimed cheerfully as

he took his place at table, "and as for a few stripes, what do they mean? If a man goes free, 'til all done."

MacTavish stood at the head of the table; and there was Johnny Lynch the mason, and Williams the joiner, with Talbot the weaver sitting close. The cobbler, Green, was there, and two other artisans, workers in brick and wood, who had come recently to Queen Anne's Town from Virginia to work on the Government House, were guests for the evening. One or two others came in, wild rollicking youths who despised town life, and lived by hunting. They roved the woods along the Sound and the tributary rivers. Trappers were not attracted to Carolina to plant fields of corn or till the soil. They hunted for skins, wolf and fox, otter, beaver and deer. In the autumn they gathered wine grapes that grew wild in the woods, the tawny round Scuppernong, the purple fox and the James. They made wine from the Scuppernong, amber and sweet like the old world Malmsey, and peddled it from door to door in the village. These men gave a tang to the Two Penny Club, a breath of the north wind.

MacTavish hit the long oaken table with his calloused fist. "The supper is on the table. Let every man say his name and give his trade; then sit and fill his belly with good food and drink. Supper being over, we may fill our pipes of the weekly gossip. Every man may have five minutes to talk, make his argument or his complaints."

He took his seat at the head of the table. There was a scuffing of heavy boots and the scrape of the long benches as the men moved close to the table. MacTavish took first meat, and the rest fell to. He was a mighty man, the farrier, with a face cut from his own Craig of Cairngorm. He wore a shirt of fine Garlex, woven by his wife Jinnie, a linen jacket and blue wool breeches. He was a surly man at times, and free to speak his tongue, not as Tom the Tinker when he was drunk, but soberly, with strong words. He was a Knox follower of firm belief, one of a little band who, without kirk of their own in the Carolinas, joined with the other Dissenters. He had little to say about kings and queens in the old country, plenty to say about government here. MacTavish was always against whoever had the power, Glover and Cary in turn. Now he was against the new Governor, Hyde, and the Albemarle aristocracy with their display of dignity and power and their land-grabbing proclivities.

Land grandees, MacTavish called them, taking up all the bottomlands and the rich lands along the river, leaving the barren soil for the poor yeomen and peasants; getting their fashions from London, their square-cut coats and long-flapped waistcoats with great pockets, their full-bottomed wigs; strutting at their house dances in square-toed slippers with red heels, their hats with curled plumes, as if parading in the Mall or at Windsor Court; spending their time hunting and fishing, cock-fighting and horse-racing, leaving wrestling and bowls and low dancing to common folk.

MacTavish was off on his hobby tonight, after a few tankards of ale. Only tonight it was Madam Hyde who was in his black books. "Coming out from London wearing her fine silk dressing, carrying her little muff, setting a bad example to the womenfolk of the village whose husbands could not afford to indulge their wives in changing fripperies."

No one made answer to his accusation and after they had all done justice to the meal the meeting began. The floor was first given to the two guests from Virginia, the carpenter and the mason. The mason told them the foundation for Government House was finished, and the great chimney on the west was completed. He had only the east chimney to do, and he would return to Willliamsburg to work on the great palace Governor Spottswood was building.

"A small bit of work I have here. I would not take it but that Governor Spottswood had lent me to Governor Hyde, as no one here could do the work proper and make the chimney draw, without smoking."

Instantly there came loud-voiced protests. Long-legged Johnny Lynch, the local mason, gave the Virginian a kick on his shins. The man cried out. MacTavish quieted the protesting mason. " 'Tis all fair," he said to the stranger. " 'Tis a rule of our club that a lie calls for a kick on the shins. Let the carpenter speak now."

The visiting carpenter, subdued by the swift punishment upon his friend, was conciliatory. He reported the work in progress: sills all laid, uprights joined to cross beams, roof partly covered. "I have seen the draught of the building in the drawing-board papers," he said. "The London man has made a nice plan of a building, small but elegant, with a wide hall below and a great room with elegant mantelboards."

"Will it have a tower?" one artisan asked.

"No tower, but a fine round cupola, and a circular stairway upside. There'll be elegant carvings of acanthus leaves to lie under the overhang and to mark the King's Point in front."

The Virginian stopped a moment to take a drink, then added, "A slave of Mr. Mainwairing is carving them now, and the Governor's lady will bring the great brass lock and hinges when she comes home from England."

"When will this fine building be finished?" Tom the Tinker leaned over the table to ask. " 'Tis not as fine as Williamsburg mayhap, but it will be fair good for Rogues' Harbour folk."

MacTavish banged the table. "Have done with your whittle-whattle, Tom. We are not Rogues' Harbour folk. 'Tis a lie, and I ask Cobbler Green to give punishment."

Tom laughed and thrust out a skinny shank. "It's glad I am that it is the cobbler who kicks with his fine handmade shoes, not your great jackboots, MacTavish."

Everyone laughed. Tom was a wit, they exclaimed. It was too bad he was always in boiling water with the town marshal and the goalers, some man said.

Each man spoke in turn. The farrier was disgrunted over the lack of putting law into force, he said. "We came here, lawabiding people. What do we find? No law at all. Quakers and Dissenters and Church of England fighting each other so hard no man preaches the word of God."

"Mr. Hyde, he's for law!" someone cried.

"How do you know that?" MacTavish scowled at him. "He's showed no sign yet. Him with his smiling ways and his soft voice and his high head. What does he do? Why, he takes orders from the Governor of Virginia—that's what he does. How do I know? My boy Jamie runs messenger for him—that's how."

"Cary will come before long," one man said slyly. "Cary has boats and cannon and plenty of shot."

"Cary won't do no better for us, for all his free whisky and fine promises," MacTavish said bluntly, "and as for Mr. Hyde—"

" 'Tis treason to talk so," Tom the Tinker interrupted loudly. "treason to our good Queen, the only ruler we've had who loves common people like us. I drink to our lady Queen!" he cried, draining his mug and handing it to the potboy. "Fetch another," he shouted. "I'll drink to all of the Stuarts—a fine strong toast to King William, the foreigner. May his soul lie in torment!"

The men looked one to the other. Tom was getting out of hand again. They didn't want the marshal's men to come in on them and break up the club meeting. Green got up and closed the door to the ordinary, first looking about to see who was at the tables. Only passing drovers and a few farmers from up the creeks who had come early for tomorrow's market-day.

The Great Court was sitting tomorrow, and Justice Moseley would sit, and Thomas Relf and John Blount. Court would bring many strangers to town, not all of them law-abiding folk. Tomorrow night the goal would be filled without Tom's company, MacTavish told him.

"Keep a civil tongue," he told the Tinker, "and mind your words about kings and nobles."

Tom promised. "I'll say naething," he said, lifting his glass. "Nae wanton thing against man, woman or child, except that whore Silvers. A fiend she is. She raised her price a shillin'. Where's a man to get two shillin's these days? She will not take trade. I've mended every pot and pan in her kitchen— long since."

This sally of Tom's raised a shout of laughter. A moment after, the door was flung open and a swarthy man dressed in sailor clothes stood at the entrance. "There's too much jollity in here," he said, scowling at the men. His dark face was flushed by drink, and the scar on his cheek burned red.

"Who says?" Tom the Tinker cried, lurching to the door. "Tu' Penny Club don't hold with men with gold rings in their ears."

The sailor reached a long arm and grabbed him by the shoulder.

"Leave be!" shouted the farrier, rising to his great height. "Leave be!"

The sailor loosened his hold on Tom's shoulder. The tinker fell back to the bench.

"So you want a bout with Diego?" The intruder's lips slipped back over his strong white teeth. "Give way," he cried, grasping a long, pointed knife.

MacTavish slid his dirk from its sheath. "One hand behind the back, sailor!" he ordered, taking stance.

The fight began. Diego, the sailor, made up in wiry agility what he lacked in strength. MacTavish, heavier by two stone, could not move so swiftly, but a blow from him was death if it touched a vital spot. Each man, one hand behind him, hewed and slashed; blood ran from scratches on arms and neck. They fought across the small room through the door into the ordinary, to the shouts and curses of the onlookers. A thin boy with short blond hair stood far back near the door, shouting encouragement to the sailor. Others of his kind came in, brawny men darkened by wind and sun, their forearms strong. In a moment the fight was general, with fists and cutting-edged knives.

The landlord stood on a bench shouting at the top of his lungs, "Brawling not allowed! I'll call the guard! I'll call the guard!"

Suddenly the bellman walking down the street rang his bell, his voice carrying into the room. "Twelve o'clock and a fine moon! Twelve o'clock and a fine moon!"

Diego dodged out from under MacTavish's brawny arm. He caught the arm of the blond boy and they started running. "To ship, to ship!" he cried, as he dashed through the door. "To ship, sailors, or we'll miss the sailing!"

The others followed, running along the road past the bellman, who moved slowly, crying his monotonous cry, "Twelve o'clock and a fine moon! Twelve o'clock and a fine moon!"

The Two Penny Club crowded the doors and windows and the low gallery. At the foot of the long street they saw a barkentine anchored beyond the Dram Tree.

"She must be sailing at the turn of the moon," Tom the Tinker observed, "and good riddance to them.'

MacTavish said nothing. He was not happy with his wounds. How would he explain them to his wife Jinnie when he went home?

Tom the Tinker walked home with the farrier. "That lad who was running with the sailor Diego, I think I seed before. Looked familiar-like to me."

The farrier paid no heed. He was wondering whether Jinnie would punish him on the morrow by not cooking the whitehass he had purchased that morning from a countryman who lived near the Rope Walk. Jinnie could be hard. A body couldn't move her when she made up her mind.

"But I can't think where I've seen that lad," Tom continued. "His thin face puckered with the effort of thinking. "Somewhere . . ."

They had come to the end of King Street. Here they met Roger Mainwairing riding into town. He pulled up his horse to give the men a civil greeting.

"What ship is that?" he asked, pointing with his crop to the barkentine that was anchored out near the Dram Tree.

"She's the *Willing Maid* from Pamticoe," Tom the Tinker said glibly. " 'Tis said she belongs to Governor Thomas Cary."

"How do you know that?" MacTavish interrupted. " 'Twas another name she had at sundown; 'twas the *Pamticoe Adventure* then and she belonged to Mr. Emanuel Low."

The Tinker slapped his leg and let out a guffaw. "Little ye know about a ship, Mr. MacTavish! The *Pamticoe Adventure*, with Mr. Low aboard, sailed up the river before I left town for the Two Penny Club. This is another ship entirely. Can't ye see she's rigged different? Why, I can see she's different even with her sails brailed up, and she's an eighty-ton burden, she is, and she's set up with ordinance like a guard-ship, but she ain't no guard-ship either." He laughed again slyly.

Roger thought, What does he know?

MacTavish said, "For all your talk, Tom, I don't think you know a foremast studding sail from a mizzen royal, so have done with your speculatin'." He looked up at Roger. "You'll have to excuse Tom, sir. He's a little over-sides, sir, what with the landlord's caudle cup and his own private drinking. I'm bound to see him home, sir, before he gets into trouble."

Roger laughed. "Just so he doesn't run afoul of the law tomorrow when the Great Court sits." With a good night to the men, he rode on towards the water.

Roger pulled up his horse and looked at the ship, bright in the moon path. An eighty-ton barkentine was near his own estimate. Heavy rigged for fast sailing, she was sitting low as if with cargo, dark except for the riding lights. That was strange for a ship in port. It was usual to have lights, and men's voices carry over the water. But this ship was silent, a ghost ship without sound.

Tom's careless words about this ship set Roger thinking. Emanuel Low ... ship upriver ... Cary's barkentine here at the village. He didn't like the look of it. Was there deviltry afoot?

He rode up to the Coffee House. Dismounting, he went inside. A dozen men were seated at the table casting dice, men from the upper river, in for court day. Some played at ombre, others at piquet. Roger ordered his rum and joined the dicers. An hour, and he had lost two pounds. His luck had deserted him. He paid his reckoning with a due bill on tobacco to Leary, the barrister. He wandered over to the men seated at a table in one corner, where Justice Relf was talking to Christopher Gale. They were speaking quietly with voices lowered. When they saw Roger they beckoned him to join them. They were talking about the ship anchored in the bay. Why was Cary here? Relf asked. Gale answered that he had a case on the docket. John Pettiver was suing him for the liquor Cary gave out at the last Assembly—a barrel of strong drink, seven gallons of rum, fifty pounds of sugar, beside the beef and pork and fowls, to the amount of twenty pounds sterling.

Roger grinned. "And it was all wasted. He'll be paying for dead cats and dogs if he pays that reckoning."

"Oh, there's more of it," Gale said, beckoning the barman. "Lodging for his people and their servants. But Pettiver's suing Glover and John Porter as well, so they're all in it."

The men laughed then. But Roger was not satisfied about Cary's ship. "Even if Cary has to come to court, must he come in an armed barkentine?"

The two men gave him their attention then. "Armed, did you say?" Gale asked. He sat for a moment, a frown on his thin face. "I believe the Governor should be advised of this," he said, his voice very low.

"Emanuel Low's ship has gone upriver," Roger added.

Gale finished his drink and got on his feet. "Come on, let's go into the writing-room, Roger. I've that matter of transporting my tobacco to take up with you." They said good night to the Justice and moved away.

Once in the small room, Gale dropped all semblance of casualness. "We must send a messenger to Balgray at once. Is there anyone we can trust?"

Roger was thoughtful. "No one that we can get at this time of night. Do you think it is important?"

"I think it so very important that I'd ride up myself, except that I have to appear in court early in the morning and I might not be able to get back."

"Do you think Cary will do anything untowards?"

"God knows. If he has made up his mind that Hyde is playing a game with the Virginians, no telling what measures he will take. I tell you, Roger, I don't like the idea of two enemy ships on the river—and that's what they are, enemy ships."

"But if Cary has to appear in court?"

Gale gave Roger a look of impatience. "Thomas Cary cares nothing for courts. I tell you we must send word to Hyde."

Roger sat a moment. He didn't relish the idea of the long ride up to White's Ferry, and crossing the Sound; but if it had to be done . . .

336

He got up. "All right, Chris. I'll go. It may be all a lot of damned nonsense, but on the other hand . . ."

Gale's face cleared. "Good. We'll go out to the ordinary. You can make some remark about riding to Queen's Gift. One never knows who stands for whom these days, so let this be done in all secrecy."

Roger said, "I've just remembered. The Council meets day after tomorrow at Balgray. Everyone will be there, including De Graffenried and the new member, Tobias Knight, who will take my place from now on."

"Tobias Knight?" Gale's voice showed his astonishment.

"Yes, he sits as representative of Lady Blake's infant son Joseph."

"God damn everything!" Gale exclaimed. "You're sure of that?"

"Yes. Mr. Hyde received the letters last week."

Gale walked up and down the room a moment, deep in thought. Suddenly his face cleared. Roger knew he expected that appointment. "That's it, Roger. You have the answer. Cary intends to take his ships to Balgray. He will be there for the meeting of the Council day after tomorrow. You must start at once. For the love of God, take care that none of Cary's men sees you ride out the North Gate."

"Any message?" Roger said, his hand on the door.

"No, I suppose Hyde has his plans made for just such a contingency. If he asks your advice, tell him to send to Virginia for the marines without delay."

Roger mounted his horse in the courtyard. He noticed several strange men loitering near the trough. He let his horse drink her fill. She would need it before he reached Balgray.

One of the men lounged up to the trough. "A good mare, sir," he said, his eyes on the horse.

"Good enough to carry me," Roger answered easily.

"Going far?" the man questioned.

Roger said, "No, only to my plantation."

The man seemed satisfied and walked away. Roger rode down to the end of King Street, to the Rope Walk, and took the road that led to Blount's Bridge. Outside the town he first made sure no one was following him. Then he turned and rode north by a short cut. He heard shouting from the water front, angry voices raised. As he left the village a red glow showed through the trees. Avoiding the North Gate, he crossed the open fields until he bisected the main road to

White's Ferry. He pulled his hat low when he passed a group of farmers coming to town with produce. The moon was bright, which made riding easy, but it also gave any lurking follower of Cary an equal chance to follow him. He knew a wood path or two that took him away from the post road. By good fortune he would be at Balgray before daylight. One thing bothered him. Where was Emanuel Low's brigantine anchored? Had it sailed up to Bennet's Creek on some legitimate mission, or was it anchored across from Balgray, hidden by the trees of the swamp?

The air was soft and balmy. The sun would bring midsummer heat, but the night was cool and quiet. Too quiet, thought Roger Mainwairing. He was skirting the long pocosin now that followed Heath Creek. He avoided the middle of the road and set his horse close to the edge in the deep shadow of the forest. Once he saw a shadow moving through the trees. He stopped his horse and loosened his pistol in the holster. A twig snapped loudly. A buck, he thought. His horse gave no sign of fright, so it was not a bear.

The moon was behind a small cloud when Roger came into the main road, a few hundred yards from White's Ferry. Something caused him to draw up his horse and take refuge in the shadows. He must have heard an unusual sound. Roger was enough of a woodsman to take immediate notice of the unusual. He listened, but heard nothing. Still he had that sixth-sense warning that something was amiss. He must have sat quietly for five minutes or more, his hand on the neck of his mare to quiet her. The Arab blood in the horse responded to its master's warning signal and she stood as quietly as a bronze statue.

Roger was at the point of riding on when he heard the rattle of a chain. An anchor chain, he thought, instantly on the alert again. Emanuel Low's brigantine might be anchored here, although he thought it would be farther upriver. It might have been the sound of a chain on the ferry.

He dismounted cautiously and dropped the reins to the ground. The mare would stand quietly until he came for her. He moved through the shadows, screening himself by bushes that grew along the ditch beside the road. The river could not be more than five hundred feet from here. After he made the turn he would be able to see the little cabin at the ferry landing.

The moonlight was dimmer now, but it was bright enough for him to catch the light of the moving water. The road

338

spread fanwise at the landing. Where was the toll house? Roger passed his hand over his eyes and looked again. It was not there. Could he have mistaken the crossroad and come in too high? No, he was sure he was right. He moved slowly and cautiously, using all his knowledge of woodcraft to approach the river without being seen. As he came close to the landing, he smelled wood burning. He saw the faint glow of embers, where the toll house had been. The road opened; through a vista in the trees he saw the black bulk of a large vessel, anchored not far off shore.

Roger moved close to the great pine tree, protected from view from the water. His mind moved swiftly, searching the answer. First, it might have been a normal fire that had levelled the toll house. This was improbable, for there would be no fire in the hearth at this season, and the cooking house was still standing, close to the river. Second, it might be Indians, for he was within a few miles of the Indian village. Third, the house had been burned by someone from the ship. The last stuck in his mind. But why? There must be some reason. Whatever it was he must find out, for there was no doubt that it had bearing on Cary and his plans.

Crouching low, he moved in the protecting shadows of the bay thicket until he was close to the smoldering ruins. Only silence greeted him. He could see nothing beyond the dull glow of embers. The house must have been burned some hours ago. He could see no sign of anyone. Nor was the ferry in the wooden slip. That too was destroyed. He saw no sign of the boat. It must be on the south shore of the river. He crept along the edge of the clearing. It was too dark to get a good view of the spot, but nothing remained of house or ferry slip.

He did not dare to go down to the little building by the water, which was used as a cook-house, for fear someone on watch on the brigantine would discover him moving in the shadows.

Roger turned to go back to the road. Suddenly he stumbled against something and fell to his knees, his body sprawled across a soft object. It took only an instant to realize it was the body of a dead man, lying face down in the dust. Still on his knees, he turned the man. The moonshine shone on the white face of old Jason, the man who ran the ferry for White. As Roger moved him, the wooden pipe, still clenched in the dead man's teeth, fell away. Roger ran his hand over the man's body. There was a gaping knife wound in his side under his arm. Old Jason had been stabbed from behind. Roger wiped his hand on the grass to take away the blood.

It took him some time to get back to the place where he had left his mare. By the time he was in the saddle his plan was made. He would ride on to Indian Town. If it were possible to get a boat he would try crossing the river at that point; if not, he would have to go on to Bennet's, or even to Sarum Creek before he could cross to the south shore. That would mean a long ride downstream. He might get a fresh horse from Bryan, or Maule, to take him down to Balgray. That would mean a number of extra miles. He would be lucky if he made it before daylight. One thing was clear: the men from Low's brigantine had destroyed the ferry so that no one could cross at that point, which was the shortest road to Balgray. It did not take much imagination to work out the answer. They would isolate the plantation. One boat at the village to keep help from embarking from there; the second boat in the river.

He came to the conclusion, as he rode through the dark wood road, that Cary would wait until all the Council had assembled at Balgray. Then he would spring his trap, whatever it was.

That was before he came to Indian Town and heard Chief Blont of Tuscarora making his speech before the chiefs of the Chowanokes at their campfire.

The Governor was drinking his morning tea on the north gallery at Balgray. He had the habit of rising early so that he could finish dictating his reports and land papers before the heat of the July day was upon them.

He was engrossed watching three cardinals and a Carolina wren fighting for grain a slave had scattered on the garden path. The early morning song of a mocker caught his ear and he took up a spyglass from the table to search the branches of the great pine that grew on the river bank for sight of the songster.

Instead of the bird, a lone canoe, moving swiftly downriver, came into his field of vision. He adjusted the glass and looked more closely. Without being able to see the face of the man, something in the movement of the broad shoulders and the way he carried his head reminded Hyde of Roger Mainwaring. That was not likely, for Knight had taken Roger's place on the Council.

340

He saw Thomas Pollock and Anthony Lovyck coming across from the stables. They were in riding dress, evidently just returned from a morning gallop. When they came up to the table, Hyde handed the glass to Anthony.

"Can you make out the face of the man in the canoe?"

Lovyck levelled the glass, holding it against a pillar. "Why, it's Duke Roger! He looks as if—wait—he looks as if he were hurt—he's leaning forward—" He put the glass on the table and ran down the steps towards the landing.

Pollock looked then. "The lad's right—I can see his arm hanging limp." He too laid the glass aside. "I'll go down," he said, hurrying away across the lawn.

The Governor finished his tea and waited. He could not see the float from where he stood. The landing was hidden by the high bank. After a time the three men came into sight, walking slowly across the lawn. Pollock's face had a grave expression as he listened to Mainwairing. Anthony left them and ran to the gallery.

"Your Excellency, he's hurt—shot in the arm by one of Cary's men. He's fit to drop. Whisky—I'll get it." He disappeared through the front door. Anthony was back with a decanter and glass by the time the others reached the steps.

The Governor got to his feet, an exclamation of surprise dying on his lips at the sight. Roger's clothes were sodden, covered with slimy swamp mud. His face was scratched and bleeding in half a dozen places, and the sleeve of his white shirt was thick with blood. He looked exhausted, scarcely able to hold himself erect. "Your Excellency, Cary—"

"Wait until you have swallowed this," Pollock said, forcing the glass of whisky into his hand.

The Governor pushed a chair forward. "Sit down, Mainwairing," he said.

Roger took the whisky at a gulp. As he drained the glass, the colour seemed to flow back into his white face. It took him only a moment to tell of the events of the night from the time he had left the village until he came to Indian Town.

Pollock started to interrupt when Roger told of finding the murdered ferryman, and the brigantine anchored across the river, but the Governor held up a warning hand.

Willie Maule rode up as Roger was talking and came up the steps. Anthony silenced him by a gesture.

"I knew something was wrong when I saw the circle around the fire," Roger said. "I recognized Chief Blont and some of his young braves. There were Nottaway Indians and

341

Meherrins, besides the Chowanokes. I got as close as I dared." He looked at Hyde. "I speak the Tuscarora tongue but not the other dialects. I could understand only Blont. He was saying that it was not good to make war now, before they had time to test the new Governor." Roger stopped and Anthony pressed a glass into his hand.

Pollock was rolling Roger's sleeve back, looking at his shoulder. He finally said, "I'll tie this up and stop the bleeding. Go on."

Roger resumed. "The young men argued against Blont, but the older Chowanokes stood by the chief of the Tuscaroras. . . . I got away then and crawled to the river. It was coming day, and I could make out canoes pulled up on shore. I turned my horse loose and switched her flanks sharply. It frightened her so that she crashed off through the bushes. I wanted her to engage their attention while I got the boat to the water and set off. The ruse worked well enough. I heard shouts and yells and the sound of a musket shot. I hope she got away." Roger was silent a moment before he took up the story. "Everything was working. I crossed the river and came down the south shore, hugging the bank. I had an idea that there would be trouble at the south end of the ferry."

"Had they sent a guard there?" Hyde asked.

"Yes. Three men—slaves of sorts, though they looked more like rascally pirates."

"Did they get away?" Anthony asked, leaning forward in his chair.

"One did," Roger said grimly. "Only one, and I think he has a bullet in him."

Hyde got up and walked to the gallery, his back to them.

Pollock sent Willie for hot water and linen cloth. "You've got a bullet in your forearm," he said. "It's a matter for Parris' knife, but I can stop the blood. What do you think we'd best do now, Duke?" Pollock asked, his eyes on Hyde's quiet figure.

"Gale says—" Roger did not finish. Hyde crossed the gallery and stood beside them. His face was grim and determined. All the gentleness had gone from his dark eyes. He addressed Lovyck.

"Anthony, please bring me Moseley's map from the office. Then get your pistols and a packet of food for your saddlebags. I want you to start at once for Williamsburg. Present my compliments to Governor Spottswood, and ask him to send a company of her Majesty's marines to Queen Anne's Town. You may say it is urgent."

Anthony went quickly into the house and returned in a moment with Edward Moseley's map of the Albemarle, which he handed to the Governor. "I'll be ready to go in a few moments," he said.

"Come back before you start. We will have your route planned."

Anthony turned towards the steps.

"Wait," Hyde said. "Perhaps Maule will go with you. Yes, two will be better. You can separate, if there is trouble; one may get through."

Hyde pushed the teapot and cups out of the way and spread Moseley's map on the table. "Which road will be best?" he asked, including Pollock and Roger in his glance.

Roger said, "Best avoid White's Ferry and cross the river farther west." He put his finger on the map. "Here, at Cheshire's Ferry—what do you think?" he said to Tom.

Pollock nodded. "Yes, then they can cut across and reach the Somer Town Road to the north." Pollock frowned, looking at the map closely with his shortsighted eyes. "I'll send a woodsman with them. He can lead them a short way along the river. Best avoid Bryan's and Maule's plantations and come in above. I'll see about horses." He left them and hurried across the lawn to the stables.

Roger leaned back against the chair. He felt fatigue through all his aching body.

Hyde sat looking at the map without speaking. "He plans to trap us, with a boat across the river and one between us and Queen Anne's Town," he said after a moment.

Roger nodded. He was a little astonished that Hyde had grasped the situation so quickly.

"Do you think they will attack today?"

Roger said, "No, sir, I believe they will wait until all the men of the Council are here before he shows his hand. I've no good reason for this surmise, sir."

Hyde nodded. "I've thought the same. When Pollock returns, we will order the men to their stations."

Roger raised his brows.

"You are surprised that we have a plan? We have it all down on paper: what is to be done in case of attack. But the plan is predicated on a force of militia with ammunition and sufficient weapons." The Governor smiled wryly. "The militia is not fully organized and our shot has not come from

343

Charles Town, nor has Captain Gregory returned from the Ashley River Settlements."

In the silence that followed Pollock came out of the house and spoke to Hyde. "I sent messengers to all the upriver planters to ride at once to Balgray, and I've set the men at their stations. No one will try landing without being seen."

"Good, very good," Hyde said, and turned back to the map.

Roger got up stiffly. "With your permission, sir, I think I'll clean myself up." Hyde acquiesced without raising his eyes.

Pollock said, "Your room is ready in the cottage. My boy has gone over with the hot water and linen. He'll dress your arm better than I can. Perhaps he can dig out the bullet."

Roger went down the steps to cross the garden. As he passed, he overheard Hyde say, "It's a good thing we had the cannon mounted when we did. At least it is ready."

"Right," Pollock answered. "A little surprise is an advantage even in a sanguinary engagement."

A slave was waiting at the cottage to show Roger to his room. He stripped off his slimy damp clothes and bathed, while the slave cleansed the wound in his forearm. He watched the slave as he probed with a hot wire for the bullet. The pain was intense for a moment. Then the man gave a grunt. "He not go deep," he said with satisfaction, holding up the ball for Roger to see.

A drink of hot tea and Roger got into bed. The cool linen sheets seemed to rest his tired body. One thought kept recurring to his weary brain, as it had during the long ride through the dark forest. "I have taken my stand," he muttered aloud, "taken my stand ... cast my lot with the government party and Hyde...."

He was dropping off into sleep when he heard horses galloping down the driveway. Anthony and Willie Maule had begun their long ride to Virginia.

"God with them," he said sleepily. "God with them."

Chapter 28

DEATH
TOKEN

CAPTAIN Zeb Bragg was engaged in packing his kit bag for his return to sea on the *Golden Grain* when Marita rode up to his little house on the banks of Albemarle Sound. He had spread his belongings on the grass, trying to make up his mind what gear he would take with him. He greeted Marita with enthusiasm and helped her dismount, calling a slave to place a chair near by.

"You don't mind if I go right on, do you? It takes a bit of figurin' to know what to carry and what to leave behind. 'Tis a small ship, Duke Roger's *Golden Grain,* and my cabin is no more than a cupboard. Now when I was sailing on the old *Lusitania,* I was but a second mate, but I had a cabin twice as big." He paused, holding up a short sabre with a Damascene hilt.

"See this? 'Tis all I have left from Morocco. I have a notion to give it to Miss Mittie as a keepsake." He sat down on a stump and filled his pipe. "I had some fine jewelry when I got away from there that a Moorish woman gave me, bangles and rings set with red and green stones . . . but the gals got them. Every port a man goes into there's always a gal looking for presents." He sighed loudly. "Ah, well, that's the way it goes. Now that I want the trinkets to give to a lady, there's nothing left." He balanced the sabre in one gnarled hand. " 'Tis a good weapon. Do you think she'd take it asmiss?"

Marita tried not to smile. "Can you spare it?" she asked, wondering what little Miss Mittie would do with a sabre.

"It's a fair stabbing blade," Zeb said, taking it out of its sheath and examining it carefully. "Much blood has run down that groove. I got enough weapons without that one." He put it in the pile of things to leave behind with reluctance.

"Now, as I was saying to Duke Roger, I've sailed most every one of the trade-ship fleets, but the old *Lusitania,* she was the finest of them all. She's not like the victualling ships, or the trade guard-ships, 'tis true, but . . ." He lighted his pipe the second time. "It's a fair come-down for Zeb Bragg to take out a forty-tonner to Jamaica with a dirty load of tar. I'd rather sail on Governor Spottswood's *Enterprise* or *Garland,* and go chasing pirates down the coast."

"I think taking out a load of tar for the Navy is splendid," Marita said, hoping to encourage him. "Do you want our Navy to be at the mercy of the Swedish Company for their tar?"

Captain Zeb's face brightened. "You're right, girl. I never thought of it that way. Of course, you're right—naval stores is mighty precious cargo in times like these. War on the seas everywhere, Frenchmen and Spaniards marauding like they do."

He blew a few puffs on his pipe and went back to work, well satisfied that taking out a cargo of tar was not beneath the dignity of a man who had been an officer on the *Lusitania.*

Marita was thinking about riding back to the manor house when the Captain discovered a small sailing boat entering the cove. He stood for a moment, his hand against his forehead to protect his eyes. "It's Edward Tomes. I know his fishing boat," he said. "He must have been up to Queen Anne's Town."

Marita walked down to the float with the Captain and waited for the boat to put in. When Edward lowered the sail, they saw that Lucretia was sitting in the stern. Marita had not seen her since the day at Bat's Grave. Once since that time, she had been over to the Tomeses', but Lucretia and her mother had gone to a women's meeting near Pequimans Court House. She dreaded to see Lucretia, for fear she would say something about Michael. Marita was determined not to make any explanation of the Anne Bonney revelation that she had been on Michael's ship. What could she say? Nothing, unless she told Lucretia that she and Michael were married.

Marita pressed her hand against the gold chain Michael had placed about her neck. It seemed to bring him close, to make her forget the horror of that day when the leet girl shouted the defiant words that exposed Marita's secret love for Michael before them all. Not one had spoken to her of Michael. Not even Anthony Lovyck. She was sure no one had spoken to her aunt, but one day someone would say something to arouse Lady Mary's suspicions.

She wished Michael would come back. Sufficient time had passed for him to make the journey and return to Pamticoe. She was aware that the Captain had spoken to her, but she was too deep in her own thoughts to heed him. A moment later Edward's boat came alongside the float. Marita saw from the expression in Lucretia's face that something disastrous had happened.

Edward stood up to reef sail. Before he jumped ashore he called out to Zeb, "There's been brawling in the village and two men killed." His voice showed his excitement.

"And a fire," Lucretia said at the same time. "A fire on Water Street, and Tom the Tinker was stabbed, and is like to die; and Mr. Cary's boat—"

Captain Zeb interrupted, "One at a time, please. Edward, suppose you tell us what's happened—who was rioting and when?"

Edward said, "It happpened last night. Sailors and townsfolk—" he hesitated a moment—"sailors from Thomas Cary's ship, the *Willing Maid*."

Marita lifted her eyes from the water. She glanced quickly at Lucretia. Lucretia's eyes met hers for a moment before she turned her head. They held no look of anger as they had the day at Bat's Grave. Now they were questioning and very sad. Marita was motionless, but her pulse beat quickly. Michael had returned. She would see him again. Joy and fear struggled in her heart. Edward had resumed.

"With knives," he said, fighting and brawling, cutting and slashing. Tom the Tinker was standing on the tongue of a waggon, shouting something ribald about King Charles the Second."

"He was very drunk, then, if he'd got back to Charles' reign."

"Yes, but not too drunk to get into a fight with a seaman named Diego—"

"Diego," Marita caught the word before it passed her lips.

"A pirate, from his black looks and the gold rings in his ears. He had a lad with him, young, with yellow hair to his shoulders, and two pistols in his striped sash. It was the lad who started the fight with Tom the Tinker."

"What happened then?" Zeb asked.

Edward shrugged his shoulders. "How does one know what

happens in a brawl? Some say it was the lad who stabbed the Tinker."

"Did he die?" Marita said.

"Not yet, but it may be mortal hurt. After that the guards came and the sailors ran to the landing. Some say they fired buildings near the water to give them time to reach their ship."

"And then?"

"They got away. Mr. Moseley's issued a warrant for the man Diego and that lad that started the trouble, but the Constable couldn't make them prisoners for the ship sailed away upriver. When the guards took after them, they saw the big guns mounted on the decks—so they did not follow."

"That is bad," Zeb said thoughtfully. "Cary should have turned them over to the officers. Bad things come of evading the law."

Edward didn't speak for a moment. Then he said, " 'Twas Michael Cary who gave orders to sail."

Marita's throat constricted. Fear made her motionless and speechless. No one else spoke until Zeb said, "I think I will go into the village. I'm in need of a kersey coat to take on my trip; mayhap the tailor can sew one up in a hurry."

Marita regained her poise. She made a little friendly gesture. "Come to the house, Lucretia. I know my aunt will want you and Edward to dine with us."

"Thank thee, Marita, but our mother expects us home. She would worry if we did not get home by the dinner hour."

Marita wanted Lucretia's friendship, but Michael stood between them. She went to Lucretia and took her hand. "You must come soon to Greenfield, dear Lucretia," she said. The girl veiled her eyes. She was withdrawn and distant.

Marita stood watching the boat move slowly out of the cove. She knew that she had lost Lucretia, who might in time get over the first hurt, but would never be her friend again. Michael would come between her and her aunt; that would be next. She shivered, as if a chill wind had blown over her. Would it always be so? Would the shadow of Michael come between her and all those she held dear?

She walked slowly up the path to the house. Captain Zeb was leading out his horse to be saddled. He helped Marita to mount.

"I don't like this," Zeb said as they rode up the lane. "I can't figure what Tom Cary's up to, turning his ship's guns on

348

officers of the law. He'll lose friends, he will. Well and all, Tom's a good fellow but his judgment's poor."

Marita spoke impulsively. "May I ride into town with you, Captain Zeb? I need muslin for the maids' uniforms, and . . ."

Zeb shook his head. There was a look of pity in his shrewd eyes. "The village is no place for you today with men drinking and brawling." They rode to the gate in silence. As Marita turned towards the house, Zeb said, "I'll stop by when I come home. There may be more news to tell you. Don't you fret, Miss Marita. Everything always turns out for the best."

Marita tried to smile. "I hope you are right."

Lady Mary was sitting in the little drawing-room, her chair placed to catch the slight breeze that came from the south. She wore a ruffled white mull dress trimmed with little blue silk bows, and she had left off all but one of her petticoats.

"If it grows a degree warmer, I shall take off everything and put on my night rail," she said, as Marita came into the room. She regarded her niece for a moment. "I don't see how you can look so comfortable wearing that Holland habit. Come here, child; let me see if you are really cool." She inserted her finger between the collar of the riding coat and Marita's neck. "Even your skin is cool," she said in surprise. "Sit down. Desham is ordering a sillabub with limes; it may be refreshing."

Marita untied her hat and took it off. "There's been rioting in the village. Men have been killed."

Lady Mary turned her languid eyes to her niece. "Men are always rioting and killing, my dear. What was this about? How did you hear of it?"

Marita's forehead furrowed in a slight frown. "I don't know exactly. Edward and Lucretia stopped by on their way home from the village. Edward said it was sailors off a ship and townspeople. Tom the Tinker was badly hurt."

Lady Mary lifted her arched brows. "I'll be sorry if he dies. He is a fine lusty fellow with a racy tongue." She smiled, amused at something unspoken.

"Why do you smile?" Marita asked. She was puzzled that her aunt could be so unfeeling about death.

"At something Tom the Tinker said the other day when he was very drunk. Something about King Charles the Second. It was very amusing and very true. It showed a certain shrewd sagacity in the fellow."

Marita said primly, "I'm quite grown up, you know. I think you can tell me."

Lady Mary lifted her drooping lids. Her deep blue eyes went over Marita slowly. "No, my dear, your mind hasn't caught up with your years. Your contacts with life are too young, too very young." She sat looking straight at the young girl without seeing her. "Too young," she repeated. "It is a pity we had to leave London at this time. You are of an age to appear at Court and show yourself at the 'Marriage Parade.'"

Marita felt the blood recede from her face. "I don't want to think of marriage." She spoke quickly with unusual emphasis. "I'm too young," she added lamely.

"A year older than I was when I married," Lady Mary said quietly. "Yes, I must find out who the young eligibles are now. Perhaps we might make some suitable arrangement even at this distance. I'll write home this very day. It will take my mind off the heat."

"Please, don't," Marita said. "Why do you think of marriage? I thought we were happy living here."

Lady Mary smiled. "My dear child, we are not living; we are existing."

Marita thought a moment. She must get her aunt's mind off this idea of hers. "Mr. Mainwairing told me he liked it here better than London. He says people live better. They have more freedom."

Lady Mary laughed aloud. "Duke Roger has more freedom, but he would be free any place—even in gaol."

"I don't understand what you mean?"

"I mean that if a man has freedom of spirit, the body does not matter. That is the kind of freedom Roger Mainwairing possesses: an integrity that is unassailable."

Marita's expression showed that she did not comprehend what Lady Mary was talking about, but it did not matter. Her aunt had ceased for the time being to think about arranging a suitable marriage for her. Marita knew the subject would come up again. Lady Mary was like that, once she had made up her mind to something.

Marita went to her room. She wanted to be alone with her thoughts of Michael.

Yesterday morning a bird had tapped at the window three times. Beulah, who was in the room at the time making the bed, had screamed and covered her head with her apron. "A death token—a death token! We shall hear of death!" Perhaps Michael was in danger. She threw herself on the bed face downward. There Miss Mittie found her and tried to comfort her. But what comfort could there be without Michael to reassure her that all her fears were groundless?

Captain Zeb was back by teatime. "There's wild talk at the village this day," he told them. "Yesterday Tom Cary came into court and defied the Justices. He would not pay the bills for liquor and lodgings before the last Assembly, for which John Pettiver had brought suit. No more would Cary give over money paid for quitrents and land fees during the time he held office. He stood up in the Great Court before three Justices and defied them to force him to give accounting to Governor or Council or Assembly. He was accountable only to the Lords Proprietors in London, and on that right he would stand."

"What will happen?" Lady Mary asked, aroused to interest.

The Captain shook his head. "That I can't say, but Moseley ordered a warrant issued against Cary for contempt."

"Moseley?" Lady Mary said in astonishment. "I thought Moseley was Cary's ardent supporter."

The Captain paused to take a glass of rum punch from a tray that a slave brought to him. "Edward Moseley stands for law first before friend or foe or devil—or God Almighty himself. He's that way. He stood up in court in his red robe and his white wig and said the Common Law would be enforced here in the Province as it was in England, because it was a just law for all the people. The time had passed for lawless living, he told them. Then he spoke some Latin, *Silent leges inter arma.* Chris Gale told me it meant 'The laws are silent in time of war.' What Moseley meant was we'd best have done with war and rebellion and be law-abiding folk. That's what I make of it in Queen Anne's English."

Marita listened, hoping the Captain would say something about the *Willing Maid,* yet she feared to ask. After a time her anxiety for Michael forced her to speak. "Where is Mr. Cary's boat?" she asked, hoping her voice did not tremble.

Captain Zeb carefully avoided her eyes. He took another glass of punch and drank half of it before he spoke. "The village has it that she is sailing upriver to join Emanuel Low's vessel."

"What does all this mean?" Lady Mary asked impatiently. "What is Cary doing now? I had understood he had given

351

over his seal of office and retired in a gentlemanly manner in favour of Governor Hyde."

Zeb spoke slowly, choosing his words. "The talk is that Cary is not satisfied with the Governor's treatment of the Quakers, although Tomes still supports the Governor. I don't know what's in his mind to do now, but it will be devilment. Cary had a band of the most rascally followers ever seen in the Albemarle. I can't think where he got them unless he 'pressed them off pirate ships."

He stopped at the sight of Marita's white face. He had let his tongue run away with him. He didn't want to hurt the child. He had not forgotten the accusation of the witch girl—that Marita had gone aboard the *Willing Maid* with Michael Cary.

"I used to like Tom Cary. He is a bold, fearless man, but now he's fair crazy for power—a doom for a man if he hasn't the right on his side."

No one spoke. In the silence Marita heard the dull drone of the great black and gold bumblebees in the honeysuckle vine that twined the pillars of the gallery.

After a little, Zeb got up. He wanted no supper, he said; he must go to his house for something, then return to the village. Marita knew without his telling that it was arms he went for, his musket or his pistols. The Captain smelled trouble. He would be ready and more than willing to get into the fray, whatever it was.

Marita stood on the gallery watching the Captain ride down to the lane. The fields and the pasture were green and lush, the young corn waving in the soft breeze, turning silvered leaves to the sun. In the meadow the Black Angus cattle grazed or chewed their cud in the shadow of the forest. The herdboy watched them, playing a mournful tune on a reed pipe. Two cardinal birds perched on a bush at the gate and a wren hovered over her nest in the roof of the gallery. So tranquil and so quiet, yet in the village a few miles away men were fighting and bringing death. A shiver went over her as if from the grave, a remembrance of the death token that beat at her window that morning.

Chapter 29

CORMORANTS' BROOD

ROGER MAINWAIRING slept like a drugged man. When he woke, the sun was well down, and the long shadows lay on the grass in front of the cottage. He found his suit, cleaned and in order, hanging in the clothes press. A slave was waiting to help him dress. The gentlemen of the Council had all arrived, the Negro told him. Nothing had happened, but men were standing guard with guns. The Baron de Graffenried had come up from Bath Town by boat, not an hour before.

"The Baron, he brings he servants, all dressed up in fine clothes and yellow caps," the boy told Roger as he held Roger's coat. "He livery finer than the Governor's and hit got gold braid up the front of de coats."

When Roger crossed the garden one of the Baron's servants in gold-braided coat and yellow cap was hurrying from the cooking house, carrying a tray of food towards the manor house. He smiled to himself. De Graffenried required the good service customary for a man of consequence. In truth he had set up a barony of no mean style at his town of New Bern. In spite of hardships and sickness among his people and the constant danger of Indians the Baron never descended from his own standard of living or neglected the amenities of good living. A stickler for form, he held a close rein on his people in his position of Landgrave.

Roger had a certain respect for De Graffenried, for his orderly mind and his adherence to his chosen code. Without humour or the light touch, the man had managed to draw loyalty from his people. For he was fearless, and took the hardships as they came without complaint. He ruled his little kingdom with military precision and strict justice.

A sentry, a roughly dressed boy from upriver, was walking back and forth along the bank, and another was posted on the gallery watching the river through the spyglass. Roger spoke to him and took the glass from his hand. Low's brigantine, the *Pamticoe Adventure,* had moved down river and lay almost opposite Balgray. There was no sign of activity on deck. Perhaps the very lack was ominous.

"Do you make out the guns, sir?" the sentry asked. "I think I can count six, although I'm not sure of the one near the prow. It might be the capstan instead of a mounted cannon."

Roger looked more carefully. "You're right I make it six cannon. She could rake us properly if she moved close in."

Roger handed the glass to the man. A servant came to the door to tell him that Mr. Pollock wanted him to come to supper in the banquet room.

The men of the Council were already seated at the table when Roger entered the room. He took a vacant chair between Blount and William Reid. A moment after he had taken his place the Governor bowed his head and said a short grace.

The attention was centred on Roger when Hyde asked him to repeat the story of the night before. Every face was grave when he finished. Foster Tomes spoke to the Governor. "I hope thee understands, Excellency, that not all the Friends agree with Thomas Cary."

Hyde was pleased, Roger could see by his expression. He made some appropriate answer which Roger did not catch.

Nicholas Crisp said, "There is nothing we can do but wait for Cary to make a move. After that we can determine what will be best and most expedient. Is that your Excellency's idea?"

"Quite, Mr. Crisp. As I told you earlier, when you first came, we have posted trusted men along the river at the possible landings, both on the Chowan and the Sound. Our men have reported that Cary's second ship, the *Willing Maid,* is anchored near the mouth of the Roanoke, opposite the south-shore ferry."

Pollock had not opened his mouth to say a word since the meal started. He laid down his knife and fork and glared around the table, his eyes bright and angry under his beetling brows. "It's an outrage, a damnable outrage! I won't have Tom Cary bringing his ships up our river and besieging me on my own land." He banged his fist on the table. "Damme, I won't submit to it! A man's house is his castle."

Hyde quieted the irate Scot. "You aren't besieged yet, Tom. There's no law against a man sailing his ship up the Sound and into the river. Suppose he says he is fishing?"

354

"He'd better not fish on this side of the river," Pollock muttered, sinking back into his chair. "If he does, I'll treat him as I would any poacher, with a blast of shot in his breeches."

The Governor addressed John Blount. "Do you know how much ammunition there is on hand in the village, Mr. Blount?"

"I don't know how much powder there is in the powder house, but we have nine hundred fifty-eight pounds of shot and twenty-five hundred flints. We've had most of the powder for some time, sir. I doubt if it will all be explosive."

Nicholas Crisp sat with hunched shoulders, his eyes fixed on the table. At Blount's words he raised his eyes. "I know where there are a few hundred pounds—"

Pollock broke in. "Why do we spend time talking and talking? Why not act? I'd have a cannon trained on that ship right now—a well-placed shot amidships and we'd send her to the bottom of the river." He half rose from his chair.

The Governor spoke quietly. "Tom, have a little patience. It's much better if we let Cary make the first overt act. Then we will know what step to take."

"I'm fair weary of waiting," Pollock answered. "Fair weary. It gives the man too great account to let him do what he pleases. Why can't we let Roger take my sloop and a few men and sail over alongside the *Pamticoe Adventure* and put a boarding party on her?"

"No," Hyde said sharply. "No, and if you make such a move I'll put you under arrest." The Governor meant what he said, and every man at the table knew it. "I can understand why you want to take action, Tom," Hyde said more kindly, "but I think my plan is the one to follow." His eyes went around the table. They were all in agreement except Roger Mainwairing.

Hyde glanced at Roger. He could read nothing in his face. "What plan would you follow?" he said abruptly.

Roger answered reluctantly. He glanced around the table. Every man present was older than he, but with the exception of Edward Hyde not one of them had had any military experience. For a moment Roger thought he would evade an answer. He found himself more deeply involved than he wanted to be. Not that he objected to making war on Thomas Cary and his men, but before committing himself he would have liked to talk with Edward Moseley and heard

355

his opinions. Hyde's deep-set eyes were boring into his. He realized that he must express his views.

"I would send a long boat with eighteen or twenty men to the ship, with orders to put the cannon out of commission."

"How many cannon have they, do you think?" Nathaniel Chevin asked.

"Six. Four are swivels," Roger answered.

Hyde said, "Twenty men wouldn't be enough, Mainwairing."

Roger said, "Ten would do if they were the right men, sir."

Nothing more was said, for Baron de Graffenried came into the room with Tobias Knight, the new member of the Council. Knight had come overland from Bath. The Councilmen greeted him with some restraint. They were not sure where he stood in regard to Cary. The men sat down after De Graffenried had made a suitable apology for their tardiness at supper, due to his changing uniforms.

"Mr. Knight has some news of importance," he told the Governor, "news concerning Thomas Cary's plans—or perhaps I should say threats. Will you tell the Governor and these gentlemen what is being rumoured in Bath Town?"

Before Knight could speak, Foster Tomes got to his feet. His benign face showed his distress. "With your Excellency's permission, I beg leave to go to my home. I think it wise that I do not listen to discussion of these matters in which I can take no part."

The Governor frowned a little, then his face cleared. "I understand, Mr. Tomes."

The Quaker hesitated a moment. "If I do not know what thee plans, it is better, since I must remain outside all thought of war or rebellion."

He made his way out of the silent room. In a short time Roger saw him walking across the garden to the boat landing, followed by his servant.

The Baron was first to speak. "If all the Quakers were of his opinion, we would have no troubles."

Hyde looked up quickly when De Graffenried said "we" but he made no comment; instead he spoke to Knight. "May we have your news, Mr. Knight?"

Knight answered readily, almost as if he enjoyed repeating Cary's words. "Cary intends to capture the Council and your Excellency and hold you prisoners."

356

Pollock's harsh voice boomed out, "I knew he was a traitor! Capture the Governor, would he—and after that?"

Knight's thin, crafty face was solemn. He hesitated before replying. "It was said in Bath Town that Tom Cary threatened to treat Governor Hyde as the people of Antigua treated their governor—tear him limb from limb—"

A stunned silence followed Knight's words. Everyone there knew what had befallen Daniel Parke: tortured and dismembered while he still lived, thrown over the walls of the city for wild animals to gut.

Roger looked at one after the other of the Councilmen. Their faces were white with fear or anger, he was not sure which, save for Thomas Pollock. He was livid with rage but he waited for the Governor to speak.

Hyde rose from the table. He spoke without a tremor in his voice. "Perhaps it will be well to double our guard and tighten our defences. I have no wish to share the fate of Daniel Parke."

De Graffenried walked out into the garden with Roger. It was not dusk, although the sun was down. Across the river lay the *Pamticoe Adventure*, caught and held by the fading light, a gaunt bird of prey, perched ready to spread wings. "Cormorants' Brood" had been a term applied to Cary's men more than once these past years. It came to Roger that Cary might put his threat into action, if his men got ashore to the Governor. He gradually became aware that the Baron was talking of Cary.

"I tried to be friendly but I found it impossible. He came to me in New Bern, in the place of my residence, where he dined with me. After the meal we drank a bottle of Madeira wine and spoke seriously, as he was supposed to supply me with all necessities by order of the Lords Proprietors."

"And then?" Roger asked.

De Graffenried's voice rose as his wrath rekindled. "At first he refused to do anything. He tried to wheedle me and get my promise not to work against him. I would not commit myself. Then he promised to deliver to me in another three weeks, in partial payment, five hundred sterling in cattle, grain and other provisions."

The Baron puffed his long pipe for a moment as he and Roger walked towards the water. "When he pressed me about siding with him against Governor Hyde, I said I would leave everything *in statu quo*. Later he tried to incite my colonists against Governor Hyde."

357

Roger thought, All this is working in Governor Hyde's favour. He did not speak or interrupt the Baron's train of thought.

"Cary is a rebel. He has got together the greatest gang of tramps and rioters I ever saw. He promises them plenty of good drinks. He will work by trickery and infamous methods, so I fear for this good gentleman, Governor Hyde."

Roger said, "We will guard him closely tonight."

"Yes, yes. We must do that. I have eight of my men here. By tomorrow you will have many planters on guard along the river. We must remember that Cary has eighty or a hundred men on his boat."

A light flared up in the darkness, a signal rocket from the ship. After a time there was an answering flare near the confluence of the Chowan and the Sound.

"The two ships will make juncture," De Graffenried said. "We may look for trouble in the early morning when the wind is downriver."

Roger agreed. His respect for this young Switzer was growing. Certainly he was not without knowledge of military and naval tactics.

A few moments later they went back to the house. They found the Council gathered in Pollock's office, studying a map of the Sound. Pollock had marked the position of his landings, and the spots where sentries were placed.

"All we can do is wait," the Governor said, as Roger and the Baron came into the room. Hyde had requested Roger to continue to meet with the Council, until the trouble with Cary was over.

Pollock moved about the room impatiently, first to one window, then to another. He started to speak, but catching John Blount's eye, he remained silent.

After a time the Governor looked up from the maps. "I am going to ask Mr. Mainwairing to take ten men and protect the east landing. Baron, will you be responsible for the one at Salmon Creek?"

The Baron stood up, clicked his heels together, and made a stiff salute. "Shall I take my own men, sir?"

"I think it would be advisable."

Roger waited a moment to see if there were other orders before he spoke. "The Baron and I think Cary will attack at dawn."

The other men stopped talking and gave their attention to Hyde.

"What are your reasons?" Hyde asked.

Roger told him of the position of the ships and the rocket signal.

Pollock said, "The wind will be downriver; that is what they need."

Hyde drummed on the table with a quill pen. "I see no reason to alter our plans, even if this be true. I would suggest that the rest of you get some sleep—before dawn," he added grimly.

The moon came up late. In his hiding place in the belvedere at the confluence of the rivers Roger waited for moonrise. His men, good stout country lads, handy with firearms, were stationed along the upper bank. Four of Pollock's trappers chose the beach landing, well hidden behind the long frame fishing house.

From his position Roger had a wide view of the stretch of the river and the Sound. Presently it would be light enough to see the position of Cary's *Willing Maid*. He made himself as comfortable as he could. The wound was troubling him. He had made a support of a silk scarf to carry the weight of his useless arm. Fortunately it was the left arm. He could fire his pistols, although he couldn't load them. His sword arm would have to be his defence.

A long path of silver shone on the water, widening as the moon cleared the trees on the south shore. Roger moved a little as the light spread on the water. He heard a slight sound at his elbow. One of the trappers moved out of the dark wood into the shadow of the belvedere. "They are making ready to land," he said. "I think I hear the sound of paddles."

Roger cupped his hand to his ear. "You are right. Are the men ready?"

The trapper chuckled. "They've spread the seine its full length and hitched it to trees. Cary's men will run into it in the dark and bang the cowbells we've strung along the border."

Roger gave a low laugh. "Good fellows," he said. "If we capture their first landing party, they may not send out a second. No shooting, mind you, unless you're in straits. Bind and gag them. Those are the Governor's orders."

The trapper spat. "It's killing they need. To my way of thinkin', the Governor's too easy on them."

"Even so, orders."

"I know, Mr. Mainwairing."

There was a faint tinkling sound; then a louder jangle. The trapper disappeared. Roger made his way along the bank to the head of the wooden steps and waited. He heard the sound of cursing and muffled shouts, the low whistle of the woodsmen; then silence. They've got them, he thought—probably not more than six or eight to a small boat. If they only could take them one boatload at a time!

The moonlight fell on the ship. She stood clear and straight in the water not far off shore. Then he was aware of the stooping figure of a man running towards him. He came up the steps swiftly and turned towards the summerhouse Roger had just quitted. As he passed, Roger thrust out his boot to trip the runner. He sprawled, but was on his feet almost at the instant, and turned. Whipping out his sword, he faced his unseen enemy.

"Come out in the moonshine, damn you!"

Roger knew that voice. It was Michael Cary.

"Come out, Lovyck," Cary shouted, "or are you afraid to cross swords again?"

Roger stepped out of the shadow. A muffled curse came from Michael's lips.

"Mainwairing!" he said, the braggadocio gone from his voice. "I thought it would be like Lovyck to hide behind a tree."

"On guard, Cary," Roger said. "This time I'll not let you off so readily as I did at the Red Lion."

Cary fought savagely. The sling on Roger's left arm set him off balance. Once he almost lunged forward on his opponent's sword, but he caught himself in time. He spread his feet a trifle and gave himself firmer footing. Little by little he forced Michael back until he stood in front of the summerhouse.

Suddenly it flashed into Roger's mind that that was what Cary wanted. He could barricade himself behind the door. If he had a pistol, Roger would have small chance to get out of range.

They were both breathing heavily. Cary lunged. Roger parried, and Roger by a quick upward stroke caught Cary's arm a glancing stroke; but it must have pierced the flesh, for Michael cursed and lifted his speed. That was what Roger wanted, for Michael could not attack and keep himself covered. Roger waited his time, suddenly countered and thrust. A moment later he was through Michael's guard.

"Damn you!" shouted Michael, as his sword flew from his

360

hand. "Damn you, Mainwairing. I swear you are Satan himself!" He put his finger to his lips and gave a shrill whistle.

Out of the tail of his eye Roger saw a figure detach itself from the gloom of the forest and cross the stretch of ground that lay open to the moon. He recognized the Indian servant he had seen with Cary. The Indian paused, lifting his arm above his head. Roger saw the light strike the flat head of a tomahawk. Instantly Roger crouched, and the weapon passed over him and sank into the door of the summerhouse.

Michael started to run, but Roger caught him with the point of his sword. "Stand back," he said quietly. "If you move or your Indian makes a move, I'll run you through. This is not child's play. Call off your Indian. Tell him to get around where I can see him."

Roger saw the trapper had come up from the beach. "No need, Mr. Mainwairing; we've got the fellow. I'll truss him up like a fowl and carry him to the spit, the red devil!"

"Thanks, you came just in time. I don't believe I could have held both of them with one arm in a sling."

Michael swore then, long and with violence.

Roger laughed silently. He knew Michael could stand capture better than being disarmed by a man who had one arm bound to his side.

Michael Cary was alternately sullen and defiant when he stood before Governor Hyde, but speak he would not. After a time the Governor grew weary of questioning him, and Pollock led him away to the slave dungeon under the house.

"Rest you here for a while, my fine fellow," Tom said. "Perhaps you will find your tongue before morning. The Governor's given you every chance, as he has that rascally uncle of yours. Now things will be different." He turned the key in the lock and, having set two men on guard, he went upstairs.

"I've put the young cockalorum in the slave dungeon," Pollock said when he came back to the room.

The Governor showed signs of anger. "We can't do that: put a gentleman in a slave's dungeon. It's unthinkable."

"It's right enough, sir. There's never been a black slave in it, or any other, since the place was built."

Hyde sank back in his chair. "I suppose it is all right," he said doubtfully.

Roger made sure that the Indian was bound and in a safe place before he went back to his post. He was certain, now

361

that he had time to consider, that Michael's plan had been to carry the Governor, and perhaps Pollock, to his ship, while his uncle made ready to attack the manor house at daylight. At any rate the surprise attack had been broken up.

He found when he returned to his post that his men had put their prisoners in the fish house. The beach head was clear, and no other boat had put out from the *Willing Maid*.

"Keep a keen lookout, Grimes," he said to the trapper. "I think they mean to attack before morning."

The attack came at sunrise. As soon as it was light, Roger saw that there was activity on the deck of the *Willing Maid*. His men on the beach were ready. Now that it was light, he could see them. They had taken positions along the shore, hiding behind the fish house, driftwood logs and in the woods.

Grimes came up to him, stooping behind bushes to cross the cleared spot near the steps. "Colonel Pollock has sent us twenty-five new men, sir," he said as he stretched out on his stomach beside Roger. "He sent a slave with hot tea and bread an hour ago. Every man knows his place and every man can shoot."

The words had scarcely died on his lips when the dull boom of cannon fire broke the quiet. From the direction of the sound, Roger knew the *Pamticoe Adventure* had opened the Battle of the Chowan. After that he had little time to think of what was happening at the manor house. In spite of the sniping by the trappers, two long boats managed to land on the beach. Roger watched his men, hoping they would not be tempted to rush out and engage Cary's mob in hand-to-hand fighting. Grimes had them in hand, and they continued to use woodsmen's tactics—sniping from safe position.

The landing party, surprised, halted as one or two of their men fell upon the sand. They had not expected opposition, thinking to land under cover of the cannonading from the Chowan position. Now they hesitated, uncertain whether to go forward under the fire of the unseen enemy or to return to their boats and retreat to their ship.

Roger saw the sailor Diego jump from the second long-boat, followed by a tall slender lad with blond square-cut hair flying to his shoulders. The lad had a pistol in his hand, and a second thrust through the striped scarf about his midriff. He started up the bank, unmindful of the bullets. Diego shouted for him to come back, but the boy kept running, his body bent. He made for the steps, calling for the others to follow, but they had already turned towards the boats. Diego ran after the boy, yelling for him to come back.

Roger ran along the bank. He would cut off their retreat at the top of the steps. He saw Grimes behind a tree at the edge of the forest, the barrel of his long musket trained on the head of the flight of steps. Roger signalled for him to hold fire. There was something familiar about the quick sure movement of the boy's body as he ran along the beach. Halfway up the steps he raised his head. It was as Roger suspected. This was the leet girl, Anne Bonney, her long flaxen braids cut square like a boy's, tricked out in sailor clothes. Roger remembered then the day of the County meeting at Newby's Ferry, when the swarthy sailor Diego wooed the girl with tales of the Indies and pirate ships.

She raised her voice, calling to Diego. "We must be sure the Captain is safe," she shouted. "Something may have happened—" She raised her eyes and stopped suddenly. "Duke Roger!" she exclaimed.

"Put down your pistol," Roger said. "Grimes, disarm the man. I'll take care of the boy."

Anne screamed, "Run, Diego, run for the boat!" She turned and ran after him, her slim body between the sailor and Roger's pistol.

"Damn her!" he muttered. "She knows I won't shoot her in the back."

A boom of cannon split the air. Roger thought: Let them escape; I can't shoot a woman. Grimes was loading again; his first shot had been over the heads of the running figures.

Roger called to him, "Wait, what's that noise in the woods?" He could hear shouting and dogs barking. A voice rang out, "Diego, hold the boat."

Before Roger could turn, Michael Cary, his face blackened with dirt, his clothes torn, dashed by him, followed by his Indian. Michael saw Roger. He laughed and waved his sword. "No time to fight you now, Duke, but I won't forget."

Bullets splashed in the water about the boat. He heard Anne's voice, "The Captain! Wait for the Captain," followed by Michael's "Push off, damn you. Push off! I'll make it."

Before Roger's men could reload, the longboat was far out on the water. Michael Cary and his crew had made their escape.

The sound of cannon was continuous from the river. Roger gave orders for his men to watch the landing, and ran towards the manor house. He wondered how Michael Cary had escaped from Pollock's dungeon. When he neared the house he understood. A cannon ball had hit one wing of the house, tearing through the wall, making a great gap in the heavy brick foundation which formed the dungeon. All Cary had to do was to walk through the breach, cut the cords that bound his Indian and disappear into the forest. "Damn the fellow!" he found himself saying aloud. "Damn him and his charmed life!"

Roger ran around the corner of the house. Here all was confusion, men hurrying back and forth, slaves rolling cannon balls across the garden. A slave was tending a man who had been injured and lay on the grass groaning in agony, his lower leg shot away. The Governor, wearing his uniform of the Queen's Guard, stood glass in hand watching the *Pamticoe Adventure*. Pollock, his red face dripping with sweat, was urging Hyde to give the order to fire the cannon, which was hidden behind the shrubbery.

"Not yet," Hyde said. "Let them enter the creek. Let them think they have everything their own way, then . . ." He laid the glass on a table. He saw Roger and called to him. Roger gave his report.

"Michael Cary got away, your Excellency." For some reason he kept silent about Anne Bonney. Pollock cursed viciously, swearing he would have the ears of the guard. In the confusion no one had noticed Michael's escape.

"I'll send Crisp out to the Point to take your place," Hyde said to Roger. "I need you here. As soon as the ship crosses the mouth of the creek we'll open fire on her."

Roger took the glass. A moment later he returned it to the table. "I would advise changing the position of the cannon, your Excellency. As it stands, you will not be able to command the entrance with your fire. See this." He pointed to the map.

Hyde was silent for a few moments, as Roger indicated on the map the arc a cannon ball would make. "You are right, Mainwairing," the Governor said. "I failed to calculate the curve. Will you take charge? Change the position of the gun and be ready to fire the moment the ship passes that line."

Roger had little time to make the change and drag the cannon up to the bank. Men worked stripped to the waist, their bodies shining with sweat. He did not want the men aboard the *Adventure* to see that they had cannon, so he ordered slaves to cut small trees and hold them upright between the spot and the ships. Presently they were in readiness, cannon well set and loaded, men ready with fuse and rod. As the brigantine under full sail swung into the little bay, it let loose a broadside. Roger waited for the smoke to clear. No damage had been done for the shot was short of the mark. Roger made a hasty calculation, waiting a few moments for the ship to pass a second invisible line. Suddenly he realized that Cary planned to anchor ship and send a party ashore. He held fire until the anchor was over the side into the water; then he dropped his extended arm to his side, the signal to the gunner to open fire. A moment later the heavy boom of the cannon sounded, fire spurted from the barrel, and the smoke belched forth and hung over them like a heavy pall. When it cleared away, Roger saw the ball had found its target on the deck of the *Pamticoe Adventure*, where the forward gun was set. The deck was confusion— sailors slid down the ropes, foremast and mizzen, orders were shouted, barefoot sailors ran across the deck, ready to touch off the fuse for another broadside.

Roger's men were loading feverishly. He took careful sight before the *Adventure* could fire another broadside. This time it was a clean hit which cut away the mainmast at its base. It fell to the deck, carrying the foresail with it.

The third ball struck the ship near the water-line. Men were swarming overside now, swimming for shore or taking to the boats.

De Graffenried's men took up their positions behind a row of bushes on the shore of the river. The rebels, seeing the Baron's servants in livery, took them for the Queen's marines from Virginia. They dared not land but pulled away, bent double with their exertions to get out of range of De Graffenried's muskets.

Without delay the Governor sent men out in pursuit in longboats and canoes. Some of Cary's force escaped by swimming and taking to the woods, pursued by Pollock's men; others in the boats rowed downstream to be picked up later by the *Willing Maid*. Thomas Cary was among these, and Emanuel Low.

The Governor's men captured the brigantine and its ammunition, and those of its crew who were trapped between decks. In spite of rejoicing over the capture of the *Pamticoe Adventure* Hyde was despondent, for the leaders of the rebellion had all escaped.

The Governor sat on the gallery at Balgray, his writing table pulled up in front of him. The members of the Council strolled about the garden or sat on iron benches near the river bank.

De Graffenried and his men had started for home. He told the Governor that he was obliged to leave at once since he had made arrangements to join Mr. Lawson at Bath Town two days hence. From there the two men and their servants planned to take a three weeks' journey westward into the Indian country. Three of De Graffenried's men sailed his boat to New Bern.

Tobias Knight joined the Baron in the march overland to his home on the Pamticoe, while the others only waited for the Governor to finish his proclamation before departing. Pollock had set his men repairing the brigantine, and a mason was laying brick in the shattered wall. Roger sat on the steps holding his arm against his side. Nicholas Crisp had poured half a pint of turpentine in the wound to keep it clear of mortified flesh, and it burned like St. Anthony's fire.

Presently the Governor finished writing. He rose and walked to the edge of the gallery and stood by the balustrade. The Councilmen, seeing him, got up from their benches and crossed the lawn.

The Governor stood for a moment without speaking, his eyes on the roll of paper in his hand. His face was quiet but his mouth was unsmiling. "Gentlemen, we have been fortunate today," he said. "We have in our possession a fully equipped vessel capable of carrying eighty or a hundred men. That is not enough. I want you to go to your homes and arrange your affairs so that you can march with me to Bath Town and rout Thomas Cary from his stronghold. I will expect each of you to provide a levy of ten men. We will start the journey from Bell's Ferry on Monday next at ten in the morning, three days from now. I am determined to apprehend the traitor Cary and crush his rebellion."

Pollock said, "Glory be to God! At last we'll march on the rebels. By Monday her Majesty's marines will be here." Pollock's tone implied a question.

Hyde did not heed Pollock. Instead, he spoke to Roger Mainwairing. "I want you to deliver this proclamation to the marshal at Queen Anne's Town. Ask him to have it placed on the board on Government House and in other public places where people congregate, so that all may read."

His eyes went slowly around the little group. "I am invok-

ing an ancient Act of Hue and Cry against Michael Cary,
late prisoner under our hand, and against Diego, a sailor, and
a youth by the name of Bonney for attempted murder on the
body of Thomas Cockburn, commonly known as Tom the
Tinker."

Chapter 30

HUE
AND CRY

THE PEOPLE OF Queen Anne's Town were in turmoil. The
events of the past two days had awakened them from their
apathy and galvanized them into immediate preparation to
defend the village against attack. The Constable called out
the militia, which consisted of twenty men. The market-
place was deserted, countryfolk hurrying to their homes, and
the Great Court recessed for the two days.

The excitement started when Cary's ship, the *Willing
Maid*, anchored in the bay. The burning of the fishing wharf,
the stabbing of Tom the Tinker by two seamen from the ship
brought half the village to Water Street, angry and calling
for the arrest of the troublemakers. The early morning cannonading upriver put fear and anxiety into the hearts of the
villagers. Very few planters wanted another outbreak of the
Cary Rebellion. Men in the Albemarle who had secret hopes
that the rebel would succeed in disrupting the new government under Edward Hyde held their tongues. The villagers
resented the arbitrary way that Michael Cary had defied the
Marshal and Constable in sailing away with the two miscre-
ants. They were weary of strife. They had hoped Edward
Hyde's appointment as governor would bring them peace.

Many set to work to repair the stockade that surrounded
the village. Idle men, women and children crowded Water
Street and the shores of the little bay, looking up the Sound
with anxious eyes, hoping to see the ships that were bom-
barding Balgray. The taverns were crowded with men calling
for ale and strong drink, speculating with their neighbours
what the outcome would be. A few acknowledged Cary men
met on the Common with the Church adherents and battled
367

with bare fists, until the militia was ordered to patrol the streets to prevent bloodshed within the village.

Roger sailed into the bay in William Reid's boat late in the afternoon. He smiled when he saw the press of people along the shore. "It looks as if we will have to act as the Queen's messengers, bringing the tidings of battle," Roger said.

Reid grinned and let the sail run. Roger ducked his head to escape the boom. "You are Queen's messenger, Duke. After I set you down, I'm sailing on. With this wind I'll make Pequimans Landing by dark."

Roger made a wry face. "I don't know to whom I'll report. Certainly I'm not going to stand on the dock and make a speech before the populace."

Roger made the speech, but not on the dock. Instead he stood on the steps of the half-finished Government House and told the people of the village of the capture of the *Pamticoe Adventure*. They listened in silence. Edward Moseley and the Constable stood behind Roger as he told his story.

"The *Willing Maid* escaped with all the leaders," Roger finished. "Unfortunately we had no ship fast enough to overhaul her."

There was nothing more to say after that. The Constable dismissed the people telling them to go to their homes; that guards would be placed at the gates and along the water entrance to the village.

Roger went into the unfinished hall, followed by the Constable. Roger handed him the Governor's proclamation. The Constable looked at it, then gave it to Edward Moseley.

"Perhaps this is for you, Justice Moseley," he said doubtfully. "I do not know that I am the one to attend to this in a legal way."

Moseley took the paper, read it carefully, and handed it back to the officer. "It is your duty to post the proclamation, Constable."

"But, your worship, Hue and Cry is what we use for escaping slaves!"

"No matter. It is legal. You must post it."

"There is no mention of the real leaders," Roger commented when the officer had left the room. "I confess I don't understand the Governor."

"It is a devilishly clever move, that proclamation. As it stands, the whole of the country will be searching for the offenders; not just the officers of the law. As for the real leaders of the rebellion, they will be charged under another Act, High Treason to the Crown. Do you see how well he has thought it out? Suppose we walk over to the Coffee House and have a drink. I feel the need of one."

"And I," Roger agreed.

MacTavish stopped them as they were crossing the Green. "Begging your pardon, Mr. Mainwairing, but my Tammy found your bay mare straying outside the gates last night. I took the liberty to wash a cut on her hock and put on the new shoes I finished yesterday."

"Splendid," said Roger, pleased that the horse had got away from the Indian village. "Where is she now?"

"In back of my shop, sir. If you care to step over, my boy will saddle her for you."

Roger said to Moseley, "I'll join you shortly. Perhaps you will dine with me at the inn." Moseley left him then and Roger and the farrier walked down Water Street to the shop.

"It's Hue and Cry they'll be putting out against those fellows who attacked Tom," the farrier said.

Roger bent down to lift the mare's leg. He examined the cut before he said, "How is Tom?"

MacTavish's eyes twinkled a little. "He's hurt fair enough, a bad cut in the leg that'll keep him off his feet for a fortnight, the doctor says. But he's enjoying it, Tom is. Every man and boy in the village has been to his house, and many of them bring him a pint. When I saw him he was back to Willliam and Mary, with signs he'd reach King Charles the Second before sundown."

Roger smiled. "I'm glad the wound is no worse."

The farrier threw the saddle over the mare's back and tied the cinch. Roger noticed he had dropped his usual churlish humour and was eager to talk.

"Is it rebellion we're going into, Mr. Mainwairing?"

"I hope not. We've had enough of rebellion. Bloodshed and killing will not help the people of this country," Roger answered, testing the girth. "If it's fighting a man wants, he can get it in the Low Countries."

MacTavish spat. "I'm agin a fight if it's only to please one man's vanity. Like as not that's what's behind this. Tom Cary wants to be governor so much that he'd drag us all into a war to get his way."

Roger did not answer this. He did not see the need of discussion.

MacTavish went on. "Still and all, I've noticed each time

there's a rebellion or fighting the common man gains a little—mayhap we willl gain something this time."

Roger said, "When a man's ready for freedom he gets it." He flung himself onto the back of his horse. "Thank you, MacTavish. I'll send my steward in to pay the reckoning. It's good work that you do, so set a good price."

MacTavish touched his cap. "Any time, Mr. Mainwairing. Any time. If all the Albemarle planters were as quick to pay, I'd have nae trouble at all."

Roger rode off down the street. When he reached the corner he heard singing and the sound of men's laughter. Tom the Tinker was sitting in a great barrel chair in front of his little hut. A dozen of his cronies were squatting on the ground or leaning against the wall, each with a pot of beer in his hand. A keg of beer was just inside the door, covered with a wet tow sack. From the colour of their faces and the way laughter slipped easily from their lips, they had been tapping the barrel freely. Tom was talking.

"It's a miracle of the Blessed Mother I'm here to speak to ye. A little more and that varmint would have slashed my innards—and me saying nothing at all to them save only, 'God Bless King Charles, a bold man, who always kept one hand in the Treasury and the other in some whore's placket.' "

A shout went up. The audience beat their caps on the side of the house to show their approval of Tom's wit.

". . . And before you could say Jemmy Jessamy, the young lad with the yellow hair was at me with his knife, and the black one followed. I'd have been a dead fish if Mac hadn't heard me yelling and come tromping to my rescue. Now I'm sitting on this chair for a fortnight to pay for it. Damn them for vipers!"

Roger turned his horse and galloped off. He had heard enough of Tom's bawdy talk. But he smiled as he rode along the lane. The man was an amusing one. He always knew what was going on in the village and the countryside. Moving as he did from house to house peddling his wares, he picked up gossip of many varieties.

Roger found Moseley waiting in the coffee room. They called a boy and ordered a meal. Moseley was quiet. He spoke little, giving his attention to his victuals and drink. After a time he raised his eyes and met Roger's inquiring glance.

"I can't imagine what has come over Thomas Cary," he said. "This escapade is too much for me to stomach. It will stigmatize all North Carolina in the eyes of decent people. For a man to attempt to abduct the governor is worse than treason. People may well cry 'Shame'." He poured a heavy drink from the decanter of whisky. "I remonstrated with Cary. I begged of him to give Hyde time to show us what he intended. A man cannot create order in a few months in a country where there has been no order for years. I tell you, Roger, we Carolinians have thrown out so many of the Lords Proprietors' Governors, we think we have that right. This move of Cary is infamous, Machiavellian! If he is not careful he will overstep himself. Then it will be Hyde's War—not Cary's Rebellion."

Roger knew what these words cost Moseley. Moseley had been Cary's steadfast adherent. He had defended Cary and stood behind him even when it lost him good friends. Some people had gone so far as to accuse Moseley of being behind Cary's dark crimes, of being as faithless to the common good as Cary. Roger knew this was false. Moseley wanted order above all things. He saw that Moseley expected him to speak, to give his approval.

"I think you are wise, Edward. Cary must be a little mad to threaten the Governor with Daniel Parke's fate."

Moseley looked as if he had not heard aright. "So that was the plan? The blackguard!" he said. "The blackguard!"

A servant came to the door and waited for Roger to give him his attention. "There is a lady in the little parlour. She says will Mr. Mainwairing come at once."

Roger followed the maid to the ladies' parlour. He had no idea who it was that had sent for him. The thought that it might be Lady Mary crossed his mind, but he was unprepared for a frightened Marita with white face and tortured eyes.

"Look," she said, thrusting a paper into his hand. "Look, I tore it down from the posting board. I . . ."

Roger glanced at the paper she had put into his hand. It was the Governor's proclamation of Hue and Cry.

"See what it says," she cried, her voice rising. "See!"

"Don't read it again, Marita," Roger said, trying to restrain her. But she had snatched the paper from him. Her hands were shaking.

Roger took the paper from her and read:

"Whereas: On the 30th of June a complaint was made by the members of the Lords Proprietors Council that one Michael Cary, a lusty young man, fair of speech and feature, wearing uniform of Cary's Company of Dragoons, a seed-coloured frieze coat and breeches, a grey cloth waistcoat, a broad belt and silver buckle diagonally over his shoulder, and high leather boots, ran away from the jurisdiction of this government after having been captured by Mr. Roger Mainwairing in an attempt to carry away the person of your lordships' Governor, and escaped on the barkentine *Willing Maid*. You will require all the people of Albemarle and Bath Counties to make a diligent search by way of Hue and Cry after said runaway, Michael Cary. Having been found, convey from Constable to Constable until he is brought to the Sheriff of the Chowan Precinct, County of Albemarle, Province of North Carolina.

And Whereas, Diego, a seaman, and Bonney, first name unknown, escaped on same ship, *Willing Maid*. To be apprehended for attempted murder of one Thomas Cockburn, commonly called Tom the Tinker, of above village.

All Sheriffs, Constables and all persons to be careful and diligent in their search as they shall answer contrary at their peril.

Given under my hand and seal at Chowan River, the 30th day of June, 1711."

"What does it mean?" Marita caught at his arm. "What a terrible thing for Edward Hyde to link him with criminals ... a common seaman ... Bonney," she whispered, "Anne Bonney! Is it true?" She looked up at Roger, dull anguish in her eyes.

"I am afraid it is true, Marita." The pity he felt for her was in Roger's voice and in his eyes.

"What must I do?" She spoke vaguely as if she were bewildered.

"First, sit here in this chair. I will bring you a glass of wine. Promise me you will not move or go outside the room until I return."

Marita did not reply. In the great chair she seemed no larger than a child, a pitiful, frightened child.

Roger went swiftly from the room, closing the door behind him. He went back to Moseley. Thrusting the proclamation into his hand, he explained briefly, shielding Marita as well as he could. Moseley's face had a grim look.

"What do you want me to do? It is against the law to destroy—"

"Let us not go into that now. Order the Constable to post it again. It will not be necessary for you to explain."

372

Moseley was reluctant. "No doubt half a hundred people saw the girl tear the proclamation from the board."

Roger was angry now. "God's death! You can't always be the judge and the jury. Give it to Roberts to post. Let the common people clack and chatter. Be a little human for once!" He went out of the room back to the parlour, carrying a glass of port. Marita had not moved. She sat huddled in the chair, her face drawn and anguished.

"Come, my child. You are going back to Greenfield now."

"I am afraid," she said without looking at him. "Afraid of all those people who saw me tear the paper down."

"We will go out the side door. Where is your cart?"

"In the yard at the back. My Indians are waiting."

Roger helped her to her feet. She leaned against him as they made their way out the north entrance to the stable yard. Only a few stable boys and grooms were in sight. They were busy playing with dice on the hard ground in front of the stable. They did not even look up as Roger and Marita walked past them.

Roger sent the Indian, Quis-la-kin, to get his mare, which was tied in front of the inn. "You will ride my horse. I will drive in the cart with your mistress."

Roger helped Marita into the seat in the high-wheeled cart. The Indian woman crawled in and sat down on the floor. Roger took up the reins and they drove down the street towards the East Gate.

The sun was down when they came to the gates at Greenfield. The quiet of twilight clothed the fields and the forest. After a time he had felt Marita's head against his shoulder. Roger leaned forward to look under the little scooped hat she wore tied beneath her chin, so he could see her face. Her eyes were closed, the traces of tears remained on her cheeks. She was asleep.

"Damn the fellow!" he said to himself. "It's a pity I didn't finish him when I had him at the point of my sword. She is so young, so defenceless. A man would be dead to all honour . . ."

The girl at his side stirred and sat erect as the keeper swung the gate open. She turned her pleading eyes on Roger. "Please, please, don't let her see me—not like this—not tonight."

Roger thought of the meal he had just eaten at the Coffee House, but he smiled encouragingly. "I think I shall ask your aunt to invite me to supper tonight, and later perhaps she will do me the honour to play a game of piquet with me."

Marita went directly upstairs. In the hall she met Miss Mittie, who looked worried and distressed.

"Captain Bragg stopped by on his way back from the village," she told Marita. "He said there had been a battle up the river near Balgray and many people were killed. He said everyone in the village was alarmed because a number of Cary's men escaped and are roaming about the woods. A great ship sailed right down past here. I saw it myself this afternoon."

An exclamation from Marita stopped the flow of talk. Miss Mittie peered at her with her nearsighted eyes. "What is the matter, Marita? You're as white as a sheet—and where have you been all this afternoon? Your aunt was so cross. She wanted you to stay with her and you weren't here. You'd better hurry and go down."

Marita said, "I have a migraine. I think I'll lie down. Will you ask my aunt to excuse me?"

Miss Mittie stood for a moment looking at her. "You do look pale. I'll send your Indian up with a dish of strong tea. I'll tell her to put you to bed," she said kindly.

When the door closed behind her, Marita sank in a chair, her hands covering her face. The circumstance of her behaviour in the village rose before her. How could she have done such a thing—pushed her way through the throng about the posting board? The words of the proclamation burned in her brain like fire. Michael Cary, Bonney, both on the ship *Willing Maid*. A dry sob shook her slender frame. How could he take Anne Bonney with him? She remembered Muster Day, when she had seen him with his arm over the shoulder of the girl.... Why had he not come to find her? He had sailed his ship so close....

Kikitchina knocked at the door and came in carrying a tray with tea. She set it down on a small table in front of Marita.

"They all eating supper," she said. "Cook say she had nice piece of breast meat if you like."

"Thank you, Kikitchina. The tea is all I want. My head aches so badly."

The Indian woman stood in front of her, looking at her with black opaque eyes. "Kikitchina thinks it is the heart that aches, mistress."

Marita did not speak. There could be no pretence with the

374

Indian woman. She could understand thoughts better than spoken words.

After Kikitchina had taken the tray away, she came back in the room to help Marita undress. Bathed and lying between cool linen sheets, Marita felt quieter, the ache in her heart dulled. The Indian woman's light fingers on her forehead were soothing. She was almost asleep when Kikitchina said:

"Atonga come from ship. His captain say, 'Do not be worried. I will come for you before many days.'"

Marita sat up. "Oh, Kikitchina! When did Atonga come?"

The Indian woman pushed her back to her pillows gently, smiling one of her rare smiles. "The sun was high when the ship anchored a little to get water from the Yaupim. Atonga comes swiftly in his canoe. Quis-la-kin was fishing off the pocosin, and to him he says, 'Tell mistress my captain says, "Do not be worried. I will come for you—before many days".'"

Marita closed her eyes. Michael's words blotted out all other thoughts. Michael would come for her. She should have known. She should have trusted him.

The Indian woman watched her a few minutes. She left quietly and took up her nightly station near the door of Marita's room.

Marita wakened once, when Roger Mainwairing was leaving. She heard Lady Mary's question, "You think there is no danger here at Greenfield?" and Roger's voice, answering, "No, they have taken to the woods back of Balgray. No doubt they will get boats to ferry them across to the south shore. By now they are on their way to join Cary at his stronghold near Bath Town."

"I understood Captain Zeb to say that some of Cary's men were captured west of the village."

"There may be a few between there and Indian Town. But the marines will clear the country when they come."

He dropped his voice. Marita heard no more. The Queen's marines would come and clear the forests of Cary's rebellious men, but Michael was safe, safe on his ship. For the moment she forgot the Governor's proclamation of Hue and Cry, forgot the staring eyes, the questioning faces of the villagers when she tore the paper from the board. One thing filled her mind and her heart: Michael would come for her. In a few days he would come and take her with him. Nothing else mattered.

Chapter 31

ISLAND
STRONGHOLD

THE march to Bath Town was tedious. The heat was terrific
and the men were exhausted by the end of the first day. They
camped in the Wild Deserts. The stream was dry, and they
could get water only by digging in its bed. Roger set up the
camp for his men near a thicket of myrtle, under a cluster of
spreading oaks, to wait for the Governor's force. He was not
too sanguine about the outcome of the march on Cary's
stronghold at Romney Marsh with fewer than ninety men.
Cary had all the advantage—more men, heavy guns of at
least one ship, and a fortified camp.

Hyde was bitterly disappointed with the result of Lovyck's
quest to Virginia. Governor Spottswood had sent him only
twelve marines. When Roger arrived at Balgray early that
morning Hyde had handed him Governor Spottswood's letter
without comment. Spottswood had written at some length
from Kiquotan on the 28th of June:

"I have ordered our frontier counties to draw together some
men and march to the assistance of North Carolina. At the same
time I attempted to obtain a reinforcement of marines from her
Majesty's ships of war here, to be sent in boats to the Sound of
Chowan for securing the brigantine and armed vessels with which
Mr. Cary has been able to insult the government and overawe
your people.

"But the commander of our homeward-bound fleet, judging it
the least part of his duty to do any service to this country, posi-
tively refused to afford me any assistance either of men or boats;
though upon my first communication of that project to him he
seemed to approve of it. I also represented to him how service-
able his boats might prove in transporting the pork I had ordered
to be brought up from Carolina for the Queen's service.

"I had already sent a letter to Mr. Cary asking to know what
his demands are. He replied that he wants the severity of your
laws against the Quakers and his dissenters mitigated. If the laws
of the last Assembly are not revoked, he threatens to declare himself again President, and attack you in your own stronghold.

"I shall still endeavour, notwithstanding the insuperable diffi-
ulty of marching forces into a country so cut off with great rivers,
ithout any convenience of carriage, to put effective stop to these
onfusions. These rebellions in your government give great appre-
ension to her Majesty's subjects in this colony. They feel that a
ıtal rebellion raised here would cost the Crown a great expense
f treasure to quell, especially since Mr. Cary threatened my rep-
esentative that another Antigua tragedy would result. This we
elieve to be his firm resolve, prompted by his own desperate cir-
umstances, and that of the wretched crew and rabble he has got
gether. This must not happen, since it would be destructive to
l government and established law.

"I am sending what marines can be spared from our guard-
ıips for the assistance of your government, and hope by that
ıeans to satisfy the people that they are mistaken in what the
uaker politicians (led by Cary and Emanuel Low) have infused
ıto them."

Roger read the letter with care. The situation so clearly set
own by Governor Spottswood was a true representation as
e, Roger, saw it. He said as much to the Governor. Hyde
ut the letter into his desk before he spoke.

"Pollock is inclined to think Governor Spottswood over-
autious. I am not sure of the wisdom of attacking Cary with
ur little band—but I have given the order. . . ."

Roger was sitting in front of his tent when the Governor
nd Pollock marched up, followed by their columns. He was
eartened to see De Graffenried with his eight sturdy sol-
iers. He had been overtaken by the Governor's messenger
nd returned to give aid, he told Roger while the men made
amp and prepared a late supper. Hyde joined them and
homas Pollock, and the four men partook of the warm
ıeal Metephele had prepared. De Graffenried had picked up
ews from some farmers he had met on the road, and he had
ith him one of Cary's soldiers who had deserted and been
ıken prisoner.

"After supper I will send for him, your Excellency. He will
ılk," De Graffenried said. "He is sick of Roach, the mer-
hant who came from Bristol and brought a ship and ammu-
ition for Cary. Roach is a fierce man who would carve out a
ıan's heart as readily as he would cut up a pullet, so the
eserter told me. They have now three vessels, brigantines of
ze, and a barco longo that carries forty men."

The Governor set his cup down on the ground. The light
f the campfire playing on his thin, dark features gave him a

sardonic, almost malevolent, look. Roger thought his voice when he spoke was cool and unscrupulous.

"I am determined to drive Thomas Cary from this Province, no matter what it costs. Baron, suppose you send your servant for the deserter and we will question him."

In a short space, two of De Graffenried's sturdy Switzers came into the firelight with the man. Roger at once saw that he was a woodsman, probably a worker in the turpentine forest by the smell of pitch that clung to his clothes. From the look in his half-open eyes and his tousled hair he had been wakened from a deep sleep. He stood before the Governor, shifting from one foot to the other in acute embarassment.

The Baron, at a nod from Hyde, opened the inquiry. The man answered questions. Mr. Roach, he said, had come recently from Bristol. He had at once set about winning the people of Bath and the country round to the side of Cary, and against Governor Hyde. He went on to tell the number of ships, of men. He himself had been employed in the woods, cutting young trees for the stockade and shelters for the guns. He told little that De Graffenried had not already reported.

"Where is the stockade—at Romney Marsh?" the Governor spoke suddenly.

The fellow stuttered and had trouble making his words come. Respect for one greater in station showed in the uneasiness of his glance. "No, sire. No, your High Mightyness. No. The new stockade is on Machapunga Bluff east of Romney."

"Is Roach's camp at the same place?"

The man's eyes shifted. The uneasiness in his glance as he looked over his shoulder put Roger on guard, though none of the others appeared to notice a change in the man's demeanor. Roger thought back swiftly. Nothing in the question or the woodsman's answer accounted for the change. An owl hooted somewhere down the long aisle of pine trees. He remembered then—an owl had hooted before, just as the fellow was about to speak. There was some connection. An ignorant fellow, he might possibly be fearful of the owl as a bird of ill omen . . . still . . .

Roger rose quietly from his place in the shadow and moved stealthily back of the oak. He waited there for a time, as immovable as the tree itself. After a few minutes the sound came again, this time closer, from the ground—not from a tree. He was sure now that it was no bird that made the signal. Moving cautiously from tree to tree, he neared the place from where the signal seemed to come. He wondered if the woods were bare of Indians. His woodcraft told him that no white man could imitate a bird call so perfectly. As he waited, sheltered by the tall trunk of a pine, he saw a shadow moving towards him. He waited until it passed and was between him and the campfire. Then he jumped, catching the man around the middle. The man, surprised, uttered a low guttural sound as the breath exhaled from his lips. It was the slippery, oiled body of an Indian squirming in his grasp. Roger had his arms pinned to his sides as in a vice. Holding him was difficult. All he could do was to bend his body backward until the Indian was off balance. He could throw him then, face downward, Roger's knee in the small of his back. The Indian lay still, the breath knocked out of his body by the fall.

Roger raised his voice and called for his *capita*. A few moments later two of his men, headed by Metephele, reached his side.

"Truss him up," Roger said briefly. "Stuff his mouth so he can't call. See that he has no knife. When I signal, bring him into camp before the Governor. Do you understand?"

"Yes, Master, yes," Metephele said.

Roger went back to the camp. The whole affair had taken not more than five minutes. Pollock was talking. He was more canny in his questions than the Governor. Had Cary stocked the new place with food? Mounted guns? Was it approached by water only? Was it surrounded by marsh land or was the ground firm?

The man hesitated before answering. His uneasiness was increasing.

Roger stepped into the circle of light and spoke to the Governor. "Your Excellency, may I question this man?"

"Certainly, certainly, Mainwairing, but I think we have heard all he knows. He appears a dull fellow without much power of observation."

Roger might have said that a man trained to life in the woods could not survive without powers of observation, but he held his peace. He had an idea that the man was not what he appeared to be, but he was not certain yet.

"You work in the turpentine woods?" he asked.

The man answered promptly. "Yes, sir."

"Whose woods do you work?"

"Mr. Neville's, sir, below Bath Town on the south shore."

"Do you score for two years, test or cut?"

The man looked at Roger, his mouth open.

"You were lying when you said Cary had fortified Machapunga Bluff. Where is his camp?"

"Good sir, I swear—" The words tumbled from the fellow's lips.

Roger turned to the Governor. "This man is no woodsman, nor is he a deserter from Cary's camp. He has been sent out to mislead us."

"I swear this is not true. Upon the Holy Bible I swear—"

"Silence!"

Pollock spoke first. "You're imagining things, Duke. The fellow's a yokel, a dumb yokel."

Hyde remained silent.

The Baron said, "Perhaps we can find out who sent him." His voice was cold and sharp. "There are ways to make a man speak the truth."

"We don't need force," Roger answered. "I think he will want to give us true information. Stand close, men so that he does not attempt to get away." He gave a short whistle. In a few moments Metephele and one of his slaves came into the light circle. Between them was the Indian, his arms bound back of him, his mouth stuffed and bound with a piece of cloth from Metephele's robe.

A muffled exclamation came from the woodsman's lips. Sweat broke on his forehead and beaded his upper lip.

"I thought so," Roger said shrewdly. "Take the Indian away. Watch him, Metephele. Call me if he tries to escape." He turned to the woodsman. "Now, fellow, you will speak the truth to Governor Hyde. The truth, no more and no less. It will not be necessary for you to answer the call of the owl—or any other signal. Always remember that I am here behind you with my pistol ready."

They heard the truth then. He had been sent out to mislead them. Cary had no stockade at Machapunga Bluff. His fortress at Romney Marsh was heavily manned and guns were mounted.

"And Mr. Roach?"

The man's answer was less ready. From his reluctance to speak, Roger felt sure he was Roach's man, not Cary's. Roger set the cold muzzle of his pistol at the man's back.

"Roach has fortified an island at the base of the Bluff," he said. "If you had marched to Machapunga you would have

380

been trapped among Roach's island forces, the guns on his barkentine, and Cary's cannon, set behind a stout stockade. Before God, sir, spare me! This is all I know."

Roger turned to the Governor. "Your Excellency, I recommend you have the man shot."

Hyde said, "Aren't you overly severe, Mr. Mainwairing? The man has confessed. I think leniency is indicated."

Roger took a step forward. His face was hard, his mouth set. "This is war, your Excellency." The Governor glanced at the other men. He saw that they held the same opinion, but he must have their word.

De Graffenried got to his feet. "A spy who comes to our camp with the confessed intention of leading us into ambush deserves no mercy. I will have him executed since I am the one he first deceived."

Hyde looked at Pollock then. He repeated Roger's words: "This is war." The Governor nodded to the Baron.

De Graffenried's men marched the deserter off, struggling and kicking, crying for mercy. A few moments later they heard the shot.

"What will you do with the Indian, Mainwairing?" Hyde asked.

"Release him, sir."

"Release him when he is as guilty as the other?" There was surprise in the Governor's tone.

"No, your Excellency, not as guilty. The Indian is here as a messenger only, to take the word to his master, Roach, of the success of the mission. Let him take the message that the plot has failed and that we have nothing but contempt for treachery."

The Governor was silent for a long time. Finally he said, "As you will, Mr. Mainwairing."

Before morning Lovyck and twelve marines came into camp. They had taken a wrong turn, and had marched all night through the forest. They drank their tea with relish, threw themselves on the bed of pines the other men had just vacated and were sound asleep in no time.

After breakfast Roger had the Indian brought to the Governor's tent. The gag had been removed from his mouth, but his arms were still bound behind his back. "A Tuscarora," Roger said, and spoke a few words in the Indian tongue. The red man made no answer. He looked at Roger with hate-glazed eyes.

"What will you do with him?" the Governor asked, leaving the decision to Roger.

"Loose him, untie his hands."

Metephele hesitated a momment. A look from Roger and he cut the thongs that bound the man's wrists. Roger spoke in the Tuscarora tongue: "Go back to your master. Tell him to send another messenger, this time with a better disguise."

The Indian stood without moving, flexing his fingers and wrists to get the feeling back into them. Suddenly he sprang forward, knocking over one of the Negroes, snatched up his tomahawk which was lying on the ground near the tent, and hurled it. Realizing the Indian's intention, Roger had jumped aside. The axe whizzed by his head a few inches from the Governor and was buried into the trunk of the oak tree. Pollock and De Graffenried leapt to their feet.

"Let him go," Roger shouted, as the red man raced towards the forest. "Let him go!"

But he was too late. One of the troopers took aim and fired his pistol. The Indian spun around and slowly toppled over.

"It is better so, I think," De Graffenried said. "It is better so. He cannot tell Cary of our numbers, and our equipment."

Roger did not answer. He knew that Cary or Roach would send others to find out what had happened. Even now the woods might be peopled with Indians—that was what he did not like, they had enlisted Indians. But he said nothing of his thoughts to the others. They were intent on marching. When the marines had their sleep, the columns would move forward to find Cary and his men—perhaps to give battle, perhaps only to lay siege against their stronghold. These were Hyde's orders.

De Graffenried walked beside Roger. "Mr. Mainwaring, how did you know the man was not a deserter?" he asked, curiosity in his bright, searching blue eyes.

"I had several reasons to doubt him," Roger answered. "First, his hands. He was not a worker in tar or pitch. Second, his story was too glib. Third, the owl."

"Owl? I heard no owl!" the Baron exclaimed.

"It hooted twice. The first time I took no real notice of it. The second time I realized it was a signal because it came from the ground, not from a tree. No owl would stay so close to a camp, with men moving about, and remain on the ground. In fact an owl would not be close at all, even in a tree."

The Baron walked on in silence for some time. Then he said, "I have much, much to learn in this science that you call woodcraft."

Roger replied, "It won't take you very long, Baron, for you are observant. You are going out with a master of woodcraft, John Lawson. When you come back from that journey you will know more than half the people in Carolina do."

"But our trip is postponed until September. Mr. Pollock brought me a letter. Mr. Lawson and Mr. Moseley have gone to Virginia on the Boundary Commission."

"Oh," Roger said, "I did not know that."

They walked along through the deep forest in silence. Behind them the columns were straggling along. De Graffenried glanced over his shoulder several times. A frown wrinkled his forehead. Roger knew he thought the marching without form and needlessly unmilitary. That did not disturb Roger. He knew every man could shoot with accuracy, and every man was a fighter. What troubled him was the dead Indian lying in the sun on the bank of the dry stream. A Tuscarora brave, one of Chief Blont's young men. Only a few days ago Chief Blont had risen in council and prevented the Indians of the Chowanoke and his own young men from joining Cary's Rebellion against Governor Hyde. Now Governor Hyde's men had killed a Tuscarora.

When this thought occurred to him, Roger dropped behind and let the columns march past. With his men, he went back and buried the Indian in the forest, and carefully concealed the grave. Perhaps in that way his death would not be discovered by his people and lead them in any untoward reprisal against Governor Hyde. There was enough danger ahead without creating enmity with the Indians.

The columns reached Bath Town the second night, dusty, foot-weary, their grimy, sweating faces bitten by a plague of flies and biting insects that left great red welts wherever they touched. They camped on the river near the village, which had no more than nine or ten houses. They got food and supplies here, but the people traded with them reluctantly. It was Cary's town, whether from choice or fear was hard to tell.

Roger swam in the river at sundown and felt refreshed. He would have moved on to Romney Marsh by moonlight, but the Governor hesitated, fearing ambush. Half a hundred men joined them, men from the south shore and the country that lies between the two Sounds. There was no thought of a surprise attack. The woods were filled with Indians and people who carried the news of their arrival to Cary's camp.

The Governor sent to Tobias Knight, whose house was near the village, for boats to take his men downriver to attack Roach's fortified island, but Knight offered no hope.

"There isn't a boat in Bath Town, sir," he said to the Governor. "Not even a canoe to be had."

"That is very strange," the Governor said. "Where are the fishermen's boats? Indian dugout canoes would do to transport my men."

Knight shook his head. "It is impossible, your Excellency. There are no boats."

Pollock asked, "You mean all the people side with that damned rebel Cary? Isn't there any man of you who is on the side of the Government?"

Knight hesitated a moment. "If there is, he would be hard to find now, your Excellency. The laws passed by the last Assembly have angered the people of this Precinct. Cary and Roach have convinced them that if Cary gets power again, he will revoke the bad laws and in their place—"

"Take the quitrent money for himself," Pollock said hotly, "and give out false land-patents."

Knight shruggged his shoulders. "Cary's convinced them all that he is their salvation. He's kept the pirates' ships from looting the town and the plantation—"

"Yes, damme, because he's one of them himself!" Pollock broke in. "I've nae doot there's a pirate ship in Teach's Hole at this moment; if truth were known."

A strange look came to Knight's sallow face. He shifted his eyes. Roger thought, Old Tom hit the nail on the head that time.

De Graffenried took no part in the talk. He sat a little apart, his servant busy mending a rent in his tunic. Roger felt from his silence that he was not pleased with the dilatory measures taken by the Governor. He wanted to move on, attack quickly, and retreat to a safe haven. Test the strength of Cary's stronghold and estimate the number of men. He looked up now.

"No doubt there are brave men here who are mortally afraid to show their colours for fear of Cary's swift punishment. If I may be so bold, your Excellency, I suggest that

384

you allow Mainwairing and me to take a few men and make a night attack."

Hyde's lips tightened to a fine line. "I have other plans for you and Mr. Mainwairing, Baron. I'll speak of them later."

The Baron's face flushed angrily, but he made no answer. Pollock's glance at the Governor was troubled. He was too canny not to realize that the Switzer could at any time march off in a huff. That would not only weaken the little party, but would have a demoralizing effect on the countrymen that made up their army. Hyde was still a stranger to them. He had not yet proved his leadership.

After Knight had departed from the camp, the Governor got up and walked towards the river. He stood for a long time looking down the Pamticoe, eastward.

Roger went back to his own camp, where his men were cooking the evening meal. One of his slaves, Primus, had killed a wild turkey with his bow, and was roasting it on a spit over a low fire. Two of the Negroes were fishing from the river bank. Roger walked over to see what their catch might be. Slipping and sliding down the bank, he came to a small cove. There, hidden under the drooping willows and tangle of fox grapes, he saw an Indian canoe. He examined it carefully. It was water-tight and would hold five men. He looked about for paddles, and found them carefully wrapped in a strip of canvas and lodged in the crotch of a sycamore tree that grew at the edge of the bank.

He stood staring at the canoe for some time. Then he went back to camp, his plan already formed in his mind. Whether the Governor liked the idea or not, he would go down river after dark. From the water he should be able to spy out Cary's strength at the Marsh and discover which island Roach had fortified. He was reasonably sure that Cary's *Willing Maid* would have had time to return to her harbour, upriver or at the Deep Hole, protected by Ocracock Island. If he could not get back before morning, he would continue on downstream and seek protection at his hunting lodge or at Moseley's on Ocracock.

By the time Roger returned to camp the meal was ready. He sent half the roasted turkey and a bottle of wine, with his compliments, to the Governor's camp. Then he sat down to enjoy his meal, finished off with a small bottle of Madeira Metephele had commandeered somewhere in the village. Roger smiled with satisfaction as he lifted his glass to his lips. His boys were good foragers.

About dusk the Governor sent for Roger. He found Pollock and De Graffenried with Hyde. The Governor thanked him for the turkey. "Your men do you well, Mainwairing," he said with a smile. "I wish my servants had the same training."

"I've had my men a long time, your Excellency. That makes a difference."

De Graffenried said, " 'A just master has loyal servants' is one of our proverbs."

Pollock fired his pipe with a sliver of lightwood and settled himself comfortably, his back against a tree. Lovyck, who had come into camp, lounged full length on the ground. Hyde sat on the stump of a fallen tree, while De Graffenried stood, stiffly erect, his eyes fixed on the Governor.

"We have been talking plans," Hyde said to Roger. "We differ somewhat in the method we must take to win our objective. Pollock wants to move forward and besiege Cary's camp. De Graffenried wants a swift attack. I feel we must wait here for reinforcements."

"Here?" Roger said, trying not to allow his surprise to show in his face or his voice. "Wait here?"

"Yes, this is a good camping spot. We can get supplies from the forest and the village."

"Where will your reinforcements come from, your Excellency?"

"Virginia. I propose to send to Governor Spottswood for more marines."

Roger calculated. "That would mean ten days' wait at least, providing the Governor is at Kiquotan, and if he can spare a guard-ship. Lovyck did not have much success."

Lovyck gave Roger a black look.

"I intend to ask the Baron to undertake this delicate mission. Governor Spottswood might refuse Lovyck, but I do not think he will refuse any request you make of him, Baron." Hyde bowed slightly in De Graffenried's direction.

The Baron bowed, with undisguised pleasure in the compliment. "A fair plan, your Excellency, very fair indeed. I have been thinking that we should have a naval force to conclude this battle in our favour, since the enemy's strength lies in his ship, not in his land forces."

Hyde was suave. "I am delighted that our ideas are in accord, Baron. I had thought it would be wise for you to sail the brigantine *Pamticoe Adventure* up the Chowan. The mast and decks have been repaired. Pollock can doubtless give you sufficient men."

"Aye, I can do that," said Pollock.

De Graffenried said, "My men and I will be ready to start in an hour. I prefer night marches. We will rest from the heat by day."

Hyde assented, well pleased with the result of his move.

"And the rest of us sit here on our breeches until the Governor of Virginia deigns to send help and succour to North Carolina?" Pollock broke in. "Why can't we fight our own battles without calling in the neighbours and having them say we're too weak to squash our own rebellions?"

"Aren't we?" Hyde's manner was cool.

"We haven't that reputation, sir. 'Tis said that the Carolinians are stout men who fear nothing. That's what the Lords thought when we sent back some of their governors."

This won't do, Roger thought. Fighting among ourselves won't get us out of this fix. He agreed with Pollock in his heart. He saw no reason to sit around waiting for favours from the Governor of Virginia, even were he really disposed to help the Carolinians out of their confusion and disorders.

"We have nearly a hundred men and twelve marines, your Excellency," he said aloud.

"Not enough to attack." The Governor was angered now, his face was dark, his mouth stubbornly set. It was no time for Roger to speak of his plan now. He felt no loyalty to a weak leader. He would do what he considered best. It was important to know Cary's strength. Attack might be possible immediately.

The Governor stood up. "Fetch lights, Lovyck. I will dictate my letter to Governor Spottswood now." He walked away towards his tent. Lovyck got up stiffly, dusted the sand from his clothes, and followed Hyde.

Pollock sucked at his pipe. After a time he said, "He's a stubborn man, Duke. I do not know if he be right or we, but I'm bound to think he's wrong. He may be a thoughtful man in the office, but he's nae general in the field."

Roger moved over and sat down by Pollock. Dropping his voice, he told him the plan he had conceived. He would go downriver to Romney Marsh, spy out the camp, and either bring or send word to Pollock.

Pollock nodded his head approvingly from time to time. He said, "You're thinking as I do, that the Governor's too timid to attack?"

"That's what I fear. There is no use losing ground because one man of us is too cautious to take a chance."

Pollock said, "The Governor's thinking in terms of regiments, Duke. We think in terms of companies—where each man fights."

Roger nodded. "Yes, eighty or ninety men would be sufficient."

"Go, and good fortune to you, my lad. We'll be sitting here with the chigres eating our rears, waiting for your messenger."

Roger grinned at that. "I've found raw turpentine a specific, after my man has burned the beastie with the hot point of a knife."

"Get you going," Pollock chuckled. "I'll stay here and bear his Excellency's temper when he finds you've deserted."

"And sit in the drumhead court martial?" Roger said with a laugh.

He made his way through the dusk to his camp. It took him no more than ten minutes to make ready for the journey downriver. He took Metephele with him, and Primus. He wanted no more. The rest of his men crowded around him begging to go with him. "If there is danger, we must stand at your side," one of the older Negroes said.

Roger was touched by his devotion. "There will be other dangers, so stay here, and take orders from his Excellency, Governor Hyde. We will be back in a few days' time."

He stopped for a moment at the marines' camp. The soldiers were seated about the fire, polishing their muskets. The young lieutenant had a word in private with Roger. "If there is an attack, we must be allowed to lead," he said. Roger nodded. "I'm sure the Governor will give that order."

Metephele had the canoe in the water, the gear stowed, when Roger reached the river. He stepped in and took up a paddle. Primus took the second, while Metephele shoved off.

"We will cross the river and keep in the shadows along the south bank," Roger said, as they swung into the current. "This is silent work, that the enemy may not know of our coming or of our going."

"It is good, master." Metephele's voice had excitement in it. "It is good. We are silent. We will slip quietly as a fog on the breast of the river."

There was time for thinking as he paddled. The canoe was well balanced. It moved swiftly. There was no danger yet. As they moved along the south shore a sudden wave of depreson came over Roger. Here he was involved in the war of two men striving for power, caught up and held. He had had no desire to remake the New World. It had suited him well enough. A new raw land took men who could fight. It called for strength, for lusty thews and sinews, for a strong grip on life. He was ready to fight Indians, or pirates, or put down lawlessness. But it seemed to him that Governor Hyde was bringing some subtle change. The suave playing of one force against another, of one man's vanity against another's greed—Roger didn't like that. Let men stand up and face life squarely. Subtlety was not for a new land—it belonged to an old decadent world that had lost virility and force.

They were well past the village now, about opposite Jewell's plantation. Roger knew this river almost as he knew the Albemarle. He had sailed his shallop up the Pamticoe often when he came to Ocracock for the autumn shooting. A little time and they would be nearing Romney Marsh. If they could get there before moonrise! He raised his stroke. Primus followed his lead. The canoe shot ahead along the shallows. After a time he signalled, and headed the boat across the channel. From midstream he saw the sights of campfires stabbing the inky blackness—Cary's camp at the Marsh.

Roger eased his long body and gave the paddle to Metephele. He loosened his pistol in the holster and buckled his short sword to his belt. His flints were in the box hanging from his belt. Metephele and Primus each had a musket and their curved knives of Africa. All was in order. He would use his weapons only in case of discovery. He hoped to slip by the Marsh. He had an idea that the ships would be downriver. There were several small islands below Machapunga Bluff.

Metephele brought the canoe close to the north shore of the Pamticoe. Cautiously they inched their way along until they came to a cove where a small stream emptied into the river. A lone sentry was walking along the narrow beach. It was deep water here. Roger tapped the side of the canoe with his finger, a signal to land. He had made out half a dozen canoes and small boats anchored in shallows. The sentry turned and walked towards them. They must wait a few moments, hidden behind the overhanging bushes, until he turned. Metephele went ashore, Roger following. The sentry had no chance to make an outcry to warn the camp. To cut boats adrift was the matter of a few moments. They did not dare destroy them, for fear other guards would be alarmed. Six

389

boats were pulled out into mid-channel and allowed to drift. It took some time to reach a point opposite Machapunga Bluff. Here they crossed two long bars to deep water. The moon was above the horizon by the time they were in line with the island which Roach had fortified. Here Roger saw the outline of a large ship, its riding lights well up. They would have to cross the river and bring the canoe in near the shore.

Roger took a mental sight. A shallow curve would bring them to the Deep Hole back of Ocracock. He dare not cross this stretch of water in the moonlight. He determined to investigate the ship. It might be possible to get some information that would benefit Hyde. He stripped off his shirt, unbuckled his belt, and removed his high boots—no easy task in a canoe. He lowered himself carefully over the side.

Swimming under water, he came up near the anchor chain that moored the boat. He swam in the shadow, until he touched a mooring rope. He went up hand over hand until he reached an open porthole. He heard a voice say, "If you had manned your ship properly, Low, we need not have lost her. I told you to lay off shore and not enter the Salmon." That would be Cary, of course. Roger twisted a long leg around the rope to ease his hands.

Low grumbled something. Then young Michael said, "No use talking about what was not done—that's water under the bridge. What are we going to do now? I swear I don't like this. I was not told we were going to attack. The plan was to take the Governor quietly, force him to agree to our terms, then let him go."

Someone laughed. "You are gullible, Michael. Why do you think we had the swivels? To shoot wild geese?"

Thomas Cary broke in. "No use talking about that. You made a pretty mess of things at Queen Anne's Town, with your drunken sailors burning buildings and murdering a man. Hue and Cry out against you. What are you going to do with your Diego and his strumpet dressed in man's clothes?"

There was a silence, then the sound of a chair scraping over the floor. Michael was close to the opening. "Let them rot in hell for all I care."

Thomas Cary answered, "No doubt the girl will make you a good bedfellow, but I advise you to put her ashore before the men get to fighting for her favours."

A moment later the door banged. Roger heard heavy steps on the deck above him. This was getting too warm for him. He slid cautiously down the ropes. He was almost to the

water when a shout challenged him from the deck—Michael
Cary's voice commanding him to halt. Roger let go and
dropped into the stream, as a shot whizzed by and ricocheted
along the surface of the water. He swam silently towards the
spot where the canoe lay. He knew the moonlight was not
bright enough to make a target of him for Michael. He was
pleased as he swam deeply in the cool water. If they were
having differences of opinion among the Governor's forces,
so were Cary's men quarrelling and making recriminations.
He located the canoe in the deep shadow and pulled himself
up the side and crawled in, dripping with water.

A second shot sounded. There was shouting. Michael's
voice came clear over the water, "I saw a man sliding down
the rope."

Someone laughed loudly. "Or a woman dressed as a man!"

"To the opposite bank," Roger said in a low voice to his
men. "We'll hide there until the moon goes down. Then we'll
head straight for the Banks."

Chapter 32

HURRICANE

No word of the aftermath of the capture of the *Pamtico
Adventure* reached Greenfield for more than ten days after
the river battle. The heat was deadly. The three women at
the manor house did not leave the plantation, nor did any
visitors come. Even Captain Zeb had been gone for a week
or more. He was up on the Pasquotank River, overseeing
repairs that were being made by the shipwright on Roger
Mainwairing's shallop *Golden Grain*, but he was expected
back any day.

Marita spoke once or twice of sailing over to see Lucretia,
but she put it off. She told herself that it was because of
the heat, but deep inside she knew it was because she did not
have the courage to meet Lucretia's accusing eyes. Nor did
she want to visit the village. The hot blood surged through
her when she thought of her conduct and the things people

must be saying about her after she had torn down the Governor's proclamation of Hue and Cry.

But more than all it was because of Michael. He had sent word that he was coming for her. When he came she must be waiting for him. She tried not to think of Michael with the terror of the hunted on him; only as he had been before that terrible day, gay with his bold, reckless laugh and his shining eyes.

Sudden waves of depression seemed to dry up her spirit. The deadly knowledge that men were out searching for him to hunt him down made her nights horrible with wild dreams. She went about silently, her face pale, with sooty shadows under her great tawny eyes. More than once she felt Miss Mittie watching her, saw the look of pity in her kind, short-sighted eyes.

Only Lady Mary did not seem to notice. Marita was grateful. She did not want to make explanations. For that reason she was glad that no visitors came to the manor house. Someone might drop a word that would start a conflagration. But no one came. The only break in the quiet routine of their living was the arrival of two gillies from her aunt's estate in Scotland, bringing the highland cattle she had sent for and the Black Angus bulls for the herd. The men had driven the cattle down from the James, where their boat landed in Virginia. In their clan plaids the two Highlanders caused a stir on the plantation among the slaves. Watkins setled them in a house not far from Captain Zeb's place. On a still night, when the wind was from the south, the sound of the pipes playing laments could be heard at the manor house, sad wailing tunes that made one close to tears.

Every day Marita rode over the plantation. The corn was high and the garden prospered. Watkins was pleased with the wool clip. The cotton was well leafed, the bloom plentiful. By September the bolls would puff out, white and heavy on the plants.

Marita rode down the lane, as she had done every day, to watch for Michael's ship. Every day she closed her eyes as she made the turn from the lane, hoping to see the *Willing Maid* anchored off the island when she opened them. Today, as on other days, the Sound was empty of ships; from the pocosin to the heavily wooded Drummond's Point, only the unbroken sweep of sluggish water. Even the Black Angus herd was motionless, standing knee deep in the water in the dark shadow of the cypress trees. The air was heavy. Not a af stirred in the thick crown of the oaks and tupelos that ringed the high bank. Birds were silent. A king snake lay inert in the rut, moving slowly out off the way of Blenheim's hoof.

Marita looked at the sky. It was a brass bowl, reflecting the intense heat of the sun. Along the eastern sky a few white cuffs of clouds lay close to the horizon. If the Captain had been there he would have said, "Weather-breeding clouds rising off the Banks of Hatteras"—the turbulent cape of Hatteras where storms were made.

She rode back to the house. Lady Mary and Miss Mittie were on the gallery at breakfast. One of the gillies stood below on the ground, his bonnet tucked under his arm. He was talking to Lady Mary.

"We had little trouble, your leddyship. The cattle stood the sea trip well enough, better than the hunters. They fretted and kicked and were off their feed. The grooms had a bad time, but the horses picked up when the ship docked in the James River, and they had a day of green pasture before we started for Carolina."

"Hunters? Is someone having hunters sent down here?" Lady Mary spoke idly.

"Yes, your leddyship. They are for Mr. Mainwairing's plantation. But the grooms belong to Miss Chapman, a lady that lives in the Midlands of England. A great horsewoman she is. The grooms boasted all the way over about her huntin' and ridin'."

Lady Mary set down her cup. "That will be all, Dougal. I hope you and Black John will not be fretting for Glen Orchy."

" 'Tis glad we are to be with your leddyship in the grand big country. Good day to you, ma'am. I'll be getting back to the herd now." The gillie set his bonnet firmly on his head and walked off briskly, his kilts swinging.

Miss Mittie said, "Isn't Rhoda Chapman the name of the girl that Mr. Mainwairing is going to marry?"

Lady Mary pushed her cup away and got up from the table as if she had not heard Miss Mittie's query. "Come to my room when you have finished breakfast, Marita. I want you to write one or two letters for me." She walked across the gallery and into the house, her head erect. Marita and Miss Mittie exchanged looks. Neither spoke. She really cares for Duke Roger, Marita thought.

Miss Mittie looked down at her plate. "It's going to be

very hot today," she said quietly. "Beulah says we'll have a storm by tomorrow—a real storm, perhaps a hurricane."

Marita scarcely heard her words. She was thinking of her aunt's face when Dougal spoke of Rhoda Chapman's hunters.

Lady Mary was seated at her escritoire when Marita went to her room. Since the weather had grown hot Lady Mary had moved her bedroom from the second story to the wing off the sitting-room. Marita hesitated for a moment at the door. Evidently her aunt had not heard her knock. She was sitting with her back to the door, and the carved mirror that fitted into the red Morocco case lay at her elbow. She was intent on the heavy parchmentlike paper in her hand. The paper was stamped with red wax and two ends of faded ribbon fell below the large signature scrawled across the bottom of the page. All this Marita saw at a glance before Lady Mary folded the page and laid it in a little compartment back of the mirror. She had closed the glass down with a snap before she turned and saw Marita in the doorway. For a second Marita thought her aunt was angry. But her face cleared. She put the mirror into the Morocco case and laid it in a drawer of the escritoire, a secret drawer; when it was closed there was an unbroken panel of wood across the front. Marita took a seat at a small table near the window.

Lady Mary said, "I think we may as well begin at once before it gets too hot and your hands sweat to the paper." She turned over a pile of letters and took out one or two, laying them on the desk in front of her. "I want you to write to my mantuamaker, Mr. Selby, at Seven Stairs in King Street, Covent Garden. Tell him to send me two Mademoiselles, straight from Paris, dressed in the very latest fashion. One in a gown suitable for me, for a large formal function, and one for a girl under eighteen, with tawny eyes and hair. Amber gauze with a twisted sash of emerald taffeta would be suitable."

She smiled as Marita looked up from her writing. "For you, my dear."

"Let the Mademoiselles be the jointed kind and completely dressed, even to underwear, so they can be used as models. Have them tinted in the fashionable complexion shades with their hair dressed as the court ladies are wearing theirs at the moment—Selby will cut the gowns to measure and Miss Mittie and Beulah can sew them to his measurements," Lady Mary commented as Marita was writing. "Tell him also that

394

I want some rolls of rich India silks and tissues and embroidered gauze."

Lady Mary got up and moved around the room as she talked. "I want one stamp dress with variegated flowers, and elbow sleeves and a hooped petticoat; and a roll of yellow damask silk, dress length. Ask him to order slippers of the same material from my bootmakers."

Lady Mary took up a memorandum from the desk and studied for a moment. "I need a new habit. I want it made with the coat and waistcoat of blue camlet. He knows the shade of blue most becoming to me. Have it trimmed and frogged with silver braid. A smartly cocked beaver hat would go well with that, I think. Tell him he is to make it more sprightly by a feather, hair-curled, hanging down to the shoulder to give it a rakish air." Lady Mary's full red lips curved in a smile as she envisaged the new habit.

"Let me see what else I need. One or two fine patch boxes, a modish little Swedish fan with ivory or tortoise sticks. A gay bonnet or two for cool-weather wear. A packet of fine Holland handkerchiefs, and a sable-skin ruff."

She tapped the desk with her pencil for a few moments while Marita waited, her pen poised above the paper. "Let him select a few pairs of earrings, and some lengths of fine brocade for turbans. Six bolts of finest white linen for underbodies and night rails. A few bolts of real Mechlin and Flemish lace, narrow, for trimming." She waited a moment, considering, before she said, "And I want one snuff box, gentlemen's size. This box must be true gold with a sapphire or emerald clasp, marked with my cipher.

"Tell Selby the Mademoiselles must be his most exclusive new fashions, for we must make a very fine appearance when the Governor formally takes office in Queen Anne's Town."

Lady Mary leaned back against her chair, a smile of satisfaction on her lips. "Selby will outdo himself, now that I've told him it is for the Governor's inaugural. He loves pomp, and I am sure he will send us handsome patterns on his little Mademoiselles."

Marita said, "It all sounds so lovely, Aunt Mary. Will the gowns be too grand for Queen Anne's Town?"

Lady Mary did not heed Marita's question. She was looking out the window, the little secret smile in the corner of her lips. "Yes, Marita, Selby will outdo himself for me."

Marita folded the paper while Lady Mary lighted the taper and melted the wax for her seal.

"Now one more letter, my dear, if you are not too exhausted."

"No, no certainly not. Please go on. I'm not in the least weary."

"This letter is to Mr. Edward Moseley, Esq., Moseley Point Plantation, Queen Anne's Town:

"My dear sir: Mr. Roger Mainwaring has suggested that you might be persuaded to let your shooting lodge on Ocracock for the months of August and September. I feel the need of change from this protracted heat, and I am sure my niece—Marita—will be better for a little sea air. If we can come to some satisfactory arrangement I will be glad to lease the place from you for that period. In so doing you will greatly oblige—"

Lady Mary broke off suddenly. Marita had dropped the pen and was leaning against the chair back, her eyes closed. "What is the matter?" Lady Mary cried, looking at Marita. "You are as white as chalk. I hope you are not going to have the vapours."

She crossed the room and pulled the bell cord. When Desham came she said, "Bring my smelling salts. I think Miss Marita is overcome by the heat."

Desham ran into the bedroom carrying a crystal salts bottle. Lady Mary took it from her and held the bottle under Marita's nose. She gasped and tears ran from her closed lids.

"It's the sun!" Desham wailed. "Riding around without a hat, her hair flying. I told her only this morning she ought to wear a beaver hat with a damp sponge under it to keep off the sun. I once knew a man who died from the sun—"

"Will you be quiet, woman!" Lady Mary cried, exasperated at Desham's ineptness. "Bring some cool water in a basin."

Miss Mittie came into the room, attracted by Desham's voice. She took over in an instant. "Lay her on the couch, with feet higher than her head. Desham, ask cook for vinegar. Bathe her head and wrists in vinegar. It's very cooling."

When Marita opened her eyes a few moments later, Lady Mary was sitting beside her bathing her temples. She had never seen her aunt look so distressed.

"You have given us a fright," Lady Mary said, when Marita tried to sit up. "Do you feel better?"

"It must have been the heat," Marita murmured. "I am still a little giddy. Things went black before my eyes."

"Yes, the heat," Miss Mittie said. "The air is so heavy."

Marita was ashamed to have caused so much disturbance.

396

"I'll finish the letter to Mr. Moseley now." She got up and walked across the room. "Oh," she said, "I am so sorry." There was a great blot across the page where the quill had slipped from her hand. "I'll copy the letter."

Lady Mary stopped her as she took out a fresh sheet of paper from the writing case. "Don't bother, my dear. It's of small importance. Perhaps Mr. Moseley will stop in one day soon and I can talk to him. That would be more satisfactory."

Marita lay on her bed in the darkened room. How could she have been so foolish? It all happened so suddenly when her aunt spoke of taking the lodge at Ocracock. How could she leave Greenfield now, when she expected Michael to come? She must find some way to stay to divert her aunt. She tried to think of a way, but she could not concentrate. Her mind kept drifting off on some unimportant thing . . . the cattle the gillies had brought from Scotland . . . the hunters . . . her aunt's face when Dougal mentioned the name Rhoda Chapman. Suddenly it seemed to Marita that the tranquil peace that was so much a part of the Albemarle was slipping away. What lay ahead? Michael, hunted, fleeing from the law . . . leaving her behind, waiting . . . sick with fear and loneliness?

The storm which had been brewing all day broke in the late afternoon. Marita, wakened by the wooden storm-shutters of her east windows banging against the frame, jumped hurriedly from her bed and ran to the window to close and fasten it. The sky overhead was a sickly green. Heavy wind clouds blew across the sky. The eastern horizon, obscured by a film of green mist, had the pale colour of the moon. The air was cool. The wind blew strongly from the southeast, carrying small twigs and slivers of branches, and treetops swayed and creaked with the rising wind.

In the barn-lot the slaves were shouting, hurrying the animals across the pasture to cover. She saw the bright plaid kilts of the gillies flying in the wind as they drove in the herd from the meadow. The sheep were huddled in the corner of the barn-lot and the horses stood under trees, turned away from the wind. Cattle lowed and bellowed, the chickens and geese squawked, and the doves fluttered into the cockloft as if it were night.

Miss Mittie came in hurriedly as Marita was dressing.

"Watkins says a hurricane is on the way," she said breathlessly. "He's having the storm-shutters put up and set with heavy bars. Your aunt said we had better all stay downstairs until the wind dies down." She smiled feebly. "Watkins says the roof may go off. Last year in August they had a storm and dozens of houses and dependencies were flattened to the ground—people killed, too."

Marita finished buttoning her light muslin sacque. "Are you afraid, Miss Mittie?"

"No—no—but I wish Captain Zeb were here. He's like a great rock for comfort."

A knock sounded at the door. Marita called, "Who is there?"

"One," was the answer. She recognized the voice of the house boy. "We come to close storm-blinds, Mistress."

It took the strength of two strong boys to close the heavy shutters and place wooden securing bars into place.

They found Lady Mary in her sitting-room, her Patience cards spread on the table before her. She drew Marita to her and kissed her forehead. "You look better, my dear, but you must not tax yourself. Desham," she said to her woman, "make the lounge comfortable so that Miss Marita can lie down."

Marita protested. "I am quite all right, now that it is cool again. Do you think it will be a real hurricane this time?"

Lady Mary turned back to her cards. "Watkins tells me that the wind will be a gale by morning. A gale is preferable to the terrible heat, even if it sours all the beer in my cellar," she said indifferently.

Miss Mittie walked about the room restlessly. Lady Mary looked up at her once or twice without saying anything. Finally, exasperated by the older woman's nervousness, she said, "Do sit down and compose yourself, Mittie. Why don't you knit or read a book—anything? Only do be quiet."

Miss Mittie sat down in a straight-backed chair. She was quiet for a moment, but soon her thin-veined hands began to clasp and unclasp.

"There's a *Spectator* on the table," Lady Mary said. "Why don't you read something to occupy your attention? There's an interesting piece called 'Beau's Receipt for a Lady's Dress.' It made me laugh when I read it."

Miss Mittie shuffled through the pages until she found the place. She began:

398

"Make your petticoat short,
That a hoop eight yards wide
May decently show how
Your garters are tied.
But mount in French heels,
When you go to a ball.
'Tis the fashion to totter
And show you can fall."

Lady Mary's laugh tinkled through the silent room. "Your face, Mittie! Your face!—You look so bewildered. I must laugh at you."

"But why is the piece funny? It isn't amusing for anyone to stumble and fall from wearing French heels."

"Of course, Mittie, you would be literal." Lady Mary laughed. "The lady doesn't fall from wearing French heels, my dear Mittie, but from showing how her garters are tied."

"I don't understand," Miss Mittie mumbled. "Do you, Marita?"

Marita coloured. "Lady Mary was teasing, Miss Mittie." She didn't quite understand Lady Mary, unless she was trying to quiet the older woman's fear by taking her mind from the storm.

"I might have known you've never had a gentleman untie your garters, Mittie!" Lady Mary added.

Miss Mittie was indignant. "I should think not, Mary. How can you talk bawdy before a young girl like Marita?"

Lady Mary only laughed the louder. She took out a fine lace handkerchief and wiped her eyes. "You are an innocent —" She broke off suddenly. A great crash of thunder split the air.

Miss Mittie shrieked and hid her face in her hands. Desham rushed in from the bedroom, wringing her hands. Beulah ran in from the back of the house crying, "It's the day of doom. It's the day of doom. Ring the bell of the dead!"

Lady Mary screamed, "Be quiet or I'll have Moses' Law for the lot of you!"

Marita went to the north window. The shutters were still open, for the wind was from the southeast. Black clouds covered the sky. The eerie greenish light that turned to yellow near the horizon made the whole landscape unreal. A bolt of lightning zigzagged across the heavens, followed by another roll of thunder.

"Better stand away from the open window, Marita," Lady

Mary said quietly. "Mittie, go get on your bed and pull the feather pad over you if you are so afraid of lightning. Desham, quit wringing your hands. Go back to your mending."

"I can't, my lady, I am afraid." She began mumbling a charm:

> "Came three angels out of the east,
> One brought fire, one brought frost,
> In the name of the Father, Son and Holy Ghost."

Lady Mary looked at her, her eyes cold and angry. Marita thought for a moment she would strike the woman, but instead she spoke quietly. "A pox on you! You are like a spinster with the vapours, always seeing apparitions and hearing the death watch. Go sit in the corner of the room there behind me. I don't want to look at you until you compose yourself. Marita, have Beulah bring us tea. I think we would all be better for a dish of hot tea."

Marita left the room and found the frightened Beulah crouching under the dining table. She saw it was hopeless to try to get the girl to go across the porch to the kitchen. It was easier to go herself. She found Dougal on the back gallery sitting on a bench, his eyes on the sky. He stood up when Marita came out.

" 'Tis a blow coming up," he said, nodding towards the east. "An east wind brings no good to anyone."

"Where is Black John?" Marita asked.

The gillie pointed over his shoulder to the barn-lot. "He's releasing the horses and cattle. It's better. Let them fend for themselves in the storm. They'll find their own protection. 'Twould be a pity to have the barn fall over them if the wind gets high."

Marita started across the gallery. The wind caught her at the turn and forced her back. Dougal sprang forward and saved her from being blown against a gallery pillar.

"Beg pardon, miss, but a wee thing like you canna buffet the wind."

"Lady Mary would like tea. I was going to tell Cook."

"Stay inside the doors, miss. I'll see that her leddyship has her tea."

Marita waited on the gallery, watching the lightning play across the dark clouds. Peal after peal of thunder followed, cracking the zenith and dying away along the water. She looked towards the wood to see if the lightning had struck any of the trees. She thought she saw a figure moving slowly down the wood road, but she could not be sure. It might be one of the horses running for shelter in the woods, or perhaps it was Black John taking the cattle out. She pointed out the object to the gillie when he returned.

" 'Tis a man," he said after a moment. "A man struggling against the blow. It's help he needs." He settled his bonnet firmly on his head and started off. "Her leddyship's tea will be in presently"—the words came drifting back in the wind— "but it's whisky the man will be needin'."

A crash of thunder seemed to break directly overhead, followed instantly by a blinding flash of lightning. Marita jumped backwards through the doorway. The great oak tree near the barn toppled and fell with a crash, the long branches grazing the cowshed. For a moment she thought the tree had fallen on Dougal, but she saw him running down the wood road, driving a horse before him to break the wind.

Her aunt came swiftly down the hall, her wide skirts flying behind her. "What was that noise? Was one of the houses struck?"

Marita pointed to the tree that had fallen. "There's a man down there near the woods. Dougal has gone to help him."

Lady Mary went to the end of the gallery, shielding her eyes as she looked down the road. "I wonder who it can be," she said quietly enough, but her eyes were alight with excitement.

"I believe you love the storm," Marita said suddenly.

Lady Mary laughed. "Anything I welcome, anything—even a cataclysm of nature—to break this damnable monotony!"

Marita felt a cold shiver go over her. "How can you say that? Some terrible thing might happen God will punish us!" she cried.

Lady Mary laughed again. "You are a silly child. Will you never grow up? Do you suppose the Almighty creates a storm to punish us poor mortals? He creates a storm to show His power, to show how puny we are against His wrath."

A sudden gust of wind caught her then. Her words died on her lips.

"Come inside—do come into the house," Marita cried, her voice lost in the noise of the wind. A great dark object flew past them, the canvas that covered the hayrick. The air was filled with whirling straw, and small twigs from the fallen tree. Marita caught her aunt and pulled her inside the hall, where she leaned against the wall, her breath coming swiftly.

"It is glorious," Lady Mary said, "glorious. If we only had its power ..." She walked away to the front of the house, Marita following.

In a little time Beulah came in with the tray. Lady Mary drank her tea with relish and ate two full slices of bread and butter. She picked out bits of straw and little twigs from the bread and butter and laid them on the saucer without comment. When she saw Marita was taking her tea as quietly as if the heavens were not breaking up over their heads, she nodded approvingly.

Miss Mittie came into the room, her Bible in her hand.

"Tea will help you," Lady Mary said. "After that you can return to your prayers."

Miss Mittie didn't answer. She wore a dazed look and she was muttering a prayer under her breath: "Good Lord, deliver us. Good Lord, deliver us."

Desham sat in the corner of the room on a stool. Lady Mary went over to her and struck her sharply on the cheek. "Get up, you fool, and bring fresh tea. It's better to die standing up than to sit snivelling in the corner."

The woman staggered to her feet blindly. But she went about her accustomed task without protest.

"It's the Day of Judgment," Misss Mittie said suddenly. "The Lord is re-creating a new world about our ears."

"For the love of God, Mittie, quit talking nonsense. Desham, take the keys of my wine closet and bring us a bottle of sack. Sack is an innocent cordial. It might put some courage into you, Mittie." She said to Marita, "Thanks be to God, you show the blood. We Stuarts may have a doom upon us, but we have never lacked courage."

Marita had not time to think of what her aunt was saying. There was a sharp knock and the door swung open. Captain Zeb stood at the threshold. His face was scratched and bleeding. Water dripped from his torn clothes and formed a little pool on the oaken floor.

He said to Lady Mary, "There's a ship aground off the Point. Two dead men have been washed ashore. I've come for help." He stopped, mopping his face with an immense red kerchief. "We'll need all your men."

Lady Mary spoke to the gillie who stood in the hall behind Captain Zeb. "Ring the plantation bell, Dougal. Find Mr. Watkins. Ask him to get the slaves and all the available men to help the Captain."

Miss Mittie struggled to her feet when she heard the

Captain's voice. "Oh," she whispered, "oh, I was afraid that you were out in the storm."

Captain Zeb's hearty laugh cleared the air. "What's one storm or another to a seaman?" he cried. He took a step forward; then, conscious of his dripping garments, he backed off. "You poor little woman," he said pityingly. "Don't you worry about Zeb Bragg."

The bell pealed out, sharp and insistent, ringing above the noise of the growing wind. Rain had come now. The wind took it from the clouds, levelling it, holding it parallel to the ground, driving it forward as it drove the straw and the branches of trees and the flat shingled roof of the cowshed, sending it whirling across the flattened field of corn.

Marita turned from lowering the window. Captain Zeb was speaking to Lady Mary. "She's aground—breaking up. Sound's blowing heavy as a sea."

Marita, hands behind her back, caught at the window sill for support. His words crashed about her ears, surrounding her, louder than the roar of thunder overhead.

". . . Not sure . . . I think it's Cary's ship, *Willing Maid*."

Chapter 33

STORM CENTRE

THE first thought which came to Roger was that his head was splitting, and the ground rocking under him. Then he heard the swish of water and the howl of wind in the rigging, and the heavy tramp of hurrying feet over his head. He was on a ship.

He opened his eyes and tried to sit up. His arms were tied, and his feet. Then he remembered. He had acted like a nincompoop, trying to move close to Roach's island in the moonlight. He might have known they would be watching more closely after Cary had seen him sliding down the ropes the night before. Metephele had cautioned him to wait until the light was dim.

Well, they had him now—trussed up and thrown below

403

decks of some stinking ship. He lay on his back and tried moving, but he had no leeway. His legs were loose but his feet were tied to the footboard of a narrow bed. His wrists were bound together, lying on his stomach. Well, here he was, and here he would stay.

His wrath rose when he thought how easily Cary had tricked him. He had walked—swum rather—into the trap that sly young fellow had baited for him. The only thing that consoled him was that his men had gone away in the canoe, with orders to report to the Governor. At least he hoped they had managed to elude Cary's men. He was a dotard in fact and in action, and now he must pay the price.

He heard footsteps coming down the stairs, the sound of a key grating in the lock. Michael Cary stooped as he entered the low door. He held a candle so he could see Roger's face.

"So you have come to your senses?" he said harshly.

Roger did not answer. Cary's tone irked him.

"I suppose you know what happens to spies," Michael went on.

Roger glanced down at his bare chest. He had taken off his shirt and boots to swim. He still wore his soggy breeches. "I did not come in disguise," he said shortly.

Michael gave an exasperating grin. He sat down astride a wooden chair. "My uncle and Emanuel Low and Roach were for stringing you up last night, but I claimed you. Since you were my captive, they turned you over to me."

Roger made no comment on this. He asked, "What ship is this and where is it headed?"

Michael looked at him a moment as if he were weighing the question, whether or not to answer. Finally he said, " 'Tis the *Willing Maid,* but I'll not say to which port we sail. Enough that she has outsailed Spottswood's guard-ship."

Roger kept all expression from his face. The guard-ship had come! That was the reason Michael Cary was taking his ship out of its safe harbour. Roger would have liked to ask about the other ship, Roach's vessel, and the disposition of the Governor's trooops, but to question Michael Cary was futile. Instead, he watched him without appearing to do so. A handsome, carefree young devil. Just the kind to catch a young girl's fancy.

Finding he could not drive Roger into asking questions, Michael left the room, saying he would send food shortly. "After your long sleep you need something, even if it's only bread and water."

404

Bread and water it was. Diego, the swarthy sailor with gold rings in his ears, brought the bread. "A pretty sight you are, lying in your filth," he said, looking down at Roger, his thin lips drawn back over his teeth. "Sit up if you can manage. I'm supposed to feed you."

He set the water jug down on a wooden bench and tossed the loaf of bread on the rude couch where Roger was lying. Moved by some impulse, Roger did not reach for it. The sailor leaned closer, a subtle change on his face. He passed his hand quickly in front of Roger's eyes. Roger, foreseeing something of the kind, did not change expression or make any movement. Satisfied, the sailor sat back, a look of bold cunning in his bright black eyes.

He untied Roger's hands. "You are to have the freedom of the room," he said. "The Captain says no tricks or he'll put you in the hold."

Roger raised his hand to his head. There was a great lump on his forehead. He tried to sit up but fell back again as if he had no strength. This was easy to counterfeit. He ached in every joint. "Everything is black," he murmured, allowing his hand to drop.

"Here, drink this," Diego said.

Instead of water it was rum the sailor put to his lips. Raw and harsh, it burned Roger's palate, but he felt the warm blood flowing in his veins. Diego took the loaf of bread, broke it in pieces and put it in a bowl, pouring water over it.

"Eat this yourself. Damme if I'll feed any man his pap."

Roger felt for the bowl and spoon. With an effort he raised his body, so that he could swallow the unsavoury mess. The sailor watched his awkward efforts to eat. From the look on his face Roger knew he was planning something evil. "The belaying pin the Captain laid on fair blinded you," Diego said presently.

Roger said, "I am dizzy, that's all."

Diego pulled the stool closer and dropped his voice. "I can get food from the galley if you have money to pay."

A faint hope rose in Roger. The man was full of greed from the look on his face. "I have no money and you know it."

"The ring you wear is heavy with gold."

Roger was silent a moment before he answered, "If you are caught with this ring on you or you try to sell it, you will be taken for a thief, for it bears the crest of my family, but I can use it to your advantage."

"How?"

"If you can get a piece of paper and a bit of wax, I can write a bill to pay you fifty pounds. Sealed with my ring, the bill will be honoured, on my agent in London, at Messers Wycroft in Jamaica, or in Virginia, or any merchant in the Albemarle will give payment."

The man thought this over a while. "Your word is good," he said reluctantly. "If I help you I'll cause Cary trouble—that will please me. I hate Michael Cary's innards."

"What happened when the guard-ship came?" Roger asked.

"It sank Roach's vessel, and the marines chased Tom Cary and his crew back to the Marsh. Some say they headed for Virginia, same as we."

"How long have I been here?" Roger asked.

"Five, six days. Captain is worried. He's got enough on him without being charged with murdering Mr. Roger Main-wairing—and there's plenty of witnesses that saw him smash you with a belaying pin."

He pushed the stool aside and stood up. Roger kept his eyes blank, staring straight ahead. "I'll be back with food when the Captain is off watch. Mayhap we can make a trade. You can get up and move around if you like. I'm going to leave the ropes off and lock the door."

Roger said, "I must get some strength first."

Diego smiled at this and left the room. Roger heard the key turn. What devilment the man was up to he couldn't fathom. But Roger was determined to play the part he had started. A head blow could easily dim the eyes. Let Diego think he was without strength and could not see. Later there might be a chance to catch him off guard.

Roger slept for a time. When he wakened, the ship was pitching. He could hear the wind howling. This was no ordinary blow. He tried to sit up, taking it slowly, for fear Diego watched through some crack in the door. He moved slowly, stumbling across the room by the aid of chairs and tables, but once out of range of the door, he moved more easily, though he was stiff, and his head went round with dizziness. He came to the square window. He was tall enough to see out, and though there was nothing in range of his vision but the water and a small strip of sand with a few scrub pines, something familiar in the point of land made him almost sure the ship was pointed north.

He would have to wait to find out what Diego had in

406

mind—nothing but evil, he was sure. Roger did not think the man would kill him. He was too valuable to him alive. He did not intend to give Diego any paper until he set him ashore.

Late in the night Roger wakened. Someone was opening the door cautiously. He lay without moving. After a moment he felt someone bending over him, touching his shoulder.

"Don't speak. It is Anne Bonney." She pressed a long knife into his hand. "Hide this under you. Don't trust Diego or anyone. I will try to get you ashore."

Roger caught her hand. "Where are we?"

"Behind Roanoke Inlet, almost at the entrance of the Sound. There's a hurricane coming. We may have to anchor."

"What are you doing here?" he said. "Why didn't you get away? Don't you know they've Hue and Cry posted against you?"

"God curse them!" she said bitterly. "They can't leave me alone. I didn't knife Tom the Tinker. It was Diego. But I should have. He was one of the devils who strung Susannah and the Turk on the gibbet."

Roger didn't answer this. "Perhaps I can get you off if you surrender," he said.

She laughed shortly. "Let the leet woman go? Never. They'd hound me to my grave if I let them. Diego has promised to get me on Rackham's ship."

"A pirate ship—are you crazy?"

"Why not?" she asked shortly. "I'm sick of being hunted. From now on I'll do the hunting, and there'll be no quarter asked or given."

Roger could answer nothing to that. He pressed the girl's hand. "I am sorry," he said.

After a moment she said, "I don't know what Thomas Cary's orders were to Diego. He hates you. He thinks you are the one who had the guard-ship brought down from Virginia. He doesn't believe the Governor has enough sense to think of that."

"Where is Thomas Cary?" Roger asked, wanting to confirm what Diego had told him.

The girl laughed. "He and Emanuel Low and that devil Roach are running through the marshes. The marines are after them hot foot."

Roger wanted to ask other questions, but he thought better of it.

407

"Don't trust Diego," she whispered. "He'd cut a man's liver out of his body for money."

"Anne, I wish you were not . . ." he began.

"That? Don't worry. I can take care of myself. I'm on the same footing as a man now." She laughed disagreeably. In the dark he could not see her, but he could imagine the ice-blue of her eyes. "I'll fight like a man. What do I care for a man's life? Kill or be killed . . ."

When she had gone, locking the door behind her, he found she had laid a flask of whisky on the bed. Good whisky. She must have stolen it from Cary.

Whatever hope Roger had of escape from the ship fell as the wind gathered force. Men tramped the decks, shoving, cursing and shouting orders. He could hear the creak of masts, the shifting of cargo. He got up and looked out the opening. The sky was the peculiar yellow green that goes with hurricane weather. He heard Michael Cary's voice, "Heave anchor!" Roger knew what that meant. The anchor was dragging. They would have to run for it or the ship would be driven against the Banks. Cary wouldn't dare venture out to open sea through Roanoke Inlet. His best chance was to put half-about, run up the Albemarle Sound under small canvas, and take shelter in some river or cove where there would be protection against the force of the gale. That suited Roger Mainwairing well, very well indeed. He smiled as he stretched his arms above his head. No trouble now except with his forearm, stiff from the unhealed gunshot wound.

He went back to his bed. If Diego came he must pretend to be weak and dizzy from the blow on his head. He wore no clothes save his close leather breeches, good enough for swimming to the shore. When the time came, he was positive that the leet woman would unlock the door. That was all he wanted of her or anyone. There was nothing now but to wait until the full fury of the storm was upon them. The wind was his friend, and the enemy of Michael Cary and his ship.

By daylight, Roger recognized Durant's Neck. Michael Cary would make for Little River or the Yaupim. The Yaupim, of course. Why had he not thought of it before? "Blast his dark soul!" Roger said aloud. Even with the danger of the hurricane, and the added danger of the pursuing guard-ship, he would try to see Marita Tower.

Roger got out of bed and tried the door cautiously. It was

408

still locked. He slipped the knife the girl had given him into the belt of his breeches. He might have a chance. . . .

Diego came with a bowl of hot soup. He set it down on the bench without comment and went away. After an hour he returned and brought paper, quill and wax. He lighted the candle stub.

"Make out the bill," he said gruffly.

Roger said, "I see dimly, but perhaps . . ." He fumbled with pen and paper. "Show me when I come to the edge of the sheet," he said. "See that I do not write line upon line."

While he was setting his seal on the wax, the door opened and Anne Bonney came into the room. She did not glance at Roger. She came swiftly across the room, snatched the paper from his hands, and turned on Diego. A string of oaths came from her lips as foul as Roger had ever heard.

"Fool, blundering fool! You let this fellow talk you into setting you free for fifty pounds. A hundred would be cheap— and half for Bonney!" She tore the paper into shreds. "I'll write," she said. She scrawled something on the paper and pushed it in front of Roger.

Roger said, "Where must I sign? My sight is blurred." He saw well enough what she had written: "Diego cannot read. Put your seal on." He signed and set his seal.

She thrust the paper in the bosom of her blouse. "I'll keep it." She glared at Diego. "How do I know you will divide when you collect the money in Virginia?"

Diego returned her black look but he did not protest. She went out the door without a backward look.

Diego said, "Tonight your door will be unlocked. At the stern of the ship a rope will be hanging, with a rowboat tied to it. That is all I can do."

"A knife," Roger said, "to cut the rope?"

Diego hesitated. "I'll bring one later."

He left but came back within a few minutes. Thrusting a knife into Roger's hand, he went quickly away. Roger was puzzled. Perhaps the man was honest. He went to the table where the candle still burned and examined the knife. The handle was loose. When he drove it against the table the blade snapped into three pieces. He smiled grimly. He would be watching for Señor Diego. . . .

The fight on the deck was never clear to Roger—the creaking of the masts, the shouts and oaths of the sailors, and over all the roar of the wind. In the darkness he made his way toward the stern, trusting that if he were observed he would be taken for one of the crew. A rope was hanging over the side. He was ready to go over when Diego caught him unawares and by a dexterous movement pinned Roger's arms to his sides.

"Captain! Captain!" Diego shouted at the top of his lungs, "the prisoner is escaping!"

"Damn you for a traitor," Roger said, gasping for breath.

Diego's teeth shone. "The Captain pays me well!" he laughed. "Both pay Diego."

Roger, by a great effort, wrenched himself loose from the Spaniard's encompassing arms. Diego tripped over a rope and fell backward to the deck. In a flash of light Roger saw him gain his knees and creep forward, a bared knife in his hands. Roger's knife, which Anne Bonney had given him, was in his belt. He had no time to draw it. He hit out savagely at Diego's shadow, again and again, sometimes striking, sometimes missing by inches. At last luck came to him and Diego dropped to the deck, after a crashing blow of the bare fist. Roger scrambled over the side, the rope burning his hands as he slid. Halfway down he realized that the rope was swinging. There was no boat below.

Shouts from the deck told him Cary had been roused. A pistol flashed. Roger let go the line and fell into the water, the breath almost knocked out of him. He kicked his arms and legs, the instinct of a strong swimmer. A second shot struck the water somewhere ahead of him. He altered his course. It was hard swimming against the current. He was all but done when he saw the solid shadow of land.

He did not know how long he lay on the thin strip of sand. In time he breathed more normally and his mind cleared. He got to his knees, then to his feet, and looked about him. The first light of dawn was breaking in the east, but there was no cessation in the strength of the wind. He walked along the warm sandy shelf below the wooded bank, hoping to see some familiar object to tell him where he was. A bend in the river gave him a long view. Then he knew. Before him was the pocosin, jutting far out into the water. Beyond the swamp was the little cove, and Captain Zeb's small house. He walked on with more vigour. He could get food here, and one of the Captain's shirts to cover his bare torso.

When he reached the house he turned. Far down the Sound he saw the masts of the *Willing Maid*. Young Cary had set a course for the mouth of the Yaupim River.

Roger knocked. The Captain was not there, nor any of his

slaves. He went inside and threw himself down on the bed. He would rest for a little while before he went to the manor house. A moment later he was asleep.

Captain Zeb wakened Roger a few hours later, shaking his shoulder violently to bring him out of the sleep of exhaustion. "Get up," he said. "There's a ship off the Point. Looks to me as if she's in trouble."

Together they scrambled down the bank to the shore to get a better view. A dark object lay on the beach. "A man," the Captain said, hurrying as fast as the damp sand permitted. When they turned the body over, Roger recognized the sailor Diego—a bullet had plowed through his neck, severing the jugular vein.

"Bled to death like a stuck swine," Zeb said.

Roger thought of the last pistol shot he had heard. Had Michael Cary killed Diego because he had allowed Roger Mainwairing to escape the ship? Or had Anne Bonney fired the shot? Roger looked down on the fierce, treacherous face, frozen in angry death.

"A rascal, better dead," the Captain commented. "I'll send a slave to bury him in the swamp, or the swine will root him up."

A little farther on they saw a second body, a sailor, the side of his head crushed.

"Seems to have been trouble on the ship," Zeb remarked, looking at Roger with his shrewd bright eyes.

Roger said, "If it's the *Willing Maid* out there, there was trouble enough. She's put in here to clear the storm, and perhaps shake off the guard-ship."

The Captain listened to his brief recital. "It's plain as pikestaff that Tom Cary's done for, and good riddance. I'd not grieve over him no longer than some widows grieve—three days at the most. But I don't like that young devil, Michael, being around—with Hue and Cry against him." He did not speak of Marita but she was in the minds of both men. "Mayhap he'd not be so harsh if he was away from Tom Cary," he added, wanting to be fair.

A heavy gust of wind drove them to the shelter of the bank. The Captain stood with his legs apart to give balance while he watched the oncoming ship. Suddenly he explained, "She's wind driven. She is without rudder or steering gear. She'll go into the bank there by the pocosin. Stay here and keep watch, Duke. I'll send a boy with pistols. Watch for that young devil, Michael Cary. Hold him if he comes ashore. I'm going to the house for help. Its men we'll be needing when she strikes the beach."

Roger was glad that the Captain and a dozen men from the manor house came back before the ship grounded. Hidden in the trees, it was easy for Watkins and the two Scots to cover young Cary when he swam ashore. Anne Bonney was with him. Dressed in her seaman's breeches and boots, a bright scarf bound at her belt, with a knife and pistol, she looked a proper pirate. Roger did not wait to hear the Captain's orders. He started through the woods to the manor house before the swimmers saw him. The presence of Michael Cary, prisoner or free, meant trouble.

The rain had stopped, but not the wind. Out from under the shelter of the trees, he was driven forward. More than once he stumbled over a fallen limb of a giant tree. It took all of his strength to move in the direction he wanted to go—to the manor house.

Roger entered the house through the little office. There were no servants about to announce him, so he walked through the hall to the open door of the sitting-room where the women were sitting out the storm, Miss Mittie, Marita and Lady Mary. Lady Mary saw him before the others. She rose from her chair, looking at him as if she saw an apparition.

"Roger," she said, "Roger, where have you come from?"

"From the sea—a deserter from the Governor's army, looking for sanctuary." He was smiling, trying to be casual, all the time trying to think of some way to tell Marita of Michael Cary. But he could think of no way to ease the shock. "I've been a prisoner on Cary's ship, *Willing Maid*," he said bluntly.

In the silence that followed his words, Marita came towards him. She was moving past him through the door when he caught her arm to detain her. "Do not go," he said quietly. "Captain Zeb has Michael Cary. He will hold him under the Governor's order of Hue and Cry until the government takes him into custody."

Marita unloosed Roger's hold on her arm. She walked across the room and sat down.

Lady Mary looked from one to the other, a puzzled frown on her smooth forehead. She moved swiftly across the room to Marita and caught her shoulder. "What does this Michael Cary mean to you?" she said, anxiety sharpening her voice.

Marita got to her feet, facing Lady Mary squarely. "Ev-

412

erything." Her voice was almost inaudible. "Everything in this world. He is my husband."

Lady Mary shook Marita's shoulder. "She is daft! She has lost her senses in fear of the storm." She turned to Roger. "She is daft—"

She stood for a moment looking at Roger without seeing him. Then she walked across the room and sat down in her chair, her fine strong features without expression.

Chapter 34

"...IS A FAMILY'S HONOUR"

"I TELL you I will see Marita." Michael Cary's voice was raised and full of purpose. The fighting Quaker strode into the room, Captain Zeb following. Cary's hands were tied and his clothes were disheveled.

Marita crossed the room swiftly and took her place at his side, her hands clasped about his arm. "Michael, Michael!"

He looked down at her upturned face. His stormy eyes softened and his black scowl disappeared. He said in a low voice, "I must speak to your aunt."

Roger Mainwairing watched Lady Mary. She did not look at Michael. Instead she nodded her head, almost imperceptibly, at Miss Mittie, who got up and went out of the room through the door that led to Lady Mary's bedchamber. Before Lady Mary opened her mouth to speak Roger saw, through the open window, the two gillies coming up the walk. Between them, struggling, fighting, was the leet woman. Things would come to a head in truth now. The girl was screaming invectives. But the two stout Scots were impervious to her kicks and screams.

"What is that disturbance?" Lady Mary said, not taking her eyes off Michael Cary.

The Captain answered, "It's Dougal and Black John. They've got the leet woman—that blasted witch girl."

Roger saw Marita's face pale, but she said nothing.

Lady Mary said, "Let them bring her in. It will be refreshing to see the two outlaws together and hear what they have

413

to say, before I have Watkins turn them over to the Constable—Mr. Michael Cary and his light o' love."

"That is not true!" The words burst angrily from Michael's lips. "She's no woman of mine. She's the sailor's harlot."

The Captain said, "Watkins found her hiding in the 'cosin after he had captured Cary."

Anne Bonney and her captors came into the room then. She looked defiantly around and took a position on the other side of Michael. "They won't believe you." She laughed harshly. "You're tarred with the same brush, black as I am."

Lady Mary nodded to Dougal. "Take her out to the hall. Keep her quiet."

For some reason the girl went quietly. Roger saw her sit down on a long bench on the opposite side of the hall.

Lady Mary sat very erect in her high-back chair, her blue silk gown falling about her in soft folds. "You have something to say to me, Mr. Cary?" she said quietly.

"I have come to talk to you about Marita," he said. He was at a disadvantage. He recognized it.

Lady Mary allowed her cold blue eyes to fall to Michael's bound wrists. She said nothing, waiting for him to go on.

"Marita is my wife. When I came back from the Indies I intended to come for her and take her away. But the war had broken out. You know the rest. A man fleeing from the law cannot ask his wife to follow him."

Lady Mary ignored Michael's explanation. "You say you are wed. By what ceremony may I ask? Over the broomstick?" she said cruelly.

Marita drew a gold chain from her neck with trembling fingers, trying to open the large locket that hung from the chain. "I have the paper," she faltered.

"The Quaker James Thurlow married us right enough," Michael said.

"Oh, a Quaker ceremony, before a Quaker meeting, with Quaker witnesses?" Lady Mary's eyes were boring into Michael. "Why don't you speak?" she demanded. When he hesitated she asked, "Who were your witnesses, Foster Tomes and his good wife, or Lucretia, perhaps? Or were you wed in open meeting?"

"No," Michael answered, as if the word was dragged from him.

Lady Mary let the scorn she felt come to her voice. "You are a dastard, Cary. You beguile a young and innocent girl. By a pretence of marriage. You are contemptible."

414

"I swear it is a true marriage in sight of God. I love Marita. I would not harm her. I—"

Lady Mary cut him short, holding up her long slim hand to silence his protests. "But not a marriage by law, even of the Quaker creed."

Michael hestiated. He glanced towards Marita. He could not meet the agonized appeal in her eyes.

Lady Mary leaned forward slightly. "If you had come to me as a gentleman would have come, or an honest man, asking permission to marry, I would have told you—"

Marita moved across the room. "It is my fault. I told him not to come. I told him that you would be angry. I—"

Lady Mary silenced her. "A true man defends himself. He does not hide behind a woman's skirts. Sit down, Marita." She turned back to Michael. "I would have told you, had you come to me, Mr. Cary, Marita is not of age and she cannot marry without permission. Not even I have the right to give that permission."

Roger looked at the faces of the three people—Marita, worry showing in her trembling lips, Michael, defiant and angry. That is what Lady Mary wants, Roger thought. She will make him lose control of his temper. She herself remained calm, almost judicial, sitting quietly in her high-back chair. What was going on in that clear brain of hers behind the calm, unfurrowed brow, he had no idea.

Michael said, "We do not ask your permission, nor do we need it. We want only each other."

"Marita is a ward of the Court," Lady Mary continued as if he had not spoken. "She can marry only by permission of the—"

Michael's anger broke through his attempts to control it. He shook off the Captain's restraining hand and took a step towards Lady Mary. Her calmness goaded him toward violence. He did not seem to hear Marita's warning, "Michael! Michael—"

"You are a cruel woman, Lady Mary. You sit there and laugh behind that mask. You want to torture, to put me on the rack."

"If you were a man you would have come to me openly. Only a sneak comes by night stealing."

"By God, I could kill you!"

"No. You might talk of killing, but you would not kill." The cold scorn in her voice filled the room. "Words are your weapons, soft, honeyed words to destroy young women."

Michael broke then, cursing and fighting against the bonds that held him. Lady Mary watched him, a contemptuous smile on her lips. His rage subsided under her words.

"You are making a spectacle of yourself, Mr. Cary. Captain, take him out and give him over to Watkins. Let him put Mr. Michael Cary and his woman into safe custody until he delivers them to the authorities tomorrow."

Marita ran to Michael. "Don't, don't, Michael. Don't let her defeat you. . . . I love you. I shall not give you up."

Michael shook her hand from his bound wrists. His voice was controlled now and very quiet. "Your aunt is right, Marita. I have played the part of a coward. A hunted man, with a price on my head, I have no right to speak now. I will come for you when I have a clear name to offer you." He leaned toward her, his eyes fixed on her. "Marita, I love you so deeply that I can think only of your happiness, not my own." There was some of the old recklessness in Michael's voice as he faced Marita. "What if you are a ward of the Court? What matter if Lady Mary is your guardian and refuses to give her consent? We are married, you and I. Not even the Archbishop of London's words can part us. I am your husband. You are my adored wife in the sight of God. I do not ask you to wait for me. But I want you to know that if I live, I will come for you."

He left the room. Marita, silent, watched him go, her face drained of colour. Roger got up and closed the door. He wished he had not been a witness to this scene—a strong, bold man beaten by a woman's words. There was something terrible in Michael Cary's defeat and Lady Mary's triumph. Yet she showed nothing of triumph in her face or in her voice when she spoke to Marita.

"Sit down, my dear, and calm yourself. The man is beneath your tears."

Marita did not move. She kept her bewildered eyes on the closed door. Roger led her to a chair and stood beside her, his hand on her shoulder. Lady Mary was motionless, looking at the floor.

The silence was long. Outside the wind was dropping. It seemed to Roger that the tempest within the room and the tempest without died at the same time.

Lady Mary rose. She walked across the floor and stood in front of Marita. Her voice was very quiet, even kind, as one speaking to an unruly child. "You must not grieve for a man who is unworthy. He could bring you only a life of agony and despair."

Tears rushed from Marita's eyes, shaking her body. Roger walked towards the door.

"Don't go," Lady Mary said. "I have something to say to Marita that I want you to hear. Please sit down."

Roger took a chair across the room from the two women. Lady Mary went back to her chair, waiting quietly for Marita to gain control. Presently the girl dried her eyes and sat up, facing Lady Mary.

"When you are of legal age, Marita, these things will all be explained to you. You will receive your inheritance, take up your obligations, and accept your responsibilities. There are times when it is necessary to forget your personal life. That is a tradition of your family—you cannot do otherwise."

She stopped talking and sat for a moment looking out of the window. She glanced at Marita. "I had not intended to tell you this until you reached the age for you to receive your little inheritance and take your proper place. There are other reasons too involved to go into now. My father, and your grandfather, Marita, was a ruler of a kingdom—King Charles the Second, of blessed memory."

She turned to Roger. "You will understand my first interest in you when you told me that you fought in Monmouth's rebellion. My name is not Mary Tower, but Mary Tudor."

Suddenly everything was clear to Roger . . . so much was explained . . . the woman herself, her assurance, her eagerness to talk of Monmouth, her knowledge of his rebellion. He spoke quickly, "Monmouth was—"

"The Duke of Monmouth was my eldest, my adored brother. We did not have the same mother. His was the actress Lucy Waters. My mother was Mary Davis, a beautiful woman with the most beautiful voice in England."

Marita stood up, her eyes burning, her voice harsh. "So you are a bastard, just as that girl, that leet woman, is a bastard. I am . . ."

Lady Mary rose. The two women faced each other, standing close, almost touching. "I am a natural child, my dear, made legitimate by my father, the King, so recognized by the State." A small smile dented the corners of her red mouth. " 'A King's bastard is a family's honour,' " she quoted.

Marita was very still. Her eyes fixed on the older woman were unflinching. "A bastard, like the leet woman," she repeated, "and you say Michael Cary is not good enough

417

for me! Why can't you see it is I who am not good enough for Michael?" Her voice broke. She was near to tears. She turned and left them. They heard her swift footsteps running up the stairs.

Lady Mary walked across the room and pulled the bell cord. When Desham came in answer to her ring, she said, "Go up to Miss Marita. Wait outside her room to be ready if she should need you. Do not allow her to go away without letting me know."

She turned to Roger. "Sit down, please. I want to talk to you, Roger. I have said too much not to say more. Perhaps there had been too much mystery here, but it was not my doing." She moved about aimlessly, then sat down again. The calm had gone from her. She looked troubled and very weary.

"It was the Queen's wish that I remain away from Court for two years. Someone, one of my enemies—my husband perhaps—had convinced her that I was in a plot to return Jamie to the throne. You already know that was not true, Roger. We wanted only to be assured that a Stuart would succeed the Queen, not a Hanoverian, a foreigner." Her voice showed only concern. "That would be unthinkable, the end of everything." She moved about restlessly.

"No one but Edward Hyde knows the reason I am here," she continued. "We are distant cousins. When heard that Edward was coming to Carolina as governor, I thought it was the solution, because it was advisable for me to remain out of England for a time. Lost here in the wilderness, I could wait . . . and forget." She paused, folding the riband of her sash. "I thought the change would be good too for Marita. But it would have been far better to go back to Normandy, even though there was war. . . . When I think of that man," she said passionately, "I could kill him with my own hands."

Roger watched her inner emotions play their changes across her beautiful face, understanding, never condemning her. After a time she was quiet again.

"From the first I loathed it here. I was planning to go away to Jamaica or to one of the other Plantations. Then I saw you that night at Balgray"—she spoke calmly, not looking at him—"wearing Monmouth's uniform . . . the decoration he had placed on your breast."

She got up and moved back and forth across the room. "How is one to know which is the best road to choose?"

418

Roger went to a small table and poured a glass of whisky from a decanter. "Here, drink this, my dear. You must be very weary."

She took the glass from him obediently.

"Sit down and rest," he said. "I will come back in a short time. Try not to think." He left the room and closed the door quietly.

He found Captain Zeb sitting on the rear gallery. "We're past the worst of it," Captain Zeb said, squinting at the sky. "This is the lull in the storm unless we're in the centre. Then she'll come back at us worse than ever. So far it's been only the fringe of the hurricane that struck here."

Roger said, "What did you do with Cary and the girl?"

The Captain jerked his thumb over his shoulder towards a small brick building with little barred openings at the top of the wall near the roof. "Watkins locked them in the dairy house where they're safe. He says he's going to take them to town, come morning. He'll turn them over to the Constable and claim reward. Dougal and Black John will see that they're up to no mischief out there."

Roger felt Captain Zeb's keen glance fixed on him inquiringly. Roger strode the length of the gallery a time or two. As for Anne Bonney, she'd got herself into this, he thought. Let her get out. True, she tried to help him get away from the ship, but he knew this was in return for that earlier time when he had carried Susannah's dead body to Queen's Gift. "No quarter given or taken," she had boasted to him. As for Michael Cary, Roger wasted no sympathy there. It was of Marita he was thinking.

He stopped in his stride and faced the old Captain. "We must protect her. She is so young, so unprepared."

The Captain nodded his head once or twice. He was in complete agreement with whatever Roger had to suggest.

"I will pay Watkins the amount of the reward," Roger remarked.

Captain Zeb spat tobacco across the rail. "The Quakers of Pequimans have an underground to Virginia," he said. "Cary has plenty of followers still."

Roger was satisfied that was the solution. "I'm going out to the lot to see if Watkins can give me the loan of a saddle horse and I'll ride home. I am anxious about my crop."

Zeb laughed. "You're stuck here for the night same as me, Duke. My cabin's flatter than a hoecake, and the horses have taken to the timber. Watkins just told me it would be morning before they'll be able to round them up and chase them to the stables."

Roger walked out to the meadow and looked around. Tobacco and corn lay flat to the ground, the silver of the under leaves turned upward. Trees were down, lying across the road, small buildings razed, debris clogging the fields between the rows of corn and tobacco. Only the low cotton plants had withstood the devastating violence of the wind.

The bell ringing for dinner found Roger still walking in the fields. Whatever damage had been here would be duplicated at Queen's Gift and the other Soundside plantations, in the village as well.

He found Lady Mary and Miss Mittie seated at the table in the long dining-room. Captain Zeb came in just ahead of Roger. As the old Captain was mumbling grace, Marita entered and slipped quietly into her chair. Servants brought in the food; the joint was cold and also the sliced pullet, but the grits were steaming and the cornbread hot. The talk was of the storm and the havoc it had wrought. Marita did not say anything until Roger spoke of the flattened fields.

"Will the corn be lost," she asked, "and the tobacco?"

Roger couldn't tell yet, he said. Sometimes the corn would come back, but a rain now was hard on tobacco. It wanted warm, dry weather while the leaf was gathered.

Marita left the table with the others and started upstairs. Lady Mary asked her to come into the sitting-room. "I have something I want you to see," she said. The girl hesitated, her hand on the newel post. Her eyes were expressionless, but she followed Lady Mary into the room. "You too," Lady Mary said, as Roger and Miss Mittie hesitated.

When they were seated, she went directly to her escritoire. She slid her fingers along the panel and a drawer opened. From this she took a red Morocco box about twelve inches square. Roger saw a small light gleam in Marita's eyes as Lady Mary opened the box and took out a mirror with a carved gilt frame. She pressed something and the mirror swung open. Back of the glass was a small painting of King Charles the Second. The same long, thin face, the bold, drooping eyes, the full, passionate red lips reproduced in the woman seated before them.

"This is yours," she said, putting the paper in Marita's hands. "It bears the signature of my father—a record giving me my legal name, Mary Tudor, and my order of precedence, outranking every Duchess in the Court. Examine

420

t carefully, Marita. Now you can understand why—" She did not finish the sentence. "If you were in England, my dear, you would be living at Hampton with other wards of the Court."

Marita folded the paper and laid it down on the desk without reading it or displaying any interest. She sat for a few moments looking out the window. Then she rose to her feet. "I shall be of legal age within a year. Then I shall take the husband of my own choosing." She spoke quietly. "I am young, I can learn patience and how to wait." For the first time Roger saw in her something of Lady Mary's spirit and indomitable will.

"If you will excuse me now, I will go upstairs."

Miss Mittie got up and followed her from the room, a look of deep concern in her kind eyes.

Lady Mary watched Marita go, her face a white mask without expression. When the door closed, she said evenly, "I have lost my girl. I fought with every weapon at my command but I lost."

"She will obey you," Roger said. "She will do what you will."

"I know. I will take her home with me, but I have lost just the same. Lost to an inferior person." To his surprise the eyes she turned to him were filled with tears. "My poor, poor child! I wanted to save her the agony and heartache that I endured. I have done what I could." She shrugged her shoulders. "But she will not heed me. From now on she will go her own way . . . she is a woman now."

Roger said, "Are you going to turn Michael Cary over to the authorities?" He wanted to know what she would say.

Lady Mary shook her head slowly. "No, I am going to ask you to set him free. Cary and his leet woman—but it will be your act of mercy, not mine, Roger."

Roger did not tell her of his talk with Captain Zeb. Let her have the salve of one act of leniency and gentleness to remember after her anger and disappointment had passed.

When Roger came back Lady Mary was sitting by the window, the light breeze playing over her pale gold hair, stirring the soft muslin ruffles of her gown.

"They have gone," he said. "I extracted the promise from Cary that he would not try to see Marita again."

"What did he say?"

Roger did not answer at once, not caring to repeat Michael Cary's word or his own, or speak the violent anger of

421

Anne Bonney. "He said he would come for her in England. In London his uncle has power. He is a Lord Proprietor. He will come to you when his name is clear and he has his own inheritance, and Marita is her own mistress. I have promised to say this to Marita."

Lady Mary's expression softened a little. "Perhaps I have underestimated Michael Cary," she said slowly. Then she shrugged her fine shoulders. "'Let the gods decide.'"

Roger said, "The child did not die, as you told me."

She looked quickly away.

"You are alike. I saw it as you faced each other—not in looks but in strength of will."

She turned towards him. The calm indifference had fallen from her. "He shall never have her—never!" she said fiercely.

Roger knew she was not speaking of Michael Cary. She recovered herself quickly. A feeling of desolation swept him. She seemed remote, as far from him as the new country from the old. Something of his thoughts showed in his face, for she came to him and put her arms about him.

"Do you remember the night I came to you and you told me that love ruled the night? No matter where our lives lead us, whether we are together or apart, we have that to remember. Two lonely souls who had wandered far before we found each other."

He took her in his arms then and said to her the things a man says to the woman he loves.

Chapter 35

THE COMMON LAW

IN THE days that followed the Governor's abortive effort to trap Thomas Cary, Roger farmed. He had no thought in his mind but to save what crops he could after the devastation of the storm.

Fortunately, none of the dependency houses was wrecked, and the new stables were intact. Rhoda's hunters got through with only a few minor scratches, though the grooms had a difficult time keeping them from bolting.

Metephele and his men were home. His *capita* spoke of the siege as of no account. Never once had the Governor cried *Chipomera mchemo,* and what was a war without a war cry? Only sitting and then marching away, and no *wa-m'goli.* This was not intelligible to the old African warrior—marching to a fight without bringing home captives, each one's neck held in a *goli,* a slave stick of forked wood. This great man, this Governor, had marched many days with many men. He had guns also, and swords.

"What kind of man is this, Master, who sits down before the enemy, but moves not forward to make the kill?"

Roger had no answer for Metephele.

In the village and along the Sound, white men asked the same question. Thomas Cary, sly as a red fox, had outrun Hyde. He had outrun the Queen's marines in their fine red coats, although the marines had taken many of the lesser leaders and held them captive. They had cleared the swamps of rebels, chased them from Romney Marsh and along their Pamticoe hideouts, a few at a time, so that no rebellion was left. But the rebels' chief, Cary, and Emanuel Low and half a dozen others had their liberty.

Sending to Virginia for help did not sit well with the people of Albemarle. Hyde had not proved his mettle, either as a governor or as a general.

In tavern and in ale house, discussion was rife. Heads were broken by flying ale mugs, swords were drawn, in defence of or against the new Governor's policy. The common man was angered most because the Governor had appealed to Virginia for aid.

"Let us fight our own fight," thundered MacTavish at a meeting of his Two Penny Club.

"Hear, hear!" shouted Tom the Tinker, beating the table with his stone mug. "He's right; the farrier's right. Be we men or slaves? If we be men let us do our own fighting. Now in the time of King William . . ."

"Shut his mouth for him," came from a dozen lips.

"Tom Cary's gone and there's no leader fitten to take his place," Johnny Lynch, the mason, cried.

"Who wants Cary?" MacTavish's voice rose. "Mister Hyde's good enough for me. But let him cease to call for help. One day Spottswood's soldiers will come marching down Somer Town Road, and we'll be Virginia, and not Carolina."

In the Coffee House the talk had the same tone. Hyde should have marched on Cary and wiped out his camp. "A weak governor will not help us now," one planter argued with Edward Moseley. "Crying for help like snivelling children! What has become of our fighters? Has our independent spirit sunk to so low a level we cannot stand firmly on our own feet to repulse an enemy without calling for help from our neighbours?"

Moseley stood on a chair in the taproom and answered the hecklers. "Gentlemen, gentlemen," he called, "listen to me for a moment! You all know I've been for Thomas Cary against William Glover. Why? Because he was the stronger man and I hoped he would use his strength to establish law, the law we so sorely need in this land of ours."

A burly farmer from upriver cried out, "What we need is men who'll fight for their rights. We don't need law—let every man be his own law. What we want is our rights."

"Be quiet, Larigan!" half a dozen men called. "Let us hear what Justice Moseley has to say."

It was market day and the town was crowded. As Moseley talked, more and more men slipped into the room. Men crossing the Green heard his voice and walked closer. There were a hundred or more farmers, herdsmen and drovers, besides the town artisans standing near the open windows.

"Come out on the Green, Mr. Moseley. Let us all hear what you are saying!"

Edward Moseley hesitated a moment. He had not sought this chance to talk to the people of the Albemarle of their responsibility in upholding the law. This occasion had been thrust upon him. Perhaps it was the hour.

Moseley took his place on the steps of the new Government House facing the Green. Behind him stood the sagging scaffolding and wrecked chimneys, all that was left of the Governor's new dwelling when the hurricane passed.

Below, standing on the ground, were a great press of people, roughly dressed men with weather-beaten faces, men in faded blue smocks and homespun, leather-legginged yeomen, and men in buckskin, for it was market day for men from the great rivers and the smaller streams and little creeks. The wharf was crowded with their craft, and the village hitching racks and the inn stables were lined with their horses and carts. As he looked at them, a feeling of deep humility came over him. His mind envisaged the little cabins set in the timber by streams and rivers, a small opening cut into the dense wilderness of trees. And these people, hardened by wind and sun, worn from fighting against the winds and

424

he rains and the blazing sun. Sickened by fever, facing a onely death, from wild beast or red man or ravishing plague, far from their kind. It seemed to Moseley that every face urned to him bore the stamp of fortitude and high courage. Who was he to tell them that they must live under a law that had been made for them by men far across the sea? These men were their own law—that was their power and their protection. Every man who stood on the Green with his two feet planted firmly on the solid earth had law in the palm of his hand, in the barrel of his long rifle, in his unflinching gaze strengthened by looking boldly at danger.

The faces of the men blurred before his eyes. It must have been like that when the nobles stood before John and watched him sign the Great Charter.

Something happened to Edward Moseley at that moment. Here was his answer.... *Each man in himself was a law. United, they made the common law by which they must live. That was the power they had brought with them from their homeland. That was their inherited power. That was the power they would leave to their children, and their children's children—the common law for the common man.*

His way was clear before him now. He must show these wilderness men where their power lay. He opened his lips and began to talk.

"I wish my words would make you see the Thames that day four hundred and ninety-six years ago. On one side of the river the crafty Angevin King, furious but impotent among his trembling foreign counsellors—on the other side the embattled host of Barons great and small, the bishops and the clerics, the mayor and the citizens of London.

"It was the voice of the English nation speaking at Runnymede—a great formless voice that grew in sagacity and power, demanding a reign of law. Under that freedom we still live, and under that law our children shall live.

"It was no theoretical freedom that the Barons at Runnymede claimed for themselves and the whole nation—a true freedom that comes from the enforcement of law for all, without regard to privilege or power—for the certainty of just and speedy decisions from the courts, for protection against arbitrary taxation.

"Liberty is indeed a meaningless thing except as a right adjustment between all the forces of people and land. The common law for the common people—and that, my friends, is our vast heritage."

Roger rode into King Street at sunset. As he made the turn along the Green, he saw a great crowd of people near the government building. As he rode closer he recognized Edward Moseley's voice before he saw the speaker. Moseley's coat was off, his dark hair fell over his forehead. He was striding up and down the platform that had been the entrance to Government House. His strong, vigorous voice carried over the crowd.

"Go home and think about the things I have said. Talk to your wives. Talk to your neighbours. Do not make war against your neighbours over the loss of a shoat or a fowl, or the way a road lies, or quarrel about who does the most road work. Work your land. Take your troubles to court. No matter if there be a thousand cases on the docket, that is better than that a man should kill his neighbour over some small difference of a boundary line or a mare's marking. We have a Great Court, and a Court of Oyer and Terminer for small cases. We have a free Assembly—we make our own laws and we will abide by them."

A rough voice shouted, "What about land, Mr. Moseley? Tom Pollock's got all the land—fifty thouand acres. What chance has a small farmer against that?"

Moseley answered quickly, "Every man has a chance to better his condition in this country. Mr. Pollock brought money to buy land. He develops what he patents and seats. He imports cattle. He plants crops. He clears timber. He fishes the streams. He pushes back the wilderness from his door. Thomas Pollock and his kind give substance to our country—and every man jack of you has the same right to patent and seat land and push back the wilderness."

Another upriver farmer, emboldened by the questions raised by the first man, called out, "You've got a powerful lot of land yourself, Mr. Moseley!"

"Not so much as I intend to have by half." Moseley's answer was bold. "I came to Carolina for the same reason you did—to better my condition. My advice to all of you is to get more land, patent and buy, and don't sell an acre. Every man here is living better than he lived in England.

"You have forests full of game. You have rivers teeming with fish. For your safeguard and your protection you have the common law. Let us look back again to the slow growth of ordered freedom over the centuries and see how far we have already come, and think how far we may go in the future in a new and vital country under an ordered freedom.

426

In this let there be no compromise, no truce, only victory—the victory our fathers won for us when they forced King John to sign the Great Charter four hundred and ninety-six years ago. I have no more to say. God save our gracious lady, Queen Anne!" The crowd shouted, "God save the Queen."

Moseley took his coat from the rail and walked away, mopping his face with a silk handkerchief.

Roger rode to the Coffee House and left his horse at the stable. When he went inside Moseley was seated at a table, a glass of whisky in his hand. A purple bruise shone angrily on his white face.

Roger said, "I rode in as you were finishing. You seemed to have the crowd with you."

Moseley's dark, deep-set eyes were dull, without sparkle or life. "At the first, and at the last. But there were hecklers who came near breaking it up."

He sat silent for a moment, intent on the glass he held in his hands. "It was MacTavish who kept order. I don't understand that. Usually he is the worst heckler of the lot."

Roger filled his glass from a bottle the barman set on the table. "Something has come over MacTavish of late. I've noticed it before. He's not for tearing down. Maybe something is happening to the whole country, Edward. Do you think we are ready to settle down and build a country?"

Moseley made no answer. Other men entered the Coffee House and came to the table—Frederick Jones, the Judge, Christopher Gale, the lawyer, and young Beasley.

"You never made a finer talk, Moseley," Gale said. "But it was over their heads. What do those farmers care for law as long as they can shoot their way out of all their difficulties? A man's life is worth nothing here. As for law, as it is administered here, it is a travesty, and has been for the past eight years."

"It will be different from now on," Moseley spoke, suddenly roused from his abstraction. "Mark you, it will be different."

"Not while Tom Cary and his crew are loose among us," Gale answered. "As long as he is free, there'll be no law." He went off to join friends at the far side of the room.

A boy came to Roger to tell him that Mr. Lovyck was waiting for him in the small room. Anthony was seated at table, a plate of cold meat in front of him, a mug of porter in his hand. He got to his feet when Roger came in, a small

427

courtesy which always made Roger feel relegated to an older generation. Roger had carried his glass from the other room and sat down opposite him.

"The Governor wants you to sit with the Council at a meeting here in the village tomorrow. He has sent messengers to Pequimans and Pasquotank to the members. He has had a post from London, and he wants to talk over the situation regarding Thomas Cary and his leaders, and the battle."

Roger swallowed his whisky and filled his glass from the bottle. "What battle?" he asked.

Anthony grinned. "The great battle of Romney Marsh."

Roger glanced through the open door. Tables were filling now—a dozen planters and men of the village were in the room. Moseley sat alone.

Roger dropped his voice. "You are close to the Governor, Lovyck. Can you tell me why he turned around and marched his men back to Balgray without attacking Tom Cary?"

Anthony downed his drink before he answered. "If it were anyone but you, Mainwairing, I'd not answer that. To tell you the truth, I think he is afraid of a fight for fear he may lose the little he has gained. I'm worried about H. E. Ever since we came back, he's shut himself up in his room, writing and writing, using reams of paper. He hasn't once called me in." Anthony's tone was aggrieved.

"What is he writing about?" Roger couldn't imagine anyone spending his days letter writing, when there was a wilderness to tame, towns to garrison, men to arm and train, an enemy to be taken or killed.

"God knows! Some sort of report to the Lords Proprietors, I suppose, or to Spottsswood."

Roger got up and brought a fresh clay pipe from a rack over the fireplace. He took some time to crush the leaf and tamp the bowl. Anthony waited, without speaking. He did not always understand Roger Mainwairing's lack of interest in the government of the colony. A successful planter was well enough, but why not be both planter and politician? That was what he intended to be. He wished he had Roger's standing in the Albemarle. People respected him. For what? Because he was a successful planter, or because he was a good swordsman, or because he carried his head high and spoke his mind, come dick, come devil? He sat sidewise at the table now, his long legs straight out before him, his hawk face brown as an Indian, making his blond hair more blond, his blue eyes deeper and more penetrating.

"De Graffenried persuaded Spottswood to send the guard-ship. I wonder how?" Roger said, blowing the first smoke cloud.

"He'll tell you quick enough when he comes," Lovyck said. "He'll be glad to explain how he, the Baron de Graffenried, in his office as Landgrave, duly appointed by the Lords Proprietors, was able to negotiate with the Governor of Virginia, where the simple messenger, Anthony Lovyck, failed." Anthony's tone was bitter. The failure rankled.

"Spottswood was afraid the rebellion would spread," Roger said in a matter-of-fact voice. "He can't afford any extra trouble in Virginia; he's got half the Assembly against him as it is."

Lovyck's face brightened. "I hadn't thought of that, Duke. Of course, you are right. I've been thinking that it was because the Baron had an official position."

De Graffenried joined them shortly. He had come by boat from Balgray. His uniform was as fresh as if it had just come from his tailor. His smile was friendly.

It took little arguing on Roger's part for De Graffenried to tell his experiences: how the hurricane had overtaken them when they were well up the Chowan.

"Never have I seen such violent winds," the Baron remarked. "But I managed to make my way to Virginia, for our need was great. Fortunately I found his Excellency, Governor Spottswood, at Kiquotan, which saved time. It did not take me long to convince him that he must send help to Governor Hyde, else his own colony would be overrun by rebels and fighting Quakers."

Anthony's eyes met Roger's for an instant. The Baron had used Roger's argument very effectively.

"There was some opposition from William Byrd, but you know he is in an ill humour against anything Spottswood wants. Fortune favoured me indeed, for a guard-ship lay in stream ready to sail—and you know the result."

Lovyck said, "I understand Thomas Cary is making for Virginia now."

The Baron raised his arched brows. "So? I had not heard. It will do the traitor little good. At my suggestion, Spottswood issued Hue and Cry against him there. I think the Quakers in Virginia will be afraid to give him or his followers aid. They are not happy over his actions, for it brands them as fighters, when their religion forbids them to take up arms."

429

The Baron went to the door and ordered supper and a bottle of the best Madeira. "I feel that I have served Governor Hyde to his advantage," he said.

Anthony's face darkened. A warning look from Roger kept him from an unwise retort. De Graffenried did not notice. He continued:

"The Rebellion is over. Cary's power is broken. I am very glad that I have played my part in bringing peace to the Carolinas, after eight long years of disorder and rebellion."

Roger got up then. "I must be riding in," he said. "I want to get to Queen's Gift before dark."

"I understand you have had some fine hunters sent out from England?" De Graffenreid said, a rising inflection in his voice.

"The horses belong to Miss Chapman," Roger said.

"Your affianced?"

"Yes."

"That is so nice. Queen's Gift will be a gay house from now on."

Roger said, "I hope so certainly."

"And the hunters? I am a good horseman, a very good horseman, myself. Perhaps some day . . . ?" he paused.

"Indeed, Baron, I shall be delighted to have you try the horses," Roger said heartily. "My men are setting up trial fences and gates and a small track. Perhaps you will put into my place on your way down Sound after tomorrow's Council sitting."

"Thank you so much, Mr. Mainwairing. I shall be delighted."

Roger found the ordinary crowded. Edward Moseley sat alone, staring moodily at the table. Roger knew what had happened. Moseley had been too close to Cary to gain the confidence of the opposition. The talk that he had made would be regarded with suspicion by both sides. The Cary faction, what remained of it would call him a turncoat, a renegade. The Government party was not ready to accept him. Roger went over to the table. "Come, Moseley, let's be riding home."

Moseley looked up at him with dulled eyes. "Yes, of course, I must ride home. I'm not welcome here."

Roger accepted Moseley's invitation to supper. They sat in his book room and waited, while his servants prepared the meal. Roger glanced about the room, shelf after shelf of books, ranging as high as the ceiling. It was said that Moseley

430

had the best library in the colony—law books, books on gardening, Sir John Mandeville's travels, and Shakespeare's plays in folio.

Roger took up a book, *Tragedies and Comedies* of George Chapman. He looked through the pages with interest, for the writer was Rhoda's ancestor. On one side of the room was a long drafting table. Moseley said, "I'm at work on a map of Albemarle County. I want to set every farm and every mill and plantation in its right place."

Roger moved over to look. He was attracted by the heavy boundary line between the Province and Virginia. "Is this your idea of where the line is to be located?" he asked.

Moseley smiled. "Yes, but we will have the Devil's own time placing it there. Spottswood's Commission wants all this land in Virginia."

Roger watched him trace a line with his finger. "You mean they will try to include the Albemarle Sound in their colony?"

"Yes, that is their idea, so Lawson tells me."

"But you won't allow it?" Roger said earnestly. "I don't want my land in Virginia. I want it in Carolina."

Moseley didn't speak for a moment. He was intent on the great map in front of him. "Lawson and I would like to have the line run straight west from Norfolk Town. That would give us a deep waterway. People will settle here from north to south, not east to west. We should have a deep harbour for Albemarle."

This was a new idea to Roger. He thought of it again when he was riding home. He thought of the other thing Moseley had told him, his own personal tragedy—the still-born child, the continued illness of his wife, Ann. "Parris tells me she will never be well again," Moseley had said. "She was too far in years to bear another child."

"Will she be able to come back to Moseley Point?" Roger had asked.

"I've talked it over with my father-in-law, Lillington, and my wife's mother," Moseley had answered. "We think it best for her to stay with them. She can have better care. While I finish my time on the bench, I must be away from home."

Roger recalled the discouraged tone in Moseley's voice.

"You're not resigning?"

"Yes, I have told the Governor that I wish to be relieved. He will recommend Christopher Gale to their lordships. That will be wise. Gale has an excellent legal mind and good

431

training and he has the confidence of the people." Moseley's voice was flat.

Roger had asked, "What will you do then?"

"Look after my land, Roger—and other people's. You must remember I am a surveyor as well as a lawyer. There is still room for me to do my share in developing this country. We must have a right adjustment between all classes, a declaration of our rights, so every man stands free. For that is the temper of our people. We can arrive at this only by the establishment of the common law."

When Roger left, Moseley was standing in the lighted doorway, looking after him. Roger wondered how long he had stood looking out into the darkness, a lonely, misunderstood man—the fate of men who think ahead, out beyond their own times.

Metephele was waiting for his master. He took Roger's coat and brought the boot-jack. The whisky decanter, a quarter full, stood on the little elbow table by his chair. Roger smiled. Metephele was watching him carefully these days.

"Post come today, Master. A mess of letters and papers in the office." He turned his eyes to the table. Roger followed his glance. One letter lay under the rim of the candle lamp. He saw the writing; it was from Rhoda.

Metephele remained standing near the table. His eyes were turned, looking straight ahead, but Roger knew the black watched him. How did these strange dark people sense what went on? He knew as well as if Metephele spoke that he was waiting for him to open the letter. He broke the seal.

"Your letter found me when I arrived at Jamaica," it started. He read on until the end without looking up, lingering over the last paragraph. He folded the paper and laid it on the table. Rhoda had written that she would come up earlier than she had first planned. She would come to Virginia early in September and stay with her cousin Russell at the Governor's Palace. Her cousin wanted her to be married there, a small wedding of course.

Roger raised his eyes to find Metephele looking fixedly at him.

"Your new mistress will be in Virginia in two months' time," he said. "I will go to Williamsburg to meet her and be married there. You will go with me, Metephele. Does that meet with your approval? Do you think you can have the house ready for her by that time, *capita?*"

432

"May can," Metephele said. Then he poured a full glass of whisky and handed it to Roger. "May can," he repeated.

Roger raised his glass. "To the new mistress of Queen's Gift," he said.

A smile of satisfaction crossed the Negro's broad face. He crossed his arms over his chest and bowed his head. *"Moyoni,* Master, *moyoni."*

His slave's salutation touched Roger strangely. "May you see life, Master; may you see life."

Chapter 36

INTERVAL

SCARLET trumpet ran rank along snake fences that enclosed meadow and pasture, and the mid-August air was heavy with the fragrance of jasmine and wild honeysuckle.

Roger walked to the float in early morning to attend to the last loading of the *Golden Grain.* Captain Zeb was standing on shore, watching the slaves roll the barrels of tar on the deck. He glanced up as Roger came down the path, and glowered at his fresh white suit and his wide West Indian hat. Bragg's clothes were mussed, covered with dirt and pitch. "A fine cargo I've got me," he said glumly.

"Fine indeed. It will bring you a good penny," Roger answered, disregarding the Captain's mood.

"You may laugh, lying in your comfortable bed until now, taking your bathe and strolling down here to see an honest man toil and sweat in the broiling sun."

"It's little you know about my hours, Captain," Roger said, grinning. "I was up betimes this morning. I was at my dispensary by sunrise, and gave all the Negroes wormseed and oil from the caster plant mixed with bark."

"God save them!" Zeb muttered. "I'll lay three shillings to one you sat up late last night drinking burnt brandy, and found yourself in an evil humour when you woke."

Roger said, "On the contrary, I am in excellent spirits. I drank little last night, and ate a fine dish of tripe for breakfast."

The Captain cursed a man who put a barrel in the wrong place. He sat down on the float and filled his pipe. "I'm sorry to sail at this time, Duke. There will be sorrow down there. The young miss is not so meek as her ladyship thinks."

"What do you mean?" Roger was at once apprehensive.

"Someone is working on that ship by night. The talk is that the Quakers are helping Michael Cary, perhaps Thomas himself—that I can't say. Mayhap Michael aims to go to Virginia. Mayhap he'll turn freebooter and sail to the Indies." He blew a cloud of smoke to keep off the stinging gnats. "Bat's Grave is a place to hide. The leet woman knows that."

"Michael Cary gave me his oath he would not attempt to see Marita again."

"A man is not obliged to keep an oath given under duress," Zeb remarked sagely, "and Marita did not give a promise to anyone."

This talk stuck in Roger's mind, long after the *Golden Grain* had sailed down the Sound. He would have gone direct to Greenfield, but there was the Governor's Council meeting, nor did he care to put the Captain's vague fears into writing. When the Council was finished he would ride down the Shore Road.

The Council sat in a parlour-cabinet in the East Gate Inn. All members were present. The day was incredibly hot, and every man removed his coat and sat in his Holland shirt and breeches, all save the Governor, who seemed not to suffer from the heat. He had not even removed his full-bottomed wig, as Pollock had done. "He has snow water in his veins," Nicholas Crisp whispered, mopping his brow, "or he is a fish, without blood. I can't fathom him, Duke."

Roger thought the Governor was fatigued. His thin face showed lines that had not been there when he came to the Albemarle a year ago. His hand shook nervously when he sorted the papers Lovyck had spread before him on the table. He brought the Council to order with a sharp tap of his gavel. The silver seal of the Albemarle lay on the table in front of him, an ensign of authority, as a mace might be in a great parliament. Hyde was a stickler for form, and well enough, for it gave dignity to the Council proceedings.

Roger wondered idly whether the Lords Proprietors sat with as much circumstance when they met in Whitehall to discuss the affairs of their domain in the Carolinas.

The Governor did not mention the events of the past two

weeks, the victory in the Chowan, or the inept failure of Romney Marsh. Instead, he took up routine business. A list of patented land again thrown into public domain, for lack of seating. A bond-woman delivered of a bastard child—a matter for the Vestry to administer, the stocks and flogging indicated as proper punishment. Several lashes to Weeks, a bondsman, at the public whipping post for stealing a pair of shoes. For seditious speech, Tom the Tinker to stand in the pillory in the Public Parade from twelve until two. Mary Colton, runaway bondwoman, to be sold by the Provost Marshal to the highest bidder.

Roger's mind wandered, as he sat looking out on the turgid waters of the Sound, where the tree-lined shore curved to a point at Frederick Jones's plantation. The Green was empty of people. The shops were shuttered to keep out the blinding glare of the midafternoon sun. Roger's interest lagged. Instead of listening to the words of the Councilmen, his mind went to Greenfield. He hoped that Michael Cary would keep his word, but the Captain's hints made him uneasy.

"We will call for a vote of the members." Anthony Lovyck's voice broke in on Roger's meditation. "The Governor suggests that the names of the men fomenting the rebellion shall be posted in the order mentioned: Thomas Cary, John Porter, Emanuel Low, Michael Cary, Challingwood Ward, Edmund Porter, Richard Roach. If any of the above be apprehended he shall be under five-hundred-pound bond until such time as he or they can be sent to England for trial.

"Is there any man present against this motion?"

Roger rose to his feet. "I am in agreement with his Excellency, with one exception. The name Michael Cary is mentioned among the rebels. He is a young man, and it is easy to imagine that he acted under the influence of his uncle, Thomas Cary. I suggest that he be given leniency."

The room was silent. Hyde waited for someone to speak in support of Roger, but his own hostility was apparent. "I am afraid we cannot give leniency to Michael Cary. In my own mind he is one of the most dangerous of the rebels."

Pollock said, "I agree with your Excellency. It was Michael Cary who attempted to carry you off—to lay hands on your person with evil intent."

De Graffenried was eager to add his word. "If your Excellency will permit me, I will say that the name Cary is an anathema to Governor Spottswood and to myself. After I had shown Thomas Cary every courtesy, he and his nephew

435

repaid me with double dealing, by refusing to supply my people with food, according to the Lords Proprietors' orders— food for which I had already paid in pounds sterling in London."

Foster Tomes rose. "I would like to add my voice to that of friend Mainwairing, and ask thee for leniency for young Michael Cary. He has been led into evil, not knowing. I think he is young to bear the stigma of rebel."

The Governor's expression remained cold and unbending. "Most rebels are young, friend Tomes."

The Governor waited for others to express themselves, but no one spoke. "I am afraid, Mr. Tomes and Mr. Mainwairing, that we shall be obliged to leave the names as they stand. High treason to the Crown will doubtless be the charge." He turned to his papers. "But, gentlemen, for the others, the lesser folk, the common men dragged into wrong-doing by these fellows, I pray for leniency for their crimes, for they were misled. Threfore, I beg you vote for their complete pardon." There was not a dissenting vote.

The Governor suggested that a letter be written to the Lords Proprietors, that "steps would be taken at the next Assembly to impeach Thomas Cary, Michael Cary, Richard Roach, and several other evilly disposed persons, such as Emanuel Low, for raising an insurrection against the peace of our Sovereign Lady the Queen, who have endeavoured to carry on rebellious purposes, by promises of reward, to neighbouring Indians, and did outfit with great guns and warlike stores two vessels, and sail in a warlike manner with a flag at the masthead, to the great terror of the inhabitants, to the house of Thomas Pollock, where the Council sat. But which advance, by God's assistance, was repelled. All this against the peace of our Sovereign Lady the Queen."

After Lovyck had completed the writing it was passed around to the Council, the Governor affixing his signature first, then Thomas Pollock, Boyd, Nathaniel Chevin, De Graffenried, Crisp and Knight. Roger watched them. The paper seemed of little importance, since neither Cary had been found, but it seemed to give the Governor a certain satisfaction.

That was the only way in which the fiasco was mentioned in the Council. It would have been better to make a report to the Council only instead of to the Lords Proprietors, Roger thought, but he made no comment to any of the members. There was work enough ahead of them.

436

The Governor glanced through his papers and rose. "I have only a few words to say to you, but it seems to me that they are important to us and to our country. With this rebellion at an end, so end eight troublesome years. From now on we may look forward to a new and wider life in North Carolina, with the Queen's peace assured." He bowed to the Council, and with "God Save Queen Anne," he left the room.

Foster Tomes walked across the Green with Roger. "I have wanted to speak with thee, friend Roger. It is a private matter, and I hesitate, but for the good of several persons I think I have the right."

"Let us sit here," Roger said. They sat down on a bench in the shade of an oak tree.

"It is of Michael Cary that I wish to speak. Thee defended him just now in Council. That was kind, and what I would expect of thee. The lad is young, and under the influence of Thomas, as thee has said. I hoped there would be support from some member of the Council, but none came forward. I have long raised my voice against friend Thomas. His conduct has not been that of a Friend. He is worldly and filled with evil ambition, and he has led good men away from the Word."

The Quaker paused and looked down at his feet, clad in heavy, coarse shoes. "The young girl, Marita, came to our house in great distress of mind. She told my good woman and my girl that Michael Cary had wed her. She showed us a paper, signed by a preacher of our faith, James Thurlow." He looked up at Roger, his eyes full of sadness. "The old preacher is a daft one, kind and harmless, but he has not the right to have a man and woman stand up before him."

Roger said, "Do you think Cary knew that?"

Tomes did not answer Roger's question. "Banns must be spoken in meeting and witnesses present before a marriage becomes law among the Friends. This was not done."

Roger said, "I do not think that Michael Cary would willfully deceive a young woman."

Tomes waited a moment before he replied. "Nor I. Doubtless he trusted Friend Thurlow and did not seek to learn more about the Friends' rules concerning the marriage ceremony. My girl Lucretia loves Michael also. She had hoped that he . . . perhaps he did not mislead her willfully . . . but until the young Marita came . . ." Tomes paused. The conversation was painful to him.

437

He got up slowly. "The good God cares for these things in his own way, friend Roger. One must not allow doubts to arise. I have told Lucretia she must forget Michael Cary. I have told her also that she must remain friends with Marita Tower. The child was wearing a Quaker garb. She had some confused idea that she must become a Friend. She said because her grandfather had persecuted the Quakers she would make an atonement. I think my wife convinced her that one does not become a Friend by atonement, but because one sees the light."

Roger knew what was in Marita's mind, but he could not explain to Tomes that it was because King Charles had dealt cruelly with the sect. He said, "Thank you, Tomes. I hope these matters right themselves. Youth is resilient."

Tomes hesitated a fraction of a second. "Word has come to me that Michael is in Pequimans and that he has hauled his ship out of the sand. Before many days she will be ready to sail. There are men in my district who are still loyal to Thomas Cary."

He walked away, his shoulders stooped, as if weighted by a burden. Roger thought of the bright dark eyes of Lucretia Tomes. "Damnation to Michael Cary!" he said aloud.

Roger stopped at the farrier's on his way home. MacTavish was shoeing a horse, the anvil ringing with the sound of his hammer as he bent the glowing iron into shape. Lady Mary's man, Black John, was standing at the head of the horse Blenheim, waiting for MacTavish to curve the shoe. He and MacTavish were talking together.

"My wife Jinnie said to me, the same night she saw her leddyship on the Green, ' 'Tis a Stuart she is from the look of her and the easy way she talks with us common folk. No highty-tighty airs, just plain and friendly-like.' "

Black John put his hand on the mare's neck to calm her. "That's right, Mac, they all 'ave a wye with them. So 'tis with the real gentry, and it's good to be serving her leddyship out here, same as we did in the Hielands."

MacTavish slapped the horse's flank and lifted his leg to place the shoe. "Aye, it's good to have real gentry coming to this New World. It shows we've settled ourselves to make a fine country. With leddies bringing good hunters, soon we'll be hearing the sound of the horn on a cool November mornin', and the horses'll be thundering across the fields amongst the straw stacks, and they'll all be shod by MacTavish, the farrier."

438

"That they will," agreed Black John, "and there'll be Hieland cattle roaming the fields. If your good wife will make a haggis for us, Dougal will do the piping."

MacTavish set the horse's foot to earth and wiped his black hands on his leather apron. When he looked up he saw Roger waiting at the open door of the shop. "I was speakin' together with Black John about the new hunters I've heard you have at Queen's Gift," he said, touching his forelock.

"That is why I stopped by,'" Roger answered. "I want you to come out and look them over tomorrow or the day after. They will need shoeing. Black John will tell you they are good stock."

"That I will, sir, since I lived alongside them in the ship for all of three months. The bay mare will be foaling before long, I'm athinkin'. If you should want help, sir, Black John's a master hand."

"Thank you, I will remember."

He rode off direct to the North Gate. He would take the River Road home, to be there by the time De Graffenried's boat put in at his float.

They sat long at the table that night. It was not hard to persuade the Baron to break his long journey. Roger sent Metephele to the cellar for some of his best Madeira and a bottle of choice brandy.

The Baron, mellow with wine, was talkative, not averse to telling of the mishaps his colonists had encountered since landing in the New World. The settlement at New Bern was not to his liking. The people were afraid, terrified of Indians. They refused to settle the more fertile lands of the interior.

"I am, myself, going to make the journey into the Indian Country with Surveyor Lawson in September," the Baron said. "We will endeavour then to conclude an extended peace treaty, to relieve my people of their fears and appprehensions. Mr. Lawson assures me that the Indians are friendly when treated in a friendly manner."

Roger remembered some earlier Indian massacres. He remembered also the night at the Chowan Indian Village, when only the eloquence of Blont, Chief of the Tuscaroras, kept the younger men from attacking Balgray with Thomas Cary. "I am afraid I do not agree with Lawson, Baron. I think the Indians are a constant menace to our outlying settlements and planters."

De Graffenried watched Roger moving restlessly about the

room. "You think we are being lulled into false security, Mr. Mainwairing?"

Roger's lean face showed concern. "Yes, that is what I think, and there is another thing more serious: The Governor's display of weakness in not attacking Cary will have its effect on the Indians. They will think that we are weak and—"

"You believe they will attack?" The Baron leaned forward, his sharp blue eyes fixed on Roger's face.

"Yes, but perhaps I am wrong. No one else shares my views. But I have travelled among Indians. I think I know them. They are cunning and treacherous and shrewd."

The Baron poured himself a glass of brandy. "The only other person I have heard voice this opinion was Governor Spottswood. He is much concerned over the situation here. He talked to me at length when I was at Kiquotan. He showed me a letter he had written to the Lords of Trade and Plantations. He told them that North Carolina was the common sanctuary of runaway servants and others that flee from law. Since there was a lack of law and religion here, it was a safe harbour for criminals. The Quakers were numerous; they had taken up arms and had a large share in administering government. He emphasized that in North Carolina it was a common practice to resist and imprison their governors."

Roger's lean face was in shadow, but there was amusement in his voice when he spoke. "Spottswood is quite right in that, but he doesn't go far enough. We throw out *unworthy* governors."

The Baron was silent a moment, his eyes fixed on his glass. "There was one thing more. I do not know if I break a confidence, but knowing you, Mr. Mainwairing, I am sure it will go no farther. The rest of the Governor's letter concerned a plan to put North Carolina under the Crown, under royal authority."

"What the devil!" Roger said. "What right has Spottswood to meddle in our affairs? Damn it to hell, it's all a part of Hyde's writing to him, begging for help." He banged the table with his fist. "The blundering fool!"

The Baron did not inquire whether Roger referred to Spottswood or Hyde. He waited for Roger to quiet down, then continued: "His Excellency, Governor Spottswood, went so far as to write the Lords that if they want the Queen's peace to exist here, they cannot lose ground, but must gain tranquillity for the people under due obedience to the estab-

440

lished Church and to royal authority in North Carolina as it is in Virginia."

"God damn them for fools!" Roger ejaculated. "I thought no good would come of Hyde's dilatory ways. To rule in a new country a man must have courage and force. He must show strength if he wants to lead. Hyde is too gentle, too timid to give us what we need now."

The Baron watched the tall lean figure of Roger Mainwairing striding angrily about the room. His own face was inscrutable. After a time Roger threw himself into a chair, his long legs stretched out, his head sunk on his chest. De Graffenried made no attempt to speak, sensing that Roger's discouragement was stronger than his anger.

After a time Roger said, "I should not be angered. These things are no concern of mine. I am a planter, not a politician, but by God, sir, I can't brook weakness in a man who calls himself a leader."

"I subscribe to that statement, Mr. Mainwairing." The Baron raised his glass, smiling a little. "There is a saying in my country, 'Strength for a man, softness for a woman.' Let us drink to that—yes?"

Roger saw Miss Mittie riding up the drive on Blenheim when he crossed the garden after seeing De Graffenried off on his shallop. He quickened his stride. Nothing short of a catastrophe could put Miss Mittie on that great horse.

"You must come," she said, her voice quavering in spite of a valiant effort to keep it steady. "Marita is gone—we cannot find her." He thought she was going to cry but she pulled herself together.

Roger did not wait to question her. His horse was saddled, ready for his early-morning ride to the fields. "We save time riding through the woods," he said, as they issued from the gates. When they had gone a mile or so, he asked the question that had been in his mind from the first, "In Cary's ship?"

Her answer was what he expected to hear. "It is gone. The farm men said it sailed in the night."

A curse formed on Roger's lips. Why had he not gone to Greenfield last night? Surely Foster Tomes had told him that the ship was ready to sail. But Mary had been so sure Marita would obey her. Fool that he was, he should have known not to trust a woman in love! He was aware that Miss Mittie was speaking.

"I was afraid. I told Lady Mary but she laughed at me. She said Marita was too timid, but I knew she is not timid, only quiet. She has a will too, a strong will." Her face puckered up and she dabbed at her eyes.

"For God's sake, don't drop those reins!" Roger said.

Miss Mittie turned an agonized face towards him. "Oh, I forgot. Blenheim is so strong." As if he recognized her fear Blenheim tossed his glossy head and broke into a gallop.

Roger called to him, trying to quiet the animal. He dared not try to overtake him for fear he would race the faster. "Sit tight and draw in the reins slowly. Don't jerk. Talk to him quietly."

They were almost to the gates of Greenfield before Roger overtook Miss Mittie. When he came up she was leaning forward, patting Blenheim's shiny neck. She turned to Roger, her face radiant. "I did it! I quieted him myself. Oh, Mr. Mainwairing, I'll never be afraid again!"

Roger, who expected only terror on her face, was dumbfounded. "Women," he muttered, "women! One can never tell!"

They saw Lady Mary walking up and down the long gallery when they turned the lane. She saw them and came down the steps into the garden. Anxiety had ravaged her face. He lifted Miss Mittie from the saddle. He knew, without asking, that there was no news.

"Her bed was not slept in," Lady Mary told him, speaking slowly.

"Perhaps she went to Lucretia," Roger said.

"I have thought of that. I sent a slave with a letter. There has not been time . . . Oh, Roger, what must I do?"

He put his arm about her shaking shoulders and led her to a bench. "Now tell me what has been done. It is necessary for me to know. Then we will think of the next step."

"I cannot think. My blood has turned to water. I no longer live," she said in violent anguish. "I have lost her!"

"Suppose she has gone away on the *Willing Maid?*"

Lady Mary fumbled for her handkerchief. The shadow that lay over her cleared. She rose. "We will search for her, Roger. Every place . . . everywhere. If she has chosen to go with him, there is nothing more to do. It is the other thing I fear. . . . Perhaps she has hidden herself. Oh, my dear, you do not think she . . . ?"

Roger sat still, not saying a word, thinking: Where would

she be likely to go? "Go to the house, Mary. Rest if you can. I have thought of something." He mounted his horse and rode down the lane to Captain Zeb's place.

Roger tied his horse at the split-rail fence and walked along the shore to the pocosin. He knew the narrow path that led through the swamp water. It was dusk in the swamp, although the sun shone hot outside. Tense expectation crowded out fears as he walked swiftly along the narrow path made by the cattle. Wild fern grew by the black water, and small squirrels chirped and made quick, flirting movements of their tails as they bounded up the rough bark of an oak tree. A moccasin lay along a trunk of a bay that stretched far out over the water, its immovable beady eyes turned towards him. The place was demon-haunted, the dwelling place of evil. He was gripped with fear that Marita had lost her way in the darkness. He was glad when he came through to the brightness of the hot sunshine. Then he saw the print of a small shoe along the bank of the river. . . . Who but Marita would come here, where she could watch Michael's ship from the Point?

He leaned forward, challenged by fear. Then he saw her. She was lying in the shadow of the cypress tree by the river. The Indian, Kikitchina, sat beside her. Quis-la-kin was there also. He fished from a boat in the river. Torn as Roger had been with anxiety, the sudden tranquillity of the scene before his eyes was unreal, as a painted canvas is unreal and without life.

When he came near, his anxiety róse. He saw Marita's face was flushed, her lips mumbling some meaningless phrase. Her eyes, wide open, glittered with the brilliance of fever, but they had no recognition in them.

The Indian woman saw Roger and rose to her feet, the anxiety in her face diminishing. Roger spoke to her and called to Quis-la-kin to bring the boat to shore.

He lifted the slight figure from the sand and waded out to the canoe. The grey skirt of her dun-coloured Quaker dress dragged in the stream. The Indian woman knelt, holding Marita's head against her knees. Roger and the man took up the paddles.

No word was spoken. No sound but the dip of paddles. High above, an eagle planed across the intense blue of the sky. Once Marita's mumbling formed into words, "Do not leave me behind, Michael, Michael!"

"God damn him to eternal hell!" Roger muttered.

443

The Indian woman looked up; her eyes flickered. "She would go, but the ship sails without her. Since morning she has been like this. It is not good."

For weeks Marita lay in that half-world between life and death. It was better when she was ravaged by fever, for then a red spot glowed on her sunken cheeks and her eyes burned bright. No one served her but her Indian. Under her deft hands Marita was quiet. When Lady Mary touched her she drew her head away and muttered incoherent words. A heavy golden chain with an oval locket lay on her breast, shining under the thin linen of her gown. Once Miss Mittie tried to take it from her neck, but Marita cried out, trying feebly to lift her hand to clasp the locket.

"Leave it alone," Lady Mary said, her voice bitter. " 'Tis the chain that binds her to Michael Cary."

Sometimes when she lay unmoving, glistening tears forced their way from under her strange gold and white lashes, and lay on her sunken cheeks. When this happened, Lady Mary would rise from her constant vigil at Marita's bed, and walk away, her face a white mask.

One morning two doctors came, the old one, Parris, and young Allen. They sat a long time with the senseless girl. Beside the bed, crouched on her knees, Kikitchina watched them with her unfathomable obsidian eyes. The older doctor shook his head. "It has been a month now."

The younger man, Allen, looked at the Indian woman keenly. He had noticed how she quieted the sick girl with a touch of her hand. He spoke to Kikitchina in her own tongue. "What can we do for her?" he asked.

"The sea," the woman answered. "The sea brings life."

"By the living God," Parris exclaimed, "the woman is right! You must take her to the sea."

And so it was arranged to have Moseley's lodge on Ocracoke. Anthony and Sarah determined to spend their honeymoon on the Island also. Roger sailed them down in his shallop. It was like moving a small army—Lady Mary, Miss Mittie, Desham, two house slaves, and the kitchen boys. At the last moment, Black John brought two goats, "otherwise where would they find milk for the sick lassie?" Dougal stayed behind to mind the herd, and Watkins to mind the slaves.

Roger rigged an awning on the afterdeck, and, made comfortable by pillows and a soft mattress, Marita lay in the shadow. The early morning sun blazed with heat, and the wind was light. The moon was well up before they tasted the salt air on their lips. Next day they sailed south behind the Banks in a quickening breeze. By nightfall they reached Ocracock and heard the roar of the sea.

At his camp at Kiquotan Alexander Spottswood, the Governor of the Crown Colony of Virginia, wrote a letter to Edward Hyde, Gentleman, the Lords Proprietors' Governor of the Province of North Carolina.

He told that the marines were home again and the prospects of peace were good. Also, that her Majesty's ship *Enterprise* had the good fortune to take a French privateeer with eighty-eight men off the capes. This was good news, since the French privateer had done great harm to trade from the capes to the Indies.

"If only King Charles had not sold Dunkerque to the French, we would have a jumping-off place for our invasion of the continent."

At the very end of the letter, he wrote: "I have captured Colonel Thomas Cary and his leaders and have sent them to England on the *Tyger* and the *Reserve*, men-of-war, for fair trial before the Board of the Lords Proprietors. The ships sailed on the thirty-first day of July. In three months' time they will be on trial before a jury of their peers. Praise be to God! Now you may look forward to an era of Queen's peace and prosperity."

Appended to the letter were the names of men captured. Michael Cary's was not on the list.

But along the Neuse and the Trent and the upper reaches of Pamticoe, throughout the deep forests, war drums were beating.

Chapter 37

RHODA

SEPTEMBER continued hot and dry. Almost two months had passed since Thomas Cary had been captured in Virginia ana sent to England. Rebellion over, the county settled down to the pursuits of peace.

Roger Mainwairing stayed close to Queen's Gift. Cotton was heavy in the boll, ready for picking. Corn was stacked in ricks, vegetables were dug and laid away in root cellars, leaving the bare fields to be plowed and turned, ready for October rains.

Towards the end of September, Roger sailed his small boat up to Balgray. He found Hester had come back from her long visit to Maryland and Virginia. She was in full blooming health, and bursting with gossip from the other colonies and from London.

She greeted Roger warmly and told him that she had heard of his approaching marriage to Rhoda Chapman. "She is co-heiress with her brother, Thomas, to those great collieries in Wales, isn't she? Is it true that she is a magnificent horsewoman and that her hunters are already at Queen's Gift?"

Hester was delighted with Roger's answer. She went on: "Now we will hunt properly, as they do in Maryland and Virginia—none of this scratch pack chasing the fox in farmer fashion. We will organize a real Albemarle Hunt now. I'll order a new habit at once."

"Hist, woman," Pollock said, "your mind is too full of vanities and fripperies!"

Hester laughed and kissed Thomas' cheek lightly. He beamed. It was easy to see he was proud of his handsome wife.

"Williamsburg is full of gossip," she confided to Roger when the men came into the drawing-room for brandy. "The women tipple so much and are very gay. Society is almost as profligate as London." She sighed a little. "We are really quite provincial here in Carolina."

"But we are rather nice people, don't you think?" Roger's eyes twinkled a little. Hester was always amusing.

"Well, I suppose so. I understand the Williamsburg young women are quite put out that you are going to wed a girl from home. . . . Is it true you will be married at the new Palace? 'Tis said Miss Chapman is a relative of Mrs. Russell."

Roger said yes to her questions. He did not need to enlarge, for Hester went right on.

"Did you know that Mrs. R. has been in Pennsylvania? She has been ill. . . . It is said that she will rid herself of her great

446

stomach before she returns." She laughed slyly. "It is an open secret that she acts in another capacity to Governor Spottswood than that of official hostess."

A servant came in with coffee. Roger noticed the service was new, very elegant silver, with the Pollock crest on the pots and the great tray.

Hester smiled proudly. "It is sterling, very heavy in weight," she whispered. "I was weary of using pewter, when all the world of fashion serves tea and coffee from silver."

The Governor joined them and the conversation changed. Hester no longer gossiped. Instead they spoke of Cary's arrest and transfer to England, until the Governor excused himself and went to his room.

Roger left shortly after the Governor. It was well past four o'clock. With a light wind he could be home by supper.

Roger said nothing to Pollock or Hester, but he had told the Governor that he was leaving for Virginia the following day to meet Rhoda. Her ship was due to arrive in York River on the twenty-third. They would be married the following day, so that Tom, her brother, could go back to Jamaica on the return voyage of the ship.

The following morning Roger and Metephele started on their journey to Williamsburg. They stopped that night at the Border Inn and rode up to the house of Roger's friend, Clayton, by nightfall the second day. That was pushing it hard, but two changes of horses along the road made the fast trip possible. He found when he arrived at York that the vessel, the *Andrea Doria*, had been spoken off the Cape and would be upriver sometime the next morning.

Roger, instead of resting, got into fresh clothes, called on Governor Spottswood, and had tea with Mrs. Russell, who was full of the plans she had made for the wedding. "It will be just as Rhoda directed in her letter. I should have liked to arrange a larger wedding ceremony, with some of the first-rank people," she added a little regretfully.

Afterwards Roger went to the Coffee House. There he met friends, with whom he diced and drank brandy until near dawn. Even then he could not sleep, for the inn room was hot and the bed without a net, so that stinging insects made rest impossible. Or perhaps it was his own thoughts that drove him early from his bed. He sent Metephele for the horses and rode through the forest to York before breakfast.

When he came to the brow of the hill, with the broad river

447

at his feet, he saw that Rhoda's ship lay anchored off shore, customs lighter anchored alongside.

How the hour passed, he did not know. He sat in a coffee shop and waited, watching through the window for the first shore boat to put off. A thousand questions came to his mind as he sat, immovable, his long body slumped on a wooden settle. After a time he saw a boat leave the ship. Roger got slowly to his feet and walked down to the wharf.

When he saw Rhoda coming towards him his fears slipped away from him. She was taller than he remembered. She moved forward with easy grace, her dark blue eyes alight, her lips smiling. Her dark hair bound her head like a turban of shining satin, and her light flowing skirts gave her the illusion of walking without touching the earth.

She came directly towards him with both hands outstretched. "Roger," she said. "Dear, dear Roger!"

Roger bent and kissed her hands. "Dear Rhoda, you are here at last."

She turned to her brother, who was a step behind her. "I remembered. I did indeed! He looks exactly as I expected him to look, only nicer."

Tom said, "I made a wager with Rhoda that she would not even know you when she saw you at the wharf, but I seem to have lost."

Roger had engaged a coach to carry them to Williamsburg, but when they walked to the end of the wharf the Governor's coach was there waiting to take them to the Palace.

"How nice of Cousin Russell!" Rhoda said. "I really would like to gallop along with you, Roger. Wait! I have not asked you how my hunters fared. Did they suffer from the long journey?"

"They are in perfect condition," he assured her, "waiting to be exercised."

Roger tried riding beside the open coach, but the horses stirred up too much dust, so he galloped ahead.

"I will be over by five," he said, when they reached the Palace gate. "You are sure you haven't changed your mind?"

She gave him a flashing smile. "And want to go back with Tom? No, now that I am in America I shall stay. . . . I like America"—her low voice trembled a little—"and I love Roger Mainwaring."

"God give you happiness, my dear," he said. He stood, hat

448

in hand at the gate, while the carriage drove up to the great doorway.

The ceremony in the little red parlour took only a few moments. Six sat down to supper, served by the Governor's footmen in scarlet livery, but Metephele, in his long white robes, his embroidered white cap on his head, stood back of Roger and allowed no one else to serve him.

Rhoda wore a white gown and a little lace veil on her shining hair. Next to her sat Parson Blair, then Tom, and Mrs. Russell. Roger's blue coat looked very dull beside the Governor's splendid uniform, a red coat braided in gold, and white breeches. They toasted the newly weds in fine Rhenish wine, and Mrs. Russell wept a little when Rhoda went upstairs to change into her travelling suit.

Tom moved over and put his hand on Roger's shoulder. "I wouldn't be satisfied to leave my sister with anyone but you, Roger. She worships you." He laughed. "I hope she never finds out that you are common clay like any other man."

Roger didn't smile. The words Parson Blair had said had new meaning to him, "until death do you part . . ."

"I swear to you, I shall think of nothing but her happiness, Tom," he said. The two men grasped hands closely for a moment.

"I am content, Roger," Chapman said.

The Governor came up to them. He had a paper in his hand. "I do not like to be the bearer of ill news at this moment, Mainwairing, but I had a message from Governor Hyde earlier today. There has been an uprising of Core Indians, and some Tuscaroras, on the Pamticoe. He has written urgently for help."

The shock of the Governor's words left Roger dazed for the moment. Ocracock Island . . . what if Mary—? His mind refused to think past that point.

Spottswood was talking. "I took up the matter with my Council and some of the Assembly this morning. They think it inadvisable to send any of our troops. If this is a general uprising, we need our militia here." He hesitated a moment. "Some of our Council suggested that we might vote you a thousand pounds sterling if your Council would secure it by a mortgage on the land as far south as the Roanoke."

The disputed territory! Roger felt blood rise to his face.

Spottswood said quickly, "I know how you feel. I told them it was an indignity to propose anything of the kind. But

449

I do not have the control of my Assembly, Mr. Mainwairing, or my Council."

Roger heard Rhoda's voice. The two women were coming down the stairs. He said quickly, "Please say nothing of this before the ladies, your Excellency. It will only worry them."

"I understand," the Governor answered. "I hope you appreciate my position. I have only good intentions toward the Carolinas, but my power is limited."

Rhoda came in. She was wearing a close-fitting habit of deep brown, and a small three-cornered hat with a tan feather curling to her shoulder. She threw herself into her brother's arms, and put her head on his shoulder for a moment. Then she stood off from him.

"You will come up for Christmas, as you promised? We are neighbours, dear Tom, very close neighbours. From Jamaica to the Carolinas is a short journey. Please don't forget."

Parson Blair wished them godspeed. Mrs. Russell touched her large dreamy eyes with a lace handkerchief. The Governor walked to the gates with them. The coach Roger had engaged was filled with boxes and small luggage. The large boxes would come by waggon under Metephele's guidance. Two fine saddle horses were led up to the block. Rhoda mounted easily, almost without assistance.

The Governor said, "I have sent men ahead to Kiquotan to have my house made ready for you. You are welcome to stay as long as you like, Mainwairing."

"Thank you, your Excellency, that is very thoughtful of you and we shall be happy to accept your hospitality for the night, but we must ride on early in the morning. I am sure my wife will want to get to the end of her journey, at Queen's Gift."

Rhoda's eyes sought Roger's as they trotted along the pine-shadowed road. "The end of my journey," she repeated slowly. "No, not the end of the journey . . . only the beginning, Roger."

"Dear Rhoda," he answered, "I want more than anything to make you happy. I hope you will love this country as I love it—that it will be your home, your real home."

They reached the river at nightfall, and found the Governor's house in readiness for them. They stayed the night and went on early the following morning.

The second day they crossed the border and followed the Dismal Swamp. Then Roger began to pick up rumours about the uprising of the Indians. By the time they stopped at

450

Newby's Ferry that night, he could not keep the news from Rhoda any longer.

Her face cleared when he told her. She said, "I knew something worried you, Roger. I thought perhaps . . . well, I thought you were disappointed in me—in my looks, or . . ." A dull red rose to her cheeks.

"How could you think that, my dear? I have nothing but gratitude in my heart."

"And love?" she asked softly.

"Love," he repeated after her, "and hope that I may give you happiness." He drew near and took her hand. "I am sorry that our homecoming should be like this. I planned something quite different."

They were riding through the woods at the Narrows of the Pequimans. Rhoda pulled up her horse and sat looking at the lovely prospect on river and forest. After a few moments she raised her eyes to Roger. "What will this mean to you, Roger? Does it mean that you must go to war against the Indians?"

He hesitated, wondering whether he could tell her how serious this news was—how desperate the condition of the settlers would be if there was a long Indian war or an uprising. There was no alarm in her eyes; her clear-cut features were calm, her lips did not tremble.

"You need not try to shield me, my dear," she said. "Whatever must be, must be. I prefer to know. Knowing what one has to meet is better, is it not?"

He leaned across his horse and put his hand over hers. "Let it always be like this, Rhoda. Truth between us." Roger told her then what he must do.

"They will be mustering now in Queen Anne's Town and upriver. I will take my best-trained men. Some will be left here to guard, in case our Indians join with the others. I can leave you at John Blount's, the next plantation to ours, or I can take you up the Chowan to stay with Madam Hester Pollock."

Rhoda smiled. She is not beautiful, thought Roger, but I've never seen a lovelier smile. "I think I will stay at Queen's Gift, Roger. In a few days my luggage will come and the carter will bring the heavy pieces of furniture. By the time you come back from the wars, you will not know your Queen's Gift."

Roger stopped his horse and hers. Leaning forward, he put

451

his arms about her and drew her to him, until her fresh warm lips met his.

His people were waiting to greet them when they rode up the long driveway to Queen's Gift. Rhoda did not speak. She sat looking from the house to the water, and back to the slaves, who were smiling and bowing and calling out their welcome.

"You make me very happy," she said, including them all in her radiant smile.

Before Roger could get off his horse and to her side, she had slipped down and started up the wide steps to the gallery. She was almost running when Roger overtook her.

"Wait, Rhoda, wait!" He gathered her up in his strong arms and carried her across the threshold of her home.

Moseley came in through the garden while Rhoda and Roger were eating supper on the south gallery. His face was haggard and he looked as if he had not slept. He greeted Rhoda cordially, in his stately well turned phrases. Then he spoke to Roger.

"I am sorry to be the bearer of bad news, but we are starting tonight for Bath Town to relieve the garrison there. We plan to cross the Sound and be ready to go south at daybreak. We must do what we can until help comes."

"We will get no help from Virginia," Roger said shortly.

Moseley nodded. "I know. The Governor has had a messenger from Spottsswood. It was no more than I expected."

"His hands are tied," Roger said.

Moseley made no comment. "Hyde has sent Christopher Gale to Charles Town to get help from South Carolina. He left day before yesterday—as soon as we had word that the Indians were on the warpath. I am going overland to Charles Town, in case Gale does not get through."

"Has there been any word from Bath Town or Ocracock?" Roger feared to ask the question or hear the answer.

Moseley shook his head. "Nothing. Fifty of Pollock's men have already marched. We'll have fifty more. But what can we do against twelve hundred savages who have tasted blood?"

Rhoda sat quietly looking from one to the other. They had forgotten her. They were thinking only of the people who were in such danger.

"There is trouble in New Bern, also," Moseley said. "De Graffenried and Lawson may have started upriver to the Indian towns—we do not know."

452

Roger remembered Rhoda then. He explained to her about the slaves living in the quarters line. "I will have two of your women sleep near you. And I will leave trustworthy slaves here. My overlooker, Jeb Vescels, will send a man or two to guard the house. He and his wife live within call. Do you shoot?"

Rhoda smiled. "Of course I shoot—rather well, if I do say so."

Moseley looked at her as if he saw her for the first time. "Roger is to be congratulated," he said. "I wish we might have given you a different welcome to the Albemarle, Mrs. Mainwairing, but I can see that you understand."

Rhoda said, "My father was a soldier. He died in the Low Countries. I have one brother in France now. Roger must not think of me. I have things to do here—my horses . . ." She looked at Edward Moseley. "War is everywhere, I think. All Europe is aflame. In the Indies, in Antigua, revolt in Haiti—now here, in this lovely soft land where there should be peace, there is war."

Moseley listened gravely. "I wish it were war as we know war. This is different. This is massacre—horrible—with knife and with torch."

Rhoda put her hand on the table to steady herself. Her face was white, but when Roger came into the room she smiled, and her voice was steady when she bade him goodbye.

She was in Roger's mind as he sailed across the Sound before daybreak and during the long march south. The vision of her dimmed, as he thought of another woman who was either dead or in mortal danger.

They were obliged to rest in the woods that night, for they dared not approach Bath Town in the dark. Roger had sixty men under his command, and he formed them in a hollow square, facing outward. Guards at each corner of the square kept sentry duty while the others slept.

Roger himself walked sentry with his men. His duty ended at two in the morning, but he had no desire for sleep. The forest had voices that made him uneasy. He tried to make himself believe that nothing untoward had happened in Ocracock. They must be safe, protected as they were by water. The Indians would be more likely to come down the rivers, murdering and torturing the planters along the river highways. But his reasoning was outweighed by his fears.

Tomorrow they would march to the Bath garrison. After

that he would find some way to get down to the island. His thoughts went back to Rhoda. How easily she had taken hold, made her plan and carried it out. His heart warmed to her.

It was almost morning when Roger noticed the dark figure of a sentry coming towards him, hurrying along the little path. "Mr. Mainwairing, there are two men in the road, coming this way—I can not make them out. They seem to be staggering, fit to drop in their tracks. Want that I go meet them?"

Roger got up. "No, go back to your post. I will see who they are. Be on the alert. It may be Indians employing some trick."

The two men staggered forward, scarcely able to put one foot in front of the other. When he saw they were white men Roger called the guard to hurry forward to meet them. Roger recognized the first man.

"Christ!" he whispered. "De Graffenried . . . !"

Men hurried forward and laid him gently on pine boughs. Roger had never seen a face so ravaged by horror. The man was shrunken, his skin pasted against the bones of his face as the flesh had evaporated. His clothes were in shreds, his bare back criss-crossed with welts where the skin had broken. A great cut curved from his ear across the neck to his shoulder. His eyes, sunken deep in the sockets, burned with some strange light, as if they had witnessed things too terrible to endure.

When they were placing him on the bed, Roger saw his ankles and wrists were cut deep from thongs. A little colour came with the drink. His eyes closed; not a word had been spoken. For one horrible moment Roger feared the Indians had slit his tongue. He looked, prying open the sleeping man's teeth with his knife.

The man with him was almost as bad off. Like De Graffenried, he reeled with giddiness. The moment he touched the pine bed he was asleep.

Roger remembered the last time he had seen the Baron, dressed so handsomely in the uniform of his own guard. His servant, splendid in yellow livery. Now . . .

Tom Pollock rode up at dawn. He saw De Graffenried. "God's blood! What does this mean?" Then he remembered. "Where is Lawson?" he cried. "Weren't they going up to the Indian towns together? We must waken him, Duke, and find out if Lawson has been taken prisoner."

454

De Graffenried moaned and attempted to sit up. His dazed eyes were slow in focussing. "Mainwairing!" he said. "Thank the good God!" He sat without moving, his face a death's head of horror. "Lawson—" he said. His teeth began to chatter and his thin body shook as if he had an ague.

"Where is Lawson?" Pollock asked gently, to try to bring back De Graffenried's wandering senses. "Where is Lawson?" he repeated.

Roger forced more rum down the Baron's throat.

"Lawson is dead . . . they burned him . . ."

"God Almighty!" Pollock's lips were stiff, his face was drawn, his eyes hard. "Try to tell us," he said, with an effort to be calm. "Try."

Fortified by the strong drink, De Graffenried made a great effort. Somehow they got the story. He and Lawson had gone upriver to visit the Indian towns and try to get a treaty made. "Lawson was confident," he said. "All the way up he talked about the kindness and gentleness of the Indians. 'They will respond to kindness as children respond to kindness.' He kept saying that over and over."

They came to the villages. They noticed a strange thing. They saw no young men nor any older men, only children and women who ran when they appproached. He saw that Lawson was troubled. Many times he had been to the towns before, always welcomed by a chieftain.

"I recalled something that had happened before I left my house. A little boy ran in to tell that he had overheard two Indian servants talking, saying that there would be war, and the Indians would fall on the whites, and we sent the boy away for telling tales.

"We waited half the day. Towards night the forest seemed to be suddenly alive with Indians, painted and oiled and ready for war. Before we had time for the courtesies, they had bound us each to a tree, the rawhide thongs tight on our wrists and ankles."

De Graffenried took another draught of rum. For a moment he seemed unable to go on. "I do not know how it was—a miracle of God—I talked the chief into letting me go. I said I was a king, a ruler, and kings did not burn kings at the stake. I was obliged to swear I did not belong to Governor Hyde's party. . . ." The Baron looked from one to the other. "The Indians hate Hyde," he said.

"Lawson?" Pollock said, tight-lipped and stern at the recital.

"I do not want to tell but I must. If I do not, I shall see his tortured face until I die." His voice rose, out of control. "The barbarians! They slit his skin, and stuck him full of little splinters of torchwood, like hog bristles, and gradually set fire to him until his whole body was a giant flambeau lighting up the forest about us and the shouting savages who danced around him. He died without sound—I could not even call to comfort him, for I was bound and gagged, and savages pried at my eyes to hold them open so I could see his dying agony."

De Graffenried covered his face with his thin hands. "After that they tortured me," he said more quietly. "They drove me between two rows of young men who flogged me with willows as I passed down the line."

Metephele brought hot tea and food. Roger ordered litters made from young saplings thrust through the sleeves of leather jerkins. At sunup they took up their march towards Bath Town.

Roger walked beside De Graffenried's litter, his horse's bridle over his arm. Now and then the men carrying the poles gave over to another pair, to make the travelling easier. He laid a cloth wrung out of cool water on De-Graffenried's hot forehead, and spread another cloth to protect his raw and bleeding back from flies and crawling insects.

"My poor people, my poor people, God help my poor people." The Baron repeated the words over until they were like a litany. "They wanted so little," he said to Roger once, when they stopped by a stream to rest. "They faced every hardship to come to this New World of promise. Crowded into filthy ships, dying for want of proper food on the long journey, crops withered in the sun, sickness and discouragement. Everything they have met with courage. Now this comes to them. No one can continue under such terror and live. . . ."

Roger could not find a word of comfort. What could he say to a man who had seen the safe living of hundreds of people wrecked and broken before his despairing eyes?

"They had wanted so little, my poor people—only to work and live in peace in this new world. So good, so patient . . ." De Graffenried's voice was muffled.

Roger felt humble before the sorrow of this man who had no thought of his own wounds. His mind was shadowed with

456

the tragedy to the men and women and children committed to his care.

Roger walked in silence. "It is always so in a new land," he said to De Graffenried after a time. "Men and women suffer and give their lives for something they cannot define, some intangible thing that leads them beyond themselves and makes them selfless. Perhaps it is their destiny—or the destiny of the land itself. Perhaps it is so with your people. Whatever it is, they have moved one step nearer the gods."

The Baron made no answer. Presently he put out his thin hand and grasped Roger's firm brown fingers. Roger knew then that he had found the right words.

They moved quietly through the dark woods that bore such hidden menace. Roger's anxiety for the safety of Lady Mary and her people increased with every step. De Graffenried's condition told him that this was a war without mercy. What would they find at the village and at the plantation along the river—only smoking ruins and devastated homes and mutilated bodies?

Chapter 38

KNIFE
AND TORCH

BLACK JOHN was working outside the lodge, cutting wood for the small oven he had set up for cooking fish. He was humming a mournful dirgelike tune as he broke the twigs and tied them into bundles with bits of seaweed.

"I wish he would stop," Miss Mittie said dolefully. "He's been singing, 'Why does yer bran' sae drip with blude?' ever since daylight."

"Why don't you ask him?" Lady Mary asked lazily. She sat in a low chair of woven reeds.

Marita lay on a couch just inside the door. The sea air had brought colour to her cheeks. She made no effort either to move or to speak, but the fever had burned itself out.

"Three gulls landed beside the window, and it was all I could do to drive them away," Miss Mittie continued. "It's an ill omen or death token."

"Black John has been feeding them with scraps of fish," Lady Mary said matter-of-factly.

"And I dreamed of a black owl," Miss Mittie went on. "We'll hear bad tidings before long."

Black John sneezed three times—a mighty sound, fit to wake the dead.

"May God bless you and the Devil pass you by."

Lady Mary turned quickly and ran into the house, closely followed by Miss Mittie. Marita had spoken the old blessing. It was her voice they had heard, weak and trembling, but a natural voice—not one built of ravings and mutterings of fever.

From that day Marita began to improve, until she could walk to the beach and back to the lodge without sitting down to rest.

One morning Kikitchina did not come to dress her. She was missing all the day, and Quis-la-kin also. No one thought anything of it, for they had always come and gone as it suited them, to fish or to hunt. Two days passed and they had not returned.

Black John came to the door to speak to Lady Mary. "The canoe is gone," he said. "I wanted to fish in the Deep Hole, but the boat was missing."

"Do you think the Indians took it?" Lady Mary asked.

They let it go at that, but as the day went on, apprehension grew in Lady Mary's mind. She had never liked the Indians, nor could she understand them. The Indian woman's devotion to Marita was beyond her comprehension.

Shortly after dinner Anthony Lovyck came over from the other side of the island. Lady Mary was alone at the house. Marita lay on the sand under a leaf shelter the gillie had made to protect her from the sun. Miss Mittie was walking a short way up the beach.

Lovyck said, "I am glad you are alone. I don't want to seem needlessly alarmed, but every boat on the island is gone."

Lady Mary sat up in her chair. "Anthony, what are you saying?"

Lovyck repeated, "Every boat on the island is missing with exception of the fishermen's and they are fishing off Hatteras, a nine-day cruise."

"What shall we do?" Lady Mary asked. "What do you think is happening?"

"I don't know, but last night with the wind from the south

I thought I heard drums, and there were fires burning on Core Island."

Lady Mary asked the question, "Indians? Do you think there is an uprising?" Her voice was quiet and steady.

"Yes—at least we must make some preparation. Where are Marita's Indians? Perhaps they can tell us something."

"They are gone. They disappeared day before yesterday."

The boom of the surf against the sand sounded like thunder in the room. Anthony got up and walked the length of the porch and back. "I want to talk to Black John. He seems a sensible fellow. I've an idea it would be well to keep a sentry on that high point and make preparations to defend ourselves here."

"With what?" Lady Mary asked flatly. "We have three men and one musket here to defend four helpless women."

"I know. I am in like case. I have only pistols and my sword."

They called Black John then and put the situation before him. He listened without speaking, pulling at his bristly beard.

"'Tis bad, verra bad, and me with no weapon save the dirk in my belt. Mr. Lovyck is right. I will put a slave on the hill to keep watch."

He left the room quickly. A moment later they saw him climbing up the little hill. The slave that followed him carried the curved horn used by Black John to call the cattle home at evening.

Lovyck said, "Sarah is coming over here. I think it will be safer if we are all together."

Lady Mary nodded absently. She got up and walked into the bedroom. A moment later she called to Anthony. There was a hint of excitement in her voice. When he went into the room she was standing beside a small cupboard secured by an iron hasp and lock.

"Do you think this could be Moseley's gun closet?" she said, rattling the lock.

Anthony crossed the room swiftly. "It might be that he keeps his fowling guns here." He looked for something to smash the lock, but there was nothing available.

"Black John's wood axe!" Lady Mary cried. "Come quickly, Anthony."

Anthony smashed the iron hasp and pulled the door open. On the rack was one light fowling piece, a cup of shot and a powder horn partly filled.

Anthony turned the piece over in his hand. "Nothing, nothing at all, against a hundred—or a thousand Indians."

Lady Mary sat down on a chair as if her knees had given way.

Anthony walked to the window. Sarah was coming across the sand, her slave carrying a heavy bundle. He turned to Lady Mary. "I think we had better bring everyone to the house. There are some things to be done. Everyone should have a little bread and a flask of water. If we had a boat . . ."

"What would you do then?" Lady Mary asked.

"We would try to get to the garrison at Bath Town. It can't be more than a few days' journey. By God, I would take any chance rather than sit here and wait to be killed with poisoned arrows."

Lady Mary got up and walked through the sitting-room to the gallery. She stood for a few moments looking out at the sea. It was very blue and calm. A ship under full sail was visible on the far horizon. If a ship would come . . . but there was no use to build false hope. Many ships passed them, all far out following the sea lane between the Virginia capes and the West India Islands.

Their danger lay from the west. If help came, it too would come from the west. She turned away from the quiet sea.

"Let us call the others," she said quietly. "They must be told of the danger which we all share."

The day was endless. The hours dragged along without change. After the first shock to all, the women were quiet. Even Desham. She packed up a few things necessary to her mistress' comfort and tied them in a silk square. After that she went to the kitchen to direct the cook.

Everyone attempted to eat a full meal at suppertime.

"God alone knows where we will have the next one," Lady Mary said. Miss Mittie stifled a shriek and got up from the table hastily. Black John came up to report that there had been no movement at all on the Sound. Not even a canoe broke the stillness of the water. He had been over part of the island hoping to run onto a boat, but not one was to be found. The island was deserted. Even the few people who lived at the far end for fishing had taken flight.

"If we are attacked, it will be at night," Anthony said.

Black John agreed. "We will keep special watch about the house. It is the quarter of the moon, and we can't verra well see the devils if they creep up on us."

Miss Mittie came back and joined the others on the porch. Her skin had a jaundiced look. Marita lay back in a long chair, her eyes on the sea, taking no part in the discussion that was going on. Lady Mary felt her antagonism but she was too concerned with their danger to give much thought to anything else. Marita would get over her infatuation for Michael Cary in time. She would not worry about that now.

"Perhaps they won't come to this island," Miss Mittie ventured her opinion timidly. "Perhaps they will only attack along the river plantations and the villages."

Black John said, "I'd thought of that, madam. Mayhap they do not know we are here on this lonely island."

"They know everything," Marita said, "everything. But I cannot believe that Kikitchina would desert me and let me be murdered. I think she will come for me."

Lady Mary looked at Marita, her eyes filled with tenderness. "I wish I had your faith, child."

"I think she will come," Marita repeated stubbornly. "She loves me. She will come because I need her."

Anthony got up and went to the window. The sun was gone from the sky but great floating clouds covered the western horizon. The afterglow caught them and changed them to crimson. "The colour of fresh-spilled blood," he muttered aloud.

"Oh, don't!" Sarah cried. "Anthony, don't say such things or I shall scream." She buried her face in her hands.

Anthony put his arm over her shoulders and whispered something. After a moment she sat up, a tremulous smile on her lips.

"I am so sorry," she said to Lady Mary. "I'm not really afraid, but the sight of blood always makes me a little sick."

Black John knocked at the door and came in carrying a long musket, two pistols and several knives. He laid them on the dining-table and departed without a word. After a short time he came again. This time he had with him one of the young slaves who carried a woven basket. The gillie added to the weapons on the table several long knives, such as are used in the kitchen, a butcher's cleaver, a mallet with an iron end, two small axes, a knife used for cleaning fish, and a broken scythe.

He spread them out until the table was a museum of weapons. "This is the lot of them, your leddyship. If anyone has knife or pistol, it would be well to put them in the common pool."

461

No one had anything to add excepting Miss Mittie. She went out of the room, and soon returned bringing with her a pair of heavy cutting shears. She glanced about the room to see if anyone was laughing, but everyone was deep in his own uneasy thoughts.

Anthony and Black John stood the watch in turn, four hours, then rest. Storm shutters were up and barred, and doors barricaded. The others went to their rooms to sleep or to pray. The slaves lay on mats on the floor of the gallery. Black John had found two dogs that had been left behind at the fishing hamlet. He staked them out near the cabin with his goats, hoping they would bark if intruders came.

The watch after two o'clock fell to Anthony. Dawn was showing faintly in the east when he heard the dogs on the shore side of the house give a sharp bark that seemed to end in a gurgle. Swiftly and stealthily he went to the window. Then he looked out the peephole in the door. He thought he saw a shadow moving. Perhaps it was only a bush swaying in the wind.

"Do you see anything?" He turned to find Marita beside him, whispering her question. She was still dressed and had a man's leather jerkin over her shoulders, one she had found in the gun closet.

"I'm not sure. Damn my shortsighted eyes! I thought I saw the bush move. That one, there to the right of the little scrub pine."

"Let me look. I have cat's eyes for the dark." She stood quietly looking out. Lovyck felt her hand touch his arm. "I think it is a man creeping towards us. Is your pistol primed?"

Lovyck took her place, pistol in hand. Unmistakably a man, creeping on his belly. He waited until the man lifted his head. It was light enough to see the gleam of his eyes. Anthony took aim and fired.

The pistol went off with an ear-splitting explosion, but it did not drown the shriek the Indian gave as he leapt into the air and started running. He did not run ten yards before he began to stagger; another five yards and he fell to the ground and did not move.

The sound of the pistol going off brought everyone into the room. Anthony cried, "Everything is all right!"

"Go back, go back to your places," Black John said. "There may be more of them Watch every tree and shrub that moves."

Lady Mary came in but went back to her room when

Anthony reassured her. The one candle cast a dim light. She did not see Marita sitting in the corner.

"He must have killed the dogs," Anthony said to Black John. "They barked only once. Or they may know the Indians. Perhaps the savages on this island. If there is one, there will be more."

Black John's bearded face was grim as he glanced over his broad shoulder. "It's fire I'm afeerd of, Mr. Lovyck. I've got buckets of sand ready to throw on the roof, but it's not much good it will do if they cast burning torchwood at this wee house."

"What will we do then?" Anthony asked, not moving from the peephole.

"I've fixed a place in the dunes. We can run there. We could stop as long as we've the shot and powder. After that it's with knives and the broad axe."

The gillie heaved a mighty sigh. "I've been wishin' and wishin' for my claymore and Dougal. He's a brave lad and would be a help to us now with all these wimmen folk to watch over."

"Do you think we should go out to look at the fellow?"

"No, no, don't do that. Wait until light is better."

A small sound made the men both turn. Marita was sitting on a chair, her face intent. She said, "I can shoot and shoot straight, if you need me. Captain Zeb taught me to use a pistol and a musket too."

"Good," Anthony said, "good; that gives us three fighting men instead of two."

Marita said, "Don't forget that Aunt Mary has been shooting in Scotland for years. I don't suppose it's much harder to shoot a man than it is to shoot a pheasant—or a stag."

"No," Anthony said, "I suppose not."

"'Tis nae a mon, 'tis a savage, miss," Black John said. "Now go to yer bed and take yer rest. Ye've done verra well indeed."

Marita got up and left the room, walking steadily.

When daylight came they found the Indian was quite dead. The gillies had two slaves drag the body down to the sea, and the dogs he had killed with him. Black John brought in the tomahawk, the only weapon the Indian had. He scouted the ground but he could find no footprint of another Indian. The fact that the dogs let the man come close made Anthony think he was an island Indian, not one from the mainland or from a large war party. That gave him fresh hope.

The second day passed without incident until almost dusk. Then the lookout on the hill gave the signal—three short blasts on the horn. From the small window in the attic Black John watched the Indians come up from the water. Seven warriors were in a long canoe. The Scot watched six of the painted savages creeping towards the lodge, using scrub growth and sand mounds to conceal themselves. From the attic he had a good clear view of the water. There was no other canoe in sight. If they could overcome these men . . . He whistled softly.

Anthony Lovyck came up the ladder. Black John pointed to the Indians. They were spreading out now, creeping low, sliding like venomous moccasins over the ground. They were still a considerable distance away.

"They'll surround the house and rush from all directions," Anthony said.

"That's what I thought, sir. They have nae gun that I can see."

"You're right, John. Praise be to God for that. Listen, we will have Lady Mary take one window here in the attic— Miss Marita the other. Give them the fowling pieces with Desham and my wife to load for them. That leaves us the pistols and the light fowling piece. Miss Mittie and one of the slaves will load for us. The others we will arm with knives and axes."

"Good, sir, good, and well spoken. It is surprised they will be when they come on us."

Black John had the first shot and Anthony the second. Both men made their target. At the sound of gunfire the Indians broke cover and ran toward the house, shouting and screaming. But a shot from Anthony's second pistol sent them back to the bush, dragging a wounded man with them. That left only three.

"We'll dash after them now, I'm thinking," Black John said, making for the door. Anthony followed, shouting to the slaves to stay out of range for fear the Indian in the boat had firearms. But he had none. It was easy then for the two men to pick off a man apiece. The man in the boat jumped overboard and started to swim. Anthony sent a shot out in the water, but they could not tell whether it struck its mark, or whether the Indian swam away under water.

Black John said, "Well, Mr. Lovyck, we've got a boat now. We can think about putting out for Bath Town during the night."

464

They pulled the boat up into a small inlet and hid it under he bushes. It was not a bad canoe—a dugout that would hold ten people. They set one slave to watch the inlet so that no wandering Indian would find the boat, and the others dragged the Indians away from the landing and dumped them into the ocean.

"We don't want other war parties landing here and finding bodies," Anthony said when they went to the house.

They all voted to try to get away from the island and attempt to reach the Bath Town garrison that night. There was an alternative, Roanoke Island to the north, but as no garrison was kept there, it seemed wiser to travel up the Pamticoe. Not one among them had ever been on the river, but they must take the chance. Any effort was better than to sit waiting.

They made the boat ready. There was room and to spare. The slaves were strong and could paddle. Anthony took the stern, Black John the bow, each with a slave to spell him at the paddles. The women sat in the bottom of the canoe at either end.

The moon rose early. It was on the quarter. Not much light but enough, with the North Star to set the course. The water was quiet. Once they all but hit something that looked like a log, but it moved off with a snap of its great jaws. They had not been gone more than an hour when Black John looked back. Cautiously he called Lady Mary's attention, and she whispered to Marita. A great light burned in the sky to the east. The island they had so recently quitted was aflame. Farther north fires were burning.

"Glory be to God!" whispered Miss Mittie. Desham sobbed quietly, alternately mumbling her prayers and making signs to keep off evil spirits.

Once they heard voices shouting and the heavy beat of drums. They stopped the canoe under overhanging bushes until all was quiet. A war party must have passed close above them. Fires were burning on the south shore of the Sound. Separate fires, some miles apart—that meant plantation houses burnt, people killed and mutilated.

Lady Mary said softly to Marita, "Lean against my back, dear. You will be more comfortable and so will I."

"I am not tired," Marita said. "I am not tired at all. I could take a paddle if need be."

They went a long time in silence, paddles dipping quietly. The pull was slow and difficult against the current. Nothing

465

was said, but they all knew they must make as much time as they could during the night, then find safe hiding throughout the day. On the north side of the stream the bank was high. They must find a place by daylight where they would be out of sight from the river.

The night was still. After the moon was down the stars were bright. The great sweep of the Milky Way shone out across the heavens. Anthony's back was breaking, but his pride would not allow him to pause. After a time they came to a small inlet where a stream flowed from the bank into the river. He turned the canoe inward. The vines hung low, making a curtain. Into this refuge they guided the canoe.

All day they rested, taking turns at watching while the others slept. They saw thin columns of smoke rising across the river, but the birds in the trees and the fish leaping in the water made the only sounds they heard. The slaves, frightened by the sight of the Indians, crouched close to the boat, afraid to move. Towards dusk Black John made his way cautiously up the bank until he stood on firm ground above them. The forest was silent. The acrid smell of wood smoke was in his nostrils. He moved past a small thicket and came to the edge of a clearing. He heard a slight noise and flattened himself against the trunk of a tree, his knife ready.

Lady Mary came from behind him, moving silently, a musket in her hand. She might be stalking stag in the highlands. Together they moved in, screened by the thicket. A squirrel ran by them and sat up on its legs, its bright eyes curious. Black John swung his arm to bar the way. "Don't look, your leddyship. 'Tis a terrible sight." He was too late. Lady Mary had already seen the burnt spot where a house had been. An old man and an old woman lay spread out on the ground.

The woman's body, with its hairless head, was bent so that she knelt, leaning against a log, her clasped hands held up in prayer, her head held in position by a forked stick. Lady Mary could not see the woman's face. The old man lay on the ground, his arms and legs placed decently, his hands clasped. A bunch of small green leaves made into a bouquet was laid under his chest covering his lower face to his high-bridged nose. His silvered hair was streaked where a red stream had trickled from a wound.

"We must go back," the gillie whispered, the horror he had just seen breaking in his voice. "Come quickly."

"We must bury them," she said, holding back. "We cannot leave them."

"Have care for the living," the Scot said sternly.

Lady Mary went after him, walking lightly. She was white to the lips with what she had witnessed, but her step was firm.

They waited until the sun was down and the shadow deepening along the river. Marita had taken her place in the prow of the boat. Anthony was kneeling behind her, his paddle ready. As she lifted the curtain of vines, heavy with purple fox grapes, three canoes of painted Indians shot across the opening where the stream emptied into the river. The two canoes went forward; the third turned and headed straight for them.

Anthony said, "Lean over, Marita, let me shoot."

Marita caught his arm. "Don't, Anthony! Can't you see it is Quis-la-kin? He sees me . . . he . . ." Her voice died away.

Cut off from view by the curtain of vines, the other occupants of the boat did not know what was happening until the Indians were upon them. The two canoes came back then. There was no chance to load and fire—even for Black John to use his dirk. The curtain of vines which had been their protection all day became their doom.

Thongs cutting cruelly into their ankles and wrists, they lay on the ground—thrown together, negro and white, like cartwood. Marita lay on one side. She could count a dozen Indians or more sitting on the ground near a small fire they had kindled. She wondered where Kikitchina was, or if Indian women went out with war parties or stayed in the Indian towns. Quis-la-kin's eyes had gone over her as if he had never seen her before.

They were talking in low tones. Presently, when it grew dark, some of the men went to the beach. She heard the hollow sound of one canoe hitting against another. She moved her head as much as she dared, but she could not see how many got into the boat, or whether one boatload or two paddled on downstream.

Miss Mittie was on one side of her, Lady Mary on the other. When it was dark she felt a hand touch hers. Miss Mittie whispered, "I have the shears in the pocket of my skirt. If you could reach them . . ."

Marita's wrists were tightly bound—or were they? She moved one hand a little, first to one side, then to the other. The thong moved. She had not seen the Indian who bound her. Could it have been Quis-la-kin? Could he have left the thong loose so that she could free her hands? She was afraid to move for fear some leering savage was watching her feeble struggle to free herself. She must wait until the darkest time came, shortly before the moon arose.

Miss Mittie whispered again, "I wish Captan Zeb were here. He would save us."

Lady Mary's back was towards her. Marita moved ever so little until her lips were close to Lady Mary's ear. "Are the thongs on your wrists loose?"

After a wait, Lady Mary whispered, "Yes."

"I think Quis-la-kin may have tied them so for a purpose. When it is dark, loose your hands; then untie the thongs on your feet."

Lady Mary was thinking of the two old people lying in grotesque death, and the burned house. "I do not think it is worth the risk. I will help you, darling. As for me, it is not hard to die."

"Don't say that!" Marita moved close. "We must try. Perhaps in the dark we can get up the bank."

"No, no, not up the bank!"

"Sh! Sh!" Marita cautioned.

When it was dark, Marita moved her hands until the thongs fell away. After a time she succeeded in freeing her ankles. She rolled a little towards Miss Mittie, reaching for the shears. They were stout; they would cut through leather.

Miss Mittie had loosened her hands and was working on her bound ankles. Marita raised herself on her elbow. She saw only one Indian seated near the fire facing them. She hoped she was in the deep shadow when she bent down to free her aunt.

"Who is near you?" Marita whispered.

"Anthony."

Marita put the shears into her hand. "Perhaps you can cut through . . ."

While she was working, a second Indian came and stood between them and the fire. Marita thought, Aunt Mary will free Anthony and he can help Black John. Where was De-sham? It was too dark now to see—only the glow from the fire sent little tongues of light out into the darkness. She tried to think about Anthony, cutting the cords for Black John . . .

Waiting was so long, she could not keep her eyes from closing. Would she ever see Michael again? His face rose

468

before her eyes. He seemed to beckon her. She got up to walk towards him. It was not Michael she followed, but a great lunar moth, its delicate green gossamer wings marked with mauve, the long tail fluttering as it poised on the dark trunk of a tree. The forest was very dark now. No light came through the heavy crown of leaves. She tried to move but her feet were held firmly, caught in some great morass that was dragging her down. If she could only reach the light . . . the moon had light . . .

She woke suddenly. A cool hand touched her forehead gently. Kikitchina was leaning over her whispering, pressing a knife into her hands. "You are all free," she whispered in her own tongue. "When Quis-la-kin jumps upon the Indian sitting by the fire, your men will rush them. Then we will take you to your boat."

"Oh, Kikitchina, where shall we go? Your people are all about. They are mad. They are killing the——"

The Indian woman said quietly, "I know, you must follow me . . . perhaps——"

There was a commotion at the fire. Marita sat up. It was like boxing night, a pantomime played out before the fire, dark shadows moving in and out of the light. Presently there was no more movement at all. Kikitchina's voice said quietly, "We must go quickly." They stumbled down to the sand. Quis-la-kin was waiting, the boat ready.

"We will go also. You are our captives," the Indian woman said. "Lie low in the floor of the boat like dead." They all huddled together trying to hide. They moved out of the stream into the darker river. Twice they passed war canoes. Twice Quis-la-kin's voice was raised in some strange greeting. No one stopped them. Each separate party was out on its own assigned district. Fires burned strongly on the south shore.

They were going west—Marita knew this, for she put her hand over the side of the boat and felt the pull of the current. She was bodily weary, but felt none of the mental fatigue she had felt during the long weeks of illness. She knew now she must live. Life was desirable; she must not again give way. She was not like her aunt who had lived long and richly. All was before her.

Towards morning they came to high ground near a marsh. Kikitchina leaned back to speak to Marita. "We will leave you near the Romney Marsh. One day, two days' march, and there will be Bath Town."

She said no more until the canoe entered a small stream and all the people were out of the canoe on the shore. Marita caught the Indian woman's hand and held it to her cheek. "Kikitchina, what can I ay?"

"Say nothing, mistress. Go quietly, not speaking, one behind the other, watching, watching, always west. Move as Kikitchina has taught you, one step in the footprint of the other. Bird calls . . . listen carefully." She looked at Marita sorrowfully. "It is only evil to kill. Tell them what I tell you. Yesterday Indians south of river—tomorrow north maybe. Go fast, but very quietly."

She looked at Marita a few moments and walked away. Quis-la-kin came and stood in front of Marita for a moment without speaking, and he too went away towards the river. Tears were streaming from Marita's eyes.

A night and half of another day they stumbled through the forest. Sometimes there was a short path, beaten hard by the passing of many feet. Sometimes they followed a stream for a little way, obliterating their tracks as best they could. Once they heard a bird call. Marita stopped the little party by a signal. They hid in a haw thicket. Three Indians went by them moving swiftly towards the east. The thorns of the thicket slashed cruelly but they remained hidden till the forest was again quite still.

Late in the afternoon of the second day they caught sight of Bath Town garrison. They would have hurried forward, but Black John stopped them. There might be Indians outside the stockade—or the men in the garrison might shoot, not knowing. One must go ahead to the town. The rest would hide in the woods.

Anthony went on. Black John lay on his stomach near a great oak tree and watched while the rest stretched flat on the ground under the shelter of low bushes.

Lady Mary's clothes hung in shreds; her long pale hair was tangled and dishevelled. Desham had tried to make it tidy, but her hands trembled so that her mistress pushed her away. The poor distracted woman moved as if she were in a trance. Miss Mittie proved wiry and resilient. Sarah was quiet but she kept watch through the trees for Anthony. Marita seemed to gather strength. She was grateful for the teachings of her Indians. She walked through the forest as if it were a friend, not an enemy. The others looked at her in wonder, not knowing that it was the earth and the forest that gave her strength.

At dusk an armed party came out from the garrison. They had litters but no one wanted to be carried through the gates. When they neared the stockade they heard the welcoming shouts and greetings, people crying out, "Praise be to God!" The heavy wooden gates swung open. They had come through.

Chapter 39

MASSACRE

LADY MARY lay on the bed of pine boughs under an oak tree inside the stockade. Weary as she was, she could not sleep. Marita lay beside her breathing quietly. Miss Mittie and Desham lay on the other side of the tree, exhausted. They slept as if danger were far away, instead of hiding in the forest that surrounded them and on the river below.

A hundred people were crowded in the compound. They were the men and women and children who had escaped massacre and fled to safety in the Bath Town garrison. When they came through the gates that afternoon, men and women rushed forward to help them, to bring them food and hot drinks, to prepare beds of boughs for them to lie upon and rest their tired bodies. All along the Pamticoe the Indians had burned and killed until no house remained on the south side of the river. Horror piled upon horror—Indians mad with blood-lust, killed and tortured and burned.

Lady Mary got up quietly and walked to the fires where Indian and Negro slaves were heating great iron cauldrons of water. A shiver passed over her. She knew why they kept the fires going and the water hot. They would use it if the savages tried to scale the walls. Across the compound were other fires and other kettles filled with tar that sent off an acrid smoke that filled the nostrils.

A woman offered her a cup of hot broth and made a place for her on the wooden bench. Her name was Anna Ponly, she said. She was one of Baron de Graffenried's Palatines who had stopped at Balgray on their way to the colony at New Bern. She was a spare, gaunt woman, her skin

471

toughened to leather by the sea and the wind. Her thin, pale hair lay closely about her head. In the firelight her eyes shone strangely. She lived at the ferry, she told Lary Mary. The Indians had come down the river at night. She had seen them, their red painted faces pressing against the frames of the windows. She called to warn her husband. He ran for the ferry. They killed him before he could come to her. She had seen them rush to him and strip the hair from his head with knives. She ran to the woods, carrying their little girl in her arms, but a naked savage, his body reeking with oil, snatched the child from her arms. He beat her with a club and she fell to the ground. She saw him dash her child to death against a tree. Her voice was toneless.

Lady Mary could not speak. She wanted to say something, anything that would bring comfort.

The woman got to her feet. "They are dead. They are dead. How can I live when they lie unburied?" Her voice rose to a shriek. She ran across the compound to the heavy wooden gate, beating against the barricade. *"Annya, my little Annya!"*

Women came out of the darkness and led her away, trying to quiet her. Lady Mary got up and followed them into the hut.

The woman's cries had awakened Marita. Miss Mittie came to her a moment later. "What can anyone do for these poor people?" she said sadly.

"I don't know," Marita answered. A woman in a faded cotton dress with a shawl crossed over her flat chest came and sat near them. The lights flared up when an Indian slave put torchwood on the fire. Marita recognized her. It was the old woman she had seen at Balgray, the Baron's Katherine Shaffer, who had cheered his people on their long hard journey.

Her lips moved silently as if she were praying. "We must not despair. God will not let us die."

A young woman with long braids of black hair hanging over her shoulders stopped when she heard the word "God." "You talk of God now? How can he find us in this cruel country? In the Old Country people were kind and gentle and God was everywhere about us." She walked away, not waiting for the old woman to answer.

"Her husband was the first of our people to die. They cut his head from his body." Katherine went on talking. "We are

472

plain folk. We want little—only to live and be free and worship God."

Marita put her hand over the gnarled, work-hardened fingers of the good woman. For a long time they sat quietly, not speaking.

"This must be the time of our testing. We must be strong and have faith God will not forsake us," old Katherine said.

Miss Mittie moved near. "There must be something we can do."

"Yes, in the morning we will find work for our hands, food to be cooked, the children cared for. Yes, in the morning." She got up and moved quietly away.

Marita groped for Miss Mittie's hand. They clung together in the darkness.

Anthony went over to the headquarters hut. He found Tobias Knight in charge of the defence. With him were planters from up and down the Pamticoe, who had managed to escape in time to reach the garrison at Bath Town. He found Willie Maule there, and Porter from upriver. They had a harrowing tale to tell of their escape. They had managed somehow to hold off a war party of twenty Indians, while six women who had fled to Porter's plantation escaped to a boat. Four men were killed while they were covering the retreat of the women. Rowing as hard as they could, they managed to get the boat out of the range of the arrows. They had come into the garrison only an hour or so ahead of Anthony.

Every man had a similar story of horror to tell. Every hour brought in a few more people who slipped through the forest or crossed the river.

Porter said, "There has never been such killing or such violence. The mutilation of the dead is beyond expression. I myself saw scenes I can never forget. One young woman, big with child, was killed with an axe. She had been placed on the ground head down, her skirts turned back, exposing her naked limbs, with a great stake driven through her body to hold it in place, leaving it bent like a jackknife."

"For God's sake, Porter, don't tell any more." The man who had spoken jumped to his feet and rushed from the hut, his face livid, his hand pressed against his mouth.

Anthony looked sick.

"That's not all, Lovyck. A child lay beside her, its head smashed beyond recognition."

473

Knight said, "Stop it, Porter! We've had enough. All hell is loose and we know it."

Two men left the place and went out. Both of them had come home to find their families killed, their bodies dismembered and thrown to the vultures.

Porter, dazed, almost out of his mind, left the hut. Willie Maule followed him to take him back to his wife, who lay ill in a hut.

Anthony turned to Knight. "Is there a chance to save this garrison?"

Knight leaned against a rough pine table. His eyes were black-ringed. He had been almost without sleep for the past three days. "I don't know, Lovyck. We sent messengers to Virginia, to South Carolina, and to Governor Hyde, but we have no way of knowing whether any of them got through. We do not even know how far this uprising extends or how many of the tribes are involved."

He got up and took his hat from a peg. "Come with me. I'm going up to inspect the sentries. From the platform you can see up and down the river."

They crossed the compound, walking among sleeping women and children stretched on the grass. The women who sat near them were nursing their babies or watching the small children playing in the dust of the compound. All had the same look of terror in their eyes.

Anthony followed Knight up the rough stairs to the watch post, a large platform set under a great oak tree, protected from sight by the drooping branches and leaves. Anthony looked in the direction Knight pointed. He saw a dozen long canoes filled with red Indians. Each canoe held, at the least, twenty or thirty braves. The canoes seemed almost stationary, not far from shore but out of range.

Knight said, "We have a cannon, but only a few balls left. We must hold those. Now we try to fend off each attack by shooting from the platform along the stockade. So far we have been fortunate. We have not been attacked by a large party."

"How many women are here?" Anthony said, looking down at the figures moving about the enclosure.

"A hundred, perhaps, women and children. We try to keep them towards the centre of the compound. There is added danger at night when the savages throw lightwood torches inside, hoping to set fire to houses and tents."

474

Anthony said, "I am confident the Governor will send help to reinforce this garrison."

Knight's expression changed, his voice was bitter. "Hyde help us? God's death! It is he who put us here."

Anthony said, "What are you saying, Mr. Knight?"

Knight's voice was sharp. "I'm saying what every man on the Pamticoe says. If Hyde had shown himself a soldier instead of showing his weakness by not attacking Cary at the Marsh, we would not be sitting here now."

"I don't see what that has to do with an Indian uprising, Mr. Knight," Anthony said, showing his anger.

"You would if you knew anything about Indians, Lovyck. They are sly and vengeful. They were afraid of Cary. He kept them in check. Well, he's gone now. The Indians know the Governor is no soldier."

Lovyck was silenced. As they crossed the platform he said, "I'll take the same station I had last night."

Knight nodded briefly and went back to his hut.

Lady Mary came out of the hut where she had been most of the day helping take care of the injured. She sat down beside Marita's bed under the oak. Desham brought her broth. Lady Mary drank it, without noticing the gourd cup. She said, "I've just talked with Mr. Knight. He says they hope for help to come tomorrow or the following day. They expect another attack tonight."

Marita said, "I shall ask for a musket."

"You are not strong enough yet, darling," Lady Mary said. "I have told Mr. Knight that I will take a post this evening. Black John will stand guard with me and we will take turns at the opening."

Miss Mittie and Desham both protested. Marita said nothing.

"Nonsense," Lady Mary said. "I can shoot as well as most of the men. I've shot often enough for pleasure. Why should I hesitate when it's to save my skin?" She put her hand on Marita's brow. It was cool and moist, not burning with fever as it had been. "You must all stay close together tonight. Black John will give you his pistol, Marita."

"I have my shears," Miss Mittie said eagerly. "They were useful last night."

"They were indeed, Mittie." Lady Mary put her hand on Miss Mittie's thin shoulder. "I count on you to look after Marita, you and Desham."

She walked towards the stockade, where Black John was

waiting with her musket. She sent the Scot to take the pistol to Marita for their protection. Presently he returned to Lady Mary and they took a station on the south wall not far from Anthony Lovyck.

Sarah stayed close to her husband, loading for him, cleaning his musket and pistol. She did not allow him out of her sight, excepting when she went down from the platform to the cooking fires and hurried back with gourd cups of hot broth for Anthony and his men.

Sarah's quiet devotion did something for Anthony Lovyck. It lessened his selfishness. It made him think of her and her comfort. He covered her thin shoulders with his coat when the chill wind blew off the river, wiped a smudge of powder from her chin, and touched her cheek with his lips.

The attack came after midnight, when the garrison was worn out with waiting. They were awakened by the alarm and the war cries of the savages that surrounded the stockade. The attack was from the land but the canoes stayed out on the water, a constant menace.

Time after time the Indians threw burning torches at the stout wooden stakes that formed the stockade. One came hurtling over the walls. It fell on a pine bed—the boughs blazed up. A woman's dress caught fire. Terrified, she ran screaming across the compound, until a man caught her and flung her to the ground, rolling her in the dust to put out the flame.

Outside the walls the savages screamed their terrible cries, and beat on the gates with a battering ram made of heavy poles lashed together. The gates buckled but they did not give way. After a time the attackers retreated across the open space that surrounded the stockade, driven back by the gunfire.

An oiled, naked savage climbed up a tree close to the stockade. He carried a lighted torch in one hand. Mary saw him from the opening. She looked for Black John, but he had gone to the next opening. There was no time to call him for the Indian was halfway up the trunk of the sapling. In a moment he would be high enough to throw it over the piling that formed the stockade. She steadied the barrel of the musket against the opening. Taking careful sight, she fired. The flint struck fire; the recoil against her shoulder sent her back against the tree; but the Indian screamed and crashed to the ground. The torch flamed through the darkness and fell athwart the Indian's naked body. She braced herself against

476

the oak. She thought her trembling knees would not hold her.

Black John's calm voice steadied her. "Verra gude shooting, your leddyship, but ye should hae called to me. It's dirty work shootin' savages."

The Indians disappeared with the dawn. All day the men worked feverishly repairing damage, doubling the stakes inside the stockade. The women and children filled tow sacks of sand to barricade houses where the injured lay.

Marita sank back in her bed of boughs. The false strength, born of necessity, which had carried her the long journey from the island, had gone, leaving her weak, almost unable to stand. Desham and Miss Mittie took turns sitting beside her while the others worked at tasks that must be done, preparing food, caring for the injured.

Lady Mary still insisted on standing her watch with the soldier. Occasionally she came down to sleep for a short time and to be assured of Marita's comfort.

Miss Mittie said, "Mary has always had the courage of a man. How can she be so brave? She stands there firing her gun at Indians as if she were shooting over the moor." Mittie dropped her voice. "She told me she had killed an Indian—more than one, perhaps." She shuddered violently. "I do not see how she could."

Marita said nothing. She could not bring herself to speak of Lady Mary. Even in the face of death she felt no forgiveness.

"Marita, are you in pain?" Miss Mittie cried. "You look so white. Is there anything I can do?"

"It is nothing," she said, "nothing, nothing anyone can do."

Miss Mittie watched the girl with her kindly eyes. She began to talk of other things—of the cotton picking at Greenfield, of the new colt. She said, "There will be a post from England this week. The little Mademoiselles should be there when we get back to the manor house. It will be nice to sew the new clothes."

Marita made no response, but Miss Mittie continued, hoping to draw her out of her dark mood: "I shall love making the gown for you, Marita; the one Lady Mary has planned of gold embroidered tissue, cut with a skirt twenty yards around the bottom, and a lovely long sash of green taffetas—"

"Please don't talk of it." Marita's voice was harsh. "I don't want worldly clothes ever, ever again. How can you talk of such thing now?" She turned her head away.

"I am sorry, Marita. I only thought to speak of something to distract us. I love to see pretty cloth. To make beautiful clothes is joy to me. I love to slash into pieces of velvet and satin and fashion them into beautiful garments."

Marita did not answer. Desham came to take her turn watching. Miss Mittie walked slowly across the compound to the kitchen. Her mind was troubled. She loved them both so much. Lady Mary and her proud, imperious ways. The child Marita, so quiet and loving. But the child had changed. She was a woman now, a woman who could be hard and unyielding. Miss Mittie sighed. It seemed trivial in the face of the tragedy that was all about them.

When she came back with a cup of broth, Marita's eyes were closed and she was breathing easily. Desham put her finger to her lips, nodding her head towards the sleeping girl. Miss Mittie sat down. She would have liked to go up to the leading platform and look out at the river, but she might see Indians.

The compound was quiet. The sun was down, the cool wind of evening blowing upriver. People were seated on the ground in little groups under trees or beside buildings, eating their frugal meal.

Anthony walked along the platform to where Lady Mary sat drinking a cup of hot tea Black John had brought to her. "I distrust the quiet," Anthony told her. "I do not think the savages will give up so readily."

"Perhaps they are afraid of the noise and have run away," Lady Mary said.

Black John laughed shortly. "More like they are making ready for a rush. They know there's only one loading left to the ship cannon."

Anthony took alarm. "Why do you say that? How could they know?"

The bearded Scot jerked his thumb in the direction of the ground, where a dozen Indians sat eating the leftovers from the table. "I dinna' like savages inside the stockade. Mayhap they are loyal, and mayhap not." He took the cup from Lady Mary's hand and walked away, a dour expression on his face.

Anthony laughed. He was no longer alarmed. "Trust a Scot for gloom," he said.

Lady Mary watched her servant go down the ladder. Her face was grave. "Don't forget that Scots have common sense

478

also, Anthony. They do not have fears without a good reason."

A young captain came up. Anthony mentioned Black John's fear about the Indians in the garrison.

The soldier laughed. "No fear of that," he said. "All our Indian slaves are loyal. They belong to another tribe anyway." He went away to give orders to the next sentry on the platform.

Not long after Anthony had left Lady Mary heard a bugle. It came from the west. A little later there was the sound of a drum beating a double-quick. The weary, frightened people inside the stockade rose to their feet looking from one to another, hope rising in them. The Governor had sent the militia to their rescue. Children shouted. Men rushed up the ladders to the sentry posts on the platforms to see with their own eyes the troops that were marching in to relieve the garrison. The road from the west was clear. The little party marched across the opening and into the stockade.

A sudden hush fell when the gates were opened. It was not Governor Hyde's militia that they saw. Instead of a rescue column ten or twelve men, exhausted and weary from fighting their way through a hostile country, entered the compound.

The people from New Bern and the planters on the Neuse ran forward when they recognized on a stretcher their leader, De Graffenried. The old woman, Katherine, came from the cooking fires wiping her hands on her white apron. She lifted the Baron's hand to her lips. "God is thanked! God is thanked!" she said. "He would not take you from us."

"My good Katherine." The Baron's voice was weak from suffering. "Come with me. Only you know how to heal this poor body of mine."

When he turned on his side she saw his back, where the Indian whips had made deep gashes. The old woman walked beside the litter, her eyes bright with tears.

Roger Mainwaring was the last man to come through the gates. He had stayed outside, his musket ready to fire, until the men were all inside. They had seen no Indians since they had separated from the main body of troops under command of Pollock, two days before. He distrusted the unusual quiet, but none was seen, though they travelled a main road through the forest. Pollock and his command had crossed to the river to get boats. They would stop at the river plantations on the way down to Bath, to pick up any planters who had not sought safety in the garrison.

Lady Mary was seated on the platform standing watch, while Black John was at a cooking fire eating his evening meal. The night was still—not a breath of air to stir the leaves. The forest that surrounded the stockade seemed tranquil, without danger. A few sentries watched the darkening river. There were no canoes in sight, although many had passed during the day, going downriver. Lady Mary shivered, pulling her plaid closer about her shoulders. She heard confusion about the gates and the shouts of the guards. Troops were arriving. She got up quickly. The gates opened and men came into the stockade. It was too dark to see their faces.

She had turned to go to her post when she heard Roger Mainwairing's voice giving a brusque order to his men. She stood without moving, her hand against the rough wood for support. "Jesu, Maria, shield him well," she whispered. A moment before she had been ready for death, red death from the forest. Now . . . she turned again to the square opening in the wall and took up her vigil.

Roger found her kneeling at the loophole, watching the dark shadow of the river. The lights from the cooking fires below flamed. The moving shadows played across her white face. He took his place at her side. "Mary," he said, his voice shaken with emotion. "Mary!" They looked at each other as if they could never turn away. "Every plantation we passed added a new horror. I do not know how you escaped death."

"You thought of me, Roger?" Her voice was soft.

"Every hour, knowing your danger. If you were not here I would have gone down the river to the island. I think I would have cut my way through red hell to find you."

He lifted his hands from her shoulders. "Mary, I have something I must say to you."

Something ominous in his voice frightened her. "Don't, Roger. I cannot stand any more horror. I have seen enough for a lifetime—blood and death—death without dignity—horrible. . . . I cannot clear it from my mind, day or night."

He said, "It is not that. What I must say to you cannot wait." He paused, trying to find a way. "Rhoda is here. She is at Queen's Gift."

She did not move or speak. In the silence the movement of people below them rose—voices, the sound of children's laughter, the short bark of a fox in the forest. He could not endure the silence.

He said, "I went to York to meet the ship. We were married a day later and I brought her home with me." He waited a moment, then went on. "I wanted to be the one to tell you."

She spoke then, her voice toneless. She spoke from a great distance that now separated them. "I am glad you were the one to tell me, my dear."

She sought no explanation. He gave none. When she spoke again she said, "When you have cared for your men I will be waiting for you here. I think there will be work for us before the night is over."

Roger went away, down the steps. He looked back at her when he reached the foot of the stairs. She had turned and stood motionless looking out over the dark river.

He talked with the men who bore the burden of defence. No one spoke of danger, but fear was in every man's eyes—not for himself, but for the helpless fugitives within the gates.

Knight said, "I think there must be a thousand of those devils loose with the massacre spirit in their blood."

Maule and Porter came in to report. One charge of the cannon, they said, was all they could spare. The powder must be for the muskets.

Maule turned to Roger. "How long will it be before Pollock can get here?"

Roger hesitated. He did not want to raise their hopes. Pollock might not come. He might run into trouble on the river. Knowing that the light from the lanthorn fell on his face, Roger hoped it did not reveal his anxiety. He said, "Pollock could get here by morning if he found boats and there was no interference along the river, but—"

Knight rose. "We must not count on what may come. Let us consider ways to use what we have. I shall double sentries tonight."

Towards midnight Roger went up to the platform after he had seen that his men were in their places. He spoke to Black John who was kneeling at the opening. The moon was rising, casting a silver shadow along the river. "Go take your sleep, John. I will stand your watch."

The gillie protested. " 'Tis her leddyship that should be resting, sir. She will not stir. It is not good to sit lookin' and lookin' at the water."

Mary turned her head at the sound of their low voices. "Go, John. Rest near my people. I will feel safer if I know you are near them."

"Aye, I will go since you ask me, but I have no wish to rest if there is danger abroad."

They heard him move along the platform and make his way down the creaking ladder. Anthony and Sarah were asleep somewhere in the compound. A stranger had their place.

Roger sat down beside Mary. Along the south shore of the river fires burned, marking new depredations and bloody massacre.

"Do you think we will get out of here alive?" Mary inquired, breaking the long silence.

"I don't know. Knight expects an attack before morning. All day canoes filled with painted savages have gone down the river. He thinks they are going to join with the Indians from the lower islands for attack." Roger knew there was no need to evade or ease Mary's anxiety. She had seen too much. She realized the danger. "Pollock and his men may come in time. Fifty men with firearms would turn the Indians away."

"I am not afraid," Lady Mary said. "To die now, here, with you near me would not be hard. It is living that takes courage."

Roger put his hand over hers. He knew she spoke the truth. She would face danger as she faced life, without fear. As for himself, it was not death he wanted—it was life—a new life that was opening for him.

She moved so that her shoulder touched his. The moon was high. In the pale light he saw her great eyes turned to him. "I am content," she said softly. "I have made my demands on life, and life has given me you and your love."

He took her hand and lifted it against his lips. "My dear, my very dear." The silence closed in on them. They were a part of the quiet night—the silent river and the deep forest. He thought of another night when they had sat together on the gallery at Queen's Gift and watched the slow movement of the stars across the sky. They were in a breathless suspended world, waiting for life or for death. He raised his eyes. Through the treetops the white light of Vega shone down on them, transcendent and eternal.

Marita lay with eyes wide open staring into the leafy

482

crown of the oak that sheltered them. The thought of impending danger bore down on her. The still night filled her with terror, and she moved closer to Miss Mittie, who lay beside her on the bed of boughs. Miss Mittie touched her hand. She too was awake, oppressed by the same dread fear. Only Desham slept, making queer noises in her throat.

Marita was about to speak to Miss Mittie when she noticed two figures moving in the shadow. They spoke quietly in Indian tongue. Marita understood a few words that turned her sick with fear. "When the moon lies there by the tree, the gates will open." She knew what that meant. The Indian slaves inside the compound would open the gates. The savages hidden in the forest and on the river would swarm into the garrison. What must she do to warn the garrison? She could not cry out. That would only make confusion, and gates would be opened before the men could prevent it. She thought of Black John, who was sleeping on the opposite side of the tree.

She put her lips to Mittie's ear. "Wake Black John quickly. Tell him the Indians inside the garrison are going to open the gates and slaughter us!"

Mittie gasped but made no outcry. With infinite caution she moved slowly through the shadow. Marita's eyes were fixed on the moonlight spreading towards the tree in the centre of the compound. When the moonlight was on the tree they would strike. Was there enough time for Black John to reach the little hut where Knight slept—rouse the sentries before the gates were thrown open to the horde of blood-lusting savages?

The delay was interminable. Without realizing it, Marita found herself on her feet, her back pressed against the trunk of the oak tree. The shadows were too dense for her to see Miss Mittie.

The alarm sounded—one sharp stroke of the great plantation bell—then rapid strokes, faster until it was one long continuous sound. Women wakened from sleep screamed. Then a man shouted, "The Indian slaves, the Indian slaves are opening the gates!"

At the alarm, hellfire broke, outside the gates and on the river. Demons with knives and torches rushed forward to attack. At the gates men fought silently. Women and little children cried out and died. Men fought and died, cursing. The infernal cries of the attacking Indians covered the sobs of motherless children and childless mothers alike.

Marita had not moved from the protection of the shadow of the tree. Desham was kneeling at her feet. "Mother of mercy! Mother of mercy!" she cried aloud. Miss Mittie was not in sight.

Men fought by the gates and by the cooking fires; knives and swords flashed in the moonlight. The Indians were flinging torches of pitch pine over the walls. The sharp explosion of firearms and the smell of powder hung in the still air. Fires blazed up outside where Indians were trying to burn the walls of the stockade.

Suddenly, above all the wild turmoil, a war trumpet sounded an alarm. It came from the river. A moment later a drum beat a rapid tattoo.

The people inside the garrison shouted and yelled and rushed towards the river gates. Sentries from the platform cried out, "Boats on the river." Help was coming from the river. An officer's voice cried out an order, "Cover the landing! Stand ready at the gates!"

Marita heard Lady Mary calling, "Marita, Marita ..." Marita started forward. When she left the shadow of the tree, Miss Mittie's voice, vibrating with terror, rose above the beat of Indian war drums that pounded against her ears. "Marita, Marita—run—run—run! Behind you—"

She whirled sharply. An Indian with an upraised knife was coming towards her, his oiled, naked body glistening in the moonshine. She could hear his swift breathing—see his cruel shining eyes. Then she saw Miss Mittie running towards her. She had her shears clutched tightly in her hands. Terror gripped Marita. She could not move. She heard Miss Mittie scream; saw the Indian whirl around. Miss Mittie sprang forward at the Indian with all the might of her strong, wiry body and drove the heavy cutting shears deep into the naked belly of the savage. A long way off Marita heard a pistol shot. She saw Miss Mittie fall. The Indian's knife had reached her before Black John's pistol found its mark. Darkness descended on her. She did not hear the creaking gates swing open or the shouts of welcome, as Pollock's men marched into the stockade.

When Roger Mainwairing and Lady Mary reached them they found Miss Mittie lying over the body of the disemboweled Indian. Black John lifted the fainting Marita in his arms and carried her away.

Mary knelt in the dust beside Miss Mittie. Roger had

carried her to the shadow of the walls, where half a hundred fugitives who had sought sanctuary within the walls of the garrison lay dead. The fighting had ceased, the forest was quiet, the river clear of Indian canoes.

Mary closed Miss Mittie's eyes and laid her thin wrinkled hands across her flat breast. She rose and stood beside Roger looking at the dead woman's tranquil face. "Mittie never gave a thought to herself in all her life—" she leaned over and touched Miss Mittie's cheek gently—"or in death."

The night before they started their journey back to the Albemarle the slaves dug a grave on the river bank near the shelter of the walls. Roger and Black John put the coffin on their shoulders and set it deep in the earth. Black John stood for a moment looking down on the flat levelled earth. " 'Tis a pity to go awa' and leave her alone. She was a brave wee lass. God rest her soul!"

"With God," Roger said softly. "Go with God."

A few days after Lady Mary and Marita got back to Greenfield, the English post came. Lady Mary took the packet of letters which were addressed to her and went to her room and closed the door. Marita sent for her horse and rode down the lane towards Captain Zeb's house. Watkins' men had been working, and the damage done by the hurricane on the house had been obliterated.

She dismounted and went slowly up the walk to the stoop. Almost without thinking she put her hand on the bell cord. The door opened and Captain Zeb stood in the entrance. When she saw his eyes Marita knew that someone had told him. He stood aside for her to come into the room.

"Ma'n'ring told me," he said, putting out a chair for Marita. "I was there with my ship when he got to Queen's Gift last night. I was waiting to tell him the good news, that I had given Rackham the slip. I was in high good humour, waiting to tell him my good fortune in bringing in his cargo of sugar and spices and pineapples."

Marita didn't know what to say. The words she could have spoken choked in her throat.

The Captain didn't notice. He went on talking. "I was sitting having my little drink of rum toddy when I saw Duke coming down the path from the house, his fine young wife walking beside him. I knew something was wrong when I saw Duke's face but I didn't wait to hear what he had to say. I

485

was so quick to tell him about seeing the leet girl, Anne Bonney, aboard Rackham's ship, dressed for all the world like a pirate, with pistols in her belt and a knife in her hand, ready to lead a boarding party.... Duke Roger stopped me. He told me about the brave woman."

Captain Zeb sat very still, his arms hanging loosely, his strong body bent forward. After a time he raised his tired eyes to Marita. "She was such a little thing, too good for this world—far too good for Zeb Bragg."

Marita left him standing beside the door, looking out on the water, his unlighted pipe locked in his teeth.

Lady Mary called to her as Marita was crossing the hall. She was smiling and very pleased. "I have read my letters—I have good news, very good news," she said. "We are going home to England in December. A ship of war is coming to Virginia and we are to go back on her. The Captain has his orders."

Marita said nothing. She sat looking at Lady Mary with blank, uncomprehending eyes. Go back to England? She was never going back! She was going to live here, on her own plantation. She tried to speak. Lady Mary was not looking at her. She was concerned only with a letter she held in her hand. She looked as she always looked, beautiful, well cared for, just out from under Desham's skilful hands. How could she be so calm? It seemed only yesterday they were walking through the forest, with savage Indians everywhere about them, Indians who had snatched babies from the arms of their mothers, driven stakes through tortured bodies.... Rage and anger rose in Marita, blazed from her eyes. She steadied her voice.

"How can you smile and think about England? How can you talk about going away and leaving Miss Mittie alone in the forest?" Her voice broke, her eyes filled with tears. She started blindly for the door.

"Marita." Lady Mary's voice was sharp. "Marita, control yourself. I was fond of Mittie when she was alive, but I can do nothing for her now.'

Marita faced her, her eyes blazing. "I'm not going to England with you," she said. "I'm going to wait here until Michael comes for me."

Lady Mary watched her walk across the hall and mount the stairs. With a sigh, she went to her writing box, selected a quill, and sat down to write. For some time her pen

486

scratched across the heavy paper that bore her cipher at the top. When she came close to the bottom of the page she paused, the quill suspended. For a long time she looked with unseeing eyes out of the window. She turned again to the page.

"When you next have audience will you please tell her Majesty that I am grateful to her for her kindness in remembering me, and suggesting I come home again? To you, my dear friend, I say the exile has been long, but not without its compensation. You will find Marita changed. She is mature and has a will of her own; not unlike her mother, you will say! Perhaps. You will see what you think of her when we get home. As for the other matter, I feel great hope now that you are in power again." She wrote a few words and signed "Mary Tudor" across the bottom of the page.

Marita paused at the door of Miss Mittie's bedchamber. The door was open and she walked in. Someone had unpacked the boxes that had come in the post from England. The room was filled with rolls of silks and gowns that Selby, the mantuamaker, had fashioned for her aunt. A length of gold tissue was on the table, and seated on the bed against the sham-pillows were two gay Mademoiselles, dressed and coifed and painted in the latest fashion. Marita took up one of the elegant little figures. She seemed to see Miss Mittie sitting beside her in the besieged stockade, to hear her voice saying, "I love pretty cloth. I love to slash pieces of velvet and silk and satin and fashion shimmering garments."

Marita dropped to her knees beside the bed and buried her face in the mass of gauze and satin. Poor Miss Mittie—at the end she had found a different use for her clever cutting shears.

Chapter 40

GOD REST YOU MERRY, GENTLEMEN

THE Christmas season brought new life to the Albemarle. Roger Mainwairing came home the middle of December. Now that the Governor had raised new levies of militia he was home to stay. He would remain at Queen's Gift to farm and enjoy the home which Rhoda had made while he was away.

Roger found, as Rhoda had told him, that it would be a new Queen's Gift when he returned. Furniture had arrived from England. Turkey carpets and woven hangings for the windows, comfortable elbow chairs for the great room, and wing and barrel chairs for the fireplaces. Chelsea china and a set of white bone with scenes in India ink; plate from his old home and from her place in the Midlands.

Roger walked through the house, his arm over his wife's shoulder. He was pleased with what he saw. He had built well the strong exterior, sturdy and firm, but she had added grace. Something of her vitality and charm touched the rooms.

"I am glad you are pleased, Roger," she said, as she stood in the long yellow drawing-room. "You have been so long without a home, I want you to have one now—a home that has comfort and warmth and happiness."

He drew her close to him. "I pray God it will always bring happiness to you, my dear."

While they were at supper, Rhoda told him of the plan for Christmas Eve. "Madam Catha is home," she said. "She is in excellent spirits. She is full of woman's gossip from London, and the Governor is pleased at her news that the Lords Proprietors gave him credit for bringing Cary's Rebellion to an end. Madam Catha and Hester Pollock came to call one afternoon. Madam Catha is eager to have the season's festivities from Christmas Eve to the Twelfth Night. We, my dearest husband, will open our new home on Christmas Eve!" She laughed, her eyes sparkling with pleasure. "Oh, Roger, people are so kind here, and so hospitable, and so curious to see what we have done with Queen's Gift!"

Roger smiled at her eagerness. "We must satisfy their curiosity, Rhoda. I think the idea is excellent. I suppose you have plans?"

"Oh, yes, certainly. It is all planned. We will hunt in the morning and have breakfast at Greenfield. . . ." She paused the fraction of a second. "In the afternoon the men will have a sailing race on the Sound, and in the evening we will have a supper and dance."

"It sounds very gay indeed." Roger did not want to dampen Rhoda's gaiety, but somehow his thoughts went to the horrors he had witnessed the past two months.

488

She seemed to read something in his eyes, for she said soberly, "I know, Roger, it seems heartless. But it is the Governor's wish. He thinks the people deserve some gaiety this year."

"Perhaps he is right," Roger said.

They had had coffee in the drawing-room. Rhoda talked of her plans, the way she had spent her time while he was gone. "We hunted all October and November, the Blounts, Anthony and Sarah (they are at Sandy Point now), and some people from Queen Anne's Town. One morning we started at Anthony's place and rode through the woods to Greenfield, where we had breakfast."

Roger said nothing. He was occupied tamping a clay pipe.

Rhoda said, "I recognized Lady Mary at once. I had seen her any number of times in London, at Court and riding in the Mall. Anthony Lovyck said there was some mystery about her—that no one here knew who she was but the Governor."

"Did you tell Anthony you knew her?" Roger asked.

"No. No, certainly not. She wanted to remain unknown. But everyone knows, now that Madam Hyde is back. Everyone in the village knows that Lady Mary Tower is Lady Mary Tudor. I believe she still refuses to use her husband's name," she added as an afterthought.

Roger said, "So Madam Catha told?"

"Well, not exactly. She hinted. She said, 'It is said that Lady Mary is the youngest sister of the Duke of Monmouth, a natural daughter of King Charles the Second.' That was enough, of course."

"Does Lady Mary know of this gossip?" Roger asked, after a long silence.

Rhoda poured a second cup of coffee for him and one for herself before she answered. "I don't know, really. . . . They are so different, those two, Lady Mary and Marita. Two women alone down there. Roger, I think . . . well, I feel there is something very strange between them—almost as if they hated each other."

"Nonsense," Roger said sharply. "They couldn't; why they—He paused abruptly.

"Not that it matters," she said lightly. "They are leaving the day after Christmas. They are going back to England. The Governor and his wife are going to stay at Greenfield until the Goverment House is finished."

Roger set down his cup. It rattled against the saucer. "I hadn't heard," he said. His voice sounded natural, almost indifferent. "I did not know Lady Mary and Marita were going home."

"Yes, in a ship of war. Isn't that rather nice? It is said that Lord Bolingbroke himself has made the arrangements."

Roger got up and poured brandy from the decanter on the coffee table. He walked to the fire and sat down in the wide chair. If Mary were going back, it meant one of two things. Her husband was dead, or the Queen had sent for her. In either case she would go away. There would be nothing to bring her back—ever.

Rhoda got up from her seat behind the coffee table. She crossed the room and sat down on the arm of his chair. "I know, Roger," she said. "Madam Hester hinted so strongly. That was the reason I wanted to go to the plantation. I wanted to see Lady Mary. I—" she paused, searching for the right word—"I think she is the most beautiful woman I have ever seen."

Roger thought, Damn Hester and her meddling! But he knew it really didn't matter. If it hadn't been Hester it would have been someone else ready to hint and make sly allusions. He took her hand and looked into her frank blue eyes. His voice was honest. "Whatever is past is past, Rhoda. You are my wife."

Rhoda sat twisting a lock of his hair. She laughed suddenly. "Tom loathes to have me twist his hair. I forgot for the moment. I love to tease Tom—dear, dear Tom. Oh, I almost forgot to tell you. He has written me he will be here on a ship that arrives in the James River on the twentieth, and he will stay with us through the Twelfth Night."

"That is splendid, Rhoda. We must do what we can to make things pleasant for him while he is here."

"I've already started. I've asked Marita to be extra nice to him, and I told Lady Mary how you and he had followed the Duke of Monmouth. She was pleased, I think." She slipped off the arm of the chair and walked back to the coffee table, her yellow gown sweeping across the polished puncheons. She sat down. For some moments she was silent. Roger knew she had more to say, but she was choosing her own time.

"Roger, I don't want you to think me bold or unwomanly. Tom says I am too frank for my own good, but I cannot help that. I don't want anything between us that might in time grow to be a barrier. What I am trying to say is' that I understand. I have had a season in London and I know what goes on among fashionable folk." A delicate flush rose to her cheek but her blue Irish eyes were steady. "I do not want you to think I am a jealous woman. What is between us must be always frank and open. We are friends now, Roger, good friends and comrades. After a time, I think that understanding will grow into love."

Roger got up from his chair and went to her. Taking her in his arms, he kissed her forehead, then her lips. His arm about her, he leaned across the table and poured two glasses of wine. He put one in Rhoda's hand and touched the rim with his own glass. "We will drink to our long and happy life together, my dear wife."

Rhoda smiled. Her eyes met his, clear and untroubled. "And to our children."

All the Albemarle danced at Queen's Gift on Christmas Eve. Roger stood in the hall watching his guests. The house was fragrant with pine and cedar, and festoons of smilax. Mistletoe hung over the doorways, and red berries from the holly tree in the garden hung over mantelboards and windows. It was gay and it pleased Roger well to see the new house open its arms wide to receive his friends. The long galleries were waxed for dancing, and the drawing-room had been cleared. Candles shone on the bright gowns of the women and the dark brocades of the men's coats. Those who had hunted that day remained as they were, their scarlet coats adding a bright touch to the scene.

Madam Catha was elegant in wine-red velvet trimmed in miniver. Hester Pollock chose scarlet. The Governor was very grand in his dark brocade square-cut coat that came to his knees, almost covering his satin smallclothes, and a silver embroidered waistcoat. He wore shoes in the new style, soft suede, fitted high over his instep, and the red heels added height. Tom Pollock wore kilts of his old regiment, and Edward Moseley's slim, elegant figure was clothed in sombre black.

Even Lucretia's pale, Quaker grey had a festive look with fresh white ruffles at her neck and wrists. She was walking with young Cathcart Phillips, she told Marita proudly when they were alone in the powder-room. They would stand up

491

and be wed some time in the spring. She said proudly, "All my linen is ready—enough for a house with two guest rooms."

Marita said, "Oh, Lucretia, I am so happy for you!" Lucretia returned Marita's impulsive kiss.

"My mother says it is so wise to marry Cathcart. She is pleased that I have chosen a Friend." She smiled demurely. "My mother says young girls are very likely to let their thoughts run away with them at times."

Marita pinned back a stray curl and smoothed her amber tissue skirts. Because of Miss Mittie she had not wanted to have a gown made from it, but Lady Mary had sent for the village seamstress, who had somehow managed.

Lucretia gave Marita a sidewise glance. "Michael Cary was never a true Friend. Now he is no longer one of us, since he has letters of marque and goes fighting up and down the sea. Some people call it privateering, but my mother says it is no more than pirating." She went out of the door, a small smile on her lips.

Marita sat alone in front of the dressing-glass. Michael's name quickened her pulse. She had not heard of him since that terrible day when she went to his ship and begged him to let her go with him on the *Willing Maid*. The thought of her boldness sent the hot blood to her cheeks. Now she would go away and never see him again. In spite of her angry, impetuous words to her aunt, she knew she would go back to England with her. There was nothing else to do. But she would not stay. She would come back to Carolina, to Michael.

Rhoda found her there. She came swiftly into the room, her white bride's gown floating behind her. Her eyes were blue and sparkling and she wore pearls wound in her glossy-dark braids. She could not wait to tell her news. "Tom is on the way," she said, breathless. "His messenger has just arrived. He's bringing guests, Mr. Christopher Gale and the captain of the ship who rescued them both from the Frenchmen. Think of it! Mr. Gale and my brother captured by a privateer between here and Charles Town. Why, the seas aren't safe for travel here any more than they are in Europe! Let us go down. Roger has a surprise."

Marita caught some of her enthusiasm. "What is the surprise?"

"I don't know," Rhoda said. "Something Roger has planned after we have had supper." She caught Marita's hand. "Come, let us go downstairs. I want to be there when dear Tom comes."

Lady Mary sat in Roger's library talking with the Governor and Thomas Pollock. Edward Moseley joined them, and a few minutes later Metephele came in with a tray of glasses and a decanter of whisky.

The Governor said, "This Indian war may drag on, but we have no civil war within our great county of Albemarle. I believe at last we are on the way to peace and a stable government."

"And the return of law," Moseley murmured, lifting his glass to his lips.

Tom Pollock said, "Always harping on the law, Moseley, but I'll grant you that it is coming. What pleases me most is that I see unity among our people now that that rascal Cary is out of the Province for good."

Lady Mary spoke. "But it took an Indian massacre to unite the people—horrible bloodshed and suffering among innocent people. It seems to me, gentlemen, that it would have been far better to find some other way to draw the people together!"

The men turned their eyes towards her grave face. She was leaning against the back of a tall chair, the firelight playing on her face. She wore a gown Selby had sent her, with a little card pinned to the basque: "This is for your ladyship when you review your own Scottish regiment." The gown was made of taffetas, stamped with the royal Stuart tartan on a white ground. The skirt was long, pleated like a kilt. The basque was close-fitting red cloth, braided to the chin in silver with the insignia of a colonel on the collar and shoulder. A light plaid swung from one shoulder, secured with a great coronet of silver, set with stones.

Roger came and stood in the doorway. His eyes met hers for a moment before he turned away without speaking.

"Moseley," answered Lady Mary, "what you say is right. We should settle differences in the court, not on the battlefield."

The Governor frowned. "What can you expect, with all Europe at war, Mary? We feel that conflict here, even in this backwater. Tonight we have heard that a French privateer raided our coast and sank a ship between here and Charles Town. When Christopher Gale comes we will hear more of that."

Pollock leaned forward, his keen eyes and his craggy brows turned to Lady Mary. "When you go back to London, your ladyship, you can speak to the Lords Proprietors. If they would take more interest in us, it would be better. As for wars on the Continent, I think the old rule would be a help to us. If they made friends with the Spanish and war on the French, we'd soon clear our seas."

No one spoke for a moment. The sound of fiddle and flute and the steady throb of the Negro's drum drifted in through the open door.

Rhoda came to the door between two men, a hand on the arm of each. She was smiling. "Your Excellency, Lady Mary, Madam Catha, may I present my brother, Thomas Chapman, who has just been rescued from French privateers; and Michael Cary, the brave captain who rescued him?"

Michael Cary stood easily, his quick, bright eyes going from one to the other.

The interval that followed seemed interminable. Roger Mainwairing came into the room, Christopher Gale with him.

Lady Mary broke the silence. "How d' you do, Captain Cary." She extended her hand to Tom. "Mr. Chapman, I am delighted to see you. Your sister has told me that you fought beside my brother in his rebellion." Her voice, quiet and poised, broke the tension that had gripped the men seated in the room.

Roger spoke then. "Metephele has announced supper. Will you all join us in the dining-room?"

Michael stepped up to Lady Mary. "May I have a moment with your ladyship?"

Lady Mary hesitated only the fraction of a second. She sank back into the chair. "Yes, Captain Cary, if you are not too long in what you have to say."

Michael stood before her, his hand resting on his sword belt. His face was grave and thoughtful. "I am ashamed when I think of my words to you that day at Greenfield. I was angry because I was wrong. Being in the wrong is not an easy position for a man of spirit."

Lady Mary made no comment. She continued to look directly at him, her eyes cool and watchful.

"I was wrong when I did not go to you in the beginning. I was wrong, and I will not try to excuse myself. I saw Marita when I came in tonight, but I have not spoken to her alone. Nor would I speak to her until I had spoken to you."

"Very noble of you, Captain." Her lazy voice was edged with scorn.

Michael's face flushed but he held his temper. "My uncle has written to me that there is hope that this sorry business of ours will soon be cleared. Then I can come to you with a fair name and ask for Marita."

Lady Mary sat for a moment looking down at the point of her buckled shoe. After a moment's deliberation she said, "We are starting for Virginia tomorrow on our way to England. Marita will have a season in London. She will meet eligible young gentlemen and live a life far removed from her life here in the Albemarle. In October she will come into her little inheritance."

Michael said, "I have land—my father's plantation in Antigua and one in Jamaica. I like it here in the Albemarle, but now I think I can best serve my Queen and my country at sea. After the war is over, I can think again of the land."

Lady Mary's eyes softened a little. "I find that my anger towards you has moderated somewhat. The past weeks have made me see a great many things more clearly. When one has been so close to death—" She broke off suddenly. After a few moments she said, "I believe you will not break your word of honour. I ask you, when you talk to Marita later this evening, not to try to persuade her to go with you now. It is unfair to her not to allow her to understand what her responsibilities are in the Old World before she makes her choice."

Michael bowed his head slightly. "I know what is in your mind, Lady Mary. You think the London you know will keep Marita from me. I know better. Marita belongs to the New World, not the Old. I pledge my word, because you have the right to ask."

"Then, sir, will you give me your arm? I think we are already late at supper. I do not wish to inconvenience our charming hostess."

At midnight the slaves came up from the quarters line. Rhoda saw them first. The men were still lingering in the dining-room over their port. The women were in the small sitting-room. Some of the young girls were in the long drawing-room, where Madam Catha was showing them a new dance step.

Rhoda was standing near the window when she noticed the wavering lights. As they drew near the house, she saw the

495

plantation slaves walking slowly, each man and woman carrying a blazing pine knot, and every child a small piece of burning torchwood. Someone was beating a little drum as they walked along.

Rhoda went to the door of the dining-room and signalled to Roger. "What is it?" she asked, as they stood on the gallery waiting.

"It is your surprise, my dear. It is the habit of our people to come to the house Christmas Eve to bring greetings. After that they feast in the tobacco barn and drink their native beer."

"It is a pagan festival!" she said, her eyes bright with excitement.

Roger gave an order to Metephele, who returned in a few moments with a large paper tied with a riband, and sealed with Roger's crest.

They waited on the steps of the gallery for the procession to approach. By the lights, they were thirty-five or forty slaves.

Edward Moseley and Lady Mary stepped out and stood in the shadow, joined in a few moments by the Governor and Thomas Pollock. Other guests came to the windows, but the young people continued to dance on the long gallery that faced the water.

An old woman, the Ancient One, walked at the head of the procession, beating a small drum, which was suspended from her wrinkled neck by a thong of leather. When she reached the foot of the steps she stopped, and Metephele and Primus stepped up and took their places on either side of her. The others made a crescent behind her, their black faces shining, their eyes gleaming, in the light of their torches.

The Ancient One held herself erect with dignity. She seemed no more than a child in stature, between the giant bodies of Metephele and Primus.

Roger came down a step to greet his people. He spoke a few words in their language to make them welcome. He held out his hand to Rhoda. She stepped down beside him, her white bride's gown glistening like silver in the flare of the torches. Roger put the paper into her hand. In a low voice he said, "Give it to the Ancient One."

To Metephele he said, "The paper your mistress has given to the Ancient One brings each man and each woman a plot

496

of land on the road. It is for a garden, so that everyone of you shall have a piece of ground to plant and to harvest. The paper gives something more. It makes you free."

Metephele spoke rapidly, repeating "*Ufulu,*" freedom, several times. Men stepped forward gesticulating, asking rapid questions.

Metephele turned to Roger. "Master, they ask, 'Is our master tired of us? Does not our labour please the master, that he turns his face from us?' "

"No, no," Roger said, going down the steps until he stood beside Metephele. "No, explain to them that they will still work for me, but I will pay for their labour, so that each man may have an ox or a mule to work his land. They will still work for me in my fields and in my forest."

The Ancient One listened to Metephele. She nodded once or twice; then she clapped her hands and spoke to the people. She moved a step nearer to Roger and spoke slowly— soft liquid words that came rhythmically from her lips. Metephele repeated the old woman's words and put them into English almost as she spoke. He said, "The Ancient One says '*Nda-kuta,*' I thank you. '*Ufumu wache sabuka nawoe a-to-bisa zakudia.*' He is not a chief that is generous and feasts his men. '*Kum'funda ufumu, ku-m'loweza ufumu.*' To make him chief there must be more. He is hospitable and does not forget to give to strangers. A great chief is thinking of his people." Metephele paused a moment, waiting for her words.

" '*Ndiwe mfulu?*' Are you a free man? the chief asks. Then and then only is a chief clothed with sovereignty."

Roger looked at the dark upturned faces of his people, moved by the words of the Ancient One. Tears were in Rhoda's eyes. She took her place beside Roger. The Negroes passed before them, each one giving his greeting, "*Nda-m'monika, ndi-muone.*" May you see life.

After the negroes had gone away, walking down the driveway, Tom Pollock said, "Roger will get us in a peck of trouble if every black wants to be made free. Is it a legal document, Moseley?"

"To the best of my knowledge, Tom. I drew it up myself. If it is not legal, it should be made so. A man should have the right to dispose of his property."

Hyde walked back into the house without speaking. His face was grave and thoughtful. As Roger joined them, he said, "Do you think it was a wise thing to do, Mr. Mainwairing?"

The guests departed. Michael Cary and Tom had horses saddled to ride as escorts to the Greenfield carriage. The young people stood outside the house. Anthony and Sarah, arm in arm, started the carol that had been sung on Christmas eve since ancient times, "God Rest You, Merry Gentlemen." Marita's clear voice rose above the others.

The Governor and Madam Catha took up their bed-candles and went upstairs.

Roger kissed Rhoda good night at the foot of the stairs. "I am going to walk down to the tobacco barn. I must be sure that our people have feasted well and had their beer." He handed her her bed-candle and watched her walking slowly up the stairs. At the landing she paused and kissed her fingertips to him. Dear Rhoda! In this short time she had made a place for herself in the life of the plantation, and in the larger life of the Albemarle. Rhoda would be a part of the New World he and his neighbours were building. She would throw herself into creating a new life for him, with the same vital enthusiasm that she did everything. Rhoda had a quality which Mary lacked. She welcomed change. Mary looked backward, to the old—Rhoda forward to the new. On this basis their life together would be built.

When Roger came back from the quarters, all the bed-chamber lights were out. He hesitated a moment, his foot on the steps of the gallery. When he looked out at the moonlit waters of the Albemarle, he could not go in. He told himself he would smoke one more pipe before he went to bed.

He walked across the garden to the shore, and sat down on a bench with the water lapping at his feet, pulling his heavy cape about him. Familiar things took strange forms under the moon. His own thoughts went out beyond the horizon set by daylight vision.

More than once in the year that had passed he had been conscious of some intangible force rising—some change that was enveloping them all, moving them swiftly forward. He realized that the land itself did something for people. The fight against the wilderness all about them gave stamina to the weak, added stature to the strong. He saw a change in Anthony Lovyck. He was sloughing off the London veneer. . . . He thought of Michael Cary. He liked Michael's frank acknowledgment of his errors, his enthusiasm over sailing his ship out to do battle with the Frenchmen and the

498

Spaniards under letters of marque. He wondered if these were the natural developments of men taking their adventure in the New World, or if it were something more profound that had to do with the destiny of the land, and the part they played in it.

Tonight as the men sat talking at the table after the women were gone, he had felt this force clearly. He seemed to see them all in their places, a part of some pattern from which their lives were being fashioned. Hyde was confident that the trouble and confusion of the years were over. His government would hold and function and his power grow. Pollock was the strong link between the past and the future, clinging to the old ideas, giving way slowly to the new, helping to hold the balance of the middle way. Moseley saw something that the rest of them could not envisage. In his dream of the rights of every man under law he went beyond known horizons, looking boldly into a future world of ordered freedom.

Roger tried to think back to when the change had taken place within himself. It must have been the day Moseley talked to the people of the village and told them of their rights under the common law. The old days were gone, the days of each man his own law, to administer as he saw fit. A new force was sweeping down upon them. As Roger saw it now, even Thomas Cary had his place. Cary might have given them the thing that Moseley dreamed, had he not lost himself in the morass of his own ambition and love of power.

Then he thought of Mary. From the first moment he saw her at Balgray to the last night, when they sat close together watching without words the dark silent flow of the river to the sea. In the poignant silence of those last hours, the cycle of their living was complete, always to remain a part of him, the centre of his secret life, a life that had passed.

A fox barked sharply in the distance. In the cypress tree that grew far out into the water, a great owl hooted, its heavy wings beating as it dropped on its screaming prey. In the dark woods life was awakening.

He watched the long dark cloud bank rise, covering the moon. What did it all matter? Men lived and died and went back to the earth again. Only the eternal things remained—the sun and the moon and the stars, the restless power of the sea, and the ever-renewing earth beneath his feet.

Roger rose and walked slowly towards the house. The dawn was breaking in the east, a thin rim of yellow light. Metephele was waiting for him at the door. He spoke quietly, "The moon brings strange thoughts, master—the sun climbs and gives a new day."